"How much jousting have you done?"

"A little," replied the young troubadour.

"A little!" the Templar said ironically. "In tournaments all over Europe, Count Amalric has bested hundreds of knights. Many times he has killed men. Of course, it is against the rules. But he is a master at making it look like an accident." He looked at Roland with an almost fatherly kindness. "Indeed, messire, the best advice I could give you would be not to enter the tournament at all."

Roland laughed. "Such cautious advice from a Templar?"

"We fight for God, messire. Have you as great a motive?"

"Yes, I do," said Roland, seeing Nicolette's eyes shining in the darkness before him. "I fight for love."

ALL THINGS ARE LIGHTS

ROBERT SHEA

BALLANTINE BOOKS • NEW YORK

Library of Congress Catalog Card Number: 86-91088

ISBN 0-345-32903-1

Folio V from Illuminated Manuscript of King Rene's "LeCueur d'A-
mour Esptis" with permission from the National Library, Vienna,
Austria.

Printed in Canada

First Edition: May 1986

TO YVONNE

"The real world, that was what I lived in with you."

Acknowledgments

Many people helped me with the writing of this book in a great many different ways. I would especially like to express my gratitude to Jeanne Bernkopf, Bernadette Bosky, Frances C. Bremseth, Gerald Bremseth, Ric Erickson, Christine Hayes, Dave Hickey, Dr. Joseph R. Kraft, Mary Kaye Kraft, Neal Rest, Michael Erik Shea, Morrison Swift, Robert Anton Wilson, and Al Zuckerman.

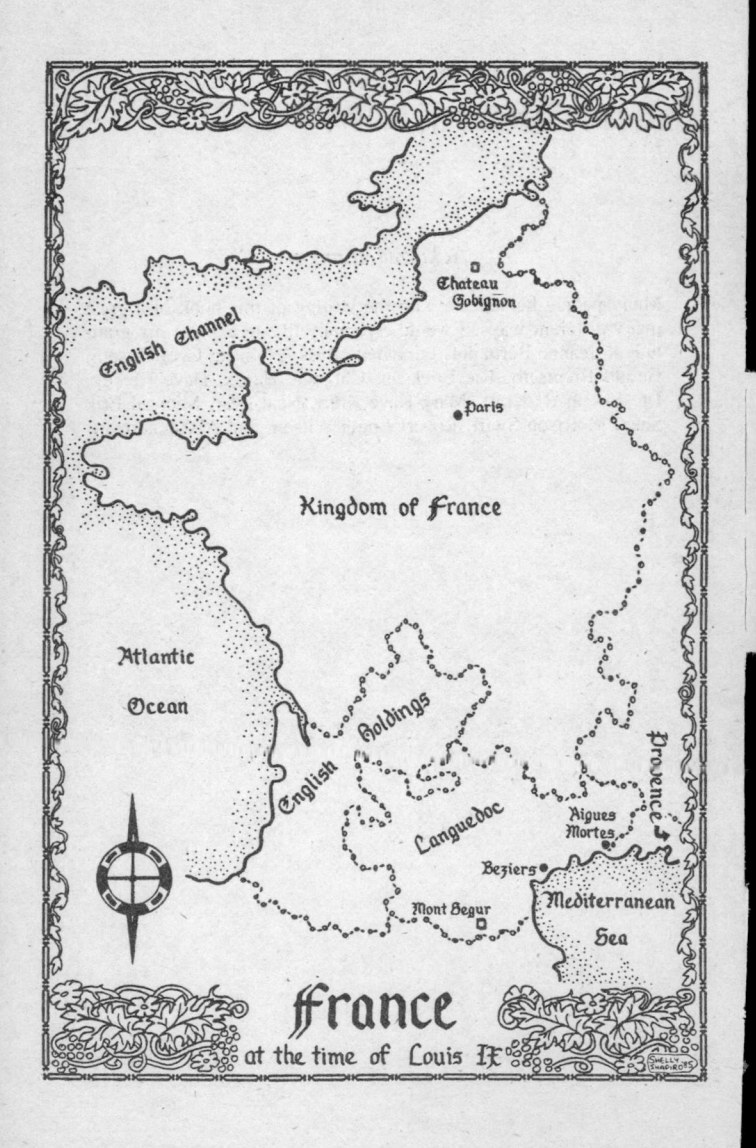

Chateau
Gobignon

English Channel

Paris

Kingdom of France

Atlantic
Ocean

English Holdings

Languedoc

Provence

Aigues
Mortes

Beziers

Mont Segur

Mediterranean
Sea

ffrance
at the time of Louis IX

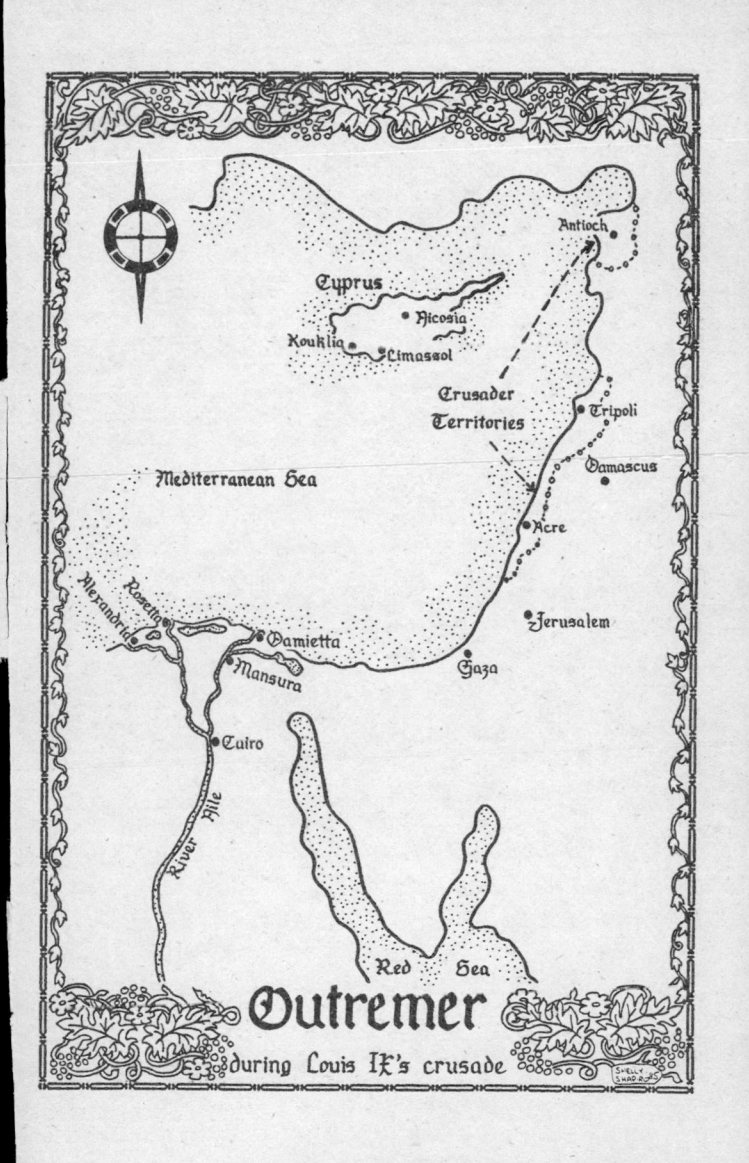

Outremer

during Louis IX's crusade

PART ONE

FRANCE

Anno Domini 1244–1248

I

ROLAND NARROWED HIS EYES AND STARED UPWARD INTO THE DARKNESS, across the top of Mont Ségur toward the Cathar fortress. Standing on a high walkway of planks behind the palisade of the crusaders' small wooden fort, he heard faraway voices and saw torches moving on the Cathar rampart.

The two men on watch with him that night, a sergeant from Champagne and a young man-at-arms from Brittany, were talking in low tones about the women to be had far below, at the foot of the mountain. They seemed not to see the activity about the Cathar stronghold on the upper peak of the mountaintop opposite their own fort. But Roland, knowing Diane was in the besieged fortress, could not take his eyes from it.

He knew he had to act soon. Each day the crusaders grew stronger and the Cathars weaker. Once the Cathar stronghold fell, the crusaders would slaughter all within, including Diane.

The sergeant, chuckling, was offering his young companion a wineskin. The Breton never received it.

From behind the Cathar wall came the sound of a huge thump, as if a giant's fist had pounded Mont Ségur. Roland recognized the sound, and fought panic as he thrust his arms out, trying to push the other two men toward the ladder. But there was no time for them to climb down to safety. The thump was the counterweight of a stone-caster, and the whistling noise that followed fast upon it was the rock it had thrown.

A shape as big as a wine barrel blotted out the stars. The stone hit the parapet beside Roland, and the whole palisade shuddered. Roland caught a glimpse of the sergeant's horrified face and heard his scream as the boulder struck him, crushing him to the ground.

Roland and the young man-at-arms clung to the wooden wall, saving themselves from falling twenty feet to the yard below. Right beside them was the gaping hole in the palisade left by the stone.

3

Roland knew more stones would soon follow, and wanted desperately to jump for the ladder. But he forced himself to stand still long enough to see what was happening at the Cathar fortress. He watched the wide main gateway swing open. A blaze of red torchlight gleamed on helmets and spearpoints—fighting men were pouring out on the run. He waited a moment, counting. A hundred or more.

His breathing quickened and his heart pounded. Here was the diversion he needed.

He shouted down into the darkness, adding his cry to the shouts of men waking up within the crusader fort. "To arms! To arms! The Cathars are attacking!"

Pushing the man-at-arms before him, he hurried down the ladder. The young Breton was blubbering.

"Alain. The damned Bougres got Alain."

"Mourn him later," Roland advised. "Just try to keep yourself alive."

Roland hesitated at the foot of the steps. The stone had knocked the logs apart, leaving an opening at the base of the wall wide enough for a man to step through.

"I am going out there to get a better look at them," Roland said, sliding the two-handed sword, almost as long as his leg, out of its scabbard. "You report to the commander."

"God go with you, Sire Orlando," the man-at-arms said to him.

Roland hurried out into the darkness, alone with his excitement and fear.

The ground shook as a second Cathar boulder landed somewhere inside the fort. He heard splintering wood and shrieks of pain and terror. Then came another massive thump, this time a counterweight of the crusaders', sending a huge stone screaming overhead to answer the heretic missiles. Behind him rose the clamor of the French knights struggling into hauberks, buckling on swords, shouting names of their patron saints and their crusader war cry, "God wills it!"

A cruel God, if He wills this, Roland thought.

The Cathars had to cross a rock-strewn ridge, barely wide enough for two men abreast, that connected their stronghold on the main peak of Mont Ségur to the lower peak, where the crusaders had their hastily built siege fort. If any Cathars had spied Roland coming out, by the time they got to this spot, he would be hidden among the boulders farther down the slope. Having no intention of fighting the Cathars, he sheathed his sword. He took his sword belt off and buckled it across his shoulder and chest, so that sword and dagger hung down his back.

With the tips of his fingers Roland touched the red silk cross on the left breast of his black surcoat, wishing he could tear away the symbol he hated. But only by joining the crusaders had he been able to get here. And this night he would bring Diane out safely, or he would die.

He stood in the darkness breathing deeply, gathering himself for the effort. Despite his chain mail and his helmet, he felt vulnerable, frightened.

Crouching, he slipped away to the left. Beyond the narrow rim of the ridge, the slope fell steeply. A misstep would send him hurtling to the rocks below. He made his way down carefully, painstakingly, over the large boulders for long minutes until he arrived at a narrow ledge about thirty feet below the top of the ridge. He took cover behind a row of charred huts where Cathar hermits had dwelt before the siege began. This whole mountain stank of burnt wood. As he began to work his way around to the other peak, from behind him issued shouts in the dialect of Languedoc: the Cathars, raising their war cries. They must have reached the crusader fort. How wonderful if they managed to drive the crusaders off the mountaintop!

The sharp rocks jabbed and bruised Roland's feet through the thin leather of his boot soles. He wore as little mail as he dared. As it was, the work of clambering around a peak in the Pyrenees weighed down by his fifty-pound shirt of steel mesh was bound to exhaust him soon. His best protection, he hoped, was the black cloak that would hide his movements from the men of either side.

The battle cries of northern crusaders and Languedoc Cathars were now so mingled that Roland could not tell one from the other. Swords boomed on wooden shields and rang on steel helmets. Screams pierced the night, some fading into the darkness below as men plunged off the mountaintop to their deaths.

But the clamor of battle diminished as Roland on his ledge crossed to the north side. The limestone wall of the fortress glowed faintly under the stars, rising above Roland like the hull of a ship. Like the Ark atop Mount Ararat, he thought. Only this ark could not save those who sought refuge in her. Against the pale background of the wall a sloping boulder stuck out, huge and black. Roland's father, who had visited this place years ago, had written him saying, "The top of the great stone is only ten feet below the top of the parapet, and an agile man can make it over the wall there. You should be able to do it, if you have not let the wine and women of France ruin your body ere now.''

Roland could make out cracks and crevices in the century-old wall where he might dig in with fingers and toes. Still, it would be a far more fearsome climb than his father had made it sound. Taking a running start, Roland scrambled up the huge rock. Atop the boulder, he threw himself flat against the wall and reached up high, finding a fissure that afforded him a grip. Then he felt about with his right toe until it slipped into a crack between stones. Maybe now he would have the leverage to push himself upward. His limbs ached from clinging to the wall, but he could only inch his way up. He dared not look over his shoulder. Behind and below him, he knew, was black, empty space. Right hand up, right foot, left hand up, left foot, he crawled upward until at last the palm of his hand touched the blessed flatness of the top. He let out the breath he hadn't even been aware he was holding. He raised himself up a little further and slid both arms over the wall and hauled himself to lie flat along the top.

Now at last he could let himself look down into the chasm. Hundreds of fires flickered like stars in the crusaders' main camp at the base of the mountain. The dots of brightness wavered before his eyes. Dizziness swept over him. Fright made his heart thud like a stone-caster, and he gripped the wall under him so hard that his fingernails broke. He had to use all his remaining strength to force himself up to a kneeling position. He made no effort to conceal himself.

He heard at once a shrill cry of alarm from the darkness within the wall. A woman's voice. He could just barely see a wooden platform about four feet below. He dropped to it and raised his empty hands as three dark figures approached.

"I am one man, not the crusader army, madame," he called. "I come in amity."

He heard a murmur of women's voices and strained to look about him, but the only light came from a vertical slit in a stone building some distance away. A shift in the breeze brought an animal stench that assaulted him. How these people have suffered, Roland thought, overwhelmed with pity even as the smell made him almost ill. Under siege for nearly a year, the Cathars could spare no water for bathing.

"May I come down?" Roland called to the huddled figures he could faintly descry in the darkness below.

"Drop your weapons to us and we will let you live a bit longer, at least," one of the women called.

Roland unbuckled and dangled the heavy weapons over the side of the platform. A slender figure stepped out of the shadows and caught the longsword's scabbard. Roland found a ladder and moved gingerly down it until his feet met flat paving stones. He turned and stood with his back to the wall, facing a row of low wooden buildings a few feet away.

Three gaunt women gathered around him. Two brought the points of their spears within inches of his face. Another aimed a crossbow at him. A twitch of her finger and that bolt would pierce him through as if his hauberk were no more than a cotton shirt. More danger here than clinging by his fingernails on the face of the mountain.

He stood very still, towering over the women, staring down at them. They looked aged, probably far beyond their years. Their eyes glittered with hate.

The crossbow woman spoke. "If you are a friend, why are you not out there fighting beside our men? Why are you wearing the sign of a crusader?" She hissed the last word.

"There is someone here whom I have come to rescue."

"Rescue? Nonsense," another said contemptuously. "We are going to die very soon now. Any among us who hoped for escape gave it up months ago. Death is our escape—from the power of the Evil One."

"Still, I want to try." Inwardly he reproached himself. He'd imagined they would welcome him like a hero. He should have anticipated how they would feel.

"Liar!" the second woman spat. "Spy!" Her spear point was almost at his right eye. He had to call on all his strength of will to keep from flinching back. Were all his pains to reach Diane going to end, absurdly, here?

"How can we know that you are telling the truth?" said the woman with the crossbow.

"Look within yourself," Roland said, keeping his voice calm, though inside he was in turmoil. "All things that are, are lights. The light shines in each man and each woman."

He noticed the spear points wavering a little, and a deep gratitude flowed from him to Diane. She had long ago taught him those sayings.

"Satan himself can quote the inspired word," the first woman said. "What do you know of the true meaning of what you are saying?"

Roland shrugged. "I know it expresses one of the deepest teachings of your faith."

"Is it not also your faith, then?" asked the woman. "Are you not one of us?"

"If I were a liar and a spy as you think, I would claim to be one of you. But since I am an honest man and a friend, I tell you I was raised as a Catholic. I am Roland de Vency, born here in Languedoc. You may have heard of my father, Arnaut de Vency."

"De Vency? The Sire Arnaut? I remember him. A Catholic, but as fierce a fighter against the crusaders as any of our own men." The woman lowered her crossbow.

Roland expelled a long, relieved breath. "My father loved Languedoc," he said. "So do I. The crusaders are our enemies, too. And I am here because I love a woman here."

"Let us take him to the perfecti, Corba," said the second woman. "They shall decide. But, Sire de Vency, if you make a single move that puts us in doubt of you, we will run you through."

They walked through an alley between darkened wooden buildings. The suffocating odor and an eerie silence told Roland that behind the shut doorways people were listening, waiting.

He saw no guard at the entrance to the stone keep. Doubtless every able man had joined the attack on the crusaders. Roland's escorts leaned their weapons beside a tall double door and pulled it open. As he stepped within, he blinked. Only a few candles lit the room, but his eyes had gotten used to the night's darkness.

The keep of Mont Ségur, he knew, was a most sacred place of the Cathar church. Yet, as Roland looked around the large room, he could see no adornments anywhere, save for white candles in black wrought-iron candelabra. As a place of religion it seemed strangely bare. He was used to churches resplendent with brightly painted statues. Yet the plainness spoke of humility and peace.

The room was crowded with men and women, intermingled, standing with heads bowed. Some prayed aloud, some silently. All were bareheaded and wore black robes. Roland was awestruck. He had seen Cathar perfecti many times before, but never so many in one place. His parents, though they were Catholics, had taught him to admire the holy ones of the other religion as saints, almost angels, because of their heroic virtue and simplicity of life. The spectacle of so many of these good men and women gathered together was overwhelming.

Even though the room was full of people, the smell of unbathed bodies was fainter here. Roland did not doubt that the perfecti shared the hardships of all within this fortress, but their austerity seemed to have purified their flesh.

Roland saw beyond them, at the far end, an ancient, white-haired man who sat in a plain wooden chair on a stone dais. Roland knew he must be their spiritual leader, Bishop Bertran d'en Marti, sometimes called the Pope of the Cathar church.

Diane would not be here, Roland thought. She probably would be out there in the wooden building with the credentes, those men and women who had not taken holy vows and who were seeing to the defense of the stronghold. The perfecti, Roland knew, never bore arms.

A young man came over, his black robe swirling around a body that seemed no thicker than a lance pole. The woman called Corba told him about Roland's climbing over the wall. The perfectus stared at the cross on Roland's chest.

Roland sensed his revulsion. "Forgive me for offending you. I had to wear this to get through to you." He dug his ragged fingernails in under the red silk and tore away the cross. The sound of ripping cloth in the quiet room made heads turn. Roland dropped the strips of silk to the floor.

"Who is that?" said Bertran d'en Marti in a voice that was soft yet carried across the room. "Does he bring news?"

Roland strode across the room before anyone could stop him and knelt at Bishop Bertran's sandaled feet. He reached for the old man's hand. It was as light and small as a bird's wing, and Roland's large fingers held it with care as he pressed his lips to the shiny knuckles. When he was growing up, Roland had often heard stories of Bishop Bertran, especially how, years ago, he had debated and won against the famous Catholic preacher Saint Dominic. The bishop must be over ninety, Roland thought. His face was skeletal and wreathed by wisps of white hair. His dark brown eyes glowed with an inner illumination.

"I wish you had not treated the cross with such scorn, young man," Bishop Bertran said in a voice that was like the rustling of parchment. "Our greatest failing has been disrespect for the religion of our opponents. We cannot build a sound church on hatred. Who are you, my son?"

"Your Holiness, I am Roland de Vency. I am a troubadour and a knight. I have also been a faidit, an exile from this land. My parents, my sister, and I fled with a price on our heads. Now I have come back to Languedoc."

The bishop's penetrating eyes held Roland's "You are dark and have a Roman face, like our southern people. But you are tall and blue-eyed like the men of the north. I sense in you a mixture, a union of north and south, of Frank and Gaul. A tormented union, even as this land is tortured by war between northern and southern Frenchmen. You are a sorrowful man—you wear somber colors, for a troubadour. You have trouble living with yourself, my son. You do not know who you are.''

Roland's chest ached at this reminder of the secret shame of his birth. And he felt fear as well, at the power of this mind that could so easily penetrate his heart.

"Doubtless you are named for the ancient hero Roland, whom *The Song of Roland* tells us died fighting Saracens in these very mountains," the bishop went on. "And the name, perhaps, has inspired you to perilous deeds. Why have you come to this place, Roland de Vency?"

"Your Holiness, I seek the woman I love, Diane de Combret."

A buzzing murmur came from behind Roland, and the bishop's eyes widened.

"Diane is of your faith, Your Holiness, and I was raised a Catholic, but before I fled into exile we loved each other and were betrothed. The war tore us apart. I took a new name and came back to look for her, but it was as if she had vanished. Then I learned that she is here, and I pretended to join the crusaders. I entered the camp of my enemies so that I could rescue her from them.'' He spread his arms wide. "If I could save all here, I would. But I am only one knight. If all the gallant warriors who defend this place cannot defeat your enemies, can I? But perhaps I can save this one woman's life, which is precious to me above all others.''

Bishop Bertran gazed kindly and sadly at him. "Diane? She is here, my son. She has heard all of your brave speech." He gestured with a frail hand.

Roland felt himself starting to tremble. Diane, here in this room? Unsteadily he rose from his knees and turned.

He saw her before him, tall, pale in a long black robe. The candlelight suddenly seemed to grow brighter. The subtle flush in her cheeks, her long shining hair, her huge eyes—Diane had appeared, and color was reborn in the world.

"Roland, Roland," she said. "How did you get here? Roland, I am so happy to see you."

The sound of her voice came to him like the most beautiful of songs played on a well-seasoned vielle. He could not speak. He was stunned, yet more fully conscious than he had ever been.

Diane was crying now, tears streaming down her cheeks. She reached out to embrace him.

Then she checked herself. With an obvious effort, she pulled her arms down to her sides and stepped back, her eyes still fixed on his but now full of misery.

He fell to his knees. "Diane, I love you." The crowd of perfecti was watching him, but he didn't care.

"It is no longer possible"—she shook her head—"for you to speak so."

He knelt there, desolate. His mind had finally grasped what had already penetrated his heart.

He knew now what he had suspected from her presence here. She had taken the consolamentum. She was a perfecta. She could no longer know human love.

His heart weighted his chest like a lump of iron. Pain spread from that crushing center to fill his body and limbs with anguish.

He stood up. "Your people's stone-caster just missed me a while ago. I wish it had not."

"Oh, Roland, if only I could share my joy with you," she said softly. "No man could have won me away from you. Every day I heard your voice singing in my heart. But even your songs could not rival the sweetness of God's own music."

Diane wore no ornament, but her long red-gold hair, hanging in ringlets to her shoulders, adorned her more gloriously than any jewelry might have. Her eyes, neither blue nor brown, were a mixture, a catlike green. Her face had always been fine-boned; now months of fasting had put shadows in her cheeks that made her look like an angel on a cathedral pillar.

"I must bow to what you have done, Diane," he said. "But if you will not come with me as my beloved, come as a perfecta. I can smuggle you through the crusader lines. Let me save your life."

Before Diane could answer, the door crashed open. The shrieks and wails of women assailed his ears. From a distance came the shouts of men in combat. The stone floor under Roland's feet vibrated, and he heard the crashing of rock on wood.

A group of women staggered in bearing a wounded man wrapped in a blue cloak. Roland stepped aside as the women laid their burden gently before the bishop. The cloak fell away, and Roland saw that a sword had cleft the man's shoulder. His arm hung by a thread. The women tried to stanch the flow of blood by pressing cloths against the wound.

"Your Holiness," the dying young man gasped. "I beg the consolamentum."

"You shall be saved, Arnald my son, and return to the One Light." The bishop got up from his chair with surprising agility, then knelt. He pressed his hand to the dying man's forehead and whispered words over him.

Roland felt himself moved by the simplicity of the ritual. Yet this was the very sacrament, he thought with bitterness, that had taken Diane from him.

"Arnald de Lantar," Diane whispered to Roland. "One of our best."

Roland felt pity for the dying man. That could be me. I could take this man's place. I could join these people in their good fight. I could kill many a crusader, and joyfully.

But more good would I do if I saved this one lady.

When the bishop's soft words ceased, Arnald de Lantar spoke again through his pain. "I am sorry, Your Holiness. We have failed you. Bernart Roainh and Peire Ferrier . . . killed. Our men . . . many fell. Fell from the mountain as we retreated. Too many crusaders . . . too strong." His eyes closed.

One of the women put her hand on his heart. Then, weeping, the women who had brought him in rose up and carried the body away.

Bishop Bertran turned to Diane with a sigh. "My child, do you wish to go with Sire Roland? I fear these are our final free moments."

"No, Your Holiness," Diane said firmly.

Roland felt himself slump in despair.

"Please, dear Bishop Bertran," she went on. "To leave here, to be safe, while my brethren are dying? It would destroy me. It would hurt me as much as if I were to commit the gravest of sins."

"How can it be a sin to want to live?" Roland pleaded.

"For us death is victory," said Diane, her green eyes shining. "But if the life of anyone should be saved, there are many of more value than mine. Your talk of spiriting me through the crusader lines is only a frivolous troubadour fancy." She turned away as again the doors to the keep opened.

Roland stood alone, burning with shame and anger.

More wounded were carried in and laid in rows on the floor. Calmly, lovingly, the black-robed perfecti, Diane among them, moved along the lines of fallen men. Bishop Bertran walked slowly past them, giving instructions. "Treat this wound at once," he said. "That man will be all right for a time." To those who appeared near death he gave the consolamentum and walked on. Any of the perfecti could have administered the Sacrament, but Roland sensed that it was a special joy for these dying men to receive it from the bishop's hands.

Watching Diane attend the wounded, Roland brooded. He had come all the way from Paris, risking his life over and over again for her, giving up all other women for her—including the beautiful Countess Nicolette. How could she scorn his effort? How could she dismiss his plan because a troubadour thought of it? Yes, he was a troubadour, a maker of songs, and proud of his art. She had loved his songs once.

How old had he been when Peire Cardenal came to Château Combret?

It had been August of the year after the eighth King Louis died and the ninth was crowned. That would make it one thousand two hundred twenty-seven. Seventeen years ago, so Roland was ten—two years younger than the new boy-king. Roland's family, in flight from the crusaders who had invaded Languedoc, had been guests of the de Combrets, a prosperous Cathar family, for many months. Their château was in Provence, east of Languedoc, where the crusade and the persecutions had not yet penetrated. A score or more people, the de Combrets and the de Vencys and their retainers and gentlefolk from the countryside around, sat at tables in the great hall. Dozens of candles lighted the hall for the occasion.

Diane usually sat beside Roland's sister, Fiorela, but tonight, for some reason, she had placed her chair next to Roland's. He was aware of a tingling excitement in his limbs.

It was partly anticipation of the songs of the great troubadour, Cardenal. But Roland knew these strange feelings had also to do with the slender girl, only nine years old, who sat beside him, her hair so red that it seemed afire.

"Will you sing for Peire Cardenal?" she asked him.

He felt as though a rock from a stone gun had gone right through him.

"Why would the greatest troubadour in the land want to hear me?" Roland shrank his skinny frame down behind the trestle table, as if someone had already called on him to play. "I am lucky just to be hearing him." The Combret jongleur, Guacelm, who had taught him the lute and promised to start him on the vielle, had said Roland's was a gift from God. But how much could Guacelm know? He was only a jongleur, not a troubadour.

Roland worked as hard as he could under Guacelm, but he never admitted, even to his teacher, that sometimes, alone in the hills, singing to rocks and trees, he dreamed of being a troubadour. He saw himself commanding words and verses as kings commanded their barons, holding seigneurs and their ladies fascinated by the power of his voice, drawing intricate music from lute and lyre and gittern by the skill in his fingers. Sometimes he forgot he was the son of a hunted outlaw and imagined himself welcomed and honored everywhere.

"I think your music is lovely." Diane's green eyes held his. He loved Diane as much as he loved Fiorela. She was another sister to him, a sister whose fragile beauty inspired protectiveness. But more. When he looked at Diane he understood why men wanted to be knights.

His sister would grow up and marry and part from him. Diane need never part from him.

The servants had cleared away the bread and meats and were bringing around silver basins so that all could wash their hands after dinner.

The Sire Etienne de Combret asked Peire Cardenal, seated at his right at the high table, if he would favor them with a song.

Cardenal took his place in the center of the hall. He was a stocky man with iron-gray hair and a battered nose that spread over his seamed face. He beckoned, and Guacelm came out and sat with a vielle between his knees. The hall fell silent, and Cardenal sang a lament for a lady who had died young. The sweet notes of his voice soared above Guacelm's bowed accompaniment, and when the song died away at last, Roland glanced at Diane and saw there were tears in her eyes.

The applause was vigorous, but Cardenal smiled and cleared his throat. "I get merrier as we go along," he said, and everyone laughed.

And he did. He sang songs of heroic deeds in battle, and comic songs. A servant placed a silver goblet set with jewels on the table within his reach and kept it refilled, Cardenal drinking deeply after each song. He began to sing sirventes about happenings of the day, about the rumor that the widowed Queen Mother of the present King of France had taken the Count of Champagne as a lover, about the Pope threatening to excommunicate Frederic, the Holy Roman Emperor, for failing to lead a crusade to the Holy Land. He sang a tenson with Guacelm, a debate on whether a man could truly love two women at once. Cardenal took the affirmative, and the applause of the de Combrets' guests declared him the winner. Much as he admired Cardenal, Roland, who shyly abstained from applauding either side, was sure that a man could love—truly love—only one woman. Roland's own father, he knew, had never loved anyone but his mother.

The wine affected Cardenal's singing not at all. If anything, it sweetened his baritone voice. He sang a duet with Diane's mother, Madame Maretta, who wrote poems of her own and had taught the forms of rhyme and meter to Roland.

Then Cardenal sang of love, songs which, Roland knew, were of his own making. He sang of love that lasted forever, love that defied human laws and even the commands of God, love that consumed men and women like a fire, love that blinded with its light.

Roland found his hand tightly gripping Diane's delicate fingers.

When Cardenal had sung his last song, the applause was muted, but only because all were so moved. Roland felt limp, drained. His hand, still holding Diane's, trembled. Reluctantly he released her, afraid someone might see, and tease him.

After a silence Sire Etienne pushed the jeweled goblet across the table toward Cardenal.

"Drink from this tonight and keep it with you always, Master Peire. A poor thing, compared to your music. But a remembrance of one of the most beautiful evenings of my life."

Cardenal bowed. "A handsome present, monseigneur."

What a power he has, Roland thought. He must have sung for hours, and everybody wishes he would go on for the rest of the night. I could never hold people spellbound like that. It is foolish of me to dabble in music.

The diners stirred. Sire Etienne, Sire Arnaut, and Cardenal stood talking at the table. Guacelm, the jongleur, joined them.

And then Roland saw that Guacelm was pointing down the table at him. The terror came back, and he wanted to run out of the room.

Arnaut de Vency, his dark face creased in a smile, beckoned. Roland sat paralyzed.

"Go, Roland," Diane whispered. "You must go."

Dragging his feet, he went to where the men stood. Peire Cardenal fixed him with fierce eyes.

"I am told you are learning to sing and play, my lad. Are you any good at it?"

"Indifferent, monseigneur," said Roland in a small voice.

"Do not 'monseigneur' me, boy," Cardenal growled. "I am a baker's son, nothing more. What claim to respect I have is here and here." He touched his hand to his forehead and his throat.

"To me, that means a good deal more than gentle birth," said Arnaut de Vency. Embarrassed, Roland could not look at his father.

"Too many of our good troubadours spend their lives—and lose their lives—fighting the so-called crusaders who have invaded Languedoc," said Cardenal. "There are but two or three practicing the art now. We need new blood. Let us hear what you can do, boy."

Roland's mother, Dame Adalys, joined the group. "Roland, sing a song of your own—the one about the pines."

Roland thought he would rather face a host of Frankish crusaders with drawn swords.

Sire Etienne called for silence, and everyone sat down to listen. Guacelm thrust the lute and a plectrum into Roland's hands, and his father gave him a gentle tug, starting him toward the center of the floor. He had to walk around the table. He passed Diane.

She squeezed his arm and whispered, "You will be wonderful!"

In a semi-trance he walked out into the center of the room, the lute big and heavy in his hands. With his head lifted as Cardenal had held himself moments ago, he stood briefly silent as he strove to collect his wits. He prayed he would remember all the words to his own song. He had sung it, mostly without audience, many times, but still he felt unsure. He let the melody begin rippling through his mind. Then, holding the plectrum tight between thumb and forefinger, he picked out the introductory notes.

He looked at Diane, her green eyes shining in the candlelight. He took a deep breath and began to sing. His fingers moved on the lute of their own accord. His soprano voice vibrated in his throat. He let his gaze sweep the room, but he sang for Diane alone.

"The trees on the mountains in summer are green
But are stripped of their robes in the fall.
When the snow shrouds the hills,
Then the whole world seems dead,
But the pines remain green through it all."

It was a short song, only three verses, and even as he sang them he felt he could hear with Cardenal's ears the echoes of other tunes, the trite lyrics. But when he thought he could not go on, he looked at Diane and felt better about his song.

The applause and cheers were louder and longer than he had expected. They are kind to me because I am Arnaut's son, he told himself. He bowed deeply.

He left the lute and plectrum on the table. He was too embarrassed to face even Guacelm. People were starting to talk to one another again. Mercifully, his song was forgotten.

He hurried through a side door and up a spiral stair to a battlemented lookout tower two stories above the main hall. There he went out and breathed deeply of the cool air, scented of the sea whose shore was not far from Château de Combret. He leaned against the hard edge of a merlon.

The oak door creaked behind him. A broad figure appeared in the starlight.

"Well, what the devil did you rush off like that for, boy? Think yourself too good for us?"

Roland shrank inside. "I could never be as good as you, Master Peire."

"To the devil with comparisons. I do not know how good I am, and neither do you. The thing is to know yourself good enough to be a troubadour."

"But how can I know that?"

Cardenal's face came close to Roland's, and Roland smelled the wine on his breath. "You know you are because I tell you, and it takes a troubadour to recognize another troubadour."

The stocky man clapped him on the shoulder. The heavy blow hurt, but it made him think of the moment when, at the touch of his seigneur's sword, a squire becomes a knight.

"I could be a troubadour?" Roland felt light-headed, as if he were floating above the balcony, drifting toward the stars.

Cardenal snorted. "Do not be so quickly overjoyed, boy. It is not an easy life. Singing for your supper, that is what it comes down to."

"Yes," said Roland in a small voice, wanting to disagree but afraid to.

"There is something more important to a troubadour than singing and playing," Cardenal went on.

"What is that?"

"Love. Even before he is a maker of songs, a troubadour is a man in love. You are too young to know love. But you will, and your love will be as vast as the ocean. Sometimes it will hurt worse than the torments of the damned. Love unlocks the deepest places of the heart. You need a lady, a goddess, to inspire you. Without her, you will be nothing.''

Roland had heard countless love songs, sung them himself. He had some sense of what it was that drew men and women to each other. But this talk of Cardenal's confused him. He said nothing.

"In love is the highest happiness known to man," Cardenal said. "And it is given to troubadours, of all men, to see deepest into this mystery whose laws have been in the keeping of women since time out of memory. Remember what I say, but think no more about it for now. Your father will tell you when you are ready."

Moments later, Roland wandered through the darkened great hall on his way to bed, his head a melee of thoughts, frightening and joyful. I must love always, he thought. Yes, I understand that much. A troubadour is a man in love.

He saw in his mind a girl-child with red hair and transparent skin looking at him and saying, "You will be wonderful!"

Yes, he thought. It is Diane. I may be too young, but I love her even now, and when we are older I will tell her. I will be her troubadour, and I will love her for all of my life.

But now Diane had taken herself from him, had chosen to become one with those who lived between this world and heaven. Her choice was the consolamentum, not the song of the troubadour. And as he watched her moving among the last of the wounded, he realized how much finer her goal was. He had no right to feel any claim upon her now.

His attention was drawn to the bishop, who had finished his ministrations and returned to his chair. Spreading out his arms, he beckoned the men and women who were the flower of his church.

"My children, this battle we have lost tonight must be our last. The time for fighting is past, if ever there was such a time. Our people should never have taken up arms. It only provoked our enemies to greater violence. Now I intend to order our knights to surrender."

From everywhere around him Roland heard sighs, groans, quiet weeping. But he heard no protest. They have accepted their fate, he thought. Perhaps they even welcome it.

With a sad smile Bishop Bertran looked about the hall. "Diane. Please come to me, my child."

She approached, lovely and stately, and Roland felt the breath stop in his throat. She bowed her head, her flame-red hair glowing.

"Diane," he said softly, "perhaps God has sent this brave man for a purpose. There are messages we must send to the outside world. We have hidden much of the wealth of our church, and word of the hiding place must be carried to our brethren who will survive us. You must carry it, Diane."

Diane opened her mouth to protest, but Bishop Bertran silenced her with a gentle wave of his hand. "You will also take with you our Holy Vessel and the ancient books that were brought to us from the East. Prepare to leave, my child."

Diane again bent her head. "Your will must prevail over mine, good bishop. But I envy you your martyrdom. And perhaps because I envy you I am not worthy of dying with you."

But Roland's heart gave a mighty leap. Diane would be coming with him.

II

DIANE'S HEART FELT LEADEN AS SHE PREPARED TO LEAVE. EACH FACE she looked at, she knew she was seeing for the last time. As if *she* were dying and *they* all were going to live on. Oh, why must I leave? Now, when all of you are about to put on the martyr's crown, how can you cast me out? I want to die with you. I do not want to go on, stumbling through this world alone.

For years these people had been her only family. When she was a child, her faith was preached and practiced openly all over the south of France. The crusade was already twenty years old then, but the perfecti still taught crowds of people in the streets of great cities like Toulouse and Béziers, still won converts away from the Church of Rome. From the lords and ladies in their castles to the peasants on the mountainsides, over half the people were Cathars. Now this year, one thousand two hundred forty-four, might come to be remembered as the year Catharism in France disappeared. From now on there would be nothing but a remnant in hiding, having to sneak about. No, she didn't want to live that way. She longed to throw herself down and beg

Bishop Bertran once again to let her stay. But duty pressed down upon her like a mail shirt. It was burdensome, but it protected her from error. She quietly made ready.

Before long, Diane and Roland were standing on the northeast wall amid a group of perfecti. From a family that had taken refuge on Mont Ségur had come a red and green costume for Diane, the tunic and hose of a well-to-do boy, an equerry. They had cut her hair short and tucked it under a cap topped with a long partridge feather. They had sewn the red cross back on Roland's black surcoat, and had made one for Diane's tunic from a gentlewoman's crimson scarf. A rope to form a sling was tied around her waist and another around her knees. Roland was similarly tied.

"I am as helpless as a baby," he whispered to her with that one-sided grin she remembered so well.

Tears welled up in her as she looked at the black-robed men and women here to bid her farewell. Dear Bishop Bertran reached up to her. She bent, made awkward by the ropes, and kissed the back of his hand, her tears falling on his white skin.

"I do not want to leave you. I want to die with you."

"Your death will come to you when it is time. May it be a happy one. Go with grace, my child."

Diane felt Roland reach out and squeeze her hand. His firm strength comforted her. But his touching her was against the rule by which she lived. A new anxiety chilled her. She was in Roland's care now. What would happen? What might being close to him do to her? She had loved him greatly. If he had not fled, become a faidit, she might never have taken the consolamentum. She had to be vigilant.

Roland tugged at the separate ropes that held them, making sure they were secure. Then he gave her a gentle push. She felt a choking fear. Whispering the Lord's Prayer to hold her terror at bay, she stepped off into the emptiness beyond the mountaintop. She could see no lights below to show her where the bottom was.

Her life was in the hands of those above holding the rope and slowly paying it out. The rope cut into her waist and thighs. To ease its bite she pulled her body upward with her hands, thankful for the deerskin gloves that would save her hands from being rubbed raw. Her arms ached. She was fortunate, she knew, that she carried very little extra weight. Only a small pack strapped to her back for the plain gold chalice called the Holy Vessel. A most sacred object, it could be borne only by one of the perfecti.

She looked up and, against the torchlight cast from above, saw Roland descending with his weapons and his mail shirt and the large pack holding two big books. He must be in much greater pain than she. And what a dreadful weight, too, for those above to hold, with their starvation-weakened arms. She prayed they would not drop him. She prayed, too, for God to give Roland and her the fortitude to bear whatever might befall them.

As she swung farther down she could barely see Roland. She tried to stay close to him and called softly to him from time to time. She felt better whenever she heard his deep voice answering.

Gradually she could discern, outlined by a diminishing field of stars, the black shapes of other peaks surrounding Mont Ségur rising over their heads. She felt as if she were being lowered into the pit of Hell itself.

She pictured herself hanging in midair, hundreds of feet above the forest in the valley, and her stomach clenched. Her body swung slowly from side to side, and she hugged the creaking rope with desperate terror. Stabbing pains in her wrists and arms made her doubt she could cling to it much longer.

From above, she could still faintly hear crashing and clanging, screams and shouts. At any moment the crusaders might break through and find the perfecti holding these ropes, while Roland and she dangled helpless above the rocks.

She pictured her brethren being cut down by those huge longswords, their blood running out over the sacred stones. She sobbed aloud. She heard Roland say something in a low voice, some word of comfort, no doubt, but she could not make out the words.

She lost track of time. It seemed just minutes ago that she had said her goodbyes. And, equally, it seemed an eternity. Would they never reach bottom? The rope around her waist felt as if it might cut her in two.

Suddenly her feet kicked loose rocks and then struck solid ground. Her legs were too weak to hold her up, as if there were no blood in them, and she collapsed. But she didn't mind the bruising fall, so good did it feel to have the earth under her. Roland, who had also fallen to his hands and knees, crawled over and knelt beside her. She wanted him to hold her, but she was terrified of his arms.

Then she looked up and saw that the mountain peak wore a crown of flame. "Oh, dear God, no," she whispered. The fire arrows of the crusaders must have ignited the wooden buildings.

"We called it Mont Ségur, the Safe Mountain," she said to

Roland, gazing up at the fire. "We thought God would protect us up there. We should have remembered that God—the true God—does not rule this world. His Adversary does."

Unwillingly, she looked up again and saw that the flames had grown paler, and the sky beyond them was not black, but violet. A rose glow, not fire but the rising sun, appeared behind the tops of the pine-covered hills east of Mont Ségur. Their long descent from the mountaintop, she realized, had taken from the middle of the night until dawn.

Under her thin silk tunic she trembled, partly from the cold. She rubbed her hands together to warm them, and when she blew on them her breath was a frosty cloud. Spring was still a few weeks away, but the people on the mountaintop would never see it.

With cramped fingers she began to undo the knots around her waist and knees. Roland helped her, and she quivered anew at his touch.

"Come away, Diane. Do not look up there anymore. We need your eyes on the path ahead."

She forced herself to stand. She looked at Roland and could see in the faint dawn light that he, too, looked exhausted.

But she knew it would do them no good to stay still in this cold when they were soaked with sweat.

"You know this forest," he said. "The crusaders' camp lies beside the village at the base of the mountain. You must lead the way."

She sighed and gestured to him to follow her.

As they turned their backs on the heights from which they had just descended, the ropes came whistling down, coil upon coil. There was little chance that the crusaders would venture down here and come upon these ropes at the edge of the forest; they would never know anyone had escaped from Mont Ségur. Gratitude welled up in her to the faithful ones above who had held those ropes till they were safely down.

She walked beside Roland into the deep pine forest. She glanced over at him. His face was darker than she remembered, and bonier. The nose seemed as sharp and thin as an ax blade. He had pushed his helmet back, and his thick black hair ringed his face. He turned and looked at her, and his vivid blue eyes, so startling in his dark face, sent a thrill through her. My God, she thought despairingly, help me. This is going to be so very hard.

"Why must we go to the crusader camp, Roland?"

"My tent and my jongleur are there. I really had to join their army, you see. It was the only way I could get up there." He gestured toward the mountain.

The thought of being among the crusaders filled her with dread. "Roland, I cannot."

"You will be safe there. No one would expect to find a Cathar in the midst of that army." His tone soured. "Especially not a perfecta."

He will never understand what my faith means to me, she thought sadly.

They walked along in silence for a time. The air was filled with the fragrance of pines. Her lungs drank it in. She had almost forgotten, after nearly a year trapped in the fortress, the sweet smell of clean air. But that her lost people could not share in even this small pleasure only redoubled her pain.

She moved on, holding branches for Roland so they would not fly back in his face. She stepped nimbly over roots and rocks. Her body moved briskly, but her soul was heavy.

"You walk so surely," Roland said suddenly. "Like a deer. And going down the side of the mountain—few women could endure such an ordeal. When I last saw you, Diane, you were a delicate lady. Now you are a mountaineer."

His words made her feel a glow inside. "Among us there are no ladies. Women work the same as men. The holy work, too. Before the siege I was traveling all over Languedoc. I preached, Roland. I brought the Sacrament to people who needed it."

He stared at her in wonder. "How do your mother and father feel about the work you do now?"

She halted abruptly. Roland, startled, stopped just behind her. She turned to face him.

"I am sure they are very happy about me. They both died, you see, last year. The inquisitors made them wear the yellow cross of heretics and turned them out on the roads to beg. They were too old to survive the winter. But they had a good death. I reached them in time and gave them each the consolamentum."

"Oh, Diane!" He held his arms out to her.

She managed a backward step and a warning gesture, despite her grief.

He turned his back on her, his hands to his face. "Will you not let me comfort you?" he cried.

"It is all right." She felt choked all through. "It is all right. Let us walk on."

She pushed on before him for at least an hour. Boughs slapped her face, and she slipped sometimes on patches of snow that remained in the cold, low places of the forest. Her leather boots were soaked through, and her toes were numb with cold. Just when she thought she could not take another step, she felt a tap on her shoulder. Roland, tired out, too, gestured toward a fallen tree trunk, and she sat down.

She took off her cap, wiped her forehead, and shook out what was left of her chopped-off hair. Her head felt strange and light. She shrugged out of her pack and set it on the ground with gentle reverence. Roland did the same.

She looked at him and saw a yearning in his eyes that frightened her. It reminded her of days when he and she were much younger. She remembered a mountain meadow and white poppies, the taste of his lips. And a poem he wrote for her:

> That which delights both woman and man
> Is praise to Him who made them.

She was swept by a sudden wave of longing, and with it came the unbidden thought: If only I could be that girl of fifteen again.

The strength of her feelings shocked her. She had always been proud of her maturity, felt blessed that she had been able to grasp the deep truths of her faith and to turn her back on this world. In Roland's presence, was she succumbing again to illusion?

Surely I would be better off facing death on the mountain, she thought.

She laid her head on her folded arms and wondered what was happening to all those she loved on Mont Ségur. Perhaps even now they were being tied to stakes for burning. She wanted to weep, but she reminded herself that those who died were fortunate. The body was like a clay vessel inside which a ray of pure light was trapped. Death was the breaking of the clay and the liberating of the light.

"Are you crying, dear one?" Roland said gently.

"For those who must die up there on the mountain," she said, with a catch in her voice. "And for myself, because I will not die with them."

She looked up at Roland as she said this and saw the look of exasperation on his face. It is true, he cannot understand, she thought sadly. Never. I must leave him as soon as I can.

"Why do you want so much to sacrifice yourself?"

It was hopeless. He believed God made his body, that it was precious. He was a troubadour—devoted to love expressed through the body. His years as a faidit seemed to have left him unchanged.

"I am not sacrificing myself at all, Roland. Everything I do is *for* myself. Death is only going back to the Light we came from. When I see the Light, as I do from time to time, I am as happy as anyone can be. Such happiness . . . you cannot imagine how great it is."

"Greater than Love?"

She remembered how he had tried to instruct her in *l'amour courtois*, the religion of Love, before he and his family fled. If he had stayed, she wondered, what would I be now? How fortunate that I was left free to discover the Holy Light.

"Yes, the happiness I have found through my faith is greater than what you call Love."

"I do not believe that." He shook his head angrily. "By calling yourself a perfecta you pretend you are not human."

"I know how very human I am, and that word is a burden for me—for all of us," she answered gravely. "We do not claim to *be* perfect, but we try to live *as if* we were free of all attachment to the material world. And if we fail to live so, there is no forgiveness for us, no second chance."

He closed his eyes in pain, then turned them on her again, burning. "I cannot believe that God wants people to live like statues—or bodiless spirits. This life you have chosen, what is it but fear and hiding, knowing one day those pigs will catch you and burn you alive? Diane, I will take you anywhere you want. You will be safe with me. I will take you away from this war, to Italy. It is beautiful in Italy. There are places there where the Inquisition has no power. You can live as you like. Think of the children we could have."

Despite herself, again she yearned to stretch out her arms to him. More memories came back to her—listening to him sing and play the vielle in her father's great hall, roaming the pine-scented countryside with him, their kisses by a mountain stream. She fought down the sweet wave of tenderness.

"Roland, no. Never. I have taken a vow never to touch a man except, if need be, to save his life, or his soul."

His blue eyes stared at her, bright as the heart of a flame. If she kept looking into them, she feared, they would melt her. Her own soul was in peril.

"You made that vow not knowing that we would meet again. Be just to yourself."

"Even if I could change my mind, I would not want to." She put into her voice all the finality she could muster.

She saw his lips press together and his eyes grow moist.

She reached out to touch his shoulder, then drew back her hand before it came to rest.

"It is true I never thought I would see you again. Believe me, Roland, when I saw you standing there in the fortress I felt almost as much joy as in moments with the Light. The last I heard, you were in Avignon. Where have you been?"

"In Italy, in Sicily mostly." Roland's voice sounded as if he were dragging himself up out of a deep well of sadness. "The Inquisition was about to catch up with us at Avignon, so my mother and father and sister and I all journeyed on donkey back along the coast into Lombardy. From there we took ship to Palermo, where my father found work with Emperor Frederic."

A fond smile warmed Roland's sharp features. "The Emperor needs men who can read and write well, yet are not members of the clergy, to serve him in his endless quarrel with the Pope. So my father rose quickly in his service. He now holds high rank in the Imperial Chancery. He is very busy, but he finds time to write me many letters."

"I am glad for him," Diane said with feeling, though she thought again of her own father's death in a shepherd's hut. "What of your sister, dear Fiorela?"

"She married well, after I left them, to one of Frederic's noblemen, a Lorenzo Celino, knight of the Holy Roman Empire. My mother writes that he is a thoroughly *virtuous* man, which is rare for one of the Emperor's courtiers."

She had heard bad and good of Emperor Frederic—that he was dissolute, but that he allowed people to speak their minds.

"And you?" she asked with a smile. "Were you thoroughly virtuous while you were at the Emperor's court?"

He smiled back and shrugged. "I did what I like to do best. I had brought that dear old lute with me, the one I played before Peire Cardenal. I set myself to become a master troubadour. The Emperor has surrounded himself with some of the greatest poets and singers of our time, and I offered myself to them as a humble apprentice. They thought they could teach me something, and soon enough they had me performing my work before Frederic himself. I must have been a success, because after that I dined more often with the Emperor than my father did."

Diane remembered how many times Roland had sung to her alone, how his voice had seemed to draw her soul out of her body. So it was not love alone, she thought. If Emperor Frederic liked him, he really must be very good.

"Was it not hard for you," she said, "keeping up your skill while traveling from place to place?"

He shrugged. "Traveling is what troubadours do most. And wherever we stopped for any length of time, I made it my business to meet any other troubadour who might be in the district and to try to learn from him."

"And so at last the Emperor made you part of his court?"

Roland's face darkened. "He made use of me in other ways as well. Now that he rules southern Italy and Germany, he seeks to control northern Italy as well, and the Pope is determined to prevent him. I fought in the cities of Italy as one of the Emperor's Ghibellines in their battles against the Papal Guelphs. Frederic even knighted me himself. But even when I was in the thick of battle, lines of poetry were always springing into my mind. I would have been happier if I could have just written my music and sung it. The world would not let me do that. Any more than it will let *you* practice your faith."

"But surely you were better off at the Emperor's court than you are here. Why did you not stay there?"

"I love you," he said glumly.

Her heart wept for his pain.

"I love my country, too," he went on. "I dreamed constantly both of you and of Languedoc. I came back, and the first thing I did was look for you. But all my friends were dead or in exile, and people even told me that you were dead."

"Protecting me," she said. "The Inquisition is everywhere in the south of France. Picking the perfecti off one by one."

He nodded. "It was impossible even to find out whether you were alive, and sooner or later the inquisitors would have found out that Arnaut de Vency's son was back in Languedoc. So I moved up to Paris, where the inquisitors are not plying their trade as yet. And there I am known as Orlando of Perugia, an Italian knight. Trying to make my way as a troubadour. Then a letter came from my father. The Emperor had received an appeal for help from Mont Ségur. It gave names of those trapped there. Your name was on the list. My father, who knows this country well, also wrote how I might get into the fortress. I joined the Albigensian Crusade for you. And now I have found you again, and lost you. All I have left are my songs."

He stood up suddenly. "If we meet any crusaders here in the forest they will question us, and it will be hard to think of good answers. We must get to the camp, and that will take us most of the day."

His voice was bleak, Diane thought, that of a man trying to hide his feelings, perhaps even from himself.

Diane, terrified of going into the midst of thousands of enemy soldiers, felt an urge to run from Roland and hide herself in the depths of the forest. But she steeled herself to remember: *God is within me, and I need fear nothing.*

Many hours later, as they walked onward through the valley in the deep shadow of late afternoon, Diane looked up at the peaks to the west of Mont Ségur. They were jagged black silhouettes. Turning her eyes to the besieged mountain itself, she saw its top glowing golden in the light of the setting sun. Now Roland was leading the way, and they followed along the banks of a little mountain creek. The last time she had seen it, it had been clear as spring water. Now she was revolted by its brown color and the stench it gave off, like a town gutter.

She spied figures moving in the woods and froze.

"It is all right," said Roland. "That is just the camp of the rabble. The merchants and whores and thieves. They live on the army as fleas live on a dog."

Only partly reassured, she stooped and picked up some dirt and rubbed it over her face, roughening her skin to make it appear more like a man's. She insisted, too, on taking the heavy pack from Roland. It would seem odd for a knight to be burdened with anything other than his weapons.

Farther on, a lank-haired girl standing ankle-deep in the stream stared at Diane with glazed eyes. *She thinks I am a man,* Diane realized. The girl couldn't have been more than thirteen, but her belly bulged under her torn skirt. She pulled open her blouse to display pregnancy-swollen breasts in pathetic invitation. Diane turned away, unable to bear the sight. Life had crushed the child's spirit and left her little more than an animal. Could there be a worse crime than to get such a creature with child, forcing her to bring a baby into this suffering world? She heard a jingle and looked back at Roland. He had taken a silver denier from his belt, and tossed it to the girl.

After they had walked on, he said, "My mother might have been such a one as that if Arnaut de Vency had not rescued her. Carrying some crusader's get."

She heard the torment in his voice and pitied him. She knew the source of his pain. In the old days, when he had been courting her, he had confided that his natural father was not Arnaut de Vency but a crusader lord who had raped Adalys,

Roland's mother, and left her pregnant. Hating his origin, Roland seemed at times to hate himself.

"Do not speak so of yourself, Roland," she said to him now. "All of us are born of shame, whether our parents are married or not."

Roland eyed her angrily. "And so that is why you perfecti despise human love. Sometimes I do not wonder that the Catholics persecute you."

She felt as if he had struck her.

She walked behind him in silence, apprehensive over the increasing noise in the distance: men's rough voices, the whinnying of horses, the clatter of steel. When, following him, she stepped out from the shelter of the trees, she stopped, her heart pounding with terror.

She was facing the power of the Evil One.

Before her rose a high wall of sharp-pointed logs. A forest of banners of silk and rich samite fluttered above and beyond it. Many of them bore bloodred crosses, some thin and long, some stout and square, some tipped with multiple points. Other banners displayed the arms of the nations and baronies that had joined together at the Pope's call for an Albigensian Crusade, to make war on Diane's religion.

Men in steel helmets wearing long coats of mail strode back and forth before the wooden wall or exercised huge war-horses covered in brightly colored silk coats. The palisade seemed to enclose leagues of rolling hills. On the hills, stretching as far as Diane could see, tents were massed—thousands of them, their pointed roofs clustered together on the hilltops, the biggest tents at the very top of the hills, the smaller ones of the poorer knights lower down.

Thick columns of smoke from cooking fires spiraled up through the clear mountain air, and Diane's stomach turned over as the odor of roasting sheep reached her. Forbidden by her vows to eat meat, she had come to loathe its smell.

The noise was terrifying now, thousands of voices echoing against the walls of the valley in a raucous, deafening clamor. How could she force herself to walk into that camp?

Roland led the way to the main gate, and she made herself follow. A sergeant with a long black mustache came forward to challenge them.

"I am Sire Orlando of Perugia," Roland said.

The sergeant touched his hand to his pointed helmet in deference to Roland's knighthood. "And this young man with you, messire?'' He spoke in the *Langue d'Oïl*, the harsh speech of the north.

"My equerry, of course," said Roland airily. "Guibert de Saint-Fleur."

Diane gave the sergeant a perfunctory bow.

"Why did your seigneur allow you to leave camp?" asked the sentry. "Were you not told that Monseigneur the Count de Gobignon ordered everyone in the camp to stand to arms?" He studied Roland with narrowed eyes.

Diane's heart pounded against the wall of her chest. She prayed that the guard would not look too closely at her. Everything she feared about the crusaders was now embodied in this one mustachioed man.

"Why a general alert?" Roland asked, his voice incredibly calm.

"Something is happening up on the mountain, messire." The sergeant gestured to Mont Ségur, towering above them. "Nobody knows what. We may be winning, or the Bougres may be counterattacking."

Diane restrained an urge to wince. They are always making up names for us, she thought. Calling us Bougres—what an ugly sound it has!—because our faith came to us through Bulgaria; or Albigensians, because our first center in Languedoc was the city of Albi. As if to name us gives them power over us. They do not like what we call ourselves—Cathars—the purified ones.

"The Count himself has gone up there, but we have no news," the sentry went on. "It takes half a day to get up."

How well we know! Diane said to herself bitterly, overcome with weariness.

"This is the first I've heard of any of this." Roland smiled. "I was in a place where no heralds could reach me, visiting the daughter of a little local seigneur. She lost all her suitors in the war. Now she is past marrying age and hungers for a man. It was my duty to try to make her happy. Report me if you will. I will take my punishment. Honor forbids me to reveal her name."

How easily Roland lies, Diane thought. Would the sergeant believe him, or would he suddenly arrest them?

But the sergeant only grinned. "Your knightly pursuits are between you and your confessor, messire. What is your man carrying in those packs?"

"Trinkets the lady pressed upon me." Roland again smiled. "One sometimes finds that unmarried ladies of uncertain age are very grateful."

Dear God, thought Diane, what will I do if he asks me to open the packs?

The sergeant laughed. "Well, it does me good to see our gallant knights prosper. It is no wonder the women hereabouts need real men. All those damned Bougres giving it to each other up the arse."

Diane felt her face flush hot with anger.

The guard stepped back and bowed Roland into the camp.

"Sorry," Roland said when they were beyond the man's hearing. "You are going to hear many a vile remark about your people."

Roland led her along a winding, muddy path through the tall, four-sided tents, each topped with a pointed pennon bearing the badge of the knight who dwelt in it. The tents were arranged helter-skelter, each knight's set up wherever it pleased him.

At the sound of chanting, Roland seized her arm and pulled her off the path.

Soon she saw a dozen priests of the Roman Church in red vestments carrying gilded crosses and silken banners. Young boys in black-and-white robes followed them down the path, ringing bells and swinging smoking, incense-filled thuribles. The robes of the priests looked hideously gaudy to Diane.

She felt overwhelmed with hatred. Priests such as these had instigated forty years of bloodshed in Languedoc. They believed they were serving God, but she was convinced they were doing the work of the Adversary. She listened to what they were singing, *Salve Regina*. They were praying for victory over her people with a hymn to the Virgin Mary. How could God have a material mother? Blasphemous!

She felt a tugging on her arm and saw that Roland had dropped to his knees in the mud. She resisted. She would never bend her knee to such priests. But if she refused she risked being found out. If only she'd been allowed to go openly to death as a Cathar! She swallowed hard, knelt, and made the sign of the cross.

After the procession passed on, she struggled to her feet, shouldered the two packs, and trudged beside Roland along the twisting path. But she was overcome with fear, convinced that every one of the thousands of men around her could see right through her disguise. Roland pointed out the different companies they passed: Normans, Bretons, knights from the Ile de France, England, Flanders, Germany. But she kept her eyes on the ground, not daring to look up at the cruel faces of the crusaders,

and she stumbled along half a step behind Roland, terrified of
being separated from him.

"Many of these men are second-generation crusaders," Roland said in a low voice, trying, she sensed, to distract her from
her fear. "Their fathers came when the Pope first called for war,
and their sons are still at it. Count Amalric de Gobignon is
himself one."

"Who?" she managed to ask in a strangled voice.

"You look frightened to death. Try to walk more as if you
belonged here. De Gobignon is the commander of this army. But
look—here is where the knights from Italy and Aragon have
pitched their tents. There are even some few knights of Languedoc
camped hereabouts, who have made the crusader cause their
own."

The sound of a strong voice singing interrupted Roland. The
voice was mellow, and there was laughter in it. Even in her
terror, it made Diane feel better.

She followed Roland through a circle of closely spaced tents
and then saw an open area, a low hill covered with men seated
on the trampled grass. Small fires burned against the February
chill. All the men had their swords buckled on, their helmets by
their sides.

Only a small part of this army was up on Mount Ségur, she
suddenly realized. The entire host was huge; this Count de
Gobignon had not even begun to throw his men into the fight. It
had always been hopeless.

Now she spied the singer, a short, stocky young man with
curly blond hair. The golden wood of his lute gleamed in the late
afternoon sun. He was standing before a plain black tent. Above
its pointed roof a small black pennant flew, bearing a silver
griffin pawing the air.

The song he sang was a rollicking one:

"The King of Cats cried, 'Where is that mouse?
He has left no virgins in our land.'
'In the palace,' the Pussycat Princess cried,
'Sinning, like Onan, with his hand.' "

The crowd howled with glee, but their shouts renewed Diane's
terror, and the heavy smell of wine sickened her.

Roland had stopped and stood at the edge of the crowd,
watching the grinning jongleur.

Why are we staying here? she thought. Why don't we go on to

some place where it is safe? Someone in the crowd handed the jongleur a wineskin, and he squirted a red stream into his throat. Then Diane saw his eyes flicker in their direction, first at Roland, then at her. The jongleur's face lost its gaiety and became apprehensive.

Diane hurried after Roland as he stepped forward. The men hastily got out of his way. Something about him frightens them, she thought. Perhaps his height, or the long black cape he wears. The men moved away to fires around the side of the hill as he strode through them.

The jongleur bowed to Roland. "I thought it would be a kindness to entertain these fellows, master, while we wait for news." He looked curiously at Diane.

"Did I ask for an explanation?" Roland snapped. "Come inside, quickly."

Diane followed Roland into the black tent. It was as stark within as without. Its main furnishing was a chest of reddish-brown wood studded with brass nails.

No Cathar, but Roland keeps himself as simply as we do, she thought.

Roland silently stretched out his hand, and the jongleur gave him the lute. Roland smiled at it, strumming it lightly with his long fingers and stroking its polished wood, before he wrapped it in its white silk cloth. Diane was unable to take her eyes off his hands. They were still as beautiful as she had remembered them.

The jongleur threw himself on his knees.

"Master! Thank God you made it back safely. I could not sleep for worrying about you. That is why I was out there singing for those louts, to take my mind off my fears." He glanced again at Diane.

Does he know who I am? Diane wondered. Should I fear him, or is he a friend?

Roland seized the young man's arms affectionately, drew him to his feet, and hugged him. "I am glad to see you again, Perrin. But why these fears for my welfare? Have you no faith in me?" Before the youth could answer, Roland turned to Diane.

"This is Perrin. He really is from Saint-Fleur. He sometimes accompanies me when I sing. Also acts as my equerry, and little help he is. Just now, for example, he should realize that we have been climbing down the mountain all night and walking all day, and that he should immediately spread out a blanket for you."

Perrin smiled tentatively at her. "Is this—"

"Yes, Perrin, this is the lady we were expecting, Madame Diane de Combret."

"Excellent disguise, madame." Perrin smiled, quickly unfolding a blanket and patting it smooth for her. "Pray sit here. Also, please forgive me if my song offended you."

Roland laughed. "It is loyal of you to take the blame. I wrote the song, Diane."

She saw no shame in Roland's eyes. Bawdry amuses him, she thought. He is at home in this world and in his body.

"But how marvelous, master!" Perrin was shaking his head. "You actually crossed the battle line, got into the Cathar stronghold, and whisked out your beloved. What a song this deed will make!"

Diane felt her cheeks burn at being called Roland's beloved, and immediately felt further shame in remembering how she had tried to belittle the same deed Perrin praised.

"If need be, you will lay down your life for hers, Perrin," said Roland. He was a head taller than Perrin, Diane noticed, and he stared gravely down into the jongleur's eyes. Roland is taller than everybody else in this world, she thought.

"Madame." Perrin bowed. "Let me tell you in all honesty that I do not hold with heresy. But I would die for this man, and he has risked death to bring you here. I shall not only die, I shall let my immortal soul be damned to help you, if I must."

Now she felt her body grow rigid with anger. Damnation in helping her? How dare he? Heresy, indeed! It is Rome that is rotten with error.

Without answering she took off her cap and laid it beside her on the chest. She combed her fingers through what was left of her hair. They had cut it so it fell just short of her shoulders, like a man's. She heard Perrin sigh and looked up to see him staring. She knew many men found her hair beautiful, but that no longer pleased her.

"I find such wild talk of damning souls troublesome," she said coolly.

Perrin blushed and turned away.

Roland stared at her angrily. "When a man lays his soul at your feet, do not be so quick to spurn it, Diane. He who would save his soul must lose it. That could be true for you, too."

Diane's face grew hot, and tears stung her eyelids. She felt ashamed. How could I speak rudely to these two, who are risking their lives for me? I am guilty of pride. I do not deserve to be called perfecta.

Roland turned away and held out his arms before Perrin, who helped him off with his surcoat and began to unlace the mail hauberk. The equerry hung the heavy coat of mail on a rack beside the chest. Roland gave a deep sigh and flexed his arms appreciatively in his quilted shirt.

She felt sudden panic. Is he going to take his shirt off, too? Then she wondered why that should frighten her. Diane had lived much in close quarters and seen many partly clad men. But she knew the reason for her fear. Somewhere inside her she felt a hunger to see his body. She stood up and turned from Roland in shame.

"I know how filled with sorrow and pain you must be, Diane," Roland said gently. "Yet you have not uttered a word of complaint. There is true steel in you. Forgive me for speaking harshly to you just now."

Diane was on the verge of tears. "There is nothing to forgive. I deserved it."

She started at a sudden commotion outside, men bellowing, cheering. Oh, dear God, it must be the worst.

"Sounds like a crier going through," Roland said. "Perrin?"

After the young jongleur had left, Roland said, "Diane, you can trust that man as you would your brother. Do not get a wrong notion of him because you heard him singing a coarse song. He has a conscience as strong as a war-horse."

"If you say I can trust him, Roland, I will trust him."

"Good. You will have to, because I am sending you with him up to Paris immediately. I have a small house outside the walls of the city, in the faubourgs, where you will be safe. The sooner you leave here, where they thirst for Cathar blood, the better. I must stay or be charged with desertion."

She saw pain in his eyes and knew that he did not want her to go.

Roland turned away from her, undid the laces of his shirt, and stripped it off. She commanded herself to turn away, but she could not. As he walked over to the rack and hung the shirt over his hauberk, her eyes devoured the wiry muscles that moved smoothly under his olive skin.

He turned to face her. A white scar ran like a streak of lightning from his right shoulder across his chest and belly. She gave a little gasp. He smiled at her, raising only the left corner of his mouth. That crooked smile she knew so well.

And loved.

Yes. Her body went cold and her heart fluttered. She tried to make herself picture the blackness of Hell, the abode of the Adversary. If I break my vow I am lost forever.

"Diane," he said softly.

"Please, Roland," she choked, "do not destroy me." She turned her back to him.

There was a long silence. She trembled, dreading his touch and longing for it.

"I have done nothing to you and I will do nothing," he said.

"I am weak," she said. "I did not know how weak I was. I am at your mercy."

She heard him move behind her, and tensed.

"Look at me, Diane."

Slowly she turned. He had thrown his cape over his shoulders. She saw suffering in every line of his face.

"I, too, have my code. As long as I love you, your will must be my will. If you believe that yielding to me would be weakness, that accepting my love would destroy you, I will not touch you. You must come to me with the whole of your will, or not at all."

Relief—and disappointment—swept through her. She sat down again on the chest.

Perrin pushed his way through the tent flap. "The news has just come down from the mountaintop." His eyes, full of pity, met Diane's. "The Cathars sent men out to parley this morning. Terms are agreed. Mont Ségur has surrendered."

Diane put her head on her arms and began to whisper the Lord's Prayer. She had known when she left the mountaintop with Roland that this terrible news would come to her.

She felt Roland's comforting hand on her shoulder, and she left it there, for in her grief she desperately needed a human touch.

In her prayer she came to the phrase "Lead us not into temptation," and she whispered it fiercely to herself.

Then she wept, not only for the fall of Mont Ségur, but in confusion and despair over her own plight.

III

ROLAND HELD HIS BODY STIFF AS HE FACED THE CATHAR FORTRESS and watched the tall wooden doors swing open. He saw now that the fire of that final night's battle, now fifteen days past, had left no structure standing but the stone keep. Inside the limestone walls stood forlorn, crude shelters made of tent cloths spread over blackened beams.

Cries of farewell and loud wailing came from the battlements above and from the open gateway, as the condemned emerged from the fortress, a long line of men and women in black. Roland's heartbeat broke its rhythm.

During the fifteen days of grace granted under the terms of surrender, he had waited in camp with the other crusaders. Now that Diane and Perrin were safely off on the road to Paris, he felt impelled to be with the Cathars in their final moments, to bear witness. He had volunteered, despite his dread, to help escort the prisoners to their execution. Those Cathars who joined the Catholic religion would now be allowed to leave in peace, though they would be forced to give everything they owned to the Church and wear the yellow crosses for the rest of their lives. But those who clung to their faith would die.

As the Cathars emerged, a man-at-arms directed each to stop at a table beside the doorway, where two Dominican friars sat with parchment scrolls. The friars recorded the name of each person about to die. This meticulous record-keeping, Roland thought, was one source of the Inquisition's power.

At the head of the procession was the Cathar bishop. Bertran d'en Marti's head glowed with the red-gold rays of the low afternoon sun striking his white hair, as if it were already enveloped in flames.

"Form around them," called the leader of Roland's party.

Roland reluctantly stepped forward with the other crusaders. His longsword and dagger swung heavy at his waist. He wore them only because, as a knight, he was expected to. He had left his helmet and mail shirt back in his tent. To escort these perfecti, he knew, he would need no weapons or armor. And they were all perfecti now, the believers who chose to stay and die having received the consolamentum.

Roland and the crusaders fell in beside the doomed people as they began to climb down the western face. At first Roland kept his eyes on the ground. He could not look at the Cathars. Walking with them, hurting for them, he felt ashamed that he was to live while his own countrymen died.

He heard little but the shuffling of hundreds of pairs of feet over rocks and gravel. He listened intently as now and then a voice was raised in prayer or a hymn.

When finally he did raise his eyes to look at the procession, he found himself staring with shock into eyes he recognized. They belonged to the woman called Corba, who had greeted him with a crossbow when he had scaled the wall. She was walking hand in hand with an elderly lady and a severely limping young girl whose long hair veiled her face. Images of Roland's own mother and sister rose before him, and tears burned his eyes.

Is this, he asked silently, the terrible enemy against whom Pope after Pope has called out all the knights of Christendom? Roland looked at the perfecti, fragile, black-robed, many of them women, many old men. Catharism, he thought, is really too gentle for this world.

As Roland watched the prisoners pick their way down the steep, rock-studded path descending from ledge to ledge, he admired the way they helped each other. A strong young man swept the lame girl up in his arms and carried her. That young man and that girl could have long lives ahead of them, Roland thought. Lord, why must they give their young bodies to be burned?

Roland looked downward toward the meadow that would soon hold all the perfecti. In the final days of the grace period, he had watched, sickened, as crusaders built a fence of logs about six feet high around the edge of the meadow. Within it they had heaped bundles of wood cut from the forest. Though the wood was still damp from winter, the bales of straw the soldiers had mixed with it and the pitch they had poured over it would, he thought bitterly, ensure a fine bonfire.

Roland stared down at the fighting men and clergy who had gathered around the fence and who thronged over the mountainside below it. They are happy, he told himself. Here is the fulfillment of their outpouring of toil, treasure, and blood, of nearly a year of siege.

A small group, arrayed in tunics and caps of blue, purple, and red, detached itself from the crowd and began to climb to meet the descending procession. The great seigneurs, thought Roland, the masters of these revels. For what they do this day may they all burn in Hell.

One of those approaching was taller than all who accompanied him. Though powerfully built, almost burly, he moved with ease up the precarious path. As Roland recognized the man, the hairs prickled on the back of his neck. His fingers twitched and his muscles contracted. Amalric, Count de Gobignon, head of this army, destroyer of Languedoc.

The knight in command of Roland's party hurried down the mountainside to meet the Count and bend the knee before him.

Amalric stood with his thumbs hooked in his jeweled belt, and they exchanged a few words. The ash-blond hair that fell in waves to Amalric's shoulders was as beautiful as a woman's, but his long, straight nose and square jaw gave him a strong, manly look.

After de Gobignon had spoken, the knight he had addressed scrambled back up the slope. Amalric and his party followed at a leisurely pace.

Upon rejoining Roland's group, the officer raised a hand to halt the Cathar procession and its knightly escort. "Monseigneur the Count requires that the prisoners be roped together and their hands and feet bound."

Roland felt a surge of anger.

"Many of these people," he spoke out, "are old and ill. All are weak from lack of food. This is a steep path. How can they manage it if we bind them?"

He sensed the others of the escort party staring at him.

The officer did not look Roland in the eye. "Monseigneur requires that the prisoners be roped together and dragged the rest of the way."

Roland was stunned. He looked at the long line of Cathars patiently standing on the mountainside. His gaze met Bishop Bertran's. Was there a warning look in the old man's eye? No matter. He could not draw back now.

"What contemptible cruelty!" he said loudly.

Amalric heard the protest and a hot wave of anger swept through him. How dare a lowly knight question an order of his! But he knew that a good leader does not act on impulse. Begin

easily, he told himself. Find out what is happening here before
you make a move in front of the whole army.

Continuing his climb up the slope, he inquired almost pleasantly, "Who is it who calls my command contemptible?"

Though he had reined in his anger, he felt the pleasant stirring
in the blood he always enjoyed before combat, great or small.

Now he saw a knight step boldly out from among his fellows
in the escort. Amalric sized him up. Tall. Might even be as tall
as I. But stringy. I've got the weight on him. The face looked
swarthy, and so thin that the large, curved beak of a nose seemed
huge. Probably Spanish or Italian, perhaps even from around
here.

Amalric prided himself on knowing as many of the men under
his command as possible. This man, he was sure, he had never
seen before. Whoever he was, he was no one of importance.
That was obvious from the thinness of his black cape, his worn,
dusty black tunic, and his unadorned belt and sword hilt. A thin,
dark, purseless fellow, thought Amalric. A shadow of a knight.

Amalric studied the knight's bearing. He held his head and
shoulders proudly, daring to regard Amalric as if they were
equals. And those eyes—they were surprising. Bright blue. As
blue as my own, Amalric thought. They do not seem to belong
in that brown face. It was as if another man looked out at
Amalric through a mask. And the look in those blue eyes was
more than defiance. Was there hatred in it?

"Who are you, messire?" he said, keeping his voice low.

"I am Orlando of Perugia," answered the knight, firmly and
calmly. He made no obeisance, addressing Amalric as an equal.

Amalric felt his body turn hot. He had heard of the knight-
troubadour Orlando. He cursed himself for having neglected to
go over the rolls of his army of late. If he had known, he would
have dealt with the man before today.

So this is the man who had the audacity to address a song to
my wife.

Amalric smarted, recalling the letter he had received months
ago in his tent at the base of Mont Ségur, from the steward of his
town house in Paris. At the beginning of winter, Amalric learned,
a man had appeared outside the garden wall just before dawn,
singing. When the guards went out to drive him off, he was
gone. Later an equerry came to the house bearing a copy of the
song for Countess Nicolette. But it fell into the hands of a
steward loyal to Amalric, and the man quickly dispatched agents

to follow the equerry. They tracked him to Orlando of Perugia, a troubadour newly arrived in Paris. The steward sent the song on to Amalric. It was titled "In Praise of Fair Nicolette," and Amalric had torn it to bits without reading it.

He had resolved to punish the man when the campaign was over. And now here was the same Orlando standing before him, ridiculing his orders.

"I do not give orders lightly, Orlando of Perugia. What is your objection to my command?"

"These people are going to their deaths peaceably. Why add needless suffering to their final moments?"

Amalric glanced at the long line of heretics extending from this spot on the slope almost to the gate of the fortress that had sheltered them. By Saint Dominic, how he loathed those Albigensians! They were like a flock of vultures, with their sharp faces and black robes. He could bear to look at them only because he knew he would shortly destroy them. He wished he could go among them swinging his sword like a harvester in a field of wheat, cutting down each and every man and woman himself. They could never be made to suffer enough to pay for the harm they had done to Christendom.

And to me. For it was creatures like these who killed my father.

"Mercy becomes a chivalrous knight, Sire Orlando. But these heretics deserve not your pity. Most of them are the so-called perfecti, the preachers and leaders who seduced countless others from the true faith. They are worse than murderers. They are killers of souls. To let them keep their dignity in death would give them a last opportunity to mislead their foolish followers. Do we want people from all over Languedoc to hear that these Bougres strolled down the mountain, laid themselves on the pyre, and serenely gave up their lives, just as if they were honest Christian martyrs? No, let it be said that they had to be dragged to their deaths and thrown upon the faggots."

"Men are often cruel in the heat of anger," said Orlando, his voice trembling as if he himself were possessed by fury. "But the foulest cruelty of all is deliberate, calculated cruelty."

"You have had your explanation, Messire Troubadour, which is more than you deserve. Why such tender concern for these imps of Satan?" Amalric grinned contemptuously. "What sort of man is it who prefers simpering with a lute to wielding a sword? I have heard somewhat of your sweet songs, but naught of your brave deeds. Perhaps you feel a kinship with that old

Bougre sodomite there?'' Amalric pointed to the black-robed ancient at the head of the line of Cathars, their so-called bishop.

As he intended, his words brought guffaws from the listening knights.

"What sort of man is it," Orlando said slowly and clearly, "who takes delight in tormenting helpless, unresisting old men, women, sick people, starving people? Perhaps I will write a song about the brave deed *you* do this day."

Amalric felt rage rise in him. As his lips drew back from his teeth, he raised his gauntleted fist and lunged at Orlando.

The troubadour seemed to step into the blow, yet it did little more than graze his cheek as he grabbed Amalric's wrist and elbow. A twist of his body, and the troubadour held Amalric's forearm locked tight.

Amalric felt a surge of panic, sensing that the bone was about to give. He was forced to drop to his knees.

Suddenly he felt himself released. The troubadour stepped quickly away from him.

He scrambled to his feet, staring into the astonished faces of a circle of knights. His own face burned with shame.

"Shall we kill him, monseigneur?" Amalric's aide, Guy d'Etampes, called out.

"Do you need others to settle your quarrels for you?" the troubadour taunted.

"No one has ever spoken so of me," said Amalric. "Let it be trial by combat. I am commander of this army, and by the power vested in me I will mete out swift and final justice." He drew his dagger, a three-edged basilard of Toledo steel, ten inches from its triangular base to its needle point, and began to stalk the troubadour.

Slowly Amalric circled to the troubadour's left, expecting that the dark man would draw his own dagger with his right hand. Amalric moved on the rock-strewn slope so that he was on higher ground than the troubadour. He felt strength and agility flowing through him.

He saw a spot of sunlight, reflected from his basilard, dance on the troubadour's black cape. He shifted the dagger slightly so that the beam of light struck Orlando's eyes. The troubadour winced and sidestepped, but Amalric caught him in the eyes with the light again.

He crouched, shifting the basilard from hand to hand, and gathered himself to rush his enemy.

The troubadour, with the setting sun behind him, was a fea-
tureless shadow.

Amalric saw his opponent undo the clasp of his cape and wrap
it around his right arm.

"Draw dagger or sword, messire, I care not which," Amalric
said. "I would not strike down an empty-handed man."

"I am as well armed with my hands empty as you are with
that skewer," the troubadour mocked.

Amalric felt his face burn with fury.

He sprang at Orlando.

The troubadour raised his cape-wrapped right arm, but Amalric
shifted the direction of his thrust and drove the basilard in under
the right arm straight toward his enemy's chest.

The troubadour tried to shield himself with his left arm.

Amalric grunted with satisfaction as he felt the steel sink deep
into flesh. Snarling, tugging hard, he yanked the dagger out of
the troubadour's arm.

The troubadour, his face stiff with pain, stumbled over a rock
and fell to one knee. As if searching for a friend, he looked up at
the ring of crusaders that had gathered to watch the fight. No one
spoke to encourage him; no one moved to help him. His sword
and dagger were still sheathed.

"Draw your sword, God damn you!" Amalric roared, making
sure all onlookers could hear.

Instead of reaching for a weapon, the troubadour unwrapped
the cape from his right arm.

Amalric rushed him.

He saw the troubadour's hand flick and the cape fly out.

He felt something wrap itself around his ankles. Helpless,
horrified, he knew that he was falling. He had just time to turn
the point of his basilard away from his body before he went
down on his face.

By Saint Dominic, the cape was a weapon. It had weights in
its corners.

He felt pain stabbing all through him as his enemy landed
heavily on his back, the troubadour's knee grinding between his
shoulder blades, the sharp rocks on which he lay pressing into
his chest.

Amalric raised his arm to strike with the dagger, and felt the
troubadour clutch at his wrist, but the man's hand was slippery
with blood, and Amalric pulled his arm free.

A burst of pain shot through Amalric's right hand and arm and he bellowed in agony. A big rock, in the troubadour's other hand, had crashed down on his knuckles.

Amalric's hand was empty, and he felt the sharp point of his basilard pressing against his throat.

"I can kill you now," said the voice above him.

"Go ahead."

"I do not wish to," the troubadour said. "Your comrades would surely repay me in kind. But if you move I will cut your throat. I shall release you on one condition, that the Cathars are permitted to go to their deaths on their feet like human beings. Give me your word of honor."

Amalric turned his face to look up at the troubadour. He had no choice unless he wished to die, that steel spike driven into his throat. His hatred burned his enemy's hawklike face into his memory.

"You have my word, but know that what is between us only begins here."

"It began long ago," the troubadour almost whispered.

Amalric felt the man's weight lifted from his back. Slowly Amalric pushed himself to his feet, favoring his right hand, which hurt abominably.

The troubadour had already turned his back on him and was walking away, blood dripping from his left arm.

Without looking at Amalric he let the basilard fall, clattering on the stony ground. D'Etampes hurried to pick it up and brought it to Amalric.

Weighing the dagger in his hand, Amalric thought, I could have him killed now. No, not in front of all these men. It would not seem knightly.

He watched the troubadour go. One day, he thought, I will have that man flayed alive. Slowly he sheathed the basilard.

But a small, cold question, coiling like a worm at the base of his brain, unsettled him. Why has he done so much to make me hate him? Who is this man to me?

Roland walked away slowly. His left arm felt numb. Blood from his fingertips spattered on the rocks. Men moved grudgingly aside, their hands on their sword hilts. At a word from Amalric, they would cut him down. Roland sensed their hatred for the upstart knight who had defeated Count Amalric with outlandish tactics. He had never in his life felt so alone.

He continued to walk amid the heavy silence, tensely waiting for an attack, watching from the corners of his eyes for sudden movement. But none came. Instead, Roland heard Amalric speaking in a low voice and then heard his aides call orders for the procession again to get under way. He heard no further word about binding the prisoners. The Cathars at least were going to be permitted to walk to their deaths under their own power.

The black-robed men and women avoided looking at Roland as they made their painful way past him down the mountainside. They understood that to show him any gratitude would put him in still more danger. He felt a wave of love, as palpable as the crusaders' hatred, from these people who were so soon to be destroyed.

I should go down to the camp now, saddle my horse, and get out of here, Roland thought. I am badly hurt. I need help, and I will get none here. Once Amalric has done these poor people to death, he will turn his full attention to me.

Yet Roland could not bring himself to leave. He had to be able to tell Diane how these people died. But more than that, he felt there ought to be one friend to the victims here in their last moments, even if his love and grief must remain hidden in his heart.

With his own dagger he cut two strips of cloth from his cape and bound one around the wound and one above it to slow the bleeding. His arm was throbbing from wrist to shoulder.

He looked down to the field of martyrdom. The long line of dark figures now extended almost to the stockade. Roland slid down the slope awkwardly, cradling his wounded arm to keep it from striking rocks.

Some of the men in the crowd recognized him and moved away as he came near, but most of them were too interested in what was about to happen to pay him heed. He took a position against the wall of rough-hewn timber, near the gateway.

Not ten feet from where he stood a bonfire of big logs crackled. He could feel its heat. Around it stood a circle of men holding unlit torches.

The Cathar procession stopped as they neared the open gate, and they clustered together in a large group. Roland saw Bishop Bertran, still in the forefront of his people. On a low hill looking down at the Cathars stood a row of men in dazzling vestments, a few with tall, gilded miters on their heads. Those, he knew, were prelates of the Roman Church. The fat one in gorgeously embroidered purple, with two or three jeweled rings on each finger, must be the Bishop of Albi, who had commanded troops in the siege. This must be a special triumph for him, since the heresy was said to be so strong in his city.

In the midst of all the red and purple finery one man caught Roland's eye. His black woolen cloak and white tunic were almost as stark as the robes of the perfecti. Roland recognized the garb of the Dominicans, the leading inquisitors. Pale, shining blond hair wreathed the Dominican's thin face, and the top of his head had been shaved in the priestly tonsure. He approached the Cathars alone, then stood a moment in silent prayer, his eyes gazing heavenward. Roland had seen him before and been told that he was Friar Hugues, the younger brother of Amalric de Gobignon.

As the young Dominican began to speak to the assembled Cathars, Roland watched them intently. Were they grateful for the few additional moments of life this sermon provided, or did this just prolong their suffering?

"Though you have denied God all your lives long, He still loves you, even at this moment," Friar Hugues said pleadingly.

As he went on, he showed himself a mighty preacher, roaring like a lion, whispering like a gentle breeze. He was so enthralling, Roland almost forgot the pain in his arm and the suffering in his heart.

Darkness was falling, and the sun had dipped below the western peaks when Friar Hugues, his face lit by the flickering glow of the bonfire, ended.

"It is a painful death you are condemned to. You know, of course, that it is not the Church that punishes you. The Holy Inquisition has merely proven that you are guilty of heresy. It is the secular authorities who will decree that you must be burned to ashes."

Like Pilate washing his hands of the blood of Jesus, Roland thought.

"Yet this death by fire is not imposed out of cruelty," Hugues went on. "We permit the State to burn your bodies as a sign that the Church must be utterly cleansed of false teachings. Think again about your heresy. Search your hearts. Are you so very sure you are doing the right thing in choosing the flames? Is there not one among you who feels some doubt? Do not be afraid. That doubt is the voice of God in your heart. He is trying to save you. Come forward now. Come forward, come to God. Save yourself, for His greater glory. This is your last chance. I beg you. Jesus Christ begs you. Come forward." Weeping, Friar Hugues dropped to his knees, repeating his pleas.

Among the Cathars no one moved or spoke.

Shivers ran across Roland's back. What a people, who could withstand such a sermon, with the sight of torches before them and the tarry smell of pitch in their nostrils.

Friar Hugues fell on his face on the trampled grass of the meadow, sobbing.

Now another voice rose above the crackling of the bonfire. "You have said the Church must be cleansed."

Realizing that the voice came from among the Cathars, Roland looked there and saw that it was Bishop Bertran speaking. His voice was not faint, as it had been when Roland last met him, but strong, clear, as it must have been forty years ago, when he debated Saint Dominic.

"The Church shall be cleansed," the Cathar bishop went on. "From the flames you light today will fly sparks that will kindle a great fire of purification. The corruption and tyranny and superstition of the Church of Rome will be burned away."

The Bishop of Albi waved fat fingers glittering with rings. "We have not come here to listen to heretical sermons. You have wasted your last chance to repent. You are hereby delivered to the secular power." He turned to a young friar seated at a table, scribbling industriously on a roll of parchment. "Let it be recorded that the accused died unrepentant."

The Bishop held out a jeweled hand. Roland's eyes followed the gesture, and he saw Amalric, seated on a big chestnut horse, holding a roll of parchment. The Count's silver coronet and his purple and gold mantle proclaimed his power, the power to put two hundred people to death by fire.

Amalric read the sentence of death for all the perfecti, pronounced in the name of Louis, King of the Franks, with a cold serenity that was more chilling than any outburst of passionate hatred could have been.

Men with spears began pushing the condemned through the gateway of the palisade. Roland's heart beat hard with the dread of what he was about to see. Even in peril of his own life, facing an enemy's naked steel, he had never felt such tormenting fear.

He looked up at Mont Ségur. The broken Cathar fortress and the crusaders' wooden fort, now abandoned, were still bathed in sunlight, though the shadows of the nearby mountains had crept over the meadow here below. Roland saw small figures standing atop the walls of the fortress. They were those who had chosen to renounce their faith and live, those who would now be left behind. This must be worse for them to witness than it is for me, he thought pityingly.

He turned back to the Cathars in the stockade. As when they were descending the mountain, they helped each other to take their places for death. Within the stockade the bundles of brushwood were piled high, higher than the height of a tall man. Bishop Bertran and the other elderly perfecti were pulled and lifted to the top of the pile by younger perfecti in black robes. Then, crawling over the mass of faggots that shifted and quaked under their weight, they moved to make room for those who came after. Having to burn so many at once, the crusaders had not bothered to erect stakes.

For Roland it was still hard to believe this really was happening. He had heard of people being killed by the thousands, but that was after sieges, when the blood lust of battle was still on men. Here there had been a respite after the siege. The crusaders and inquisitors had had time for calm reflection, and this is what they had chosen to do. It was the deliberateness of all this that made him despair of humankind.

Roland saw the woman called Corba tenderly lift the elderly woman she had been walking with to the top of the pile. Then Corba and the soldierly young man supported the lame girl as she climbed up. There was a family resemblance among the three women. Were they grandmother, mother, and daughter? Roland felt tears burn his eyes and a sob gather in his throat. His helplessness was maddening.

I should have killed Amalric.

That would not have stopped this.

When all the perfecti were inside the palisade, six men-at-arms pushed the gate of half-logs shut and propped more logs against it to keep it closed. Men carrying burning torches of pine soaked with pitch climbed ladders leaning against the wooden walls. The red flames glowed in the twilight. From within the enclosure rose the sound of over two hundred voices reciting the Lord's Prayer in unison.

Roland looked at de Gobignon. His handsome face composed, Amalric lifted his bare right hand. Even at this distance Roland could see, with a faint satisfaction, that the Count's hand was swollen and purple. Amalric dropped his hand again, decisively. The men on the ladders threw their torches into the stockade.

For a moment the Lord's Prayer could still be heard. Then the flames shot up with a roar. Roland heard screams, for though they were called perfecti, these were human beings, and they would die with cries of pain. The gold banners of fire leaped so high they hid Mont Ségur behind them.

As it grew, devouring its victims, the fire was merciful to the executioners and onlookers. Most of the screams were drowned out by the deafening clamor of the ever-fattening flames, like the continuous thunder of a huge waterfall, and the thick black smoke drifted upward into the windless violet sky, so that the dreadful stench of burning flesh was fast carried away.

Roland heard no word from the men around him. As the log wall itself caught fire, the onlookers backed slowly away. The heat was fierce on Roland's face and hands, but he knew it was nothing to the fire claiming the bodies of the Cathars.

Roland looked at Hugues. The friar's face was wet with tears. *Is he really grieving for those he thinks of as lost souls?*

Bishop Bertran, the lady Corba, all those good people whom Roland had known too briefly, must already be dead.

Overcome, he sank to the ground and, sitting, buried his face in his hands and began to sob. The pain of the wound in his arm, forgotten for a time in the horror of what he was seeing, overwhelmed him, piercing the whole left side of his body, as if a lance had impaled him.

"If you are so damned sorry for them, why not jump into the fire with them?" said a harsh voice above him. Roland stood up wearily. He felt a sudden urge to draw his dagger and strike. The impulse vanished as quickly as it came, drowned by another wave of grief.

Roland reached out with his wounded arm and touched the man's shoulder gently. "You do not know what you have done," he said.

The man shrank from him.

Roland turned his back on the great fire and walked away. He could not bear to watch any longer. *How can I ever know a moment's joy in my life again? How can I love another human being, when I know that men can do this?*

As he stumbled down the mountainside toward the main camp, the hideous image of three charred skeletons—Corba and her mother and daughter—arms entwined, arose in his mind and made him feel faint. He was dizzy, too, from the pain in his arm. He knew he could lose his left arm, or even die, if this wound was not treated. But there was no one in the camp he could trust to help him.

I must get to my horse, try to get help for my arm on the road.

Maybe find people who remember my father. Now, before Amalric
sends his men after me.

In his despair, though, he walked slowly, because he could
not make himself care whether he died of his wound or whether
Amalric killed him.

Diane wanted to stay here and die. I did not understand you,
Diane. But I do now.

He spoke also to the dead: I vow to your memory that I will
do whatever I can to put an end to such evils as this.

A hopeless quest, perhaps. But if I cannot live for Diane, and
if life is to continue in me, this is a good purpose for it.

An armed man stepped into his path.

Roland tensed himself defensively.

The man looked like any other crusader, but when he spoke it
was in the *Langue d'Oc*. "Your wound needs attention, Sire
Roland. There are those who wish to help you, as you have
helped those they loved. Will you come with me?"

"I have many enemies," Roland said, realizing that the man
had called him by his true name.

"You have friends as well. All things that are, are lights."

Looking closer, Roland saw that tears were running from the
man's eyes. He must be one of the many spiritual children of the
perfecti left orphaned by this day's horror.

Despite the darkness of this moment, he felt despair give way
a little. Yes, there were armies that could put people to death
mercilessly, led by barons like Amalric and priests like Hugues.
But there were men like this as well, and people such as the
burnt ones had been.

Now, Diane, I, too, have a vow to live by.

Feeling stronger, he said, "Yes. I will go with you."

IV

Countess Nicolette de Gobignon pressed a wet cloth to the
King's brow. Though he lay there helpless, still she found him an
awesome figure, like a fallen cathedral tower.

Only two other men are as tall, she thought. Amalric and
Orlando.

She felt a pang of guilt. How could she be thinking about the troubadour here where her royal master lay slowly dying.

She fixed her eyes on Louis, and on the ivory and wood crucifix that rose and fell on his chest with his labored breathing.

Nicolette felt as if she, too, could hardly breathe. Across the crowded room a fire roared in a huge stone-lined fireplace. The air was stifling. She resented all that made it so, down to the woolen draperies and wall hangings and the thick carpets that sealed in the heat. But she knew that this northern château, Pontoise-les-Noyons, a day's ride from Paris, had had to be built to withstand cold, its walls thick and its windows tiny—so totally unlike the bright, airy Languedoc manor she had grown up in.

Sweat trickled down her brow and stung her eyes. Her breath was coming in little gasps. She felt as if she would faint if she couldn't go outside soon.

Dozens of people, the King's family and courtiers, had packed themselves uselessly into the room, making it even more suffocating. Their whispers, like the buzzing of mosquitoes, irritated Nicolette.

Almost all of them, she was sure, worried more about their own welfare than about the King's. And even Louis's wife and mother, though they grieved for him, were too distracted to do much to alleviate his suffering.

She saw the King's lips quiver, and quickly she bent close to him. Any last words could be terribly important.

"Jerusalem," he mumbled. "Towers—golden. Gates of pearl. Crystal waters." Then he panted heavily.

"Hush, sire," she whispered. "Rest easy."

Louis's heavy eyelids lifted slightly, showing only the whites of his eyes, as if he were already dead. He's delirious, she thought.

"The trees bear fruit all year round." He said this distinctly. Then he lapsed into wordless muttering, and then silence.

She took a fresh wet linen cloth from the silver basin beside her, squeezed out the lukewarm water, and laid it on Louis's high forehead.

Why Jerusalem? The Jerusalem he was mumbling about, she knew, existed only in his fevered mind. She had listened to crusaders who had been there. There were no golden towers or gates of pearl. There were no towers or gates at all now, because the Turks had destroyed them.

She caught her breath. Perhaps it is not an earthly Jerusalem. Could he already be seeing Heaven?

Her body turned cold and her stomach churned as she imagined Louis closing his eyes forever. As a girl, she had seen the village near her father's château burned to the ground by marauding knights. Now she saw those flames again; heard the screams of bleeding men, terrified children, women being raped. What had been happening in Languedoc all these years would happen now all over France. War. War had killed her dear father, trapped her in marriage to an enemy. What horrors would she have to endure this time?

There would be factions, and she would have to decide which to join. What side would Amalric take? She had no idea. And where should she go—stay here in Paris, flee north to Château Gobignon, or try to get back home to Languedoc?

She felt the urge to weep for Louis as if he were already dead. She liked him so much. When she had first come to court, a stranger and almost a foreigner, he had gone out of his way to be kind to her. And how gentle he was with his Marguerite.

So good not only to those close to him, she thought, but to everyone—merchants, townsfolk, peasants. How they cheered for him as he passed by! What would become of them all if he died?

Amalric should be here at a time like this.

But he considered it more important to visit the properties the Church had awarded him after his victory over the Cathars, take inventory of each one, put down any local disorder, and appoint men to occupy and govern each château and town for him. All the spring, summer, and autumn he had been journeying about Languedoc. It might be dangerous for him to be away from Paris and his own holdings if the King died, but he also stood to lose a great deal if he did not fully secure his new lands. He was always at the edge of a precipice, always juggling one danger against another. And how he enjoyed it all!

But not all men were like Amalric.

A wave of grief washed over her, darker than the sorrow she felt for dying King Louis. She had hoped for so much from Orlando. She had loved him so. And now that love was dead.

It hurt to think about him now. But perhaps it was better to feel pain than to feel nothing. The King was quiet as she sat by his bed. He breathed evenly, seemingly sleeping, and as she sat with her eyes fixed on him, her mind wandered. She let herself dream.

*   *   *

How she had trembled when her eyes first met the troubadour's. His sky-blue eyes, so strange against his dark complexion, compelled her to look at him, as if he were a magician and had her under a spell. It had been early in September, over a year ago, and the King and Queen were holding court in a field outside the château at Chinon. Amalric was far away, having begun his siege of Mont Ségur.

The troubadour's first words were not to her, but to the King.

"If it please you, sire, I will sing a ballad of Peire Cardenal's."

Even as he spoke, his eyes flickered to her, and he seemed to be asking for her approval as well as the King's. She felt herself nodding and smiling before she knew what she was doing.

He sang, and his voice washed over her, a warm, rich baritone. She felt full of a sweet confusion, certain that it was really to her he was singing. She watched his long, slender fingers on the strings of his lute, and it was as if those fingers were holding her hand and stroking her.

Her gaze lingered on his glossy black hair, memorized his high, narrow forehead, his brilliant blue eyes, his large, slightly hooked nose and sharp chin. No, she thought, not the features of a handsome man as convention would have it; but having seen him, her idea of handsomeness abruptly changed.

Rapt, she kept her eyes fixed on him all through the song. And her heartbeat quickened with delight each time his gaze strayed to meet hers.

She was filled with a longing that was intensely painful, yet somehow she felt happier than she had been in a long time. She wanted to hug the world to her, as if until this moment she had been sleeping, and now for the first time she was awake and fully alive. And as she listened, she found herself imagining him singing to her alone, songs he would create for her. His lyrics would speak to her of a secret kingdom of love. There she would be the ruler and he the adoring subject. She envisioned herself in some secret silken place lying in his arms.

All too soon for her he finished his song. He bowed deeply— and how gracefully, she thought—to King Louis and Queen Marguerite, and accepted their praise and thanks. Then he walked, with the proud carriage of an Arabian stallion, across the open grass, to stand among the courtiers.

It was only then that she realized she had not heard his name. She whispered to her friend Marguerite, "Who is he?"

Marguerite looked over to where the troubadour stood and

back at Nicolette and smiled. "He looks as if he could be a countryman of ours, does he not? A man of Languedoc. Very handsome. If I did not love Louis so much, I could almost be attracted to him myself."

"But who *is* he?" Nicolette demanded again.

"He is called Orlando of Perugia," said Marguerite with a sigh. "Where is Perugia? Northern Italy, I think. A pity he is not a genuine Languedoc troubadour."

From then on, as the feasting continued at trestle tables set in the meadow, Nicolette's eyes sought him out again and again.

She said "Orlando" silently to herself many times that afternoon, and discovered that in shaping the name slowly, languorously with her lips, they moved as they might if she were kissing him.

But she did not dare try to speak to him. Amalric had his retainers, relations, and favor-seekers scattered all through this festive assemblage, and any interest she showed in another man would surely be reported to him. How fortunate at least that Louis's mother, Queen Blanche, who watched over the younger women of the court as a falcon watches hares, was not with the royal party that day.

Nicolette had been deeply thankful, too, that Amalric was away at war.

At the end of the festive day, when the King and Queen were ready to retire, the troubadour gave her one last burning look before he left the meadow.

She was ecstatic. After eleven lonely years of a marriage she had entered into only to save her mother and sisters, she might have found her true love.

But when would she receive a message from him?

The very next day her personal maid, Agnes, handed her a roll of vellum tied with a black ribbon, and she cried out with delight. He had worn black.

She tore the ribbon loose and devoured his words:

> When I beheld you yesterday
> You were all that I could see,
> So bright your beauty shone.
> It made the castle fade away,
> And by some wondrous sorcery
> We two seemed quite alone.

Five stanzas. In her eagerness she read the lines over and over again. And what delicious pleasure she felt that they were written in her own native language, the southern *Langue d'Oc*.

*   *   *

Now, sitting by the dying King's bedside, she remembered the first time Orlando had sung only for her. It had been a year ago, just at the start of winter, after the King and Queen had returned to Paris. She was in bed in the de Gobignon town house on the Right Bank. She had fallen asleep thinking about her troubadour, and she'd been dreaming of him, as she often did.

She must still be dreaming, she thought when she first heard his voice. But suddenly she was wide awake, realizing that he was singing in the garden outside her window.

He sang an aubade, a dawn song of Languedoc, about the agony of lovers parting while a friend on watch warns of approaching morning. She slowly rose from the bed and tiptoed to the window. Though she was barefoot and wore only her shift, she hardly felt the December cold. She struggled with the fastenings of the shutters, yearning to see him.

Then she heard angry voices below, Amalric's men-at-arms up and about, and she froze in terror.

"Oh, no, let him be safe!" she prayed.

She heard running feet and the clatter of steel weapons.

In dread she pressed her hands to her breast. But then there was silence.

She went back to her bed and wept, terrified that something awful had befallen her troubadour.

Later that morning Agnes reported with a twinkling eye that the men-at-arms had chased a prowler, but he had gotten away.

Nicolette all but fainted in her relief.

A week later, Agnes handed her a folded parchment, and again she was aglow with excitement. It was, as she had expected, a plea for a tryst:

> To the lady who is always in my thoughts:
>   We are two rays of light shed by a single sun. The Goddess whom we both serve forbids us to remain apart. I beg you to join your light with mine that both of us may shine the brighter.
>   Entrust your reply to him who brings you this.

And no signature.

"His man wants to know if there will be an answer, madame," Agnes said with an amused smile.

Nicolette trusted Agnes, who had been with her since they both were children. The same age as her mistress, Agnes had proved her loyalty by giving up her home and family to accompany Nicolette when she had been compelled to marry Amalric. Both felt out of place in this northern country, and they shared an abiding love for the sweet customs of ladies and troubadours.

"Not now," said Nicolette. "I shall have to think about it."

All that day she tried to decide what to write back. She would take a worn piece of scrap parchment, start a letter, rub it out with pumice, and try again. She must have done it a dozen times.

It is too soon for a meeting, she told herself. If he has been properly instructed in courtly love, he must know that as well as I do. No, first he must woo me at a distance with songs and sweet messages. Then, after a year or so, I shall arrange a very brief secret meeting. That will show whether I can trust him to do only what I allow. Then I may let him kiss me. And then we will proceed ever so gradually, over months and years, from kissing to touching, to lying together clothed, and then with no clothing, and at last, when I have tested him fully and totally, the final sacrament of Love.

But at the thought of that union of their bodies, she could all but feel his arms around her, his hard, lean body pressed against hers. Her hands tensed, as if they clutched his shoulders, drawing him closer still.

Why must I wait? Why must I draw it out as they do in the old romances? In a week or a month he could die, and then I would never know the glory of lying in his arms.

How awful!

She took a fresh piece of parchment and began to write, inviting him to set a time and place for a rendezvous.

It was hard for her, though, to hold the quill firmly, because suddenly she was hearing the voice of her mother, dead these three years, exhorting her.

"You will want to yield to him at once, because to sleep with a man you love is the closest thing to Heaven we can know here on earth." Her mother had held up a warning finger. "But do not do it. If you give yourself to him right away, the love he feels for you will lose its force sooner than you would think possible. You must use the power of unfulfilled desire—his and yours—to teach him. In the world, man rules woman, but in the kingdom of Love the man must call the lady *mi dons,* 'my lord,' because he is ruled by her. So my mother told me, and so, in our tradition, mother has taught daughter, in secret, since before the time of Christ. And I know it is true, because I have lived it. Remember, when it happens to you, you are not the first woman to feel this way—although it will seem that way to you. This teaching has stood the test of many generations. You will never know the true magic of Love unless you follow its rules."

Since her marriage at thirteen Nicolette had known what bodily union with a man was like. She even remembered a spring night, two years after her marriage, when, after an evening of merry dancing, she had been able to forget her resentment of Amalric, forget who her husband was, and had enjoyed his body so thoroughly that she had been left trembling from head to foot, exhausted with pleasure.

But she knew deep down that Love could be far more than that. From what her mother had told her, from what friends whispered, from innumerable poems, she knew what glories Love promised. At its best Love could carry lovers to heights of bliss that the priests claimed were reserved for the saints in Heaven.

She clenched her fist so hard she broke the quill and left a big blotch on the parchment.

She might have only this one chance in all her life. Twenty-four was no longer young. Still, the happiness they would know in the end would be worth the delay. She wrote:

> Messire:
>   Press me not for favors yet. I must know if you are true, and only time can tell me that. Desire is overhasty, but Love is patient.

Days followed days, stretching into lonely weeks. But no answer came back to her. She grew sorry, then bitter. Why had she not acted on her first impulse and arranged a secret meeting? At home and at court she went through her routine with a constant, aching hollow in her stomach. The thought that she might have ruined it all filled her with anguish.

She shared her pain with Marguerite, who insisted that Nicolette had done absolutely the right thing in postponing a rendezvous. But what did it matter whether she had done the right thing if she had lost Orlando forever?

She worked hard to convince herself that if he really cared about her, one such note from her should only have spurred him to greater ardor. She repeated to herself again and again what she had said in her reply to him, wondering if he had perhaps misunderstood her chiding tone and taken offense.

One day she saw that the ice in the Seine was melting. Winter was ending. The word from the south was that Mont Ségur must soon fall. Then perhaps Amalric would be back, and a meeting might then be impossible. And still there was no word from her troubadour. She stood on the riverbank and prayed to the Goddess of Love that she would hear from him.

When the trees in Paris were budding, she overheard gossip at court. The troubadour had ridden off to Languedoc. She felt as wretched as if the inquisitors had pronounced her death sentence.

Why? Had he fled Paris to forget her? Was he, as she suspected, a man of Languedoc only pretending to be Italian, and had he gone to fight against the crusaders?

She felt his loss constantly, but oddly this pain made her happier than she had ever been since she married.

For she continued to hope. One day he would come back from his mysterious journey. One day she would see him again. Whatever she had done wrong, whatever had cut him off from her, she would not make the same mistake twice.

During the summer that had followed, as a lady-in-waiting to Queen Marguerite, she had again accompanied the royal couple and their court on a tour of the kingdom.

Because Louis was unwilling to burden his subjects with a huge expense, his retinue was a small one, as such parties went—the King and Queen and a dozen noble companions, two dozen equerries and pages, twenty or so clergymen (so that Louis should not lack for the theological conversation he loved), and fifty servants headed up by Isambert, the palace cook. The King felt such trust in his subjects that only a hundred knights escorted him. At each château and abbey where the royal party stopped they were lavishly feasted and entertained, and their mounts stabled and fed. Every man and many of the women of the entourage took three horses. There were mule-carried litters for the ladies, but Nicolette and Marguerite both preferred horseback.

They journeyed through the northeastern lands—Champagne, Picardy, Artois, and Flanders—and, along with other castles, they visited Château Gobignon.

Amalric, flushed with pride in his conquest of Mont Ségur, made a special trip north to play host to the royal party. Nicolette's private reunion with him was bleak and empty of feeling. When the King and Queen moved on, and she with them, she was relieved. So, she suspected, was Amalric, who hurried back to oversee his new holdings in Languedoc.

Summer in the north of France was usually the happiest season for Nicolette, because then it was most like home. But that summer, almost a year after she first saw the troubadour, there was a veil of sorrow between her and the warmth of the sun and the green of field and forest.

"There is news from Paris, Nicolette," Marguerite said gravely one morning at Troyes when Nicolette had come into the Queen's bedchamber to help her dress for the day. "A certain troubadour has returned."

Nicolette's body went hot, then cold. Why was Marguerite reporting this good news so solemnly?

"Tell me everything you know!" she cried.

"There are ill tidings, and much that only a friend who shares your secrets would dare to tell you."

"Why?" The dark look on Marguerite's oval face frightened Nicolette. Something terrible had happened.

"It involves your husband."

In her surprise Nicolette dropped the necklace she was trying to clasp around Marguerite's neck. "Amalric! Does he know?"

"It is possible," said Marguerite, catching the necklace as it slid over her bosom and fastening it on herself. "Here, sit down."

Nicolette stared into Marguerite's large brown eyes, trying to guess what she was going to tell her.

"An equerry who was carrying letters to Louis from Paris says that Orlando returned to his house in the faubourgs badly wounded, deathly ill. Hurt as he was, the equerry said, he had ridden all alone the whole way from the Pyrenees to Paris."

Nicolette felt dizzy.

The man she loved—yes, loved—deathly ill. Would he die? Would she never see him again? It was unbearable.

"What happened to him? How was he wounded? Tell me quickly."

"He had been with the army besieging Mont Ségur under your husband's command." Marguerite put her hand over Nicolette's.

Her troubadour, ravaging Languedoc? Nicolette felt as if she had been stabbed.

"I do not know what he was doing there, but it was Amalric who wounded him, Nicolette. They fought with daggers, in front of the whole army."

The room seemed to spin around.

Amalric and Orlando fighting? Was Orlando fighting against the crusaders? Or was it because of me? Is this why I have heard nothing from him? She pressed a hand to her throbbing forehead.

And Amalric. He had said nothing at Château Gobignon about this, nothing at all.

"But why were they fighting?" she asked in a trembling voice.

"It was over an order the troubadour did not wish to obey, something of that sort. Perhaps that was only an excuse. Perhaps they really fought because your husband knows of the troubadour's attentions to you."

An order? Of Amalric's? Then Orlando had joined the crusader army. Oh, how could he!

"How badly," Nicolette whispered, "did Amalric hurt him?"

"He stabbed him in the arm, I am told. But your troubadour gave a good account of himself. He had Amalric down and had a knife to his throat. He could have killed him, but he had the sense to hold his hand."

Nicolette shut her eyes as blackness seemed to fall around her like a curtain. She felt as if she were an earthenware figure someone had smashed to bits with a hammer. Surely Orlando was now lost to her. Amalric, until he was avenged, would never rest. And how could she and Orlando ever meet, now that Amalric would be watching him, hating him? If the troubadour had escaped death at Mont Ségur, it was only death briefly deferred.

Then her mood abruptly changed. Anger blazed up in her, and she felt her body grow hot. How could Orlando do this to her? Rage drove out grief. She clenched her fists in her lap.

What kind of man was this troubadour that he would first woo her, then turn his back on her to take part in a war against her homeland? How could he be such a fool as to challenge her husband? No, no, no, he is not worthy of Love, she told herself.

But then an image of the lean, dark face, the dazzling blue eyes, and their soul-searching gaze came to her. And she felt herself aching with longing.

Marguerite tried to console Nicolette. "Orlando was a fool. You will be much happier if you forget him. Besides, all troubadours are mad."

Nicolette pretended to take her seriously, but within she kept asking herself, How can I see him?

It was only later that Nicolette realized, with amazement, that if the fight had gone otherwise, she would now be a widow. The thought of such freedom sent a small thrill through her. Then she felt ashamed. How monstrous, to wish her husband, her children's father, dead. And how would she live, a widow with three daughters, dependent on Amalric's family? Would that be an escape, or a trap far worse than her marriage?

The prospect of death . . .

It brought her mind back to the long figure on the bed before her. Louis was only thirty. What a shame. It seemed terribly unfair to Nicolette that Louis should die so young. France needs him. There is no one else.

Tomorrow is Christmas Eve, she thought. Christmas, one thousand two hundred forty-four. But there was no Christmas gaiety here at Pontoise among those gathered at the royal bedside. People stood around the huge bed, watching the King with foreboding, watching one another with suspicion. Nicolette felt uneasy among them. She felt their presence almost as a physical pressure at her back. They were breathing the good air the King needed, air she herself needed.

Closest to the bedside were Queen Marguerite, whom Nicolette loved and pitied, and Queen Blanche of Castile, whom Nicolette feared. Near the two queens stood Louis's three younger brothers, Robert, Charles, and Alphonse. They were strong young men, but Nicolette felt none of them had the ability of their elder brother. A bit farther away were the highest officials of the court. Beyond them were bishops, barons, abbots, the heads of religious orders. And in an outermost circle were still others, more than could fit into the room. Almost all the great ones of the realm had come to pay homage and witness Louis's passing. A king, Nicolette had heard it said, never dies alone.

She sensed a stirring on the bed. The King's large eyes opened, and he stared up at her. Gasping with the effort, he levered himself into a sitting position, pushing back the tentative hand she put forth to hold him down. His forehead glistened with sweat, and he trembled under his white shirt as he held up the heavy wooden crucifix, clutching it with both hands.

The buzz of the crowd faded, and a silence fell over the room.

"Jerusalem is lost," he said in a voice that was now loud and firm, no longer a delirious murmur.

"Jerusalem is lost," he repeated, "and I have seen my duty." Now he seemed to stare at the fire in the huge hearth across the room.

Why does he keep talking about Jerusalem? Nicolette wondered. Behind her she heard people whispering the same question to one another. An uneasiness came over her, a premonition that something strange and terrible might soon happen.

"Peace, my son, peace," said Queen Blanche, moving to stand beside him, a tall, thin woman in a gown of white satin. She had been wearing white, the color of mourning for queens, ever since the death of Louis's father, and people called her the White Queen. She had ruled France all alone for ten years, until Louis came of age.

Nicolette was terrified of Blanche. She would never forget what had happened last year, when Louis's first son was born, a terrible childbirth that had almost killed Marguerite. Louis had been visiting Marguerite. Nicolette, too, had been there, at her friend's bedside. Suddenly Blanche had burst in and demanded that her son leave and come with her at once, claiming pressing state business.

"Alas," Marguerite had wept. "Can I not have him with me even when I am dying?"

Blanche had whirled and stared coldly at her daughter-in-law. "You have provided us with a royal heir. My son no longer needs you."

Blanche frightened most members of the court. She was a harsh woman of strong opinions, quick to find fault and totally unforgiving.

"What duty do you speak of, sire?" Marguerite now asked Louis as she leaned over the bedside.

"There will be time enough to talk of duty when you are better," said Queen Blanche, glaring at her daughter-in-law from under heavy eyebrows.

"Jerusalem," the King again intoned, his pale blue eyes fixed on the fireplace as if in its glow he was seeing those golden towers and crystal waters.

Nicolette wondered, had the fever made him mad?

"Louis, please," his mother begged.

"Let him speak!" Marguerite cried.

The clash of the two women closest to him seemed to draw the King down from his feverish exaltation, and he spoke more calmly. "I am going to take the crusader's cross, Mother. As I lay almost dead just now, I promised God that if He would let me live I would lead a crusade to liberate Jerusalem."

Nicolette heard the whispers start up again throughout the room. He is better, they were saying. He promised God he would go on crusade, and now he is sitting up and talking. She heard the word "miracle" uttered by more than one person.

No, someone else said gloomily, fever victims are often lucid before the end.

But this was not the end.

Sitting by the King, Nicolette could see with amazement and joy that those who spoke of a miracle were closer to the truth. His color was coming back; his eyes were sparkling. He was not on the brink of death but was moving farther away from it with every passing moment. And the change was so sudden! The moment he started speaking of Jerusalem the healing had begun.

Jerusalem. Despite the heat of the room Nicolette felt as if a blast of icy wind had blown through it. She shuddered. When had there last been a crusade? A *real* crusade, not like this Albigensian Crusade, this war of Christian against Christian in Languedoc. Not in her lifetime, thank God, had men taken the cross and marched off to Outremer—the land beyond the sea. She had heard tales from some of the old veterans—of great armies going out and only a handful of men returning. Of plagues, famines, droughts. Of the fury of the Saracen Turks, slaughtering knights by the thousands. Crusading to Outremer, her father had often said, was *one* madness at least that had gone out of fashion. "And thank God for that!" Guilhem de Lumel had always added.

Yet he had once said about the invaders of Languedoc, "those so-called crusaders" against whom he had fought all his life, "I just hope that before I am through they will wish they had gone to war against the Turks instead of their own countrymen." A few weeks later he had fallen in battle. Against so-called crusaders.

Within only a month after they brought back her father's body, slung over his war-horse, Amalric strode into her life. He was everything she expected a crusader to be—overbearing, bigoted, in love with the spilling of blood. To save her family's property from being seized by the Church she had married him, but she had felt herself no more than a prisoner of war. Little wonder that the very word *crusade* filled her with loathing.

And now the King? God forbid!

Blanche shook her head, looking to her other sons for support. "It is the fever that speaks."

Marguerite, too, looked shocked. "A crusade. Oh, no, Louis. You must not say such a thing."

The King now spoke with solemnity and without a trace of feverishness. "Look at me, Mother. Can you not see I am better? God has spared me. He wants me to rescue Jerusalem for Him."

"It is true!" cried the King's brother Robert, drawing a black look from Blanche. "The fever is broken."

"Praise be to God!" cried the Archbishop of Sens, raising his beringed hands prayerfully. At this, a murmur of wonder and joy rippled around the room. Some even fell upon their knees.

Despite her sadness and fear, Nicolette, too, felt relief burst forth in her like a mountain spring. It does almost seem like a miracle, she thought. He will not die, and the kingdom will be preserved.

Blanche peered more closely at her son. Her eyes widened, and Nicolette saw joy fleetingly appear in her pale face. She clasped her hands together convulsively.

"Thank God!" she whispered. "Oh, Louis . . ." She reached out toward him, but before she could embrace him, she drew back. She would not, Nicolette realized, show her love for her son in front of all these people.

When she spoke again her voice was firm, decisive. "You are right, Louis. God has spared your life. But you can serve Him best by fighting the heretics here at home."

Has there not already been enough killing in Languedoc? Nicolette thought angrily.

"Catharism is finished, Mother," Louis said. "Its last leaders died at Mont Ségur. I want to bring peace to Languedoc."

"Amen to that," said Marguerite with deep feeling.

Nicolette felt such warmth toward Marguerite that tears rushed to her eyes. We are children of Languedoc, she thought, more like sisters than friends.

"What we need is a purpose that will draw all Frenchmen together, north and south," Louis said. "Let our young men stop fighting one another and fight to free Jerusalem."

To die in Outremer instead of in their homeland? Nicolette thought. Is that so much better?

Blanche sighed. "If God wanted us to have Jerusalem, He would not have let the Saracens capture it. What has Christendom gained from all the blood and treasure that has already been spent trying to hold Jerusalem?"

"Mother, the Egyptian general, Baibars the Panther, captured Jerusalem only last June. Do you think God intends him to hold it forever? If we were to give up trying to deliver Jerusalem, that would cause more Christians to doubt their faith than were ever converted by the Cathars."

Blanche turned and walked away, shaking her head.

The atmosphere in the room had changed, Nicolette saw. It was no longer a death watch. The King was sitting up, talking excitedly. It really did seem as if his decision to crusade had made him better.

Nicolette's heart felt another cold touch of fear. If the men go to war in the East, what will become of me? Will Amalric go, and will I have to? She remembered hearing that the kings of France and the great barons had usually taken their wives. How could she survive those burning wastes filled with savage Muslims?

But then a deeper pain seemed to blot out this new fear. She had lost Orlando, her one hope of happiness. So what matter if she were to die in the East?

Marguerite broke into the circle around the bed and held Louis's hand tightly in both of hers.

"Louis, Louis, if you had died it would have killed me, too. I thank God for your life, whatever His reason for giving you back to me. If your promise to take the cross saved you, it saved me as well. But, mark you well, I may still forbid you to go on crusade." She said this with a smile, and the King smiled fondly back at her. Nicolette saw the love between them and felt envious.

Now she could see the pink coming back into his cheeks. How powerful Love is, Nicolette thought.

"You would forbid the King?" Louis said.

"Yes, sire. Unless you promise to take me to Outremer with you."

For answer Louis reached out to her and drew her against his chest.

The White Queen turned purple as a turnip. "This is madness," Blanche fumed. "I would rather see you dead right now, my son, than to destroy yourself and the kingdom in Outremer."

What really incensed her, Nicolette knew, was the sight of Louis embracing Marguerite.

Blanche marched out of the room, eyes blazing. The lords, ladies, and prelates shrank back from her. Then they all turned to the King to see how he would deal with his mother's fury. Louis only shook his head ruefully, called for the chest of maps that always traveled with him, and began to make plans with his brothers.

Nicolette, seeing that she was no longer needed, went back to the small room she shared with Agnes on a lower floor of the château.

Agnes was waiting for her, a peculiar smile on her face.

"Agnes, the king has declared that he is going on a crusade."

"I know, madame. The servants are all abuzz about it. But everyone says it will take years before the King and his army will be ready to leave, and between now and then much could happen to change his mind. Right now I have something to show you." She held out her hand. Nicolette saw in it a roll of parchment tied with a black ribbon.

Her heart leaped for joy.

He had written. He was well enough to write.

Love was alive.

Feeling almost too weak to hold the scroll, she reached out for it and said in a small voice, "Please . . ."

Agnes understood and left her alone.

Nicolette sat on the edge of her bed and began to read.

Again the words were in the *Langue d'Oc*. They began:

> Parted from you, I wither in my need,
> A flower too long hidden from the light.
> On your clear heavenly brightness must I feed.

The King's recovery—could that be a sign? Nicolette wondered when she finished the last verse. I thought he was going to die, and he did not. I thought Love, too, was dead, but perhaps it is not. His love for me must be alive, or he would not have written so to me.

She checked herself. No, I cannot trust in him. He is a fool who will not live long. I am sure to lose him, and the suffering will be more than I can bear. I am no silly maiden. I have three children. I am a countess. I have paid dearly for the title. My husband is one of the greatest landholders in the kingdom. Am I to risk all that?

Within her a voice whispered, *yes*.

She looked down at the poem unrolled in her lap, and she hungered to hold in her arms the man who had written it. Without him, nothing is important to me.

If I die—if Amalric kills me because I bind myself to Orlando—will that be worse than having to live without him? What Mother told me long ago is true: life without Love is a living death. I need him as I need air to breathe.

And I have not the power to command Love to go away. It possesses me, and I am far too weak to disobey.

She was breathing hard, her chest rising and falling with excitement. She was suddenly acutely aware of her breasts moving against the silk of her shift.

She stood up, rolled the poem tightly, and slipped it into a secret pocket in the crimson samite belt that hung low about her hips.

I will not make the same mistake twice, she thought. This time I will meet him.

Her heart was fluttering.

With Louis better, the royal party would be returning to Paris. Then she would send him a message.

V

THOUGH HOODED AND CLOAKED, NICOLETTE TREMBLED. THE CHILL of the January afternoon pierced her through, but it was fear, more than the cold, that made her limbs shake. Having just crossed over to the Left Bank, she glanced back over her shoulder and saw the towers and spires of the royal palace across the Seine. She felt as if hidden eyes there were watching her. Could anyone on the palace wall have seen her walk over the Petit-Pont?

Not Amalric. He was still in the south, the King having just appointed him seneschal for Béziers and the surrounding country. But he had so many agents in Paris and allies at court. Except for Agnes, all the servants in the Gobignon town house were loyal to him. His aunt, Queen Blanche, was forever praising him to all who would listen. If Nicolette were involved in scandal, the White Queen would be furious, and would see to it that word reached Amalric. And if indeed he found out about her meeting the troubadour? Just a message, a song, let alone a meeting like this one, could mean death for her and Orlando.

I should turn around right now, cross this bridge, and run back to the palace. The streets of the Latin Quarter were crawling with ruffians and criminals—it was insane for her to be walking here alone after sunset. The sight of the small knife she carried under her cloak might deter an attacker, but then she would be discovered.

If I screamed for help, the whole palace would find out. Blanche would demand to know why I was here. No, she thought, her blood turning to ice, she would *know* why.

But those eyes of his, to look into them again, was that not worth any risk?

She stood, vacillating, in the shadows by a wooden house that overhung the Rue Saint-Jacques. I must see Orlando, she thought. Over a year now, and I have not been able to forget him. She longed just to be alone with him and have him take her in his arms.

But first he must answer the questions that tormented her. Why had he become a crusader? Why had he fought Amalric? Could he truly care for her and hurt her so?

He would have to explain. And even if his explanation fully satisfied her, she had nonetheless to remain firm and withhold the ultimate favor.

Sweet Goddess! she thought suddenly. I have never even spoken to him. I know nothing about the man, nothing at all.

What if he tries to get me into some sordid little room and force himself on me, like an animal? How will I fight him off? All alone, not able to cry for help.

No, it will not be like that, it could not be. I would have known if he were that kind of man, and felt repelled. He could not sing and write such beautiful verses, and look so fine if he were not the man I want him to be. Yes, when we meet, it will be as it is in his songs. He will obey, do exactly what I tell him and no more. Oh, I have hoped so long for this. Goddess of Love, let it be beautiful.

The path before her was anything but beautiful. The crooked streets seemed to hold fresh terrors at every step. It was hard for her to see her way now that the sun was almost down. The jutting upper stories of the houses had plunged the streets almost into darkness. She worried that she might not remember the directions he had written to her. She brushed against rough walls as she hurried along, trying to avoid all attention and to keep out of the mud, reeking of manure, that covered the center of these streets. She picked her way over planks laid down by the servingmen of the university, but more than once she stepped ankle-deep into a puddle. My good leather boots will be ruined, she thought, and if someone sees them before I get rid of them, how will I explain that?

From under her fur-trimmed hood she cast furtive glances at the dozens of swaggering students from all the nations of Christendom. Their heads were shaved in clerical tonsures, but they brazenly wore long daggers at their belts, even though carrying weapons was forbidden to students. Studying for the priesthood or not, she thought, each one looked as if he would like nothing better than to push her into an alley and have his way with her.

And the masters, those scholars in black mantles who walked two by two, conversing in rapid Latin, would be no help at all.

More of Orlando's strangeness, she thought, having me meet him in the Latin Quarter. He should know I have never been in these streets before. I could get lost. She looked up at the buildings leaning over her like unfriendly giants. I am lost right now.

The thought brought on a sudden access of anger. Marguerite is right. Troubadours are all mad: professing to worship their ladies, they thrust them into danger! And *I* am mad, to venture here.

But could she find her way back to the palace? The houses all looked alike. The streets were so dark now. And even if she dared approach any of these passersby, none of them seemed to be speaking a language she understood. Yet she could not just stand here. At any moment she could be accosted.

How she hated this cold, muddy city.

Resolutely, she turned back the way she had just come.

She would look for the Rue Saint-Jacques. She thought she would recognize it, because it was broader than the other streets and was paved here and there with old stones. The Rue Saint-Jacques, she knew, led right to the bridge.

Her feet began to hurt now as she hurried, uncertain as she turned corners. Then she looked down and saw a great worn slab. Never had a simple piece of stone given her such relief.

Now, which way is the bridge?

She stepped out into the middle of the street and looked both ways. Above a rooftop, she caught a glimpse, thank God, of the gold-painted spire of Notre-Dame, glittering faintly in the last rays of sunset. Oh, thank you, holy Mary. She headed toward the Petit-Pont.

Then she heard something. A fine tenor, it cut through the babble in the street and held her motionless.

> "God save Lady Eleanor
> Queen who art the arbiter
> Of honor, wit, and beauty,
> Of largesse and loyalty.
> Born wert thou in happy hour
> And wed to Henry King."

A tingling sensation ran from her scalp down her spine, and she felt herself reaching deep for breath. The voice was not one she recognized, but its sweetness and the beauty of the melody, so well wedded with the words, touched her deep inside. It was a song about Eleanor of Aquitaine, her ideal ever since she first heard tales of the great queen at her mother's knee. It was Eleanor, a woman of Languedoc, who had brought *l'amour courtois*, the cult of Love, into the palaces of kings and inspired generations of troubadours.

She stood enchanted, oblivious now of menacing passersby. The verses following one after another transported her to another world, a world in which beauty ruled and terror was banished. In this world men loved women and served them loyally. If they did bloody deeds, it was only out of devotion to their ladies.

When the song came to an end, Nicolette felt stronger, and more at peace. Her fears still lurked in the back of her mind, but they no longer possessed her.

She saw that she was standing before a tavern whose sign bore the device of two crossed gold swords on a red background.

The Two Swords, Nicolette remembered, was a sign Orlando had mentioned.

Still under the spell, hearing the song again in her mind, Nicolette asked herself, Would Eleanor have run away from such a rendezvous like a frightened milkmaid? Would she, who had been married first to the King of France, then to the King of England—and had dared to stand up to both of them—let a husband's anger stop her from meeting her lover?

Nicolette felt new strength surging through her.

Orlando's directions now came back to her. From the Two Swords, left at the first corner. After a doorway decorated with a figure of Saint Julian the Hospitaler in his boat, left again and you will be on the Street of Straw. Intently, shutting out all her fears, she set herself in motion. In minutes she spied Saint Julian.

A hooded figure blocked her path.

She cried out.

A powerful hand seized her arm.

Her fingers darted to the little knife at her belt.

"Hush, madame. You are safe. It is only me."

The voice! It was his! At the sound of it, her heart leaped up for joy.

A sudden blaze of torchlight threw their shadows against the white wall beside them, and a wealthy student strutted past, with a linkboy to light his way and another servant to carry his huge, leather-bound books.

The reddish glow enabled Nicolette to see the face deep in the shadow of the hood. Piercing eyes, an arching nose that gave him the look of a bird of prey.

"Sire Orlando."

"I have been following you ever since you crossed the bridge. Now we are this close to our destination, I thought it time to make myself known." He spoke low, in a voice like velvet. It recalled his songs to her.

She shivered, and realized that he was still holding her arm, that this was the first time he had ever touched her.

"You were about to turn back, were you not?"

"Yes." She answered automatically, and then thought, All that time I was stumbling around lost, he was watching me. Why did he not help me? Again she felt anger well up within her.

"And if I had elected to leave this charming quarter?" she challenged him. "Would you have tried to stop me?"

He did not answer, but looked deep into her eyes as he held out his arm.

She took it and they started walking together down the Street of Straw. Suddenly dizzy with excitement at being with him at last, she leaned heavily on his arm. The strength she felt in him enthralled her.

"I would have wanted to stop you," he finally said. "I would have wanted to kneel down in the street and beg."

His response melted the last of her anger, and she realized suddenly that he was speaking in the *Langue d'Oc*. How could he be from Italy?

"But I would not have done as I wanted," he went on in a thoughtful tone. "I know what a chance you are taking. I wanted to see whether you would come to meet me all on your own, without any more persuasion, whatever the obstacles."

She shivered at the reminder of her peril. She had been in danger before, but now that they were together she knew she had crossed the threshold. If ever they were seen together, she was doomed.

Yet she felt delight, not in spite of the danger, but because of it. The hollow sensation in her stomach, her cold palms, were not making her miserable. Quite the contrary. To *choose* danger, to embrace it and not just suffer it, felt thrilling. Now, she thought, I understand a little why men go to war.

They stopped, and she looked up at a handsome, three-story building, its timber exterior coated with plaster.

"The house of Guillaume the Bookseller," said Orlando. "In the back there is wine, and good talk for those who love books."

"I have heard of it," said Nicolette. Guillaume's was whispered about among the younger courtiers. A place where the most rebellious students gathered and heresies were openly discussed. Just now it seemed the perfect place for her adventurous mood. She took a deep breath, and when he opened the door for her, she went in.

She was dazzled by the light of many candles. When her eyes became accustomed to the light, she saw hundreds of volumes stacked on tables. Two brawny apprentices, she noticed, were standing guard over the expensive books. Quickly she dropped her eyes and reached up to draw her hood closer about her face.

Orlando led her to another door, and she stepped into a darker room. Here there were no windows and few candles. People sat in the shadows at small tables drinking and talking softly. Nicolette had heard that the people who frequented Guillaume's actually dared to exchange ideas on sorcery and even to accuse the bishops and the barons of robbing the poor, talk that could land a person in the dungeons of the Inquisition.

A young man strumming an Irish harp leaned against the far wall. He had blond hair in tight curls and an impish grin, and seemed to give Orlando the faintest of nods as she and Orlando moved quickly to a table in a dark corner. Was the young man, she wondered, one of those scurrilous poet-outlaws of the Latin Quarter known as *Les Chiens Enragés,* the Mad Dogs?

The blond man struck a chord, and the room fell silent.

Nicolette, pleasantly tremulous, listened intently.

> "Our Lord had nothing to His name,
> He had to beg for shelter and for meals.
> Our Pope, he tries to do the same,
> And lives exclusively on what he steals."

Nicolette found herself joining in the almost furtive laughter that rippled softly but pervasively around the room. Surely the singer was one of the Mad Dogs.

But what a joy. I have not heard that kind of song since I married Amalric, she thought. No one would dare make such sport at Château Gobignon—or, for that matter, at the royal palace.

This bookseller's back room reminded her of her childhood home, of the free talk at her father's table.

She turned and smiled at Orlando. He smiled back at her, and her skin tingled.

I must not let myself be swept away. Not yet.

"What would you say if I told you that man is my jongleur, and that is my song?" Orlando asked her.

Just then a stout, bearded man, perhaps Guillaume the Bookseller himself, brought two big earthenware cups of the local pale-gold wine of Paris. Setting the glasses down, he left without a word. Orlando's privacy, she saw, was respected here.

Now I must question him, Nicolette thought.

Still, she hesitated. The moments since he appeared out of the shadows on the street had been so deliciously exciting. Now, if his answers proved to be unworthy, all her love and hope would turn to dust.

But she saw a warmth in his eyes that gave her the courage to begin.

"I find it strange that a man who writes songs mocking the Pope also crusades against the Cathars. Just where do you put your loyalty, Sire Orlando?"

His blue eyes burned at her. "Let me tell you at once that my name is not Orlando but Roland. Roland de Vency. Like you, I was born in Languedoc."

She was amazed. And yet she wasn't. Nervous laughter bubbled up in her throat. She put her hand to her heart. "Why are you telling me this?"

"To place my life in your hands, *mi dons.*"

Mi dons! A wave of joy overwhelmed her. By those words in the *Langue d'Oc* the troubadour was declaring his total submission to her.

Then a ripple of fear erased the joy. "Why do you use a false name?"

His answering smile appeared. "I am a faidit. My father, Arnaut de Vency, was like so many knights of Languedoc. He fought for his homeland against the crusaders and the inquisitors. So did I, when I got old enough. But then they were coming too close to capturing us. And every time we killed one of them, they would hang ten village boys. We could not go on. We could not stay in Languedoc. The name de Vency is on the lists of outlaws. So, were I to use my real name now, I would suffer for it—for my deeds *and* my father's."

Orlando's—Roland's—father was just like mine, she thought, feeling a new warmth of kinship with the troubadour. *If I had been a man, my story might be the same.*

"But why did you come back to France?"

Roland shrugged and smiled sadly. "I have many ties here." He looked up at her suddenly, his face shadowed with pain. "But now I know that it is not enough for me to be just a troubadour. After seeing all those good people die at Mont Ségur, I have vowed that I will do whatever I can to work against such things."

Her head began to ache. In answering her questions, he was only adding to them. He was at Mont Ségur. And wearing the cross. But how could he, after what he just told her? Was he playing with her, enjoying her confusion?

"Well. Once again then, messire, what were you doing at Mont Ségur in the first place?" she said sharply. "If the crusaders are truly your enemies, how could you have joined them?"

He drained his cup, set it down hard, and stared at her. "Will you trust me?"

His eyes held hers, and she wanted to stroke his cheek with her fingertips.

Could she trust him?

"What do you ask of me?" she said, and was worried by the uncertainty she heard in her own voice.

"Come with me where we can talk in greater safety. I have had a room prepared for us above. Will *mi dons* go there with me?"

She had been expecting such an invitation. When she heard his voice speak the words, a sudden warmth flooded her loins. She was shocked by the eagerness of her body.

But suspicion darkened her mind. He has told me little, and now when I press him he refuses to allay my confusion. Could he just want to get me alone and take advantage of my weakness?

"I have already granted you more than you deserve under the laws of Love, which you yourself have invoked," she said, trying to keep her voice steady. "It is time I left now. Will you escort me back to the bridge?"

Now she saw pain in his blue eyes.

He looked at her, speechless.

Say something that will make me stay! her heart begged him.

He bowed his head and spoke in a choked voice. "Certainly, if it is your wish to go."

Regret washed over her like a sudden incoming tide.

No, no, I have wanted this so much, she thought. I cannot turn my back on him now and return to living the way I have been. I might never see him again.

She made no move to get up from the table.

"How can I know," she said hesitantly, "whether you will deal honestly with me?"

He leaned toward her, and his eyes were bright and compelling in the candlelight. "Risk it."

She regarded the grave face before her.

No, his was not the face of a liar. And he felt as she did about Mont Ségur. Heretics, yes, but *our* people, people of Languedoc. Had not Amalric burned them? As he would burn me if he could see into my heart.

She felt strange and tremulous as Roland's gaze held hers. Am I going to let my fear of Amalric stamp out every bit of life left in me?

His hand slid across the table till it rested on top of her own.

His audacity knew no limit!

But had she not left her hand lying there to be taken? And could he have seen anything but invitation in her eyes?

His palm felt warm and dry. Fire traveled up her arm. She could not move her hand. The thought of intimacy with him thrilled her. She felt as if she were riding a hunting horse at full gallop through an unknown forest.

Suddenly she stood up and said in a low voice, "I will go with you." Their hands were still joined.

As they went to the flight of stairs near their table, the jongleur struck a brazen chord on his harp and sang.

> "Let wine to my lips be nigh
> At life's dissolution.
> That will make the angels cry
> With glad elocution,
> 'Grant this drunkard, God on high,
> Grace and absolution.' "

Nicolette glanced back as she left the room, and saw that their departure was unnoticed. Everyone was enjoying the jongleur. Roland gestured to her and she climbed the steps ahead of him.

On the second floor, Roland pushed open a heavy door. She saw the golden glow of a small fire within. He went in ahead of her, lit a taper, and touched it to the candles of a large brass candelabrum on a table.

Her legs trembled as she crossed the threshold. Now, she thought, I will find out what he really is.

Light by light as the candles flared up, the chamber revealed

itself to her. It seemed for a moment as if she had walked into a
silken pavilion. No window was visible. Walls and ceiling were
covered with heavy draperies embroidered in complex Saracen
patterns, mazes and whorls, vines of crimson, green and gold
twining together invitingly. On one side of the room a huge bed
strewn with brightly colored cushions stood raised on a carpeted
platform. At the sight of it her heartbeat quickened, whether with
fear or desire she was not sure.

Roland went back to the door and slid a thick wooden bar
through two iron brackets. "In the great days of Languedoc such
meetings as this would take place in the secret chambers of fair
châteaux," he said with his wry smile. "Now we must hide in
wine shops."

He took her hand and started to lead her to the bed.

She felt herself panicking. This was happening too quickly. In
Love the lady must be the *dons*, the master.

She pulled her hand out of his grasp.

"Wine shop or no, messire, this room has its own consider-
able beauty. How much do you pay Guillaume to keep it ready
for your use?" she asked lightly.

"There has been no woman in my life since I met you. No
woman I can love as I love you."

Odd, *No woman I can love as I love you.* He seemed to be
correcting himself.

"I am afraid that you may not understand what Love means to
me, Sire Roland. Love cannot be like a wild spring flood that
destroys and is gone. It must flow like a kindly river. It must
nurture what grows beside it. It is the union of soul with soul
that the lady and the lover must strive to attain. Must earn."

"Your soul enchants me," Roland said, taking her hand and
looking deep into her eyes.

She felt dizzy.

"But the philosophers," he continued, "say the soul is the
form of the body. I adore the beauty of your soul made visible in
your lovely body."

"If you would love me, you must be ruled by me."

"I *will* be ruled by you, *mi dons*," said Roland, his dark head
bowed. "I will dedicate my art to you. I will make and sing a
hundred songs to your beauty." He knelt before her.

She wanted to bury her fingers in his thick hair, to press his
head against her, but she fought the urge. She must maintain the
commanding air called for by the code of Love.

"You will have a chance to make good that promise, Sire

Roland. On the first of May the Queen holds a singing contest to celebrate the King's return to good health. Every notable troubadour and trouvère in Christendom is to be summoned. You may be sure I shall see you get an invitation. You shall be my champion.''

Roland smiled, raising one dark eyebrow. ''Delighted, *mi dons*. That is the kind of battle I like best.''

Battle. Mont Ségur. She still did not know why he had gone there. He had dared to avoid answering her question; she must dare to persist in asking it.

''Since it did not occur to you to provide chairs when you had this room prepared, I will sit on the bed and you will remain where you are.'' She turned from him with a swirl of her long skirt and sat primly on the edge of the great bed. The ropes cradling the down-stuffed mattress creaked faintly.

''As you wish, *mi dons*.'' He stayed on his knees.

''You may stand if you would be more comfortable.''

Silently, he got to his feet. His mouth was solemn, but she could see a twinkle of amusement in his eyes.

''I hope you did not think to distract me by taking me to this Turkish paradise, messire. I still must know what you were doing at Mont Ségur. And what possessed you to challenge my husband to a fight with daggers.''

''Ah, your husband.'' His broad smile showed that he took no offense at her haughty tone but well understood that it was part of courtly custom.

''Yes, my husband. It is a miracle that you stand whole and hale before me. Do you know how many men he has killed? What were you thinking of, messire?''

''Not of myself, *mi dons*.'' He shrugged, and a sadness came into his face. ''The Count de Gobignon ordered that all the Cathar perfecti, old men, women, people exhausted from starvation, be dragged by brute force down the rocky mountainside to the pyre. I protested. I did not challenge him. And I never drew a weapon against him. If you had talked to anyone who saw the fight you would know that. In the end I got his dagger away from him and forced him to take back his order.''

''What you say agrees with what I have heard. But did you have to humiliate him like that?''

The troubadour spread his hands as if to show surprise at her question.

''Madame, when you are fighting for your life you do not worry about the other fellow's pride.''

"He must hate you more than any other man on earth. Do you not realize that?"

The troubadour shrugged. "It has been almost a year since that happened, madame, and he has yet to try to avenge himself."

His seeming obtuseness made her furious. He was a fool who had been lucky once. It was that simple.

"Apparently you have no idea what sort of man you have made your enemy. He owns enough land to be a king in his own right. He has to deal with a thousand matters, great and small, every day. But he is not one to forget an injury. He will get around to you."

"I know the house of Gobignon much better than you think I do." The troubadour gazed at her with that infuriating, calm amusement. "What would you have me do? Flee the country again?"

"What would I have you do?" She was clenching her teeth. "There is nothing you can do. It is too late. It was already too late when you protested his order. Why did you provoke him so, if you wanted to pay court to me?"

"You are right." Roland shook his head. "It would have been wiser for me to hold my tongue. But it would not have been human."

She drew a deep breath. "If the Cathars are so dear to you, what were you doing in the crusader army? What darkness lies here, Sire Roland, that you have thrice answered this question with evasion?"

He groaned softly.

She waited.

After a long silence he said, "I cannot tell you."

Every muscle in her body went rigid. "You call me your *dons*, and yet you would keep secrets from me. You are trifling with me, messire." She stood up. "Let me out of here at once."

He held up a placating hand. "Wait, please. You must try to understand."

Rage boiled up inside her. Understand? He all but spat in her face and then asked her to understand. Did he take her for an idiot?

"I do not care to put my life in jeopardy only to hear your lies—to be told I must trust you even as you refuse to place your trust in me."

His brows drew together and his eyes flashed blue fire.

"If I wanted to lie to you, do you not think I could invent a tale that would satisfy you better? When I say that I cannot tel you, it is the simple truth. It is not a matter of trust between us—other people's lives hang on my silence. If you knew the full truth about Mont Ségur, you would be in far more danger than now.''

"From whom?" she snapped.

"From the Inquisition," he said through bared teeth.

The word quenched her anger with fear. All her life she had lived in dread of the white-robed friars with their pale, pinched faces, their eyes ever greedy to feast on the evil they seemed to see all about them. Their anonymous spies, their secret torture chambers, their power to order people burned alive. When she was a little girl the inquisitors had prowled through her night-mares more often than wolves or dragons.

"Now do you understand?" Roland pressed her. "I told you I have vowed to do all I can to put a stop to such horrors as the Mont Ségur massacre. Do you think I wore the crusader's cross to fight against my own people? Me, a faidit and the son of a faidit? Why do you think I go under a false name? You know enough about me now to guess at what I was doing at Mont Ségur, and that must suffice. You know enough to send me to the flames. I am in your power." His grin was humorless; only the left side of his mouth turned up.

What is he trying to tell me? she asked herself. That his crusader's cross was a disguise, like the name Orlando of Perugia? *You know enough about me to guess at what I was doing at Mont Ségur*. He must mean that he was on the Cathar side. Could he have been carrying a message to those in the stronghold? Or from it, to someone outside? Other lives hanging on his keeping silent—whose lives? Had someone survived the massacre?

Uncertainty—and despair whether she might ever know who Roland was—were two rough hands wringing her heart. Perhaps this, perhaps that! Anything was possible. He could make any claim he liked, and how would she know? Until, perhaps, too late. No, she had best get out of here. Now.

"From the moment I saw you at Chinon I believed in you, and you repaid my trust by vanishing without warning. For almost a year, I had not the slightest sign that you cared for me. Then to hear, not from you but from others, of these mad deeds—joining the invaders of Languedoc, dueling with my husband. And now you expect me to accept you as my lover even though you still offer me no explanation? Do you think I am such a fool as that, Sire Orlando—Roland—whatever your name is?"

His crooked smile again. "I do not think you are a fool, *mi dons.* I think you *know* I am telling the truth.'' He advanced toward her a step at a time. ''You will accept me as your lover because you love me.''

She stood paralyzed. His hungry stare had turned her to stone, like the gaze of that monster of the bestiary books, the basilisk.

''Stay where you are, messire. No, open the door for me. I will not love you, because I cannot trust you.''

''*Mi dons,* you cannot help loving me, whatever I am. I see you, and I know you. Love is your master. As she is mine.''

Nicolette felt heat rising in her body. Her breath quickened.

''I will fight you,'' she said. ''If I cannot be sure of you, I will drive you away.'' But she felt about to fall backward. Her calves were pressed against the soft, yielding bed.

Roland took another step toward her, smiling. ''Have I asked *you* to explain why you are married to the enemy?''

His words struck like a blow to the pit of her stomach. She was first shocked, then furious. How cruel! How unfair! I had no choice. She sprang at him and slapped him across the face with all her strength.

She saw with satisfaction that she had staggered him. His face reddened, but his hands remained hanging at his sides.

Instantly, tears filled her eyes.

''Roland, I am sorry. Forgive me. Will you forgive me, please?'' She threw herself at him again, this time wrapping her arms around him.

His answering embrace was gentle at first, then tightened about her as she held him more fiercely.

She wept into his chest. ''You are right. I betrayed our people when I married Amalric. I have no right to question you.''

''I know you had your reasons for marrying him,'' he said softly, ''and I am sure that they were good ones. Forgive me for mentioning him. As for me, it is true that I am withholding much from you. Believe in me, and some day, when it is safe, I will tell you all you want to know.''

Desire made her legs weak. She pressed her body against him.

''It is just as you said,'' she whispered. ''I love you, whatever you are.''

To her amazement, he held back.

''You know that I want you, *mi dons,* but you did not mean to lie with me today. When you entered this room''—he smiled—''this Turkish paradise with me, you instructed me in the course our love must take. And I know you were right. It is too soon. I *want* to earn the right to hold you naked, body and soul, in my arms. When our love ripens, our passion will be all the stronger and our union all the sweeter.''

She stepped away from him, breathing as heavily as if she had climbed the spiral steps of a high castle tower.

"I am yours, now as I will be then," she breathed.

He dropped to his knees before her and took her hand. "I am *yours, mi dons.* I am your true troubadour, now and forever. Command me in all things. I will live from this moment as you wish. By Love I swear it.''

Her heart turned to molten gold in her chest. Tears streamed down her cheeks.

He held his hand up to her, and she took it.

"I will always be your lady and live for you and love you through eternity. By Love I also swear it.''

Gently she raised him to his feet and held up her arms to him.

His kiss was like a hot coal on her lips.

VI

ROLAND FELT HIS STOMACH KNOTTING. HAVING RIDDEN OUT OF THE city through the Saint-Denis Gate, he now was nearly home, and the hurt inside was cutting so deep that he thought it would drive him mad. He repeated again and again the pledge he had just made to Nicolette: *I am your true troubadour, now and forever.* It felt like a knife stabbing into him.

I do love her, as I have not loved any other—except Diane.

Under his fur-lined mantle he was sweating, despite the bone-deep chill of the January night.

Was my pledge to Nicolette a lie?

No, not now that Diane has vowed herself to God.

He had always believed that a man or a woman could love but one person. For all the years he had loved Diane, he had accepted that as a sacred law of Love. It was the way things should be. But it was not the way they were. Not for him.

What if I had known, that day I saw Nicolette at Chinon, that Diane was still alive? I would have wanted Nicolette just as much, but I would not have begun this. There would have been no messages, no song in her garden. But I was sure Diane was dead. There was nothing but a memory of a younger time to check my feelings for Nicolette.

And then, when I found Diane again, I could not have her. I had lost her forever. So at last I wrote again to Nicolette.

But tonight, when Nicolette would have let me make love to her—and how I want her!—I could not go beyond an embrace and a kiss.

Not as long as I still love Diane.

When he had set out, a full moon had hung low above the huddled rooftops of the university town. Now the silver disk was high overhead, and he could discern the small house he had bought two years ago with money he brought with him from Sicily. My little château, he thought fondly, with bare poplars and fruit trees rising above its crumbling wall. He especially liked the three-story watchtower, built in the days when Northmen raided Paris. Diane had been living in the circular tower room, her presence here a daily joy and torment.

He saw a dark figure glide through his gate, just under the lower branches of the bare trees, and he reined his palfrey up sharply. A rectangle of yellow light glowed as the shadow entered through the front door, then the front yard was dark again. He felt fear in his chest. De Gobignon? *He will get around to you,* Nicolette had said. This very night?

He slid down from his horse and hastily tied her to a tree stump before a neighbor's darkened house. He slipped through the same front gate the figure had entered and then went around to the rear. Noiselessly he opened the back door and stepped quickly inside, his hand hovering near his dagger.

Lucien, the cook, his wife, Adrienne, and their son, Martin, were huddled for warmth around the kitchen fire. They started and stared at him, and Adrienne gave a little cry of surprise and put her hand to her heart. Roland was relieved to see that they, at least, were unharmed.

"Did you hear someone come in at the front?" he asked, quietly.

"It was your sister, messire," said Lucien. "Madame Diane is in the hall, talking to Master Perrin."

Roland relaxed. His limbs trembled a little as the tension eased.

But then he realized he did not want to face Diane. Nicolette's kiss was fresh on his lips, and guilt clawed at his heart. He just wanted to be alone, perhaps to sleep, if he could.

But unless he left again there was no avoiding Diane. He took a deep breath and pushed open the door.

Perrin was seated at the trestle table, facing Diane. His blond head swung around toward Roland when he entered. Diane's delicate lips curved in a small smile, and Roland's insides twisted painfully. The lovely face that had delighted him so was now a reproach.

"Go on, tell him," Diane said to Perrin. She stood straight and tall in her hooded cloak of coarse wool, her feeble protection against the winter's cold. She had refused the fur-lined cape Roland had offered her, as she had refused his love.

Perrin expelled his breath angrily. "Very well, madame." He turned to Roland, his eyes troubled. "I have to whisper it, master. We do not want them to know." He jerked his head toward the kitchen.

"What the devil is it, Perrin?"

"Madame claims," Perrin said almost inaudibly, "that she has your permission to preach to secret Cathar meetings right here in Paris."

Fear constricted Roland's chest. He could still see the flames at Mont Ségur.

True, Diane had warned him that if she took refuge with him in Paris she was going to continue her work among the Cathar faithful. And he worried each time she had quietly slipped out after sunset.

Diane's eyes held his. He stood immobile, feeling as if nails were being driven into his temples.

"Diane, the friars are not going to stop just because Mont Ségur is gone. Now they are more active in Paris. Only last week they burned a woman and two men in front of Notre-Dame. Some day you will get a message that someone needs the consolamentum and you will go, and instead of a dying person there will be a Dominican."

"Yes, I knew the people they burned," said Diane, bowing her head in sorrow.

Then she looked up, and he saw defiance in her clear green eyes. "But that is exactly why I must redouble *my* efforts. They are determined to stamp out our religion, but we are not going to let them."

She turned to Perrin, smiling gently. "Still, Master Perrin is

in the right. I have been endangering you two and those innocent
servants. I should leave here. I should have left long ago.''

No! Roland's heart cried out.

Perrin looked as if Diane's suggestion pained him also. "No,
madame. Please do not talk of going. That is not at all why I
waited up to speak to you tonight. It is as the master said—if you
keep on going to meet your Cathar people, the Dominicans will
catch you. I could not bear to see that happen.''

"Would you not risk everything for your Catholic faith, Perrin?'' she asked.

The jongleur cast his eyes down. "I do not have that much
faith, madame.''

She is finer, more spiritual, than anyone else I have known,
Roland thought. And with all that, so beautiful.

He felt the pounding in his temples again, the nails being
hammered in deeper.

"Diane, walk with me in the garden.''

He saw apprehension in her look. She had still not gotten over
her fear of him.

Inclining her head, she preceded him through the door leading
to the kitchen.

'It is the middle of the night—you should all be in bed,''
Roland growled at the little family in the kitchen. He did not
wait for an answer, but followed Diane into the garden. He drew
his squirrel-lined cloak tighter around him against the frigid air.

"The only house that has any privacy is one where a man
lives alone,'' he said. "In spite of Perrin's caution, I think the
servants must know all about you.''

"They seem like good people,'' she said. "Not the sort who
would inform. But if they do know what I am, it must frighten
them terribly that I am here.''

Yes, Roland thought, and if anything happens to them, that,
too, will be my fault.

It was too cold to sit on the stone benches. So they stood
facing each other beside an old apple tree with gnarled black
branches.

"I suppose you think your nightly wanderings are none of my
business.''

"No,'' she said. "Because if you are caught harboring me,
you would probably spend the rest of your life in a dungeon.
That is the penalty these days for protecting heretics. Do you not
fear that?''

He tried to picture himself in a tiny stone cell, no light, unable to move, no one to talk to, buried there for months, years, till he died. I would go mad, he thought. I would much rather be hanged outright. Or even burned.

But all he said was, "A knight must know how to live with risks."

"Send me away, Roland. Tell me to go. For the sake of everyone here. Please."

"Do you want so much to be away from me? Why not just leave? I cannot stop you."

"I have been ordered to stay here."

Her answer hurt him. He had not known that.

He turned and studied her face, like marble in the moonlight.

Would she stay if she knew I am paying court to another woman?

"I want you to know where I was tonight, Diane," he said through clenched teeth. "I met in secret with Nicolette de Gobignon."

She gave him a quick, frightened stare, like a startled deer. "The Countess de Gobignon? The wife of Count Amalric, who almost killed you at Mont Ségur?"

Roland laughed sourly. "Come, Diane. Give me some credit for my accomplishments. I could have killed him if I had chosen to."

"Roland," she said softly, "everything you have done is for love of me, I understand that. You risked your life to rescue me. And risking it again with de Gobignon to spare my people some pain, that too was probably partly for my sake. Now you shelter me in your house because you do not want to part from me. But, Roland, you, in chains for life? I do not want to be the cause of that."

"I did not go to the Countess de Gobignon this night for your sake," he said angrily.

"Are you so sure of that?"

The question gave Roland pause and somehow drained the anger from him.

"Do you think my evening with Nicolette de Gobignon is a way of wooing you?" he asked her.

"I hope not, Roland." He could see tears sparkling in her eyes. "You have got to find someone you can fully and honestly love."

"I see," he said, an edge in his voice. "I may court Nicolette with your blessing, then?"

"You are a troubadour," she said. "You must find an approachable lady to give your heart to. I know what *l'amour courtois* means." There was a fondness in her voice. "You did your best to teach me. But why Nicolette de Gobignon, Roland? Surely the count already hates you. Pursuing his wife could mean your death." She drew in a sudden, frightened breath. "That cannot be your reason for choosing her, can it, Roland? Have I disappointed you that much? Are you courting the countess, or death?"

Yes, you have disappointed me that much! he wanted to shout.

"If I were looking for my death, why would that horrify you? How do you think I feel when you go out on one of your missions and I wonder whether you will come back?"

"Ah, dear Roland, can you not see the difference? I believe with all my heart that if I die—if the Inquisition catches me and burns me—I will be happier, go to a better world. I will be united with God. But you do not believe that. For you, death is the worst thing that can happen to you. So, please, you must not go looking for death. You must not, *must not*, let my vows be the reason for your giving up life. I could not bear that."

"Diane, I believe that I love Nicolette de Gobignon. And I believe that Love is the only thing worth living for. To love her might mean my death. But if I die for Love, it will be a sweeter death than most men meet."

A cold wind rattled the black, leafless branches, and she huddled in her cloak.

When she spoke again there was a quiver in her voice. "How can you say you love Nicolette de Gobignon? You have told me that you love me. Have you turned to her because I will not—cannot—have you?"

Roland turned away and began slowly pacing the garden as he thought back to that day at Chinon when he had first seen Nicolette.

Even as he bent the knee to the royal couple he had felt his eyes drawn to the dark young woman beside the Queen, the woman wearing the silver coronet of a countess. She seemed to glow with a radiance that cast everyone else into shadow.

He sang his song for the King and Queen, but in his heart he sang it to the dark lady whose name he did not know. And his heart swelled when he saw that her gaze returned to him as often as his did to her.

Diane, as far as he knew that day, was dead. He had sought

her everywhere in Languedoc and had failed to find her. Her entire family had vanished. Many of the people he questioned declared that she had died. He had seen no proof, but thousands of deaths had gone unrecorded in that war-ravaged land. Grief-stricken, he had rested for a time at Avignon. Then he had made his way back to Paris, where he plunged into study, writing music, singing and seeking a patron. The sharp edge of mourning gradually was worn down, and his heart began to be free again—although there was an empty space in it where Diane belonged.

Now, for the first time since he had accepted that loss, he felt himself drawn to a woman. Powerfully drawn.

Later that day at Chinon, when he returned to the crowd of courtiers, he pointed out the dark young woman with the coronet to a pleasant-spoken young knight named Jean de Joinville, a member of the King's entourage.

"Ah, that one. She is very pretty, but you had better forget her, my friend."

"I shall listen more patiently to your advice when I have heard her name, Sire de Joinville."

"You are an Italian knight, Sire Orlando? Tell me, then, is the name de Gobignon much mentioned in Italy?"

De Gobignon. The name he had learned to hate above all others. Stunned, Roland had turned to stare at the woman who so fascinated him. She was strolling arm in arm not far away with the Queen. There was a vigor in her stride that delighted him. Even as he looked at her their eyes met, and there was a bold twinkle in hers. He looked away.

She could not be a daughter. As far as he knew the Gobignons were all tall, blond, and blue-eyed. Perhaps she was only distantly related. He prayed it might be so.

"Then is the lady a Gobignon?" he asked de Joinville.

"By marriage. Perhaps you know that Count Amalric owns more land, fields a larger army, and has killed more men than any other baron of France. You would be wise to pay no attention at all to Countess Nicolette, messire."

Defiance surged up in Roland. But no fear.

Nicolette. Nicolette de Gobignon. All day she had fascinated him. As Amalric's wife, her fascination became irresistible. He felt challenged, as if a gauntlet had been thrown down before him.

He stared across the grassy field crowded with gaily dressed courtiers. The setting sun threw the long shadows of the château's towers across the meadow, and the Countess de Gobignon and the Queen walked from light into darkness.

Now, over a year later, standing in his garden, he said to Diane, "I was drawn to Nicolette de Gobignon at a time when I thought I would never see you again. I left her to go to your rescue. But when you rejected my love, I found myself thinking of her again."

Since then I have talked to her, seen her courage and her wit, held her in my arms, kissed her, he thought. My love for her could never have taken root if you had occupied the central place in my heart, Diane. But now my love for her has grown strong, and even you cannot drive it out.

"What about her husband?" Diane asked. "Are you attracted to her because you want to injure the count?"

What is between de Gobignon and me is complicated, Roland thought. The thought of her in his arms is unbearable, makes me want to kill him. But I do love her for *her* sake.

"I felt love stirring in me before I even knew her name. She is all life and high spirit, Diane. When I was with her tonight the whole world seemed brighter and happier. No, I would not make love to her to spite her husband. But I will make love to her *in* spite of him."

"Then your love for me—you have renounced it? I know you have too much honor to pursue two women at once."

Roland stared at her, and his temples were pounding again. He still—even now!—yearned to take Diane in his arms.

He held his body rigid as he forced himself to speak. "Yes, Diane. From now on Nicolette de Gobignon is the lady who rules all my thoughts. What I feel for you now is what I feel for my sister."

Even as he spoke, the words sounded hollow on his lips.

He stood looking up at the night sky, feeling his soul as scarred and pitted by doubt as was the moon's face.

"I am glad for you, Roland," Diane said. Her voice was so low he could barely hear her.

"It is what you want, is it not?"

"I do not want anything to happen to you, Roland," she said. Her green eyes seemed to shine in the dark. "If you must court her, be careful. Do not make a public display of your feelings."

"That might be difficult. She is going to have me invited to the Queen's singing contest on May Day."

"Oh. You must do as you think best. I cannot advise you

about that. But, Roland, send me away from this place, because
I, too, am a danger to you.''

Perhaps it would be easier if I let Diane leave. But I cannot.
The Dominicans would find her within the week.

"There is no need for you to go. The world thinks you are my
widowed sister, and I told you I love you as a sister now. Would
I turn my sister out?''

"Oh, Roland!'' She turned her back on him, her shoulders
shaking with sobs.

"Diane, do I make you so unhappy?'' He put his hand out to
rest on her shoulder.

She pulled away violently.

"Do not touch me!'' It was almost a scream. She covered her
face with her hands and shrank away from him.

He staggered back, stunned. To hear such fear of him in her
voice was unbearable. He turned away from her.

She drew away from him into the shadow of a pine. "Just
leave me alone, Roland. I want to pray.''

"Good night, then, Diane.''

He was exhausted and trembling as he went into the house.
The kitchen was dark. The servants had gone to bed. So had
Perrin.

His head was throbbing. He put his fingertips against his brow
and pressed hard.

I made a choice. Now I have to live up to it. If I can.

As she waited to meet her superior, Diane felt herself in
turmoil. At one moment she loved Roland, the next she hated
him for what he was doing to her. I enjoyed inner peace before
he came back into my life, she thought. Hunted by inquisitors,
besieged by crusaders, still I led the life I wanted, and I found
joy in every day. Now every hour is a torment. If only, she
thought for the thousandth time, he had let me die at Mont
Ségur.

It was late at night, and she was hidden in deep shadows. She
stood, in an agony of suspense, amid scaffolding and blocks of
masonry outside the unfinished south portal of the cathedral of
Notre-Dame. She had met her superior only twice before. She
had no idea who he was. Each time it had been at night and he
had been cloaked and hooded. That way she could not, even
under torture, reveal his identity.

I must make him understand the torment I am going through,
she thought. He must let me get away from Roland.

Since the night before last, when Roland had told her of
Nicolette de Gobignon, she had been wracked by pain. As
jealousy ate at her, her desire for Roland mounted. It grew ever
fiercer, until she felt as. if her very skin were on fire.

It had been bad from the time she first had settled in Roland's
house. Her body betrayed her incessantly with lustful feelings
while she was nursing Roland's wound. It was agony living
there, with Roland sleeping a mere flight of stairs away. Every
night she had to protect herself against love by repeating, "Lead
us not into temptation."

When she first met her superior, soon after arriving in Paris,
she had begged him to send her to some other place of refuge,
but his answer was that the peril was too great, there was no
safer place. So she had obeyed and remained. She had tried to
distract herself. She had insisted on helping Lucien and Adrienne
with household tasks. She spent hours every day making copies
of Cathar texts. These she distributed to the little groups of the
faithful whom she served in Paris. Night after night she went
out, sometimes walking the length of the city, to speak truths to
six or a dozen huddled in small rooms, to answer their questions,
to try to help them with their problems. Twenty or more times
now she had hurried to the bedside of a dying person to confer
the consolamentum. She did all these things until, deliberately,
she exhausted herself. She fasted far more than she was required
to, until her superior ordered her to stop. He reminded her that
the Cathar perfecti were well known for their asceticism, and a
too-gaunt look would invite suspicion. Indeed, she sometimes let
herself hope that the Inquisition *would* catch her, was even
tempted to be careless, to make it easy for them. But her
conscience would not let her actually do it. In spite of her
unfulfilled longing and the severity of her efforts to control
herself, she had endured. She had remained in Roland's household, and she had not fallen into sin. But now, knowing about
Nicolette de Gobignon, the agony was a hundred times worse.

I *must* make my superior understand, she thought.

Her reaction to Roland's announcement about Nicolette had
terrified her. She felt something that she had not experienced
before—jealous rage. She hated Nicolette de Gobignon, a woman
she had never seen. And she hated Roland.

She was forced to face what she had tried not to think about
for months: she could not stop loving him.

*   *   *

After he left her that night she had fallen to the cold earth and lain there sobbing. What seemed like hours later, she had gone up to the watchtower and remained sleepless all night on her pallet, crying silently, biting her knuckles so he would not hear her.

It could not have hurt her more if her mother and father had turned against her. If Bishop Bertran had cast her out of the church, could she have felt more lost?

She had been able to control her desire for Roland only because, in a way, he was still hers. She could both have him and not have him. Now he was turning to another woman. She really was losing him. She could not stand it.

Shivering because the cold penetrated the two blankets she allowed herself, turning over and over on her pallet, she felt thankful when finally she saw gray light filtering through the shutters. Now, exhausted after a sleepless night, she could get up and start the morning fire.

That day she had given a note to the believer who carried her secret messages. She had to see her superior, in person, soon. The following day the go-between brought back instructions. He told her to wait just outside Notre-Dame's south portal. She thought the cathedral the strangest of places for two Cathars to meet, but probably that was why he had chosen it.

She was distracted from her thoughts by the sight of two men wearing heavy fur-lined cloaks of deep blue embroidered with gold fleurs-de-lis marching slowly past the cathedral. A torch-bearer walked before them, and the tall halberds they carried glinted dangerously in the light of the flame. Sergeants-at-arms of the royal watch. Such men might come one day and conduct her to the stake. She drew deeper into the shadows of two tall stones just outside the temporary door of the cathedral. Accidentally, she pressed her bare hand against one of the stones, and the cold of it burned her palm.

"All things that are, are lights," said a low voice at her side. Her heart stopped beating, he had surprised her so.

"There is one Light, and it shines in each man and each woman," she responded automatically.

She turned to look at her superior. Even though her eyes were well adjusted to the darkness, all she could see was a shadow darker than the shadows of the rough-cut stones around them. A frosty puff of his breath glowed faintly in the starlight.

"We are relatively safe here, Diane," he said. As he always

did, he spoke to her in a whisper. "The stonemasons' guild is friendly to us. Still, it is dangerous for us to meet at all. Not just dangerous for you and me, but for our work. Why did you send for me?"

She trembled with the cold, but also with the same fright as when she had first given a sermon to a group of strangers. Could she make him listen? It was so important, and yet how could she convince a man she did not know, could not even see? She marshaled her thoughts as she would to begin a sermon, and took a deep breath.

"You have said that I should stay at the house of Roland de Vency because I am safest there. Now I discover that I am in greater danger there than anywhere else in the world."

"What do you mean, child?"

She told him about Roland's turning to Nicolette de Gobignon and about herself.

"Diane, you know you must resist your love for him. What is changed?"

"I did not realize how much it would hurt me when he turned to another woman. I love him so much, I do not think I can hold out. He has renounced me, but I think he would come back to me if I gave him some hope. And now I *want* him back. You must let me leave, or I will damn myself forever."

A mad thought took possession of her. If he does not help me, I will drown myself in the Seine. But she looked down the riverbank and saw the moonlight gleaming on thick ice. What foolishness! And it would be as great a sin as throwing myself into Roland's arms.

"So he is pursuing the Countess de Gobignon!" said the hooded figure beside her. "This Roland de Vency aims high. First he humiliates Amalric, and now he courts Amalric's wife. Diane, the Gobignons are our worst enemies. If you remain close to de Vency, you may be able to give us valuable information about them."

Sudden anger at this faceless man surged up in her. She was begging him for help, and he was thinking about how he could use her.

"You would have me damn my soul for some information?"

"Diane, I understand how afraid you are for your soul. You would not have risked meeting me if it were not over something you fear more than death. But think, child. How many perfecti are left in Paris? I will not burden you with the exact number, but it is less than ten. And if I told you how few in all of France, you might despair. Our enemies are relentless. They have been hunting us down for forty years, and they mean not to leave one of us alive.''

The great bells of Notre-Dame tolled for the midnight nocturn. She looked up at the great cathedral, already almost a hundred years in the building. She thought of the three who had been tied to stakes here only a week before, dying in flaming agony before a gleeful mob. She remembered Mont Ségur. Our last stronghold gone, and everywhere in Europe edifices like this are rising. Before coming to Paris she had never seen a church as immense, with such vast, jewellike windows. If she were a Catholic, she was sure, she would think it beautiful. But the power that could create such buildings terrified her. How could a handful of people like herself stand against such might?

When the tolling stopped she said, ''But why must I stay with Roland?''

''Your identity as the sister of a foreign knight whose family is unknown cannot easily be challenged. There is no other house in Paris where you would be as free from suspicion. Roland de Vency is the best protector you could have. And we want to keep a watch on him. His father has the ear of Emperor Frederic, and now there is the Countess de Gobignon. You may be able to do much for us if you stay.''

''If I fall into sin, will that not hurt the church?''

He moved closer to her, so close that she could see, under his hood, a white cloth drawn up to mask his nose and mouth. He kept his hands at his sides, and she sensed that he was being careful not to touch her, but she also sensed the trembling intensity in him.

''Diane, I believe there is forgiveness.''

Diane shrank back from him. His words shocked her.

''How can you tell me the opposite of what I have been taught ever since I was a child?''

''Diane, you know that people may believe and teach differently and still belong to our church.''

''Our church? But I have never heard any teaching like this.''

''By our church I mean the larger, invisible association of which the Cathars are but part. There are levels of initiation, Diane, with different teachings at different levels. Child, the only sheep left alive are those who have adopted the clothing of wolves. Those of us who cannot live openly as perfecti must adopt many strange guises. If I told you what my place is in the world, you would not even believe me. To deceive our enemies we must appear quite contrary to what we really are. These pretenses may even require us to sin. The things I do in my public calling *are* sins.''

"But you have taken the consolamentum," she protested. "Once you have had the Sacrament there is no forgiveness for any sin you commit. Thousands of us have died because we believe that.''

"Thousands of us have died," his voice was earnest, "not for any one belief, but because we would not believe as Rome commanded.''

"But I cannot believe that there would be forgiveness for me if I accept Roland's love.''

He sighed. "Ah, well, the voice you hear in your heart is the voice of God, even if He speaks differently to you than to me." He turned away and stared out at the ice-bound river. "The many worlds of God are stranger than we can possibly think.''

She perceived the weight of the huge stone building behind her as if it were about to fall on her. The thought of the struggle with herself that lay ahead felt even more crushing. I cannot do it! she wanted to scream.

But is it possible that I want to leave Roland, not because I fear for my soul, but because the struggle to keep from sinning is so hard? If I cannot bear pain, what right have I to call myself perfecta?

Her sigh was longer than his. "I will remain," she said. Weariness engulfed her, so overpowering that she felt an urge to sink down to the cold stones and never move again.

"Good," her superior said softly. "And please consider, should you fall, what I have said about forgiveness."

"It would be there for you, perhaps, because you believe so. But not for me.''

"God may surprise you.''

She turned to go. She could barely put one foot in front of the other. She faced either Hell in the next world or Hell in this.

"I will be following you at a distance as far as the wall at least," he said. "The worst scum of Paris haunt the streets around here.''

She walked quickly with head lowered through the district of brothels that nestled hard by the cathedral. Fear of the streets gave her the strength to hurry toward the Grand-Pont, connecting the Ile de la Cité with the Right Bank. She sensed the figure of her superior moving through the shadows somewhere behind her.

She had started across the bridge, walking down its center to avoid the dark places under the houses built along its length, when she heard a sudden exchange of angry voices. Fear clutched at her, and she started to run. But the voices sounded familiar. One was her superior, and she thought she recognized the other as well. She hesitated, then turned back.

At the end of the bridge, the two men were standing. Perrin's blond hair glowed in the moonlight. Her heart thudded in terror. He had his dagger out.

"Perrin, in God's name, what are you doing?"

"This man was following you, madame."

"I know," she said.

Her superior cut in. "You know this man, Diane?"

She turned to the hooded man and froze. She could not believe her eyes. His hand was on the hilt of a sword protruding through a slit in his robe. The sight made her heart turn over.

"He is Roland de Vency's jongleur, Perrin," she said. "How do you come to be here, Perrin?"

"I have been following you, madame, for your safety. I saw this man trailing you and stopped him."

"And at the same moment I accosted *him*," said the hooded man, a chuckle in his voice. "I had better be going, Diane. You appear to be in safe hands. Two hands too many, perhaps."

"Just a moment, messire," said Perrin angrily.

"I assure you, you do not want to know any more about me, my friend," the hooded man said.

Diane heard kindness, but just the hint of a threat, in his tone. "Say nothing more, Perrin," she asked him. "Please."

Like a magician, her superior vanished.

Who and what is he really? she wondered. I am so alone. The only one who knows all about me is a man about whom I know nothing.

God knows me, she reminded herself. And I know God.

As long as I can keep myself from sin.

"Perrin, you know this is dangerous for Sire Roland and for you," she said, angry at him in spite of the length he had gone to to protect her. "If the friars' men-at-arms were to arrest me on the street, would you threaten them with your dagger as you threatened that man?"

"I would have to," he said. "I could never face my master if I let them take you."

Dear God, this is a good soul, she thought.

"If they overcame you, Perrin, and found out you were Roland de Vency's man, then you and Roland would both have to face the Inquisition." Her vexation, though, was in her voice and not in her heart. She liked this young man, so honest and forthright. And enough courage for a dozen men.

"You are not afraid of the Inquisition," he said. The tone was almost accusing.

"Yes, I am terribly afraid of it," she said. "But I believe that I have to do what I am doing."

"Your beliefs have made my master a very unhappy man, madame."

Her heart felt heavy as a stone. "Not meaning to, he has made me a very unhappy woman."

They walked along in silence for a time. Suddenly he said, "Not just my master. All of Languedoc laid waste. Thousands of people dead. Is it really worth so much agony?"

"Surely," she said without hesitation.

"How can you be so certain of your beliefs that you will let yourselves be slaughtered by the hundreds and thousands?"

She thought of what her superior had said about dying rather than believe what Rome commanded.

"We are not always so sure of what we believe," she said. "But we know there are certain things we cannot believe."

"Such as what, madame?"

Diane sensed that he was truly inquiring. She thought, this is how it must have begun for each person who was once Catholic and became Cathar. With questions. If the questions were answered well enough, the questioners became believers.

"We have a long walk ahead of us, Master Perrin. If you are really interested, I can try to tell you where we differ with the Catholics."

"I am not interested in heretical preaching, but I would like to understand you better, madame," he said.

The eagerness to win a soul for God grew in her. If this man's curiosity becomes something deeper, I will have to be an example for him and never give in to my feelings for Roland. Perhaps he has been sent to help me.

"The first thing you should understand," she said, "is that we do not consider ourselves heretics. We are the true Christians."

VII

ROLAND HANDED THE PARCHMENT SCROLL TO THE ROYAL SERGEANT at the tall doors of the great audience hall. As the sergeant examined the invitation, Roland stood tensely, forcing his hands not to tremble. He had just heard the bell of the palace chapel chime the hour of None, and his nervousness about performing was compounded by knowing that he was three hours late. The Queen's song contest had begun at midday.

The sergeant gave Roland a puzzled look.

"I know," Roland said. "I should have been here last night for the royal banquet. But I have come from a great distance, you see."

"It is the Queen you will have to answer to, not me, messire." The sergeant snapped his fingers, and two pages in long blue tunics embroidered with gold fleurs-de-lis pushed open the doors. Drawing himself erect, Roland strode through, followed by Perrin.

The stone hall was the largest he had ever seen. It was decorated for May Day, the dark oak ceiling beams festooned with garlands of yellow, blue, pink, and white spring flowers, just as Nicolette had told him it would be.

Courtiers in bright silks and satins were seated along the sides of the room at trestle tables covered with white linen cloths. The women wore headbands of silver and gold threads over their translucent *couvre-chefs*, the men yellow or violet caps adorned with long feathers. Behind the seated gentlefolk, people of lesser degree in brightly colored smocks and frocks stood crowded along the walls.

Sunlight streamed in through high windows paned, not with sheets of horn as in so many great halls, but with real glass, of a pearly white color. The daylight was so bright that the fat yellow candles in tall brass candlesticks placed around the vast room were hardly necessary. Between the windows the walls were hung with the silk banners embroidered with the arms of the great barons of France. Roland couldn't help himself, and his eyes strayed to the purple and gold Gobignon banner, far up the

97

hall on the right. The banner beside it bore the arms of Blanche of Castile, a castle with six turrets.

At the end of the hall, on a raised dais, sat the Queen, wearing a crown of cherry blossoms.

And beside her, Nicolette.

He glowed inwardly at the sight of her.

But she must be furious at me for coming late, he thought.

An extraordinarily fat troubadour stood in the center of the room, bowing to acknowledge the hearty applause that followed his song. He was accompanied by three jongleurs. He, too, wore a garland on his head, of pink Damascus roses. His crimson mantle was cut with jagged edges. His hose was embroidered with rich fretwork, and the long, pointed toes of his green boots curled up. A bit ostentatious, thought Roland. But I wish I had heard him sing.

The fat troubadour, he knew, could be no one else but Thibaud, Count of Champagne. It was he who had brought Damascus roses back from the Holy Land. But he was more renowned, Roland recalled, as the troubadour whose love had comforted Blanche for several years, after the sudden death of her husband had left her a young widow.

And there is the old tigress herself. Roland noticed Blanche of Castile on the other side of Queen Marguerite. Blanche wore her invariable white mourning gown and, unlike the other ladies, no flowers. Hard to picture that fat man and that dried-up old woman as lovers. But who knows what I will look like when I'm old—if I live to be old.

Roland realized that now he himself had drawn attention from the dais. Queen Marguerite was staring at him and whispering to Nicolette. Nicolette was looking at him, but her face, as far as he could tell at this distance, showed no particular emotion. Others noticed the direction of the Queen's gaze and turned, too. Roland heard Perrin, at his side, give a little grunt of dismay.

The applause for Thibaud faded away. The rotund count, his present moment of glory cut short by Roland's arrival, waddled off the floor. Scowling, he took his seat at the trestle table at Marguerite's right. The contestants were seated there in a row, looking, Roland thought, like a parliament of peacocks, each one in brighter plumage than the next. Behind them, back from the table, their jongleurs were seated holding lutes, lyres, Irish harps, vielles, rebecks, gitterns, sackbuts, clarions. Pages carrying heraldic banners stood behind the more high-born contestants. One troubadour, Roland noticed with surprise, was wearing the spotless white mantle of the Knights Templar.

Roland was about to move to the contestants' table when Queen Marguerite's stern voice rang out in the now silent hall.

"Come forward, messire. Tell us who you are."

"God's bones!" Roland heard Perrin whisper to himself.

Roland wished he were back in Sicily. But he put on a brave face and marched forward.

"Madame." He made a deep bow and walked the length of the marble-tiled floor, his black cloak sweeping behind him.

As he walked Roland glanced left and right. This might be his only chance to see these great ones of whom he had heard so much. That blond man with the long face and those big eyes, in the plain robe sitting amongst the courtiers, that must be King Louis. Yes, they say he doesn't like to dress up. What should I do? Stop, bow to him? No, this is the Queen's day, and he looks as if he doesn't want to be noticed. King Louis smiled faintly and nodded to Roland as he passed.

Nicolette was frozen-faced at the dais, her hands clenched as if her fingers were in knots.

How I hope she likes my song enough to forgive me any pain my lateness has caused her. Thank Saint Michel, no one but she knows I sing for her.

Roland stopped before the dais and dropped to one knee. From under his brows he stole a glance at Nicolette. Her light blue outer tunic, thrown back over her shoulders, was fastened at the neck by a gold pin in the shape of a love knot. Beneath the tunic she wore a violet gown with a low neckline. A necklace with green jeweled pendants lay against her creamy skin. Her wavy black hair was bound in a caul of gold thread and crowned by a wreath of scilla.

It was hard to turn his mind to what he should be doing. The Queen had asked him a question, and he must answer.

"Madame, I am Orlando of Perugia, knight and troubadour. I apologize for arriving late, and I pray you that, if I have offended you, you will send me away at once. I had rather wander to the ends of the earth than cause you a moment's displeasure."

"Saucy fellow," said a voice from the dais, low but loud enough for him to hear.

Roland's gaze shifted, and he saw Queen Blanche glowering down at him. He had heard that it was she, personally, who had insisted on the destruction of Mont Ségur. If any person in this room was likely to be an enemy to him, it was Blanche of Castile.

"You are forgiven, Sire Orlando," Marguerite said. "It is a long journey from Perugia to Paris."

"Indeed it is, madame," Roland answered, smiling up at the Queen. Her brown eyes were friendly. She somewhat resembled Nicolette, though she was thinner and older. Two women of Languedoc, together at the court of Paris. Easy to see why they were close.

"But I made the journey here from Italy two years ago," he went on. "It is Love that made me tardy today. I wanted above all else to compose a song especially for the lady I serve, on this occasion. I must confess my wits deserted me until this morning. I could not come here until my song was ready."

He waited, holding his breath. For weeks he had sat, staring at his parchment, picking at his lute, making one false start after another. The phrases of melody that came to him reminded him of Diane. The images that arose were all of the One Light. But that was a concept of the Cathars, and that meant not Nicolette but Diane. He needed a song that would be altogether Nicolette's.

He knew how important it was to her that she be the first and only love in his life. Again and again during their secret meetings in the upper room at the bookseller's she had questioned him. Was there anyone else? Was he sure there was no one else?

Again and again she had come back to his presence at Mont Ségur. Why had he left Paris so suddenly, without telling her? Was a woman involved? He hated himself for not being able to tell her the whole truth.

But he had renounced his love for Diane, so was it not the simple truth that Nicolette was the only woman in his life?

He knew, though, that the truth was not simple. And that knowledge made writing this song devilish hard.

When he thought about Nicolette, nothing worthy of her came to him. It was, he understood, the very urgency of his need to write a song for Nicolette that was blocking its creation. But knowing that did not help. He sat sweating, pounding his table with his fist, edging closer to despair as May Day approached. Only this morning—when, after a sleepless night, he realized he would have to write a song at once or not go at all—did he give up and let the song write itself.

How much easier it would have been to dredge up some song he had written long ago. But she had commanded a song especially for today, and her commands were sacred, and his art was, too. Where either was concerned he could not lie. So, half in anguish because, hinting as it did at Diane's faith, his was not fully, uniquely, a song for Nicolette, half in excitement because he was making something new and beautiful, he copied the song out as he heard it in his mind. Even then it took him most of the day. He prayed it would please her.

Having spoken of the lady he served, he thought it best not to look at her.

"To be tardy for love's sake does you credit, Sire Orlando," said Marguerite with a smile. "But you must pay some penalty for being late. You shall sing last of all."

Now Roland looked at Nicolette and saw her eyes widen almost imperceptibly. She realized at once, as he did, Marguerite's gift to him. Singing last would give him an advantage. An unknown in this distinguished group, he now would be the singer freshest in everyone's mind when the judging came.

Chills of excitement raced through Roland's body. He had a chance of winning now, winning for Nicolette.

He bowed low and said, "As you command, madame. It is kind of you to let me compete at all."

He went back to the contestants' table and took a chair at the far end, next to a young knight with light blond hair.

"I had won last place by the luck of the draw, but you did me out of it," said the blond man good-humoredly.

"Forgive me, monseigneur."

Behind the young knight stood a page holding a banner bearing six horizontal bars of red on white, the arms of the Coucy family. This must be Raoul de Coucy, a noted troubadour and a baron whose family held almost as much land as the Gobignons.

De Coucy patted him on the arm. "The song that made you late had better be worth all the fuss, that is all."

They settled back to listen to the others.

At first the time passed pleasantly for Roland. To divert the company Marguerite had arranged for dancers, jugglers, and tumblers between songs. Roland glanced at Nicolette from time to time. Whenever their eyes met he felt a sweet, sad longing.

He tried to remain relaxed, but beyond the first two hours the wait began to be well-nigh unbearable. Pages kept bringing pitchers of claret and trays of meat and cheese pasties. He refused them all. A wine goblet had been placed between Roland and Raoul de Coucy, but whenever the young nobleman offered it to him he shook his head. His stomach was clenched tight as a fist. He wondered if he had any chance. Probably not, though he had won first prize at two contests in Naples, and in both he had been competing against the Emperor himself. But here he would be singing in the *Langue d'Oc*, and these people were Northerners. He could only hope that Nicolette, at least, would like the song.

He wanted to make a gift of it to her, to perform a deed that would be for her alone. He wished he could honor her publicly, as the troubadours of Languedoc had paid open homage to their ladies in the great days of courtly love.

He listened intently to the rondeaus, ballades, sirventes, and canzones as the hall grew dark and servants lit more candles along the walls and tables. It was the skill of his rivals as makers of poetry and composers of music that interested him more than the singing and playing. Often, indeed, the creator of the song was not the one who performed it. A jongleur might sing his master's song, though when the master's voice was good enough, the jongleur would provide only accompaniment.

Each troubadour or trouvère seemed to have his own band of partisans, who applauded him clamorously, to Roland's amusement. The contestants sang in every language, mostly in *Langue d'Oïl*, but also in *Langue d'Oc*, Spanish, Italian, Latin, even German. Roland understood all the songs well enough. A well-traveled troubadour had to be versed in many languages.

It was in Latin that the most unusual man present that day sang. Roland had noticed him earlier, a Knight Templar from Verona named Guido Bruchesi. Like all Templars, and unlike all other knights, he wore his black beard long, halfway down the white Templar mantle, which was sewn front and back with red crosses. What was he doing here? Roland had heard of priests and friars who also were troubadours, but a warrior monk who also sang was unusual indeed.

Roland enjoyed Brother Guido's ballade. It was pious enough, a hymn to the Virgin Mary, but it amused Roland to think he caught a number of hidden allusions to Love. The Templar's voice was a magnificent tenor, and he finished on a high note that brought many in the audience to their feet, applauding.

A Hungarian refugee from the Tartars, Sire Cosmas, sang something in his own language, which no one understood. Roland knew even Arabic, having learned it from the Sicilian Moors at the Emperor's court, but he had never before heard Hungarian. Still, Cosmas was politely applauded. Then Raoul de Coucy sang a simple, beautiful canzone. Roland was still applauding when de Coucy sat down again.

"I shall tell you a secret," said de Coucy with a grin. "I am not a proper trouvère. That was for my wife."

Now it was Roland's turn. He felt his heart beating so hard he thought people could surely see his chest throbbing. He pushed back his cloak to display the embroidered silver griffin, the insignia granted his family by the Emperor. No one here, he was sure, would recognize the griffin or, for that matter, have heard of the de Vencys. On a silver chain around his neck he wore another memento from Frederic, an ancient bronze medallion of Apollo playing a lyre. He hoped he made a decent appearance. This morning he had rubbed away at his heavy beard with a pumice stone till his cheeks felt silky to his fingertips.

He walked slowly to the center of the room with Perrin, a step behind him, carrying a lute painted in a pattern of red, yellow, and green diamonds.

Roland stood perfectly still, allowing a silence to build. Perrin tuned the lute, string by string. Everyone in the room stopped eating, drinking, and conversing, and leaned forward attentively.

Marguerite is on our side, I can feel it, Roland thought. But the rest of them? This was a demanding, knowing audience, schooled in music from childhood, skilled in judging. Many of these men and women could have performed as well as the contestants.

Perrin struck a chord.

Roland breathed deeply and expanded his chest.

He allowed himself a brief glance at Nicolette.

She looked back, and then closed her eyes.

He began.

> "What makes the sun shine less than bright?
> Why seems the moon's glow less than pure?
> Madame, look in my heart this night,
> For all life's ills here find the cure:
> One light outshines all lights above,
> The light within, the light of Love."

The melody he had chosen was slow, almost languid. While he had been working on it, he had been thinking of a boat drifting down a moonlit river. It was a gentle yet radiant tune, he thought, suggesting the afterglow of love.

He heard his baritone voice fill the hall, resonating against the stone walls and roof timbers. His native tongue rang out as a challenge to these Northerners who had sent the Albigensian Crusade and destroyed his country.

But in his words and tones, highlighted by the rippling notes of the lute, he tried to convey the secret ecstasy of *l'amour courtois*. Nicolette, he hoped, would hear echoes of the words he had spoken in her ear. This song is for you, Nicolette.

> "I lie sleepless all through the night,
> I walk by day but still am dreaming.
> She who appears in my mind's sight
> Is truth. This world is but a seeming.
> One light outshines all lights above,
> The light within, the light of Love."

Roland had finished his song, and for a moment he heard not a sound anywhere in the hall. Then a thunder of applause beat at his ears, and he felt his face grow hot. Some of the applause, he knew, was for all the contestants, some for the contest itself, but he could feel that much of it was for him. He bowed and walked back to his seat. About half his fellows at the trestle table were applauding vigorously. The others applauded, too, but with little enthusiasm. Keeping his eyes down, Roland dropped into the chair Perrin held for him.

De Coucy squeezed his arm. "I doubt I have heard better singing in my life. You were the best, my good fellow. The best all day. No question about it."

The words were very pleasant to hear, but what Roland felt most of all was relief. He sat limp in his chair and thanked Saint Michel that for good or ill he had done what he had to do, he had not dishonored his lady, and it was over.

"And now, gracious ladies and seigneurs," said Queen Marguerite, standing up, "we invite you to feast, while we struggle with the impossible task of deciding which of these splendid artists has earned the prize." She held it up, a dark blue silk scarf of Palermo, patterned with gold crescents. Roland joined in the applause. The King rose and bowed from his great height, and all the men followed his example. Marguerite then led half a dozen ladies from her high table.

Now Roland could drink. He held out the empty goblet that stood between him and de Coucy to a servant, who filled it with bright red wine. He drained the goblet at a gulp, had it refilled, and turned to Perrin.

"What did you think?"

Perrin grinned. "Not bad, master. Not bad."

"The Devil roast you."

Perrin laughed.

After what seemed like hours, a blast of trumpets stilled the audience. The ladies filed in from the side and again took their places. The hall stood silent.

Roland's heart was pumping frenziedly.

I must not let it matter, he told himself. The main thing is that before all this hall I proclaimed my love for my lady, and that *she* knows it is she.

As Marguerite was about to announce the winner, Roland noticed that Blanche was not beside the young Queen but was standing off to one side of the head table. As if to show that she does not support their decision, Roland thought.

Fear chilled his spine, not so much for himself as for Nicolette. Knowing how dangerous Blanche could be, he almost hoped for a moment that it was not he who had won, that her displeasure was directed elsewhere.

His eyes then met Nicolette's, and he actually felt faint.

Marguerite spoke. "It is the judgment of the ladies of the royal court of France that the highest prize has been won fairly and fully by the knight of Perugia, Sire Orlando."

Roland felt as if his heart had stopped altogether. His face went hot as a blacksmith's furnace.

Cheers and applause rang all around him, but the sound was faint, as if he had gotten water in his ears. He felt hands pushing at him. They wanted him to get to his feet.

"Look alive, master!" Perrin was saying. "Get up and claim your prize."

"Good fellow!" de Coucy was shouting, clapping him on the back. "I knew it would be you."

In a daze, Roland forced his limbs to carry him out into the center of the room. Perrin, hurrying after, shoved the neck of the lute into Roland's hand. Roland made his way to the dais one deliberate step at a time, feeling the continued cheering as if it were a tide through which he had to push his way.

He saw Nicolette sitting beside Marguerite, motionless, her eyes bright.

If only I could take you in my arms, he thought.

He knelt and laid the brightly painted lute on the floor before the Queen.

"Sire Orlando," said Marguerite, "I hope you will continue

to sing—and your jongleur to play—as well as you did tonight, bringing honor to this prize and to the ladies who award it to you.'' She unfolded the square of blue and gold silk so that everyone could see it, and then released it to float down into Roland's outstretched hands.

"May you never regret bestowing this prize upon me, madame,'' said Roland, raising his head.

Again he looked at Nicolette, and had to fight an urge to show everyone here what she meant to him.

As Roland stood up, a crowd of ladies and troubadours pressed around him, introducing themselves and congratulating him. His hands cold, holding the silk as if it were fragile as a cobweb, he looked past the people near him, trying to see Nicolette.

The Templar clapped him on the shoulder. "Magnificent, Sire Orlando. You sing in the *Langue d'Oc* quite without accent,'' he said in Italian. "When I speak it or sing in it, anyone can tell I am Italian.''

Roland, feeling exposed, stiffened. He had to make an effort not to clench his hands on the scarf. He felt immediate distrust for Bruchesi. The eight-pointed cross on the monk's white mantle was a blatant reminder that the Templars were crusaders. Still, their order had held aloof from the rape of Languedoc.

"The *Langue d'Oc*,'' said Roland carefully in the southern speech, "has been the tongue of all the great troubadours, and so I prefer it.''

And then Nicolette was standing beside him.

This triumph is yours as much as mine, Roland wanted to tell her.

Nicolette moved toward him, almost protectively, as if she, too, feared there might be enemies in this crowd.

Barely whispering, his lips formed the words, "*Mi dons*.''

The circle gave way to admit Queen Marguerite, who came to him and said, "About the *Langue d'Oc* I quite agree, Sire Orlando. I, too, will always love the speech of my Provençal childhood. Though now that the north has triumphed, I fear we will always have to say *oïl* instead of *oc* when we mean yes.''

Roland then bowed to Queen Marguerite. "A lady's 'yes' has a sweet sound in any language, madame.''

"Spoken like a troubadour, messire.'' Marguerite laughed. "Yet I fear the torch of poetry has passed, perhaps''—she nodded graciously to him—"to Italy, and from Languedoc we shall never again hear the like of Arnaut Daniel or Bernart de Ventadour.''

"Yes, but surely," said a new voice, "the beauty of a language is created by the poetry written in that language. If beautiful songs are sung in the *Langue d'Oil*, it will become great."

Everyone turned. The King stood before Roland in his plain dark robe, the red cross of a crusader sewn on one shoulder. Louis towered over everyone.

Roland dropped to one knee.

"Please stand up, messire," said the King, patting Roland on the shoulder. "I merely wish to thank you for that exquisite song. And to congratulate you on winning this lovely prize."

Roland rose and studied Louis's face. How innocent he appeared. Thirty-one, but he could as easily be twenty-one. The cross on his shoulder, Nicolette had told him, came from some mad notion the King had of delivering Jerusalem from the Turks.

A thought struck Roland. If I were at home, I would not hesitate to honor *mi dons* publicly. Why not here? Certainly the Queen would understand, perhaps the King, too.

What holds me back, then? Amalric de Gobignon? A hot anger rose in his chest. Shall I let him stop me from paying *mi dons* the tribute she deserves? After all, it will seem to be nothing more than the customary tribute a troubadour pays to the distant lady who inspires him. And I know Nicolette has the wit—and the courage—to respond as she must before King and Queen and court. Only we two will know the true meaning of the gesture. Let me do it, then.

Roland turned to Louis. "Permit me to put a question to you, sire. Who deserves this prize more, the one who made the song, or the one who inspired it?"

Louis smiled, his large blue eyes focused searchingly on Roland. "An interesting question, Sire Orlando. Well, in my opinion many have the skill to write songs, but only a few are inspired to make the best use of that skill."

"I agree, sire. Therefore I shall present my prize to the lady to whom I dedicate my art." And with a smile he turned toward Nicolette.

Suddenly, for him, the King, Queen, Blanche of Castile, the seigneurs and ladies, even the great stone hall, all seemed to vanish, and there was no one and nothing but the dark young woman in violet. He knelt before her, holding up the blue and gold silk.

Her fingertips touched his as she took the scarf from him and touched her lips briefly to it in a ceremonial kiss.

Keeping his eyes on her, Roland heard disapproving whispers from the sides of the hall. But there was also friendly laughter and a spattering of applause.

One man's voice said clearly, "Charming!" It might have been Raoul de Coucy or Guido Bruchesi; he could not be sure.

But those whispered remarks undermined his confidence. Had he acted too rashly and endangered Nicolette?

There was no turning back now. He must carry it off.

"Madame," he said with a smile and a bow, "I hope you will forgive the ignorance of an Italian *trovatore*. Perhaps, as Madame the Queen has suggested, the torch of poetry has passed to Italy, and what is still a respected custom among us is no longer done here at Paris. If I have been too bold, if I have offended, I beg you to forgive me."

"Not at all, Sire Orlando," Nicolette replied airily, and loud enough for the whisperers to hear. "Whatever is done or not done here at Paris, I am a lady of Languedoc, and it pleases me to accept this tribute from a troubadour."

Nicolette turned inquiringly to Marguerite, as if to confirm that she had spoken aright, and the Queen smiled and nodded approval.

Roland sensed, rather than saw, a stirring at the edge of the circle around them. A flash of white, and suddenly Blanche of Castile was in their midst.

An avenging angel, she turned first upon Nicolette.

"This is scandalous. You must return the scarf to this presumptuous knight at once."

"To give back this scarf," Nicolette answered in a voice so low Roland could barely hear it, "would itself be a discourteous act, madame."

"He has compromised you. The honor of your good husband is in danger."

And her good husband will be sure to hear about it, Roland thought. He began again to regret his audacity. It would be best for Nicolette, he thought, if she yielded to Queen Blanche and rejected my gift. He saw Nicolette turn to Marguerite with a look of appeal.

The young queen herself was trembling with controlled anger. She took the King's arm and held it tightly.

"Who is a better judge of honor than the King?" she said. "Tell us, sire, is the Count de Gobignon's honor threatened? Should the Countess return the scarf?"

"Take a moment to think, dear Mother." The King spoke

softly but firmly to Blanche. "For a troubadour to choose a lady and dedicate his achievements to her is an old and pretty custom. To quarrel over this would indeed cause scandal. The gesture seems to me without harm."

Silently but fervently Roland blessed King Louis for his good will.

"You cannot imagine how these supposedly harmless gestures can spread rot," snapped Blanche. "When I ruled this court I protected you from such corrupting influences." She looked pointedly at Marguerite.

"But, Mother," Louis protested, "it is not so many years since our good friend the Count of Champagne, who sang so well here today, wrote songs in your honor. And no one thinks the less of you for that."

Oh, do they not? Roland thought with amusement. Then he hasn't heard the rumors I have.

A lesser woman might have retired in confusion, but Blanche, though she reddened, stood her ground. "That was altogether different!"

"I am sorry, Mother," said the King earnestly. "Lovely ladies inspire poets like this knight. Much good comes of such chivalry."

"Louis, you are—" Roland guessed that Blanche wanted to say "a fool." But even Blanche, with all her years of power, could not speak so to the King. She clenched her fists, and Roland could see her checking herself.

"—too trusting," she continued. "This is great shame, my son. You should not permit it." Tight-lipped, the White Queen turned and cut through the group around Roland. Courtiers shoved one another to make a path for her.

And now, thought Roland, a messenger will be on his way to de Gobignon.

He turned to Nicolette and saw her standing composed, drawing the scarf through her fingers. If Blanche had upset her, she had recovered quickly enough. Still, he must try to protect her if he could.

He dropped to one knee and threw out his arms in a troubadour's stylized gesture. "Madame, I am overwhelmed by your kindness in accepting my unworthy gift. But I would not cause a quarrel between you and good Queen Blanche. Do not hesitate to spurn my offering if it causes you the slightest embarrassment."

Nicolette gave him a look that had just the right degree of disdain in it. "Have you not heard both the King and Queen approve the giving of the scarf, Messire Troubadour? Do not be tedious.''

Delighted with her performance, Roland bowed his head. *She has enough presence for an empress and enough courage for an army,* he thought. *What a splendid woman this is!*

VIII

AMALRIC CAUGHT HIS BREATH AS HE SAW A WOMAN HURRY IN THROUGH the open doorway. She was hooded and cloaked in dark green, but he knew her at once.

He stepped out of the shadows at the palace entry hall and faced her, fixing his eyes on hers as she gasped and turned pale.

"Monseigneur! I thought you were in Languedoc. How is it you are here?"

Her maid, Agnes, appeared then, following her, and behind the frightened-looking Agnes he saw a page carrying a small book.

It was a year since he had seen Nicolette, and he felt himself stunned by her dark, flashing eyes, her teeth so white against her olive skin when she smiled, as she did now in hesitant greeting. She was still the best-looking woman in the kingdom. He wanted to take her in his arms, but, remembering why he had come, he checked himself.

He found it hard to speak. His longing for her love fought against the suspicion that had driven him from Béziers to Paris in five days, a journey that had worn out three horses—and himself.

"Your duties here at the palace must be none too burdensome," he said, "if they give you time to wander about in the streets."

Accusations already, he reproached himself despite his righteous anger.

He had known when she married him that she cared nothing for him, perhaps even hated him. But how he had hoped that would change! His love for her, meeting with her coldness, made him feel as if he were bleeding slowly, steadily, somewhere inside his chest.

*   *   *

. . . A wound he had sustained on a June afternoon thirteen years ago in a miserable Languedoc village. He had been standing at the top of the church steps when a young woman in somber garb had ridden up to him on a tall bay horse.

She had looked him full in the face, and he had drawn in a sharp breath. By God, she was beautiful! An oval face framed by a white wimple, a short nose, a generous mouth. And an olive complexion with its promise of Mediterranean passion. He saw now that she was young, too, perhaps thirteen. Young enough to be still virginal.

"Your name, messire?" The authority in her voice bespoke gentle birth. But what was a girl of good family doing out riding at dusk?

He hurried down the steps and bowed. "Count Amalric de Gobignon, at your service, madame." He held out his hand to help her down from her horse. He addressed her in her own tongue, the *Langue d'Oc,* which he'd learned to speak passably in five years of occupying this heresy-plagued country.

She ignored his proffered hand and swung down with the agility of a boy. Amalric noticed her legs, slender but well-curved, in hose and boots under her black velvet skirt. Why is she wearing black? he wondered. For whom does she mourn? He also saw a small dagger in a jeweled scabbard, gold flashing in its hilt and guard, swinging at her slender waist.

She faced Amalric, her dark brown eyes bright with anger.

"You are holding one of my servants captive," she said. "I have come for him."

He was taken aback, almost amused by the peremptory tone of this child-woman.

"One of your servants? But, madame, you have not vouchsafed to tell me your name." He spoke with an elaborate courtesy.

"I am Nicolette de Lumel," she said. "Daughter of Guilhem de Lumel, seigneur and protector of this village."

"I see," said Amalric. This could, he thought, be serious, depending on who this Guilhem de Lumel was, and what his connections were. The name sounded familiar to him. He tried to remember where he had heard it before.

Some of the knights and men who rode with him were gathering around them. He wanted this girl to himself.

"Will madame walk with me?" He held out his arm, but she made no move to take it.

"Are you holding a young man named Daude Perella? If you are, you must release him at once."

"I must?" said Amalric, controlling his amusement. "Will you not walk with me, so that we can discuss this as one high-ranking personage to another?" The listening men laughed.

Her eyes blazed. "Do not mock me, damn you!"

Amalric stared into that small, angry face and knew he should be offended at being spoken to so, especially in front of his men. A man who said "Damn you!" to him would already be dead. Instead he found himself thinking, By Saint Dominic, how brave this little creature is! Barely out of childhood, and she rides alone into a village occupied by knights and men-at-arms to rescue some servant. And swears at me when I will not do her bidding. I must talk alone with her.

"Forgive me, madame," he said easily, and heard one of his men give a little grunt of surprise. "Just come with me, tell me in private why this man of yours deserves to be released, and I will listen with all respect."

The dark, burning eyes searched his face for a moment. He tried his best to look courteous and well-disposed.

She nodded.

He led her away from the houses of the village, clustered like gray heaps of stone on either side of the winding road. There was a vineyard near at hand, and they walked side by side along a path through the low shrubs with their new green leaves. Purposely he kept their backs turned to the stone communal barn where he and his troop were holding twenty local young men to be hanged at sunset.

He did not want to talk to her about the condemned ones. He wanted to ask her where she lived and whether she was married and if he might call upon her.

What is happening to me? he asked himself. I should not involve myself with Languedoc women. Especially ones who say "Damn you!" to me.

"Tell me, Madame de Lumel, who is this Perella, and what is he to you? May I call you Nicolette?"

"Perhaps, Count, we should begin by your telling me what harm he has done that you should hold him prisoner."

He hesitated. She was a Languedoc girl. She would never understand. How to explain?

"Look here, Nicolette." I am the Count de Gobignon, he thought, and I will call her by her first name whether she permits me or not.

"Look here," he went on. "A week ago three important men were killed less than a league beyond this village. One of them was a priest, a Dominican friar."

"An inquisitor," she interrupted.

"Yes, an inquisitor, doing God's work. The others were his escort, a knight and a sergeant. They were ambushed on the road, shot full of arrows. A foul, cowardly deed."

"Yes," she said impatiently. "I know about that. But Daude was at Château Lumel when that happened. He is the son of our head groom. His sister, Agnes, is my personal maid. I can vouch for him and so can a dozen others."

"That is beside the point," said Amalric. He was thinking, one hanged man more or less would make little difference to his purpose.

She broke into his thoughts. "Is Daude to die even though he is innocent? I am told you are holding twenty young men prisoner. Do you mean to hang them all, in vengeance for the killing of your countrymen?" Her face was pale.

"Those murdered were your countrymen, too, Nicolette," he reproved her. "There is a treaty between your Count of Toulouse and the King of France. The war between north and south is over."

"Not for everyone," she said bitterly.

Then he remembered who Guilhem de Lumel was. A band of knights had raised a rebellion at Montauban, one of those savage little uprisings that were ever and again wrecking the uneasy peace in Languedoc. The town had been retaken by the army of the Constable of France only a month ago. Guilhem de Lumel—Amalric now recalled having seen his name in a dispatch—had been among those killed. So the protector and seigneur of this village was now dead, and had died an outlaw.

"Now I remember your father's rebellion." He looked at her in wonder. "How brazen of you to come to me, to make demands on me, when your father only a month ago died in arms against our King."

Her shoulders slumped a little.

I have her now, he thought. She needs more help than having one of her people saved from hanging. Her father's estate is surely forfeit.

She looked up at him, and the desperation in her brown eyes wrenched at his heart. "I had to come, even if my father was Guilhem de Lumel. I could not stay home knowing Daude Perella was in deadly peril."

"Is there no one else in your family who could have come here?" he asked gently.

She shook her head. "My mother has been bedridden since my father's death. There are only my younger sisters and me."

Amalric spoke quickly. "Nicolette, if I let this servant of yours go, will you permit me to call upon you?"

She stared at him, the brown eyes wide.

"You would use a young man's life to force me to submit to you?"

"Submit? No, I mean no shame to you, Nicolette. I am a man of honor, a knight, a count. Perhaps I could help you. You know the danger in which your family stands."

"But, call upon me? *Why?*"

He moved his hands helplessly, wanting to reach out and seize her small shoulders, not daring to touch her. He was twenty-one, time for him to be married. But surely to court this daughter of a rebel would be a mistake. Still, he could not accept the idea of never seeing her again. He groped in his mind for words.

"I want to know you better. To be your friend."

She stood staring at him. She seemed to be struggling to come to some decision.

"Let all of them go," she said. "Release all of the young men you are planning to hang, and you may come to Château Lumel, and I will receive you. And may God protect me."

"But . . ." How could he explain it to his men? How could he explain it to his commander, Eudes d'Arcis, Constable of France? "You do not realize how much you are asking."

"You do not know how much *you* are asking," she said fiercely. "Your people killed my father a month ago. You are invaders. I cannot help but hate you. I cannot betray so much for one life alone. Even Daude, whom I have come to save, would despise me. No, messire. It must be all twenty lives."

He shook his head. "But how can we put a stop to these crimes if we do not hang hostages?"

"You will never end the killing that way. You will just make our people hate you more, and more of your people will be killed."

She was beautiful and full of fire. She was quick-witted and brave. What would she be like in bed? he wondered with a hot stirring in his loins. She was so passionate and alive that she made the women of his own country seem pale and dull by comparison.

"You cannot imagine the trouble this will cause me," he said.

"But I will do it. For you. You may take your servant back to your château with you. I will let the other young men go back to their homes. And we will just go on hunting the killers. But in a week's time you must be prepared to entertain me at your home."

For the first time since he met her, she smiled.

"Your clemency makes me very happy. I will receive you, Count Amalric. Though I must warn you, I do not think I can easily help hating you."

And I do not think I can easily help loving you, he had said in his heart as she turned away.

But now, because of the strength of that love and the pain it caused him, it was easier for him to travel about and not see her for months at a time.

"I went to the bookstalls near Notre-Dame to buy this for Isabelle," Nicolette was saying, taking the book from the page as he stood by and proffering it to Amalric. She dismissed the page with a wave of her hand.

Amalric made no move to take it.

"It is *Reynard the Fox*, a most amusing tale. Do you approve?"

He felt tormented. Was she telling the truth, or was buying the book a pretext for meeting the troubadour?

When he remained silent she gave a tiny shrug and turned to Agnes. The maid took the book and helped Nicolette off with her cloak.

An equerry in a blue tunic embroidered with gold fleurs-de-lis came to them and bowed. "Monseigneur, Madame the Queen has set rooms aside for your use where you can rest. Will it please you to follow me?"

Amalric walked beside Nicolette up the stone steps.

"How is it that Queen Marguerite knew you were coming and I did not?" Nicolette asked.

"The equerry was speaking of Queen Blanche."

"Oh," said Nicolette, as if that explained everything.

He took her arm, tentatively at first, then firmly.

She offered no resistance.

She never resists me, he thought angrily. But neither does she ever truly yield.

"Monseigneur, you have come here in great haste," Nicolette said, too low for the equerry to hear. Her brown eyes stared directly into Amalric's as they mounted the steps. "Have you heard ill tales about me? The old queen, I fear, may be trying to turn you against me.''

If only he could safely trust those innocent eyes.

The equerry opened a heavy oak door and bowed them into a spacious chamber dominated by a huge, canopied bed. Three of the walls were covered with embroidered silk hangings. Four large windows, their glazed casements flung open to the spring air, lined the other wall. Glancing through the nearest window, Amalric saw the pale early leaves of a plane tree that grew in the palace garden below.

"The Queen asks that you and the Countess dine with the royal family tonight, monseigneur," the equerry said.

Blanche had said something about dinner to Amalric just after he arrived, and added that she hoped he might talk the King out of crusading in the Holy Land. Could that be the real reason she wants me here? he asked himself.

He had a reason all his own for wanting to speak to Louis. After Mont Ségur he and Hugues had spent much time discussing how next to advance the house of Gobignon. Their next step depended on the King's favor.

"We shall be honored to sit at table with the King," Amalric answered, and the equerry left, closing the door behind him.

"Now then, Amalric," said Nicolette, turning to face him, "what is it that brings you here?"

"As you seem to have guessed, Queen Blanche wrote me that I had best come and see to my wife. She said that you allowed an Orlando of Perugia to present you with the prize he won in the Queen's song contest, that you let him pay public court to you. Is this true?"

She was so much shorter than he, and yet she managed to look up at him so haughtily. The same way she had looked at him the first day they met.

"Monseigneur, it has long been the custom among civilized people for a lady to accept the homage of a troubadour. It does not mean I have made love with him."

"Be still!" Amalric snapped, shocked and also furious that she would suggest he was uncivilized. "That is a shameful way to talk."

"Is that not what you are thinking? And how else can I defend myself?"

He dared not believe the worst of her. Or he would have no choice but to kill her. "I do not doubt your virtue, Nicolette."

"Then why this anger?" she asked coolly.

He stared at her dark red lips. How he wanted to kiss them.

"It offends me that you should show even the slightest favor to that Italian dog."

"Is he your enemy, monseigneur?"

Again, Nicolette's wide brown eyes as he stared into them seemed innocent. And how lovely she looked. He felt a fluttering in his stomach and a quickening in his heartbeat. To the Devil with this quarreling. Still, he must tell her what had really happened at Mont Ségur.

"That man is too far beneath me to be my enemy. And yet he dared insult me in front of my own men. He impugned my courage. So we fought, and he used low brigand's tricks to overcome me. He humiliated me, very nearly killed me. And this is the man you have shown favor to."

"I had heard that he fought with you," she said gravely. "But you have bested so many men in combat. Is each one, then, your lifelong enemy?"

"Many are dead," he said with satisfaction. "Of those I have spared, yes, most would like to see *me* dead. Even so, this is different. He fought dishonorably. Thus he owes me a debt of honor, which he must pay by dying at my hand. You are to have no more contact with him. You are to return forthwith any gifts he has given you, as a sign of your scorn of him."

"And if I refuse?"

That made him angry. She had grown unruly in the time they had been apart.

He advanced on her, his hand upraised.

She stared up at him, unflinching.

He swung and slapped her.

"You will show respect for me, and you will guard my honor."

Nicolette glared at him. The red mark where he struck her was bright on her creamy cheek.

"Do not ever hit me again."

He pressed her back toward the bed. "I am your husband. It is my right."

Her look was venomous. "Yes, it is your right. But never exercise it again."

"Are you threatening me?"

"I have made no threat. I demand only that you treat me with respect, nothing more."

"Nothing more, eh?"

He found himself once again thrilled by her courage, the

hardihood of a small young woman defying the most formidable knight in all of France. He knew only one way to express what he felt for her. He put his hands lightly on her shoulders and pressed her gently toward the bed.

"I will not hit you again. There is another right I would assert, Nicolette."

"Of course, monseigneur."

There was no interest in her voice, much less love. Only acquiescence. Even after all this time apart. But his eagerness for her overrode that.

She lay back on the big, soft bed, her eyes fixed on a spot somewhere above him.

Trying not to feel injured by her indifference, he stared at her breasts rising and falling under the silk of her gown. Her body could almost have been a boy's, were it not for those breasts, whose fullness he loved to hold.

He lay down beside her, unbuckling his belt and dropping it to the floor. The three-sided dagger that had stabbed the troubadour clattered on the oak boards. He moved closer, pressing his palm against one of her breasts. Touching her so after so long a time made his groin ache.

He hastily bared his loins and drew up her gown. But then he paused and tenderly stroked her cheek.

If only she would smile at him. But she was still looking past him, into the darkness above them.

Kissing her was like biting into a fruit that was beautiful but had no taste. Her mouth yielded but did not answer.

Her eyes were closed now, and she was breathing deeply, as if asleep. Her arms and legs were relaxed, unresisting.

He moved to mount her. She was closed and dry. Breathing harshly, he pressed into her again and again, forcing entry little by little. He saw her grimace with pain, and he quickly shut his eyes.

By the time he was fully within her, his striving had brought him almost to his peak. Oh, why couldn't their first embrace in so long last a little longer? The spasms of release were as much pain as pleasure, forcing a loud agonized cry from him. He let his body go limp.

He lay upon her a moment longer, breathing heavily. The room was so dark that he had to strain to see her face. Her eyes were still closed, and there was no longer any sign that he had hurt her. She looked serene, as if unaware of what had just happened.

He withdrew from her and turned on his side, his back to her, feeling sad and angry. Why must she lie there like a dead woman? He had lain with peasant girls and wives and daughters of the nobility. He could bring most women to heights of pleasure, make some so happy they ended by weeping hysterically. Why, then, could he give no delight to this one, who meant more to him than all the rest?

He wished he could talk to her about it, but with what words? The way he talked to his comrades in arms, to peasant wenches, that sort of crude speech would hardly do. The only way he knew was the way he had just tried, with his body. And she did not hear him.

If I were a troubadour, he told himself, with sweet songs and eloquent speeches, I could make her understand and win her heart. God, how I hate all those glib fops who have words for every occasion—lying words.

He lay on his back staring into the darkness and pictured the song contest, mincing, lisping troubadours beguiling the ladies. His fists clenched and unclenched.

That sneaking Orlando, trying to steal my honor through my wife.

I should have killed him after Mont Ségur, or sent men after him as he rode north. I could still have my people do it right now here in Paris.

But she would know it was me.

By Saint Dominic, I want her to know!

No, she would despise me if I did it that way. I shall have to kill him publicly, in full view of everyone who did him honor, the Queen, the King, Nicolette, the entire court. It will have to be . . . a tournament.

But I cannot challenge him openly, he is too far beneath my station. I must make him come against me. Yes, I will provoke him. Insult him, hurt him so terribly he will burn for revenge.

Then I will give him his chance. But make sure he has no chance whatever.

There are many ways to kill a man in a tournament, and I know them all.

"Nicolette."

"Yes, monseigneur." Her voice was faint, distant.

"Stay far away from that man, Nicolette. He has vexed me for the last time. Before this year is out, I shall send him to join his heretic friends in Hell."

He felt a faint movement in the bed, as if her body had stiffened. But she said nothing.

At dinner with Louis and other members of the royal family, Amalric, who had brought no clothing with him on his hasty journey, felt pleased with himself in a fine red damask mantle which Nicolette had borrowed for him from the King's eldest brother, Count Robert d'Artois. Louis, as usual, was dressed in an unornamented robe, with the crusader's cross on his shoulder. Why could not the King dress in keeping with his station?

Amalric was seated on Louis's right at the linen-covered high table in the solar on the second story of the palace. Marguerite was at her husband's left, and Nicolette on Amalric's right. Farther along the table were Queen Blanche, the King's brother, Robert d'Artois, and Robert's countess.

The chair Amalric sat in was high-backed and comfortable. At most tables in France, even those of great barons, diners sat on benches, but the King's wealth allowed him to provide a chair for each guest. Between each pair of guests was a handsome silver wine cup damascened with gold. A hum of conversation came from the guests at the lesser tables along the wall—the usual rabble of priests, friars, and poor knights Louis seemed to prefer for company. Smells of roasting meat drifting up from the kitchen on the floor below made water flow in Amalric's mouth. He had eaten little on his journey.

Louis turned his great round eyes on Amalric and bent his long face toward him, raising the wine cup he and Marguerite were drinking from. "Dear cousin, you have exiled yourself from us too long. I shall want to hear about Béziers and the Minervois country you have been governing for us. But right now I want to talk to you about something very close to my heart."

"Sire, whatever is important to you is equally important to me," said Amalric with a sinking feeling.

He turned away to wash his hands in a silver basin held for him by an equerry. He was sure Louis was going to start in on his pious nonsense.

"I speak of the enterprise of Jerusalem," said Louis, eyes aglow. "I beg you to join our crusade, cousin."

Amalric now felt rage rising in his throat. I am to abandon everything I have fought and bled for to follow you on a mad quest to Outremer, because you would rather be a saint than proper king? He tore off a chunk of the King's expensive white bread and stuffed it into his mouth to hide whatever feelings showed in his face.

"Louis, Louis, spare us this endless talk of Jerusalem," Queen Blanche cut in.

Now, there is a great woman. If only she were still ruling the kingdom.

"Please, dear Mother," said Louis quietly. "Cousin Amalric has not heard this."

"I have great responsibilities, sire," said Amalric quietly. "My conscience tells me I must remain at home."

"Indeed, you have great responsibilities," said Louis with his damnable gentle smile. "Are you not one of our greatest seigneurs, a Peer of the Realm? You would bring with you hundreds of knights, contribute immeasurably to our supplying. Whereas, if you remain behind, good cousin, our pilgrimage will be a horse with three legs."

The King's servants put platters of lobsters and new beans boiled in milk on the serving window of the solar, and equerries carried them to the tables and began to break the lobsters up for the diners. The guests fell silent as they began to eat. The royal cook, Isambert, was generally acknowledged the best in France.

Amalric felt Blanche, Marguerite, Nicolette, and the others at the high table waiting for him to speak. How could he convince Louis that the war against heresy in Europe was more important than his so-called pilgrimage to Outremer?

He reviewed the plan he and Hugues had worked out. If he could turn Louis to a war against the Emperor Frederic, the Pope's enemy, the need for unity within France would mean a wide campaign against heretics. And he, as the leader who had destroyed Mont Ségur, could ask for the power to seek out and destroy heresy everywhere in the kingdom. Working with the Inquisition, he would be the most powerful seigneur in France.

"Amalric," said Blanche, "tell my son why this crusade of his is a mistake."

Amalric turned to Louis. "Have I leave to speak freely, sire?"

"Always," said Louis.

"Sire, there is another holy city much closer to us that also is in the grip of infidels—Rome. Is it not a scandal to us that Emperor Frederic has driven our Pope out of Rome and forced him into exile at Lyons?"

Louis nodded soberly. "It is a scandal. But equally great a scandal is that the Pope is not satisfied with being Holy Father. He wants to be King of Italy as well. That is what he and the

Emperor are fighting about. I say let popes be popes and kings kings.''

"But, sire," said Amalric, "His Holiness has preached a crusade against Emperor Frederic. It is our duty to answer the call."

A war in Outremer would bring the Gobignons nothing. Just a huge waste of treasure and perhaps even death. But if Louis made war on Frederic, Amalric could take enough land in Germany to be almost a monarch in his own right.

"Frederic has not attacked me," said Louis shortly.

"Neither have the Turks attacked you," said Blanche.

"Mother," Louis sighed, "Jerusalem was a Christian kingdom for a hundred years and more, ever since the first crusaders captured it. It has been our holy city since the time of the Seigneur Jesus." He bowed his head reverently. "When Baibars the Panther took Jerusalem last year, he was attacking all Christendom."

"When the Emperor attacks the Holy Father, he makes war on all Christendom," said Amalric.

"The Pope may call his war with Frederic a crusade if he chooses," said Louis, "but really it is only a clash between two Christian monarchs."

"The Emperor is not a Christian," said Blanche.

"Absolutely true," said Amalric, grateful to his aunt. "Sire, surely you have heard about the testimony at the Pope's council at Lyons. They are calling him the Antichrist, and I believe they are right. Frederic may pretend to be a Catholic, but he consorts with heretics and Muslims. He has a whole army of Saracens. He even made a treaty with the Sultan of Cairo."

"That treaty restored Jerusalem to Christian hands for sixteen years," said Louis.

"Yes, but then the Egyptians took it back," the King's brother Robert put in. "It was a bad treaty. You cannot trust the Saracens." Robert was almost as tall as his brother, but much broader in the shoulders and chest. He was a simple soul who enjoyed war, and Amalric rather liked him.

Queen Marguerite spoke up. "I thought it was the Turks who captured Jerusalem."

Why does she not keep her ignorance to herself? Amalric detested Marguerite almost as much as he disliked Louis.

"They are one and the same, my dear," said Louis patiently. "Turks are Saracens, and the Turks have ruled in Egypt for hundreds of years. At any rate, Frederic had nothing to do with the breaking of that treaty. No, I do not think he is an enemy of religion. He is just unwilling to let the Pope have the territories in Italy that he wants."

Louis's serene stubbornness infuriated Amalric.

"The Emperor not an enemy of religion?" Amalric cried, and heads turned and bent forward at the lower tables as people strained to hear what he was saying. "He harbors heretics and rebels, and the disease spreads. They sneak into France and infect our people. Frederic has agents all over this kingdom sowing dissension."

He noticed that Nicolette, beside him, was twisting her hands nervously in her lap.

"In Béziers," Amalric went on, "I have found evidence of a network of heretics that spreads across all of Europe, like a spider's web."

Blanche of Castile gasped.

Amalric hoped he would not be asked to produce his evidence. It had convinced him, but Louis, in his present frame of mind, would dismiss it as mere conjecture. Yet there was a pattern to it: the Cathars and other heresies; the troubadours and their courtly love, which had infected Nicolette; the similar ideas advocated by Frederic; the attack on the Pope; the unruliness of students and the rebelliousness of commoners against their seigneurs. Something was gnawing at the foundations of the world. It all fit. There had to be a single plot behind it all.

And, he thought, with the cold hatred he had felt as far back as he could remember, they killed my father. I will not rest until every heretic in Christendom has been consigned to the flames.

"Amalric, Amalric," said Louis, resting his long-fingered hand on Amalric's arm. "It is possible to be too zealous, believe me. Did not you yourself overcome the last armed heretic resistance at Mont Ségur? Heresy in the future will be dealt with by the Dominicans. Good preaching friars like your brother Hugues."

Pious hypocrite! Louis's father wasn't murdered by heretics.

"The more devious heretics have survived and have hidden themselves. They are more dangerous than ever, sire. The preachers cannot prevail without the help of your knights."

"What are you suggesting, Amalric?" Louis asked softly.

"If you want me to crusade for you, I will, most gladly. Here in France. Give me the authority, I beg you, sire, to discover and destroy the enemies of the Church and the kingdom, wherever they may be found."

Louis sat looking thoughtfully at Amalric. Equerries brought platters of venison and rabbit from the serving window and began to carve and distribute the pieces at each table.

Amalric, knowing this could be the turning point of his life, had lost his appetite. But his throat was dry, and he reached for the gold goblet set on the table between himself and Nicolette.

At last the King said, "You are asking for the power to make war on our own people."

He does not understand, thought Amalric. He's too monkish for me to talk to. Hugues might be better with him.

"Not our own people, sire. I am talking about the heretic leaders. Many remain in hiding. When you pull a weed, you must get all the roots or it will grow back. The roots of heresy, the hidden leaders, are still there. In league with others who are spreading corrupting ideas throughout the kingdom. University students, guildsmen, troubadours."

Out of the corner of his eye he saw Nicolette turn to stare at him, but he plunged on. "And I think they are all working for Emperor Frederic, who is the creature of Satan himself."

If he could get Louis to listen, there would be inquisitorial courts everywhere, not just in Languedoc. Working together, he and Hugues would terrorize the evildoers and cleanse the kingdom. No one would be beyond his reach. Everyone would beg for his favor. Add that to the lands he could gain in a war with Germany, and there would be no limit to what he might achieve. Indeed, one day a member of the house of Gobignon might wear a crown, as his ancestors had.

"All who live in France are my people," Louis said. "I want to shape this kingdom so that it will be easy for every French man and woman to live as a good Christian."

"The kingdom must be thoroughly cleansed if you are to reach that goal," said Amalric.

He was exasperated. He had made his point, and yet Louis's thoughts seemed to keep wandering off into the realm of the supernatural. Yes, Hugues should be here. A priest can talk to him better than I.

"Indeed there is much to correct," said Louis. "Before I go on crusade, I intend to undo every injustice I can discover in the land. Not only those committed by the kings who reigned before me, but those committed by me and my officers as well."

He's mad, thought Amalric. All those hours of praying have addled his brain.

"Justice also means that more heretics must burn, sire."

Louis looked pained. "Is my reign to be remembered for nothing but horrors like Mont Ségur?"

Amalric felt a pulse pounding in his forehead.

I spent an agonizing year capturing those Bougres, and was almost killed at the end of it by that troubadour, and he dismisses it all as a "horror." How dare he!

"Not horrors, *holy* work, my son," said Blanche.

Amalric's rage abated a little as he saw the fervent glow in her thin face.

Blanche went on, "I have been told that no bones were found in the field at Mont Ségur after the Albigensians were burned. More proof of their ties to the Evil One. The Devil carried off his minions, body and soul."

"The Cathar credentes probably took the bones as relics," said Marguerite. "To them those people were holy martyrs."

Amalric saw loathing in Marguerite's face as she stared at him, and he felt the heat of anger rising within him again. She, like Louis, thought the mass burning horrible.

"Perhaps the believers did take the bones, madame," he said, making his voice sound matter-of-fact to outrage the young queen even more. "We broke camp immediately after our work was done, without bothering to look for bones. I was clearly remiss in not posting a guard. That would have given us a chance to capture more heretics—and their sympathizers."

Amalric hoped his meaning was clear. Marguerite might be Queen of France, but when she spoke as she just had, she, too, could be suspect. Not that there was any possibility she herself could be a heretic. But these Languedoc people all were tainted with a tolerance for heresy.

"But, in a way, I sympathize with the heretics," Louis said. "We must feel for them, pray for them. Amalric, I must say no to you. I know you care deeply about the welfare of the kingdom. But I want to put an end to discord, not create more of it."

"When you sail off to Outremer, sire," said Amalric, no longer able to keep the anger out of his voice, "you will be offering your unprotected back to your enemies. The enemies of France. The enemies of the Church."

"I told you I do not think that heresy is any longer a danger," said Louis. "I will not inflict more misery on my own people. I permit the Inquisition to do its work in France. That is enough."

"Sire, the Inquisition needs a secular military arm to investigate, arrest, and punish heretics and their sympathizers. I ask you to consider creating such an institution."

He held his breath. Would this last attempt to reach Louis succeed?

"No," said Louis with finality. "No, Amalric. Even if I liked the idea, it would divert men from Jerusalem. Forgive me for disappointing you."

Amalric's muscles contracted. The effort of controlling himself was like trying to stop a charging war-horse. But he managed it.

"I thank you, sire, for at least hearing my advice." His voice came out as a hoarse whisper.

"Both of us want what is God's will for France," said Louis. "And what of Jerusalem, dear Amalric? You are my sworn vassal, but I would never order you to join the crusade. You must come of your own free will, for the good of your soul."

Amalric seethed. By Saint Dominic! He dashes all my hopes, and not content with that, he wants to drag me off to the East with him.

"Give me time to think, sire," said Amalric. "My family has been scattered far and wide for years. In your service and the service of the Church. Nicolette and I will go to join our kinfolk at Château Gobignon. There I will discuss this with my family. With your permission."

Nicolette, he noticed, had picked up the wine cup she shared with him and spilled some wine on the tablecloth. She was staring at the pink spot.

"Of course you have my permission," said Louis. "What of your position as my seneschal for Béziers?"

"I left good men in command there, sire." I know very well how to run a city or a province. Or a kingdom, for that matter.

"I will miss Nicolette," said Marguerite. "I cannot be selfish, for you have let her stay with me a long time, Count Amalric. But I charge you to restore her to me at the end of the summer."

Amalric felt a trickle of acid in his throat. To have Marguerite tell him when he could have his wife's company and when not infuriated him.

Marguerite, of course, was the one responsible for that accursed song contest. A decent king would be spending his time in more manly pursuits than song contests.

Marguerite and Louis, he couldn't help but see, were in love with each other. There is a marriage of north and south that is happy. Why not Nicolette and I?

The thought of manly pursuits reminded Amalric that he had another aim for tonight's dinner with the King—the tournament.

Louis broke in on his thoughts. "When will you return to us and let us know your decision, cousin?"

A good opening, thought Amalric. "Sire, I hear that Madame the Queen entertained your court recently with a song contest. Song contests are all very well, but your vassals should be offered a more, may I say, robust way of earning honor. Perhaps a royal tournament here in Paris in the fall? I, for one, would be happy to ride a passage at arms before you."

Louis frowned. "I hate to disappoint you again, cousin Amalric, but I have never approved of tournaments."

Amalric felt his jaw muscles trembling. Never in his life had he felt this much rage and had so little freedom to express it.

He downed the rest of the wine before continuing. A servant hurried to refill the goblet.

"I have heard that said of you, sire, but I have never understood why. Next to a battle, what any knight worthy of his spurs enjoys most is a tournament."

Louis shook his head. "Too many men are killed in tournaments, and even more are crippled. And the hatred aroused in tournaments, I am sure, deeply offends God."

Robert d'Artois spoke, thumping his wine cup onto the table. "Brother, I think Amalric's idea is magnificent. I am pining for excitement, and I know many of your knights who feel the same way. The crusade is still years off. Peace may be good for the kingdom, but it is not good for the kingdom's fighting men."

Ah, thought Amalric, feeling new hope.

But Louis shook his head. "To risk life and limb in a just war is a necessary thing, but for mere vanity, is that not a sin?"

"But it is not just vanity, sire," Amalric cut in. "A knight needs constant practice to stay in fighting trim. When there is no war on, there is no reason to practice. Unless we have tournaments. Yes, some men do get hurt. But think how many more will be injured—and killed—in a real war, if they are out of practice. If you are to take French knights to Outremer and liberate Jerusalem, you will surely want them ready for battle."

"But one tournament," Louis said slowly, thoughtfully, "would not make that much of a difference."

"One royal tournament will inspire dozens of others to spring up all over the kingdom. It will be almost as good as a war for producing the sort of seasoned warriors you need."

Louis shook his head. "Yes, I would be setting an example. A bad example."

Amalric's heart fell once more, and he could hardly breathe.

"Brother," Robert d'Artois said, "you put too fine a point on things."

"My son," Blanche spoke up, "a royal tournament would do far more for the strength of the kingdom than a song contest. I am sure if you asked any reverend father, he would tell you such a trial of arms would be good for your knights."

Louis was silent.

Amalric held his breath. He glanced at Nicolette and saw that she was studying him, puzzled. *She wonders why I want this so. She will soon understand.*

If only Louis decides as he should. As he must.

"The best fighting men, knights and barons, from all over the country, all over Christendom perhaps, would come, would they not?" said Louis. "And I could talk to them about the crusade."

"Yes, brother, yes," said Robert, half affectionately, half impatiently. "They will be all on fire for battle, and you can preach to them and they will all take the cross on the spot."

Louis nodded. "It could happen that way." He smiled happily at Amalric. "Very well, then, let there be a tournament. I am glad I can take your advice in this, cousin. I look forward to seeing you display your skill at arms before us in the fall."

"No more than I look forward to it, sire," said Amalric, bowing his head.

A wave of fierce exultation swept through him. *He would get his revenge.*

Now to make sure this Orlando of Perugia enters and seeks combat with me. I shall have to throw down an unmistakable challenge.

He took a long swallow of wine, this time with satisfaction. He leaned against the high back of his chair and imagined the scene—the great war-horse pounding under him, the troubadour in the flimsy armor of a poor knight, the lance point smashing into the skinny chest, blood gushing.

Ah, I chose a sharp-pointed lance by mistake. How could I have made such a terrible error? May God forgive me!

He almost laughed aloud.

And Nicolette, then she will know how much I feel for her. I cannot give her a song, but I can give her a man's life.

Many a woman grows hungry for love at the sight of spilled blood.

He imagined Nicolette, eyes heavy-lidded with lust, reaching for him.

God grant it may fall out so, he thought, sighing with pleasure and reaching again for the golden goblet.

IX

EVEN THOUGH THE SUN HAD SET MANY HOURS BEFORE, THE HEAT OF August lingered in the house, and Roland had gone out into his garden. A half-finished phrase of melody was circling about in his mind, and with the help of his lute he was trying to capture it. Diane sat beside him, home this evening for once, listening quietly as he picked at the strings.

The rear door of his house burst open, and Roland saw there the silhouette of Lucien, his cook.

"Master! Perrin is hurt!"

The shock in Lucien's voice struck more dread into Roland than his words.

How badly was Perrin hurt? Roland put his lute down on the bench and followed Lucien through the kitchen and into the candle-lit front room where he saw Perrin lying on the big trestle table, a blanket covering him from the waist down. As Roland entered, Perrin gave a shivering groan and turned his head toward him. Beads of sweat dotted Perrin's forehead. Roland had seen that look of agony and appeal before, in the eyes of men dying of painful wounds. God, let it not be.

After looking at Roland, Perrin closed his eyes and seemed to lose consciousness.

Adrienne, Lucien's wife, and Martin, their son, stood in their nightshirts beside the table. In the flickering shadows, Roland saw horror frozen on their faces.

At Perrin's head stood a tall man with strong, aquiline features and a long black beard. He wore a rose-colored tunic, and it took Roland a moment to recognize him. When he did, he warned himself to be on his guard. It was Guido Bruchesi, the Templar. At Queen Marguerite's singing contest he had been wearing a white mantle adorned with a red cross.

Saint Michel! What is this Templar doing here?

Bruchesi bowed his head to Roland, and Roland saw sympathy in his eyes.

"What happened? How bad is it?" Roland asked without preliminary.

Guido pulled back the blanket without speaking.

"Ah, Jesus!" Adrienne screamed and covered her face with her hands.

Perrin was naked below the waist and his belly and thighs were smeared with blood, the hair around his privates matted with it. A strip of blood-soaked cloth was tied tightly around the base of Perrin's member. Dark red blood puddled on the table between his partly opened legs.

Roland's stomach felt as if someone had driven a knife into it and twisted. He would kill whoever had done this. He had to.

Young Martin staggered out of the room, choking and retching.

"We must loosen the tourniquet soon," said Guido. "I gave him such battlefield aid as I know."

Roland turned to the Templar. His hands, as if they had a will of their own, grasped at the man's tunic, crumpling the clean linen. "Who did this?" Roland choked out.

"Time to speak of that later, messire," responded the Templar. "Let me take him to the Paris Temple. We Templars know as well the healing of wounds as the giving. I would have brought him with me at once, but he insisted I take him to you."

Perrin, even in his agony, tries to protect me, Roland sobbed to himself. He knows that unconscious he might let slip some secret of mine. God, I love this man. And this happened to him in my service, because of me, I know it. How can I ever repay him?

Guilt clawed at Roland's heart.

Diane's voice suddenly broke in, low but firm. "We can care for him ourselves."

Roland swung around. In his anguish he had forgotten that she was here.

A new terror seized him: a fugitive heretic, confronted by a Catholic monk whose order was the most powerful in Christendom. She must not stay. The danger was too great. He tried to signal her with his eyes, but she wasn't looking at him.

"Diane," he said sharply. "Allow me to present the Sire Guido Bruchesi. Sire Guido is a member of the Poor Knights of the Temple of Solomon. Sire Guido, my sister, Diane."

"Madame." Guido bowed. "I am honored to meet you."

"And I you, Sire Guido," said Diane. "Now you will excuse

me if I get on with helping this poor man." She turned to the cook. "Lucien, light a fire and heat water. Fill a brazier with hot coals and put a big carving knife in it until the blade is red hot. Adrienne, get clean cloths, and have your son bring wine—three full pitchers."

She turned back to Roland, ignoring his pleading look. "This is a cruel wound, but it need not be mortal. I need some things from my room." She hurried out.

Cold sweat formed beads under Roland's tunic. She was giving herself away. Her skill in medicine would immediately reveal her as a Cathar perfecta.

"Does the lady's husband live with you as well, Sire Orlando?" Guido asked casually.

"Sadly, she was widowed some years ago," said Roland. "She came here from Perugia to help me manage my household."

Tears had begun to burn Roland's eyes as he looked at Perrin. He knew the Templar was watching him, but he was not ashamed.

He was remembering another time, two years ago, when Perrin had come back to this house. But that time it had been early in the morning, and Perrin had been singing.

"Where the Devil have you been?" Roland had asked with mock severity.

Perrin's face was alight with pure bliss. "Nowhere near the Devil, master. All last night I was playing in the fields of Heaven. I think God's creation can hold no joy equal to helping a young woman discover for the first time all the pleasure her body—and mine—can give her."

Out of his own loneliness at the time Roland had made some sour remark about seducing virgins, but within, he remembered now, he had been touched by Perrin's simple happiness.

A happiness Perrin would never know again.

Perrin, Perrin, what have they done to you? Why such cruelty?

"A widow," Guido said thoughtfully. "That is why she wears black."

A chill of fear rippled up Roland's spine. There could be only one reason why Guido would express curiosity about Diane's black gown. The perfecti wore black.

The enemy, here in my own home. Was that the real reason he came here, to spy on us? Have Diane's meetings with other Cathars at last been noticed by the Church?

Roland tenderly put his hand on Perrin's cold, wet forehead.

It would have been kinder to kill him, he thought. Who could have done this?

De Gobignon. The answer, waiting in the shadows of his mind, sprang out. It must be de Gobignon. Sooner or later he would strike at me, I knew. But the coward, to attack me through Perrin.

Diane came back with a brass-bound cedar box. She unlocked the box and drew out bottles, jars, and white cloths that smelled of aromatics.

He watched her wash her hands in a brass basin of hot water till they were scarlet. Unable to stop her, he felt terror for her alternating with anguish for Perrin.

"You seem to know what you are about, madame," said Guido with interest and admiration.

Suddenly it came to Roland that he might have to kill the Templar. His legs trembled and his heartbeat quickened. The Templar had a longsword and a dagger belted at his waist. He himself was weaponless. His sword was upstairs.

And yet he felt no threat emanating from this man. The Templar appeared to regard Diane with the intelligent interest of one who shared her art. And he had saved Perrin's life by bringing him here. Roland wanted to feel gratitude toward him, though he dared not.

"There is no mystery to tending wounds, Sire Guido," Diane said, "as I am sure you know. If you keep them closed and clean, God heals them at His pleasure."

Roland was amazed at her calm. He knew she cared for Perrin almost as much as he did, yet she went about her work with brisk efficiency, and she spoke as calmly as if she were delivering a lecture on medicine at the university.

"Quite so, madame," said the Templar.

At least she was careful to bring God into it, thought Roland with some small relief.

Diane covered Perrin with the blanket and then put her hand under his head to raise it up so he could drink from the wine cup she held to his lips. When he emptied the cup she filled it again and gave him more.

"God's bones, the pain," Perrin gasped. "What did they do, stab me in the belly?"

He does not know, Diane mouthed to Roland.

Roland felt a dull ache in his heart. The tears kept running freely down his cheeks.

He gripped Perrin's shoulder and stared into his pain-glazed eyes. "Who attacked you, Perrin?"

"They must have followed me out of Guillaume's. I had sung

that song about the Pope. There was a girl with me. Their leader was tall, stooped over. Ugly face, pitted with pox. He said I insulted the Pope. They knocked me down. I do not remember any more than that, master. How bad is it? Will it kill me?''

"No, it will not kill you," said Diane. "Drink as much wine as you can. It will ease the pain.''

Guido drew Roland to a corner of the room and said in a low voice, "I was in the bookseller's, too. I recognized your jongleur. I also recognized the men who left when he did. A bad lot. I followed, but by the time I got out to the street the girl was screaming and your man was lying on the ground and they were running away. Some of the Mad Dogs chased them, but they had horses hidden in an alley.''

His account had the brevity of a good battlefield report. He was a knight passing information to another knight. But how, Roland asked himself, did he come first to be at the song contest, then at Guillaume's, and now here? The bookseller's, that haunt of folk of dubious opinions, was a particularly odd place for a Templar.

"Who were they?''

"The pockmarked man is called Didier Longarm. A highwayman. His face is well known in the Latin Quarter. He often preys upon students. His den is said to be in the ruins south of the abbey of Saint-Germain.''

A movement on the table caught Roland's eye. He saw Perrin's hand sliding down his body, seeking the place where the pain was coming from.

"No, Perrin," Diane said, and reached out to take his hand.

But it was too late. Perrin's hand was on his groin, touching it gingerly at first, then clutching at himself in terrified spasms.

Perrin screamed. He pounded his head on the table, and he howled again and again.

Diane threw her arms around him and held him against her breast. Her calm broken at last, she joined her weeping to his screams.

Lucien, standing beside Diane, shut his eyes and put his hands over his ears. He, too, was crying.

Each of Perrin's screams struck Roland like the blow of a scourge. He suffers this for my sake, the troubadour told himself.

Perrin's screams gradually subsided to a broken whimper.

Diane after much coaxing got him to drink more wine.

"There is nothing to be done?" he groaned. "I am . . . no longer a man?''

"You are still a man, Perrin," she whispered. "You will always be a man. But your body cannot be made whole."

"You people know how to put a stop to a man's misery," Perrin said fiercely. "You end the lives of those who cannot be cured. Well, do it for me. I cannot be healed either."

Saint Michel! Roland thought, his heart a lump of ice. In front of the Templar! Perrin might as well have called Diane a Cathar outright.

"The wine has gotten to him," Diane said. "He does not even know who I am." Would the Templar, Roland wondered, accept her explanation?

Guido stepped forward, and Roland's heart froze.

"I am a monk, my son."

Roland tensed himself for action. If Guido learned the truth about Diane, Roland would have to kill him. And the Templar looked as if he would be a very hard man to kill.

How can I get to my sword?

"You are hurt most cruelly," Guido went on. "But you must try not to wish for death. Despair is a great sin. God is testing you. He must love you very much to test you so harshly."

Roland caught the scornful look Diane turned upon Guido. In his mind he pleaded, Please, please, do not argue with him.

Perrin stared at Guido in horror. Now he realizes he has said too much, Roland thought.

Overcome with pain and fear, the young man shut his eyes and, in Diane's arms, fainted again.

"Lucien," Diane said, "the knife."

Diane seemed serene again. Roland could not tell whether he admired her for it or thought her inhuman.

Frantically, he tried to think what to do. Kill the Templar, bind up Perrin as best he could, and flee Paris tonight? Lucien and Adrienne will not betray us, I know.

No, a murder would weigh too heavily on their consciences. They could never keep silent.

Lucien gingerly drew out of the brazier a long, broad-bladed knife, its edges glowing red, and handed it to Diane. Without hesitation she pressed it between Perrin's legs.

The hissing sound made Roland's stomach heave.

The unconscious jongleur let out a long, eerie moan.

Roland's hand ached to hold his sword. Find those men. Before all else, that one thing he must do.

"Go out and get Alezan ready for me to ride," Roland said to the boy, who was being sick again. Martin ran to the door, choking, his hand over his mouth.

"The wound is sealed," said Diane as she began to anoint and bandage the burned flesh. Without looking up she said, "The men who did this will be waiting for you."

"Quite right, madame," said Guido. "Everyone knows that this unfortunate jongleur is Sire Orlando's man. And the high-waymen can be sure they were recognized. Will you permit me to go with you, messire? The rule of my order requires us to accept battle whenever the odds are three to one or better. There are, I believe, six of them, so two of us would not be one too many."

"I want no help," Roland said. "This is not your quarrel." But even as he spoke he felt a frustrated fury. He was in chains, fettered by his own ignorance. He had heard of this Didier Longarm, but he did not know where to find him. Though a moment ago he had wanted to kill the Templar, he had to have help.

"Since we met at the Queen's song contest I have come to like and admire you, Sire Orlando, and we are, after all, fellow countrymen." There was both warmth and irony in Guido's brown eyes. He seemed to be hinting the opposite of what he said, that he knew Roland was not Italian, and that he did not care. "Had I thought and acted more quickly, I might have saved this young man. Let me make amends for my lapse by helping you punish the swine who castrated him."

Roland wanted, needed, the help. But Guido Bruchesi was a member of the fighting arm of the Church. How could Roland possibly trust him?

"How do you know about these highwaymen?" he asked, still paralyzed with indecision and suspicion.

"As you may know, our first mission is to keep the roads open," said Guido. "We have been intending to clean out this lot for some time. Another month and we would have gotten to them."

How can I find and kill a band of highwaymen hiding in country I do not even know? Roland asked himself. Expecting me to come after them. I have no chance at all.

"Come with me then, if you want to," he said, speaking the words with reluctance as he searched Guido's eyes. "But you take a risk, going into combat with a man whom you do not really know."

"Can you bring a longbow, or better still, two, Sire Orlando?'' Guido said as if he had not heard the warning. "The bow is not considered a fit weapon for a knight, but I have learned from the Turks to respect it.''

"I scorn no weapon," said Roland. He sent Lucien for the bows, as well as for his belt, longsword, and dagger.

"A leather pot of oil and some rags, as well," Guido called after the cook.

Ready to leave, Roland looked into Diane's large green eyes, now openly grief-stricken and frightened. They spoke no farewells, but a new anguish pierced his breast as he wondered what would become of Diane if he were killed tonight. Would she survive without him to protect her?

And what of Nicolette, cut off from him since the beginning of the summer, far away to the east at Château Gobignon? She might never know what happened to him, should he fall to the brigands, or to a treacherous sword in Guido's hands.

Except that Amalric will see to it that she finds out, if I die. To punish her.

Roland had plenty of time, too much time, to let his fears eat at him as he rode across Paris with Guido. He had taken his best war-horse, the chestnut Alezan, who covered the miles at an easy amble. His helmet and the leather flask of oil Lucien had tied to the saddle thumped monotonously as they rode along. Guido's dark brown mare was not as big or strong-looking as Alezan but kept up easily with him.

They passed through the city wall at the Louvre tower and rode along the Right Bank. In the winding streets of the city they met only an occasional patrol of sergeants of the watch, armed with halberds, who let them pass when they identified themselves as knights. Roland, full of foreboding for himself, for Perrin, for Diane, and for Nicolette, paid little attention to the landmarks of Paris as he crossed the Grand-Pont and the Ile de la Cité.

He tried to draw Guido out. "Why do you mix yourself in this quarrel? Why does a Templar write troubadour poetry and seek dangerous company in a bookseller's wineshop?"

"I may say only that my order has wider interests than most people realize, Sire Orlando."

Roland tried to fathom his meaning. Guido seemed to be saying that the Templars were not in the same camp as Amalric and his inquisitor brother. For all their power, Roland recalled— and their castles stretched from England and Spain all the way to

the Orient—the order had never fought in Languedoc or persecuted the Cathars. Great barons like Amalric hated them because
they recognized no boundaries and acknowledged no overlord.
They claimed to serve the Pope, but in fact they seemed to do
pretty much as they pleased. They might indeed have interests in
common with Roland's. Which meant, perhaps, that Roland
could count on Guido. Still, he doubted that he would learn
much from the fair-spoken but evasive man who rode beside
him.

They rode across the Petit-Pont, through the Latin Quarter,
and out through the city's wall. They followed the Rue Saint-
Jacques, the old Roman road that led up to Paris from the south.

Now they were coming close. They passed the abbey of
Saint-Germain-in-the-Fields, and Roland stared over the moonlit
expanse of hay and rye cultivated by the monks, out into the
dark forest beyond. Somewhere in there they were waiting.
Perhaps even now arrows were aimed at his chest.

Why did I not wear my hauberk? Why did Bruchesi not
suggest it? He realized that Guido was not wearing any armor
either. For such an experienced warrior that could hardly be an
oversight. He must think they'd be better off without the encum-
brance, Roland decided. And, remembering what a burden his
hauberk had been when he was trying to rescue Diane, he
decided leaving it behind was for the best.

Guido raised his hand where the road entered the forest, and
Roland reined up Alezan. They dismounted and tethered their
horses. At Guido's gesture Roland untied the flask of oil and the
rags. He put on his helmet and laced it under his chin. It
weighed heavily on his head despite its soft leather lining.

"They think because you are a knight you will gallop straight
down the road," Guido said, donning his own battle helm. "It
has been my unhappy duty to fight many men like this. I am
certain they will be waiting farther along to ambush you. See
that hill on the horizon? That is where Didier and his men have
their 'château.' "

Roland found himself liking Guido, his humor, his intelli-
gence, his competence. I have let him take command of this little
expedition, he thought, without even realizing I was doing it. He
carries himself with authority. I only hope my feelings about him
are right.

Treading softly, carrying their bows in their hands rather than
on their shoulders so they would not get caught on branches,

they made their way through underbrush beneath old oaks with broad trunks.

If this is a trap, this would be the place to spring it. The skin crawled on the back of Roland's neck. The air was still and oppressive, even this late at night, and sweat plastered his tunic to his body.

After what seemed an hour they were climbing the hill Guido had pointed out. Through the trees he could see that the crown of the hill was bare.

Behind him the bells of Saint-Germain chimed a silvery nocturn. Three hours after midnight. Before those monks got out of their beds to sing lauds he might be dead.

But with luck he would have gotten his hands on those dogs.

As they climbed higher, still screened by the wood, Roland looked up and saw that the moon was directly overhead. At the top of the hill he could discern a cluster of stone columns, broken but still graceful, pale as the moonlight itself, rising out of a heap of tumbled stones. In ancient times, Roland knew, the Romans had built their villas here. He saw a low wooden shack huddled in the midst of the marble pillars.

"They will have left their women unguarded in that hut, and their horses tied beside it," Guido said softly. "We will attack in an unknightly fashion."

Crouching at the edge of the woods, they poured oil on the rags and bound them to the heads of their arrows. Guido struck a spark to tinder and lit a candle, which he pressed into the soft ground.

In the sudden glow, Roland saw a face in the grass. It was a fragment of a statue, the nose and smiling lips of a boy. It gave him an eerie feeling, as if they were being watched by people long dead.

From the candle they each lit an arrow. At any moment Roland expected the highwaymen to leap at them out of the trees. He nocked an arrow and took aim at the cabin, holding his breath until he let go the bowstring. He blinked, and when he looked again the ball of fire was falling upon the roof of the shack. I cannot believe my aim was that good. It has been so long since I have touched a bow. He felt a bright upsurge of glee.

Now Guido's bowstring twanged beside him, and Roland lit another. One after another the flaming missiles arched to the cabin in the ruins. It had been a dry summer, and the highwaymen's shack appeared to be built of old wood. Almost at once a flickering glow turned the marble columns orange. Women screamed and terrified horses neighed. Moments later, Roland and Guido heard men shouting and cursing and bodies crashing through the woods on the other side of the hill.

"That has flushed them out," said Guido. They crept closer to the fire, using a broken wall for cover.

In the lurid light Roland saw shadowy bodies, the women naked just as they had been roused from sleep, the men struggling with frightened horses.

"Look sharp, that knight has done this!" one of the men called.

There they were. The ones who had crippled Perrin. With only the fire and the moonlight to see by, he could not make them out clearly, but hatred welled up in his chest, burning in his throat. He wanted to charge at them with his sword.

As if he could read Roland's mind, Guido seized his arm in a restraining grip.

The black figures ran about before the blazing shack, searching for their attackers.

Roland pulled an arrow from his quiver and nocked it. From his kneeling position behind the ruined wall he aimed at a man holding two horses. He let the arrow fly. The man fell, screaming.

Roland cursed himself for merely hitting the man's side. The freed horses galloped off into the woods. Guido's bowstring thrummed again, and the fallen man jerked violently and lay still. The remaining highwaymen quickly crouched in the shrubbery around the shack.

"Now we must go in after them," said Guido softly, and Roland was glad. He wanted to meet them man to man.

Roland and Guido stood up. Roland slid his sword from his scabbard and heard the hiss as Guido drew his. The great weight of Roland's sword, balanced by the iron ball at the base of the hilt, felt good in his hands. He held it out before him and brandished it a little to warm up his arms and shoulders. "Now may you drink blood," he said to the sword.

"There!" one of the highwaymen called. "Two of them!" He pointed as Roland and Guido stepped out from behind the fallen stones. A woman screamed.

"Out of the way, you sluts!" another highwayman's voice growled. "Go hide in the woods." The pale, naked forms disappeared into the trees.

The highwaymen called out to each other and pointed at Roland and Guido.

Despite the strength his anger had given him, Roland felt a quivering in his guts. Five against two. *They could butcher us.*

Roland and Guido automatically advanced in unison, Guido's sword pointing slightly to the right, Roland's a bit to the left. The point of Roland's sword drew small circles in the air as he moved forward.

The five highwaymen spread out in a line, raising their own weapons. Two had long, gleaming daggers. They stepped slowly to either side, flanking the knights. Again Roland felt naked without his hauberk. Another man came forward slowly, gripping in both hands a huge club. The moonlight glinted on the three tines of the fourth man's pitchfork, sharpened to needle points. In the center stood a highwayman taller than the rest, brandishing a woodsman's ax as big as any battle-ax Roland had ever seen.

Roland paused to size them up, and Guido stopped with him. They were big, strong-looking young men with hard, determined, confident faces.

"Brought a helper with you, did you, Messire Lute-player?" the man with the ax called. "Good. There will be two less knights in the world before dawn."

Roland did not answer, but he thought, *You bastards will wish to God you had never laid a hand on Perrin before I am through with you.*

He resumed his slow advance, Guido beside him. They stepped carefully. There were broken stones that could easily trip them scattered all over the grassy summit of the hill.

As Roland moved closer he saw that the tall man's cheeks were pitted with old pox scars, his cheekbones and the ridge of bone over his eyes prominent and thick. Bruchesi had described him: Didier Longarm.

The fire inside Roland flared up until his very brain seemed ablaze.

Easy! he commanded himself. *I must keep my head until I have made them talk.*

Purposefully, Roland advanced on Didier.

"Come on, Messire Lute-player, come on," Didier mocked him, shaking the ax. "You will lose even more than your man did."

Suddenly a man with a dagger darted at Roland from his left, thrusting to get inside his guard while his attention was on Didier.

Dodging, Roland felt the point slash through his tunic and slice along his ribs.

Roland stepped back, planted his feet, and swung the sword two-handed, putting all the weight of his body behind the forty-pound blade.

The man with the dagger tried to duck away, but Roland leaped forward as he swung, and the edge of the sword caught the man at the joining of neck and shoulder, slicing away his head, shoulder, and arm. So sharp and heavy was the longsword that Roland barely felt resistance as it cut through flesh and bone.

He heard a distant wail of anguish from the women peering from the trees.

Then he took a stunning blow high on his back, near his right shoulder. The pain was so great he cried out and nearly dropped his sword.

"Good hit, Jean!" Didier called. "Now finish him. Smash his head!"

Roland's right arm went numb. He thought his shoulder must be broken. But he was still filled more with fury than with despair.

Staggering, holding his sword in his left hand, he turned to face his attacker, struggling to raise the sword with one hand in time to parry a second blow of the man's club. He could hear the clatter of Guido dueling with the pitchfork-wielding man.

The club knocked his blade downward. The steel's ring was like a cry of anguish, and he thought for a moment the blade might be broken. The sword's point struck the ground, burying itself in the tall grass.

Pain shot like lightning up Roland's left arm. But he still managed to keep a weak grip on the hilt.

The highwayman rushed forward, swinging his club up with both hands. Roland knew no helmet would protect his skull against the blow. His head would be crushed like an eggshell.

He tried desperately to lift his sword to protect himself.

Just then the highwayman uttered a sick, squealing noise and dropped the club.

A gleaming steel point protruded from the man's belly. The highwayman moaned again, pitched forward, and fell at Roland's feet as Guido jerked his sword out of the man's back.

Roland's pulses pounded in his temples.

He had just time to smile his gratitude at Guido when he saw Didier charging him, whirling his ax over his head. Roland gripped the sword hilt with both hands and found, thank Saint Michel, that there was still some strength in his arm. His back hurt abominably, but he made himself ignore it and lifted the sword, slowly retreating from Didier.

With a wordless roar, Didier sprang at him and swung the ax at Roland's head.

Roland raised his sword back over his shoulder and then with all his force brought the edge of the blade hard against the ax handle. There was a loud crack.

The head of the ax flew through the air. Roland heard it crash through bushes and thump somewhere in the darkness.

Didier, disarmed, backed away, flanked by his two remaining henchmen, all breathing like spent horses.

Roland and Guido were panting heavily, too, but Roland was determined to fight on.

The highwaymen's eyes were wide with terror.

"Now you know what it is to come up against knights," Roland taunted them.

Didier let the broken ax handle fall to the grass. "I cry you mercy, messires," he said sullenly.

At his action, the other two brigands dropped their dagger and pitchfork.

Roland peered into the blackness of the forest below the summit of the hill. There was no longer any sign of the women who had fled.

He turned his eyes again to the empty-handed men.

"That is better," he said, forcing himself to smile though hatred for these filthy creatures still smoldered within him. "It is not you lads I am after. Just tell me who paid you to cut off my jongleur's stones."

"I have sworn not to tell," Didier answered defiantly.

"Of course you have, and you are a man of your word, are you not?" said Roland, keeping to the friendly tone. He moved closer to Didier till he could smell the rank sweat of the man's fear.

"They call you Longarm, do they not? Didier Longarm. Let us see if they speak true. Hold your right arm out here, and let me see how long it is."

Didier hesitated, and Roland, still smiling, prodded him in the ribs with his sword.

Slowly Didier raised his arm, watching Roland fearfully.

"By Saint Michel!" Roland exclaimed in mock wonderment. "It *is* long."

In no more than the space between two heartbeats, Roland brought up his sword, two-handed, and sliced down on Didier's wrist.

The great force of the blow sent the severed hand to the ground with a thud, and Didier fell to his knees, screaming.

Roland stood over him, the sword pointed at his chest.

"Now you will tell me what I want to know, or I will shorten the other arm. Then your legs."

"I will tell you, messire," Didier sobbed. "It was the chief steward of the Count de Gobignon's house in Paris. Oh, please, messire, have pity. Do not let me bleed to death. I will give you all the silver he paid us."

Amalric. Roland could see the pale, arrogant face of the Count de Gobignon. Him. But why this way? He is no coward, to strike through hired ruffians. And why these poor, stupid brutes? God knows there are more accomplished killers in the kingdom of France.

"Why did the Count hire you to cripple my jongleur?"

But Didier was writhing on the ground, moaning.

One of the other men said hesitantly, "The steward said we were to lie in wait for you. That you would come after us to avenge your jongleur. He said you plan to challenge the Count at the King's tournament next month. The Count thinks you are too lowly for him to fight, so he wanted to get rid of you beforehand."

But I hadn't even decided to enter the tournament, Roland thought. His heart felt like a burning brand, and the blood around it boiled. I see. He must have planned that either I would die ignominiously here in the forest, or, if I were able to overcome these creatures, I would be goaded into challenging him. Either way he expected to trap me, and these men are but his pawns.

But these pawns also took away Perrin's manhood forever.

"You will not bleed to death," he said to Didier Longarm.

There was a brief flicker of hope in Didier's pain-twisted face just before Roland plunged the sword into his chest.

The man who had told Roland about Amalric's plan screamed in terror.

Roland shouted, "Did you think I would let any of you live, after what you did to Perrin?" He brought the blade down on the screaming man's head, splitting it in two.

The last of the highwaymen started to run down the hillside into the woods.

Roland sheathed his sword and drew his dagger.

In the bright moonlight, the man was a clear target. Roland took careful aim at the center of the fleeing man's back and cast the dagger just as the highwayman was reaching the big trees.

The man went down with a despairing shriek. He lay groaning as Roland came up to him. Roland stooped and pulled the dagger out of his back. He rolled the body over with his foot. In the dying man's eyes he saw the moon reflected, and the same anguish he had seen earlier that evening in Perrin's eyes.

"Please—" the highwayman choked, gagging on his blood.

"Ask God to forgive you when you see Him," said Roland. "I cannot."

He knelt and dragged the sharp edge of his dagger across the man's throat, wishing the veins he was severing were Amalric's.

He plunged the dagger into the earth five times to clean it, then sheathed it. He walked away quickly, not wanting to see the highwayman's death struggle.

Guido was waiting for him by the red coals of the shack. The odor of smoldering wood was heavy in the air.

"May Jesus Christ receive them mercifully," Guido said. "They were fools who knew no better. We can leave it to their women to bury them, I suppose. You are crueler than I thought you to be, Sire Orlando."

"No," said Roland, feeling his stomach turn over as he thought: I have just killed four men. And tortured one of them first. "If I were really cruel, I would have done to them what they did to my Perrin."

He turned away from Guido, no longer feeling comfortable facing him, and led the way into the woods on the side of the hill that sloped down toward the road.

"Do you really think that to be castrated is worse than death?" Guido asked. "I have vowed myself to celibacy for Jesus' sake, and my life is a merry one. Most of the time."

"You chose celibacy," Roland said angrily. "You still have your manhood. You could break your vow any time you wish. As most of the clergy do. So do not preach at me."

But he was beginning to loathe himself for what he had just done.

"Do you think Perrin was right to want to die, then?" Guido persisted.

The back of Roland's neck went cold. Guido was probing again. He remembered what Perrin had said, the words that damned Diane as a heretic. True, Guido had just fought beside him—saved his life—but he was still a Catholic monk, and

Roland still could not be sure of him. Would it not be better to settle this now, while they were armed and there were no witnesses?

He stopped suddenly and turned to Guido, hand on his sword hilt. "Look here. Are you trying to find out whether I am a heretic?"

Guido stopped and faced Roland, but his hands stayed motionless at his sides. "I know exactly what you are, Orlando," he said calmly. "Your true religion is *l'amour courtois*. You are nominally a Catholic, but you doubt a good deal more than you believe. I do not care about any of that. It matters to me that you are a good man and you are loyal to those you love. I have tried to be your friend tonight. I shall continue to be your friend if you will trust me."

Roland took his hand from his sword. He could see Guido's eyes in the moonlight. There were mysterious depths in them, but there was honesty as well. He felt a powerful warmth drawing him to the Templar. What they had been through tonight had made them blood brothers.

Still, there were so many questions. Questions he knew the Templar would not answer.

He shrugged helplessly. "I want to trust you, Guido. But it is hard."

"I know." Guido nodded. "We Templars have our secrets, and that makes everyone suspicious of us. All I can ask is, judge me by what I do, not by what you suspect. By our fruits ye shall know us. And I swear to you, on my oath as a brother in the Poor Knights of the Temple of Solomon, that I will never betray you and will be loyal to you unto death."

He held out his right hand, and Roland took it in his own and gripped it strongly. Roland felt so powerful a wave of affection for the man that he turned away, embarrassed.

"Let us speak of your future," Guido said as they continued down the hill. "Do you realize that these highwaymen were only the first in a series of deathtraps your enemy has set for you? Now he expects you to challenge him."

"Count Amalric has made a mistake," Roland said. "I fought him and spared his life once before. This time I will not."

"He wants you to enter the tournament and try to kill him. He wants to kill you publicly, in front of the Countess. Do you realize that?"

"Yes, I am certain of it."

"Have you done much jousting?" Guido asked.

"A little."

"A little," Guido said ironically.

"I suppose I have done less of it than most knights. To be honest, it seems a foolish sport to me. I have been fighting for my life ever since I was a boy. I see no need to make a game of combat."

"You do well enough in real combat," said Guido. "But the tournament requires special skills, and de Gobignon is acknowledged throughout Christendom as one of the great tourneyers of the age. In tournaments all over Europe he has bested hundreds of knights. Many times he has killed men. Of course it is against the rules. But he is a master at making it look like an accident. And you expect to go up against him with your little experience? That is exactly what he wants. He has made you mad with hatred for him."

"Yes, he has forced me to fight him." The yearning to strike Amalric down was so painfully strong! "I think I must hate him more than he hates me."

Guido grunted. "How do you spend your days, Sire Orlando?"

"I compose songs. I sing on invitation at the homes of great barons and men of wealth. I am pursuing studies in natural philosophy with the help of several masters living in Paris. And, of course, I am keeping up my practice in arms." The account of his days rang hollow in his ears. He did so little that sounded important. He felt sure this formidable man would despise him.

"If you plan to live, Sire Orlando, you had better give up everything else and train day and night. The King's tournament is on the twenty-ninth of September, little more than a month from now. If you like, I will spend some time with you and give you some pointers from the Templars' book of experience. I might even be able to arrange for you to use our practice yard." There was almost a fatherly kindness in Guido's voice.

Roland stared at his new friend, a man he now felt he could count on in the darkest of hours.

"I would be very grateful," said Roland.

"Forget about killing him. Consider it a victory if you merely come out of it alive. Indeed, messire, the best advice I could give you would be not to enter the tournament at all."

Roland laughed. "Such cautious advice from a Templar? I thought the Templars never retreat."

"We fight for God, messire. Have you as great a motive?"

"Yes, I do," said Roland, seeing Nicolette's eyes shining in the darkness before him. "I fight for Love."

X

LANCE POINTED SKYWARD, ROLAND APPROACHED THE ARENA, RIDING Alezan through the many-colored pavilions that had sprung up like flowers bordering the broad field northwest of Paris. Perrin walked beside him, leading the war-horse by the reins. Through the two oblong eye slits in his tilting helmet Roland saw the lists, rough-hewn log fencing about chest-high. The lists surrounded a dusty arena two hundred yards long and fifty wide.

The big cylindrical helmet turned awkwardly with his head, and he saw thousands of Parisians gathered on the grassy hills around the lists. Even the trees were festooned with spectators. A wooden gallery painted green and red overlooked the center of the field. He peered through his helmet at the hundreds of nobles and wealthy burghers in the tiers of seats, their brightly colored finery sparkling with gold and gems.

Roland breathed in deeply, smelling the cold, clean fall air mixed with the odors of oiled steel, horseflesh, and trampled grass. Saint Michel, he thought, today is your feast day. Help me to kill Amalric de Gobignon and I shall write a song in your honor.

He felt strength surging through his arms and legs. The cuts and bruises the highwaymen had dealt him over a month ago were now quite healed.

"Strike a blow for me, master," Perrin called up to him.

He is still in pain, Roland thought, and his wound will never heal, but already he manages to seem more his old cheerful self. God bless him.

Today is your day, my poor Perrin. I will strike de Gobignon dead for you. Even as that promise went through his mind, though, he felt a chill in his spine. He could be sure of nothing. Including that he would come out of this alive.

Equerries pulled back the gate on the west side of the lists for him. Alezan's hoofs thudded on turf beaten to dust by the dozens of chargers that had galloped over it in the day's earlier encounters. As custom prescribed, Roland cantered a hundred yards to the middle of the field, faced the nobles' gallery, and saluted the King.

Louis, seated on a high-backed chair beside Queen Marguerite, smiled and waved. The warmth Roland felt at the sight of Louis's long, pale face nettled him. A faidit of Languedoc, he thought, should not feel affection for the French King. But he could not forget Louis's kindness at the song contest.

Nicolette was sitting with a group of court ladies above and behind Marguerite. The sight of her made him feel as unsteady as a boat in a stormy sea. She smiled brightly at him. What courage she shows, he thought. She knows that this day she must lose either him or me, and yet she can smile.

He heard people asking one another about him. Who was this knight in the maroon surcoat, and what family's device was a silver griffin on a black shield?

Then he caught a new note of surprise in the murmur from the gallery. Ah, now they see the scarf. Doubtless many of them know its story.

Tenderly he touched the blue scarf with gold crescents tied around his right arm, over his sleeve of mail. Strength seemed to flow from the fragile silk through his fingertips, filling his whole body.

It was just a week ago that she had given him back the scarf to wear. He had held her in his arms at dusk in a cemetery north of the city. It had been their first reunion after her summer at Château Gobignon. But the joys of their embraces had ended when he told her what had happened to Perrin and of the vengeance he and Sire Guido had taken.

She did not speak. She stood, staring into the distance, her brown eyes burning with anger. Then she reached into the bosom of her gown and drew out the scarf.

"He ordered me to return this to you. Now I want you to wear it—to flaunt it—in the tournament."

Her words thrilled him. He would be fighting for her, as well as for Perrin. But the risk to her was too great.

"You know better than anyone what sort of man Amalric is. If I wear this, what will he do to you?"

"If he so much as threatens me, I shall tell the world how his jealousy drove him to mutilate an innocent man. Let him see then if the King will have him as Constable of France."

He forgot his fear for her in surprise at her last words.

"Constable of France? Is that what Amalric wants?"

"He would be King if he could," she said, shaking her head sadly. "Constable is as close as he can come. He is very close to that. Eudes d'Arcis is too old to continue as Constable. Amalric has told me that his name heads the King's list."

A black fire raged through Roland. Amalric, commander of all the armies of France? It must not be.

Now, as he sat on his horse alone in the center of the field, he felt a hollow in his stomach and he wondered at his rashness. Had he not stood just outside the lists this morning and watched Amalric conquer ten knights in a row? Three of them had been carried off the field unconscious. And later he heard that one of Amalric's victims had needed an armorer to cut him out of his crushed helmet. That is the man I expect not only to fight, but to kill?

Well, first I must earn the right to challenge him.

Roland bowed again to the King, who still wore the blue surcoat and mail he had worn this morning when he had ridden a careful passage at arms with the aging Constable, Eudes d'Arcis.

From the group of officials and musicians gathered below the gallery, a herald in a yellow and blue tabard stepped forth and asked Roland's name.

A moment later three trumpeters blew a long blast and the herald bawled, "Sire Orlando of Perugia challenges the Sire Enguerrand de Coucy."

Roland turned to look at the man he had challenged. The Sire de Coucy, who had just defeated his last opponent, sat his horse awaiting challengers at the eastern end of the tilting barrier, a low wooden wall that ran lengthwise down the center of the field. He was a broad, powerfully built man. His tilting helm sported huge bronze elk antlers.

Roland anxiously awaited de Coucy's response to the challenge. What if he refuses to fight me? The de Coucys are one of the great families of the realm, after all, and I am just a landless knight. But he cannot refuse. He is only a younger son of the house, and he has neither land nor title.

Before de Coucy, all the knights who had taken the field had been landed barons, bearers of old and famous titles. Tournament custom would have permitted them to reject a challenge from an unknown. Enguerrand de Coucy was the first likely opponent to appear for Roland.

Roland remembered Enguerrand's older brother, Raoul de Coucy, the head of the house, who had been so pleasant to him at the Queen's singing contest. All Roland knew about Enguerrand was that he had a reputation as a savage fighter and had many tournament victories to his credit. Today Roland had seen him drive two knights off the field.

Slowly, de Coucy lowered his lance, pointing it at Roland. He had accepted the challenge.

With a last look at Nicolette, Roland turned and rode into position at the opposite end of the tilting barrier from de Coucy. Alezan, impatient, stamped his hooves and blew out his breath noisily.

"Easy, my big fellow," Roland said softly.

He raised the thirty-pound shield on his left arm till it covered his body from his chin to his knees. He shook his head to settle the tilting helm more comfortably.

The nobles' gallery was quiet. Hundreds of common people pressed against the fencing. Roland stared down the field to the opposite end and saw the narrow platform on four wooden legs where knights who broke the tournament rules would be made to stand, stripped of their armor, their shields turned upside down, to endure public scorn. For now the platform of shame was empty. Saint Michel, do not let me make some blunder and end up there, he prayed.

"Cut the cords! Cry battle!" shouted the chief of the heralds from the center of the field. He turned and walked back to his place in front of the gallery. Six musicians in blue and gold royal livery stepped out and raised pennon-hung trumpets and clarions to their lips.

Roland lowered his lance and pointed it across the barrier, sighting along it at the figure of de Coucy, two hundred yards away.

At the trumpets' blast Roland settled himself deeper into his saddle and spurred Alezan to a gallop down the length of the barrier. Peering through the slits in his tilting helm, he kept his eyes fixed on the red and white bands painted across Enguerrand's shield.

He leaned forward in the saddle as Alezan picked up speed.

The center of the field seemed to rush at him. He felt himself hurtling forward, his heart beating faster than the drumming of Alezan's hoofs. The wind whistled through the eye slits in his helm.

As de Coucy's red-banded shield grew in his sight, Roland remembered Guido's instructions and turned his shield to meet de Coucy's lance point at an angle. But he fixed his eyes and his own lance point on the exact center of de Coucy's shield. He tensed the muscles of his chest, shoulder, and arm till they felt like a solid piece of iron.

Enguerrand's blunt lance point struck Roland's shield off center and slid harmlessly by, but Roland's lance hit solidly. The shock of the impact would have knocked Roland out of his saddle were it not for the high back that held him in place, and he threw all his weight forward to keep his seat. His horse gave an angry whinny.

What happened? Roland asked himself frantically as momentum carried him and Alezan farther down the length of the field. The big headpiece prevented him from looking over his shoulder.

Roland heard a metallic crash behind him. He pulled Alezan up short and turned his head toward the center of the field. He saw Enguerrand on his back in the dust as his gray charger dragged him by a foot caught in one stirrup.

My God, I did it! Roland thought triumphantly. He whooped aloud, his voice booming within the helmet. I knocked him off his horse.

De Coucy's runaway horse broke through the lists, sending men and women flying in all directions. A dozen equerries swarmed to stop the big animal and free de Coucy. The gray reared up, and two young men were sent flying by the steel-shod hooves.

This combat is over for certain, thought Roland. He not only touched the lists, he went right through them. Inside his tilting helm and his hauberk, the seventy-pound shirt of mail that hung down to his knees, he went momentarily limp with relief. He unlaced the front of the tilting helm and pushed it back from his head to get some air.

That horse was badly trained, he thought. A good tournament horse would have stopped running the instant its rider fell.

"You would have known what to do," Roland said to Alezan.

He walked Alezan to the center of the lists and waited while the crowd roared its approval.

He looked up at the gallery. His eyes met Nicolette's.

He glanced over through the gap in the palisade and saw beyond it that de Coucy was on his feet now. While equerries held his horse he was beating its back with the flat of his sword. He is more of an animal than the horse, Roland thought disgustedly.

After a time the heralds declared Roland the winner, but decreed that since an accident had ended the fight they would not make the customary award of the loser's horse and armor to the winner.

Any other day I would have been disappointed, Roland thought, slender of purse as I am. But today the only reward I want is Amalric.

At a herald's gesture he rode to the end of the tilting barrier. As he sat there on Alezan, de Coucy came walking up to him. Now that Enguerrand had his helmet off, Roland could see his face, broad and swarthy, his chin covered with black stubble. He bore no resemblance to his brother Raoul.

"I am not finished with you, fellow. Italian knights are not worth a Frenchman's spit."

"I shall meet you again with pleasure," Roland responded. "As I see it, you still owe me a destrier and a shirt of mail."

Now it was Roland's turn to meet challengers. He watched a knight with a red and blue shield ride into the lists and listened to the name announced by the heralds. From Salisbury? An English knight? Then Roland saw the red cross on the challenger's surcoat. He must be one of that English troop pledged to join Louis's crusade.

Roland had never fought an Englishman. He had heard they were doughty men and hard to beat. A fear of the unfamiliar quickened his heartbeat.

In their first clash they both splintered their lances on each other's shields. Roland studied the jagged stump of his lance and hefted it thoughtfully.

When he rode back to his end of the barrier, Perrin was ready with another blunt-ended lance.

"God's bones, master, you are magnificent!"

"Be silent," said Roland with a laugh, taking the new lance. "Do you not know it is bad luck to talk so to a tourneyer?" But he wasn't as amused as he sounded. He knew any little error could send him crashing to defeat. Saint Michel, he prayed again, do not let me fail.

The second time Roland rode at the Englishman, he feinted with his lance point at the man's head. When his opponent lifted his lance to parry the threat, Roland spurred Alezan hard, lowered his lance, and hit the red and blue shield near the bottom. Dropping his lance, the English knight toppled out of his saddle.

Roland dismounted and dashed through a wicket in the tilting barrier to attack his opponent on foot. They went at each other with blunted one-handed swords. Blade clanged against blade, against helmet, against shield.

The Englishman was a dogged battler. I will never beat him, Roland thought, almost despairing. His right arm ached with fatigue. His arms and shoulders throbbed from the bruising blows of the Englishman's sword.

Desperate to end it, Roland suddenly smashed his shield into the front of his opponent's helmet. The foreign knight staggered backward, dropped to his knees, fell forward with a clatter, and lay still.

Roland stood panting with relief as two equerries rushed to help the fallen knight.

As he watched the Englishman tottering off the field, leaning on the equerries, Roland felt a surge of sympathy for him. Having traveled from England to France to join the crusade, he probably could ill afford to lose expensive equipment.

Roland turned to face the King, pushed back his tilting helmet so he could be heard, and addressed Louis in a voice that stilled the crowd. "Sire, I would restore to the English gentleman his forfeited arms and horse, that he may use them when he accompanies you on crusade."

The audience shouted in praise of Roland's gesture, and Louis lifted both hands in a gesture of blessing.

Again Roland felt a warm glow in his chest as he bowed to the King. Absurd that I should be happy because this King, who reigns over the destroyers of Languedoc, approves of me. Or that I should be assisting crusaders.

At that very moment he saw Amalric, leaning against the lists, staring at him. Amalric's look was empty of recognition. As if I were already a corpse, thought Roland.

An hour later, the crowd was cheering wildly for the unknown Italian knight. Close to exhaustion but dizzy with excitement, Roland could hardly believe what he had accomplished. Nine more knights after the Englishman. Now, as he waited at the end of the tilting barrier for Perrin to water and wipe down the sweating Alezan, he could not remember how he had overcome them all. Two—or was it three?—had been knocked unconscious when he unhorsed them. Some he had attacked furiously on foot, driving them up against the lists and so automatically defeating them. Others he had battered into submission with his sword.

Nine war-horses, each worth a fortune, he thought. Nine helmets, nine shields, nine swords, nine hauberks. I shall keep the best two of each and sell the rest, and I shall be able to support my household for a year without help from Father. If I live.

He saw Guido, with the Templar's eight-pointed cross on the chest of his white surcoat, standing in the western gateway. Guido waved, and Roland waved happily back. By God, without that month of training with the Templars, I could never have done this. They are a wealthy enough order, but I shall give them a handsome gift.

I have surpassed Amalric, Roland thought. Now, before I am completely exhausted, it is time to call him out. His body tingled expectantly.

He remounted Alezan and leaned over to speak to Perrin.

Moments later the chief herald cried, "Sire Orlando of Perugia challenges His Grace, Count Amalric, Seigneur of Gobignon, to try conclusions with him on this honorable field."

The crowd shouted eagerly. They would like nothing better, Roland thought, than to see a passage at arms between the two knights who had fought best so far this day.

But when Roland looked up at Nicolette in the gallery, she half rose from her seat, pale and frightened.

Do not be afraid, my love. In a few moments I may set you free. Gingerly, he touched the blue and gold scarf with his mailed hand, wishing he were stroking Nicolette's cheek.

Peering down the length of the field, he saw a dun-colored percheron draped in purple and gold being led to a violet and yellow tent. He saw the flaps of the tent swept apart and a tall figure with long blond hair emerge.

Having rested from his combats of this morning, Amalric would be fresh, while Roland's every muscle ached with fatigue. Amalric's hauberk gleamed as if he had never been in battle that day, and Amalric vaulted into the saddle as if he were not wearing a coat of mail. Every move Amalric made seemed to Roland full of a terrible calm strength—the way he donned the tilting helmet with its silver wolf's head, the way he took a lance from an equerry and lifted it high, the way he spurred his charger to a trot as the gateway to the lists swung open before him.

Can I really do it? Roland wondered, full of doubt as the

glittering enemy rode into position at the far end of the tilting barrier.

In the silence that fell over the crowd Roland could hear a ringing in his ears from the blows he had taken on his tilting helm.

He felt a painful emptiness in his stomach as he thought over his plan. When they clashed, he would break his lance on Amalric's shield. Then, instantly, he would lift the broken end of the lance and smash it, with his and Alezan's full weight behind it, into the front of Amalric's helm. More than one knight had died that way, his face caved in.

But his hands were cold and damp under the mail gauntlets. There is no way I can be certain this will work. What if my lance does not break properly? What if Amalric holds his shield high to protect his face? He forced himself to stop thinking about what could go wrong.

The trumpet blared. "Do not fail me, Alezan," Roland whispered to the chestnut war-horse, and he spurred him to a gallop.

The figure of Amalric, small in the distance, suddenly loomed huge before him. Roland thought of Perrin and Nicolette. He forgot everything else. His eyes and his arms must carry out his plan.

He flung his shield wide when Amalric's lance struck, driving the point off to one side. His own lance hit the purple shield square in the middle. Roland's lance shrieked and splintered. Yard-long slivers of wood flew past Roland's head. So hard was the blow, Roland was amazed to see Amalric still in the saddle— amazed but pleased, because he wanted him there.

He was holding a seemingly useless stump the length of a two-handed sword. Spurring Alezan again, he gave him the bridle. He aimed the broken end of the lance directly at Amalric's face.

A red-brown wall of horseflesh rose up before Roland, and the splintered lance thudded into it. A hoof as hard and heavy as a mace crashed against Roland's helm. He heard a horrible scream of agony from the rearing horse before him.

He felt himself falling from the saddle and, as the Templars had trained him, pulled himself into a ball. He landed on his left side, the breath knocked out of him. He hit the ground with the impact of a rock from a stone-caster. He saw glittering lights inside his tilting helm and felt a shocking pain in his arms and ribs. Terror seized him. A blow might strike from anywhere.

Driven by desperation, he shoved himself to his feet and saw at

once what had happened. Instead of using his shield, Amalric
had saved himself by jerking back on the rein of his horse. The
horse had reared up and caught the full force of Roland's broken
lance in its throat. One of the flailing hooves had hit Roland's
head. Amalric's charger lay dying, its side heaving, blood spurt-
ing from its mouth.

The spectators murmured in pity.

I failed, Roland thought. I did not kill him. And now he is
going to kill me.

Amalric, on foot, had his sword out and was coming through
the wicket for Roland. Roland drew his own sword and stooped
to pick up his shield.

Amalric's blade struck him across the back, and a searing pain
shot through his body. He heard cries of protest from the gallery.
But he knew that did not matter. Unfair the blow might be, but it
was legal.

He brought his shield up with all his strength, smashing it into
Amalric's chest, throwing him backward. He could feel blood
soaking the quilted linen jacket under his chain mail hauberk.

His heart froze. Instead of the edgeless sword prescribed by
tournament rules, Amalric was using a deadly sharp blade.

It was an old tournament trick, even more common than trying
to kill your opponent with a broken lance. Afterward, when
Roland was dead, Amalric could always claim he had taken up
the wrong sword by mistake.

Pain spread like a fire over his back. Saint Michel, that sword
must be sharp and heavy, to cut through chain mail like that.

Amalric kept circling to Roland's right.

He was so close, Roland could see the blue eyes flashing
through the slits in Amalric's helm. He stepped backward, parry-
ing the blows of Amalric's sword.

Should I try to stop the fight? he asked himself. The heralds
would declare him the winner if they saw Amalric's illegal
sword.

Hatred stiffened his resolve. No! I do not want to end it that
way.

But can I fight with this much pain?

Gradually Roland realized that Amalric's strokes were all
aimed at his right arm. He was trying to slash away the scarf.

Jealousy has maddened him, Roland thought. He should be
trying his best to kill me, and he is wasting his efforts on a love
token. If his mind is not clear, I have a chance. He tried to stop
thinking about the throbbing wound, the blood running down his

back, but the pain was spreading through his body, and he was feeling weaker.

Amalric swung again at Roland's arm. Roland lifted his shield high, pivoted on the balls of his feet, and, with all his strength, brought the pointed bottom of the shield down on Amalric's wrist. The blow knocked the sword out of Amalric's hand, and it flew through the air.

Roland whirled and ran in the direction of the sword's flight. When the weapon hit the dusty ground, he let go of his own sword and scrambled for Amalric's. Amalric's weight crashed into him, and the broad back was in front of him. Roland sidestepped and threw himself earthward. Exultation gave him new strength as his mailed fingers closed around the haft of the deadly sword. As quickly as he could, he straightened and whirled to face Amalric. Amalric swooped down on Roland's discarded sword and leaped back, lifting the blunted sword high. Roland rushed at him.

Now I have the sword that can kill.

Roland struck with all his power at Amalric's head, neck, and chest. Amalric fought back ferociously, his counterblows driving Roland backward.

The blood thundering in Roland's ears almost drowned out the shouts of the crowd.

Amalric could save himself, Roland knew, by calling a halt to the fight, but that would mean admitting that he had knowingly used a forbidden weapon. Instead, he kept up his attack on Roland. Blow after furious blow rang on Roland's shield, on his helmet, on his shoulders and arms. Even though it was against the rules, Amalric stabbed with the point of the blunted sword at the eye slits in Roland's tilting helm. Roland was forced to cover his face with his shield and could not see to strike back at Amalric.

Roland used his shield to throw Amalric back. He stepped away to gather his strength, and over the top of the shield he saw glistening red streams on Amalric's mailed arms and red stains on the purple surcoat's shoulders. I have hurt him. I have given him more wounds than he has given me.

He swung the sharpened sword at Amalric's head, but it clanged harmlessly on his shield.

If he lets his guard down just once, I shall have him.

A high, shrill series of trumpet blasts cut into his consciousness. The call to stop fighting.

"No!" Roland roared. His fury burned white-hot.

He struck one last, unlawful blow at Amalric's neck.

Amalric's sword stopped his blade with a clang that rang like a church bell.

"Messires!" a voice called.

Roland and Amalric looked toward the gallery. King Louis was standing before his chair of state.

"Each of you has won high honor this day. Do not, I beg you, tarnish the pleasure we feel in your strength and skill by giving each other grievous wounds. Desist, messires, your King commands you."

There was an angry muttering throughout the arena. The crowd wanted more fighting and more blood.

Roland's back felt as if it had been laid open by a whip. A reminder of his failure, it enraged him all the more.

"Let all gallant knights now arm themselves and enter the lists," Louis said, as if to placate the spectators. "We call for a grand melee."

From all parts of the field Roland heard cries of approval.

Roland thrust the point of Amalric's sharpened sword into the trampled dirt. Amalric threw Roland's sword to the ground, seized his own, and strode away without taking off the helmet that hid his face.

Roland stared after him, longing to run at him and strike him down.

A team of oxen dragged away the carcass of Amalric's horse. A dozen poor families in Paris selected by the King would have meat on the table for days to come.

Perrin came into the lists, picked up Roland's sword, and handed it to him. Together they led Alezan from the field. The chestnut destrier rolled his eyes and snorted, frightened by the death of the other horse.

They walked past the tents of the contestants, clustered at the end of the lists. All around them rose the shouts of excited men and the jangle of arms as the hundred-odd knights entered in the tournament readied themselves for the melee.

"Nine chargers!" Perrin exclaimed. "You could trade that many chargers for a castle. Where are you going to keep nine big horses, master?"

"Do not collect them now, Perrin," said Roland. "Let their owners have the feeding and care of them till I am ready to dispose of them."

"Can we stop now, master? Take our winnings and go? You have earned honor enough today."

Roland stopped dead and stared at Perrin. "What the Devil do you mean? Did you not hear the King call for a melee?"

"Yes, but I think you should stay out of it, master," said Perrin. "God's bones, the Count de Gobignon is trying to kill you! You have nothing to gain by giving him another chance."

"Nothing to gain!" Roland shouted, still furious. "Can I not try to kill *him*?"

"Kill him? What for?" said Perrin angrily. "He is the injured party. It is his wife you have paid court to. This dueling is foolishness, master."

Ah, Perrin, Roland thought, you know it not, but thanks to Amalric it is you who are the injured party, and it is to avenge you, most of all, that I want to kill him.

But how good to see Perrin's eyes bright and his cheeks flushed with the excitement of the tournament. If he knew of Amalric's role in his castration, he would be eaten up with the need for revenge right now. His spirit would not have healed as it did. Let him go on thinking the highwaymen did the thing out of their own brute, spiteful impulse. Now they are dead. He can forget revenge.

But I cannot.

"I have good reason for wanting to kill him," Roland said, squeezing Perrin's arm. "Trust me, and when I can, I shall tell you why."

Roland searched out his black and white striped tent. Telling Perrin to give Alezan a good rubdown, Roland went into the tent.

To his surprise, a pair of large green eyes met his in the cool shadow of the pavilion.

"Diane! What are you doing here?" He feared for her safety whenever she was outside the walls of his house.

"Did you think I could stay away, knowing that I might never see you alive again? You are wounded, are you not? Take off your hauberk and let me help you."

Roland carefully untied the scarf. He held it lovingly in his hands, then folded it and laid it on the lid of his arms chest. Diane helped him roll up the chain mail shirt and lift it over his head. When he raised his arms the wound felt as if it were tearing open again. Stripping off his quilted undercoat to bare his back, he sat on the floor of the tent.

"It is just a bad cut," he said. "It did not go deep. The dog was using a sharpened sword."

"He might have killed you," she said, a tremor in her voice. "If he had, what good would that have done Perrin? Or the countess?" She rested her cool palm on his back.

He did not answer, just luxuriated in the relief from pain as she wound the bandage tightly around his chest and back.

The flaps of his tent parted, letting in bright light that momentarily blinded him. Squinting, Roland saw in the opening a broad-shouldered figure in a long white surcoat.

"Ah, a tender moment between brother and sister. Forgive my intrusion."

Roland heard the mockery in Guido Bruchesi's voice, but it was a kindly mockery, as if Guido knew their secret but would keep it safe. Guido had done everything he could for Roland in the weeks leading up to the tournament, working with him daily in the Templars' practice yard. The Templar could do nothing more now, but the sight of him cheered Roland. Even the eight-pointed blood-red cross on the chest of his surcoat no longer seemed threatening.

But Diane shivered slightly and lowered her eyes. A deep scarlet flush appeared on her cheeks. Quickly she finished tying the bandage.

Roland stood up and moved away from her.

"Have you not had enough, Orlando?" Guido asked. "I admit you are much better at jousting than I expected you to be. But in the lists Amalric is still your master. You did your best to kill him, and it was not enough."

Roland felt himself growing angry all over again, and his slashed back stung.

"No, I have not done my best. Not yet."

Guido grunted skeptically. "I have just taken a stroll past the Count's pavilion. He has a dozen knights gathered around him. They are professional tourneyers. The sort who go from tournament to tournament all over Christendom and live on their winnings. They know a good many more foul tricks than you do, my friend. And Amalric was talking with Enguerrand de Coucy, who bears you a grudge. We Templars hold it honorable to retreat when the odds are more than three to one."

All true, Roland thought, but there was something Guido had not taken into account. He picked up the blue and gold scarf, where it lay on the dark brown oak lid of the chest, and pressed it against his heart. A man fighting for himself can be beaten. A man fighting for Love is invincible.

"You are a monk," he said to Guido. "You know very little about Love. You do not know how powerful it makes me feel."

"It is you who know less than you think," said Guido. "I will help you all I can, Orlando, but before this day is out you may need my prayers more than my sword."

Immediately after Guido left, Perrin came in holding a folded paper. "A lady named Agnes gave me this for you, messire."

It was unsigned, but Roland recognized Nicolette's cursive script:

> As you have called me *mi dons*, I charge you that you make no further attempt on the life of him who has injured you. If you succeed, my children lose their father, and the vengeance of his family will not let you live long. If you fail, I lose you, the one most precious to me in all the world. Either way, you condemn me to a lifetime of anguish. Therefore, I command you, hold your hand. In the name of Love.

As the meaning of the note sank in, all the strength and confidence Roland had felt only a moment ago drained out of him. Groping for support, he sat down on his arms chest, holding the paper so loosely it slipped from his fingers and fluttered to the carpeted floor of the tent.

He felt as if iron hobble-gyves had fastened themselves to his ankles. A moment ago he was going to win. And now?

I must obey, he thought. I have sworn by Love to serve her in all things, and if I disobey her now my life is a lie.

Still, she did not forbid me to fight in the melee.

Maybe I shall see a way to obey her command and yet take some revenge on Amalric.

But what way?

"What is it, Roland?" Diane asked him anxiously.

"Nothing. Nothing." He picked up the paper and tore it into tiny fragments.

"Perrin, help me to arm myself."

Roland felt a chill around his heart. Perhaps he should simply ride away from this field. To risk his life in this melee was foolhardy.

But if he left, he would appear a coward. There would be no vengeance for Perrin. And Amalric still would pursue him.

He held out his right arm so that Perrin could once again tie the scarf around it. When it was in place he lifted his arm and pressed his lips to the smooth silk.

His mind empty of any plan, his hands tied by a torn letter, Roland joined the knights gathering before the gallery in the center of the arena. The marshals had removed the tilting barrier that had divided the field in half.

The chief of heralds announced that the knights must form two companies, those happy in love and those disappointed in love. Roland smiled sourly beneath his helm. The usual tournament conceit, he thought, probably Queen Marguerite's idea, a shallow borrowing from the traditions of *l'amour courtois*. The side we pick depends on who is leading it, not on how we stand with the ladies.

"A seigneur of highest rank will command each company," the herald cried, his powerful, trained voice booming out over the tournament field. "Monseigneur the Count Robert d'Artois will lead the happy in love."

The King's nearest brother, thought Roland. The other side is likely to let his side win, out of politeness. I should probably join them.

"The disappointed in love," the herald went on, "will be led by Monseigneur the Count Amalric de Gobignon."

How ironic—and how true.

"De Gobignon unhappy in love?" laughed a Gascon knight near Roland. "But his countess is exquisite."

"It must be some other lady, not the countess, who has disappointed him," said another. "It is impossible for a man to be in love with his own wife."

The Gascon answered, "I would never look at another woman if my wife were the fair Nicolette."

Mindful of Nicolette's command, Roland spurred Alezan over to a marshal and said, "I wish to fight on the same side as the Count de Gobignon."

The marshal's eyebrows flickered in surprise, but without comment he gave Roland a strip of black silk to tie to his tilting helm.

Dust clouds glowed in the bright sun, which had moved around to the west. The field enclosed by the lists was a confusion of chargers and armored men, of waving lances and fluttering black and white silk streamers on tilting helms.

Roland smiled to himself as he guided Alezan into the ranks behind Amalric and saw the blond count, his tilting helm thrown back, turn to glare at him, surprised and angry.

Amalric spoke to Enguerrand de Coucy and the other riders

near him, pointing to Roland, and they all looked in his direction. A cold feeling spread through Roland's chest.

He looked for friends, but he recognized no one among those near him, or in the company gathering at the far side of the field. Over there Robert d'Artois, riding a nervous white charger and holding a blue shield charged with three gold fleurs-de-lis, was marshaling his men.

"Form two ranks!" de Gobignon shouted.

Roland took a place in the center of the second rank. A silence settled over the tournament field.

The trumpets sounded.

Roland felt the ground shuddering under him as the knights in the rank in front of him shot forward. In an instant, all he could see in the center of the field was a whirlwind of dust, flying lance splinters, and the tumbling bodies of mail-clad men. The clash of arms and the roar of the crowd combined in a hellish din.

Now the dust settled enough so that Roland could see the combatants fighting at close quarters. He admired the expert way they guided their mounts. The gigantic chargers seemed to step with the grace and precision of dancers. Knights and destriers were like the centaurs of Greek legend, rider and horse moving as a single creature.

Roland charged with the second rank.

Almost at once four lances from his own side converged on him. The suddenness of it stunned him. He had expected to be attacked, but not so soon and not so openly.

He brought Alezan up short, and with rein and spur made the horse wheel while he swung his lance in an arc that struck aside the weapons of his enemies and knocked two of them from the saddle.

But Roland was in the center of a solid circle of mounted men, all like himself wearing black strips of silk on their helmets. *Now that Amalric has seen me joust, he has decided he needs help. Who the Devil are these bastards?* he thought angrily.

Some of the men pressing him wore nondescript helms and carried plain shields. Others were elaborately, expensively arrayed, doubtless in captured accoutrements. On the edge of the ring he saw the silver wolf's head, also with a black ribbon tied to it. Among the shields facing him was one painted with the red and white bands of de Coucy.

There were no longer any questions. It was simple now. They

were trying to kill him, and there was only one thing to do—
strike down as many of his attackers as possible.

And if Amalric joined the attack, surely Nicolette's command
did not mean that he must die rather than defend himself.

Three lances stabbed at him from the right. One slid past him,
but two struck him hard in the side under his lance arm, knocking the wind out of him. He managed to club one of the attackers
with his own lance, bringing him down, but he felt himself
losing balance and toppling out of the saddle.

He hit the ground on his feet and drew his blunt-edged tournament sword. He chopped at the lances jabbing him from above
and slashed at the hooves of the war-horses trying to trample
him.

"Beauséant!" The deep-voiced shout lifted above the din of
battle was the war cry of the Templars. Guido Bruchesi was
riding through Amalric's men, cutting a path with his longsword.
He wore the white silk ribbon of the happy. The professional
tourneyers Amalric had recruited to help him fell away from
Guido. Roland's heart leaped thankfully.

Then Enguerrand de Coucy engaged Guido. The tide of battle
swept between Guido and Roland, and he was once again fighting for his life, alone.

Riders wearing white silk, followers of Robert d'Artois, were
attacking Amalric's hirelings. Among the attackers Roland
glimpsed the shield of the English knight whose arms he had
returned. The professional tourneyers ignored the knights who
were supposedly their opponents and continued to strike at Roland.

Roland heard cries of "Foul play!" from the stands as the
crowd began to see that something was amiss.

Beyond the steel ring closing in on him, Roland could see
Robert d'Artois riding against Amalric. Amalric was armed with
a mace. He swung it at Robert's shield, and the King's brother
fell and disappeared from Roland's view.

The fighting had driven Roland and his attackers to the edge
of the field. Roland knew that he could touch the wooden barrier
and thereby be allowed to leave the field in safety. But he was
sure that Amalric's men would never let him escape that way.
He was close enough to the spectators to hear their shouts of
encouragement for him and their angry protests at his enemies.

Feeling that the crowd was with him gave him fresh strength
as he hammered furiously at his attackers, driving them back
inch by inch.

He took a stunning blow on his helmet, where it covered the

back of his neck. He blacked out momentarily, and when he could see again he was lying full-length on his back. From all sides the heavy blades hammered at his body, not sharp enough to cut through his mail, but hard enough to break his bones.

Only half conscious, he sat up, despite the merciless shower of sword strokes.

A momentary break in the ring of enemies around him gave him a glimpse of the gallery. He looked for Nicolette—this might be his last sight of her—but saw only King Louis on his feet, gesturing and pushing his way down the gallery steps. Then the dust and the forest of mailed legs closed in again.

The outcry of the crowd, shouting at Roland's assailants to spare the fallen knight, drowned the clangor of arms.

Above the screaming of the crowd rose a clarion blast. Roland heard the heralds calling for a stop to the melee. Am I saved?

Amalric roared, "Fight on! Fight on! Kill him!"

As Roland struggled to get up he saw heralds riding in among Amalric's men, trying to drive them back. The trumpets and clarions shrilled again, in vain.

A pair of steel-encased legs appeared before him. He lifted his head, and there, in the small oblong of sight permitted by his tilting helm, was Amalric, towering above him, mace upraised.

The thick staff, topped with its spiked iron ball, was coming down on Roland's head. Desperately he tried to twist out of the way, knowing there was not time.

From somewhere a figure struck Amalric's legs. Roland heard the shout, "Stop! He is fallen!" and glimpsed Perrin, unarmed and unarmored, at Amalric's feet.

Then the mace smashed down on his shoulder. Agony shot through him. He felt bones shattering.

His shoulder was crushed. He collapsed. The pain, sweet Jesus! The pain in his shoulder filled his whole body. He could barely cling to consciousness.

Lying on his back in the dirt, he saw Enguerrand de Coucy send Perrin flying with a blow of his red-striped shield.

Amalric raised his mace again, gripping it with both mailed hands.

For the third time the trumpets shrieked for a halt.

A man was standing protectively over Roland. Amalric shifted the mace to bring it down on the bare, blond head of this newcomer. Roland heard cries of horror from the spectators. Amazingly, Enguerrand de Coucy threw himself between the two men, his arms up to deflect the mace.

Roland turned his head. Through a haze that drained all color from his vision, he recognized the King.

Louis drew his longsword and put the point of it against Amalric's chest. He thrust with it, pushing Amalric back from Roland.

Roland propped himself up with his left arm. The right one was useless. All feeling was gone, from shoulder to fingertips.

He was able to see over the top of the lists. On the other side a line of royal sergeants stood with crossbows loaded and drawn, aimed at Amalric.

"You have used me, Count, used me ill," said Louis in a low voice that carried in the sudden silence that had fallen in the arena.

Amalric lifted off his tilting helm. He was standing beyond Roland's feet, and Roland got a good look at his face. It was flushed and full of hate as he stared at Louis.

"Forgive me for menacing you, sire," he ground out. "I was possessed by my angry mood and did not see that it was you who barred me from my enemy."

"Possessed indeed," Louis replied. "If you had struck me it would have been an accident. But what you were doing to this man was no accident."

"It is my right to defend my honor as I see fit, sire."

"How dare you speak of honor, you who persuaded me to hold this tournament so that you could use it to cloak murder? You have made a fool of the King and a mockery of chivalry. You will be stripped of your armor and will stand until vespers on yonder platform, like any other recreant knight."

"I am the Count de Gobignon. I am a Peer of the Realm. You cannot treat me like some ordinary knight."

Another figure moved into Roland's line of sight. Roland saw through the wavering film over his eyes that it was Enguerrand de Coucy.

"Sire, if you do this to de Gobignon, you insult all of us of noble birth." His face was as red as the stripes on his shield.

"God's justice is the same for everybody, highborn or lowborn," said Louis. "For the crime of attempted murder I could punish the Count much more severely if I chose."

"I should have let him brain you," Enguerrand de Coucy muttered.

Roland heard Robert d'Artois's voice cut in suddenly. "Silence, de Coucy!" he snapped. "How dare you speak so to the King?"

Waves of pain rippled out through Roland's body from his shoulder, cresting and ebbing in time to the rhythm of his heart. With each beat, it seemed sight and hearing faded momentarily and then came back. This felt worse than any other wound he had ever suffered. In a lucid moment he thought, I may never use this arm again.

He heard the King say, "Amalric, will you take your punishment like an obedient knight, or must I have you bound?"

I must try to witness this, Roland thought. With a supreme effort he fought the pain and raised his head a little higher. He managed to see Louis and Amalric staring at each other. Both men were golden blond, the King's hair falling fine and straight from his receding hairline, Amalric's thick like a lion's mane. The King was slender, Amalric broad and powerful. Trembling with anger, the King seemed ready to seize Amalric himself, while Amalric's chest heaved with suppressed fury.

At last, in a cold, controlled voice, Amalric said, "I will submit, perforce. You do me a great wrong, sire, and not me alone. You undermine the very foundations of this realm. In exposing me to public scorn, you tell the men of rank that they cannot rely on you. In the end, it will not be I who am shamed by this day." Amalric turned and strode out of Roland's sight.

Perrin's dirt-streaked face, a rivulet of blood running from nose to lip, appeared before him. Gently lifting Roland's head, he unlaced the tilting helm and pulled it off. Roland gasped as a new wave of agony shot through him. Anxiously Perrin peered at him.

"Do I still have the scarf?" Roland whispered.

"Yes, master."

Louis dropped to one knee beside Roland. "How fare you, Sire Orlando?"

Through clenched teeth Roland gasped, "I live. Thanks to you, sire."

Louis smiled and laid his hand on Roland's forehead. "Be it God's will that you be healed, to fight again as magnificently as you fought today."

At Louis's touch the terrible pain that throbbed through Roland's body seemed to diminish. It is said anointed kings have power to heal, Roland thought with awe.

"M-may I have help to get him to his tent, sire?" Perrin choked out, his voice tremulous.

It is not every day, Roland thought, that a jongleur speaks to a king.

"He shall be in my care," said Louis. "My own physicians shall tend him. Orlando of Perugia, I must have a man like you as my companion in arms." He stood up and beckoned to the royal equerries. "Take him to the palace." He turned to the heralds, standing in a small group nearby. "This tournament is now at an end. Let it be proclaimed." Then he passed from Roland's sight. He heard a cheer for the King go up from the spectators. They do not yet know he has cut short the fighting, Roland thought.

God, what has happened to my shoulder? How can I still be awake? I would rather be dead than feel so much pain.

Then in the midst of his suffering his heart lurched with dread. The King's companion? What on earth . . . My life is my own, not his.

Yet, were it not for him I would be dead now.

Saint Michel, what if he wants to take me crusading?

Ah, well, if I live I won't be able to do any fighting anyway. If I live. In his pain Roland hardly felt the hands that lifted him, as his consciousness slipped away.

XI

THE SPARKLING OCTOBER DAY AWED ROLAND, AS IF HE HAD NEVER before seen sun, blue sky, and trees. Out for the first time since the tournament, he was walking with Perrin in the garden of the royal country estate at Vincennes. His feet felt uncertain on the dirt path. Leaning on Perrin's arm, he made an effort to walk upright despite the weight of the wooden frame and the bandages Louis's physicians had wrapped around his right shoulder. After weeks of lying in bed wearing nothing but a nightshirt, he felt his clothing rough against his skin. But the bearskin cloak over his back was a welcome protection from the autumn chill. The light of the morning sun poured strength into his limbs.

"Good day, Sire Orlando."

Roland recognized the voice and turned. The King had come up behind him.

Roland tried to get down on one knee, but Louis stopped him

with a wave of his hand. Roland looked for some token of kingship on Louis's apparel, but the sovereign wore only a mantle of black silk trimmed with red squirrel fur, such as any country gentleman might possess, and his head was bare.

He knows what he is. He does not have to proclaim it.

Saint Michel, can this really be happening to me? Roland wondered. A moment ago, walking with Perrin, he had felt that this royal garden and this beautiful day were as real as the continuously throbbing pain in his shoulder. But now, staring at the tall, large-eyed man before him, he asked himself if this could be yet another one of the feverish dreams he had been having since the tournament. Louis had appeared often in those dreams, along with Nicolette, Amalric, and a great mace always descending but never striking. *Can I actually be a houseguest of the King of France?*

"Dear Sire Orlando, I heard you were up and about. Praise God, your health is coming back. Come walk with me, and we shall enjoy the fall colors in the forest together."

"Sire," said Perrin nervously, "he tires quickly."

"Nonsense, Perrin," said Roland testily.

"I shall prop him up, if I have to, my good fellow," said Louis. "You have been watching over him day and night for a month. Be off and have a cup of wine with my equerries. Let me care for your master for a while."

Walking slowly beside Louis, Roland realized with surprise that the King had no attendants. There were just the two of them strolling through the manor garden. Roland looked back and saw Perrin in the doorway of the two-story stone mansion, looking anxiously after them. Lifting his left arm, the one he could move, Roland waved him away irritably.

"I like to walk alone, or with just one companion," said Louis. "I never get enough solitude. That is why I enjoy Vincennes."

Roland inhaled deeply. The air felt sweet as water from a spring.

Louis cheerfully pointed out some especially brilliant splashes of gold and red in the foliage around them.

"When did you bring me here, sire?"

"About two weeks after the tournament, when the friars said you were well enough to travel. I thought being away from the dirt and noise of Paris would speed your recovery." His face fell. "But then it seemed I might have made a terrible mistake.

We took you in a litter, and the ride was bumpy. You got much worse for a while. My queen was very angry with me.''

And Nicolette? If only I could ask about Nicolette, Roland thought anxiously. Where is she? And how does she fare? Will Marguerite let her know I am better?

They were following a path to a clearing, where Louis showed him a huge, twisted oak.

"That is my favorite tree in all this forest. I like to sit under it. Sometimes the people who live nearby come to me here with their troubles, and I try to help them.''

Louis took Roland's left arm and helped him seat himself under the old tree.

Embarrassment made Roland's face burn. The King helps me to sit down?

Slowly he leaned back until his weight was resting against the tree trunk. The ache in his shoulder subsided a little.

Louis folded his long body down beside Roland. "Now, Sire Orlando,'' he said with a wry smile. "If I can urge the matter of your taking a crusader's cross, without being answered in the language of a Parisian guttersnipe . . .''

The crusade? Uneasiness made Roland want to draw away.

"I do not understand, sire—about the language, I mean.''

Louis smiled, but his fair cheeks reddened. "While you were very ill, just after we got here, I laid a crucifix on your chest and told you how God had saved my life after I promised to go on crusade. I suggested that He might spare you if you made the same promise. You . . . you . . .'' Louis hesitated, then looked away. He rattled out the rest of the tale in a voice so low Roland had to strain to hear it. "You threw the crucifix on the floor and told me to stuff my crusade up my arse.''

Roland stifled an impulse to laugh. This was no laughing matter. He went cold with mortification—and with dread. Any suspicion that he was irreligious might provoke an investigation. And that could lead to Diane.

Saint Michel, was I that sick? No wonder Perrin was afraid to let me be alone with the King. Dear God, I hope I did not let anything slip about Nicolette.

"Sire, I do not know how I can apologize enough. I beg your forgiveness.''

Smiling, Louis shook his head. "As my good mother might have said, it was the fever talking. I mentioned it only in jest, but I should not have embarrassed you. It is you who must forgive me.''

What a strange man. Roland felt himself becoming more and more intrigued. He may have been trying to joke, but he actually blushed at repeating my coarse words. Yet he has led knights in battle.

"Sire, for me to forgive you would be an impertinence. I owe you my life."

"I saw what was happening in the melee, and I did the only thing I could, Sire Orlando," said Louis. "Besides, I could not let such a man as you be lost. I saw you knock down one knight after another. I saw you hold off a dozen or more professional tourneyers. Jerusalem needs men like you to fight for her."

Roland felt cold despite the high sun. His heart was being pulled in two directions. He wanted to give this man, to whom he owed his life, anything he asked. Yet this was the same king whose armies had pillaged Languedoc.

Roland had worn the crusaders' cross as a disguise to rescue Diane. But to wear it in earnest?

He looked off into the forest and saw a figure prowling through the trees. Sunlight glinted on a steel helmet. Off in another direction, he glimpsed the blue tunic of a royal sergeant behind some scarlet-tinted shrubbery. The forest was full of the King's guards, he realized, keeping far enough away to give Louis some privacy. The sight of the guards sent a little tingle of fear down Roland's spine, reminding him that this man sitting companionably beside him wielded enormous power.

This is the king who unleashed the inquisitors on my poor people. In his name Amalric burned hundreds at Mont Ségur.

If only I could tell him flatly, no, I will never go on crusade with him. But I dare not.

"Sire, with this arm of mine, I probably will never be able to fight again." He raised his right hand from his lap, and a lightning bolt of pain shot from neck to fingertips. He winced and let the hand drop again.

Louis's face shadowed. "Your suffering is my fault. I let Amalric persuade me to allow maces in the melee. I know as a Christian I should forgive Amalric. But he does not feel any remorse. Those few hours of public shame only hardened his heart. And to think I was considering him for one of the highest offices in the realm!"

Was! Roland's heart leaped. That at least I accomplished. Amalric will not be Constable of France. That much I have done for the martyrs of Mont Ségur.

But what of Nicolette? Amalric must be furious. What if he

took it out on her? If only I could ask about her. But that would compromise her even more.

"Well, sire," he said, "if the tournament changed your mind about the Count de Gobignon, it may have been a good thing, saving you from placing such great trust in the man."

"A shrewd point," Louis said with a small smile. "Yet I cannot afford to lose Amalric. He is strong, a good general in the field. You should have seen him riding down the English at Taillebourg. And I need his army, the vassals of the house of Gobignon. And his treasure."

It dazzled Roland to realize the position he was in. Discussing Amalric with the King of France.

He looked up at the sky through the brown leaves of the great oak. God, it is good to be alive.

"Sire, it is no help," he said carefully, "to have a man on your side whom you cannot fully trust."

"Oh, he will be all right," said Louis confidently. "I told him to stay away from Paris for six months, till my anger cools. By then his feelings toward me will have improved, too. His family has served mine for hundreds of years."

Perhaps they've resented it for hundreds of years, too, Roland thought.

Did Amalric take Nicolette with him when he left Paris? I must get a message to her.

"I need you as well, Orlando," said the King. "Let us suppose you are lucky and God gives you back the use of your arm. Will you come on the crusade then?"

How can I escape this king? Beneath his gentle manner, what an iron stubbornness!

Roland tried to imagine himself using his right arm again. It hurt even to think of moving that crushed shoulder. I will never be well enough to go on crusade. But I will not make him any promises, not even empty ones.

"Sire, a crusading knight needs a string of horses, arms and armor for war, a following of men-at-arms. I have none of that. I am so light of purse, I could not even pay my own passage to Outremer, much less for a whole retinue."

"A crusading knight need only be a great fighter," said Louis quietly. "Without that, all the rest is worthless. You can fight. I saw that. And do not forget, you won arms and horses in the tournament. Also, as your jongleur tells me, you have a little house outside Paris. You must have a bit of income."

"My father sends me a little money. I have nothing of my own."

A hollow feeling in Roland's stomach warned him that he was stepping close to the edge of a cliff. If the King asked who his father was, he would either have to lie—or reveal that his family were enemies of the French.

But then, the truth might be the very thing. If Louis knew I was a faidit and the son of one, surely he would not want me with him.

The hollow of dread grew till it became piercing physical pain. He wondered if he could trust himself to take such a risk with the King.

If I tell him, he might have me beaten, turn me over to the Inquisition.

No, he is not that sort of person.

"Sire, I must confess all and throw myself on your mercy." He felt like a rider who had come to a dangerous jump and made up his mind to try it.

Louis eyed him, startled.

There was no turning back now. "I am not the person I have claimed to be."

"You interest me, messire. Who are you, then?"

"My name is Roland de Vency, and I am a man of Languedoc." He went on to tell the story of his family. "My father is now in the chancery of the Emperor. If he were to come back to France, he would be executed for his crimes."

Finished, Roland waited for Louis's response. His shoulder throbbed, and a jackdaw on a nearby branch cawed derisively.

Louis's large eyes held Roland's. "Are you a good Catholic, messire? You had the last sacraments while you were sick, you know."

"Then my soul is whiter than it has been in many a year, sire. No, I am no heretic. My father was not fighting against Catholicism. He was fighting for his homeland."

Louis was silent for a long time.

"I will have to ask you many more questions," he said finally.

"Of course, sire."

Louis leaned back against the knotted bark of the immense oak and gazed up at the sky.

"So your father is with Frederic. You cannot possibly know how much I wish I could be friends with Frederic. My France and his Germany are the two largest realms in Christendom. We should be like brothers. And his fight with the Pope—how I hate to see that! If only I could bring them together. Everybody, everywhere, is hurt by the war between those two, and nobody is thinking about Jerusalem. Except me.

"Your connection with the Emperor could be helpful. And it would please me to give a post to the son of one of our former enemies. Such a position would give you income enough, too, for the crusade."

Roland's heart sank. This beautiful day was turning darker and darker.

"Sire, I am just not the sort of man you want. I do not believe in crusading. I have no wish to make war on the Turks."

"But," said Louis, his big eyes shining, "are you not named after Charlemagne's paladin Roland, who died a glorious death fighting the Saracens?"

"Sire, if you recall, Charlemagne's Roland was fighting Arabs who had invaded France. I promise you, if the Sultan of Egypt attacks France, I shall be among the first to go to war against him. If I can ever hold a sword again."

"Jerusalem *is* our land," said Louis. "It belongs to Christendom."

"Sire, as you know, the Emperor has Muslim servants at his court. They told me Jerusalem is a holy city for them, too."

"Yes, well, they may believe that," said Louis imperturbably, "but they are mistaken. Islam is not the true religion."

Roland's eyes burned, and he felt an ache in his temples. He really had been out of bed too long, he thought.

"Sire, Jerusalem is too far off for us to hold it."

Astonishingly, Louis merely laughed. "You are in good company. My mother and two of my brothers say the same. With God's help I hope to change their minds. I think we can liberate Jerusalem, and I believe it is worth the sacrifice."

Roland's headache became worse, and a dull anger pulsed in his chest. The man is impossible. This sweet, patient determination—it wears me down.

It is like trying to fight the tide, he thought. Each wave seems no higher than the last. But slowly, irresistibly, one is overwhelmed.

"It was a crusade that destroyed my homeland. I would be a traitor to my people if I wore the cross."

Louis's large eyes remained sympathetic, and Roland felt doomed. "That is it exactly, do not you see, dear Roland? Now that I know you are a son of Languedoc, I must, I *must* win you over. The Albigensian Crusade—I cannot say it was wrong, because the Pope commanded it and my grandfather and my father both supported it. But it is time to write an end to all that. I want all France, north and south, united." Now his eyes were alight with fervor. He held up clenched fists. "Think of it—men of Languedoc and men of France fighting side by side to recapture Jerusalem for Christendom. I believe God wants that. He wants France *healed*."

Despair pressed heavier on Roland than the wooden frame on his shoulder.

What is there left for me to say? I do not give a fig who holds Jerusalem! Let the Sultan have it. I should say *that* to the King; it might get me out of here.

But I do not want to offend him. I like him.

He accepts me even knowing that I deceived him, that I come from a faidit family.

Louis broke in on his thoughts. "I can see you are thinking about what I have said. That is good enough for now. I have tired you out with all this talk. Forgive me for that. I do forget myself sometimes. I should not be preaching at you when you are still suffering so."

And if he keeps on so, he will have me altogether in his power.

Louis stood suddenly and gave Roland both his hands to help him up. An excruciating pain shot through Roland's right side, and he bit his lip to keep from crying out.

Louis gave Roland his arm. "Here, lean on me. We shall walk back to the manor together."

Roland's pain gave him an excuse for silence on the return walk. The royal mansion, built as a retreat by Louis's grandfather, Philippe Auguste, soon rose stout and square ahead of them. Its stolidity was redeemed by the graceful spire of a chapel which, Louis told Roland, he had added to the manor house a few years before.

As they reached the gate leading from the forest into the walled garden, Louis said, "If your shoulder does not let you return to the warrior's life, there is plenty of other work for a knight of talent who can read and write. A post will be yours, whether or not you go on crusade. I need men of your quality around me, Roland de Vency."

There was such affection in Louis's voice that Roland felt an answering warmth in his heart.

He had come to France seeking a patron, and now the King of France himself was offering him a post, practically demanding that he take it. True, not as a troubadour, but was it not better to have serious work to do? He could always write songs. Even kings wrote songs.

Nicolette spent much of her time with Queen Marguerite. A post with the King might bring him closer to her.

And he liked this king. Here was a man so free from pride that he would half carry an injured, unknown, penniless knight through his royal park. Honest, generous, he cared about his people. Of course, when it came to the crusade he sounded dangerously mad, but now that Roland had heard the King explain it, he understood the notion at least a little.

He is like a wizard, Roland thought wonderingly. I was so sure I knew my mind, and yet he is changing me.

But perhaps if I take his post, I can move him as well.

But then if the war in Languedoc continues? What would Diane say?

I want to be a free man. But no man is free in this world. And at least under Louis I might have the power to do things.

Yes, but to wear the cross?

Rarely had Roland thought about his soul, but that day he began to fear he might be losing it.

XII

HER STOMACH TIGHT WITH APPREHENSION, NICOLETTE STOOD IN THE center of the empty great hall of Château Gobignon. Rows of old banners hanging from the ceiling rustled faintly as she watched the broad staircase leading to the château's chief tower.

A heavy door closed above. Footsteps approached the stairs.

A white robe appeared at the head of the staircase, ghostly in the light of the torches set around the gray stone walls. The beads wrapped around his waist rattling, Hugues de Gobignon descended.

Nicolette bowed politely. "Good evening, Friar Hugues."

Hugues gave her a malevolent look, blue eyes glittering.

"Madame," he said curtly and turned quickly away, walking in the direction of his own chamber.

He hates me because I am a woman of Languedoc, Nicolette thought. He would love to see Amalric put me away in a convent—or a dungeon. The de Gobignons think of me as Amalric's great mistake. Especially since I have had three daughters and no sons. But Amalric has always refused to listen to them—so far.

She knew Amalric was alone now, up there in his council chamber in the tower. She took a deep breath and started to climb the stairs, fear and nervousness weakening her knees.

She had prepared herself carefully for this interview, spending an hour before her silver mirror braiding her long black hair because Amalric had said he found her lovely in braids. Her face in the mirror looked anxious and pale, though she had pinched her cheeks to give them color. She pinched them again now. She wore a long green velvet gown that clung to her figure, with a belt of gold links that emphasized the slenderness of her waist. She wanted to look her best for Amalric, though she knew it would be useless to try to be seductive with him. Not because he did not desire her, but because he knew she did not desire him.

In the seven months we have been here, she thought, I doubt he has had me seven times. Just as well; I do not have to drink that awful herb concoction so often to be sure I do not get pregnant again. He has had peasant girls and the daughters of villeins in plenty, I am sure.

Strange, I do not care how many women Amalric goes to bed with. But if there were another woman in Roland's life, I would die.

Sweet Goddess, I must get away from here. I am so unhappy in this place.

She caressed the folded parchment she held in her hand, its heavy red wax seal broken. He must yield to this. He cannot refuse a royal request. But what if he does not let me go? I will run away. I will take the best horse in his stables and just head south and not stop till I see the Mediterranean.

She reached the top of the staircase and the oaken door of Amalric's council chamber. The knocker was an iron wolf's head. Repelled by it, Nicolette struck the door with her knuckles. At his answering command she turned the black iron ring that unlatched the door and entered. She had been trembling as she climbed the stairs, but at the sight of him her fear was tempered by amusement. He looked so out of place, seated at a long, heavily carved table covered with piles of paper and parchment, half-opened scrolls, and even a few books. He was reading by the light of fat candles burning in cressets on the walls of the circular room. The windows were shuttered, and the smell of melting wax was heavy in the room.

"Madame," he said, without getting up, "how may I serve you?" Sarcasm was heavy in his tone.

Her heart quailed. He was still bitter over his disgrace at the King's tournament, and he blamed her for it. He hates the King and Queen, he hates Paris, he hates Roland, she thought. He'll never let me go back there.

"I received this today, monseigneur." She held out the parchment.

"Read it to me, if it is something I must know about," he said brusquely. "I am half blind from all the reading I have had to do tonight."

Yes, she thought, he loathes this sort of work. He does it only because he has to, to administer his domains. For people like me—and Roland—reading is a pleasure. I am lucky that I learned to read. So few of the women here in the north seem to know how to.

The letter was from Queen Marguerite:

> The winter here has been twice as long and twice as cold, owing to your absence. There is no one who laughs with me at the same things, no one to share gossip in the tongue of my childhood. The King is my dearest friend, but he speaks only in the accents of the north, and he is preoccupied with matters of state and religion. Dear Nicolette, I need you, who are so like a sister, to make me merry. Do beg your husband to spare you most kindly for his Queen. After all, the six months are up.

She glanced uneasily at Amalric after referring to the term of his banishment.

From the day the King stopped the tournament and saved Roland's life, she had felt a new reverence, and an even greater love, for Louis. She would never forget what he had done.

Amalric would never forget it either.

He would never forgive Louis for those hours he had had to stand, stony-faced, on the platform of shame, the de Gobignon shield of which he was so proud hanging upside down from the wooden railing. What vengeance had he begun plotting, she wondered, as he stood there?

During their two weeks' ride after the tournament from Paris to the Gobignon possessions in the northeast corner of France,

she had sensed in him a fury more terrible than anything she had
known before.

Only when they rode over the crest of a hill and caught a
glimpse of Château Gobignon—still a whole day's ride off—did
a grim smile cross Amalric's face. But her own heart sank when
she saw the gray drum towers and battlemented walls crowning
the distant rocky hillside. In all the years of their marriage she
had spent as little time as possible at Château Gobignon, staying
at court with Marguerite or visiting Amalric's holdings in the
south. The château frightened and depressed her, now more than
ever. It was an edifice dedicated to the power of the Gobignon
family as a cathedral was dedicated to worship. But to Nicolette
it had always seemed nothing more than a huge prison.

The next day, much closer, she saw that the château was
wearing gay finery in honor of its master's return, dozens of
purple and gold Gobignon banners fluttering from the tall round
towers. Amalric might have left Paris in disgrace, but his family
and vassals, she knew, would treat his return as a triumph.

In Gobignon-la-Ville, the walled town that nestled at the base
of the château's hill, she rode beside Amalric past a crowd of
cheering burghers, craftsmen, men-at-arms, and serfs. She glanced
at Amalric and saw that he looked almost happy as he waved to
them. They shouted for Nicolette, too, as she rode through the
town, but the closer she came to the château walls the lonelier
she felt.

When she rode through the barbican and into the courtyard,
she saw Amalric's whole family lined up to greet him, and her
heart felt heavier still. None of them even looked at her. She had
just spent the summer with these Gobignons, and now she
dreaded a winter in their company. Countess Marie, Amalric's
mother, was the daughter of King Philippe Auguste and the sister
of King Louis VIII, and she never let anyone forget it. Amalric's
brother Hugues was there, of course, his fanatical eyes piercing
her. And there was a pack of ambitious, powerful relatives and
vassals, who dropped to their knees before Amalric.

Their greeting should make him feel better, she thought. In
Paris he had to yield to the King. Here he was king.

Amalric hoisted his eldest daughter, ten-year-old Isabelle, to
sit in front of him on his horse. She thrust into his hands a little
pillow she had embroidered for him, and Nicolette saw how
moved he was.

As she watched the younger girls, Alix and Blanche, greet
Amalric and hardly more than glance shyly at her, guilt jabbed

Nicolette. Because they came from *him*, her children brought her
little joy. She remembered how she had loved her own mother. It
was terrible that such a wall must stand between her children
and her. *It was my fortune to meet and marry their father, and
they are the innocent consequence. I am a bad mother*, she
thought, and grief and guilt made her heart heavy as stone.

How long can I stay in this place? she wondered.

Now she handed Amalric Marguerite's letter, which might be
the key to her escape. He dropped it to the paper-laden table
without a glance.

He said harshly, "Visiting the Queen is out of the question. I
need you here."

Rage and rebellion boiled up in her.

"Good God, what do you need me for?" she burst out. "You
got everything you wanted from me when you took my family's
estates."

"I did not marry you for your lands, Nicolette."

There was suffering, a look of yearning, in his face. She saw
it but did not want to admit that she did.

"The King had it in mind to appoint me Constable of France,
something I wanted more than anything in this world. And I lost
the post because of that damned troubadour. Do you think I
would ever have made such a sacrifice if it were not for you?"

Agree with him, she pleaded with herself. *Tell him you
appreciate him.*

But before she could stop herself she said, "You never meant
to sacrifice anything. You planned to kill that man in a way that
would leave you looking blameless. But you lost your head when
it turned out he was not as easy a victim as that poor jongleur."

"By Saint Dominic, madame! Your innocent Italian troubadour was trying to kill *me*."

"It was your jealousy and cruelty that started it."

Suddenly his eyes narrowed. "How did you know about the
jongleur?"

Her body went cold.

My God, she thought, *I have destroyed myself.*

Amalric stood up, looking huge to her, stalked around the
table, and seized her wrist.

Desperately she tried to pull away, her heart thudding. As his
face drew close to hers, she felt faint, could hardly breathe.

"Only he knew about the jongleur."

She had to clear her head. Her life might depend on her saying the right thing. He could strangle her right here.

"His whole household knew about it, and they made no secret of it," she said. "Servants gossip, and it reaches one's ears eventually." She summoned all her strength to look calm.

"How did he get the handkerchief?" Amalric was a wolf with teeth fastened in a deer's throat, unwilling to let go until his prey is dead.

"You *told* me to return it to him," she answered, her guts churning. "I did as you commanded. I never thought he would be so mad as to wear it, much less at the tournament. I have told you again and again, this man has done nothing but pay me the harmless honor a troubadour offers to the lady he has chosen. A troubadour does not talk to his lady, he worships her from a distance. I have never given him permission even to speak to me."

Breathing heavily, he still held her wrist. There was a strange blankness in his eyes, as if his rage had blinded him.

After a silence he said, "Do you swear that you have never known this man, that you have never been with him in secret?"

"Of course," she said hastily.

" 'Of course' will not do, madame." His hand still clamped on her, he dragged her out of the chamber. He pulled her down the spiraling stone stairs to the bottom level of the tower.

She did not dare struggle against him. Her hand was going numb, and pain was coursing through her body. She could hardly keep her footing on the steep stairs.

They emerged into the small chapel, so dark that its round, vaulted ceiling was barely visible, the only light a tiny, flickering candle burning at the altar. The Blessed Sacrament is in the tabernacle, she thought. He would not dare kill me here, in the presence of Jesus.

As her eyes adjusted to the dim light she saw with an inward shudder the seven stone boxes around the walls of the chapel that held the remains of earlier de Gobignons. Most frightening of all was the carved figure of Amalric's father, Count Stephen, on his black marble sarcophagus. One leg was crossed over the other as a sign that he had been a crusader. The stone eyes seemed open, staring at the chapel ceiling, the eagle's face still alive with rage. She looked away quickly.

Dear Goddess, Amalric is going to make me swear before the altar that I have never been with Roland.

A new fear struck her, the fear of Almighty God. She shook

inwardly at the thought of what God's vengeance might be. He might strike her dead—or kill Roland.

But if I refuse to swear, Amalric will surely kill me.

"Swear now!" Amalric bellowed at her, his voice booming against the cold stones. "Swear before the Seigneur Jesus that you have not conversed with this man, that you have not met him secretly, that you have not"—he choked the words out— "bedded with him, that you do not love him."

He waited, blue eyes burning like the heart of a flame.

She stared up at a painted wooden statue of the crucified Savior above the altar, bleeding profusely, eyes rolled up in exquisite agony. She felt a closeness to Jesus unlike any she had ever known before. As He was alone and forlorn the day He died, she was, too, at this moment.

I will tell him the truth, she thought suddenly. Why not? I will never see Roland again anyway. Why spend the rest of my life as a prisoner? If he kills me it will all be over.

No! Anger and defiance flared up inside her. I am the daughter of Guilhem de Lumel. This man has crushed my country, my people, and I am not going to lie down and die at his hands.

Standing at the altar, she clasped her hands before her breast. "I swear. Before Jesus Christ, I swear to all of it, monseigneur."

Amalric was silent for a moment. Then he shut his eyes and expelled a deep sigh.

"Thank God," he whispered, and she felt a stab of guilt at his heartfelt relief.

He held out his arms to her, and she let him embrace her. The gold threads in his embroidered tunic scratched her cheek. She could hear his heart beating hard and fast.

He believes me because he wants so much to believe me. He wants to believe me because he loves me, and there is nothing I can do for him.

After he had held her desperately for a moment he released her and said softly, "Come with me, Nicolette."

She cast one last look at Jesus, and then let Amalric take her hand and lead her out of the chapel.

I may have damned myself to Hell for all eternity, she thought. But she did not know which she feared more—God's judgment or Amalric's rage.

Back in his council chamber Amalric held a chair for her, then sank into his own. His fury now spent, he seemed worn out. His manner was almost apologetic, though Amalric de Gobignon would never apologize to anyone.

"Did I hurt you?" he asked.

"Not at all, monseigneur."

"I am glad. Nicolette, I have much to offer you. And there will be more in years to come. I want you at my side. Let us be better friends."

She writhed inwardly. She loved Roland, and that made any closeness with Amalric impossible. She wanted to offer Amalric some comfort—the wrongdoing was not all on his side—but she did not want to utter another lie.

"I shall try to be a better wife, monseigneur."

His smile was warm. "You will have the opportunity. We are going on a long journey together, you and I."

The thought of a journey with him chilled her heart.

"A journey to where, monseigneur?"

"Call it a pilgrimage, if you will. That is what our psalm-singing King calls it. A pilgrimage to Outremer. I told Hugues earlier this evening, and now you are the second person to know. I have decided to go on Louis's accursed crusade."

She stiffened in surprise. "But why?"

"That tournament changed everything. I have been turning it over in my mind all winter. And I have had the advice of some good men—Enguerrand de Coucy, Thibaud de Champagne, and several other great barons."

She felt a tingle of fear along the back of her neck. Amalric had always disliked the King, but since the tournament his hatred for his sovereign lord had grown venomous. And these same barons, she knew, also hated Louis for his attempts to check their power and improve the lot of lesser folk.

"What sort of advice have they given you?" she asked uneasily.

"It might indeed be better if Louis went to Outremer. Queen Blanche would rule as regent, as when Louis was a boy. Did you know that Louis has been planning to meddle in how each baron rules his fiefdom?"

She remembered listening raptly when the King talked about having royal inspectors, *enqueteurs* he called them. The idea had struck her as bold and admirable.

"Yes, I have heard something of that plan."

"Well, my royal aunt knows it is a dangerous innovation. She will have none of it while Louis is away. She is our friend. He is not. He now forbids us barons to make war on one another. He says he will settle all our disputes himself. As if he were man enough to be my master. Altogether, the kingdom will be in better hands with him gone."

Nicolette suppressed a shudder. What he meant was that the same marauders who had plundered Languedoc would be free to ravage any part of France. And Blanche would allow it. But what would Amalric gain from this?

"But you will be on crusade, monseigneur."

"There will be reliable men here to look after my interests. *Our* interests, since you will accompany me."

She felt another terrible chill, as she had when she let slip her knowledge of Perrin's wound. So that was what he had meant when he said they were going on a long journey together.

Outremer, that graveyard for countless Christian men and women! She recalled her horror when she had first heard King Louis proclaim a crusade. But then her fear had been for others, for the men who would be victims of "the madness," as her father had called it. She had never thought before tonight that Amalric might go. He had been so against the idea, had even tried to argue the King out of it. The possibility of her having to go could not have seemed more remote.

Bad enough that she had been forced to spend so many years in the cold, hostile north of France. Now must she follow this man to a war in Outremer, endure the heat, the disease, the hunger and thirst? Risk death or capture and enslavement by savage Turks, should—as had often happened—the war go against the crusaders?

But how could she oppose Amalric? What reason could she give for not being willing to go? Kings and barons usually brought their wives with them on crusade rather than endure separations that must last years. And she had just promised to be a better wife.

A short time ago, Amalric had seemed ready to kill her. She could not face his rage again.

"I am entirely at your disposal, monseigneur," she said with resignation.

"I am pleased to hear you say so, madame." Amalric paused and smiled at her.

"I have just decided to let you return to Marguerite," he said.

Joy and wonder made her feel dizzy. She knew how a prisoner felt, unexpectedly released from his dungeon. The prospect was overwhelming, almost too much to bear, as if all the candles in the room had suddenly blazed up.

Then I will see Roland! It took all her strength to remain standing decorously, eyes down, to hear what else her seigneur would say.

"Granting the Queen's request for your company will be a step toward healing the breach between Louis and myself," he went on. "I, too, have received a letter from the palace, you see." He shuffled the papers on his table and held up a parchment decorated with a huge, beribboned royal seal. "He makes overtures. When he finds out I have decided to take the cross, I will gain back much of the favor I have lost."

"I shall do my best to make peace between you and the King," she said, hoping that was what Amalric wanted to hear.

But she knew that Louis would do better to invite a viper into the palace than to renew his friendship with Amalric.

"Since you have had a letter from the King, too, will we go to Paris together, monseigneur?"

"I am still the King's seneschal for Béziers. Time I resumed my duties there. And I do not think I could stand the sight of Louis, even after six months away from him. Just the thought of that papelard and his preaching makes me wish Enguerrand had not stopped my mace. Ah, well, the East is far off and perilous. Who knows what might happen to the King there?"

She heard wild anger in his laugh.

She felt a sudden horror, as if she had been sleepwalking and had wakened suddenly to find herself at the edge of a high rooftop. She saw now why Amalric was willing to go on the crusade.

What did he have to gain? The King's death.

Her life and perhaps Louis's, depended, she realized, on not letting Amalric see that she understood him.

"We must pray he comes back safely," she said in a soft voice that she hoped sounded calm.

Amalric looked at her intently for a long time. The yellow light from the cressets cast deep shadows on his face but she could see a faint smile playing about his mouth.

"Of course we must," he said finally. "His return might be delayed for many years, though. That would give our people, those who think as we do, time to set the kingdom to rights."

"I do not really understand what is wrong with the kingdom now, monseigneur." As soon as she said those words she regretted them.

"Nicolette, I know your father was killed, and by our side, and that hurt you deeply." His mood seemed to have changed. She heard a melancholy pensiveness in his voice.

"But perhaps, having lost your father, you can understand what it is to be five years old, just old enough to know and love your father, and to be told that he was murdered. It was like waking up to find this whole château—my home all my life—vanished."

He looked at her, his face full of pain, and she could almost see that small, orphaned boy he spoke of.

"I found out, when I was a little older, that it was the heretics who murdered my father." His fists clenched. "They fell on him when he was sleeping and hacked him to pieces in his bed. Dirty, sneaking Bougres!"

Sleeping in a stolen bed in a stolen castle in a land he had invaded, thought Nicolette. But she bit her lip and said nothing. This story, she understood, was sacred to Amalric. And though she knew his father had been killed in Languedoc, this was the first time he had told her about it in a way that helped her feel something of what he felt.

He spread his hands. "So, you see. Later I learned all the reasons why we must destroy the heretics—how they worship two gods, they say this world and our bodies are made by the evil god, they murder sick people, they lie man with man and woman with woman—all of that. I know it is from them that the rabble get their ideas of communes and charters. It is they who spread the disguised paganism called courtly love. It is they who instill ideas of rebellion in the university students. Most knights and seigneurs, priests and bishops, they only know these things here." He tapped his forehead with his fingertips. "But what the heretics are is burned into my heart." He struck his chest with his fist "I know in my very blood that this kingdom will never be safe until heresy and all that springs from it is stamped out so that not a trace remains. I look forward to going back now to Béziers, to Languedoc,-where this evil has its roots. Hugues and I, we shall light a few fires."

Her flesh crawled as if in the grip of ice-cold hands. How false, how twisted, were his ideas of the Cathars and of courtly love. And of Languedoc. I am one of those he would destroy.

What if I have so offended God by my false swearing in the chapel just now that He wants me to be destroyed?

"And so you want to purify the entire kingdom? To do that you would almost have to be King yourself, monseigneur."

He raised his square chin with pride. "I am almost a king. Attend, Nicolette—do you know that one of my forebears was one of the seven great barons who helped Hugues Capet seize the crown? That makes me a Peer of the Realm. Where do you think the King gets the right to rule? From the Peers of the Realm, the descendants of those seven barons who placed Louis's ancestor on the throne. Every time a new King is to be crowned, we must consent. Did you know that?''

"No, monseigneur, I did not," she said, and was dubious.

"It is true." Amalric nodded solemnly. "We can make kings and unmake them."

And you want to unmake a king. She shuddered inside herself. When Amalric had exulted at the thought of what might happen to the King during the crusade, she had felt as if she were standing on the edge of a high roof. But now she saw, far below her, not the ground, but Hell itself. Hell was burning cities, dismembered bodies, men and women straining at the stakes, the screams of innocent sufferers. Hell was made by men like Amalric.

We shall light a few fires, he had said.

I must try to stop this man. I must find a way.

XIII

NICOLETTE TREMBLED WITH IMPATIENCE. SHE LOOKED UP FOR THE sun, but it was too low to be seen, though a late-afternoon glow suffused the canopy of leaves and branches over her head. If he kept to the promise in his letter, Roland would appear at any moment. Her black mare, tied to a nearby elm sapling, stamped her hoofs restlessly.

Seated between the twisting roots of a huge oak, Nicolette leaned back on her arms and tried to relax. After the August heat and the dust of the road, this glade was as cool as the interior of a cathedral. She stretched out her legs, encased in red hose, and pulled off the page boy's cap that hid her coiled-up hair. Some page in the Queen's entourage was in luck. For these clothes Agnes had paid him twice what a new outfit would cost. She unpinned and shook down her hair, enjoying the feeling of freedom.

She could not believe that it was almost a year since she had last seen Roland. And would she see him today, after all this time? The tension inside her was so strong she was ready to burst. She had endured the long months, but now she could not stand another minute.

He had many leagues to travel to make this rendezvous. Would some mischance of the road delay him—a storm, an accident to his horse, an encounter with highwaymen?

What if, absurdly, she were waiting in the wrong clearing, under the wrong oak? She reread Roland's unsigned letter, which Agnes had put into her hands only yesterday, while they were visiting the cathedral of Our Lady at Chartres. She had followed all his directions exactly.

But when would he come? And when he came, if he came, what would he be like? Weak and sickly, perhaps, after his long convalescence. His clerkish work as an *enqueteur* could have done little to restore his strength.

No sooner had she arrived at the royal palace, on a sunny day last May, then she sent Agnes to inquire about Roland. As she waited for word she sang. She had not always loved this city, but today all Paris seemed to shine with new life. How wonderful to be far from that gloomy Château Gobignon! She was still unpacking her gowns, humming to herself, when her maid came back, looking crestfallen. Nicolette seized her by the shoulders.

"Tell me, tell me! What has happened to him?"

"He is well enough to get about, madame," Agnes said with a weak smile. "But the bad side of that is he is not here. I talked to a clerk in the royal chancery. Your troubadour has joined the King's service as an *enqueteur*, and he is touring through Gascony just now. He will be gone most of the summer."

"Oh, God!" Crushed by disappointment, Nicolette sat down on her bed and started to cry.

"Something else you had better know, madame," Agnes went on, sitting beside her and taking her hand. "He is not Orlando of Perugia anymore. He is Roland de Vency."

He is using his real name, then? She wondered at that, but she was too miserable to think. She threw herself full length on the bed and wept.

Now she asked herself, as she had so many times since that unhappy day, what if he does not love me anymore? What if he has been hurt too badly? We should have possessed each other in body and soul in Guillaume's room when we had the chance.

What if he has met someone he loves better than me? Her hand went to the dagger she wore to protect herself while traveling. When she realized what she was doing, she let go of the hilt as if it were hot. *What is the matter with me? This waiting is driving me mad.*

She could no longer rest under the tree. Eagerness to see Roland goaded her. She stood up, the better to peer through the forest to see if he was coming.

She heard the footfalls of a horse picking its way through the trees and held her breath as she glimpsed a man walking his mount.

It was Roland. He was the only man she knew so tall and dark.

He was tying his horse to a tree near hers. He turned and strode toward her.

Dear Goddess, there he is, with that beautiful hawk's face.

"Oh, my love!" She held out her arms to him.

"Nicolette."

She hurled herself at him, the whole length of her body pressed hard against his. He was holding her so tightly she could not breathe, but she did not care; she would happily have died in his arms.

When at length he released her, she stepped back to look at him. He was as thin as ever, but he seemed well—except for something about the way he held himself, his right shoulder hunched forward and bulking larger than the left.

Amalric had crippled him. She saw again the tournament field, Amalric's mace crashing down upon him. Hatred for her husband raged within her.

"Come, let us sit down," Roland said. He held her arm as she seated herself, then dropped down beside her. There was no awkwardness in his movements. But his poor shoulder still looked huge to her. Timidly she reached out to touch it.

Roland chuckled softly, but there was pain in his eyes. "The King's physicians had an impossible task, like trying to piece together a smashed pot inside a pillow. I hope the sight of it does not . . . distress you."

She sensed the anxiety in him.

"Oh, Roland, I will never forgive myself. I stopped you from fighting Amalric, and so you placed yourself on his side in the melee."

"He and his men would have attacked me whichever side I was on."

"Yes, but you would have had the knights on the white side fighting with you."

He stroked her cheek. Her skin tingled at the touch of his fingertips.

"It all worked out well for me. Amalric lost favor with Louis that day, and I became a friend of the King. True, I cannot play the vielle any longer. You need the full use of your right arm for that. I still do well enough with the Irish harp and the lute, though. But if I am ever going to fight again, I shall have to learn to fight left-handed."

"Oh, Roland!" She sobbed his name and pressed her face against his chest.

"Do not feel sorry for me. As one of the King's *enqueteurs* I have no need of a warrior's skills. I do my fighting with ink and parchment. And I can use my injury as an excuse to stay out of the crusade."

She heard the undertone of bitterness in his voice, and she felt desolate. She would have traded her life to restore the power to his right arm.

He has suffered this because he loves me.

"I hate Amalric for what he has done to you."

He shook his head and gently touched her lips with his fingertips.

She took his hand in hers and kissed the hard palm. "And for what he did to Perrin," she went on. "Is Perrin with you?"

"He is camped near the road. He will stand watch for us. He is far enough away not to be able to hear anything we say—or any sound we make."

She looked up at him. His gaunt face was in shadow, but his meaning was clear.

The thought aroused an aching yearning in her belly. *Yes, I want him. I have wanted him so long—I cannot go on denying him, and myself, any longer.*

"Forget Amalric," Roland said suddenly. "Forget hatred. This moment is for us. Let us shut out the rest of the world."

She knew he was right. The beauty that was possible here and now must not be spoiled.

She heard a bell tolling in the distance, a country church sounding the Angelus, calling the people to sunset prayer. Bright light no longer fell in their glade, and the sky overhead was a pale violet.

Sitting beside him, she held his strong hand in both of hers. The trunks of the great oaks were growing indistinct, merging with the darkness. A choir of the night's little creatures, birds and insects, sang vespers. *This grove of oaks is our cathedral of Love,* she thought.

"When must you go to Paris?" he asked her.

"Tomorrow. I have packed some ladylike finery in my saddle-bags. The Queen's party will be coming up the road from Chartres, where I left them, and I shall simply rejoin them at Rambouillet. If anyone has been trying to spy on me, they will be quite mystified."

"We have this whole night?"

"Yes," she whispered happily, feeling her hunger for him mount.

Roland raised her hand to his lips and kissed it, as she had kissed his. "Will *mi dons* wait here a moment?"

He stood and went over to his tethered horse, grazing beside hers among the trees.

He returned with a mandolin. He sat beside her and began to pluck the strings.

She closed her eyes and let her head fall back against the tree trunk. To hear him sing to her after all this time—it was ecstasy.

After a few measures he began, his voice soft, yet strong as ever:

> "I stand in my lady's sight
> In deep devotion;
> Approach her with folded hands
> In sweet emotion;
> Dumbly adoring her,
> Humbly imploring her."

She recognized it as a song of Bernart de Ventadour, a song she had loved even as a little girl. With each chord her joy in him grew more overwhelming. By the time he reached the last verse she was weeping with happiness. She looked up through the black leaves overhead and saw a small, blue-white star twinkling in an opening in the foliage where there had been sunlight not long before.

"That was beautiful," she said. "But, Roland, why did you not sing a song of your own?"

"I have had no inspiration these many months."

"You shall have inspiration enough tonight."

He laid aside the mandolin and turned to her. She pressed her weight against him, bearing him to the ground as her arms wined around his neck.

Her mouth fused with his, warm and liquid, his tongue velvet-soft and hard all at once. His long arms wrapped around her, and even in the heedlessness of desire she noticed that the pressure of the left arm was stronger than the right.

Roland wants me, and I want him even more. With that decision her whole body felt suddenly as hot as if she were standing before a fire.

Savagely she whispered, "I will end my marriage to Amalric this night by loving you."

She discovered her hands moving as if they had a will of their own to the laces of her page's tunic. She pulled it over her head. Under it she wore only a linen shirt.

Roland drew away from her and rose to his feet. He threw off his black cloak. He pulled off his tunic and undershirt, baring his chest. In the twilight his skin gleamed like old ivory. His muscles were hard, ridged and braided like the coils of a rope.

She rose and went to him and put her hand on his arm. There was a long scar across his chest and belly, and another, a triangular white scar, on his left forearm. She bent over his arm and kissed the scar.

She sat down again with her back against the huge oak tree. He knelt before her and drew off her boots and her red hose. She quivered as his fingertips grazed the calf of her leg.

Standing again, she turned her back to him and raised her arms over her head. He lifted her shirt so gently she hardly felt it leave her body.

Never had she felt so secure, so free. At night in this huge forest an army could never find them.

He drew back into the deeper shadows and quickly slipped out of his remaining garments. He stepped close to her and stood before her as naked as she was. He was beautiful—dark and powerful. He stood gravely with his hands at his sides, letting her look her fill at him. Then he moved toward her.

She felt a sudden need to pause. It was happening so quickly.

"Roland, I am frightened."

He stood still. "Whatever happens here, happens as you will it, *mi dons*. If you want to stop now, we will. You have already given me more joy than a man has a right to expect, this side of Heaven."

His worshipful words overwhelmed her last fragments of caution. "I want it to be so beautiful. I want it to be everything Love can be at its best." Her words came out between little gasps.

"Looking upon your body, *mi dons*, I feel as if I see God."

"Then come to me," she said, sinking to the ground at the base of the tree.

They lay side by side. His naked length along her body made her arms and legs feel as if they were melting like wax in a flame. His hard chest rose and fell powerfully against her, and she dug her fingers into the muscles of his upper arms.

Her hand crept up his right arm till she touched the shoulder. She slid her naked body higher against his. As a mare licks a newborn colt, she licked the broken shoulder.

He groaned softly. Then his musician's hands began to travel lightly over her body. Waves of pleasure rippled through her.

After they had lain together for a time, she gently drew away from him and sat with her back against the rough tree bark. He, too, sat up and faced her, drawing back his knees and crossing his long legs.

The sight filled her with delight. He knows the secret position of Love, she thought. He must know the entire rite. We can enter the gates of Paradise tonight.

She drew herself toward him, and he put his big hands under her. She helped him to first lift her, then lower her to his lap. As he entered her, a deep groan escaped him. She answered with a cry of pleasure at the sweet, ultimate closeness.

Nicolette had so often dreamed of a moment like this that now it seemed like still another fantasy. But this was real.

He is here, his flesh is solid inside me, he sees me, holds me, loves me.

He said, "This is the best moment of my life."

"Oh, my troubadour!" She clung to him, her legs embracing his hips, shuddering with pleasure.

"This song, I want to sing to the end, *mi dons*. And yet I long for it never to end."

She knew what he meant. As her mother had explained it to her, in the sacrament of courtly love the man was expected, difficult as it might be, to deny himself the ultimate release. The woman, however, need not resist the passion that sweeps her along. In moments, Nicolette rose to the crest of a wave that made her scream and bite Roland's neck.

Roland seemed to her like a man in the throes of fever. She felt a fine coating of sweat on his skin. She could see faintly in the dark that he grimaced as if in pain, but she knew it was the agony of pleasure controlled.

She ascended peak after peak until she lost count of them. She was panting and sobbing until she thought she might die of her passion. Then she felt transformed. It was beyond bodily pleasure, but still it *was* bodily pleasure, of the same stuff, yet finer.

She looked into Roland's eyes and they glistened in the starlight, seeing her and yet not seeing her. Something was lifting them up. The forest shadows about them disappeared.

They were rising together through an ocean of golden light. There was no top, no bottom, no shore to this sea of light. Innumerable tiny white lights, brighter than the golden glow, twinkled around them. And they themselves were glowing.

Roland was saying something. "Everything is light. You and I, we are lights. We are stars."

As he spoke, the light grew brighter, changing from gold to the white of molten metal.

"You are the lady of all my visions."

Brighter than the sun now.

"You are my true self."

Brighter than a thousand suns.

"We are in the presence of God."

Now she spoke. "We are God."

The light that was Nicolette and the light that was Roland became one, and the body of that one was this whole infinite sea of light. They could not see the light, not because it blinded them, but because they were the light.

Then she felt Roland gasp and clutch at her, and she could see him, as Roland, again. She saw the gleam of his bared teeth as tremors shook his body. From deep in his throat came a growling sound. She held him close, stroking his hair, until his spasms subsided. The light shattered into glittering fragments that drifted down around them as they sank back to the dark forest floor.

Nicolette felt such joy that she was seized by a storm of weeping.

"Forgive me," he whispered.

"There is nothing to forgive," she said, smiling even as her tears trickled down his chest. "The happiness I feel is beyond description."

"You might conceive," he said.

"I will not." But, of course, she knew it could happen. Her mother had imparted to her a secret no man, even one's lover, was permitted to share, the recipe for a concoction which would prevent a man's seed from planting itself in a woman's body. But it had to be drunk within a day of the event, and she could never gather all the herbs and brew them properly in time. Still the chances were in her favor, she thought. Out of a hundred arrows fired, only one hits the mark.

She was back at Chartres, standing before the Virgin of the Crypt. She knew the time-blackened statue was thousands of years old, made by Romans. She realized suddenly that it was not a statue of Mary, but of the Goddess of Love.

Smiling serenely, the Virgin—or Goddess—spoke to her in Latin: *"Amor vincit omnia."*

Roland's voice awakened her. *"Mi dons.* Have we succeeded in ending your marriage?"

She opened her eyes. Thank the Goddess it was not yet dawn. They did not have to part. She felt deep happiness at waking beside him, but it was tinged with sorrow. If only she could waken with him every morning of her life.

"For this time, but not for all time," she said. The sadness weighed on her as she thought how she must leave Roland and go back to her everyday life, perhaps not to see him for months.

"If only I had killed him at the tournament last year. Your bondage would have been ended forever." The pain in his voice made her reach out and touch his cheek.

"What is it, Roland?"

"He forces you to couple with him, does he not?"

"I have not lived with him since last spring. I have been with the royal household since then. And he has gone back to Béziers, to inflict more misery on our unhappy people of Languedoc. Even when I was with him, the mood was rarely on him. He has other women. Let us not speak of it. I have no choice."

She felt his anger like a wave of heat.

"He desecrates you. Just as his father desecrated my mother."

She strained to see his face in the moonless dark.

"Your mother?" He had never spoken of his mother before. "Who is your mother, Roland?"

"My mother is Adalys de Vency—now. Once, years ago, she was a frightened, helpless girl in the power of . . ."

He stopped. She could hear his heavy breathing, almost as loud and as fast as after love. She felt the hammering of his heart.

"Of whom, Roland?"

"My father!" He spat the words. "Who died the death he deserved at the hands of Arnaut de Vency."

"But is Arnaut de Vency not your father?"

He did not reply, and she sensed him struggling for words. Bursting with impatience, her mind swirling with half-formed questions, vague efforts to make sense out of what he was saying, she waited.

"Amalric's father, Count Stephen de Gobignon, was a leader of the first crusaders to invade Languedoc at the Pope's call. After a few years of warfare, he captured a certain castle and seized for his bed the young girl, orphaned by the war, whose home it was. One night a band of Languedoc patriots led by Arnaut de Vency, to whom she was betrothed, broke into the castle and killed him. But Dame Adalys, my mother, was already with child, you see."

A sudden light broke in her mind. But it was a harsh and terrifying light.

"You said Arnaut de Vency killed *your* father. That means—"

"Amalric's father was also my father."

"My God!" She felt as if the turf beneath her had opened up suddenly.

His fingers clamped, hard as chains, on the flesh of her upper arms. "I am the bastard son of Count Stephen de Gobignon, begotten of rape. What does that mean to you? Tell me. I have to know. Do you hate me for not telling you before this?"

She recalled how Amalric had spoken of heretics having killed his father. He has no idea, she thought, who really killed his father or who Roland is.

Dear God, she thought, I have been making love to Amalric's half brother. The shock was making her heart beat furiously. She was almost too frightened to speak.

"Roland, I love you," she said.

She felt his grip on her arms ease a little.

He, too, must be terrified of what this truth could do to us.

But *can* it be true—the same father? Yes, the blue eyes, the tall frame.

"Yes," she said, trying to sound as if it did not matter. "One can see the Gobignon blood in you, if one knows enough to look for it."

"If you were to go to Naples and see my sister Fiorela, you would know we could not have had the same father. She is your height and has dark brown eyes. People in Naples sometimes looked askance at me, but one does not ask embarrassing questions of Arnaut de Vency."

Ah, thought Nicolette, that was what she must make him understand—it did not matter to *her*.

"Arnaut de Vency," she said, "must be a very good man. For you have been reared with a father's true love. A man's father is the one who shapes and educates him—who forms his soul—not he who sires his body."

"Even so, I must know." There was pain still in Roland's voice. "Does it not repel you, disgust you, to learn that I am Amalric's half brother?"

She searched herself, knowing she must speak quickly to save their love.

She pressed herself against him.

"Father, half brother—those are only words. They do not change the man I have known, and held in my arms this whole night long. What do begetters mean in the face of Love? What power on earth can command Love? If I learned you were *my* brother now, it could not stop me from loving you. Love has spoken."

It was growing lighter. She could see his face now as he smiled crookedly at her. Daybreak must be near. She looked up. The sky was a deep purple. She felt all the pain of all the parting lovers in all the aubades she had ever heard.

"You sound like the King when he talks of God," Roland said. "You are both so certain."

The King. She hated to tell him, but she must.

She tightened her arms around him. "Roland, my darling, we shall have to say adieu soon. Before we part, I have to tell you—the time is coming when we shall suffer a far, far longer parting."

His pained, questioning look wrung her heart. She went on quickly. "Amalric has decided to go on crusade. He is taking me with him."

"No!" Roland struck his fist into his palm. "Why? I cannot believe he is mad enough to risk his life in Outremer. And even if he is, why must he drag you with him to share that risk? Damn him!"

"The King and all the great barons are taking their wives."

"The fools. What do they think it will be, another sort of tournament? Every Christian army that has gone up against the Saracens in the last hundred years has been slaughtered." He seized her by the shoulders. "Nicolette, I will not let you go."

Forlorn as she felt, his rage pleased her. She put her hand on his to soothe him.

"The King aims to depart in the spring of twelve hundred and forty-eight. That gives us nearly two years. Until then Amalric will be in Béziers and you and I will be in Paris. We shall have all that time together.''

He looked into the distance, still trembling with anger. ''I will take you away with me.''

For a moment she saw a glimmer of hope, but then the reasons why she could not run away with him came crowding to over-shadow it. ''He might hurt my sisters. My children, I cannot abandon them. Besides, he would track us down. He has a whole army. And how would we live? What would we do?''

And, she thought, there was Amalric's plotting against Louis, which only she knew about. She had to stay near Louis and Marguerite, to try to protect them.

He turned to her again, his face hard. ''Do you really want to die in the desert? A good many women have gone out there with their crusader husbands and perished with them. And more ended up in Turkish slave markets.''

''I will not be anywhere near the fighting.''

''How are you so sure of that? Perhaps the fighting will come to you, eh?''

That angered her. ''Stop trying to frighten me. I do not want to talk about the crusade anymore. I want to hold you and kiss you. To talk about Love.''

The distant church bell tolled for matins.

''Amalric must know how dangerous it is,'' Roland said. ''Whatever else he may be, he is no fool. Why is he going?''

There was nothing Roland could do about Amalric, but at least she could share the burden with him.

''Roland, I think Amalric means to harm the King.''

Roland frowned and shook his head. ''No one can hate Amalric more than I, but I doubt that he would commit treason. Besides, Louis's mother and brothers would tear Amalric to pieces if he harmed the King.''

She drew away from him a little. ''That may be exactly why Amalric is going. Hoping that far away in the East, in the midst of war, whatever evil he does will go undetected. And he does not see it as treason. He believes somehow that he has the right to become King.''

Roland sighed and said nothing. He let go of her and bowed his head. A shadow of pain crossed his face. She knew he was struggling inside himself, but she could not guess what was in his mind.

Suddenly she felt ill at ease with her nudity. She stood up and began to gather her clothes.

Roland seemed unconscious of his lack of clothing, and of her. He sat between the ridges of two of the great oak tree's roots, staring into the misty forest.

When she was finished dressing he turned to her suddenly, his face full of resolve.

"I will go. I shall take the cross."

His words were like a blow to her heart. "You cannot."

"But I can. I will go along with all the rest of the fools. I will sew the cross on my tunic, even though it will burn my flesh beneath it."

"Not you, Roland! You hate the crusader's cross as much as I do. You have said all along this crusade is a foolish dream. How can you talk of going?"

His smile was taut, bitter. "Amalric changed his mind. So can I."

"But why?"

The anger faded from his face, and a tender light came into it. "If you will not flee with me, I have to go where you are going. Do you think I could let him take you to the other side of the world while I stay behind?"

"Oh, Roland!" She felt a surge of love for him so powerful she felt almost dizzy. She knelt beside him and pressed her head against his bare chest.

"I tried to kill Amalric once and failed," he went on grimly. "Instead he crippled me. I still owe him a death. If he has joined the crusade in the hope that he can kill the King in Outremer, I will join the crusade in the hope that I can kill him." He clenched his right fist so hard it trembled. "To take the cross will betray what I am, but I will do it. I will do it for vengeance."

She raised her head and looked up at him. "Roland, you have been badly hurt. If you think the King and his army are doomed to defeat, what chance have you if you go along with them?"

He sighed. "You mean I am too crippled to defend myself, much less protect you, is that it?"

His words cut deep, but she had to be honest with him.

"You cannot wield a sword."

His mouth tightened. "I do not know that for certain. As you said, it will be nearly two years before the crusade departs. I seem to be getting more use of my arm as time passes. Guido, the Templar whom I met at the song contest, helped me avenge Perrin and train for the tournament." He smiled wryly. "He might be able to show me how to fight as a left-handed crusader."

She shook her head sadly. "A dream, like the King's dream of recapturing Jerusalem."

He shrugged. "Each man needs his dream. No matter how well or poorly I can fight, I would rather die than see you go off to Outremer without me."

He must not drag his broken body to a war he despises, wearing a symbol he hates, all for my sake.

She echoed his earlier words. "I cannot let you do it."

He glowered at her. "Do you command me, *mi dons*?"

"Command you?" she said, remembering her ill-fated order that he not fight Amalric at the tournament. "No, I shall never do that to you again."

"Then it is settled."

"Oh, Roland!" She was terrified for him. She was angry at him. And she loved him.

"Let us say no more for now," he said. "Whatever happens in Outremer, we shall meet many times before the crusade departs. And we shall take joy in each other as we have this night."

He rose and began to dress while she sat under the tree and watched him.

Now, though still fearful for him, she admitted to herself that all along she had desperately wanted him to go on the crusade. She could not bear to be so long parted from him again.

Then a frightful doubt crept into her mind.

He had said he was going because he wanted to avenge himself on Amalric.

Why, out of all the women in the world, had Roland chosen her to love? He must have learned hatred of the Gobignon family at his mother's knee. What a perfect revenge—his mother is raped by Amalric's father, so he debauches Amalric's wife.

No! she shouted in her mind. *I will not believe that. I must not even think it. Else my whole life is lost. We entered the light together last night. In that ecstasy he must have experienced what I experienced.*

I must trust him.

XIV

DIANE SAT CROSS-LEGGED ON HER STRAW PALLET IN THE TINY WATCH-tower room, rocking back and forth, a ball of anguish in the very center of her body. *I know this world is a place of torment, but never have I suffered so much as these two years and more with Roland.*

True, there were days, even weeks, when she was almost able to forget her agony. Life had been much easier all last summer, while Roland was journeying about the country on the King's business. But this September afternoon her longing for Roland had been very strong. Ever since his sudden departure a few hours ago.

At noon a messenger had come for Roland. The servants had left the house for a long-planned visit with relatives living north of Le Marais, so Perrin had let the man in.

After the messenger left, Diane heard Roland swearing. She went downstairs to see what had angered him.

"De Joinville—the new seneschal for Champagne—needs me at Troyes. There are irregularities in the accounting of the summer fair they hold there, the Hot Fair. Perrin and I have to leave at once." His fists were clenched, and a scowl darkened his face.

She did not know why that troubled him so. "It is not a long journey, and Troyes is a pleasant city," she said.

"I agree," he said impatiently. "But I was to meet Nicolette tomorrow, and now I have no way of getting word to her."

Diane's heart fell. The naked look of disappointed love on his face crushed her. But she knew she must not give way to jealousy.

"Could Martin take a message to the palace when he gets back tonight?" she asked.

He shook his head. "I have always used Perrin as a go-between. The fewer people involved, the safer the secret. But I have to take Perrin with me now."

"Martin is very discreet," she said.

She knew Roland would be surprised at how discreet Martin could be. Martin and his father, Lucien, had joined the Cathar faith the year before, and Roland knew nothing of it.

Roland shrugged. "All right. I will write a letter to Nicolette, and I will tell you how Martin can deliver it to her maid."

And now, she thought bitterly as he left the room, I am involved in his affair.

By None Roland and Perrin were packed and ready to leave. Roland had handed her the sealed letter. And when the door closed behind him, she had pressed the folded parchment against her breasts.

Oh, dear God, how I wish this were for me!

Now it was nearly evening, and she felt an aching in her groin as if there were knots tied inside her. Sweat was breaking out all over her body. She pushed the heavy book of Cathar scripture she had been reading to the floor.

God forgive me. I have got to get control of myself.

She tried to think clearly about her feelings. I love the power of Roland's mind to understand and to create, and his courage to think his own thoughts even when those around him think only as they are permitted. I want to be one with Roland's beautiful spirit, even as I long to be one with God, but my body tricks me and turns this noble longing into a yearning to know his body. My flesh burns like a soul in Hell. Indeed, my soul would be safer if I were in the hands of the Inquisition's torturers than it is here where I am tortured by love. God, give me the strength to contain myself in his presence.

Brushing away the straw caught in her long blue tunic, she picked up her large, leather-bound volume again and laid it in her lap. This book, kept behind a concealed panel in her room, was all she had left of the holy objects she and Roland had rescued over two years ago from Mont Ségur. All the rest—including the whereabouts of the stored-up wealth of the Cathar church—she had passed on to her superior. Now she was trying to prepare, by reading this scripture, for the sermon she would preach tonight to a small group of the faithful.

But she was unable to concentrate, feeling so unworthy to teach others.

Adrienne knows. She is a woman, and she senses what I am feeling. She looks at me so skeptically when I talk to her about the faith. That is why I have not yet won her over.

If my faith weakens, I am nothing. I can only escape this

agony by leaving him. Oh, God, why do You not hear my prayers? Why does my superior not listen?

I want to go back home to Languedoc. There are hardly any perfecti left there now. Oh, please, I want to go back to my people.

Sadness overwhelmed her. She wept for her own pain. She wept, too, for her church, which was dying, and for the lost souls who would never know the truth because there were so few left to teach it.

They have arrested Guillaume the Bookseller, she recalled with horror. They must be very close to the rest of us. She shuddered.

She barely heard the knock at the front door of the house, three stories below.

When it was repeated, a little stronger now, her heart stopped. She clasped her hands together in prayer that it would not be the Inquisition. If they must find me, let it not be here. If I am caught in this house it will mean the end for everybody—for Roland, for Perrin, for Lucien and Adrienne and Martin.

But if it is the Inquisition, it is better if I let them take me when no one is here. Then the others will have some warning and may be able to save themselves.

The knock came again.

Diane lifted the Cathar book into the hollowed-out place and shut the panel that hid it. She hurried downstairs, smoothing her tunic.

She opened the door and saw a lone woman standing in the September dusk, dressed in a robe, a dark veil over her head. Diane let out her breath in a sigh of relief and opened the door wider. There was a donkey tied by the gate.

The woman looked as startled as Diane felt. She gasped and stared wide-eyed at Diane. After a moment, she put her hand to her mouth and shook her head, as if to deny what she was seeing. During this long, silent moment Diane took in the woman's brown robe, tied at the waist with a white cord, and the black veil over a white wimple.

Terror seized Diane. The woman was wearing the habit of the Poor Clares, the order of nuns founded by Friar Francesco of Assisi. She could be an agent of the Inquisition—Franciscans sometimes were.

Diane stammered a greeting.

Without replying, the woman lurched forward, putting her

hand on the doorjamb to steady herself, and took a few steps into the front hall. Is she ill? Diane wondered.

"Who are you?" The woman's voice was hollow. Strangely, she spoke. in the *Langue d'Oc*.

Automatically answering in the same language, Diane murmured the lie she had repeated so many times in the past two years. "I am Roland's sister Diane, madame. How may I serve you?"

She was angry at herself for being so frightened. Why should I tremble before a lone nun as if she were Blanche of Castile herself? She is probably just here to beg.

As she calmed herself she began to scrutinize the strange nun. Franciscans, she knew, never traveled alone. As with the perfecti, their rule was "two by two." On foot, too, not on donkeyback. And this one hardly looked like a beggar. She was young and very pretty, with huge dark brown eyes, which now narrowed in apparent anger as she stared at Diane.

"That is a lie," she said. "Roland has a sister, named Fiorela, who is presently living in Naples. And she has dark hair and brown eyes."

Taken aback, Diane could not speak. Her heartbeat quickened painfully.

"Where is Roland?" the young woman snapped, her voice suddenly sharp and imperious. "Where is Perrin?"

Diane suddenly recognized her. Nicolette! The day of that terrible tournament, she had seen her from a distance, sitting in the gallery reserved for the nobility. She must have come today thinking to visit Roland. Instead she finds—

"You speak the *Langue d'Oc*, but I know you are not his sister," Nicolette said again. "Why do you claim to be? I demand that you tell me who you are at once."

Diane struggled to control herself. She was trembling, sick at heart. She felt herself in a trap that could destroy the lives of Roland, Nicolette, and herself.

She stared at Nicolette. So beautiful, with her great, flashing eyes, that flawless olive skin. The loose-fitting brown robe did not quite conceal Nicolette's proud breasts.

"I know that you are the Countess de Gobignon, madame," she began hesitantly. "Roland has told me much about you."

She made the curtsy due Nicolette's rank.

"Indeed," said Nicolette coldly. "Well, he has not told me a word about you. Why would he have kept your presence here a secret? I thought it would delight him if I came to him unexpectedly in disguise. I never thought he was hiding *this* from me."

"Madame, if Roland were here he could explain—"

"I am sure he could." Nicolette's cheeks were flushed with anger. "He has a clever tongue, does he not? For explanations, for words of love, for other things. I am sure you know that. If he were here, though, I would give him no time for explanations."

Diane drew a deep breath to give herself strength, and then spoke.

"Madame, you must not believe evil of Roland. He has always been faithful to you. I will tell you who I am. By doing that I put myself at your mercy. You may then have me killed if you wish."

"Living with a troubadour is not a capital offense," said Nicolette bitingly.

"Please listen, madame. I am here because Roland is hiding me from the Inquisition. I am one who has received the great Sacrament of my church called the consolamentum. I am known as a perfecta, though I feel far from perfect. We never touch men. I was a friend of Roland from our childhood. He did not tell you he is hiding me here because that would make you an accomplice to his crime. So you see, now *his* life is in your hands, too."

She paused, waiting anxiously.

Nicolette took a step back, looking Diane up and down.

"A Cathar woman. Yes, you do have that look about you— pale and thin and pious. Still, I can see what Roland sees in you, with your skin so fair, and your hair like red gold. But where is your black gown? I thought the perfecti always had to dress in black."

Despite her anxiety, Diane smiled at the trivial question. "Oh, no, madame. To protect our lives we are recently dispensed from that rule."

"I see," said Nicolette coldly. "How fortunate for you, since blue looks so well on you. And what other rules can you dispense with to protect your life, Demoiselle Perfecta? Is it possible that you can make love to a man if he shelters you from the Inquisition?"

Diane opened her mouth to protest, just as Nicolette snapped, "How long have you been living with him?"

Feeling sick with fear, less for herself than for Roland and his household, Diane nonetheless knew she had to plunge on. Nothing she said now could make things worse.

"I came to this house in April of twelve hundred and forty-four, more than two years ago, madame," she began.

Nicolette stood and listened, fists clenched at her sides, as Diane quietly told her how Roland had slipped into the Cathar stronghold and brought her out safely. As Diane talked, tears ran freely down Nicolette's face.

Diane felt more and more unsure of herself. This was not the reaction she had hoped for.

"At last I understand. I always wanted to know, and he would not tell me." Nicolette's words were interrupted by convulsive sobs. "Why he went to Languedoc. Why he suddenly joined the crusading army. Led by my husband." She looked meaningfully at Diane as she said this last, but Diane did not understand why.

Nicolette went on, still weeping, "He had already pledged his love for me then, you see. I was awaiting the right moment for our first secret meeting. Then he disappeared."

Groaning, Nicolette put her hands over her face and bent almost double. Then she straightened up abruptly. "He loves you, does he not?"

A wave of dismay washed over Diane's heart.

"As I told you, a perfecta may have nothing to do with men. I swear to you, madame, I have been faithful to my sacrament. I have forbidden him to speak of love to me."

I am evading her question, she told herself, and that is as bad as lying.

"If you had to forbid him to speak of love, then he does love you."

From under her tunic Nicolette drew a dagger. With a trembling hand she held the point to her breast.

Diane screamed and reached out to her.

"Come any closer, and I will stab myself," Nicolette whispered, both hands now firmly wrapped around the handle. "Perhaps you would like to see me kill myself. You have already done so much to kill me."

Diane twitched her hands helplessly. "He loves you, madame, I know he does."

"Do you expect me to believe he truly loves me," Nicolette said, "when you have lived with him for two years?"

Nicolette threw the dagger to the floor. It landed point first and stood quivering upright in the oaken boards.

"Listen to me," Diane pleaded. "He did love me once, long

ago, when we were little more than children. He came to Mont
Ségur for the sake of that love. I told him then that there could
never be anything between us. I did not even want to be rescued,
madame. Can you understand that? I wanted to die there on the
mountain with brothers and sisters of my faith. There can be
nothing between Roland and me now, nothing.''

And how many nights have I suffered the torments of the
damned because there can be nothing?

"Then why," Nicolette demanded, "have you stayed for two
years in the house of this troubadour, this writer of scurrilous
songs, this adulterer? You, who are so pure, so *perfect*!''

"His home is only a refuge for me, madame. Only that.''

She had never in her life needed so much to be believed, and
never had her words sounded more hollow.

Nicolette peered at her. "You really expect me to take your
word," she said wonderingly, "that you have lived under the
roof of such a man as Roland for two years, and you have never
touched each other.''

Putting those two anguished years into her voice, Diane said,
"It is the truth, madame.''

Nicolette stared deep into her eyes without speaking.

Then she said, "All the Cathars I have ever known have been
scrupulously honest. And you would not have admitted that you
are a Cathar if you were going to lie to me about you and
Roland.''

Her shoulders slumped, and some of the life went out of her
voice.

"If what you say is true, that only makes it worse, you see.
Because it shows how deeply he feels about you.'' She raised
her head, and her dark eyes, full of suffering, held Diane's. "He
left Paris without a word to me and rushed to Mont Ségur to
rescue you. He found that you were a perfecta and he could not
save you. But still he brought you back here and kept you in his
house, at great peril, and for the sake of your vow he has never
touched you. So he started courting me again, as *second best*.
Only because he could not have you. That is how it must have
happened. I am not first in his heart, you are. You are the one he
really loves.''

Diane felt a terrible helplessness. Disaster was falling upon all
them, and she could not stop it.

"As a sister, Nicolette. He loves me only as a sister.''

"You have no right to address me by my first name.''
Nicolette's tone was angry, but Diane heard the despair beneath.

"Madame, the love that matters is not our love for each other as woman and man, but our love for God and for one another as spirits. That is what we are—spirits. These male and female bodies are only prisons. To love someone's body is like loving a dungeon."

"Stop preaching at me," Nicolette snapped.

"But it is the truth," Diane cried. "I have to say it."

"It is a dreadful lie!" There was hatred in Nicolette's eyes. "You deserve to be burned for saying such things."

Nicolette drew herself up stiffly. "Tell Roland that if he comes near me again, I will deliver him to my husband and his knights. I will confess to adultery and let my husband do whatever he wishes with Roland and me. Now I know that is what it was." She started to sob again. "Common, low adultery. Not Love. Not Love at all."

Nicolette reeled toward the still-open door. Again Diane put out a hand to help her, but Nicolette struck it away. She all but fell through the door into the darkened front yard.

Diane stood frozen as she heard Nicolette being sick outside the door.

After a while there were footsteps stumbling away, then the slow clip-clop of a donkey's hooves. Diane went to the door and gently closed it. She turned and stared at the dagger still upright in the floor.

XV

THE RAIN WAS NOT ENOUGH TO KEEP NICOLETTE FROM HER DAILY ride, but it was soaking through her thick brown cloak and raising a reek of wet wool. Even though she wore a broad brimmed leather hat over her hood, her face was wet.

Her palfrey did not seem to mind the wet weather. The aging mare ambled contentedly up the stony mountain road, stopping every so often to nibble at tufts of brown grass growing out the bare slope on their left.

It was midday, but it seemed like twilight. It is as miserable Paris, she thought. Languedoc is not at its best in November.

The gloom of the day was well matched to Nicolette's mood. Since that terrible moment when she had learned the truth about Roland, the whole world had gone gray, as if she were suddenly color-blind.

Foolish of me to be out on such a day. I could take a chill, and that would be doubly dangerous just now.

For though she felt dead, there was life growing inside her. For nearly two months now she had known it: she was with child. But sadness weighed as heavily on her as the thick low clouds that seemed to press down on her head. *All she could think was, I do not, for myself, care whether I live or die in childbirth.*

If I do die, I shall surely have time to confess to a priest what I did with Roland. At least I will not go to Hell.

I do not think I believe in Hell anyway. Or in anything. Not even Love. Especially not Love.

The six mounted guards, who, by Amalric's orders, here accompanied her everywhere, were probably cursing her for dragging them out in this weather. They'd rather be drinking wine and toasting their feet at a fire. But this was occupied country, and the patriots of Languedoc still struck at the invader from time to time. It would be foolish for the wife of the royal seneschal to go riding in the hills around Béziers alone, and so they must perforce don their heavy helmets and hauberks, buckle on their swords, and ride along with her.

She looked back to where Béziers crowned a cliff top over the river Orb. A mist had crept up the river from the sea and now hid most of the city, leaving visible only the red-tiled, cone-roofed towers of the city walls and the spires of the churches. She could see the upper half of the yellow stone citadel, in which she lived with Amalric. He was there now, writing requisition orders for supplies for King Louis's crusade.

The fathers and grandfathers of these men riding with her could have been among those who massacred the people of Béziers forty years ago. Her escorts were all good-looking blond Franks with straight noses and square chins. Amalric tended to favor such men.

Sire Guy d'Etampes, the young knight who was Amalric's constable, kept up a running flow of conversation. He apparently considered it his duty to entertain her. But all he could talk about was war—the coming crusade. She recalled how she had talked to Roland about going on crusade, and the ache in her heart turned to a sharp pain.

"These are good years for the peasants," d'Etampes said. "The King's agents are everywhere, buying up the harvest. It will be another two summers before we leave, but they are already stockpiling hay and wheat at Aigues-Mortes." He turned and grinned at her. "At least when it is time to embark our party will have a short journey. Aigues-Mortes is but twenty-five leagues up the coast from here."

"I know where Aigues-Mortes is, messire," said Nicolette tartly, cutting him off. "After all, I was born in this country."

"Excuse me, madame. I had forgotten." D'Etampes turned away, using a corner of his blue woolen mantle to wipe from his eyes the beaded moisture that ran down from his conical helmet. He pulled his hood over his head, protecting his face from the drizzle and obscuring it.

The young man was abashed, Nicolette saw. He wanted her to like him. He had his eye, she knew, on Isabelle, who would be an excellent match for a knight of middle rank like himself. This presumptuous knight does not realize that I have no influence at all with Amalric. Isabelle will go to whomever her father picks out.

And, she told herself, unless Amalric sires a son, he will never accept anyone below a count for Isabelle. Whoever marries Isabelle will inherit the Gobignon holdings.

What if this child I am carrying is a boy? At that thought, the pain in her heart hurt like a sudden knife wound.

Roland's baby.

There were times when she prayed that she would lose the baby. At others she wanted it desperately, for it was all of Roland she had left. Today she felt loving and protective toward it. This time she would be a better mother.

She saw a shallow cleft in the mountainside ahead. Nestled in it under bare tan cliffs was a small chapel, half fallen to ruin. She had seen dozens of such decaying churches in this country. Amalric, she thought, hadn't made Catholicism very popular in Languedoc.

As her party approached the church she noticed two men in brown robes sitting in the doorway. As she and her escort came near, they stood up. Franciscan friars. Nicolette remembered the Franciscan habit she had worn only two months ago.

Oh, Roland, now we have lost each other. Forever.

The two friars trotted out to intercept the riders, their robe flapping in their unseemly haste. You would not see perfec scrambling to beg like that, Nicolette thought.

"Dirty vagabonds," said Guy d'Etampes. "Want us to whip them out of the way, madame?"

Nicolette was surprised. D'Etampes, after all, was a Catholic, and these were friars. Ah, she realized, but Franciscans are dedicated to poverty. The respectable abhor poverty.

"These men have taken a vow to humble themselves by living only on charity," said Nicolette. "Would you be strong enough to live that way, do you think?"

The young knight blushed angrily.

Now the friars were only a few feet away, and Nicolette observed that they were indeed wretched-looking. Their hair was wild and tangled. They had short, greasy beards. Their bare feet and legs were covered with sores and caked with mud. Nicolette squirmed to think of the fleas and lice that must be crawling around in those dirty robes. But it must take character to live like that, she thought, her revulsion mixed with admiration.

The taller of the two said, "The blessing of Monseigneur Jesus on the cheerful giver, madame."

The voice stopped her heart.

Roland.

She had to clutch the pommel of her saddle with both hands to keep from falling. Dizzy, she quickly looked away, out over the hills toward Béziers, where Amalric was.

If Amalric knew he was here . . .

She looked back again at the friar. In her grief might she not have deluded herself?

No, it was he. Under the dirt, the untrimmed hair and beard, were the same sharp features she knew so well. Three months ago in the forest between Chartres and Paris, she had touched that face with her fingertips.

The deformed right shoulder bulked under the shabby frieze. Out of the dark face burning blue eyes met hers.

He must have chosen the Franciscan robe to remind her of the disguise she had worn to his house. Was he trying to provoke her? Had he come all this distance looking for death?

She opened her mouth. All she had to do was tell d'Etampes that this was Orlando of Perugia. Almost certainly Amalric had warned d'Etampes about the troubadour, possibly ordered him to kill Roland on sight.

No. She hated Roland for his faithlessness, but she could not bear to end his life.

She looked past Roland and saw that the other friar was Perrin, a faint smile playing about his lips and a question in his eyes. What a chance Perrin is taking, she thought. Roland does not deserve such a loyal companion. Shrewd of you, Roland, bringing him along. Even if I wanted to expose you, I could never do anything to hurt Perrin.

Excitement coursed all through her. Her body seemed to her like a limb that had gone numb and was waking up with painful prickings. The ache she had felt these past months was very much present, but there were now other stirring sensations, too. I feel alive again, she told herself with surprise.

She had to talk to Roland. Even if only to tell him how much he had hurt her, how she hated him. And she wanted to hear what he had to say. In the aftermath of her discovery of his perfidy, her broken-hearted flight from Paris to Béziers, the one thing she regretted was that she had not waited to meet him face to face.

And whatever I do, I will not let him talk me into forgiving him.

She realized suddenly that everyone—Roland and Perrin, Guy d'Etampes and the men-at-arms—was looking at her.

D'Etampes, she remembered, was carrying her purse. "Sire Guy," she said, "a silver denier for each of these good friars."

"Madame will be blessed a hundredfold for her kindness to Saint Francesco's little brothers," said Roland, reaching for the coins Sire Guy held out disdainfully. Roland dropped them into a leather scrip tied to the rope around his waist.

"Off with you now," d'Etampes said curtly.

"Thank you, messire," said Roland with a bow. "But perhaps I can offer some spiritual recompense for your kindness. I will gladly hear the confession of anyone in your party who feels the need to make peace with our heavenly Father."

So this is the reason he came here, thought Nicolette.

"Your pardon, reverend friar," said d'Etampes with elaborate sarcasm, "but I doubt that any of us would want to get close enough to you to make our confession. Thanks all the same, and good day to you." The men laughed.

"These soldiers of the cross may not need your shrift, good friar," said Nicolette quickly, "but I believe that sometimes God ordains chance meetings for our greater good."

D'Etampes snapped his helmeted head around to stare at her astonished.

"And I have a special admiration for the Franciscan order," she went on. "Would you vouchsafe to hear *my* confession?" she said to the ragged-looking friar who was Roland.

D'Etampes looked annoyed and anxious. "Madame, you have no idea who this fellow is. He may not even be a true friar."

D'Etampes's concern was not altogether foolish. Languedoc patriots had been known to disguise themselves as Catholic clergy.

"I am sure these friars will not mind if you search them, and you can stand near enough to protect me, as long as you are out of earshot."

"Search them?" said Sire Guy, staring disgustedly at the dirty pair in their ragged robes.

He is afraid of those fleas and lice, she thought. "Do as you think best," she said. "I shall wait in the chapel out of the rain."

Most of the chapel was open to the sky, the roof long since stripped away by wood-hungry peasants. She could shelter herself, she saw, by the altar, which was protected by a vault of stone.

She trembled as she anticipated their talk. She feared she might utter words of hatred, and she dreaded even more what she might hear from him.

Dare I tell him about the child? Her body was cold with fright. What would he do to keep his child from falling into Amalric's hands?

The rhythmic drip of rainwater echoed like the tapping of countless tiny hammers. She watched a man-at-arms, ordered by Guy d'Etampes, hastily pat Roland's ragged frieze robe. A paltry search, if Roland really were a Languedoc patriot with murder on his mind.

Then, with his hands folded before him, Roland was pacing over the flagstone floor. Sire Guy, she noticed, stood in the doorway of the chapel, glowering at Roland's back.

Roland trembled as he approached the small figure seated by the altar. He ached to run to her, kneel to her, beg her forgiveness. But he had to keep up his pretense.

Was there anything he could say to her that would win her back? She had not denounced him at once. That might be a hopeful sign.

She took off her leather hat and looked up at him, and he saw hatred smoldering in her eyes. His heart sank. Yet what delight, even in his pain, to see her face again.

He tried to smile. "You had better kneel if you want to make this look like a real confession," he said softly.

Glaring at him, she slowly dropped to her knees.

"It is you who should be kneeling to me," she whispered fiercely. "If I had seen you in Paris you would be two months dead. I could still do it. I have my dagger with me."

He felt an impulse to test her, to tear open his friar's robe and bare his chest. I would rather die here, looking at her, than anywhere else.

He thought of the blade strapped to the inside of his thigh, where no self-respecting knight would ever put his hand.

"I have my weapon, too. Your husband's vassals are not very expert."

He saw her lips twitch in a little smile. Hope leaped up in him.

He seated himself on the altar steps, a discreet distance from her but close enough so that they could talk in low voices. He could smell the dirt and stale sweat on his body and was glad of the space between them.

How to begin? He had composed hundreds of speeches in his mind as he and Perrin traveled south. At night, lying beside the road on cold stones, he had stared up at the pitiless November stars and wondered what he could say that would move her. Now the moment to speak had come, and he felt as if he were falling into emptiness. He forced the words out through a constricted throat.

"You are still *mi dons*," he said. "My life is at your disposal. I have come to let you do as you will with me. In my soul, I do indeed kneel before you, dumbly adoring you, humbly imploring you."

He looked at her and saw in the dim light that filtered down through the broken roof of the church that her face was flushed with anger.

"How dare you speak so?" she whispered. "You have betrayed every vow we made to each other." Tears sparkled in her eyes. "You love another woman."

He shook his head. "I *loved* another woman. When I learned that Diane had become a perfecta, I felt as if she had died. I do not deny that she holds a special place in my heart, but it is a niche for a saint's statue. You are the only one now."

But even as he spoke, he searched his heart, as he had so many times before. Did he really feel as if Diane were dead When he knew so well that she was living, and in his house Part of the pain he felt now rose from the knowledge that all thi was his fault. He could have sent Diane away. She had begge him to send her away. And yet he had never been able to let her go. He had clung to her, and now this was the result.

"I feel about you as you *say* you feel about Diane," Nicolette said, her voice breaking. "As if you had died."

It is hopeless, he thought. She will never understand. She will never forgive me.

But something in him would not give up.

"You must believe that I never touched Diane. I have had nothing to do with any woman since the day we met in the secret room at Guillaume's. Since long before that."

He looked away. Confessors do not stare at their penitents.

She asked, "What is to become of Guillaume?"

He was surprised at her change of subject.

"He has been lucky. They have not been able to prove heresy against him. Of course, inquisitors can find evidence to prove anything they want to, but the King himself asked them to be fair with Guillaume. I managed to put in a word. So the Inquisition only confiscated his house and his books—burned quite a few— and ordered him out of Paris. He will move to England. No Inquisition there."

"What about . . . our room?" He heard mourning in her voice.

He laughed bitterly. "I imagine it looks quite different now. The Dominicans are using the house to quarter their novices."

"So the place where we first pledged our love no longer exists." She was struggling, he sensed, to hold back tears. "Just as well. I came to believe your Diane when she said you and she had never made love, and I believe you now. But if you had been true to the laws of Love, you would have remained faithful to her, even if you could never have her. You did not have the strength for that, so you made do with me. Made do! You pretended to me that I was first in your heart."

Roland stretched out a hand to her, then drew it back. He heard a clatter of metal and turned to the doorway of the chapel. The leader of her escort had taken a step forward, hand on sword hilt. She waved him back.

Let him come, Roland thought. I would gladly die fighting.

But his battle now was for Nicolette's love.

"If I came all this way," he said, "to tell you anything, it is his: yes, Diane was in my heart before you. I knew and loved her from the time I was a boy. But you alone are in my heart now. Believe me!"

He stared unblinking at her till his eyes hurt. Would she believe him?

She looked back at him, and he saw love burning in her eyes. But then her eyes wavered, and he saw the doubt. His heart turned to stone.

"Even if what you say were altogether true," she said slowly, "what was between us must now be over forever."

There was something else, he realized, something she had not told him. What else could come between them?

"What do you mean? Why?"

"Because I am with child."

It was as if she had spoken in a language he did not understand. Then he reeled, almost falling from the stone he was seated on. Everything went dark before his eyes.

Amalric? Rage poured through his body.

No. That night in the forest last August.

His chest filled up with fear for her. What if Amalric found out? Then there was a little flicker of joy. I have fathered a child. Nicolette is going to have my baby.

He realized he had been silent for a long time.

"It is mine, of course," he said.

Her eyes narrowed and her face flushed. He realized with dismay that he had made her angry. Her low, bitter laugh made him wince inwardly.

"The baby is mine, *of course*. I am the one who is carrying it."

"Does your husband know?"

She chuckled mirthlessly.

"My husband is pleased and has no reason to doubt that he is the child's father. In my grief after the visit to your house, I begged the Queen to let me come here, and left almost at once. Where else could I go? After all, this is my country, and he is my husband."

Her voice broke, and his heart with it.

Carrying my child and thinking I betrayed her. My God, how she has suffered! If only I could take her in my arms.

"Amalric," she went on, "had already exercised his marital rights with me before I even realized I was with child. And I have tried to restore good will with him. It is not difficult. He does love me, you know, in his crude way. I will go to my sisters at Château Lumel when the time approaches for the lying in. If need be, my sisters can delay the announcement of the birth a week or two." She paused, choking back a sob. "Have I not shown foresight on my child's behalf?" she added bitterly.

She cannot do this.

It *is* mine, he thought. Not Amalric's. It has my blood. And my mother's.

And my father's. But he put that unbearable thought out of his mind.

The child of Roland de Vency in the house of Amalric de Gobignon? He felt himself growing angry. Not *my* child! Never!

"Then what?" said Roland in a strangled tone. "After the child is born?"

"Why, then, it will be reared as the fourth child of the Count and Countess de Gobignon. In the summer after next the crusade will embark, and I shall accompany monseigneur. The baby will be old enough to stay behind, with my family or with Amalric's."

The very foundations of the earth seemed to rock under him. "You cannot let Amalric have our child," he whispered. "My God, do you not see what you would be doing? If I am the father, as I must be, then this infant is my mother's grandchild. The very blood in this infant's veins betrayed into the hands of our worst enemy?"

"What you are saying makes no sense," she said. "People's fates are not decided by their blood. Do you belong to the Gobignon family because you have Gobignon blood?"

No! he thought. But I was rescued from the Gobignon family.

He squeezed his eyes shut. He had lost not only Nicolette, but the child they had given life to on that beautiful summer night.

Now I know what Hell is.

"I know I drove you to this," he said. "That is why I have abandoned my duties, traveled from Paris on foot, risked my life to talk to you in front of your husband's guards."

"You admit that you wronged me?"

He spread his hands. "I admit I should have told you the truth from the beginning. But I thought I was protecting you. You would have been an accomplice to the hiding of a heretic."

But it sounded weak even to him. Even if there had been no danger, he could not have told her about Diane. Yet if there had been no danger, Diane would not have been hiding with him. Fear, fear of the Inquisition, had caused it all.

Fear—or love?

"No," she said. "You were afraid I would refuse your love if knew about Diane."

He had now felt the pain for so long that his chest was numb.

"Perhaps you are right," he said, bowing his head in submission. "I have wronged you, and I accept the pain of losing you as my just desert. But what about justice for my . . . for the child? The child has no voice here. You are deciding its fate."

"There are many ways to look at it," she said pitilessly. "Amalric's father got a bastard on your mother. Now that bastard has gotten another bastard on Amalric's wife. The Vencys have been avenged on the Gobignons. If not on the field of battle, at least in the bedchamber."

He shut his eyes, the pain overwhelming him. He was breathing heavily, as if he were crushed under an enormous weight.

"That is the cruelest thing anybody has ever said to me."

"It is easy to be cruel, Roland, when you have been hurt as I have. When the door to your house opened and I saw that woman and knew in an instant that all I cared about in this world and the next had been betrayed, that, too, was cruelty."

Frantic in his suffering, he struck back at her.

"It is you who betray Love, not me. You are giving yourself and the child our love has created to the enemy of our love."

"Dear God, what would you have me do?" she said. "Run away with you? Two paupers—and later three—wandering the roads of Christendom, waiting for Amalric's men to hunt us down? A child needs protection, a home, family."

In his mind he saw Amalric and Hugues de Gobignon, and his heart filled with loathing.

"*Family?* The Gobignons? I would rather see a child of mine dead than raised as a Gobignon. You would sell your baby's soul, and your own, for the gold of the Gobignons? Does Love not mean anything to you at all?"

"How dare you lecture me about Love?" she snapped. "The word is sullied on your lips."

He felt the anger growing in him.

"You blame me for driving you back to Amalric. You say it is my fault that you have decided to let our child be raised as Amalric's. All this, you say, is because I hid Diane from you. Tell me, madame, suppose Diane did not exist. You would still be pregnant, would you not? And would you not still have run back to Amalric?"

Her face whitened, and the anger drained out of it. Still kneeling, she cast her eyes down at the space of floor between them.

After a while she said, "I do not know. Maybe I would have run away with you. But what difference does it make now? All

I know is I am lucky to have found out about that woman when I did. How much more awful if I had learned only when my child and I were helpless and dependent on you."

"But you and your child will be dependent upon Amalric. Do you truly believe that will be better?" Roland broke off.

"I cannot bear the thought of you in his embrace," he said at last.

He watched the struggle in her face. Her love for him and her hatred for what she thought was his faithlessness. Her fear for her baby. Her fear of the love that had hurt her so badly.

Her face hardened. She is protecting herself, he realized. Herself and the child.

"It does not matter to me," she said. "One Gobignon brother is much like another."

Though he had braced himself for the blow she would strike, he felt as if she had plunged a knife into him.

"You are reckless, Nicolette. There is a way to ensure that neither you nor my child will ever be possessed by Amalric. I told you, your guards were not very careful when they searched me."

"I am not afraid of you, Roland."

Her eyes widened fiercely and her kneeling body tensed. She was ready to fight him, he realized, for her own life and the baby's.

"And I hope you need never fear me. But I am on the brink of madness now. Do not push me over. Do not say more."

All was lost, he thought. He was helpless. There was nothing left for him but to go back to Paris. Their love was dead. The child would be Amalric's.

He made the sign of the cross over her with his right hand, slowly and almost reverently. "I bless you with the sign of suffering. Bless yourself like a good penitent. And go from me in peace." His voice cracked on those last words, and tears blinded his eyes.

Still she knelt there. "What will you do, Roland?"

He tried to take a last look at her through the tears. He wanted to reach out and stroke that smooth olive cheek. What will I do? he thought. God knows. Try to find some honorable way to die.

"Forget me," he said. "If you can."

She blessed herself with a shaking hand, keeping up the appearance of confession for the watching guards, and stood up. Roland turned his head away, gazing fixedly into the shadows of the chapel.

*   *   *

As she stumbled down the nave under the open sky, the rain on her face mingled with her tears.

She was still crying uncontrollably much later, as the horses picked their way back down the mountain path toward Béziers. Sire Guy kept casting sidelong glances at her but said nothing. He wonders what I confessed, she thought in her pain, to make me cry so much.

When they were halfway to the city he said, "Madame, I do know something of the world. If you were truly a great sinner, you would not weep so after confessing."

Her tears stopped abruptly. This is a decent man, she thought, but people are absolutely opaque to him. He can't see into hearts. Otherwise he would not serve Amalric. Leaden despair cloaked her. She had no courtesy left for Sire Guy.

"Be silent, messire. You understand nothing."

They rode the rest of the way back to her castle—her prison—in silence.

XVI

DIANE STIFFENED WITH FEAR AS SHE HEARD ROLAND'S FOOTSTEPS ON the stairs. All winter long, since he came back from Béziers and his encounter with Nicolette, he had not been himself. His speech was unrelievedly bitter. He drank, he brooded. Sometimes he would stare at Diane for long moments without saying anything.

I am the cause of his suffering, she accused herself. In spite of my superior, I should not have stayed here. I was weak, because I wanted to be safe and I wanted to be near Roland. And now I have ruined his life.

The signs of his ruin lay on the table in the front hall—a stout walking stick as tall as a man, a simple leather bag, and a cross of red silk. That Roland should possess these things meant he was turning his back on everything he had lived for. And this time that cross was no disguise, as at Mont Ségur. Feeling sick, as if the things on the table had somehow fouled the air in the room, she opened the front door and let in the pleasant spring breeze.

And yet what could be more harmless than the pilgrim's staff and the leather scrip in which he carries a few coins and a bit of food? Who is more peaceable than a pilgrim? And what could be more a symbol of love than the cross, made sacred by Jesus Christ? How do such innocent articles allow knights to bring looting and murder to faraway peoples?

Roland, she knew, had taken the crusader's oath yesterday in a great May Day ceremony at Notre-Dame cathedral. But he had not brought the crusader's paraphernalia home. She had heard him stagger into the house in the blackest part of the night. This morning a royal messenger had brought the objects, saying that Roland had left them at the palace.

Now she watched Roland's scuffed black boots come slowly down the steep stairs. At the bottom he stopped and blinked at the sunlight streaming in through the open front door. His wine-stained maroon tunic and black hose were so wrinkled he must have slept in them.

"The sun already on this side of the house?" he said. "Can it be afternoon?"

"It is a beautiful day," said Diane.

He grinned at her sourly, drawing his mouth up on the left side. "Beautiful days are the handiwork of the evil god, is not that what you Cathars say? For my part, blue skies and sunshine only make me want to go back to bed."

His face was waxen and furrowed after a night of heavy drinking. His bitterness seemed deeper than ever today. She could have wept for him.

"The King gave a great banquet for all us new crusaders last night," he said with a smile that was more a sneer. "Twelve courses. Quarter of bear and boar's head. And the Queen gave me some happy news."

Whatever the news, it was probably the reason for his drinking last night. She waited for him to tell her.

"Nicolette is delivered of a son," he said abruptly. "My son. My son will be the Count de Gobignon one day. Think of that."

Sorrow for him engulfed her. Tears burned her eyelids. The poor man. To have the only child he has ever sired in the hands of his worst enemy. She wanted to stroke his head to comfort him.

"Oh, no," was all she could say aloud.

I wish it had been me, I wish he had given me that baby. What am I saying? God forgive me!

"I am horribly thirsty," said Roland. "And after all I drank last night even a glimpse of wine would make me vomit. You perfecti are wise never to drink wine." He sighed. "But then, how do you wash away your sorrows?"

We do not, thought Diane. We live with them always.

"May I have some of that well water you drink?"

Diane went to the kitchen and got her earthenware water pitcher. Through the open kitchen door she spied Perrin in the field beyond the garden, swinging a great two-handed sword around his head. The sun glinted on the knee-length hauberk he wore as part of his practicing. So, he is going, too. He will wear the cross and kill people, because his loyalty to Roland comes before everything else. Even though he is one of us now.

She went back and poured water into Roland's tin cup. He swallowed it all and held out the vessel for more.

"Where are the others?" He was staring at her oddly, and she nervously smoothed the skirt of her blue gown.

"Perrin is in the meadow, exercising with his sword. Adrienne and Lucien are marketing. The boy is grooming your horses." She gestured at the symbols of pilgrimage and crusade. "The palace sent those."

"Oh, yes. Those."

"Perrin is in marvelous condition, you know. He made the journey to Béziers and back on foot with me with never a complaint. You would never know he had been . . . wounded."

She looked at Roland's own hunched shoulder and her heart melted. This man has been wounded inside and out. He could never wield a two-handed sword the way she had just seen Perrin doing.

"Roland, are you actually thinking of fighting in this crusade?"

He gave a short, harsh laugh. "Why does one go on crusade, if not to fight? What a strange question!"

"But you cannot raise your right arm above shoulder level. How *can* you fight?"

"I have another good arm, and there are many weapons besides the two-handed sword."

"Oh, Roland. You will throw your life away if you go into battle."

He laughed again. "I can do other things. The King found out that I learned Arabic in Sicily, and he thinks that could be useful. He has already got me teaching the Arab numbering system to the palace clerks. I doubt we shall do much talking with the Saracens, but if we do, I can help there.''

"But if you have to fight, any Saracen you meet will have the advantage.''

"I will be better prepared than you might think. Do you remember Sire Guido, the Templar who brought Perrin here that night? He has invited me to train at their headquarters over in the Marais. And the King's army leaves for Outremer not this summer, but the next, in twelve hundred and forty-eight. I can acquire great skill in that time. The Templars know more about the art of war than anyone else. Many have lost a limb to the Turks and can still give a good account of themselves in battle.''

She remembered Guido Bruchesi. He had frightened her by seeming to see right through her pretense of being Roland's sister.

"I will never forget the night Guido brought poor Perrin here,'' he said. "You were splendid, Diane.'' Suddenly he looked intently into her eyes. "How can you be such a fine physician when you believe that the body is evil?''

"We do not think the body is evil, just that it is, in a way, an illusion. Pain itself is real. We think we have a duty to ease the sufferings of our brothers and sisters, whatever its source.''

But she was not convincing herself. I am tempted, too, to believe in the beauty of the body. And I feel it in me, the power of that Love he worships.

Roland was smiling that twisted smile of his again, with as much anger in it as pleasure.

"If you do not hate the flesh, if you feel obliged to ease suffering''—he moved closer to her, and suddenly she was frightened—"why will you not be mine?''

Terror shot through her like an arrow. "Roland, you promised you would never speak of such things to me.'' She moved so that the table was between them. "You are disturbed now because of Nicolette and your son. I cannot take her place.''

"No, and she could not take your place. Well, she seemed to for a while. But she was the first to see the truth—that I never really stopped loving you. I hid it from myself. It is you whom Love has chosen for me. It is you I have loved—first, last, and always. Long ago I wrote, 'That which delights both woman and man is praise to Him Who made them.' I wrote those words for you. And what I feel for you is not evil. It is good.''

All the longing for him that had ever tormented her now rose up within her. Like a thirst, but one that she felt not merely in her throat but in her arms and legs, chest and belly, in her fingertips. It clamored to be quenched, and it would be only if she pressed her mouth against him. It was not Roland who terrified her as she backed away, but her own body.

"Diane, your faith asks too much of human beings. I saw young men and women give themselves to the flames at Mont Ségur. You, too, are immolating yourself day after day by denying Love."

My body is burning right now, she thought.

She tried to think of her faith, what Bishop Bertran would say if he could advise her.

"Roland, the love you are speaking of is only a momentary fleshly pleasure. Would you have me destroy myself for that?"

But how hollow those words sounded, against her need of him.

He was circling the table. She moved in the opposite direction.

"What *you* are doing is destroying yourself, Diane. You are destroying both of us."

"There is an afterlife, Roland. I know it."

"There can be another life for us right here on earth." He gestured angrily at the staff, scrip, and cross. "Is this my future? The stake and the flames, is that your future? There are places you and I could be safe together. The Alpine communes. England. Come away with me now."

In her mind Diane saw two paths. On one lay a long life together for him and her—talking, laughing, singing, making love, having children. All simple, human pleasures. And if she took that path?

Beautiful as it seemed, she would chain herself to evil. And when she died her soul would be imprisoned for all eternity with the evil power, the Adversary. She would be tortured with blackness and fire and cruel winds and the mockery of demons and other damned souls. Damnation would never end. No hope. No hope at all.

And she would never know God.

Down the other path, if she denied Roland, lay a life of constant fear and, surely not far off, the death that awaited the Inquisition's victims.

Once, just to see if she could bear a little of the fire she knew she must face one day, she had put the tip of one finger in a candle flame. Her flesh had hissed, the pain had shot up her arm, and she had screamed, even though she had steeled herself, and jerked her arm back. The burn blistered and hurt for days afterward. She tried to imagine feeling that pain all over her body, but it was beyond her comprehension.

At the stake, would I beg them to let me renounce my faith? She had seen a few men and women with hideously scarred faces and crippled limbs, people who had screamed their recantation when they felt the flames and had been freed at the last possible moment. Once she had pitied their weakness, but after her trial with the candle flame she had a new understanding of them.

Beyond the Inquisition's fire, though, she would know eternal bliss in union with the true God. If she were good when she died, she would know goodness and happiness forever. Happiness that would make Roland's embrace seem as a mere drop of water compared to the sea. She would walk and talk with the good God in His paradise beyond the stars.

"Roland," she pleaded, "you know this is wrong. Search your heart."

"Search my heart?" he said fiercely, moving catlike toward her around the table. "My heart tells me that I have loved you since I was a boy. I loved you these last three years while I tried to renounce my love because you demanded it. Yes, you commanded me not to speak of Love, and I obeyed you. But I love you still. I cannot help myself. I do not mean a spiritual love for all men and women. I mean a passion of body and soul. Yes, I long to hold you naked in my arms. Yes, I long to pierce your body with mine, to be one with you. With every fiber of my being I believe my desire for you is good. It is what human beings were made for. I search my heart and it tells me that you must love me, too. I know it."

As he spoke he moved inexorably toward her.

Backing away, she pressed against a wall. I could have run out the door. Why did I let myself be trapped? I wanted to be trapped.

His arms reached out to her.

"No!" she screamed. She put her own arms up stiffly to fend him off. "I do love you, Roland," she said, gasping as if she were out of breath. "Yes, I do."

His face seemed to glow. She was overwhelmed by the sudden beauty of his expression.

His eyes bright, he stepped closer, so that she had to press her hands against his chest to hold him back. Feeling him, a trembling ran through her fingers into her arms.

"But you must not do this to me, Roland," she hurried on. "You will destroy my soul forever and ever. Even while I live, even living with you, I will be nothing. A ruined thing. Vows broken can never be renewed. For me there can be no forgiveness."

The happiness faded from his face, and she grieved to see the misery that replaced it.

"There is so much fear in your eyes, Diane. I cannot stand to see such fear. Do you not know that I would never hurt you? That I would never touch you unless you let me?"

He stepped away from her.

But now it was too late. She could no longer stop herself.

She quivered, still feeling the pressure of his hard chest against the palms of her hands. She had to touch him again. She could no longer withstand the hunger for him.

She was going to him.

She moved, closing her eyes, hands reaching out.

She heard heavy steps, and someone was between them. She was so startled she screamed.

She saw Perrin in front of her, his mail-clad back to her, facing Roland. Perrin held his longsword before him, across his chest. She looked past Perrin's curly head and saw the pain and anger on Roland's face.

"You would raise your sword against me, Perrin?" he said softly.

"Forgive me, master," said Perrin, his voice full of misery. "You once charged me to guard this lady with my life."

"Do you really think I would hurt her? Do you know so little of me?"

Diane was horrified. That Perrin should lift his sword against Roland because of her.

"I am only trying to do what my conscience tells me, master." Perrin's voice almost broke.

"You can put up your sword," Roland said harshly, turning his back on Perrin and Diane. "I had no intention of forcing myself on Madame Diane. I did think that she . . . Never mind what I thought."

"I have not forgotten what it is to love, master," said Perrin quietly, sliding the sword into its scabbard.

"Diane," said Roland, "I saw the fear in your eyes just now. You said that if you were to love me you would be a ruined thing. I see now that your faith is too strong for my poor words. Forgive my presumption in speaking to you. I will never disturb you again."

He does not know, Diane thought, torn between anguish and

relief, that he had won. But now I am saved. My vow is unbroken.

She held herself rigid. I must not throw away this moment of grace. But she knew that when she was alone she would weep for what she had just lost.

"You, too, must forgive me, Perrin," said Roland huskily. "You deserve to be jongleur to a much better troubadour."

Holding himself stiffly, right shoulder higher than the left, Roland walked out toward the garden.

"I will have no other master but you!" Perrin called after him.

"My God, Perrin," Diane groaned. "What have I done to him? I drove Nicolette away from him. Now I have come between you and him."

"It is not your fault, madame," said Perrin. "Do not reproach yourself. It is the countess breaking with him, and her carrying his child. It has driven him half mad." He smiled kindly. "Do not think you have come between us, either. I know my master. In a little while I shall go with him to the Left Bank and help him get drunk again like he did last night. It is the only medicine for him just now."

She heard Perrin only dimly. Her heart was pounding, and her hands were ice cold. Regret tortured her. Will I die wishing I had let Roland take me?

"I think it is best for you to leave this house, madame," Perrin said gravely. "I hate to say it. Perhaps our church can find you another refuge in Paris. Leave, if you can, while he and I are gone tonight. As I said, he has been a bit mad ever since he talked to the countess in Béziers."

"There is more, Perrin," she said, trying to wipe away her tears with her long blue sleeve. "He just found out that she has given birth to a son. He said to me that his son is the future Count de Gobignon."

"Dear God! That would be enough to drive him altogether mad. You know that his father is . . ." Perrin stopped and eyed her narrowly. "Do you know?"

The strangeness of his words momentarily turned her mind from the sorrow in her heart.

"Know what, Perrin?"

"Ah," he sighed. "You do not know. And perhaps I should not tell you without his permission, but I have started, and this way you will understand him better. You see, his father was the earlier Count de Gobignon. Amalric's father."

For a moment Diane's mind went blank. It made no sense.

"But I know Roland's whole family. I know his father, Arnaut de Vency. His mother, Dame Adalys."

"No." Perrin shook his head. "When my master's mother was very young, she was seized by Count Stephen de Gobignon and held by him in a castle he had captured. Arnaut de Vency led a band of young men who broke into the castle and sent Count Stephen to his just reward. He rescued my master's mother, but she was already with child. So Amalric de Gobignon and Roland de Vency are half brothers."

Diane's senses reeled. The butcher of Mont Ségur, Roland's half brother? Then Nicolette's son *was* actually a Gobignon by blood.

"So you can see how he must hate the Gobignon family," Perrin went on. "And to think of his son growing up as one of them. A man might almost be better off like me, not able to have children. Yes, that is why he came after you, madame. A madness."

No, she thought. Even if that set him in motion, the real reason is that he has never stopped loving me. But Perrin is right, I must get out of his life. I shall tell my superior. Either he will help me get away from here, or I will disobey him and leave. I will not lose my soul for disobeying him, but by staying here I surely will.

"You are right, Perrin," she said wanly. "I have to leave."

Did she hear a cry, like the howl of a wounded animal, from a distant part of the garden?

I will not find another place in Paris, though. I will go back to Languedoc, where they need me. They say there are not ten of our preachers left in all of Toulouse and Aquitaine.

Maybe the Inquisition will find me quickly. Life, she thought, is too much pain. Let me die, and let my soul fly up, like a spark, to God.

XVII

STANDING IN THE MIDST OF THE CROWD OF VILLAGERS LISTENING TO the proclamation, Diane felt a sudden chill. The bright sun of Languedoc shining down on the marketplace lost all its warmth for her.

"Friar Hugues of the Order of Preachers, grand inquisitor for the County of Toulouse, will preach at mass this Sunday," the crier, a man in a black tunic with a red cross on his chest, declared. "Everyone living in Azille is required to attend."

The crowd broke up quietly, people neither speaking nor looking at each other. They all feared, Diane knew, that any comment might be reported to the Inquisition.

As she walked slowly down the street, her market bag laden with eggs, a bunch of scallions, and three small loaves of fresh-baked bread, Diane saw a group of men on the edge of town. They carried crossbows and wore polished steel helmets, and they were setting up a tent. Northern French soldiers, the inquisitors' men-at-arms. There must be guards on all the roads out of town, Diane thought with a sinking feeling. It was too late to escape.

She should not have stayed this long in Azille, but old Aleth needed her. Aleth, the weaver's widow, had wracking pains in her chest, which might kill her at any time. If Diane went away without giving her the consolamentum, Aleth might die and be reborn to another lifetime of suffering. But if Diane gave her the consolamentum, Aleth would be required to lead a perfect life from then on, or be doomed to Hell. And Aleth was a worldly woman, likely to stray from the rules if she got back on her feet for even a short time. Elderly though she was, she had admitted to having had four lovers since her husband died.

In a quandary, Diane had stayed on at Aleth's house these past few weeks, nursing the old lady. She liked Aleth and wanted to see her make a good end. But it had been a mistake, she realized now, to have remained with Aleth when she knew the inquisitors would be stopping here on their regular rounds of the villages.

Her superior back in Paris had warned her against courting death.

But I have been in Languedoc for a year now, and I have had three narrow escapes. If I were trying to die, I would not have lasted this long.

It had been a good year, and she had accomplished much since her sudden flight from Paris and Roland's house. She had slipped unobtrusively from town to town in Aquitaine and Toulouse, and she had won converts to the truth, strengthened believers in their faith, and given the dying the Sacrament that sent them straight to God. Her reward was the love and gratitude she saw in the faces that greeted her in secret gatherings. Sometimes, alone at night, she wept, remembering Roland. But often, exhausted, she sank into a mercifully dreamless sleep. Time had passed unnoticed.

So that when May of twelve hundred and forty-eight arrived, the anniversary of her leaving Roland, the realization took her by surprise. She was surprised, not least, to find herself so long in Languedoc and still alive.

Diane had never seen Hugues de Gobignon, but she had heard how he had preached to the martyrs of Mont Ségur, and a dark impulse she could not name made her look forward to seeing and hearing him.

Back at Aleth's small cottage, Diane told the widow about the inquisitors. Aleth begged Diane to go away.

"What if someone stands up in church and points a finger at you, madame? What you should do is leave town."

"Too late for that," said Diane. "The friars' men would see me, and they would guess that I could only be trying to escape because I am a Cathar."

On Sunday Diane watched people hurrying to find places in the church. They were talking in low, excited whispers. Though they were afraid of the Inquisition, most of them, she realized, would have come even if they were not compelled to. To hear a famous preacher is a great event in their lives, she thought. Whether he were Catholic or Cathar, it would make little difference to them, whatever their religious sympathies.

She suppressed a shudder as she let the crowd carry her through the doorway of the little village church. She had been in many Catholic churches, but they still repelled her with their gaudy decorations, their atmosphere of strange rites and idol-worship. This church was filled beyond capacity, so that there was not even room to kneel. The air was stifling, the smell of sweat overpowering. The Frankish crossbowmen in helmets and mailed shirts who had been watching the roads now stood against the walls, their weapons in their hands.

A friar who called himself Gerard gave a brief introductory talk, reminding the people that all were required to come to confession during the following week.

Then Friar Hugues ascended the small pulpit.

The people had been quiet, but now the stillness was like death.

Hugues began softly, in a friendly tone. He had been to this town many times before, he said. He paid his respects to the pastor of the church, to the local seigneur, a mustachioed northern knight who sat in a chair of state to the right of the altar, and then to some of the people in the congregation, whom he greeted as old friends.

"You all must know," he said, "that the King has raised the sacred war banner of France, the Oriflamme, and is now marching southward from Paris to the sea. Behind him advances the blessed crusader host. More and more barons and their men will join as they go to the sea."

Diane wondered whether Roland were traveling with the King. Her heart ached with longing for him.

"I, too, am called to go with the crusaders, as is my good brother, Count Amalric, who has all the people of this region in his care," Hugues went on. "While so many priests and knights are gone, my children, who will protect you from the plague of heresy? We must cleanse the land thoroughly now, that it may remain safe while the crusaders are gone."

He repeated the many evils attributed to the heretics: murder of priests and nuns, hastening the deaths of the aged and sick, encouragement of suicide, fomenting rebellion against lawful seigneurs, sodomy, abortion, prevention of conception, contempt for marriage vows. The list went on and on. Diane's cheeks burned with anger, and she wished she could stand up and expose these lies. She stared at Hugues. What she saw frightened her. If ever a human form was the Adversary's handiwork, surely this man's was. He had the face of an angel, thin and beautiful and pure. The crown of his head, shaved in the tonsure, was large and shapely, bespeaking the power of the mind contained within that noble skull. His voice was like a clarion, and it held the people in thrall.

He spoke for a long time, and at last came to the end of his sermon: "If there be any among you who have harbored thoughts

of heresy ere now, rise and come forward. Confess yourselves
and receive God's mercy. For those who admit error and recant
now, there will be small punishment only. Our Holy Mother, the
Church, is all-forgiving.''

He waited. His burning eyes traveled over the crowd, passed
Diane's, moved on, then came back to her again. Her heart
hammered in her chest. *What a fool I was not to leave this town
when I had the chance.* His gaze left her. *How strangely like
Roland's his eyes are. Dreadful for Roland to know he is half
brother to such a fiend.*

Hugues resumed. "If any among you know of one who holds
to the teachings of the heretics, it is both a mortal sin and a
serious crime to fail to tell us. If you do not wish to speak out
now, you may come to us at the house of the pastor at any hour,
day or night. You will not have to face those you accuse. If you
have even the smallest suspicion of anyone, come to us. If you
are mistaken and the person you name is innocent, God will give
us the grace to find it out. Better that many innocent people
should be examined—if they have nothing to hide, they have
nothing to fear—than that one guilty heretic escape to go on
poisoning souls.''

When Diane left the church she was panting heavily, as if she
had been long deprived of breath. She had tried over the years to
school herself not to feel fear, but now she was seized by an
overwhelming terror. And yet she dared show no sign of unease.
People were looking at her. In the plaza in front of the church
men and women stared at her, as if aware of her for the first time
as a stranger in town. *Someone is bound to tell them about me.
Perhaps one of the very people I preached to will tell them, to
save himself. I knew that all along, did I not?*

She hurried off to Aleth's house, feeling like a hunted animal
scurrying to its hiding place. And yet she knew, with icy cold
heart, that she was no safer there than out here in plain sight.

The next morning, Monday, Diane heard a heavy knock on
Aleth's door. Whispering a prayer, she got up and opened it to
find three of the inquisitors' men-at-arms standing there. She had
spent a sleepless, terrified night on her pallet next to Aleth's bed,
wondering when they would come for her, and it was almost a
relief to see them. *Uncertainty is more painful than certain
doom,* she thought. She searched their faces. They seemed neither kindly nor cruel. They asked if she were the woman visiting
the widow Aleth and told her she must go with them. They

showed no curiosity about who she really was. They were simply men doing their work, to bring certain designated people before the friars.

She agreed to go but protested when they said Aleth must be taken, too.

"She is very sick."

"She did not come to the sermon yesterday," said the sergeant in charge. "Everyone was supposed to come. No excuses."

"But it might kill her to leave her bed," said Diane, praying that they would leave the poor old woman alone.

"We were ordered to bring both of you, and you will both come," said the sergeant, turning his back on her.

So they walked slowly back to the center of town, Diane half carrying Aleth. The old woman was stout, and Diane felt sweat dampening the sides of her gray peasant kirtle. The streets were nearly empty. This time of day, Diane thought, most people would be in the fields surrounding the town, tending their animals or their crops. Under the eyes of the inquisitors' men-at-arms, no doubt. The few people who passed Diane pretended not to see her. Diane looked up at the yellow southern sun in a sky that was, she felt sure, a shade of blue brighter than anywhere else on earth, and thought, This is the last time I will see the sun as a free woman. A wave of sadness rolled over her. There is a better world beyond this, I know. Still, this world will be hard to leave.

They came to the small but handsome stone building where the pastor lived. Inside, the pastor himself met them, a stout man with the red-veined cheeks of a heavy wine drinker.

"Take this woman upstairs," he said, staring coldly at Diane. "The friars want to question her at once."

"Aleth, I have not seen you in church in a long time. Years, in fact. We have much to talk about." He spoke to Aleth as if she were a child, but there was a cruel insinuation in his voice. He took the old lady's arm and led her through a door to the rear of the house.

Anxiety for Aleth overshadowed Diane's fear for herself. I should have given her the consolamentum. Will that priest talk her into giving up her faith?

The guards led Diane up the stairs to the main hall on the second floor. It was a long, bare room with whitewashed walls. A black crucifix with an ivory figure of Christ hung behind the two Dominican friars sitting at a table. Five young tonsured assistants flanked the inquisitors. All the men at the table wore

white robes. Six crossbowmen in black tunics with red crosses
stood along the walls.

These priests know how the people of Languedoc hate them,
and they are frightened men, Diane thought.

Hugues stared at her without speaking. She looked back into
the sharp blue eyes, trying to guess what he was going to say. At
last he smiled cordially, pushed back the sleeves of his spotless
robe, and picked up a parchment scroll.

"I hold in my hand a list of the remaining heretic preachers
known to be at large in the County of Toulouse," he said in a
brisk, warm tone. "Let us not waste time while you tell me lies
and I try to penetrate them. I will let the old lady go home now if
you will say at once who you are."

"You will trouble her no more?"

Hugues grinned at her. "We are not after her sort. We are
looking for special people. Those whose names are on this list. I
noticed you in church yesterday, madame. You had a certain
look about you. You could be one of those special people, the
ones who preach and give the sacraments, the ones who dare to
call themselves 'perfect.' Pray, madame, are you one of those?"

"I am such a one as you are looking for," said Diane calmly.
She heard the pens of the clerks scratching furiously. She felt a
lightness as soon as she spoke. The feeling amazed her. Knowing she was delivering herself into their hands, was probably
pronouncing her own death sentence, she should be terrified.
Instead she was relieved, buoyant. It was as if, instead of
becoming a prisoner, she had been in chains and was only now
set free.

After a moment, she understood. The struggle, the running
and hiding, the endless alertness and care, the constant, nagging
fear, were over and done with. Bishop Bertran and the others
must have felt this way after Mont Ségur had surrendered. Now
she need only compose herself for death.

"Why did you remain here?" asked Friar Gerard. "You must
have realized suspicion would fall on you, as an unknown person
in town."

"I was staying to give what aid I could to that sick woman.
Will you let her go now?"

"Why did you not just give her the Sacrament, smother her
with a pillow, and get on out of town?" said Hugues. His tone
was lighthearted, as if he found it amusing to contemplate such a
murder.

She felt the same indignation as she had at his calumnies in the church.

"Despite what you claim, we do not practice mercy killing. You are killing us quickly enough."

"Not half quickly enough," said Friar Gerard.

The venom in his remark sickened her. She could not understand such hatred.

How long, she wondered, would they keep her standing here? What did they want from her now? Perhaps to get her to admit to the abominations of which the Cathars were supposedly guilty. Or they might hope she would tell them something that would lead to other Cathars, especially to other preachers. Each time a Cathar was captured, she knew, the friars did their utmost to trace the prisoner's connections to others.

I know little, Diane tried to reassure herself, and will say nothing.

But I can bear witness to the truth, she decided. Give the lie to their false ideas about my church. Who knows, there might be one among the men in this room who has a mind open enough to listen.

The hatred her religion aroused was a mystery that had shaped the course of Diane's life. She had always wanted to ask why these men inflicted so much suffering on her and her people. Now at last she might solve the riddle of her persecutors.

"Why do you hate us so?" she asked. "We have never done anything to you. Surely you know we harm no one."

The two friars laughed as if this were a good joke.

"Oh, yes," said Hugues. "We all know what good men and good women you are. Honest, hardworking, austere, a reproach to your Catholic neighbors, are you not? Your master, the Devil, makes you so."

Diane was bewildered. Surely he does not believe that.

"You harm no one?" said Friar Gerard. "Why, before the Albigensian Crusade you people had almost taken the entire south of France out of the Church. Countless souls burn in Hell because of you."

Hugues said, "Do you think it no harm to teach people that they do not need bishops and priests? That they may make up their religious teachings to suit themselves?"

Their implacable hostility was like the heat from a great fire. They mean to burn me alive, she thought with mounting horror, and they will feel that they are doing right.

"So, we have encouraged the flocks you were shearing to run away, is that your grievance?" she said bitingly.

"Runaway sheep end up being eaten by wolves," said Hugues instantly.

He is quick-witted, she thought grudgingly. I must try to understand him. Or I will die never knowing why I had to die.

"People are not sheep," she said. "They can think for themselves. Why are you so afraid of that?"

Hugues narrowed his eyes. "Runaway souls end up being stolen by the Devil. When people imagine they are thinking for themselves, Satan is putting ideas into their minds. And those whom you lead astray listen to him, instead of to their proper shepherds. You set children against parents, wives against husbands, peasants against landlords, townsfolk against seigneurs. For a hundred years your influence has been spreading throughout the kingdom, even among those who remain Catholics. Questioning authority. Delving into pagan philosophy. Speculating about nature. The troubadours with their seditious songs. Even royalty is corrupted. You are the ones behind it all."

"Surely you do not think we are all that influential."

"Do not try to play the innocent with me, madame. I know how your web spreads throughout the country. In the last few years I have spent much of my time in Paris tracing a conspiracy that may touch the royal palace itself. Little by little I have been weaving my net of informers. We know about students, booksellers, vagabonds, troubadours, and little secret groups of Cathars all working together in the very heart of the kingdom."

Paris! This man might have been on her track even there. Perhaps it was lucky for Roland and the others who knew her that she had fled when she did.

I must be very careful.

She glanced at the clerks, the tops of their shaven heads gleaming at her as they bent over their parchment, writing, writing. Every word she said was being taken down and would be studied and studied again for whatever clues it might yield.

I should turn his thoughts away from Paris.

"You do not care to know what we teach, do you?" she said. "You are only concerned that we may influence people, as you put it, and diminish the Church of Rome's wealth and power."

"We know what you teach is false," said Hugues with a shrug. "That is enough. Once we burn the last of your books and the last of your preachers, no one will know what you believed. Your religion will disappear."

His words terrified her. What if he were right? When the last few like myself have gone to the stake, what will be left of us?

Her feet, shod in rough leather sandals, were beginning to hurt. She had not sat down since leaving Aleth's house. She wanted to ask them for a chair, but she knew they would refuse and would get satisfaction from that sign of weakness in her.

I must stay strong, she told herself. And bear witness.

"You are very wrong, Friar Hugues," she said huskily. "Our faith does not come from books and preachers. The One Light is present in every human heart. Even yours, though you refuse to see it. People will always be able to look within and rediscover the truths we have taught.

"Kill all of us, but among your own people there will be those who will come to doubt what you tell them and will leave your Church. What you call heresy will arise again and again, until finally it wins free of you. You can never stop men and women from finding the knowledge of God within."

Diane realized she was trembling. The Spirit spoke through me, she thought, and was awed by this sign of divine favor. I have done part of what I wanted to do. I have borne witness. But I never really will understand these men.

The two friars looked at her, seeming momentarily at a loss.

Hugues finally said, "You are gifted. You are no ordinary Cathar, are you? Tell me your name."

She felt an instant of pleasure, glee even. Her name, perhaps her last little coin to bargain with. So many things now are the last for me, she thought.

"You have not yet released the widow, as you promised."

"Of course." Hugues pointed to a guard. "Send the old woman home."

I never did get to lay hands on her, Diane thought. She will probably die and be reborn again into this suffering world. Perhaps she will fare better in her next life.

"And now—your name?" said Hugues, stretching his pale hand toward her invitingly.

"My name is Diane de Combret, if it matters to you."

"Diane de Combret!" Hugues's eyes widened, and he smiled, baring perfect white teeth. "I thought it might be you." His index finger stabbed at a place on the scroll before him.

"Oh, your name matters much to me, madame," he went on, eyes bright. "I had hoped to find you in Paris a year ago. I am delighted to meet you at last."

Hugues stood up suddenly. "Our inquiries here at Azille are

closed for now. We will take this woman back to Béziers with us at once. If we press hard we should be there in two days."

Friar Gerard and the clerks stared at him, astonished. He ignored them and merely continued to grin triumphantly at Diane.

Does capturing me mean so much to him, Diane wondered, that he no longer wants to continue his work here?

As if he knew her question, Hugues said, "I want you safely within the walls of Béziers, guarded by my brother's army. Should your misguided brethren attempt to rescue you there, they will surely fail."

A bright light stabbed at Diane's eyes. She had been lying in total darkness in a stone room in Béziers for so long that her eyes could not bear light. The straw she lay on smelled of human droppings and urine. Her bones ached from the long ride on muleback, and she was faint with hunger, having not eaten since the morning of her arrest.

She saw Friar Hugues standing in the doorway holding a candle. Fear seized her. Was he going to hurt her now? She drew herself into a hunched sitting position against the wall. He set the candle holder on a ledge and stood facing her, hands folded. Her eyes were so weak that even his white robe was hard for her to look at.

"How did you escape from Mont Ségur?" he said suddenly.

She gasped, and now her fear became horror. How could he possibly know that? The realization had been growing in her that her terrors were not over. The worst of all was just now beginning. Dear God, make me strong. She said nothing.

After a moment he said, "What happened to the wealth and the sacred objects of the Cathars that were held in Mont Ségur?"

Again she kept silent.

"Where is the Cathar treasure hidden? Where is the vessel that some say is the Holy Grail, stolen by Gnostic heretics at the dawn of Christianity?"

She said nothing.

Hugues said, "Madame, in the lower chambers of this tower are frightful implements. Perhaps you caught a glimpse of them as you were being taken to this room. They will cripple your body and leave you alive, maddened with pain. They will splinter your bones. They will tear your joints. They will pierce your flesh. They will strip your white skin away."

She willed herself not to listen. But she felt pains shoot through her body in anticipation of the torturers' instruments.

She trembled violently and hugged her knees to keep the tremors from showing.

"Not the least part of your pain," he said softly, "will be the torment of mind and the shame you will know as your beautiful body, which you have preserved in dignity and chastity, becomes the plaything of the brutes I employ to do this work." He moistened his lips. "A pity, all of this, because you are very lovely."

Her stomach knotted painfully, and she felt she might be sick. A whimper rose in her throat, but she choked it down.

"When you go to the stake, Madame Diane," Hugues continued, "as you surely must, it is possible for us to give you a speedy, merciful death. Or you can roast slowly, taking hours to die, in such agony that you will scream curses on those who taught you your religion."

She tried to stop her trembling to keep him from seeing that she was afraid, but she knew he was not exaggerating.

He moved closer to her, and she shrank away.

"I would like to spare you this suffering, Diane." It was the first time he had addressed her so familiarly. There was something insidious in his tone.

"I will not tell you anything," she said, hearing her voice break.

"When you escaped from Mont Ségur, how did you make contact with your superior in Paris?"

Again she was appalled. How did he know of that? Dear God, have they captured *him*? Even though such prayers were futile in a world ruled by the Adversary, she prayed that her superior's life—and more important, his work—was safe.

But how did Hugues know so much? Most of those she had contacted in Paris did not even know her name. Ah, but her appearance, that was harder to conceal. And if the friars' records showed she was not burned at Mont Ségur and they knew what she looked like, they could identify her from a description given by an informer in Paris.

"How did you contact your superior?" Hugues said again.

"I have nothing to say."

"How long were you in Paris? Why did you leave?"

"I will not tell you."

Again he stepped closer. "Where did you live in Paris?"

She did not answer. Her heart was thudding so hard that she thought—hoped—it might burst. That would be the greatest blessing ever.

Hugues said, "I will repeat certain names to you. You will tell me whether or not you know these persons. The first is Guillaume Bourdon, the bookseller."

She felt as if she were hurtling down from a precipice. Oh, God, no! Not names. What if she recognized a name? How could she stop herself from giving it away? She dug her nails into her palms, praying that she would not betray anyone.

"No."

He went on through a long list. Most were people she had never heard of. Some, to her horror, were members of her little secret congregations scattered about Paris. How did he know about them? His network of agents? Yes, he had said he had almost found her, too.

But why Paris? Was not Toulouse his territory?

To each name she answered no. He held the candle near her face, closely watching her reaction.

I am a fool to think I can best him. He is a master at this. She felt despair weakening her, draining away her last reserve of strength.

Then he said, "Roland de Vency, the troubadour."

Involuntarily, her head jerked up and she found herself staring at him. Quickly she lowered her eyes and forced her face to relax. But he had seen, and when she looked at him again, he wore that triumphant grin.

Then the grin faded, to be replaced by another expression, almost like pain. She had seen that look on a man's face before. More than once Roland had looked at her that way.

"You are a beautiful, intelligent, strong-willed woman, Diane," Hugues said. "You are God's creation, even if the Devil has twisted you to his purposes. I cannot help admiring you." He moved forward and sat down beside her.

She shrank away from him along the curving wall of the chamber.

"Diane, a priest is still a man. And a perfecta is still a woman, eh?" He seemed to be trying to laugh, but it came out as a series of hoarse grunts. She saw sweat gleaming on his forehead in the candlelight. He was losing his composure.

"I know you are pure, Diane. But have you never loved a man? Wanted one? Wondered what it was like? You must have. I want you because you are so pure—so untouched. Will you let me do what I want? I can help you. Think of the power I have. I can say a word, and you will not suffer at all. If you are very good to me, I can even save your life."

His voice was soft, serpentine. And she felt disgusted, nauseated, as if she had suddenly found a snake in the straw with her.

Why had his mood changed so suddenly? Had this lust been lurking all the time under his stern inquisitor's manner? Or did he hope to learn more from her by threatening her chastity? Did he hope that if he succeeded in persuading her to break her vow, she would be so weakened that she would betray her faith and friends?

"Come, Diane," he said insinuatingly. "You have kept away from men all your life for all the wrong reasons. For a person like you to discover the pleasure of the body would be a small sin. It might even bring you closer to God."

His false reasoning made her angry.

"God did not create the pleasure of the body," she said scornfully.

He stood up. "You Cathars sin against God when you say that the body is evil. That is why God will forgive me for what I do with you."

He blew out the candle.

God help me, if this priest tries to rape me, do I have the strength to fight him off?

"Even if you think me in error," she pleaded, "you know what a vow of chastity is. Can you not respect my vow?"

"Respect the vow of a heretic?" His voice came contemptuously from the dark. "You made your vow to a false God. I may do whatever I want to a heretic. God will approve."

She heard the rattle of the prayer beads wrapped around his waist as he moved toward her.

"Truly *your* God approves of rape," she said, no longer caring how she might provoke him.

As he threw himself at her and bore her down, she realized that if only she had remained quiet, she might have, for a time at least, evaded him in the darkness. The smell of him, of sweat, meat, and wine, was hideous, sickening. He pressed his damp face against her, the stubble of his beard rasping her cheek. He pushed her onto her back and rolled on top of her. She felt his distended member pressing into her thighs like a club. He was panting like an animal. She felt as if she had suddenly become entangled with a rotting corpse.

"You disgust me," she spat at him. "Filthy! Dirty!" All her rage and pain knotted her stomach, and she began to retch. There was nothing in her stomach but its own juices, and she vomited the burning liquid into the straw beside her head. The stench of her vomit mingled with the smell of Hugues made her sicker still. He was clawing at her skirt, dragging it up, pushing his knees between her legs. Coughing, choking, she began to pray, to give her strength as she fought him.

"Our Father, Who art in Heaven—"

"Be still, blasphemer." His fingers were prying between her thighs.

"Hallowed be Thy name. Thy kingdom come, Thy will be done, on earth as it is in Heaven—"

He tried to put his hand over her mouth. She twisted her head free.

"Give us this day our consubstantial bread—"

"Shut your damned Bougre mouth!"

"And forgive us our trespasses as we forgive those who trespass against us. Lead us not into temptation but—"

His hands left her legs. They were at her throat now. He was strangling her to make her stop praying.

She seized his wrists and with the last of her strength she broke his hold on her throat.

She screamed it: "Deliver us from evil!"

Almost as if her prayer were answered, he fell away from her.

Suddenly, gasping, she was released. Relief, and gratitude to God, flooded through her.

"What have you done to me?" There was anger and panic in his voice.

"What have I done to you?" She echoed his question, bewildered, her voice quavering. Her arms and legs were trembling violently. Her stomach was still heaving. She expected him to attack her again at any moment.

"I have done nothing to you," she said after a moment.

"You took away my manhood," he said fearfully. "You shriveled me. You cast a spell on me. You are worse than a damned heretic preacher. You are a witch!"

"Perhaps," she said, sobbing, "you were more ashamed of yourself than you knew."

"Monster! Witch! You will wish you let me have my way with you. You are going to suffer much, much more than you would have from taking a man between your legs."

She heard him scramble up from the straw and fumble his way to the door. The heavy wooden door opened and slammed shut again. Then his fine preacher's voice was raised in a shout for the torturers.

She shook violently with terror and curled herself into a ball to try to still her trembling.

They are going to hurt me and hurt me. Oh, God, please let me die before I tell him what he wants to know. Do not, oh, do not let me betray my friends. Do not let me betray Roland. Let me die first. Please?

Little Simon held his mother's hand with a strong grip. Nicolette felt proud that he could toddle now, on his stout bare legs, down the halls of the citadel at Béziers. He was handsome, with a cap of hair black as a raven's wing and bright blue eyes. Looking down at him, Nicolette thought, He has Gobignon eyes.

He had made Amalric enormously happy, this child he had named Simon, after Simon de Montfort, the first leader of the Albigensian Crusade.

It was Simon's bedtime, and, as was now family custom, she was taking him to Amalric's council chamber to say good night. As she approached the oak door she heard voices, Amalric and Hugues. They would not want to be disturbed. She turned to go back upstairs.

Then she heard Hugues say, "As soon as she admitted she was Diane de Combret, I brought her back here to Béziers, where we can better guard against any rescue attempt. She is perhaps the only Cathar perfecta to have escaped from Mont Ségur. I have been looking for her ever since then."

Nicolette stiffened with shock. The woman at Roland's house. Hugues had captured her, then? Was Roland, too, in danger?

"We heard rumors that Diane de Combret was among the Cathars in Paris after Mont Ségur," Hugues went on. "Indeed, we had set a trap for her in Paris, when for some reason she left there suddenly. We lost track of her for a time, until we learned that a woman preacher answering her description was active this past year in the county of Toulouse. What is most interesting is the possibility that she is connected with your mortal enemy, Roland de Vency, he who called himself Orlando of Perugia. When I spoke his name to her, she started like a frightened deer."

Nicolette's heart beat furiously. She gripped Simon's hand tightly and crept closer.

"That man!" Amalric's voice rumbled through the door. "He could have been at Mont Ségur helping her to escape. Evil—he has the look of evil all about him."

"The woman de Combret is a witch," Hugues said in a voice

so low Nicolette had to strain to hear him. "That I know for certain."

"A witch?" said Amalric. "What do you mean?"

Simon started to giggle. It was funny to hear Papa's voice coming through a door.

Nicolette pulled him away and hurried upstairs to the seigneur's bedroom, where she and Amalric and their four children slept. She left Simon with his sisters and went back.

Even from a distance she could hear angry shouts.

"Do you not realize she could accuse you publicly?" Amalric cried.

"Who would believe her?" Hugues answered. "A condemned heretic."

What are they arguing about? Nicolette wondered. And Roland, I wonder if he knows.

"Everyone would believe her!" Amalric bellowed.

The thunder in his voice made her nervous. Servants might be drawn by the shouting and find her eavesdropping.

Amalric went on, "Everyone knows priests are forever hoisting their skirts. That is why these damned heretics have made so many converts. I expected you to be above that. How can you risk your future by violating your vow?"

"What difference does that make to my future?" said Hugues. "Bishops, cardinals, even some popes take their pleasure with women. I have had dozens since I became a priest, and still I am grand inquisitor for Toulouse."

Hugues could not have lain with Diane de Combret. If she would not lie with Roland, she certainly would never let Hugues touch her.

Roland. I do still love him, Nicolette thought. How can I not, when I see his face every time I look at Simon? How can I judge him after what I have done—taking his son from him and presenting the child to Amalric as his?

And now, what if Hugues finds out that Roland rescued Diane from Mont Ségur and sheltered her in Paris?

"You will not be grand inquisitor for Toulouse much longer if your Dominican superiors find out you tried to rape a woman prisoner," said Amalric.

Nicolette felt her body grow hot with rage. She could not help making a little sound of disgust in her throat.

But Amalric had said "tried to." Then Hugues had not succeeded.

"I will not have you lecturing me on morals," said Hugues sullenly.

"You *will* accept correction from me, messire. I am head of this family, do not forget."

"Oh, I can never forget that, monseigneur," Hugues said sarcastically. "By the luck of birth you get the title and all the land, and I must make my way as a priest. I am expected to deny my body's needs, while you have a beautiful wife to go to bed with whenever you want."

Nicolette's skin crawled, hearing Hugues speak of her so.

She jumped back as she heard a sudden, sharp crack from within the room.

"How dare you strike a priest?" Hugues shrieked.

"I dare because I have more respect for the priesthood than you do," said Amalric. "Never join my wife and your lust in your thoughts again."

"I am no threat to your marriage," said Hugues. "And I may even have found a way to destroy the man who is. Then you may regret the way you treated me."

"If she had the strength," Amalric said, "to stop you from raping her, she probably has the strength to keep silent under torture."

"She does not," said Hugues. "She used a spell to stop me. But there is no human being made who can stand up under what the skilled torturers I have hired can do. They have already begun. In a few hours I shall go back and find out everything."

"And if she does not say what you want her to say?" Amalric asked.

"Impossible. We have almost a month to work on her."

Nicolette felt sick. Amalric might be furious with Hugues for attempting to rape Diane, but he thoroughly approved of torturing her.

"When will you hold the *sermo generalis*?" Amalric asked.

"Customarily we keep heretics as long as a year to give them time to recant," said Hugues. "Since we must soon go adventuring with our foolish King, I want this lot we rounded up recently done away with before we leave. I have chosen July twenty-second. An appropriate date, think you?"

"Yes, we should be sailing soon after that," Amalric said, "but what is special about that date?"

"That day, in the Year of Our Lord twelve hundred and nine, God delivered this city of Béziers into the hands of our crusaders," said Hugues with glee. "Our own father was among the victors."

When twenty thousand men, women, and children were murdered in one night, thought Nicolette. God protect us from men like this.

"By mid-July the King and his army should have arrived at Aigues-Mortes." Amalric suddenly grew enthusiastic. "We can invite him to the last great burning before the crusade embarks. How will his delicate stomach stand the sight of rows of sizzling heretics?"

Hugues said, "Think how it would embarrass him if Diane de Combret, at the stake, named Roland de Vency, a royal *enqueteur*, as her protector."

If only I were a man, thought Nicolette, I would cut both their heads off.

"Remember," Amalric said, "a crusader receives amnesty for past crimes when he takes the cross. I have word that de Vency took the cross over a year ago in Paris."

Thank God, thought Nicolette.

"To be sure," said Hugues, "but the revelation of this crime would end the favor the King could show him."

"How it galls me," she heard Amalric saying just as she also heard footsteps coming up from the first floor of the citadel. Quickly she left and hurried to the steps leading up to the bedroom. Then she paused in the circular stairwell to listen again.

There was a knock. Guy d'Etampes identified himself.

Nicolette stayed on the landing to hear what he had to say.

"The King and his army have stopped to besiege the castle of La Roche-Glun," said Sire Guy. "The King accuses the Sire Othon de la Roche of robbing pilgrims and merchants."

"Even in his own castle a baron is not safe from this meddling King," Amalric grumbled, standing in the doorway of his chamber.

Nicolette withdrew to their bedroom. The girls were asleep on a bed on one side of the room, Simon in his cradle. Nicolette undressed to her shift and climbed into the big bed she shared with Amalric, drawing shut the curtains that created a private space.

Goddess, how can I hope to fall asleep before he comes to bed? I will feign sleep.

That poor woman.

Guilt seared Nicolette's heart like a red-hot iron. She turned from one side to the other in the bed, trying to get comfortable.

Here I am in a soft bed, and she is being broken by torturers.
Could it be my fault? What if she left Paris because I found her
at Roland's?

Tangled in the sheets, she clenched her fists. Fear gripped her.
She broke out in a cold sweat.

Roland is in terrible danger. By the time she goes to the stake
she will be mad. She will say anything they want her to.

I must warn him. How? Where are they? La Roche-Glun,
north of Valence. Soon they will be near our lands at Lumel.
Could I tell Amalric I want to take the children to see my sisters
before we leave for the East? Leave Simon there and send the
others to Château Gobignon. God only knows what the Turks
will do to us in Outremer.

What is the matter with me? How can I think of myself now,
while that poor woman is . . .

The horror that she imagined made her want to scream.

Only one thing I can do. Warn Roland. I must warn him.

XVIII

"Knights, you will surely be saved
If you take the side of God
Against the Arabs and the Turks
Who have so dishonored Him."

SINGING, THE LONG BLACK CLOAK HE HAD WORN NEARLY THREE YEARS
ago at Queen Marguerite's song contest thrown back over his
shoulders, Roland stood before his black and white tent. Perrin
and the nine men he had enlisted for the crusade had formed a
circle around him.

At the sound of the music, men stood up and began to drift
toward them from all directions, swords and spurs clinking
faintly. The bright reds and blues of their tunics were dusty from
weeks of slow travel.

As Perrin blew into the shawm, his cheeks puffed and reddened till they seemed about to burst. Martin, the son of Lucien

and Adrienne, beat the drum fiercely in time to the rousing martial song. The listening men clapped their hands in time.

Roland surveyed the tents out beyond his audience. They covered the hills so thickly that grass and shrubbery were hidden: nothing was visible but miles of peaked tent tops—white, red, purple, orange—glowing in the late-afternoon sun. Hundreds of white banners with red crosses fluttered against the intensely blue sky. Six thousand knights and ten thousand men-at-arms were camped out there, the huge army Louis had brought together for the deliverance of Jerusalem.

The army had been camped outside the city of Viviers on the Rhône for three days. It had taken them a month to get this far from Paris. The dry summer of the south had set in, and Roland watched dust motes drift through the air, flecks of gold in the sunset.

What a hypocrite I am, he thought, singing crusading songs to amuse the men, when I still believe this is all madness.

With Nicolette and Diane both lost to me, I have nothing to live for. Except the promise I gave Louis that I would go crusading with him. One does not break a promise made to that man.

> "He who goes with King Louis
> Will never have to fear Hell.
> His soul will go to Paradise
> With Christ and His angels."

He came to the end of the song and bowed his head to the applause. Several called to him to sing more, but he shook his head.

"I am tired tonight."

I am not tired, I am sad, he thought.

The men drifted away. A figure in black mantle and hood stepped out of the shadows nearby.

"Roland."

He could not believe he was hearing her voice. He stared under the hood at the beautiful oval face he had loved so much.

Nearby, he heard Perrin whisper, "God's bones!"

He looked around. The other men had gone back to their own tents. No one else saw Nicolette.

He had told himself many times how much he hated her because of the boy. But he felt no hatred now.

"Why are you here, Nicolette?"

"I have terrible news. It means your life. Will you talk with me?"

He realized that she must have feared he would refuse to listen to her, send her away.

"Good God, yes, I will talk with you."

How far had she come to see him?

He led her away from the city of tents to a huge, twisted olive tree at the edge of an orchard. He saw no one nearby.

Beneath the tree he turned and faced her, feeling a wariness. Had she come to deliver some new wound?

"Are you all right?" he asked.

She nodded quickly. "It is not me. Roland, it is Diane de Combret. They have captured her."

He staggered back a step as if struck by a stone. "Oh, dear God, no."

But he had been expecting this.

When I saved her at Mont Ségur, it was only a reprieve. I have known that for a long time.

"Is she . . . to die?" he asked. It hurt terribly even to ask it.

"It is worse than that, Roland. They are torturing her. They have been torturing her for weeks, and they will torture her right up to the day they burn her."

A black vertigo engulfed him. He reached out to the trunk of the olive tree for support.

"Why?"

Nicolette shook her head. "I know what you must be going through, Roland. I would give anything not to be the one to bring you this news. Hugues and Amalric want to force her to tell them who has helped her, whom she worked with. And they are after you especially. They suspect you are linked with her. Amalric still wants to destroy you. They will torture her until she names you."

The pain in his heart was unbearable. He struck his chest with his fists. *She suffers because of me. I saved her from death only to bring her to a worse death.*

"Hugues even tried to rape her," Nicolette said.

He groaned, unable to find words.

"Roland, you know what they must be doing to her. She will end by accusing you. You must flee now. Béziers is not even a week's ride from here."

Roland stood like an animal that had been speared but had not yet fallen.

He had to force his voice through his tightened throat. "Why do you come to tell me this?"

Nicolette started, as if surprised by the question. "Strange, I never thought about why I was doing it. It seemed I must find you and tell you. I know that you love her. I wanted to help both of you."

The pain weighed him down so, he did not know how he could stay on his feet. His mind kept edging close to images of what was happening to Diane, then veering away desperately.

He stared at the clusters of crusader tents spread out through the nearby fields and orchards. He thought, Help us? There is nothing you can do, Nicolette, nothing either of us can do.

He looked at Nicolette and thought how he had hurt her by concealing Diane from her. How he had parted from her at Béziers, hating her. Even in the midst of this crushing grief, he felt a small spark of joy at seeing her. I still love her, he thought. And she deserves a far better man than me.

"You are very good to come all this way to tell me, Nicolette." He groaned. "This is all my doing. After we parted at Béziers and I thought Love was dead, I tried to win Diane's love, and I drove her away. She left me, to go back to Languedoc and be tortured and die."

"Do not blame yourself," said Nicolette. She reached out, and he felt her touch on his hand, light as a butterfly's wing. Quickly she drew her hand back.

She said, "They would have caught her even if she had stayed in Paris. Hugues said the Inquisition knew of her there. And if they had caught her in Paris it could have been at your house."

He clenched his fists. "I wish they had. Then I could have suffered with her. Then she and I would both be happily dead by now."

"I came here to help save you, Roland. Not to hear you talk about dying."

He looked into her dark eyes, and they were fierce. How full of fire she is.

"Nicolette, for all the hurt I have done you, forgive me. Please. I know you condemn me for . . . for Diane, but I cannot help it."

"I do not condemn you," Nicolette said sadly. "How could I after what I have done? To you, to our son, even to Amalric. You did what you had to do. I did what I had to do. Would I have ridden here from Béziers if my heart was still turned against you? Love is our sovereign. We cannot alter Love's commands."

He felt greatly moved, and grateful to her in the midst of his agony. That they could still love each other seemed a small but precious gift in the face of the horror of what was happening to Diane.

But the thought of brutal hands on Diane, of flames destroying her . . .

"They shall not burn her!" he said, clenching his fist.

Nicolette put her hand to her mouth, staring at him. "Roland, you are not thinking of trying to rescue her. It is impossible. Amalric has a whole army at Béziers."

"He had a whole army at Mont Ségur."

"I did not seek you out to summon you to your death, Roland. Leave here now. Go to Outremer ahead of the King. The Inquisition cannot reach you there."

"Nicolette, they are torturing Diane. The viper Hugues even tried to rape her." Speaking it aloud sent a shock of horror through him. For a moment he was unable to go on. A sob bubbled up in his chest, convulsing him. He choked it down.

"Think you," he said then, "I can just turn my back and sail away?"

"But what else can you do? You cannot help her. No one can."

He struggled to envision some plan, but his mind remained empty, maddening him. "I saved her once. I can do it again. There must be a way."

"Amalric and Hugues may be hoping you will try, so they can capture you, too."

He pressed both hands against the tree, his head hanging down.

"Do you not understand?" He wrenched the words out one by one. "I would rather die than feel this pain."

"Do you love her so much?" Her voice seemed to him to come from a great distance.

He whirled and seized her shoulders.

"I love *you*, Nicolette. To have you come to me like this—to touch you again—is part of the pain. Knowing that love is still alive between us. Knowing that if I were to live I could sail with you to Outremer."

"If you live!" Her eyes blazed at him. "You have *got* to live."

Her hands gripped his arms so hard she was hurting him.

"I cannot abandon her, Nicolette." He sighed deeply. "I could not go on living if I did."

"You might as well kill yourself now," she said, throwing herself against him.

He groaned. The thrill of holding Nicolette in his arms again made the hurt in his heart worse.

He pushed back her hood and pressed his lips into her hair.

"I must try to help her. There is nothing else I can do."

Her shoulders slumped as she gave up trying to persuade him. "Roland, when they take Diane into the plaza to burn her, I will be there. I will be there to mourn you both, if that is how it falls out."

She pushed herself away from him and stood staring at him, her face pale with grief.

"Have you talked to Queen Marguerite?" he asked her. "Will the King go to Béziers to attend the burning?"

"He does not wish to," said Nicolette. "Marguerite says he has no desire to see eighty helpless people burned to death. He will use the excuse that he does not have the time."

"No one will believe that," said Roland, his affection for Louis making him smile in spite of his suffering. "He has found time to make dozens of stops on our march down here from Paris. Why, he has just spent the last three days here trying to persuade the Bishop of Viviers to stop coining his own money."

"At least he will not be there to see you die," she said, her eyes full of reproach.

He wanted to hold her again, but he fought down the longing.

"Promise me one thing, Nicolette," he said grimly.

"Anything."

"Do not take the boy to see the burning." He could not bring himself to pronounce the name Simon.

Roland walked with Guido Bruchesi in the kitchen garden of the Poor Knights of the Temple of Solomon outside Viviers. Around them rose a wall of square-cut gray granite, twice the height of a man. Before them was the Templars' command post, a stone house with a peaked roof and massive round towers, one at each corner.

Guido looked more monk than warrior this evening, in his white linen robe with the splayed red cross on the shoulder. He held Roland's arm as they circled the fish pond that provided the Templars, who rarely ate meat, with most of their suppers.

"Your sister is to be burned as a heretic?" Guido's bearded face was full of distress and compassion.

"You know she is not my sister." In his desperation, knowing how hopeless any attempt to rescue Diane must be, Roland had decided he had nothing to lose by confiding in Bruchesi.

Guido said, "And you know, Roland, that we Templars serve the Pope. The same Pope who has sole authority over the courts that send people to the stake. So why do you come to me?"

"Because you are my friend. A man loyal only to the Pope would not have done the many things you have for me. And, for what reason I know not, you Templars have never persecuted the Cathars."

Guido gripped his arm tighter and turned him around. They stood facing the commandery with its four towers. One of the mysterious Templar symbols, a single eye within an equilateral triangle, was carved over the doorway.

"What would you have me do, Roland?"

Roland felt like a trapped animal, throwing himself uselessly against the sides of a pit.

"I am not sure," he said, shaking his head. "I thought perhaps you would be able to tell me what *I* should do. I want to try to save Diane. I am not asking you to help me. I would not expect that. It is just that . . . I must try." He searched Guido's warm brown eyes for help as he talked.

Ever since the night when they had wiped out the highwaymen, Roland had loved and trusted this man. Guido, saying little, seemed to understand much. Even though, like all Templars, he was a monk bound by vows, he seemed to Roland to possess a unique grandeur of spirit. Next to Perrin, Guido was Roland's closest friend in all of France, the only one he could turn to now.

Guido put his hand on Roland's shoulder and smiled sadly. "I am grateful to you for not asking me to go with you. It would hurt very much to have to refuse you. My heart is with you, though. Please know that."

Roland sighed. He had, in fact, harbored a faint hope that Guido would offer to come. He had even imagined that somehow with the Templar's help he might actually rescue Diane.

"I may need quite a lot of silver," Roland said.

"You deposited the money from the sale of your house with the Templars in Paris as I advised, did you not?" said Guido.

Roland nodded.

"Good," said Guido. "Now you will see how reliable our Templar banking is. You received a note in return for your coins?"

"Yes," said Roland with another sigh.

"If you have it now, you need only present it here. I will see that delivery to you is hastened. But you will need more than silver to see you through this. How is your arm? Can you wield a sword?''

"I have been practicing the exercises you taught me with the broadsword. With the left hand, I am adequately skilled. With the right alone, I am about as good as a ten-year-old boy."

His arms and legs seemed to grow heavier and heavier as he felt their uselessness. He could no more do anything for Diane than he could drive his fist through the wall of this commandery.

He felt as if he were drowning in despair.

"Do you have any idea how I might rescue her?"

"My dear friend, there is no way. Recognize that. Do not delude yourself. And if you are going to die, do it with open eyes. But once you admit there is no hope, you must then ask yourself, why die so pointlessly?"

"There is nothing else I can do. She is there, and it is my fault she is there. I have to go."

"I have told you many times, we Templars retreat when the odds against us are more than three to one. In Béziers you will be one against thousands. It would be no shame for you to stay away. And since you ask me for advice, that is the best advice I can give you. If you go you will simply be throwing your life away."

Roland shook his head. No shame to stay away? But this had nothing to do with shame or honor.

He envisioned Diane in the torture chamber. Her beautiful green eyes held his. She called to him over those leagues that Nicolette had just ridden. Abandon her? It would be easier to die than do that.

"I do not feel I have any choice. You understand that, do you not?"

Guido took Roland's hand in his powerful grip, and there was deep compassion in his eyes. Wordlessly, Roland returned the pressure. Saint Michel, it is good to have a friend like this.

"I understand you perfectly, Roland," Guido said. "All I can say to you is, go with grace."

When Roland returned to his campsite he found Perrin had struck his tent and loaded it on a packhorse. He had saddled Regibet, a deep-chested brown stallion with more speed and endurance than Alezan.

Perrin stood by Regibet's head. With him were three of Roland's men. Two were members of the Mad Dogs who had frequented the back room of Guillaume the Bookseller. The third was young Martin.

"We have our own and five spare horses ready to travel, master," said Perrin. "The rest of our men can take our equipment on to Aigues-Mortes. As for us, we shall have to ride hard. We have only six days to get to Béziers."

Roland felt an iron ball in his throat. He had never loved Perrin as much as he did at that moment.

But, my God, he thought, I cannot drag these men to their deaths with me. He looked at Martin, so slight his sword nearly dragged on the ground. His parents must be dying of worry as it is. I cannot do this to them.

"Where do you think you are going?" he demanded.

"With you, master," said Perrin firmly.

Gratitude and guilt mingled in Roland's breast. These four good men would take on Amalric's army and the Inquisition out of loyalty to me. I do not deserve it.

"How do you know about Béziers?" He tried to keep his voice stern.

"Madame the countess told me everything while you were at the Templars' headquarters." Perrin's voice was level, and his gaze was steady. "Before she left she bade me look after you."

"Sire Guido Bruchesi has just said my going to Béziers is certain death."

"No man can foretell the future. Not even a Templar. Despite what he said, you are going, are you not, master?"

"Yes."

"Then we are going, too."

Roland felt a warmth in his breast as he gazed into Perrin's eyes. But he could not allow this. I drove Diane to seek her death in Languedoc, and now I must die. But must these men die, too, fruitlessly, because of me?

"I order you to stay here and wait for me to come back."

"It is no use, master." Perrin shook his head. "We have all sworn fealty to you. We are your men, and nothing can change that. Not even an order from you."

In his hopelessness, in his anguish for Diane, in his grief at having found Nicolette and lost her again, Roland felt as if all his strength had drained away. He could not fight Perrin, too.

I will let them come with me, he thought, but I will find a way to get them out of there before the end.

He turned his face away to hide his tears. Thank God for men like this.

XIX

ROLAND SAT UP ON THE COT HE'D LAIN ON, UNABLE TO SLEEP, FOR the past several hours. The clamor of the people of Béziers in the plaza assailed his ears like thunder. Through a window he glimpsed a bright blue sky. His four men were standing by the window staring glumly out.

Diane was to die today, and in all likelihood he was, too. He felt as if he were wrapped in iron chains.

Somehow he got up and began to wash and dress himself.

With the help of Gautier and Horace, the former Mad Dogs, he donned his hauberk, specially shaped to allow for his deformed right shoulder. Over it he drew on his black surcoat emblazoned with the silver griffin. Then Martin handed him the bronze medallion of Apollo given him years ago by Emperor Frederic. Roland lowered the silver chain over his head. *I last wore this at Queen Marguerite's song contest,* he thought.

"Bring me my sword."

Silently Perrin unwrapped Roland's belt and, in its plain black scabbard, the broadsword he could wield with one hand. Kneeling, he presented them to his master.

So full of despair was Roland that he could move only slowly, heavily.

Diane might already be dead, he thought. *Then his sortie into the plaza would be for nothing—she would not even know he had tried.*

The four men with him in the room he had rented for one hundred silver deniers were silent. No longer were any of them trying to sway him from the course he had chosen, to ride into the plaza fully armed when everyone's attention was on the ceremony. He alone would cut through the crowd and the guards, seize Diane, and ride off before anyone realized what was happening. He had ordered Perrin and his men to slip out of town and seize a boat, specifying a meeting place upriver, for their escape when he began his attack. If they obeyed, he thought, they might get away.

256

He was as aware as they that de Gobignon's archers could bring him down before he got halfway across the plaza. But they all pretended this was a daring but well-conceived plan. He felt grateful to them. This would be the last service they could do him.

He took his conical helmet from Horace and pressed the leather lining down on his head. The helmet seemed to weigh a hundred stone. I am putting this on for the last time, he thought. Everything today is for the last time.

I wish I had written a poem to leave behind. Beautiful verses that someone might sing after I am dead. Something for Nicolette to read. Something she could show our son, one day when he is grown and she tells him about me. *This is the kind of man your father was.*

Riding into that plaza, that will be my poem. Maybe some other troubadour will make a song about it. A different *Song of Roland.*

I wonder how far I shall get. Saint Michel, there will be women and children in that crowd. I do not want to trample them.

Perhaps I will get some of de Gobignon's guards. Cut the swine down with my sword. Even left-handed, I can get a few of them. If they do not see me right away. Got to keep them from spearing Regibet. I might make it all the way to the pyre before they realize what I am doing and start shooting arrows at me.

Nicolette will see me die. Why must she go through this hell, too? Dear God, please make her stay away.

Saint Michel, am I going to cry? In front of my men, when I am trying to face death like a brave knight? That would be a poor thing. Let them say I went to my death gallantly. Let me have at least that little bit of glory.

He listened to the sounds coming from the plaza. Bursts of laughter from men, the cries of women greeting one another, the shrieks of excited children. There must be hundreds out there.

Then he heard trumpets blaring a solemn hymn while drums beat slow time. This was the signal they had agreed on for Perrin to go down to the inn yard and prepare the horse. Roland's heartbeat quickened. But he felt no fear. Just great sadness, and relief that finally he was acting.

"Perrin, get Regibet."

Perrin left, and Roland and the men went out to the balcony whose fine view of the plaza had cost so much of his silver. Blinking in the high, bright sunlight that glared off whitewashed building fronts, Roland thought, It must be mid-morning, the hour of Terce. They will start soon.

Filling the center of the plaza was a mass of piled-up wood, higher than a man, square in shape and about fifty feet on each side, streaked with black pitch, contained by crude wood fencing. It is Mont Ségur all over again, thought Roland, wanting to disbelieve his own eyes. Out of the heap of wood jutted rows and rows of stakes. A spiral of thick black smoke rose from the opposite side of the square, beyond the pyre. That would be the fire from which the executioners would ignite their torches. The sight made Roland curl his lips in revulsion.

He saw people packed around three sides of the square, and their voices sounded to him like the clamor of a waterfall. Who comes to see such things? he wondered. Most of these people were probably not native to Languedoc. As their landlord, himself born in the county of Gobignon, had reminded him last night, thousands of common folk from the north had followed their seigneurs down here to take the places of dispossessed and dead Southerners. And that was especially true here in Béziers, where the entire original population of the city had been massacred by crusaders.

Looking down, he saw that the crowd was composed largely of families. Many small children rode their fathers' shoulders, to see better. Most of the people wore brown or gray, the colorless clothes of the poorer folk. Here and there in the crowd blossomed the bright red or blue of men and ladies of means.

His gaze traveled around the edges of the plaza, where the shops were all open and seemed to be doing brisk business. Entertainers performed for coins—jugglers, acrobats, singers, fire-eaters. He saw a man walking high in the air on a rope stretched from one red-tiled rooftop to another across a corner of the plaza. He saw gay green and gold banners fluttering from rooftops and windows. He even saw a dancing bear.

I will give them entertainment they are not expecting, he thought savagely, his fingers tightening around his sword hilt. He had been worried that he might hurt innocent people in the crowd. Now that he saw their glee over the burning, he no longer cared. Let Regibet kick their brains out.

The gleam of steel caught his eye. He studied the double line of men in brightly shined helmets and purple and gold tunics. Armed with long pikes, they surrounded the great pile of wood in the center of the plaza. Those pikes, Roland knew, would rip open his horse's belly if he got that far.

Now he looked at the Church of the Madeleine directly across the plaza. It was an old, dark stone building with round-arched doorways and a gallery protected by battlements. It was close to the city wall, and two of the pale yellow guard towers overlooked it. Diane might be in one of those towers, Roland thought as he looked up at the slotted windows.

Had she broken under torture, revealed that he had rescued her, protected her? *Yes*, he wished fervently. He hoped she had told them everything. Because then perhaps they would have stopped hurting her. And it no longer mattered to him what they knew about him. He would not live long enough for them to arrest him.

He saw a row of archers, their crossbows loaded and cocked, standing before the steps of the church. They are there to protect the great ones who come to see the burning, he thought. There is always the chance that some Languedoc patriot might attempt some wild deed of vengeance at a time like this.

He watched the dignitaries gather at the tables and chairs set before the open doors of the church. He saw three bishops in purple and gold robes, dazzling gold crosses on their chests, bejeweled miters on their heads, holding golden croziers, their staffs of office, in hands encrusted with rings. If wealth be the mark of God's favor, surely theirs is the true faith, thought Roland sourly. Beside the bishops stood Dominican friars, stark in their white robes and black mantles.

Seeing a man with a thin, handsome face and a tonsured fringe of yellow hair, Roland recognized Hugues. Torturer! Rapist! How I wish I could bring my sword down on that shaven skull of his. What pleasure to be the agent of his death!

He was surprised to see a group of white-mantled Knights Templar climb the steps of the church and join the high-ranking onlookers. Two of them had long black beards, like Guido's. After kneeling to kiss the bishops' rings, the Templars took places standing on one side of the steps.

Even the Templars, he thought, feeling betrayed. Everyone is tainted.

At least Louis is not here. Thank God for Louis.

The scene in the plaza filled Roland with bitterness. So much care and ceremony going into this mass murder. The spectators were awaiting it with such evident pleasure.

Let me ride through those pigs down there, then let them kill me. To the Devil with this life. There is no hope in it. No hope at all.

"You know," he said to the three men with him, "maybe the Cathars are right. Maybe the God who created this world is a bad god."

Young Martin nodded. "They *are* right," he said.

Roland turned and looked at Martin. What a strange thing for him to say. Had Diane had so much influence on him?

Now a flash of silver coronets and bright purple cloaks caught Roland's eye. Amalric de Gobignon and Nicolette were crossing the church steps to seat themselves in chairs of state beside those set up for the bishops. At the sight of Nicolette Roland felt himself melt inwardly. Will she tell the boy about me one day?

But with what pleasure Amalric will look upon my death.

This will not help Diane. It will torture Nicolette. Delight Amalric and Hugues. What am I doing?

For a moment the music stopped. Then the drums, half a dozen of them, began again, solemn, monotonous, funereal. From the balcony Roland could see along the street that led past the church to one of the city towers. He saw a door at the base of that tower swing open. A file of people emerged from it, wearing the tall, cone-shaped paper hats the inquisitors mockingly put on the heads of condemned heretics. He felt hammer blows of pain battering his heart, and he knew worse was to come. He tried to brace himself.

Led by chanting friars holding up a great golden cross, the procession of heretics, walking two by two in a long line, came down the street past the church. The doomed ones were flanked by crossbowmen and pikemen, all wearing the purple and gold livery of Gobignon. Each of the condemned carried a lighted candle. They had nothing on but the paper miters and thin white robes. Their heads had been shaved. Roland could not tell the men from the women. He searched the procession for Diane, desperate to see her and dreading to see her.

The first of the condemned disappeared behind the bulk of the pyre. Then, one by one, prodded by the warders, they climbed up ladders to the top of the heaped wood. A trio of executioners, dressed in red hoods and tunics, began tying them to stakes.

Then Roland saw Diane.

He went cold as if the blood had drained out of his body.

Her red hair had been shorn away, but her long figure and fine-boned face were unmistakable. Two guards were lifting her to the pyre. She seemed unable to move under her own power. Her feet dragged over the brush as they pulled her to her stake.

Sweet Jesus, they broke her legs. She cannot use her legs at all.

Little sobbing sounds escaped from Roland's tight-shut mouth, though he was scarcely aware of them. Only by biting his lips hard enough to draw blood could he stop himself from screaming. A wave of blackness swept over his eyes. He swayed, grasping at the iron balcony railing to steady himself.

They turned her to face the church, with her back to Roland, tying her hands behind the pole, then wrapping ropes about her body to hold her up. She sagged in the ropes as if unconscious. The back of her shift was stained with blood.

Roland wanted to howl his grief to the heavens. The pain of being burned alive could not be more unbearable than this, seeing the bleeding, still-living remains of the woman he loved.

"Oh, God," he whispered, tears running down his face. "God, God, God!" Oh, my poor, sweet, gentle Diane. How could anyone do this to you?

He put his hands over his face and wept. If I had left her to die at Mont Ségur she would not have had to suffer this.

Was I wrong to rescue her?

If I was, my death today, I pray, will make up for it.

It was all settled. After seeing this, life was worth nothing. There was only one path. To die. To die fighting, if possible. Sword in hand, at least.

He turned to the men beside him. "It is time for me to go."

"Yes, messire."

He wanted to say something to these young men, some last watchword.

"You are young men," he said brokenly.

"Yes, messire." All three were crying.

"Do not hate the world. I did not mean what I said before about the Cathars being right. In spite of what you see this day, it is a beautiful world, and I believe that a God of Love created it."

They said nothing.

Perrin was standing in the room, his face, too, wet with tears. He was holding a length of rope in his hand.

"Is my horse ready?"

"Forgive me, master." Strong hands seized Roland, and Perrin looped the rope over his shoulders. Martin took Roland's helmet off and laid it carefully on the bed.

For a moment Roland was too surprised even to try to move. By the time he started to fight, his arms and hands were bound.

"Perrin, my God! Not this from you!"

Perrin stepped away from him. Gautier and Horace still held him, but with the ropes securely around him he was helpless.

"This is no treachery, master," said Perrin, still weeping. "I am carrying out the wishes of Madame Diane herself."

"You could not have spoken to her."

"The day she left your house in Paris I had a last word with her. She knew then that if she returned to Languedoc it was only a matter of time before the Inquisition caught her. She said that even though you had rescued her once and might want to try again, sooner or later she was certain to die a martyr's death. Your efforts to prevent that would be futile. Try to understand, master, she does not need to be rescued. Even less does she need you to lay down your life. We are still your men, master, and if there had been the slightest chance of success today, we would have gone into the plaza with you—if need be died with you. But when I saw how hopeless it was, then I knew that madame's request must be honored."

Roland heard Perrin's words, but they made no sense to him. His grief of a moment ago had now turned to rage. Rage that filled him so full he felt almost able to burst the ropes that held him. He strained savagely against them. The ropes cut into the muscles of his arms through the mail and burned his wrists. He hardly felt the pain. Diane was dying out there. He was frantic with the need to fight his way through to her. Why were these fools stopping him?

"Perrin, may God damn you! Let me go. How can you betray me like this?"

"I understand your hatred, master, and I shall bear it. I love you. I love Madame Diane, too, and thanks to what she taught me I think I know her mind better than you. She wants to die. For her, as for me now, life is suffering. She said to me that all the time she lived after Mont Ségur was borrowed time that she must eventually pay back. Well, she has paid it back now, with usury. As for you, master, she believes the time for you to die will not be till you have traveled a long road, fulfilled a mighty destiny, and come at last to know peace. She wants you to help the King, and be reconciled with Madame Nicolette. This was her last message, which I was to give you should this terrible day ever happen. As for Madame Diane herself, she has won. She has remained steadfast. They could not break her spirit. Today is her victory."

Roland shook like a man with the falling sickness. His chest heaved against the constricting ropes. He could scarcely breathe.

"I shall never forgive you for this, Perrin," he panted. "From this day you are no longer my man."

"I expected that, master," Perrin whispered, wiping his streaming eyes. "But if I did anything but what I am doing, I could never forgive myself."

Perrin glanced at the door to the balcony. "Soon it will be over, master. There is nothing for us to do. No good can come of your seeing our dear lady's final agony. It is only her body they are destroying, anyway. Her spirit will live on and always be with you. Let us go away from here quietly now and not look back."

"No," said Roland. "If I cannot die fighting for her, let me at least suffer with her. Let there be one person among all this multitude who loves her. She may not even know I am here, but I must do this for her. Please take me outside."

His heart felt impaled on a barbed spear. He was sure he would go mad. But if he could not die he must make himself stay and bear witness. He had done that at Mont Ségur, but the agony of that was nothing compared to this. He had cared for the hundreds who died that day, but he loved this one woman. He would do this for her, and he hoped the sight would forever stop the beating of his heart.

Perrin said, "We will release your bonds if you give us your word you will not try to escape from us."

"I will give you my word in nothing. I will never give you my word again."

Perrin sighed. "So be it."

They helped Roland out to the balcony, where he could watch Diane as the long ritual of the *sermo generalis* began.

Diane woke to the din of hundreds of shouting voices and blindingly bright light. Something was holding her upright, but not her own strength. Ropes. There were ropes around her. They bit into her torn flesh, hurting her arms, her waist, her thighs.

But these same ropes, she realized, were sparing her some pain by holding her against a thick post so that her weight was not bearing down on her crushed legs.

All was hazy before her. They had done something to her right eye, she could not remember what, and it saw nothing. They had kept her in total darkness so much of the time that her left eye ached and saw only unrecognizable shapes.

Now I remember how I got here. They carried me from the tower to the pile of wood. Somebody started to lift me up, and there was terrible pain, and that was all. I must have fainted again. I have been awake hardly at all for a long time. Weeks, I think.

She began to see a little more clearly. There were people across from her, in chairs before the doorways of the church. The glitter of their gold and jewels, the bright colors of their raiment, hurt her eye. Above the church was a red mass, the conical roof of one of the city towers. It was a terrible effort to hold her head up. How long since she had eaten?

Then she remembered the torture and her surprise that pain could be so bad, that more pain was still possible. Even now she hurt all over. But no, parts of her felt nothing at all.

Thank God I shall be dead soon. If they did nothing more at all to me I would probably die in a little while. Surely my body is ruined past any chance of healing.

Another day of this pain and I would lose my mind.

O Lord, let me die quickly, and let my body be absorbed into the One Light as a raindrop disappears in the sea. Please accept me. I know I have not been good. I should never have wanted to give myself to Roland, that day in Paris, but do not let me be damned for that.

What is that music? Are they really playing music?

Dear God, forgive me for loving Roland. And please, let him be far away from here, and let him find out nothing about it until this is all over.

What a miracle that I managed to keep from saying his name. That I knew I had the power to endure just a little while, and when that little while was past, to endure a little more still. When did I first realize that it did not matter what they did to me—what part of my body they hurt or destroyed? My body is not me, and what I am neither torturers nor any flames can touch. My death today is defeat for them. This fire will burn away the dross that is blended into my being so that nothing is left of me but light.

She heard a voice singing. It was an old Cathar hymn, and she knew the words well:

> "I came out of God and the Light,
> And now I am exiled from them.
> A child of God was I born,
> But now I am made to know pain."

Who is singing? It sounds so beautiful.

After a moment she realized she had been singing. Whether she had sung aloud or only in her mind she did not know.

Suddenly she was in a time and place where the hurting had stopped and she could see with both eyes. She had fallen, she realized, into memory. She found herself in a candle-lit room with whitewashed stone walls. Before her Hugues de Gobignon sat at a table. As always, there were books and rolls of parchment before him. A white figure of Jesus hung twisted against a black wooden cross on the wall. Hugues waved away the guards who had brought her to him.

"You have suffered for a week," he said.

"I did not know how long it was."

"It will go on as long as I wish it to."

Wearily, grateful in a way for this moment of quiet conversation, she said, "I am your prisoner, and you can do as you like with me."

He raised a finger. "That is not true. You have power over me. I admit it. You can make the torture stop. You know how."

"No, I do not."

"Lift the spell." He turned his face aside. "Restore my manhood."

Could he actually believe she had used magic upon him when he was trying to rape her?

"There is no spell. If you cannot achieve the"—she hesitated, embarrassed—"the manly state, it is because you believe you cannot. I did nothing. You put this notion into your own head."

His face was agonized as he looked up at her. "I have tried to cure myself. If my brethren knew of the alchemists and infidel physicians I have gone to, I myself would stand trial for heresy. I have been with five different women, women I had enjoyed many times before. The spell is unbroken."

"I cannot help you."

"You are a witch. You have the marks—the green eyes and the red hair. You did this to me. Only you can undo it. I will stop the torturing. I will not ask you again about de Vency. I will even save you from death by fire. Only . . . help me. Please."

"You have done this to yourself. Only you can help yourself."

He slammed his fist down on the table. "Witch! You will suffer and suffer and suffer for this. I will torture you forever, if

I have to. I will not kill you until you have cured me." He stood up and shouted, "Guards!"

They were going to hurt her again. She started whimpering and babbling in fear.

"Oh, no, please do not."

But they had taken her away.

Her scream brought her back to the present. She found herself again on the pyre tied to the stake.

Why did I not remember Roland instead of that horrible priest?

An indistinct figure in black and white came to the center of the church steps and began to preach.

Sudden terror swept over Diane at the sight of the friar's robe. *Are they going to torture me again? Oh, no, I cannot bear anymore. I am so afraid they will make me say whatever they want me to.*

Roland a heretic? Yes, yes, yes! He is a heretic, and he knows where the Holy Grail is, only stop, stop hurting me, please.

But that friar is nowhere near me. He is over on the church steps, and he is only going to preach.

Then they are only going to kill me.

When the sermon was over, the friar—it was Friar Gerard, the one who had been with Hugues at Azille—took up a scroll and began to read aloud the names and sentences.

Why was Hugues not doing this? Diane wondered. She had not heard a word of Gerard's sermon, but she found herself now able to listen. Gerard named first those who had recanted. She saw them, a large group, perhaps two hundred, gathered at the bottom of the church steps. A huge iron basin that held glowing coals stood beside them, to remind them of what they had escaped. The friar commanded some to make pilgrimages, others to take the cross and join the King's army at Aigues-Mortes. Some were to lose all of their possessions, some to be imprisoned for long terms, some for life.

"Brothers and sisters! Do not let them enslave your souls along with your bodies. Join us up here and be free of them forever!"

Diane knew the voice. The hoarse cry came from Diane's right, from a young perfectus named Georges, whose arrest six months ago at Montpellier had been a great sorrow to their church in hiding.

"Silence, or I will gag you," growled an executioner in red hood and tunic who stood with them on the pyre.

"Bless you, brother Georges." Diane was barely able to speak through her cracked, swollen lips. "You restore my strength."

"Shut up!" snarled the executioner.

At last the friar addressed those who were to die. As he exhorted them to recant, Diane's mind wandered. He held up a crucifix, and she thought, I am closer to Jesus on the cross than that man is.

"It is you who should give up your errors," the young Cathar preacher called out. "It is you who are about to commit an unforgivable crime."

The executioner's fist thudded against Georges's jaw, and the slender man slumped against the ropes that held him to his stake.

Now a glittering personage holding a golden staff—some bishop or other, Diane thought—rose and came forward.

"Since you are unrepentant, I must with sorrow abandon you to the secular authorities for such punishment as they think fit. I recommend that they be merciful and the punishment involve no mutilation of the limbs or shedding of blood."

A tall man in a purple and gold mantle, wearing a small silver crown, stood up.

Diane's remaining eye had finally adjusted to the glare in the plaza. This must be Friar Hugues's terrible brother, Amalric de Gobignon. And there, seated at Amalric's right, was his countess, Nicolette, the woman Roland loved. Nicolette was too far away for Diane, with her uncertain sight, to make out the expression on her face.

Lord, I hope she has come this day in compassion. Nicolette, my dear, from this day on Roland is entirely yours.

Amalric spoke quickly. His voice was cold, brisk.

"By the power vested in me by Louis, King of the Franks, as his seneschal for Béziers, I hereby sentence you all to die on this twenty-second day of July in the year of our Seigneur twelve hundred and forty-eight. In deference to the request of his excellency the Bishop of Béziers, you shall die by fire." He sat down.

A movement at the base of the pyre caught her eye. A friar, his white robe billowing, took a torch from one of the executioners, lit it in the brazier, and started to climb one of the ladders.

She recognized Hugues and felt dread as he came up the

ladder, closer and closer. She trembled against the ropes that cut into her.

A surprised murmur went through the onlookers. Count Amalric half rose from his chair.

Hugues's pale face swam through the glare to come close to Diane. She could hear the torch crackling in his hand. His body swayed on the unsteady mass of bundled branches and twigs. His lips quivered, and his eyes glared at her out of dark hollows.

"For the last time, will you not save yourself from this terrible death? Say that Roland de Vency helped you, and you will live."

Diane whispered hoarsely, "Do you think I want to live any longer, in such pain?"

He came closer still and whispered back, "If you believe so in what you are dying for, then in the name of Jesus Christ, Whom we both worship, have mercy on me. Lift the spell."

What if she simply told him, "The spell is lifted. Your virility is restored." Would he believe it, and thereby be cured? She was tempted to say the words. But she could not let her last act on earth be a lie.

"Any kindness I could do for you—in the hope that it would touch your soul—I would do. I cannot help you. It is not in my power. I tell you again, you have done this to yourself. There is no spell. You are perfectly well, in your physical being. Believe that, and you will be cured."

"You are lying!" he snarled.

His haggard face was a handsbreadth away from hers. The torch, a wad of tow soaked in pitch, hissed and popped.

"I can save you from suffering even now. I can have you strangled before we light the pyre. I can even do it with my own hands."

"Just let me die in peace, will you not?"

He brought the torch close to her face. "Diane, feel this heat. Even if you have borne everything else, you cannot endure a death by fire. If I give the order, the executioners will clear away the faggots around your feet, so that you will not be in the fire but will dangle above it. It will take hours for your body to be consumed. And then long before you die you will lose your faith and beg for the chance to help me, I promise you."

"Hugues, listen to yourself. Could the worship of a good God make you do all this to a helpless woman? After I am gone, look in your heart, Hugues, for the true God, and you will find Him."

"Hugues!"

Hugues turned, and Diane looked down to the foot of the pyre. Count Amalric was standing there.

"Hugues, in God's name, what are you doing up there?" His voice was urgent, low, just loud enough to carry up to his brother. "You will get nothing from that woman. Come down and let us get on with this."

Diane closed her eye. Her body felt as if it were already on fire, fevered and filled with pain.

Yes, oh, yes, let me go, please let me depart.

As if in answer to her prayer she saw Roland in her mind.

Ah, thank You, God, for sending me this comfort. How my heart overflows with love. For Roland. For Your spirit. Now I know why Roland spoke of Love as if it were God. Roland's God is my God, too. *All things that are, are lights. And the light shines in each man and each woman.*

She heard a scream right beside her.

Against her will, she looked. She beheld Hugues's face, contorted with terror, his mouth hanging open, his eyes staring down at the long wooden shaft that jutted from his chest.

The torch fell from his dead fingers as he collapsed.

From a great distance Diane heard cries and screams. Count Amalric's shout, "Hugues!" was a bellow of anguish.

She saw an executioner hurl himself from the pyre to the paving stones.

She heard Georges's voice reciting the Lord's Prayer.

Flames sprang up around her feet. The heat felt so terrible that she knew only that something was eating away her flesh.

She heard herself screaming. Oh, God, help me, help me, please. Let me think of Roland. Let me think of Bishop Bertran, of my friends of Mont Ségur.

I am coming, friends. I am joining you now.

She felt a blow, as if a fist had slammed into her chest. She looked down. There, in the very center of her breast, was an arrow.

She had time to think only, I am free. Forever free.

PART TWO

OUTREMER

Anno Domini 1249–1250

XX

As he rode, Roland glanced up at the full moon of January, which had lighted his way along the beach all night. He hardly had to guide his mount. The mare, a patient palfrey borrowed from the Templar commandery at Kolossi, trotted steadily over the hard-packed sand, while Roland tried to recall the months that had passed.

He could not remember seeing Diane die. His mind refused to yield up the horrible memory. His first recollection was of riding out through the wide-open gates of Béziers, the screams of the people in the plaza fading behind him. All around them were other people on foot and on horseback, also running as though for their lives. What were they running from?

Later Perrin had told him people were shouting about the arrows that had killed Hugues and Diane. Their fear was not of those arrows, though, but of the wrath of Amalric.

It was Perrin who had led the party back to Aigues-Mortes. Roland had been too sunk in despair even to speak, much less command his little group.

"You are a fool" was the first thing he could remember saying to Perrin. Standing on the deck of a Genoese galley crowded with knights and men, they were waiting to set sail for Cyprus, whence King Louis would be launching his invasion.

To Roland then, anyone who embraced any religion was a fool. Catholicism was monstrous because it murdered people, and Catharism was monstrous because it persuaded people to seek death.

Perrin's reply had been to quote Saint Paul: " 'There is one body, and one Spirit, ever. as ye are called in one hope of your calling; One Lord, one faith, one baptism, one God and Father of all, who is above all, and through all, and in you all.' "

"What does that mean?"

"It means that we are all God," Perrin had insisted. "You, me, Madame Diane, even Friar Hugues. What you saw at Béziers was God returning to God."

273

"So you do not mourn Diane? Is that what Catharism has done for you?"

Perrin shook his head sadly, and Roland noticed his red and swollen eyes. The jongleur had indeed been grieving.

"I mourn, master. But my belief comforts me, a little. As I think it would comfort you."

"I do not believe anything can comfort me," Roland had answered. "But I do know that at Béziers you tried your best to be my friend. The terrible things I said to you that day—I apologize for them. I was out of my mind with grief. Perhaps I still am, but I want your forgiveness."

For answer, Perrin had gone over to Roland and thrown his arms around him in a strong embrace.

The crusade had carried him along with it to Cyprus as the tide carries a bit of flotsam. After the three gray weeks of the voyage Perrin had delivered Roland to Guido, with whom he listlessly rode to the fortress of the Templars at Kolossi up the coast from Limassol. There he had discovered that he was not just numb with grief. Like many other crusaders, he had come down with an illness of Outremer that turned his bones and muscles to water.

The Templars saw him through the sickness, and as soon as he was able to stand, Guido proceeded with the cure of his spirit. Work was the treatment—hard training, morning, noon, and night, with sword, bow, and lance, on horseback and on foot.

It hurt. Guido demanded that he use his right arm to hold his shield up, and many were the nights when the throbbing in his shoulder made it impossible to sleep. It hurt to swing heavy swords with his left arm, and yet every few days Guido produced a sword that was heavier still for him to practice with. While his body suffered, his mind remained blank.

Whether he lived or died, he still did not care, but at least he would die fighting well. He became as proficient with his left arm as he had ever been with his right. His chosen weapon now was the saber, which he could wield with one hand. He could not cut through a helmet or a mail shirt with it, but he could strike a dozen blows in the time it took to swing a longsword once, and he could thrust it into vulnerable spots.

In the moments left him between arms practice and sleep he mourned Diane with an enormous grief. The woman he had loved ever since he was a boy was gone, leaving a black place as if the moon had disappeared.

He wrote verses on the meaninglessness of life, the omnipotence of matter, the indifference of God. He sang his songs for Guido, expecting an argument, but the Templar only shrugged sadly.

Gradually Roland's mind moved from simple stunned grief to wondering how Diane had been killed. Had the man who fired those arrows wanted to spare her the pain of a death by fire, or was it really his purpose to kill Hugues? And above all, who was it?

After some weeks on Cyprus, he began to think of Nicolette. At first he felt that such thoughts betrayed Diane. But he came to realize that Diane would not feel that way. She had wanted him to be happy with Nicolette.

And so, little by little, his mind began to turn toward Nicolette as a flower turns toward the sun.

All his judgments of her—how wrong they had been! How could he condemn the decisions of a woman with a child, when he could not feel as desperately as she the need to protect herself and her baby? Nicolette is not like Diane, a woman who ran to meet death, he told himself. Nicolette hungers and thirsts for life.

As he thought more often of her, and as his body grew stronger and harder, he began to think perhaps he did not want to die.

And in his thoughts he became more absorbed with her. Nicolette is the only person alive who can make me happy, and I am probably the only man who can make her happy, and yet in our jealous anger we have parted from each other. At any moment either of us may be carried off by sickness. Since we landed here on Cyprus a thousand and more crusaders have died of disease. Why waste the little time we have? I must see her, and before the army leaves for Egypt.

In December Perrin had come to him and told him that a message had come from Nicolette.

Joy had welled up in Roland's heart like a spring suddenly bursting forth from a rock. He was amazed at the power of his feelings.

Nicolette had not risked a written message. She had sent Agnes to tell Perrin that the Queen and her ladies would shortly be making a circuit of the island, visiting monasteries and holy places. In a few weeks they would be in Paphos, to see the pillar at which Saint Paul had been scourged. Paphos and Kolossi, where Roland was, were both near Kouklia, the legendary site of the birth of Venus.

So the meeting had been set: dawn on the feast of Saint Paul's miraculous conversion, the twenty-fifth of January, by the Rock of Romios, the place where Venus—or, as he had heard the Cypriots call her, Aphrodite—had emerged from the sea.

As he rode, the thought of seeing Nicolette again raised a tingling in the pit of Roland's stomach, sent his blood racing through his body. He felt excited and apprehensive—worried that instead of a joyful reunion they might have another savage quarrel, as when he had come to Béziers as a friar.

A huge black rock, shaped like an overturned ship, loomed out of the darkness just ahead. He scanned the rock and the beach about it, but he could see no one.

He walked his horse into the forest of cedars along the edge of the beach and tethered her to a low-hanging, gnarled limb. He stopped to breathe deeply of the cedar fragrance which seemed to pervade the whole island. There were more cedars on Cyprus than there were in Lebanon, Guido Bruchesi had told him.

Then he went back to the beach. Just above the border between wet and dry, next to the giant rock, he spread his black cloak and sat down on it, staring out at the sea.

After a time he looked to the west and saw that the moon had disappeared. Eastward the sky had gone from black to purple. A pleasant sea breeze caressed his face. Looking south out to sea, he watched a line of bobbing yellow lights, fishing boats, move slowly past a second rock that rose thirty feet out in the water.

Will we love each other this time, simply and purely? Or will we waste more of our lives in anger? His heart struggled in his chest. What if she does not come at all?

He noticed a spot in the water out by the distant rock, and caught his breath. A head, moving out there? Curious, intrigued he stood up to get a better look. Arms flashed through the waves. His lips parted in wonder. It was lighter now but not light enough to identify a distant swimmer. Still, the shape in the waves had to be Nicolette. Hurriedly he kicked away his boots drew off his hose, and strode down into the foam. The swimmer was in the shallows now. Slender arms, long flowing hair—surely it was she.

Then she stood up. The rushing water roiled about her knees. Arms at her sides, she stood still, swaying slightly to the push and pull of the breakers. On his left, the red-hot edge of the su broke over the eastern horizon. The light sparkled on the drops of water besprinkling her naked body, turning them to fiery jewels. She stood, ten feet away from him, looking deep into his eyes. He was stunned, awestruck. The first worshipers of the Goddess of Love must have felt like this when Venus arose, surely no more beautiful than the vision before him, from these same waves. He stared at her high, full breasts with their nipples the color of dark cherries, at the creamy white belly, at the sweet dimple of her navel, the sea-wet shield of hair that graced her loins, and he felt faint with desire and fell to his knees in the foaming water.

She walked toward him as he knelt at the water's edge, then stood above him, her body like a Grecian statue. She took his head between her hands and pulled it to her. His cheek rested against the flat curve of her belly for a moment, then he turned his head and kissed her, tasting the salt of the sea.

"Mi dons," he said, whispering the words into her flesh, "I worship you."

"Let me worship you as well," came her answer from above him.

He pressed the palms of his hands against the small of her back and felt her trembling.

He stood and took her by the hand, leading her alongside the rock to where he had laid out his cloak, and quickly stripped himself. He embraced her sitting up, facing her in the ancient way. As the sun rose higher, it warmed his almost motionless naked body, and he felt heat rising from her, dispelling the chill of the sea. Fire swept through him, burning away all that was matter, until he was pure mind, pure light. It was with his mind, rather than his bedazzled senses, that he felt Nicolette's transports.

As for himself, he sought no release this day. This union with her was perfection as it was. When he felt she had achieved the fullest possible measure of bliss, he allowed his own tension gradually to subside. Suffering, sickness, and harsh discipline had given him a new power of restraint.

They drew apart and lay side by side on his cloak, spent, and he listened with delight to her breath whispering in his ear.

A distant church bell rang out the Angelus. "The villagers nearby must be up and about," Nicolette said. She sat up, smiling. "If they saw us lying here nude they might take us for Venus and Mars come back to earth. Or they might decide we are a pair of shameless fornicators and march us off to their priest. Perhaps it is time we dressed."

Her smile vanished, and she was suddenly crying in his arms. "Oh, my love, I thought we would never again be together like this." He held her till her sobs subsided. She raised her head, and he traced the path of her tears on her cheek with his fingertip.

She rose and walked to a niche in the great rock, where there was a small pile of clothing he had not noticed before. The beauty of her body, glowing like ivory in the morning sun, took his breath away. She put on the clothes, the costume of a Cypriot equerry, with an ankle-length tunic of lightweight blue silk, and she piled up her long hair under a yellow turban. Roland noticed, higher up on the rock, a withered bouquet of wild flowers. It looked as if it must have been placed there by devoted hands several days ago. They had not altogether stopped worshiping the old gods and goddesses on this island, he thought.

With reluctance he donned his own clothing. The cedar-scented air was so pleasantly warm he felt he could have stayed naked in it all day.

"How did you come here?" he asked Nicolette when they were sitting together. "Did you come alone? Did you fall from the sky?"

"Of course I came alone," she said with a low laugh. "Would you have wanted an audience for what we just did? I tied my horse out of sight in the forest, and then I went in swimming. I wanted you to think me born of wave and foam."

"It was perfect," he said. "How foolish you and I have been not to spend every moment we had enjoying each other."

"Oh, yes."

He read in her face a mixture of happiness and regret. "Do you understand about Diane now?" he asked her.

Her arms went around his shoulders. "Yes, truly I do. Do you understand about Simon?"

Anger surged up in him. How he hated that name.

Then, as he looked into her anxious eyes, his anger faded and sympathy filled its place, and sadness.

"I have thought much about you and . . . the boy. I think I understand now. Where is he?"

"With my sisters at Château Lumel, where he will hear nothing but the *Langue d'Oc* spoken for all the years we are here in Outremer. Amalric wanted him at Gobignon with our girls, but I had my way. So Simon may grow up to be a true son of Languedoc."

Those words made him shudder. He saw the plaza at Béziers

the white-gowned figures tied to stakes. And then, Friar Hugues menacing Diane with a torch. Hugues's body jerked suddenly, and the torch fell and flames shot up, sweeping Diane from his sight.

He put his hands over his face and began to sob.

Nicolette held him as his body convulsed, and his cries echoed against the great black rock beside them.

"What is it, Roland?"

"I remembered. Just now, for the first time. I could see it. How Diane died."

She gasped. "Oh, dear God, yes. It was awful. I had never seen a burning before."

"Who do you think fired those arrows? Did he mean to kill her?"

"I am sure of it. I was so close. I saw the arrow strike her right in the heart." She touched the red cross on Roland's black tunic. "It was well aimed. She must have died instantly. Whoever did it loved her. It is just what I would have wished for myself, were I at the stake."

"Who could it have been?" he asked again.

"I thought at first it was you. Then I saw you with Perrin, far away on the other side of the plaza. It must have been one of her Cathar brethren. We shall never know."

"A stronger man than I," said Roland, still reproaching himself.

"And what Amalric did afterwards, it was horrible—more horrible than anything I imagined he could do."

Roland felt cold revulsion as he remembered what he had heard. Hangings of hostages, whole villages burned down—the atrocities had gone on and on until the King himself had ordered an end to them.

"He did not see you, as I did, but he knows you were in Béziers when Hugues was killed," Nicolette said. "Your innkeeper described you to him. Poor fool. He should not have, but he expected to be rewarded. Amalric had him tortured, hoping to get more information, and he died."

Roland rose and stood with his hands clasped behind his back, staring out at the dark blue sea.

"Does Amalric think I killed Hugues and Diane?"

She stood beside him, resting her hand on his arm, the breeze blowing her pale blue tunic against her legs.

"No, he knows the arrows came from one of the city towers, not from your inn. But he thinks you must have arranged it."

"All his horrors did nothing to discover the killer?" he asked.

Pain shadowed her face under the strange Eastern turban. "I do not think he really was expecting to find out. He just wanted to hurt people, make them pay for Hugues's death. I thanked God when King Louis made him stop. But now Amalric has yet another reason for hating Louis. Roland, I am still afraid he may try to kill the King. I told you he lusts for the throne."

Cold water raced up the beach, engulfing Roland's bare feet. It swept the sand out from under him, and he staggered before he could steady himself.

"You mean he plans to make himself King? That would be madness."

She shook her head. "That is what I thought at first. But then I tried to think as he must think. The King and his three brothers will be leading the invasion. Suppose, then, there was a great defeat in Egypt and the royal brothers and most of the nobility were lost. It could happen. Who would rule then? Queen Blanche and the King's nine-year-old son. Suppose that Amalric, anticipating such a disaster—*or helping to make it happen*—returns to France. Would it be so difficult for him to take control? Would it be so surprising if the child were set aside, so that a strong man, a Peer of the Realm, well liked by the great barons and backed by the clergy and the Pope, might take over? Does not the royal blood flow in Amalric's veins, his mother the daughter of Philippe Auguste?"

Roland's head spun. He felt as if the world were as unstable as the shifting sand beneath him.

Unthinkable. There were four strong brothers—Louis, Robert, Charles, and Alphonse. Queen Blanche ruled securely in Paris. But if indeed all those were swept away? Who would fill the gap?

Amalric?

He felt his face grow hot and his skin crawl.

Standing beside him, Nicolette gripped his arm tighter. "Do you know what the three crowns on the Gobignon coat of arms stand for? The family tradition is that two are for the royal ancestors from whom they are descended—Clovis and Charlemagne. The third is for"—she whispered it with a shudder—"*the crown that is yet to come.*"

Fury boiled in Roland's chest.

"It cannot happen," he said, clenching trembling fists.

"Amalric has written already to the Pope," Nicolette said. "Innocent is angry with Louis for going to Outremer instead of making war on Frederic. If something happened, Amalric would have the Pope's backing. Of all the great barons, he is the one who always supports the Pope.''

Roland, filled bone-deep with wrath, clenched his teeth in frustration.

He thought how all Languedoc had been reduced to a waste-land by barons like Amalric and by the Inquisition they had brought with them. What if such men had a free hand throughout France? Only Louis could stave off that devastation. Only be-cause of him was France the strongest, proudest, most prosper-ous kingdom in Christendom. Should all that be lost?

"Perhaps," he said fiercely, "it can be arranged for Amalric to meet with calamity in Egypt."

She looked at him with a cold intensity. "Do to him as you think best. I once commanded you not to kill him. Hundreds of lives would have been saved if he had died that day. I will not make that mistake again."

He took both of her hands in his.

"I must join the King at Nicosia at once," he said.

"Are you well enough?"

"This illness of mine has been a kind of mourning, I think. It is time for me to put my grief behind me."

"We will never forget Diane," Nicolette said.

At her words he felt a warmth inside. His love for Diane no longer divided them.

"What we do will be for her as much as for France," he said. "I must become the King's shadow. That means you and I will both be in the royal household."

"And we will both be near Amalric. Your life will be in constant danger."

"He, too, will be in danger from me."

He looked at her sorrowfully as he added, "We can no longer live for our own happiness, *mi dons*, though God knows we have had little enough of that these past few years. We can no longer risk discovery. We must not give your husband an opportunity to destroy our usefulness to King Louis. Do you understand?"

Her eyes clouded over. "Yes, Roland, I do. And we will give up our joy in each other for the sake of the King and our love."

He touched a finger to her cheek and wiped away her tears. "We will meet again when the crusade is over, if . . ."

She seized his hands. "Do not say 'if.' However things may fall out, we *will* meet again." She threw herself against him.

He drew a long, deep breath. Whenever he smelled cedar, he

would remember how they had made love this morning at the place where Venus had been born.

He crushed her in his arms.

Not long ago, all I wanted was a quick and decent death in battle. Now she has given me a reason for living again. Yet I must turn my back on her.

He pulled Nicolette closer and pressed his lips against hers till they hurt, knowing this kiss might be their last.

XXI

ROLAND TENSED HIS ARMS AND LEGS AGAINST THE JOLT HE KNEW would be coming. Still, he was thrown forward, almost off his feet, as the keel of the longboat ground against the sand. His body was rigid with fear. *Egypt. This is the land of Egypt.*

"For God and the Sepulcher!" a knight shouted, and Roland heard men behind him scrambling over the side. He, too, clambered over the gunwale and splashed into the muddy water. It was cold and waist-deep, soaking under his mail shirt, and he gritted his teeth against the discomfort.

He tried to catch sight of the enemy. Anxiety made him wish for eyes on all sides of his head. Holding his lance high in one hand, long shield on his right arm, he waded ashore with the others. *Will my right arm hold up today,* he wondered, *or will it fail me?*

Farther down the beach he saw a circle of knights, and he ran toward them. Out of the center of the group rose a gold banner, the Oriflamme—the golden flame—the sacred war banner of France. It bore a red cross, and its bottom edge was cut in points and fringed with red.

A flash of gold under the Oriflamme caught Roland's eye. He recognized Louis's helmet, topped with a crown. *The King would be among the first to land,* Roland thought, and fear for Louis made him run faster to join the circle.

He jostled his way into a place among the knights. Gripping the round top of his shield with both hands, he drove the pointed bottom into the sand until it stood upright by itself. Around him

he heard knights talking about the long, wild ride in the small
boats from the Genoese ships to the shore.

How long would it take the Egyptians to ride out to meet
them?

Fear possessed him again, and he gripped his lance hard.

He had been friendly with the Saracens who served the Emperor in Sicily, had even learned their language, but that would
be no help in meeting these Egyptians in war.

He scanned the beach. No sign of the enemy yet. He saw a
long stretch of reddish sand stretching to east and west, bordered
by a line of green shrubbery about twice the height of a man.
From the brush rose the tall, snakelike trunks of palm trees,
crowned with spiky leaves. Beyond was nothing but sky. The
land seemed to be utterly flat—not a mountain, not a hill,
not even a sand dune.

Looking to the east he could make out the grayish walls and
towers of a city. Damietta, their objective. His heart sank. It
seemed leagues away. They would have to cross the Nile to get
to it.

But he understood Louis's plan. By landing on the bank of
the Nile opposite Damietta, where there were no Egyptian defenses, the King hoped to get most of his army ashore before the
Saracens attacked.

Something whistled past his head. He ducked, then looked
behind and saw an arrow half buried in the sand. Another hiss.
Nearby, a man screamed and fell, holding his hand to his head
and thrashing his legs in pain, as an equerry rushed to his aid.
More hissings. Roland felt about to burst with tension. The
attack was on.

Louis's voice rose above the shouts of crusaders and the whine
of arrows. "Commend your souls to our Seigneur Jesus, messires."

The Egyptians burst out of the green brush a hundred yards
away, a long line of horsemen in red silk cloaks. They screamed
war cries in high voices. Black and green banners inscribed with
verses from the Koran fluttered above the sand cloud raised by
their horses. Roland read the Arabic script: "There is no God but
Allah."

The helmets of the enemy were covered by yellow turbans,
their faces hidden by embroidered scarves, their bodies swathed
in long-sleeved mantles and cloaks, well designed to keep out
the heat and dust.

The sun struck white fire on polished scimitars, blinding him.
The Saracen horses were not as big as Christian knights' war-

horses but in their own way were magnificent animals, with proudly arching necks and slender legs, built for speed and agility. The riders looked formidable, invincible. And the crusaders' horses had not yet been landed. They will kill us all, he thought.

He watched tensely as the Egyptian host thundered at them, hooves a blur on the sand.

A turbaned giant with bulging white eyes in a brown face, a red scarf over his nose and mouth, rode straight at Roland. The Saracen leaned out of the saddle, scimitar lifted to strike.

Roland thrust his lance at the chest of the Egyptian, who rode right onto it, hitting the lance head with such force that the needle-sharp point punctured the chain mail under his green robe. The Egyptian flew out of the saddle like a rag doll.

Roland felt a surge of elation. It is like a tournament, he thought. He crouched behind his shield to protect himself from the hooves of the now riderless horse, and jerked his lance out of the body.

Dust stung his nostrils, and he wished he had a cloth to pull over his face as the Egyptians did. From all around him came shouts and screams. The sand beneath him trembled to the drumming of the horses' hooves.

Three Egyptians converged on him, warbling their battle cries. One threw a spear, and he crouched to duck it, lifting his lance. The lance point caught the center man's horse in the belly, and it fell screaming, throwing its rider and falling so that it tripped one of the horses behind it. The third Egyptian, as Roland still crouched, jumped his horse over Roland's shield.

The enemy was real now, no longer an imagined terror, and in the thick of action Roland had no time for fear. He knew that the horseman who had gotten by him could reach the King.

He unsheathed his saber with his left hand. He could not go to the aid of the King because two Egyptians were coming at him on foot—the two he had just unhorsed.

Putting his full, armored weight behind his shield, Roland threw himself at one of them. As the man fell beneath him, Roland, also falling, drove the point of his saber into the enemy's throat.

Roland jumped to his feet, feeling an ache in his right shoulder as he hoisted his shield. The clang of metal on metal all about him was deafening, and the crowd of struggling figures confused him. He looked wildly about for the other Egyptian.

Just in time. Fierce black eyes looked into Roland's, and a scimitar whistled at his legs. Roland danced back and then rushed in, thrusting his saber point into his opponent's chest. The saber struck mail, bending, and the Saracen fell back with a grunt, unhurt.

The man began to move forward again, one deliberate step at a time, eyes fixed on Roland, the huge, curving scimitar lifted. Which of them would still be alive a moment from now?

The scimitar came down to block Roland's thrust, and Roland slashed across the Egyptian's face. The Egyptian apparently was not used to a left-handed opponent, nor to Christians who fenced with sabers. Where there had been bright eyes in a brown face, there was a mask of blood, and the Egyptian fell back, screaming.

From behind him, Roland heard a shout of "Saint Denis!" and a loud clang. He swung to see the King standing tall and triumphant, holding his bloody two-handed sword over the cloven body of the Muslim whose horse had leaped the shield wall moments ago.

"He was about to strike at you," Louis panted. "Always remember your back, messire." He turned to rush to where mounted Egyptians were trying to break through the circle of knights.

And I was going to protect *him*, Roland thought with a rueful smile as he ran back into the protective ring of knights. He has saved my life a second time.

He glanced around. Everywhere crusaders and Saracens were in man-to-man combat. The shield wall had expanded as more and more had landed from the longboats, and the crusaders now held a larger part of the beach. In the center of the circle lay dead and wounded crusaders, about two dozen of them. Grayrobed priests tended them and gave last rites.

Roland had tasted blood, and his comrades were holding their own. When they land our horses, he thought, then we shall really start to fight.

He turned to look out to sea at the haven he had left only a short time ago. A line of ships fenced the horizon, square white sails painted with red crosses. Nicolette, he thought, is out there watching. She was on the galleass *Montjoie*, he knew, the flagship of the fleet.

The water just beyond the breakers, stained russet by Nile mud, was now crowded with barges, each carrying six or more war-horses. The barges were anchoring close to shore, where the horses could wade in. The Genoese let ramps down into the waves. Equerries jumped into the water and led the horses ashore, where knights dashed to meet them.

"Make way!" a voice roared, and Roland felt himself shoved aside. He looked up to see a destrier draped in red and silver trotting past him. The horse passed so close to him its flank seemed as big as the side of a ship, and the plumed helmet of the man mounted on it appeared to brush the sky. Another horse and rider followed, and another. Pointed gonfalons fluttered from the tips of the lances the equerries had brought along with the horses.

Roland turned again to face the enemy and found that they were falling back. Banners aflutter, still shrieking defiance, they formed a line across the beach, blocking the way to the towers and walls of Damietta. Sunlight flashed on their scimitars.

The heat was almost unbearable. It was high noon, and the sun, directly overhead, was turning his helmet into an oven that baked his scalp. And this is only June, he thought, dismayed. Even if we can beat the Egyptians, the heat here may beat us.

He heard excited cries behind him and turned. A small group of shouting, gesticulating men, most of them wearing the ornamented helmets of great barons, was gathered around the Oriflamme. In the center was Louis's crowned helmet, and near it, one topped by a silver wolf's head.

Fear flooded back into Roland's limbs. The sight of the wolf's head made him grip his saber angrily. Amalric. One small mishap and the King could be dead.

The King's face was brightly flushed. "Bring me my horse. Bring me Veilantif," he commanded. "I will ride against the infidel alone. Let them see what stuff French knights are made of."

Roland heard a chorus of protests as his heart sank.

Louis has been carried away by his first sight of the foe. He should be making plans and giving orders, not rushing out in front of his army. He will be killed today—now—if we do not stop him. And he may get us all killed.

Roland tensed as he heard Amalric's voice shouting, "Equerry! You heard the King. Bring his horse at once."

Amalric, in purple and gold surcoat and shining steel helmet, was standing beside Louis. He had his longsword out and ready, even though there were no Egyptians nearby. Perhaps to cut down any of us who contradict him, Roland thought.

Knowing it would be accounted disrespect for one of his low rank to address the King unbidden, Roland still felt the need to speak up.

"Please, do not so sacrifice your life, sire," he called out.

"One great deed of arms now will inspire our men and prove to the infidel that ours is the true God," said Louis. His face was aglow with what Roland had come to think of as his Jerusalem look.

Roland despaired as he made way for an equerry leading a magnificent white charger into the ring of knights. Louis reached for the pommel and put an armored foot into the stirrup.

Without thought or hesitation, Roland reached out and seized Louis's arm. The horse whinnied angrily.

"Please, sire! Think how our men will despair if you should be . . . hurt."

"Take your hands off the King!" shouted Amalric, brandishing his sword.

To Roland's relief, Jean de Joinville came to his aid. "Sire, this good knight wants only to preserve your life. Let us all ride together against the Egyptians."

"If I ride against them alone, God will protect me," said Louis.

A new figure pushed into the circle. He wore the white surcoat and red cross of a Templar over his mail. With a leap of his heart, Roland recognized Guido Bruchesi.

Guido looked at him but did not acknowledge him. He went directly to the King.

He spoke quietly but firmly. "Sire, what you have just said is presumption."

"I do not see how that could be, brother Templar." But Louis took his foot out of the stirrup as Roland watched with growing hope. You can always catch Louis's attention with a religious argument, Roland thought, even on the battlefield.

"Sire," said Guido, "Satan tempted our Seigneur Jesus, telling Him that if He cast Himself down from the mountaintop, angels would lift him up." Guido cast a sidelong look at Amalric. "You, sire, are being tempted to ride alone against the whole Egyptian army, expecting God's protection. You are demanding a miracle. That is presumption."

Louis was silent for a moment. "Perhaps you are right."

Roland let out a long breath.

Calmer now, the King looked around him with his usual gentle smile. "Well, then, messires. Shall we ride against the Saracens together?"

Roland felt his body go limp with relief. He would have felt better if Louis were off on one of those ships. But at least now he is not taking a greater risk than the rest of us.

Roland's steel-shod feet sank in the wet sand as he ran to the water's edge to look for Perrin and Alezan.

Facing east, Amalric studied the beach carefully, systematically, beginning at the shoreline on his left and peering long at the brush and palm trees to his right. He was let down, disappointed. The enemy had suddenly disappeared. There was no one for him to fight.

His shadow on horseback stretched far before him on the rust-colored sand. He had been fighting for so many hours that his arms and legs ached. There was a sharp, stinging pain in his cheek where an arrow had grazed it.

He sat brooding in his saddle, recalling the fighting. Many skirmishes. Three fine charges by our side. Two Saracen counterattacks. Their horses are fast, but ours are heavier. They are deadly with those damned bows, but we are better at hand-to-hand fighting.

Where the devil have they got to?

There had been an eerie horn blast a few moments ago, and then the Saracens had all ridden away. All he could see now were the dead ones, their bodies scattered over the beach, distinguishable by the bright reds, greens, and yellows of their garb. Sunlight gleamed dully on the mail and helmets of slain Christians. The friars were already moving among them.

The Saracens had not ridden toward Damietta, but south, staying on this side of the river. He squinted, looking for bridges connecting the west bank with the east bank, where Damietta stood. He could not see any.

The glare from the wide mouth of the Nile hurt his eyes. The river gleamed like a sheet of copper under the afternoon sun. On the other side of the water the dun-colored walls of Damietta looked high and solid. He studied the defenses, noting that it was a triple wall surrounded by a moat, and the inner wall must be at least forty feet high. He counted seventeen square towers along the walls. It had taken the last crusaders a year to break into that place.

But now there was no one in the towers or on the walls. Odd.

He unbuckled the iron hoop under his chin and took his helmet off, sweat gluing the separate leather lining to his brow. He touched the steel cone with its wolf's-head ornament and jerked his fingers away. The metal was so hot from the sun, it actually burned his fingertips.

Now he understood why the Saracens wore turbans over their helmets.

Though tattered, bruised, and tired, he felt at peace. During the fighting, as he had cut down one Egyptian after another with his longsword, he had been filled with an all-consuming joy. To him there was nothing in the world like doing battle. Not even his greatest pleasure with a woman.

I love it so. And it does my heart so much good to be chopping down these black heathens. I could be a hero of this crusade if it suited me. Too bad I have a different war to win.

He heard galloping hooves on the sand behind him and turned to see a rider in the blue and gold of a King's herald. Louis wanted something. Resentment burned in Amalric's chest. Why the devil can he not leave me alone?

The herald dismounted and made a deep bow.

"The King sends his greetings and asks you to attend upon him, monseigneur."

As Amalric rode in silence past the line of mail-clad knights slowly walking their horses to the bank of the Nile, he felt bile rising in his throat. If de Vency and that damned Templar had not intervened, Louis might now be with his beloved saints.

It was because of Louis—his leniency to heretics and his softness toward Languedoc—that Hugues was dead. And when Amalric had taken just reprisals for Hugues's death, it was the accursed Louis who had stopped him.

I must take the throne myself.

Louis, grimy of face, his surcoat torn, was seated on his white horse in the midst of a group of his knights. He was excited but did not seem to Amalric to be in the same wild mood that had gripped him earlier.

"Amalric," he said, "our scouts report that the gates of Damietta stand open, and no defenders are to be seen. You are the boldest of my barons, and I have decided to give you the honor of being first into the city. Will you cross the river and take possession?"

Damn! If there is an ambush I am a dead man. Amalric's hands clenched on the reins, and his face burned as he tried to hide his rage.

His glance fell on the troubadour, de Vency, sitting on his chestnut horse beside the King. He could never see de Vency without wanting to put a sword to the troubadour's throat and force him to tell who killed Hugues. De Vency's swarthy face was expressionless under his black-painted helmet, but Amalric thought he saw a glint of amusement in those strange blue eyes. He is pleased that I am being sent into danger.

Well, let him be. It is I who will come back from Egypt and he who will leave his bones here to bleach in the sand. He and Louis. Louis, I pray the Egyptians tear you limb from limb and cut you open and eat your heart.

"As you wish, sire." Amalric saluted the King and rode back to his own troops.

He ordered Guy d'Etampes to requisition boats, and selected a party of a dozen mounted knights and fifty men on foot. If the Egyptians were trying to lure the crusaders into the city, they would not want to reveal themselves by attacking so small a group.

An equerry riding behind him held aloft the purple and gold banner of the house of Gobignon. Amalric knew he would seem a hero to the crusaders for venturing into Damietta with so few men. Yet fear ran clammy fingers down his spine. It was one thing to enjoy battle, another to make himself a target for whatever Egyptians might be lying in wait.

He and his men crossed in longboats and barges to the east bank, under the walls of Damietta. The river was shallow here, and the land around the city was an expanse of soft brown mud, into which the horses' hooves sank up to their fetlocks. Farther up the river shapeless brick houses were clustered between the bank and the moat. There were small wooden docks for boats, but no boats were tied to them. Nor were any people about. The silence gave Amalric an uneasy feeling.

The drawbridge over the wide moat was down, and the main gate of the city stood open, as if this were an ordinary market day. But he smelled smoke and saw a black pall in the sky above the walls. Perhaps they really have abandoned the city. But why?

He lifted his hand and waved his men forward. His own horse clattered over the drawbridge first. He gripped the pommel of his saddle hard, so the sudden trembling of his hand would not show. Thank you for this great honor, Louis. I hope to repay you for it.

Within the triple walls he saw miles of mud-colored buildings roofed over with small domes. The streets before him were narrow, twisting, and unpaved. Most of the houses had second-story balconies jutting out so far they almost turned the streets into tunnels. Which way to go?

There was a cluster of pink spires in what seemed to be the center of town. Making the sign of the cross for protection, he chose the widest street that led toward the spires and waved his men forward.

He rode through a maze of blank, plastered walls, trying not to think about the pots of boiling oil, the arrows, the rocks, the daggers that might await him in these crooked streets. He had heard on Cyprus that the Saracens had a weapon called Greek fire, a substance that would burst into flame on striking its target, a flame that clung to its victim and could not be put out.

A city like this, he told himself, would be a perfect place to trap and destroy a whole army. But Damietta seemed empty of all life, save occasional packs of stray dogs.

After what seemed hours of riding, with his flesh sweating under his hauberk, his arm aching from holding his sword at the ready, and every sense strained, he turned a corner and found himself looking at a plaza and, beyond it, a Muslim temple. The spires he had used as landmarks rose above the mosque's majestic blue dome. The very splendor of the building made Amalric want all the more to burn it down. But, of course, our good priests will want to turn it into a church. Oh, Hugues, if only you could be here to say a mass in this conquered temple.

In the center of the plaza huddled the first people he had seen in Damietta, a small group of men, women, and children. He tightened his grip on his sword.

At the sight of Amalric and his men all the people fell to their knees, except for a gray-bearded man in a black robe, who held up a cross on a long staff. Amalric felt a stab of disappointment. Could they be Christians? Behind the people a fountain splashed pleasantly, reminding Amalric of how thirsty the heat and fighting had made him.

One man detached himself from the group in the plaza and ran to throw himself facedown in the dust in front of Amalric's horse.

"Blessed be you who come in the name of our Seigneur!" he cried.

"Who are you?" Amalric demanded, pointing his longsword at the prostrate man's back, lest he turn out to be a killer disguised as a supplicant. But would a Saracen be speaking French?

The man raised his head. His face, marked by networks of tiny wrinkles, was brown as any Egyptian's, but his eyes were pale blue. When he opened his mouth to speak, Amalric saw that he had no front teeth.

"I am called Maurice, monseigneur. I come from the town of

Vailly. I was a foot soldier in John de Brienne's army, which came here I do not know how many years ago. When we lost the war at Mansura, the damned Mamelukes made a slave of me."

"Who are these others?" Amalric asked.

"They are Coptics—Egyptian Christians—who welcome you and beg your protection, monseigneur."

His disappointing suspicion confirmed, Amalric bowed curtly to the gray-bearded man in the black robe, the priest, who moved his right hand in a gesture of blessing.

"Where is the Egyptian army?" he asked Maurice.

"Gone, monseigneur. A few hours ago they withdrew up the Nile. The authorities here—of whom my master was one—became frightened. They thought the army was abandoning them. They set fire to the arsenal, the granaries, and the bazaars, and they rode away—so swiftly that I was able to hide and stay behind. Everyone except these Christians fled with the garrison. They were afraid for their lives."

As well they should have been, thought Amalric.

Then a vast relief swept over him. Slowly he sheathed his sword and flexed the arm at last freed from that great weight. No ambush. No fight at all. The city is ours. Mine. Thank Saint Dominic!

"Damietta is yours, monseigneur," old Maurice echoed his thought, throwing his arms wide. He began laughing and sobbing all at once, tears streaking the wrinkled face. "Forgive me, monseigneur. You are the first Frenchman I have talked to since I was captured so long ago."

It occurred to Amalric that it could be useful to have a man in his service who had lived among the Egyptians for many years. Louis, after all, had de Vency and the Templars to interpret for him. One never knew when discreet communication with the enemy might be necessary.

He climbed down from his horse and beckoned to d'Etampes.

"Secure that mosque. And send a party to set my banner in the highest tower of the city, where the King and our army can see it."

In a moment, Amalric was alone with Maurice.

"Master Maurice, you may stand up. Can you speak the Saracen tongue?"

"I can," said Maurice as he slowly and shakily got to his feet. "My master put me in command of all his house slaves, because I had been a soldier. To do my work, I had to speak to them.

Tell me, monseigneur, have you come with an army great enough to conquer all of Egypt?''

"That is our aim, God willing," said Amalric piously.

"And how many are you, monseigneur?"

Amalric shrugged. "One cannot be exact. We lose some men and gain others every day. But I would say we are nearly six thousand knights and ten thousand men on foot.''

Maurice clapped his hands and laughed. "A mighty army! God be praised! No wonder the Turks fled. Are you the leader of this great crusade, monseigneur?''

"I am Amalric, Count de Gobignon. He who leads us is the King of France.''

"I suppose the great Philippe Auguste, who was King when I left France, does not still live?''

"Alas, no," said Amalric, making himself look grave. "Our King now is his grandson. As it happens, I, too, am a grandson of Philippe Auguste, on my mother's side." Maurice looked awed, and Amalric was gratified.

"This King is a rather different piece of work from Philippe Auguste," Amalric went on. "I fear you will be sorry to learn more of him. He is a friend to heretics.''

Maurice looked shocked. "To heretics? A crusading King? How is that possible?''

D'Etampes was coming back from the mosque now.

"I cannot explain more here and now, Master Maurice. I will tell you about this King when we are able to speak in private.'' Amalric turned to d'Etampes. "See that this good old crusader is treated with high honor, Sire Guy. I want you personally to escort him back to our camp. And then you can carry my compliments to the King. Say to him that it is safe to enter the city.''

Maurice of Vailly went back to the little group of Christians around their priest to tell them about his conversation with Amalric. As he did so, Amalric called d'Etampes back.

"Keep that man under your eye at all times, Sire Guy. Make sure he speaks to no one at our camp except you and me.''

D'Etampes saluted and rode off to get a horse for the old man.

Now, thought Amalric, to find the biggest mansion in the city, before the rest arrive. That is the least I deserve for taking this risk.

XXII

ROLAND STOOD WITH THE KING AND A GROUP OF BARONS AND knights on the steps of what had been, a week ago, the palace of the governor of Damietta. It was a rambling, white-walled three-story building with bright blue and yellow tile borders around its arched doorways and spacious windows. A high wall surrounded it, and within its confines were gardens and fountains. From the steps leading to the main doorway of the palace Roland studied the intricate beauty of the city's blue-domed chief mosque across the plaza.

Louis's outposts farther up the Nile had announced the coming this morning of two envoys of the Sultan, and now Roland's attention shifted abruptly from the mosque. The envoys were entering the palace courtyard.

As far as he could tell, the Sultan's emissaries rode unarmed. They wore yellow turbans, long green robes, billowing red trousers, and leather boots with pointed toes. A third man in a plain, dark robe, evidently a groom, rode behind them. He took the three horses and stood to one side. Roland observed that the ambassadors were tall, light-skinned men whose features looked more European than Turkish.

"They must be Mamelukes," he said.

Raoul de Coucy, standing beside him, said, "I have heard that word before, but I do not know what it means."

"It means 'white slave.' The Turks buy boys from Russia and farther east and train them as warriors. They are the personal slaves of the Sultan and the backbone of his army."

"What about that one?" said de Coucy, nodding his head at the groom. "He is not white."

Indeed, the third member of the Egyptian party was strange-looking, Roland thought. He was tall, like the other two, but his skin was a dark brown. His cheekbones stuck out sharply, and the inner corners of his eyes slanted downward toward a flat nose. But although most people of the East Roland had seen had black hair and brown eyes, this man's mustache was red, and

294

one of his eyes was blue. The other eye was an opaque white, probably, Roland decided, from the cut of a sword.

"Perhaps he is a Tartar," Roland answered de Coucy. "I am told they make Mamelukes of Tartars, too." He turned his attention to the envoys, who bowed ceremoniously to the King. One spoke a fulsome greeting in Arabic. They are not lacking in courtesy, Roland thought.

The emissary drew a scroll from the embroidered shawl that tied his robe at the waist and held it out. Louis beckoned him to approach, and Roland tensed himself. He is too trusting. What if there were a dagger hidden in that scroll?

The King took the scroll and broke the seal as the Mameluke, bowing repeatedly, backed down the steps. Louis glanced at the message and beckoned Roland.

"Can you read this?"

Roland examined the heavy parchment. It bore the seal of Sultan As-Salih Ayub of Cairo and his signature in thick, black strokes at the bottom. Roland quickly scanned the flowing Arabic script, reading from right to left. A chill of excitement rippled through him.

He turned to Louis. "We have won, sire. It is an offer of peace."

Louis looked surprised and troubled. "Read it aloud."

Sentence by sentence, Roland translated the flowery Arabic. After complaining at length about the French invasion of Egypt, the Sultan gave his own version of events leading up to the seizure of Jerusalem by his general, Baibars the Panther, five years ago. Then Roland came to the heart of the message:

"Leave our city of Damietta whole and in peace, O King of the Franks, sail away from our river Nile, and you shall gain all that you seek. We will restore Jerusalem to you, as well as Bethlehem, Nazareth, and Galilee. We will do this because Allah loves peace above all."

Roland was swept by a joy so powerful his hands were trembling by the time he finished reading. The Sultan truly was offering everything they had come for—all the holy places of Palestine. There need be no more fighting.

Louis could return to France. He would be safe. And the kingdom would be safe.

And I will live, too, Roland thought wonderingly. Nicolette and I can be together, and we shall find some way to deal with Amalric.

Louis took the scroll from his hand, calling Roland back to the present. The crowd had grown, he now saw, since he started reading. Knights jostled one another within the courtyard's brightly painted plaster walls. Roland could see some Egyptian men, inhabitants of Damietta, staring in through the gateway. They had come back to their homes in the week since the capture of the city, having decided the crusaders would not massacre them. The Mameluke groom was strolling about the courtyard, cocking his one good eye at the knights and their weapons and at the King himself.

After a moment of hesitation Louis said, "Sire Roland, tell the envoys I must discuss this with my counselors. Make them comfortable." Turning, he reentered the palace, followed by his brothers Charles and Robert and the other great barons.

Raoul de Coucy gripped Roland's arm. "I may be back home with my wife in a month," he said with a delighted grin. He hurried off to join the King's council.

Roland felt his joy replaced by unease. He had not seen an answering eagerness in Louis's face. The Sultan's offer, of course, had to be discussed. They must make sure it was not a trick. And there would be arrangements and guarantees to settle.

Still, Louis should have shown some pleasure.

Did he want to go on fighting?

Roland determined to go in after Louis and speak for peace, if peace needed a spokesman.

He delivered the King's response to the Mamelukes, who bowed and seated themselves cross-legged on the tiles. Politely but firmly they refused his offer of food and drink. Roland understood. They would not accept hospitality from an enemy. So courteous-seeming were they it was hard to think of them as enemies. Yet there was a strangeness in their calm that made Roland uneasy as he turned his back on them.

The audience hall of the palace was a large circular room, its vaulted ceiling held up by stone columns. Since Islam forbade the depicting of natural objects, the walls were decorated with mosaics in patterns so exquisitely detailed it hurt Roland's eyes to look long at them. Sunlight slanted down from skylights, and whatever other illumination was needed was supplied by hanging oil lamps of filigreed brass.

When Louis first took over the palace, he had a table and many chairs moved into the hall. Now he sat in the chair with the tallest back, and the barons formed a circle around the table.

Before them was spread a map of Egypt painted on a large parchment sheet. Tiles dug out of the wall rested on the four corners of the map to keep it from rolling up.

"It is only fifty leagues to Cairo," Robert d'Artois, Louis's eldest brother, was saying as Roland entered. "God has delivered the land of Egypt into our hands."

Half the barons, it soon became apparent to Roland, wanted to march on Cairo. To them the Sultan's willingness to bargain was at best a sign of weakness, and more probably he had no intention of fulfilling his promise.

Furthermore, though the avowed purpose of the crusade was to secure the holy places, these men, Roland saw, wanted more. They wanted to seize more land, to crush the Muslims.

Amalric put the views of these barons in a sentence: "Infidels are to be fought, sire, not bargained with."

As one after the other spoke, Roland's alarm grew greater. Not permitted to speak unless consulted, he struggled to contain himself.

One who urged acceptance of the Sultan's offer was William de Sennac, grand master of the Knights Templar, Guido's superior. "The fifty leagues between here and Cairo are as crowded with natural and human enemies as Hell is filled with devils," the gray-bearded Templar warned. "The Nile may flood at any time now. If we advance, we are almost certain to be mired and destroyed. If we remain pent up in this city, the summer heat and the diseases of Egypt will take many lives. It is sensible to march on Cairo only when we can be sure of being stronger than the Egyptians."

The grand master's views were echoed by the King's more cautious younger brother, Charles d'Anjou, by Raoul de Coucy, and by others.

The argument went on through the morning until the bell hung by monks in a minaret of Damietta's great mosque rang the hour of Sext, the middle of the day.

Then the King spoke. "Many lives hang on what I decide," Louis said. "It is my duty to listen to as many voices as possible. Sire Roland, you know much about the Saracens. What do you think of this offer?"

Roland felt as if his heart were swelling in his chest. Saint Michel, if ever I needed eloquence, I need it now.

He stepped forward to the table and looked at the faces around it. Amalric glared back. William de Sennac looked expectant. The King's face was unreadable. Lord, how do I reach him?

"I believe the knights of Islam are proud men," he began, "men of honor, who for the most part would rather die than break their word."

"So *we* have found them," agreed the Templar master.

Amalric snorted in disgust. "They are tricksters and thieves."

Roland felt his face grow hot, but he held his anger in check.

"Sire," he said, "I have talked with people who live here in Damietta, both Christian and Muslim. They all say that our victory here was an accident. Damietta could have held out against us for a year or more if a few officers of the city had not given way to panic when the Sultan's army withdrew. The Sultan has had thirty of Damietta's former officials strangled, I hear. So we should not think he is afraid of us or too weak to fight us."

"Are we to listen," Amalric sneered, "to rumors repeated by those who consort with infidels?"

Roland's left hand twitched, wanting to go for his saber.

"I would not put it as you do, Count," Louis said reasonably. "If one of our knights can learn from the people who live in this country, we should listen."

But then Louis turned from Roland, and Roland had a terrible feeling that he had not said enough.

Louis consulted others in the room. Roland was relieved to hear many agree that the next encounter with the Egyptians would not be so easy.

When he had listened to everyone, and some several times over, the King spoke. "I have been praying and thinking. It is true that it will weaken us to stay here in Damietta while the Nile is in flood. Not only the bodies of our men but their souls are in peril. We have been here only a week, and already I could not throw a stone in any direction from this palace without hitting a brothel."

Roland joined in the general laughter.

Louis cut it short by staring about him sternly. He had not meant it as a joke.

Louis spoke on in the silence that followed his angry look. "It is also true that we cannot expect another easy victory the next time we meet the Egyptians—though I would prefer to call the capture of Damietta a miracle and thank God that so few lives were lost, rather than say it was an accident."

Roland felt a chill. That was aimed at him.

Louis wiped the sweat from his forehead with the sleeve of his surcoat. "But we will be much stronger by the time the flood

waters go down. My brother Alphonse is coming with reinforce-
ments. We will await him, holding Damietta, and work at building river galleys and stone-casters until we can march." He
paused and looked about him earnestly.

Roland was in despair. The war was going to continue.

Louis spoke again. "I say this with a heavy heart, because it
means many good men must die. But they die for the faith, and
our Seigneur will gather them to His bosom. We do not *want* an
easy peace. Count Amalric, you said just now that the infidel
must be fought, not bargained with. I would say, rather, that the
infidel must be fought *first*, then bargained with. We must strike
such a blow that they will never dare threaten Jerusalem again.
Otherwise, no treaty we make with them will be secure."

Louis stood up and turned to Roland, who felt as if he were in
mourning. Louis's head was high and his face was flushed,
Roland saw. His Jerusalem look. God help us all.

"Tell the envoys," Louis said, "we will trade a city for
Jerusalem, but not Damietta. Tell them, when we take Cairo we
will trade *it* for Jerusalem."

Roland closed his eyes. He felt overwhelmed by a sense of
doom.

But the barons shouted their approval. All the men in the hall
were on their feet now. And apart from the grand master of the
Templars, who looked downcast, even those who had favored
accepting the Sultan's proposal glowed with enthusiasm. They
believe in him, Roland thought.

I love him. I would die for him. But I am sure he is wrong,
and the price will be terrible.

Amalric brought his fist down on the map of Egypt and
roared, "On to Cairo!" A tile fell from the table and smashed on
the floor.

Robert d'Artois echoed, "On to Cairo!"

The barons took it up, chanting, stamping their feet and
shaking their fists, while Louis stood in their midst, silent, his
hands clasped and his head bowed in prayer.

When Roland returned to the Mamelukes in the courtyard,
they were standing, their faces grave. They might not understand
French, but there was no mistaking the shouts coming from
within. Their groom held the reins of their horses, his one blue
eye bright with amusement. Amusement? Roland wondered.
Why does this man take pleasure in his embassy's failure?

Roland wanted to soften the wording of the King's reply, but to do so would be to falsify it. In Arabic he said, "My lord the King says he will trade a city for Jerusalem. However, the city will not be Damietta, but Cairo."

The tall, one-eyed groom laughed aloud. He let go the horses of the two envoys and leaped into the saddle of his own Arabian charger. He sat easily, not bothering to hold the reins. The Mamelukes mounted and looked at him expectantly.

"Our Sultan's letter said that Allah loves peace above all," said the one-eyed Tartar in a deep voice, his Arabic strangely accented. "It is not so. Islam is the faith of warriors."

He looked past Roland. He raised his hand in salute to someone there. Roland turned and saw King Louis on the steps of the palace. Here, sire, here is your enemy. Clever, resolute, fearless.

The Tartar said, "Say to the King of the Franks I shall meet him again, at the place of victory." With those words he wheeled his mount, using the pressure of his legs to guide it.

Awed, Roland felt more certain than ever that the war would be a calamity. Whoever this Tartar was, Roland had never encountered a more intimidating man.

The three envoys rode through the gateway of the palace. Roland followed them on foot. They galloped across the plaza, past the blue-domed mosque, which had been consecrated to the Virgin; it was now a Christian cathedral. The Tartar let out a war cry that made Roland shiver—a high, weird scream like the call of a great bird of prey. Long after the hoofbeats of the Mamelukes had died away, the cry seemed to hang in the air.

Roland stood staring at the dust cloud the three riders left behind. He whispered to himself the Arabic word for victory.

"Mansura."

XXIII

HEAT AND WEARINESS WEIGHED ON ROLAND AS HE WALKED THROUGH the crusader camp to the King's tent. He stopped as his path came to the river's edge. The tents of the crusaders stretched northward along the bank. Their once bright colors were faded to a muddy gray-brown after the months of campaigning, and the camp looked like a field of rust-colored mushrooms that had sprung out of the dampness of the Nile Delta. Upstream were the pathetic remains of the bridge of boats the crusaders had tried so desperately to build. Now there was nothing except a few blackened ribs of galleys protruding grotesquely above the water.

He watched the brown Nile flow, over a thousand feet wide here, oblivious to the crusaders. Across the river the yellow brick walls of Mansura curved in and out along the bank. In this flat country they looked as formidable as high mountains. Sturdy, square towers rose at intervals along the walls. To the north and east of the city Roland could see rich green fields where the Egyptian peasants, the *fellahin*, worked on as usual, ignoring the invaders across the river and supplying Mansura with all the provender it needed.

Could this truly be January? How amazing that crops here never stopped growing. The sun was as hot as August in Languedoc.

He slapped at the flies that kept settling on his face, drawn by his sweat.

It is only fifty leagues to Cairo, he could hear Robert d'Artois saying just after they took Damietta in June of twelve hundred and forty-nine—six months ago. It has taken us that long to cover half of those fifty leagues. And now they have stopped us at Mansura. A month now in this one spot.

Mansura—victory. Just as well I have not told anyone what that name means.

He came to the King's yellow and blue tent, and the two equerries on guard saluted him. He went in, grateful for the cool shade, and bowed to the King. Louis gestured him to a cushion.

The King lay, exhausted and ill, on a Turkish divan brought by river galley from Damietta. Sweat plastered his long blond hair to his brow. His eyes were a sickly pink, the lids edged with red, symptoms of an affliction that ran through the whole crusader host. Some men, Roland knew, had already gone blind from it. A small Egyptian boy fanned flies away from Louis.

"I had heard the Saracens practice witchcraft, but until I saw that fire weapon destroy our bridge today I did not believe it." The King spoke with almost no voice, feebly, sadly.

"It is not quite witchcraft, sire," Roland said. "It is a work of alchemy."

"Alchemy?" Louis asked. "What do you know of it, de Vency?"

"It is a weapon devised by the Greeks of Constantinople,"

Roland said, "a mixture of oils and other substances. The exact formula is secret. It burns hotter than ordinary fire, sticks to whatever it touches, and cannot be put out. I saw it demonstrated once at the Emperor's court."

Louis looked surprised. "You mean Frederic uses this? I never heard that."

Roland shook his head, recalling how Greek fire had shocked even the German ruler of the Holy Roman Empire, a man with neither fears nor scruples.

"He will never use it, sire. Too destructive, he says."

"How true!" said Louis, clenching his fist. "And though this Greek fire be not the work of witches, it still must surely be inspired by the Devil. I think of our poor fellows burned to death on the bridge this morning, and I cannot stop crying. Did you see it? Even the water seemed to burn." He stopped and wiped tears from his inflamed eyes. "If only I could get at those heathen savages, get across this river and meet them man to man. If there were a man who could show me a way across this river, I would declare him Constable of France. I must end this war."

Roland felt a flash of resentment. Bitter words sprang to his lips: You could have ended it half a year ago! But it was too late for that now.

They were at the turning point, he knew. The Egyptians had brought all their strength to bear at Mansura. If Louis broke the Saracens here, he could drive on to Cairo and win. But with every passing day the Egyptians grew stronger and the crusaders weaker. If the enemy could hold Louis here long enough, they would destroy him.

"We all want the war to end, sire," he said quietly.

"To think of my beloved Marguerite waiting there in Damietta, guarded by only a handful of knights," Louis said, his mind plainly having taking another turn. "Have I told you she is with child?" He smiled tenderly. "Even in the midst of war, life goes on."

And if you loved life more than your damned holy war, Roland thought, you would lead all of us out of here today.

Thinking how deep his own love of life ran reminded Roland of his last night with Nicolette. The next day—six months ago now—the crusaders had begun their march up the Nile. Amalric had already left, riding ahead with the vanguard, and Nicolette and Roland had decided that, just this once, they must break their pledge not to meet again in Outremer. These might be the last moments they would ever share with each other.

An Egyptian serving woman Nicolette had hired told her about a secret place among the islands of the Nile Delta. On a certain island, she said, were the ruins of a temple once dedicated to a great Goddess. Good Muslim that she was, she made a warding-off motion with her thumb and little finger. But despite her gesture she admitted to Nicolette that sometimes women of Damietta went to that island after dark to ask for aid in matters of love.

"The ruins are on high ground," she said. "You can see the city from there. It is easy to see if someone is coming. But the grasses around the temple are tall, and anyone within it is hidden from sight."

Roland and Nicolette took a small boat, which Roland poled through the reed-bordered canals that crisscrossed the delta marshes. The crescent moon was rising over the east as they set out. By the time they found the island the moon had traveled about a quarter of the way along its path through the night sky.

They made love against the base of a broken white column, under the huge, bright stars of Egypt. Later they felt the carvings in the marble with their fingertips, wondering what deeds of the Goddess the ancients had portrayed here.

"When you are gone, I will come to this place from time to time and think of you," said Nicolette. She took his hands in hers, and her grip on them was so tight it hurt.

"I will think of you wherever I am," he said.

"I am so frightened," she whispered.

"You will have us between you and the Turks," he said, trying to give her a reassurance he did not feel himself.

"It is you I am afraid for," she said. "If anything happens to you I will not care if the Turks kill me."

Now he tightened his own grip. "Listen well to me." A sudden anger against all the dying he had seen boiled within him. "I will not hear any talk from you of not caring. This readiness to die is a plague. Louis and his whole host have come out here prepared to die. Enough. I want to live, and I want you to live. I am going to stay alive and come back to you. And you are going to stay alive and wait for me. That is my vow to you, and I demand that you vow the same to me."

She pulled her hands free and her arms went around him again. "Yes, my darling, yes. In this place sacred to the Goddess, let us vow to each other to live."

* * *

"I have asked my counselors their advice," Louis said, breaking in on Roland's reverie. "My cousin, Count Amalric, proposed that we rebuild the bridge, using stone instead of wood."

"Stone is difficult to find in these marshlands, sire. And even if we could gather enough of it, the Saracens would bombard the workers with their Greek fire. We would lose a dozen men for every foot of bridge we built."

"The Count de Gobignon said we should force the *fellahin* to build the bridge. I declared that would be unworthy of Christian knights. Just as unworthy as this Greek fire would be, if we were to use it."

Except that Greek fire was invented by Christians, Roland thought. But he held his tongue.

Louis stood up. He led Roland out of the tent, and the afternoon sun struck Roland's head like a blast of the terrible Greek fire. They were on a narrow point of land between the Nile and a broad canal which joined it at Mansura. Here near the water greenery grew lush, but less than a league to the east or the west, Roland knew, there was only desert.

Beyond the tents Roland spied a line of huge wooden machines, like strange, long-necked beasts out of Africa, trundling on wooden wheels along the riverbank. Long lines of oxen were drawing them.

The stone-casters. Louis had sent for them a month ago, when the crusaders had reached Mansura. It had taken the engineers in Damietta this long to build and transport them here.

They were so big and powerful that at the sight of them Roland felt a new hope stirring within him. These great engines might turn the siege of Mansura—and thereby the crusade—in their favor.

"That is the only way we can strike at those devils now, with those," said Louis. "No, no bridge of stones. But we will hurl stones at them. Our machines, praise God, are bigger and more powerful than any the Egyptians have. With them we shall lay down a barrage so fierce that our men will be able to cross in boats."

"Our stone-casters, alas, do have a weakness, sire," Roland said. "They are made of wood."

And where in this marshland are we going to find enough ammunition for them? he wondered.

"True, and it will be late in the day before all six of them are in position," said Louis. "Tonight they may be terribly vulnera ble to attack. But again, my cousin Amalric had a suggestion. You, of all the knights in this camp, know most about the Saracens. That is why I sent for you. As Amalric proposed, you shall be in charge of the guard to protect our casters from enemy attack."

Roland felt a falling sensation in his stomach. Amalric had sentenced him to almost certain death. The Saracens were sure to attack.

"Sire, I shall do my best, but there is no protection against Greek fire."

Louis smiled imperturbably. "Be it God's will, we may destroy the enemy's fire-thrower this afternoon. If not, I will have our stone-casters sprinkled with water from the holy well of Saint Denis. If there is aught of the Devil's work about this Greek fire, that may help keep it off."

Roland felt a hot flush of anger rise to his cheeks. "That will do as much good as water from the river there."

Shocked at his own temerity, Roland cursed himself for his too quick tongue.

Louis looked surprised, then amused. He laughed.

"You men of Languedoc are too skeptical for your own good. Happy are we who believe in miracles."

"I will not fail you, sire," Roland promised. "But the Egyptians are all around us. An attack might come from anywhere."

Louis's smile faded. "You are overly fearful, messire. If the Saracens were minded to, they could have attacked our machines on the road from Damietta. They are less likely to attack now that the casters are safely in our camp."

"Then I would advise you to put the whole camp on alert, sire," Roland persisted, stung at having his courage questioned.

"I plan to launch a general attack tomorrow," Louis said, waving his hand irritably, "after the casters have done their work. I want the men well rested." He looked earnestly at Roland. "Sire Roland, I know Count Amalric must have suggested you out of ill will. I chose to follow his advice, however, because you *are* our best man for this task. I do not think you will be killed, but it is my duty to send men into peril of death. I will have my own men watching over you. If there is any treachery here, Amalric will pay."

"I understand, sire." He knew that if he argued anymore, he would be thought trying to shirk the responsibility.

But Roland could envision the vessels of Greek fire flying

across the river with a whistling roar. He could see the flaming liquid splash on those great wooden machines. And his body broke out in cold sweat.

Roland stared fixedly into the flame. The black ring painted around the hour-marked candle turned to gray liquid and ran down in waxen rivulets that hardened again, sullying the whiteness.

Time to visit my sentries again.

He stood up. The Nile dampness made his right shoulder ache. He stepped out of his little tent that stood on a hummock overlooking the line of casters. The stars above were snowflakes of white fire.

He felt somewhat reassured that the wooden walls and rows and rows of tents of the entire camp lay between the stone-casters and the Nile. He was pleased that he had talked Louis into having the casters dragged to the far side of the camp. Louis had ordered that the engines be grouped together for the night beyond the range of the enemy's fire-throwers. A detachment from the main camp, headed by Roland, would encircle the stone-casters, making a smaller camp to protect them.

It had been a grueling job, and Roland would have liked it better if they could have kept bombarding Mansura's walls all night, but they had run out of stones.

Still, it had been a fine feeling when they had scored a direct hit on a fire-thrower!

He smiled in the night, remembering. The thump as the counterweight smashed into the soft earth. The boulder, big as a wine cask, tumbling through the air above the river. It had seemed to fly ever so slowly. He had held his breath.

Then, at the very end of its descent, it appeared to speed up.

The Saracens never moved, perhaps paralyzed with fear.

The boulder had crashed down. Splinters of the Saracen machine flew in all directions.

Roland roared with delight, and the whole crusader camp had cheered.

Then vessels of Greek fire around the crushed machine had broken open, spilling their horrid contents, turning a troop of Egyptians into living torches.

That had made him think of Diane, and of Mont Ségur, and sorrow overcame triumph.

"Who comes?" a guard challenged him.

"The Sire de Vency."

The sergeant, one of the engineers who had built the stone-casters and were now operating them, saluted. "Still up, Sire Roland? You can rest easy now. It will be dawn in another few hours, and no infidel has dared approach our big girls." He looked affectionately up at the nearest of the huge engines. They all had names, Roland knew, Alix, Beatrice, and Iolanthe among them.

"These are the darkest hours," Roland said. "We have enemy territory on all sides. So keep a sharp watch." He eyed the line of torches, tied to high poles short distances apart, surrounding the casters. "Keep those torches burning and replace any that go out, so no one gets close without your seeing them. But remember, the light on our machines makes it hard to see into the darkness beyond."

The sergeant gestured to his men, standing with crossbows at the edge of the lighted area, and to the surviving seven of the ten men Roland had brought with him on the crusade.

"Any Saracen who tries to sneak up on us will be turned into a pincushion, messire. We can handle anything except that fire weapon of theirs. Thank Saint Genevieve, we destroyed it, and we are out of range now if they try to bring up another. In any case, I have set casks of river water near each machine."

"Water only spreads the Greek fire."

"True, but it thins out the stuff that burns and makes it easier to stamp out."

That is a good mind at work, Roland thought. This man's worth was as much in his ability to build as to fight.

A white-haired man appeared suddenly out of the blackness. He identified himself to a crossbowman and strolled toward Roland, his hand raised in greeting. Roland recognized him as Maurice, the old crusader Amalric had found in Damietta. He wore a purple tunic, as did most of Amalric's men. His belt was adorned with silver, and the scabbard of his dagger was set with colored stones. Amalric treats him well, Roland thought.

"I came to look at your magnificent stone-casters, monseigneur," Maurice said, his smile revealing shrunken gums. "They are far bigger than any we had in my day when we sieged this city. I wager we shall reduce Mansura to dust on the morrow."

"You should not be wandering around in the dark, old man," Roland said brusquely. "We lose a few men to the Bedouins every night."

Sorrow stabbed Roland as he thought of one of his own men, the second of his little company to die, his body discovered without a head outside Damietta.

"Yes, yes, the Sultan has promised them ten gold bezants for every Christian head," Maurice said. "A fortune. But the Bedouin has not been born who can sneak up on me, monseigneur. I have not stayed alive thirty years in this country without learning how to guard my back."

Roland eyed the old man with dislike. He wanted him gone. He was Amalric's man. Reason enough to distrust him.

And so fawning. He knows I am not a baron. Why does he keep calling me "monseigneur"?

Perhaps, though, I do him injustice. After all, it is not his fault that Amalric was the one to find him. And a man cannot be a slave for so long without learning to act like a dog.

Still, he could not resist speaking harshly. "We have no need of you here, Master Maurice. And go back to your quarters after you leave us. Else, if the Bedouins do not take your head, our sentries may shoot you by mistake."

"Yes, monseigneur," said Maurice, his blue eyes veiled. "Thank you and good night to you, monseigneur." He bowed and walked off, out of the ring of torchlight.

Roland stood with the sergeant a while longer. All seemed quiet enough, and he decided to go back to his tent.

"Saracens!"

The shrill cry came from the vicinity of the stone-caster at the other end of the row.

Then Roland heard the blood-chilling battle shrieks of the enemy. All night he had half expected this, that they would wait till now, just before dawn.

He drew his saber and ran toward the threatened spot. The sergeant pulled out his own two-handed sword and followed him.

The sentries had set up a wall of shields and were firing their crossbows out into the darkness. Two guards already lay dead, arrow-pierced, beside the man-high wooden wheel of the machine nearest Roland.

"Do not shoot unless you can see what you are shooting at," the sergeant shouted angrily. "Stay down behind your shields."

Roland peered beyond the torchlight. The Saracens' irregular skirmish line was only a few yards away when he finally saw them. They wore the dark, billowing robes of Bedouins, the wild desert tribesmen of Outremer. They were charging on foot. He felt a kind of helpless fury. There could be hundreds out there in the night, more than it would take to overwhelm his little force.

He turned to the sergeant. "Get help!"

But there was no time. The Bedouins threw themselves at the crusaders, shouting the names of their clans. The crossbowmen fell back to reload, while Roland, the sergeant, and a few other guards with swords held their ground.

Roland found himself dueling with a small, fox-faced man. He was quick and agile, forcing Roland back with feints of his scimitar. From somewhere behind Roland a lance darted at his opponent, who jumped back and vanished in the blackness.

As he braced himself to meet the next attacker, Roland asked himself what these Arabs were trying to do here, armed as they were with nothing but bows and scimitars. He could hear the main camp rousing themselves to come to the defense of the siege engines.

"Hell's fire!" he shouted. "A diversion!"

Even as it dawned on him, the first Greek-fire missile broke and splattered on the capstan of the machine at the opposite end of the line.

Suddenly scores of robed Egyptians were running into the lighted area around the machines. They were throwing pottery balls no bigger than a man's fist at the casters, and the balls broke and burst into flame where they struck. Nearly every guard had rushed to Roland's end, and the Saracens had overwhelmed the remaining few who had tried to resist them.

Now, along with the torchlight, there was firelight to see by.

In agony, Roland shouted again, "Get help!"

An arrow whistled out of the night and caught the sergeant in the chest. He fell facedown, that good mind extinguished more easily than these fires would ever be.

All around him Roland heard shouts, the cry for help being taken up in the camp. But it was all over. Each of the six machines was burning furiously in dozens of places.

No one had even touched the barrels of river water. And no one would. It was too late.

But he could not just stand there and watch. Even if he accomplished nothing he had to fight on.

He ran at one of the Egyptians, a bone-thin man in white robes who was calling upon Allah gleefully as he made ready to throw a ball of Greek fire. The man was not even carrying a sword. A dervish, one of the ecstatic Muslim holy men. Roland drove his saber into his heart.

As he died, the Egyptian flashed a white-toothed grin at Roland and smashed the fragile vessel on Roland's mailed chest. Roland screamed in pain and fear as the fire spread instantly over his tunic. The Egyptian, his hands burning, fell away, a beatific smile on his dead face.

I am going to die, Roland thought. Burned alive.

He dropped his saber and tore frantically at his tunic, but the flaming garment searing his chest would not come off.

He threw himself down on the sand and screamed as he felt the chain mail, almost red-hot, press into his flesh. He raised himself, and the fire flared up. Again he flattened himself, and forced himself to stay there despite the pain, beating out the tendrils of flame along his sides with his bare hands.

After a moment the pain was less. The fire was out.

He stood up, and the agony of his burns came back full force. He staggered a few steps, then looked up at the stone-casters. "Oh my God!" he cried.

The machines were frameworks of pure fire. Every stick, every timber, was ablaze. He almost wished the fire had killed him.

He fell to his knees, sobbing. He had failed his King and his comrades.

Who would have guessed the Turks could make Greek fire vessels small enough for a man to hold in his hand and throw like a rock? Even Emperor Frederic had not known that.

The orange flames shot into the sky, high as a cathedral steeple.

How many times had Diane told him death was but a release from the sufferings of life? At this moment he wanted to throw himself on the nearest fire and burn up with the casters he had failed to save. Burn as she had burned.

No, I can try to keep fighting. Then maybe the next Muslim will kill me.

He had dropped his saber when he threw himself down. Now, as he bent over to pick it up, his burnt skin creased, and the pain was so terrible he came near to screaming again. Clenching his teeth he picked up the saber and looked about for those demons in long robes.

But no Saracens were to be seen, except a few who lay on the ground, stabbed or arrow-struck, beside the Christian dead. The Egyptians had done their work well and had vanished into the night. From afar Roland heard cries of rejoicing, thousands of voices raised across the river in Mansura.

A hand gripped his arm. "My God, your whole chest is black How bad is it?" It was Guido, his bearded face lined in concern.

"It is the pain inside that is worst," Roland said. "I have lost us the battle. Maybe the war."

"Well, messire," another voice, full of contempt, broke in, "you seem to have done an excellent job of protecting our siege machines." Amalric de Gobignon stalked out of the darkness to gaze at Roland with haughty amusement. "Could you not at least have managed to get yourself killed?"

Guido swung around to stare at Amalric. "Count, this man is badly hurt. If you want to provoke a fight, I am at your service."

"You, Sire Templar, like this troubadour, have a way of turning up whenever calamity strikes. I wonder if you have some part in bringing it on."

"Just what do you mean, monseigneur?"

"I saw you at Béziers."

"You saw me do no wrong there, or you would have spoken of it before this," said Guido shortly, turning away.

Guido at Béziers? Surely I would have known if he had been there. The exchange made no sense to Roland.

Amalric was hoping I would be killed. And I, I swore to Nicolette I would stay alive and come back to her. And yet moments ago I wanted the Saracens to kill me. It *is* a disease, this yearning for death, and I can catch it as quickly as the next man.

Slowly Roland's knees buckled, and Guido held his arms and lowered him to the ground.

Roland looked up and saw Perrin standing over him.

Always there when I need him. But the fires are blazing up. And I must save Diane.

From a great distance, he heard Guido's voice say, "Get that hauberk off him, Perrin. We need to tend his burns."

I vow to your memory, burnt ones, that I will do whatever I can to put an end to such evils as this.

Who said that?

Perrin is hurt. Guido has brought him. We must help him. He is burned.

"Where is Diane?" Roland said. "She knows what to do for burns."

"Hush, master," said Perrin.

Roland's vision cleared, and he saw Amalric's face staring down at him, full of rage or astonishment, Roland could not distinguish.

I was delirious, he thought. I spoke of Diane in front of Amalric. Now he will be sure I had Hugues killed.

Perrin had his dagger out and was cutting away Roland's burned tunic and the lacings of his mail shirt. Another figure swam into Roland's ken. It was the King.

Roland struggled to rise.

"Stay as you are, Sire Roland," said Louis, "in God's name." His voice shook with grief. "Why did I not listen to you? You warned me this could happen."

Roland was weeping. "Sire, I know you can never forgive me, but—"

"Be still, Sire Roland," said Louis. "There is no blame in this for you. It is I who have been careless. I laid an impossible task on you."

"Sire," Amalric said, "an idiot could have seen that the first Bedouin attack was only a trick to draw the guards away. This fellow led his whole troop in the wrong direction. He is supposed to know so much about Saracens. I say he should be tried and punished."

Louis turned on Amalric. "How do you know all this, then, Count? About first attacks and second attacks? Were you here? And if you were, why were you not fighting?"

"My man Maurice, the crusader we liberated at Damietta, he saw it all, sire."

Maurice, Roland thought. He saw the Egyptians attack and went running gleefully to tell his master. Toothless old dog.

"The King should be punished first of all," said Louis in a dull voice, "for not having assigned more men to guard our machines." His tone changed, became brisker. "But do you know what this means, Amalric? The Egyptians were able to come at us from behind with their Greek fire in the night. There must be a place near here where the river can be forded. I say once more, if a man can find a way for me to cross this river and attack Mansura, I will make him Constable of France."

Perrin had cut all the lacings of Roland's hauberk and was about to pull the chain mail away from the burnt, blistered flesh. "Easy now, master," he said softly. Gently he began to lift the links of mail away from Roland's chest.

"Do it quickly, Perrin," Roland said, gritting his teeth.

Perrin pulled. In an instant the pain blazed up beyond Roland's bearing. Then he saw Diane and Nicolette standing together, smiling at him.

XXIV

THE SILVER WOLF'S HEAD GLISTENED, THE LANCE POINT GLOWED BLOOD-red in the firelight, the black charger's hooves shook the ground. Nicolette was right in Amalric's path. She was naked, tied to a stake, a shimmering ring of flame surrounding her. Roland struggled to reach her, crawling up an endless hill. Amalric was almost upon her, the lance aimed straight at her heart. Roland reached for his sword. His scabbard was empty. His body was all he had to stop Amalric. He threw himself in front of the black war-horse. Now the lance point was aimed at him. It struck him, pierced him.

"Master!"

Perrin was shaking his right shoulder. His tortured bones ached fiercely. Perrin was usually careful not to touch that shoulder. Something must have excited him.

"Is it an attack?" Roland's heart pounded fiercely, still in the thralldom of his terror for Nicolette. He felt the pain of the dream lance in his breast.

"No, master. The King has sent for you."

"What is the hour?"

"Past midnight, master. Dawn is still far off."

No peace in sleep, no peace waking, he thought. A melancholy had hung over him since the night the stone-casters burned. It was so deep now that he had to force himself to move.

The skin of his chest still hurt when touched, though it had had two months to heal. He wondered if Nicolette, back in Damietta, had heard about the loss of the siege machines. And if she had, how did she feel toward her troubadour now?

If only he had kept his guards spread out. If only he had been quicker to get help. If only he had tried harder to persuade the King to put more men on guard.

He cursed himself. We shall all die here in this damned Egyptian swamp because of me.

On his way to the King's tent he felt groggy. He had been sleeping for only a few hours. The night air was cold, as it always was in this desert country, but he wore only tunic, hose, and boots. Back home, the mountain passes would be blocked with snow this time of year.

Before the King's tent he descried, standing in the orange light of a big campfire, nearly two dozen figures wearing fur pellisons against the night's chill. Near the fire the Oriflamme hung, glistening gold like a dragon's skin. Roland saw figures coming out of the darkness from all directions, converging on the King's pavilion.

Louis stood bareheaded at the doorway of his tent. He had on a long white linen robe with a huge red cross sewn on the chest. To Roland he looked like a warrior monk. After months in Egypt Louis was even thinner than usual, and his sunburned skin was mottled red and white. He seemed elongated and fragile, like a statue of a Biblical king.

One of the friars who traveled with the King checked Roland's name off a list as he joined the semicircle of knights.

Shortly after Roland's arrival the friar reported that the men sent for were all present. Roland looked around the circle of firelight and saw that the men were important barons and knights close to the King. He noticed Robert d'Artois; William Longsword, the English earl; William de Sennac, grand master of the Knights Templar; and Raoul de Coucy.

Roland saw Guido Bruchesi standing near his superior. Guido waved, and Roland, feeling cheered to see him, waved back.

Louis beckoned to someone behind him. To Roland's surprise, Amalric de Gobignon emerged from the royal pavilion to stand beside the King. He, too, had grown leaner in Egypt, but he still seemed three times heavier than Louis. His face was the brown of a seasoned oak log, making his sun-bleached fair hair look almost white.

"Many of you have heard me say that I would make any man Constable of France if he could show me the way across the Nile," Louis began. "Behold now our new Constable of France."

Roland shut his eyes and forced himself to keep from groaning aloud. It was almost as if Amalric had succeeded in making himself King. Now he was commander of all the armies. His word final, his plans to be followed. No one could gainsay him.

Oh, Louis, Louis, how could you be such a trusting lamb? Amalric's hatred is not for me alone. Fear, not so much for himself, but for the army and the kingdom, flooded through Roland. Fear and hopelessness.

And anger. He almost deserves to lose his throne. I should never have come on this crusade.

The King said much in praise of Amalric, then asked him to explain how he had discovered a way across the Nile.

Amalric stepped forward with a confident smile. "You have all heard that the Sultan had many officers of the Egyptian garrison at Damietta strangled for abandoning the city. It happens that one of those executed was the former Saracen master of my man Maurice. A kinsman of Maurice's dead master holds high position in Mansura. Maurice slipped a message to him through the Saracen lines. The Saracen pigs are like us in one respect, they are loyal to family. As we hoped, this Egyptian Maurice wrote to wants to avenge himself on the Sultan. Today, before dawn, he will guide us to a place where it is shallow enough for men on horseback to cross the river. It is three leagues south of here. All of you present here have been chosen to be in the first troop of the army to go over." Amalric bowed graciously to the King.

Chosen? Who chose me? Roland wondered. Was it Amalric who selected me, as he suggested me to guard the casters? Roland remembered Amalric's face when he came out of his delirium after mentioning Diane. He wants me dead.

Then will this river crossing win us the victory we hope for?

No, thought Roland, his heart chilled by foreboding. Not if Amalric has devised this. He looked at de Gobignon, standing proudly beside Louis, his arms folded across his purple and gold tunic. Even more than he wants my death, Amalric wants to destroy the King. And Maurice, that gray bird of ill omen who appeared just before the burning of the casters. If he is in on this, there is surely doom in it.

But it may have been Louis who chose me.

In spite of his doubts, eagerness tingled through Roland's limbs. This could be my chance to redeem myself. If I were in the vanguard, if I fought well, if we took Mansura . . .

The disgrace of the burnt stone-casters would be erased.

He wanted to go. He wanted to believe that this fording of the river could lead to victory.

Then he remembered. Victory. *Mansura.*

Whose victory? Ours or theirs?

"Does any man need to know more?" Louis asked.

The men standing around the King shifted from one booted foot to another and looked at each other, their faces ruddy in the firelight. No one spoke. They were ready to go, Roland realized.

After three months of camping in the mud, they were dying for battle.

I cannot just allow my suspicions to go unvoiced, Roland thought. I owe it to Louis to speak up. It is all too easy.

But they would sneer at him, he knew. They wanted to fight. They wanted to hear nothing of doubts.

He could not bring himself to speak. The silence stretched on. He listened to the ancient Nile burbling past the camp, smelled its dank smell, heard the distant call of a Saracen guard across the river.

Are you a coward as well as a fool? he asked himself. Are you truly afraid to raise your voice in this company of great seigneurs? More men's lives could well be lost because of your silence. A cold breeze rustled the dry palm fronds overhead.

He took a deep breath. This was harder than riding out to face Saracen swordsmen. He stepped forward, out of the circle, moving closer to the fire. The ring of hard, bright faces, eager for battle, turned toward him.

"Sire," he said, his throat constricted, "what assurance do we have that this is not simply an ambush?"

He heard an irritated mutter run through the gathering of barons and knights.

Amalric glowered across the fire at Roland. "Do you think your King has not considered that? If you are afraid to come with us, by all means stay behind, messire. Tell me, have you written a song yet about your glorious defense of our stone-casters?" This brought a roar of laughter from the knights and barons, and Roland felt fire in his cheeks.

Louis stepped between Amalric and Roland, his white robe rustling. "Count, your baiting of this loyal knight distresses me. I am pleased with you tonight. Please do not do anything to mar my feeling. Remember, your appointment is not final until our army has successfully crossed the river."

Roland unclenched his fists, wishing the King had not intervened. If only I could challenge Amalric. If I could kill him it would rid Louis of a deadly danger and lift the burden of hatred that weighs ever on my heart.

He looked past the King into Amalric's eyes and knew that de Gobignon wanted to fight him, too. Amalric shrugged his shoulder, making his fur-trimmed cloak fall away from his arm and his sword.

Holding Amalric's eyes, Roland said, "With your permission, sire, I repeat my question. How do we know this is not a trap?"

Amalric answered, not addressing Roland, but speaking to the standing circle of barons and knights. "The renegade Egyptian tells us that the bulk of the Saracen army is encamped in the suburbs south of Mansura. We will be able to see them when we cross the river. If they show signs of being ready for us, we will know."

"I do not intend to send the greater part of the army across the river until I know it is safe," said Louis. "Led by Amalric and my good Robert"—he held out his hand and smiled affectionately at his tall young brother, Robert d'Artois—"you will cross as quickly as possible. A thousand mounted knights will follow you. After sunrise, when you have assembled across the river and scouted the countryside between the ford and Mansura, you will set up a defensive line at the ford to hold that end of the crossing. Then I will lead the rest of the army across."

The King raised a warning hand. "On no account are you to fight with the enemy until all our forces are across. When our army crosses, we will storm Mansura. We cannot hope to take the city from the Saracens unless we attack it with our entire strength at once." He smiled. "Today is Fat Tuesday. God willing, we shall hold carnival in Mansura."

"And then, on to Cairo!" Amalric shouted.

"On to Cairo!" the assembled knights shouted back.

A surprising feeling of hope came over Roland. A sudden attack like this might just do it. The bulk of the Sultan's army was facing them here. If they defeated these Egyptians, they could take Cairo.

He desperately wanted to believe that this river crossing would bring them victory, and that he could be part of it.

A great yearning for life seized him, and he saw Nicolette, glowing warm like the sun. They will not kill me. Not Amalric, not the whole Saracen army. Nicolette, I am going to get back to you. If I have to cut my way through all of Egypt to do it.

As Roland and his men caught up with the main body of crusaders, he felt pressing into his groin the emerald the size of a plum he had secreted in the pouch he wore under his clothing. He had taken the emerald from the turban of a Mameluke emir he had killed in a short, vicious sword fight on the outskirts of Mansura. These Mamelukes wore their fortunes into battle with them. He disliked robbing the dead, but this stone was enough to buy a castle. He could not leave it behind.

The crusaders, still nearly a thousand strong, were lined up in a marketplace before the main gate of Mansura. Above them rose the yellow walls of the city, built of bricks the size of a man's head. Huddled here at the base of the walls were the flat-roofed, gray houses of the Egyptians. Doubtless the people who lived in those houses had fled inside. As had the Egyptian army.

"God's bones!" exclaimed Perrin, beside him. "They have left the city gates open. We could ride right in."

Roland stared at the wooden double doors, reinforced with iron and about twelve feet tall. Thick as they were, they protected nothing, because they were swung wide, and between them the rutted roadway ran invitingly into Mansura.

This is impossible, Roland thought. Yes, we took the Saracens by surprise, but they cannot have lost their wits altogether. This is Damietta all over again—the easy victory, the open gate. But this gate has not been left ajar by accident.

This time I am sure it is a trap.

Roland was trembling with anger, not just at Amalric, but at all the men who were blindly following him. This was foolishness, Roland thought. Deadly foolishness. The King's plan had been ruined, and the vanguard was riding pell-mell to destruction.

As soon as they had crossed the ford and sighted the Egyptians, they had forgotten Louis's orders. Amalric and Robert d'Artois, without consulting the other barons, had led an immediate attack on the Saracen camp. In a furious battle they had slaughtered hundreds of Egyptians and driven the rest into the relative safety of the city.

Now Roland saw the leaders of his troop, still on horseback, gathered before the open gate. There was the silver wolf's head on Amalric's helmet, and next to it the gold coronet adorning the helmet of Count Robert, and there was William Longsword's blue shield with the six gold lions.

"Wait here," he said to Perrin. "I want to hear what they are saying." He gave Alezan a nudge with his knees and walked the horse over to where the leaders were gathered.

Amalric was addressing Robert d'Artois. As Roland rode up to them, Robert removed his coronet-crested helmet, and his hair, bright blond like that of his brother the King, hung free to his shoulders.

"Monseigneur Robert," Amalric said, "a greater victory than Damietta awaits us. The Saracens are routed and have fled into the city, so panicked that they did not even close the gate. We can drive the Egyptians out of Mansura and capture the city. Now is not the time to pause."

Amalric was breathing like a war-horse after a long gallop. His sun-browned face was deeply flushed. His surcoat and that of his charger were splashed with blood. Blood dripped from the double-bladed battle-ax he held in a mailed hand. He is a happy man, Roland thought. He enjoys killing as much as I loathe it.

"Now you want to enter the city, Count Amalric?" William de Sennac spoke up. "That is sheerest folly. Have you not disobeyed the King's orders enough for one day?" The Templar grand master's white beard fell almost to the red cross on the chest of his surcoat. His prominent, hooked nose gave him the face of an eagle, and he glared at Amalric with an eagle's anger.

"The King is not here to see the situation," said Amalric brusquely. "The King's brother is here, and he sees that the orders must be changed."

William Longsword, brown mustache bristling, said, "I have ridden this far with you, count, but it is one thing to attack when we have surprised the enemy and have a clear field. It is another to go into a city we know nothing about, when the enemy expects us. If we ride in there, I predict we shall not ride out again."

Roland was sure the earl was right. He remembered street fighting in Florence, during the years when he had served Emperor Frederic—the raids, the ambushes and murders, the special alertness needed and the special dread you lived with always. Most of these knights had no idea what war in city streets was like.

Amalric said, "And *I* predict the Saracens will not defend the town. They will run away just as they did at Damietta."

Robert d'Artois said, "Whatever you others decide, I shall not hold back from the enemy. I shall chase them all the way to Cairo."

De Sennac said, "We are greatly outnumbered."

"The Devil we are!" Amalric snapped. "The King and the rest of the army are on their way across the river right now." He pointed southward along the riverbank.

Roland looked back. But from here at the city wall it was two leagues to the ford, and the view was obscured by the smoke of burning tents and houses, the devastation where the crusader vanguard had passed. If the army was crossing, neither Amalric nor he nor anyone else here could see it.

"Then let us wait for the King," said Longsword.

"No need to," said Amalric. "Now that we have got the Egyptians on the run, we must take the city by storm. If we wait we shall give them a chance to regroup. And they might risk trying to block that gateway.''

Roland stared at the silent gateway. They will not block it, he thought. They want us to go in. They are waiting for us in there. Waiting. He shuddered.

"Let us go forward," Amalric urged. "Now."

Must I go, too? Roland asked himself. And lead Perrin and the others into almost certain death?

"The King's orders are to stand fast!" Roland shouted, thrusting his voice into the midst of the leaders. They turned and stared at him. Until now in their heated debate they had not noticed him nearby.

Glaring at Roland, Amalric said, "Any man who fails to follow me is naught but a crop-tailed coward.''

"Amen to that!'' said Robert d'Artois fiercely. His face, like Louis's but broader, was as full of disdain for Roland as Amalric's.

William Longsword said, "I have warned against this, but let no man say, count, that I or my English knights feared to set our feet anywhere that *you* would go."

He would rather die, thought Roland, and take all his men to death with him, than let Amalric call him a coward. War makes men mad.

The grand master of the Knights Templar shook his silvery beard. "You give me no choice, monseigneurs. If the King's brother rides into disaster, the Templars must ride with him, but truly I doubt whether he or we will return."

"Follow along, then," said Amalric with a triumphant smile.

"Forward!" shouted Robert d'Artois, his cheeks bright red, planting his gold-crowned helmet firmly on his head. "For God and the Sepulcher!"

Roland turned his horse and rode back to his little company without another word.

Grief battered at his heart. He could already see the narrow streets of Mansura choked with the bodies of men. Hundreds of good men who did not deserve to die.

This is stupid. This is ruinous. And Amalric knows it. And de Sennac and Longsword know it, too. Even if Count Robert does not. Oh, God, if only Louis would come riding up and stop them. If only he were here, and not two leagues away.

And what about me? What about Perrin and Martin and the others? Must we go into that deathtrap? Do we have no choice?

If I refuse to go, surely Amalric will charge me and my men

with disobedience in the face of the enemy. With desertion. If he survives, and if I do.

But he and Count Robert are the ones who are disobeying. Disobeying the King. But I have to obey *them*, do I not?

To the Devil with obedience! It is *my* life. And Perrin's, and the rest of them. I promised Nicolette I would preserve my life.

But the King's brother is going.

Roland looked back and saw the little group of leaders trotting toward the gate, swords held high. Count Robert's gold coronet led the way. Roland caught a glimpse of the Templar master's white mantle beside the Count d'Artois.

I feel the same way de Sennac does. I cannot let the King's brother ride into such peril without going along to fight beside him. I cannot hang back when so many good men are going forward.

He saw Louis's eyes—grief-stricken, reproachful.

And I could not face the King if I stayed behind.

He shook his head. I must go, and I must take Perrin and Gautier and Horace and Martin and the rest of my good men with me. He looked at the gates hanging open in the yellow walls.

We are like a herd of wild horses, he thought. Where the leader goes all the others must follow, even if it be over the edge of a cliff.

Amalric! he thought with sudden rage. Always Amalric! A black fury blotted out his sight of the gate of Mansura and the crusaders riding bravely and foolishly through it. Again and again Amalric rises up to strike down those I love.

If I get out of this, I will kill him. He will not live to get back to France. I swear it.

XXV

As He rode down the narrow street, sunlight suddenly struck Roland's face, dazzling him. He looked up and saw that the sun was directly overhead. It is noon, he thought. We have been struggling and dying in this accursed city since early morning.

He rode the trembling Alezan at a walk around a turning. He found himself facing a white plaster wall. A blind alley. He had no one to blame but himself. He was the first in line.

Something hit his mail-covered neck hard and fell to the ground. He saw a dagger gleaming under Alezan's hooves.

Then a heavy stone hit his helmet and bounced off, stunning him slightly. Alezan tossed his head, rolling terrified eyes at Roland through the holes in his steel chauffron. More rocks fell on them.

Roland looked up and saw Egyptians standing on the rooftops on three sides of him. Men with rage-contorted faces, women in long robes, children with slings. They screamed curses. Not warriors, just people of the town. They stood on the roof and hurled rocks, unafraid, knowing his sword could not reach them.

Why the Devil did we not wait until we could bring archers into the city with us? Why was Amalric so eager to invade the city with such a small, poorly equipped force? Only a thousand of us, on horseback, with no archers. "Drive the Egyptians out of Mansura and capture the city," he had said. Drive the Egyptians out, when every Egyptian man, woman, and child in this city has become a warrior? Capture the city, when every street of the city is risen against us? How foolish.

Foolishness, or a plan?

Roland raised his shield, and the rocks clattered on it. He tried to back Alezan out of the alley. Perrin was just behind him. In the hours of stumbling, fighting, advancing, and backtracking though the labyrinth that was Mansura, Roland had seen three of his men killed. The others had gotten separated from him.

"Make way!" Perrin shouted. "This is a dead end." But the crush of riders and horseless knights was too great. Roland could move neither backward nor forward.

Roland saw a boy dart out of a doorway. Before he could shout a warning, the boy had slashed the hamstrings of a horse with a curving dagger. The horse collapsed, screaming. Another mounted knight swung his longsword and cut the boy down.

Roland managed to turn Alezan between the building walls that pressed on both sides. The unhorsed knight struggled free and, with a cry of anguish, cut his wounded destrier's throat. Now the street was blocked by a dead horse.

"Burn in Hell, Christian dogs!" It was a woman's shriek.

Roland looked up. A woman in black was holding a smoking pottery jar over her head. Boiling oil. If it hit him it would flow under his hauberk, burning him horribly and killing him, but not quickly enough. He dug his spurs into Alezan's sides as she tilted the pot.

The golden, steaming oil splashed down. It missed Roland and hit Alezan's flank.

Alezan gave a shrill scream, jumped over the dead horse, and galloped out of the alley, all his tremendous weight charging at full speed, knocking aside the men and horses blocking the way.

"My poor Alezan," Roland said when he had brought the chestnut stallion to a standstill in a quiet street. He dismounted and cut away a portion of his own surcoat, using it to wipe down the burnt and blistered hide.

Perrin rode out of the alley, his cheek bleeding from a gash.

"I was right behind you, master, but Alezan bolted like a rock shot from a stone-caster."

He scanned the rooftops while Roland comforted his horse.

Patting Alezan's neck, Roland said, "When this battle is over, I will keep you out of any more fighting. I will bring you back home to honorable retirement." He leaned against the horse's quivering side. "I swear it, Alezan." We at least go to war knowingly and willingly, he thought, but what right have we to inflict this suffering on these poor animals?

Roland mounted Alezan again and patted his neck. "I am going to get you out of here." Alezan was more of a hindrance than a help to Roland in this kind of fighting. A man on foot would be able to move much faster through these winding alleys and to find shelter in doorways from attackers overhead.

He resolutely turned Alezan's head away from the center of town and back toward the gate. If this be called retreat or even desertion, I care not. He beckoned Perrin to follow him.

"Do not worry," he said, at Perrin's anxious look. "I am not running away. I just want to get Alezan to safety. Then we shall come back on foot."

Perrin frowned as if he did not understand, but he shrugged and followed on his own horse.

Roland heard the clip-clop of slowly approaching hooves. After another hour of backtracking he and Perrin were now near the city gate. Roland could see some greenery thrusting above the blank, pink-brown walls that lined the street. There must be large houses with gardens in this quarter, he thought. He looked down the street toward the center of the city and saw a large troop of knights.

Leading them was Amalric de Gobignon.

Roland wanted to ride at Amalric and run him through on the spot with his saber. During the morning he had seen dozens of knights die, shot with bone-tipped arrows, stabbed with daggers, lanced with javelins, crushed by huge wooden beams, burned alive with flaming oil. And he himself had nearly been killed a dozen times. Far from taking the city by storm, the vanguard had been torn to bits. And it was all Amalric's doing.

For every hour of agony in this city, for every man he had seen die, he hated Amalric more. Hated him more than the Saracens who had been raining arrows and hot oil down on him.

Many of the knights following Amalric were wounded, and some were reeling in their saddles. Many more, having lost their horses, trudged along on foot. Amalric himself no longer wore the air of excitement and triumph Roland had seen this morning, when they had destroyed the Egyptian camp. The silver wolf's head on his helmet was intact, but the nasal bar was dented, and there was dried blood on his upper lip.

But his words rang out, shrill and cruel, echoing off the plastered walls. "Still trying to run from battle, troubadour? There is no safety outside the city now, you know. We are cut off."

Anger choked Roland. The man who had led them into this deathtrap dared to taunt him? He gripped his saber so hard his hand shook.

"What are you saying?" he snarled at Amalric.

Amalric's eyes bored into his. "I have had word from guards I posted outside the city. An entire army of Mamelukes has come up from Cairo."

Mamelukes—the city surrounded by a Mameluke army.

He remembered the calm, competent Saracen officers who had brought the Sultan's letter to King Louis at Damietta, and their strange, one-eyed servant. All these months he had awaited an attack by the Mamelukes as a condemned man awaits the executioner's sword. And now, an army of the Sultan's finest, his personal slave-soldiers, had come to join the battle.

And Amalric had gotten the vanguard trapped here in this city.

"And what does the great Constable of France propose to do now?" he said cuttingly.

Amalric held up a hand. "We can take up our quarrel later. The Mamelukes have cut our army in two on this side of the river, coming between those at the ford and those in the city. We hold the south gate against them, but the city itself has turned into a slaughtering pen for us."

So, you admit it, thought Roland. If we get out of this alive you will face the King's justice for this. Or my sword.

"Why are you riding to the gate if the Mamelukes are outside?"

"It is the only thing we can do. If we remain in the city, we shall be destroyed. I intend to try to break out through the gate. The Mamelukes will be fighting the King's army. They will have their backs to us. We men can dash by the Mamelukes before they realize it." He eyed Roland with cold hostility. "You can ride with us, if you like," he said grudgingly.

"You are most gracious," Roland said sarcastically.

I would rather kill him than follow him, Roland thought. But I will wait till we are out of here before I strike at him.

"Follow along, then," said Amalric, hefting his bloody battle-ax and spurring his black destrier up the street.

The same words he used to lead us into Mansura, Roland thought bitterly. He fell in behind Amalric's second in command, d'Etampes. Perrin rode directly behind them.

The street they rode down was wider and straighter than most in Mansura. The balconies and upper stories of the houses overhung the street, just as they did back in France, but here the roofs were flat or domed and the walls were of mud brick or stone rather than wood.

Amalric's company had to pick their way around dead horses and men. D'Etampes jabbed at the bodies of Egyptians with his lance, making sure they were dead.

Where are our other leaders? Roland wondered as they rode in silence. He was about to ask Amalric how Robert d'Artois, William Longsword, and the Templar grand master had fared, when the Count held up a hand.

"Did you see, d'Etampes? A movement on a housetop. They are lying in wait for us up ahead."

Roland had seen nothing, but d'Etampes said, "It may take us the rest of the day to find another way to the gate."

"All ways are equally perilous," said Amalric. "Perhaps we can fight through here." He pointed to a heavy gate of wrought iron. It hung open, and beyond was a spacious courtyard paved with red and white tiles. In its center a fountain was flowing.

"De Vency, take a party and climb to the roof of that house," Amalric said. "We must see how many are up ahead, and how they are deployed. Perhaps we can even launch an attack across the rooftops. D'Etampes, hold here. Some of you go with the troubadour.'' His casual gesture included Perrin and three other mounted knights.

Roland felt a chill across his shoulders as he rode, saber drawn, into the courtyard. He had seen too many men die today, attacked from some unexpected direction, and the swirling red pattern on these tiles reminded him of spilled blood. The splashing of the fountain, he thought, could mask noises made by Egyptians in ambush. He looked about him carefully. This was a rich man's mansion. Shrubs bearing thick green leaves stood on all sides, and two tall date palms towered over the flat roof.

He had just time to note these things when something smashed against the side of his head. Flashing light and blackness alternated before his eyes. Alezan sprang forward under him. He heard the whoops of Egyptians. He clung to his saddle desperately as his grip weakened and dizziness made him reel. A rock. It must have been a rock from above. He struck out wildly with his saber.

A weight hit him from behind, and a man's bony forearm nearly crushed his windpipe. Rage and terror gave him strength, and he fought back, struggling to break loose. He felt many hands on him. One enemy had a grip on his saber arm and was twisting it. Pain shot through his right shoulder as his shield was jerked from his arm. He felt a sharp blow against his back, then heard a metallic snap. A knife, he sensed, had broken on his mail shirt.

Alezan, trumpeting anger and fear, galloped this way and that, trying to escape the figures that swarmed all around them.

It was here, on the roof of this house, that Amalric spotted the ambush, Roland realized. Not up the street. He saw them waiting in here, and he sent us right to them.

Rage flooded his body with new power, and he lashed out right and left at his attackers.

One of the knights who had come in with Roland galloped out. Two other men with their horses were down beside the fountain, their blood trickling in dark rivulets across the red and white of the tiles.

He threw away other men's lives to get me killed.

Frantically Roland thrust with his arms and jabbed Alezan with his spurs, furious to break loose and go after Amalric. Striking any more Egyptians hardly mattered to him at all.

Perrin, still on his horse, was at the gateway. "This way, master! This way!'' he shouted again and again.

"Get out of here, Perrin!" he roared.

The Egyptians kept hurling themselves upon him, from above and from all sides. They clung to Alezan. They stabbed at Roland and the horse with knives, and Alezan screamed in pain. My poor horse, Roland thought, my poor horse.

"God! Help me!" he cried wildly.

Perrin rode, clattering over the tiles, to Roland's side, swinging his longsword with both hands. He slashed at the man on Roland's back, and Roland felt his attacker fall away.

A huge earthenware jar hurtled down from the roof and crashed on Perrin's head. The jongleur's sword fell from his hand, and he slid from the saddle. Roland, fighting for his own life, was nevertheless agonizingly aware of the shrieking Egyptians surrounding Perrin and his horse. Roland saw a knife flash and blood spout into the dust-laden air. He heard a dreadful, nonhuman scream.

Alezan reared up on his hind legs and kicked at the Saracens. One of them flew into a corner of the courtyard to lie crumpled and still. Roland clung with his right hand to the reins, almost pulled from the saddle as another Egyptian sprang upon his back.

Rocks pelted Roland from the rooftop, hurting him, knocking him from side to side.

I am not leaving here without Perrin. I will die first.

Something struck him on the back of his head, and he seemed to be falling into a black whirlpool. He was conscious enough to feel the impact of his face hitting the tiles. After that, nothing.

His next sight was of blue sky, and his first feeling surprise. He was still alive. He lay flat on his back. He raised his head to look around, and from the lightness of his head knew he was no longer wearing his helmet.

A bare brown foot came down on his face and stamped his head against the tile. His cheekbone and jaw throbbed on the left side. He reached up to feel his nose, to find out if it was broken. A sword point jabbed his throat, and he dropped his hand.

I must brace myself to die, he thought. In an instant they will cut my throat.

A pang of sadness struck at his heart as he thought that never again would he see Nicolette.

Diane, if there is a life beyond death, I am joining you.

Everywhere around him he heard excited voices talking in Arabic. "I say the big red one is for my master. This is his house."

"Your master is a dung-eating coward who ran off and left us to fight the Franks."

"It is foolish to fight over it. By the time your master comes back, the horse would be rotten."

Roland's body trembled as he raised his head again. He expected at any moment to feel the sword driven into his throat. But this time they let him look. He saw brown legs, bare feet, the hems of short robes, and the fallen bodies of horses.

"Alezan!" he cried.

He could see now that there were four horses lying in the courtyard, and the biggest, the nearest to him, had a familiar chestnut coat. Blood was oozing from countless stab wounds. The long, broad back seemed motionless. He could not see the flanks rising and falling. Cold with dread, he raised his head a little higher.

Then he screamed.

From a huge slash in Alezan's throat a pool of blood was spreading rapidly over the muddy tiles.

"Oh, God, no!" Roland shouted, and fell back to the pavement in despair.

Alezan, my friend, I loved you. And you loved me. You saved my life a dozen times. And I brought you here to die in agony.

"Does he lament for his horse?" said one of the Egyptians curiously. "Or for his friends?"

Another shock went through Roland. Not Perrin, not him, too. Oh, dear Heaven, if it be so, give me the strength to hurl myself on these men's swords.

"Perrin!" His voice was shrill with dread.

"I live, master." The response came, tight with pain, from another part of the courtyard, beyond the dead horses.

Roland uttered a groan of relief.

"Why do we spare these two Frankish dogs?" an Egyptian voice said. "We should have killed them and kept their horses alive. The Mamelukes pay well for the great Frankish horses."

A voice directly above Roland said, "That reddish-colored horse, the one *this* was riding upon, killed my cousin Jamal. Its meat will feed Jamal's children, at least."

Roland lifted his head to look at the speaker, an Egyptian who stood over him holding Roland's saber to his throat. The man's face was dark brown and his ears stuck out on either side of his bald head. He was so small and thin the sword seemed as big and heavy as he was, but he held it unwaveringly. He glared at Roland.

Slowly and distinctly, Roland said in Arabic, "He who killed my horse, I pray that his father and mother and his grandparents and his wife and children may all sicken and die, and may his family and the very name of his family disappear from the earth. Hear me, God."

The small Egyptian looked back at him stonily and said, "Allah does not heed the prayers of Christians."

Another Egyptian said, "The Mamelukes want us to save any Franks we capture, so they can hold them for ransom."

"What is that to us?" said another. "We will not see any of the money. What do we care if some Mameluke gets richer? Kill the dog now. Silence his evil tongue."

"Yes, kill me," said Roland. A laugh forced itself up from his chest, a laugh that had nothing of mirth in it, only bitterness. "That I may haunt you ever after."

One of the Egyptians pointed two fingers of his right hand at him, a magical warding-off.

"So you managed to kill some Franks and capture some," said another voice, deeper and more commanding. "Good for you, my brave little men."

In spite of the warning prod of the saber point, Roland sat up to see who had spoken. It was an officer, his spiked helmet swathed in a bejeweled yellow turban. His accent was strange. Like many Mamelukes, he had pale skin.

Roland felt a stirring of hope in his breast. The Mamelukes might let him live.

But his heart sank again. When they find out I have no money to ransom Perrin and myself they will cut our throats.

The emerald! The gems on the Mameluke's turban reminded him of it. I do have something to give for ransom, if these common folk have not already stolen it. He moved his thighs and felt the lump at his crotch.

The men in the courtyard bowed to the Mameluke. He walked over to Roland, his red boots with their pointed toes falling lightly on the tiles.

"I heard you speak our tongue just now."

"Yes, *effendi,* I speak Arabic," Roland said courteously.

"Let him up," said the Mameluke. "Take this one and the other to the eunuch Sahil at the house of Lokman. You will be rewarded when you deliver them. All of you had better go with him. He is of great size, even for a Frank. But first take off their mail shirts and give them to me. Their armor will be my reward."

He smiled at Roland. "Does it not shame you to know that

you were overcome by a flock of servants? The rich men who lived in this quarter fled with their families. The servants they left behind helped defend the city better than many a warrior could."

The chests of the ragged Egyptians around the courtyard swelled at the praise.

"It does not shame me to be captured by servants," said Roland sadly. "These are honorable men who did their duty. Not like a great nobleman on my side who betrayed me."

His eye fell on his charger's bleeding body, and he turned away, filled with grief. At least my dear Alezan will feed poor children. Good-bye, Alezan, good-bye.

He raised his arms to let them strip off his hauberk.

It was late afternoon, after a long wearisome walk through twisted, dusty streets, when Roland stood before a mansion as big as a palace, surrounded by a high, blank white wall. Before it a crowd was gathered.

"Your mother couples with pigs!"

"We will hang your skin from our walls for banners!"

A small stone stung the back of Roland's head. He turned to see who had thrown it. Something soft and vile-smelling hit him on the cheek. He felt as if he might vomit. With the sleeve of his surcoat he wiped away the dung as best he could. The servants who had captured him hurried him past the shouting crowd.

If all these people are in the streets, Roland thought, the only Franks left in Mansura must be captive or dead.

Roland's escort was admitted through gates of black wrought iron by stolid Saracen guards in green turbans. Proud of their accomplishment in capturing a Frankish knight and his equerry, the little Egyptians swaggered as they marched Roland and Perrin into a large reception hall, its walls decorated with black and white mosaic tiles forming interlacing patterns, its floor of black marble that reflected Roland's image to him when he looked down at it.

The sides of the room were lined with columns of polished green stone supporting pointed arches. The ceiling was painted with gilt inscriptions, lines of Arabic poetry. Under the arches little clusters of turbaned Egyptians stood talking excitedly. They might be the leading citizens of Mansura, Roland thought. They grew quiet when Roland and Perrin entered, and watched, eyes alight with triumph, as the two captives were led across the room. In their silence there was as much hatred as there had been in the shouts of the mob outside.

At the end of the hall, on a marble dais, a pale, thin man wearing a white robe with a dark green cloak over his shoulders lay on a divan with slender, gilded legs. Parchment scrolls were arranged on a low table of dark wood before him, and a heavy gold chain around his neck glittered as he sipped steaming black *kahveh,* a favorite Saracen beverage, from a small cup.

This, Roland thought, must be Sahil the eunuch.

Sahil threw a small leather bag to the men who had brought them and waved them away. The servants retired, chorusing blessings upon him.

The eunuch's guards, well armed with bows, scimitars, and spears, seized Roland and Perrin and pushed them down, forcing them to kneel. They locked short chains around their ankles.

Sahil demanded their names and ranks and wrote the answers down on a scroll. His almost hairless brows twitched as Roland responded to him in his language. Then, with his quill, he pointed one way for Roland, the other for Perrin.

Roland and Perrin exchanged a look, and Roland saw despair in Perrin's eyes. They are going to kill him, Roland thought. He trembled as he tried desperately to think of a way to save his friend.

"Would it be asking too great a favor, *effendi,*" said Roland, "for us to be permitted to stay together?"

"It would." Sahil smiled thinly. "We do not let common men live. They can pay no ransom."

Roland stared into the cold black eyes. He felt the hard stone still there between his legs, and sent thanks to Heaven.

"This man is very dear to me," he said to the eunuch. "I pray you, let me buy his life."

The eunuch looked amused. "What do you possess that I could not simply take from you, giving nothing in return?"

Roland, his heart beating fiercely, decided to risk all on an appeal to the man's pride.

"Truly, I am at your mercy, *effendi,* but you seem to me a man of honor, perhaps also a generous man."

"Do not try to flatter me, Christian," Sahil said. But he looked pleased. "Show me what you will offer for your servant's life."

Roland lifted his tunic and slipped his hand into his breeches. The eunuch's guards immediately pressed in upon him, lest he draw out a weapon. He untied the pouch, took out the emerald, and held it out to Sahil.

Sahil gasped, and his guards leaned forward, wide-eyed, whispering among themselves. Sahil waved them back imperiously.

A tightness in his chest, Roland waited to see what Sahil would do.

"I know this stone," Sahil said. "There is only one like it in all the world. This is from the turban of Emir Fakr ad-Din, may he rest in Allah's bosom. He was in command of the army defending Mansura." His voice rose shrilly. "Did you steal it from his body, Frankish dog?"

Roland remembered the Turkish emir splendidly attired in flowing silks, his hair and beard dyed red, whom he had encountered on the outskirts of the city. They had caught him by surprise as he was emerging from a bathhouse, but he had fought fiercely. So that was who he was!

Roland tensed himself. "I fought him and killed him. This is booty honorably taken."

"Have you thought, stupid Frank, that it might please us to boil in oil the man who killed Fakr ad-Din?"

Roland forced himself to betray none of the fear he felt.

"Yes," he said. "But I also try to be a man of honor. Therefore I have told you truly how I got this emerald, even if it means my death."

Sahil stared deep into Roland's eyes for what seemed an eternity.

Roland held his breath.

Finally, the emerald disappeared into Sahil's white silk robe.

"I shall accept this as ransom for your servant. He may remain with you for now." He waved them away.

Roland felt his body go limp.

Sahil's guards, pushing the hobbling Roland and Perrin with the butts of their spears, took them through a series of large rooms with arched doorways, the walls decorated with painted Arabic letters and mosaic designs. The guards' boots clicked on gleaming floors of black, green, and white marble. Lokman, whoever he was, possessed a vast establishment, but all the furnishings in the chambers through which they passed had been removed. Perhaps he was one of those rich men the Mameluke officer had spoken of earlier who had fled the city with their goods when it was threatened. And now his palace had been taken over by the defenders, to be used as a prison.

They came to a room whose doorway was barred by an iron

gate. The guards unlocked it and pushed the prisoners into the room so hard they tripped on their chains and fell.

The guards laughed and locked the gate behind them.

A deep sense of helplessness came over Roland. He could hardly find strength to push himself up from the cold stone floor.

The room, he saw, was large and dim, with light coming only through a narrow, barred window at the far end. Groans and mutterings came from all sides, and Roland, his eyes gradually adjusting to the darkness, discovered that the place was crowded with men, captured crusaders like himself, most of them lying on the floor. A few tried to hobble about, despite the hampering chains.

"Name yourself, messire," called a voice. "And tell us what you know. Who has lived through this calamity and who has fallen?"

When Roland spoke his name, a delighted voice sounded from another side of the room. "By Saint Bernard, Roland, I never thought to see you walking on this earth again. Come here to me."

For the first time that day, Roland felt a leap of joy. It was Guido.

A new strength began to spread through his body. With Guido beside him, he could hope again.

But his mood quickly changed again to grief. Guido here, too?

It was better than learning that the Templar had been killed, but not much better.

Roland and Perrin hobbled across the crowded floor to Guido, who was binding a man's hand that had been pierced through by a spear. His white mantle, with its eight-pointed red cross on the shoulder, was torn and bloody.

At Guido's urging, Roland told what he had seen of the day's battle and defeat. Some of the men nearby gathered around to listen, and then told their own stories. All the tales were much the same. Pent up in the streets and alleys, their little troop had been cut to shreds.

Roland wept again as he raged at Amalric's treachery and described Alezan's death.

One man who had been listening told him he must be mistaken about the Count de Gobignon. "Next to the King," he insisted, "he is the greatest of our leaders. Why, the King has even made him Constable of France."

"Forget Amalric for now, Roland," said Guido in a soft, kind voice. "Tell me, how did Perrin get in here with you? Did he manage to pose as a knight?"

"After this day I could not manage to pose as myself," said Perrin. "It was my master who saved me."

Roland told Guido about the emerald and added, "Even though the eunuch recognized the emerald as Fakr ad-Din's, he accepted it and agreed to let Perrin remain with me."

"Is that what he was, a eunuch?" said Perrin. "God's bones, if a eunuch here can rise to such a high and mighty post, this is the land for me."

"How good that you can joke about it," said Guido, clapping Perrin on the shoulder and smiling in the depths of his black beard.

He turned to Roland, still smiling. "There is much enmity among the Egyptian leaders. This Fakr ad-Din was a favorite of the Sultan, greatly envied, and you may have pleased Sahil by killing him. Have you heard that the Sultan himself is dead of consumption, up in Cairo? The message came through to my superior, Brother William de Sennac, while we were trying to fight our way out of the city."

"Does that mean there might be peace?" Roland asked.

Guido shook his head. "The rumor is he died three months ago, in November. They have done a good job of keeping his death secret and carrying on the war. There will be no peace as long as our army is in Egypt. Which may not be long, if Ash Wednesday's fighting goes as badly as Fat Tuesday's did. Many a good man who rode with us this morning is in Paradise tonight. William Longsword, Raoul de Coucy . . ."

Roland remembered the handsome, merry young baron and how fondly he had spoken of his wife. She will never see him again, he thought sadly.

Guido went on, "Count Robert d'Artois . . ."

The shock of it struck Roland like a mace blow. His knees folded, and he let himself drop to the cold, rough floor.

"Not the King's brother!" Perrin exclaimed, sitting beside Roland and throwing a comforting arm over his shoulders.

"He fought his way to the very heart of the city and fell before the central mosque, surrounded by Saracens," said Guido sadly. "Because he wore his count's coronet on his helmet, they thought for a time they had killed the King himself. They were wild with joy."

Roland's arms and legs turned to ice. Now only the two

younger brothers remained to safeguard the throne. Amalric was one step closer.

"The news of Count Robert's death will break the King's heart," Roland said. "Have you any word of how he himself fared in the day's fighting?"

"The King and his army crossed the ford to come to our aid," said Guido. "Then thousands of Mamelukes on horseback from Cairo set upon them. They were commanded by the Emir Baibars al-Bundukdari."

Roland recalled the name. "Baibars? Was it not he who conquered Jerusalem for the Sultan?"

Guido nodded. "He is said to be the best of the Mameluke generals. The Egyptians call him the Panther. He comes of the Tartars of the Golden Horde who rule Russia. He lost the sight of one eye in a duel years ago, but that has not prevented him from rising to the highest rank. After taking Jerusalem he paraded the captured crusaders in Cairo and made them wear the heads of their fallen comrades around their necks."

Roland shuddered and shook his head to drive that picture out of his mind. A one-eyed Tartar, he thought. That man I saw in Damietta . . .

"What of King Louis?" he asked.

"The King, as far as I know, fought through the day unharmed. Hundreds of other good knights perished here in the city and out there on the riverbank. Thirty of my brother Templars died fighting. Our grand master was wounded, but I think he managed to escape. I should have happily died with the others, but a Nubian with a mace stunned me, and here I am. Well, I shall join the dead soon enough."

Roland heard men's anguished voices through the nearby window—screaming, shouting, and sobbing. Roland and Perrin stumbled to the tall slot in the brick wall and peered through the iron grillwork. Guido sighed and stayed where he was.

Other men quickly crowded up behind Roland and Perrin. Roland felt their breathing on his neck and smelled the acrid sweat of their terror.

Through the window Roland saw an interior garden, its paths paved with marble and its walls ornamented with mosaics. Its pool, lined with blue and green tiles, was dry, and the shrubs were wilted.

"Sweet Jesus," he whispered, his guts twisting at what he saw. Herded by the eunuch's guards, a line of tattered crusaders, ankles chained, stood before a black-bearded man, naked to the waist, who raised a huge scimitar over his head. As Roland watched, he swung the glistening blade down on the neck of a trembling man who was kneeling before him. Two other captives, their faces dazed with woe, dropped the severed head into a blood-streaked basket almost as tall as a man. They dragged the bleeding body to a cart standing on one side of the garden and piled it on top of others.

The guards dragged another sobbing man before the executioner, and others with spears prodded the line to shuffle forward.

Roland turned away from the window, sick with grief. He had thought he had seen so much death that day that nothing more could hurt him. But his heart ached with pity for those poor men, who were here only out of duty to the knights they served. All day he had seen men die, but this was much more horrible, the executioner working as serenely as a woodcutter.

How lucky that I was able to save Perrin from that.

He hobbled back to sit beside Guido.

"All the commoners suffer that fate," Guido said. "They are asked if they wish to convert to Islam. If they embrace Islam, they are kept to be sold as slaves. Most of them refuse, because they fear Hell more than they fear the sword. And the Saracens kill them."

Roland started as Perrin, still at the window, began to shout, "Martin! Martin! God is with you, Martin."

Not Martin! Roland forced himself to his feet and tried to get through the crowd back to the window. Martin was so young—only sixteen—and the lance he had carried was twice as tall as he. His parents had begged him not to go on crusade. After all, Martin was not even Catholic. Diane had converted him to Catharism, but he looked up to Roland and had longed to go adventuring with him. And this was the end of the adventure.

"You are going back to God, Martin," Perrin called. "We will all be together on the last—" He stopped suddenly, and Roland heard the *chunk* of the headsman's scimitar.

As Perrin turned away from the window, sobbing, Roland put his arms around him and led him back to sit beside Guido.

Anguish and guilt slashed his heart. I could have told Martin I did not want him. If I were ever to meet Lucien and Adrienne again, how would I face them?

He sighed. *And if I feel so bad about Martin,* he thought, *how must Louis feel, knowing he has led thousands of Martins to their death?*

"We might as well say our good-byes, master," Perrin said.

"Sooner or later I will be out there, too. You have no more great emeralds to buy my life again."

"Do not talk that way, Perrin," Roland said, patting his jongleur on the shoulder. "You heard what Sire Guido said. In this room we are safe."

Guido held up a cautioning hand. "Not exactly. The Saracens had already decided to kill those poor men out there. They just have not made up their minds about the rest of us."

Engulfed by despair, Roland sat silent. Of all the men he had brought with him, Perrin alone was left now. If the Saracens had killed Martin, they probably also had killed the comrades who took such care of him at Béziers. All gone.

No doubt the Egyptians will decide I am not worth keeping either.

Nicolette! Dear God, what will become of her? No one to protect her from Amalric now.

"Oh, God!" he groaned aloud.

If only I could write a poem to her, so that she could know I was thinking of her at the hour of my death. But I have nothing to write with and no way to send it.

He sat hunched over, his hands hanging down between his knees. He had eaten and drunk nothing all day, he realized suddenly, but he had not the strength to care.

The light coming through the barred window faded, and the sounds of killing ceased. They have beheaded every man-at-arms they captured, Roland thought.

Reaching Roland's ears from a great distance, the high, wailing cry of the prayer callers summoned the people to the mosques of Mansura: "Come to prayer. Come to security. Allah is most great."

Truly, he thought, today was Allah's day.

A little later he heard gay shouts, music, laughter, the murmur of happy crowds. The people of Mansura have much to rejoice about, he thought. Their city has lived up to its name.

Guido spoke in the darkness. "Roland, there is a great deal I have wanted to tell you. I may not have another chance. Come, let us find a corner of this room where we can speak together without being overheard."

They had just climbed painfully to their feet when the lock clanked and the iron gate swung open. A flare of light made Roland wince and blink. The eunuch strode in, his white silk gown rustling about his thin legs. He was flanked by two torchbearers and followed by a troop of guards carrying steel-tipped spears.

Roland held his breath as Sahil padded through the room peering into faces.

He came to Roland and Guido.

"Ah, it is you I want. The knight of the emerald." He pointed a slender finger at Roland.

In an instant a cold sweat broke out all over Roland's body, and his hands began trembling.

He was astonished at himself. Can I really still feel fear, after all I have been through today? It was his body, he thought, still eager to live when his weary soul was ready to give up.

The guards seized him and started to drag him to the door, not even giving him time to walk.

"God is with you, master!" Perrin cried after him.

"Go with grace, my friend," said Guido more softly.

XXVI

AFTER THE EUNUCH'S GUARDS HAD MARCHED HIM THROUGH A SERIES of corridors and apartments, Roland found himself in a large, brightly lit room lined with tapestries and intricately carved wooden screens.

A Mameluke officer sat cross-legged on a divan under a canopy of purple silk. His head was swathed in a yellow turban fastened by a pin of black pearls. He wore a steel breastplate inlaid with gold over his embroidered red robe, and jewels sparkled on the insteps of his pointed red slippers.

A dozen warriors arrayed in red and green silks held scimitars as they stood at ease against the walls. Slaves in vests and pantaloons crouched on the thick Persian carpet, awaiting commands.

Roland trembled with apprehension. Why was he here? Was this a trial of some kind? Would he have to undergo the Muslim version of an inquisition before he was tortured and killed?

Yet this pleasant hall was a far cry from the rooms used for imprisonment and execution. From nearby came sounds of music, the voices of men and women raised in laughter and song.

A sudden recognition penetrated his confusion. He had seen the man on the divan before.

The Mameluke's right eye was dead, the lids crossed by a vertical scar. His other eye was a gray-blue that glittered in the light of the oil lamps beside the divan. The face was flat, the cheekbones jutting. His skin was dark brown. A long mustache of coarse red hair bracketed the lipless mouth. If the one-eyed man stood up, Roland knew, he would be tall.

Then he realized who this man must be. His heart beat faster still. Baibars the Panther, Guido had said, had only one eye.

The man had seemed frightening even in his role of a mere servant, unarmed in the midst of the crusader army. Now that Roland was a helpless prisoner, guilty of the death of an Egyptian emir, the one-eyed Mameluke was all the more terrible.

"The last time I saw you, you were holding horses for the Sultan's ambassadors."

The Mameluke smiled. "Now the horse groom commands armies, and the King's interpreter is a captive."

He remembers me. Roland felt a glimmering of hope. He might want to preserve me because I speak his language. Through me he could communicate with the King.

"You are the Emir Baibars al-Bundukdari," he said.

In answer, the Mameluke took a date from a golden bowl on a low table set before him, chewed it slowly, and spat the pit on the carpeted floor.

A slave darted forward and scooped up the pit. Dry-mouthed, Roland swallowed hard.

"Are you hungry? Thirsty? Surely you are." Baibars clapped his hands. He went on eating dates and observing Roland silently.

He wants to keep me wondering what he is going to do to me, Roland thought. This is a man who knows how to control other men. He does not need armies to do that.

Perhaps Baibars is one of those Guido spoke of who are pleased that I killed Fakr ad-Din. But I must be on my guard.

A handsome blond boy brought a tray and placed it on the floor before Roland. On it were a porcelain pitcher and a cup, loaves of flat bread, and a bowl of fruit.

Roland looked curiously at the young slave, wondering where the Mamelukes had found him. Dress him in a page boy's tunic and hose and he could easily pass for French.

Baibars smiled at the boy and waved him away, then gestured to Roland to sit down.

Lowering himself to the floor with difficulty because of his hobbled ankles, Roland poured water from the pitcher into the cup and drank rapidly. He tore the bread apart and stuffed chunks of it into his mouth, chewing greedily. After he had finished one loaf, he began more slowly to consume grapes, dates, and slices of melon. When the edge was off his hunger, he sat back and bowed his thanks.

"I am curious about a Frankish knight who speaks our language, which I thought none of you Christians bothers to learn," said Baibars in his strangely accented Arabic. "I am curious about a knight who defeats and kills one of our emirs in single combat, winning a priceless jewel, and then gives that jewel to ransom a servant. I wish to know: Who is the Sire de Vency?"

Roland heard his name from the Mameluke's lips with a small shock. How strange that this man of a barbarian race should have found it out.

I must walk a fine line with this man. If I frustrate him, he will kill me. But if I tell him too much I could hurt King Louis.

"There is little I can say about myself, Lord Baibars. I am a troubadour, a maker of songs, a poor knight, a vassal of the King of the Franks."

"And as a vassal of the King of the Franks, were you obliged to invade my country?"

Roland tensed himself. The atmosphere in the room was like the air before a thunderstorm. He cast another quick glance around the room to see whether he was dealing only with Baibars, or if there were other high ranking Egyptians about. He saw only warriors and servants.

I had best be honest, he thought, *but not say everything.*

"We are here because you seized Jerusalem, lord."

"Jerusalem!" Baibars exclaimed. "It draws you Franks as a mirage draws travelers in the desert. I am glad, though, that you came to make war on us." He smiled broadly, but without mirth, baring strong teeth under the red mustache. "I was delighted, as you saw, when your King refused to bargain with our late Sultan."

Then it is true, Roland thought. *The Sultan is dead.*

Excitement flickered through his weary body. *I have not told him anything important yet, but he has just told me something very important. Perhaps I can learn more from this Mameluke commander.*

"Why do you prefer war to peace with us, lord?" Roland asked boldly.

The gaze of the single eye fixed Roland like the point of a dagger. "I commanded our army at Gaza. There we destroyed the Franks and their allies of Damascus and Jordan. And then I went on and took Jerusalem. It was I, Baibars al-Bundukdari, who took Jerusalem from you infidels. I did not like to see my master, the Sultan, offer to give the city back to you. But I want more than Jerusalem. I wish to defeat your King in battle. I wish to wage war on you Christians until I have taken all your cities in Palestine and Syria, leveled your castles, torn down your churches, and cut the throats of your priests. Until I have driven every Christian out of the lands of Islam forever."

"Christians will never stop fighting for Jerusalem, lord," Roland said. "It means as much to us as Mecca does to you."

Somewhere in the streets outside, horns, drums, and cymbals were playing parade music, and crowds were cheering. The Mamelukes who had come to relieve the threatened city today must be enjoying the applause of its people.

Baibars held up a long, tapering finger. "You are wrong. Most of you Christians have already given up Jerusalem. Tell me, when your King Louis began to talk of this crusade, did the Pope approve? Did the Emperor Frederic? What of those close to him, such as the Queen Mother and the great Frankish nobles, the lords of Couçy and Gobignon, Champagne and Toulouse? Did they greet your King's call for a holy war with shouts of joy?"

Roland was amazed at Baibars's knowledge of the Christian world. He had gone to very great lengths to learn about his enemies.

Tension knotted Roland's stomach. Am I going to add to his knowledge and make him even more dangerous?

"I think you know the answer to your questions, lord."

"Yes," said Baibars with a satisfied smile. "No one in Europe wanted this war except your King. Long ago, the first of you crusaders took Jerusalem, and you held it for over a hundred years. Then you lost it to the great Saladin, on whom be peace. The Emperor Frederic regained it by treaty. And then you lost it again, to me. By now very few Christians really care enough about Jerusalem to fight for it. King Louis may be the last. Tell me, what sort of man is he?"

Cold with fear of a misstep, Roland remained silent, thinking carefully. He must not say anything that would give Baibars an advantage over the King.

"I think," Roland said slowly, "that if he were an ordinary man and not King, he would still be one of a kind. He believes more deeply in the truth of his religion than any other Christian I know."

A sudden breeze rustled the hangings in the room, rattled the beaded curtains and made the lamps flicker. It was going to be a cold night, especially for the prisoners.

"As a Christian, such a man is wasted," said Baibars. "Go on."

"The King is not some impractical holy man, though," Roland said, "with his eyes fixed on the next world. He works at being King the way a master mason works at planning and building castles and cathedrals. In planning this war he has moved slowly and carefully, and his preparations have been as complete as he could make them. He does not want to shed blood unnecessarily. He does not hate Islam. He only wants Jerusalem, because to us it is a holy city. If you could strike a bargain with him, you could trust him to keep faith with you forever."

Baibars sat back and laughed deep in his throat. "A bargain? Yield Jerusalem to him? Every inch of Islam's soil is sacred to us, and to us Jerusalem is also a holy city. Do you not know that it is the place from which the Prophet ascended into Heaven? Until no Christian feet tread our land, we will not rest."

Roland shook his head sadly. "Think of all the lives it will cost, on your side as well as ours."

Baibars laughed again. "What better way to spend lives than in war? As I said to you at Damietta, Allah delights in war."

Roland felt his body sag. "What will happen will happen."

"What will happen," Baibars said, "will happen *as Allah decrees*, Roland de Vency. Allah will show that he is the only God by giving his people victory. You have undertaken to learn our language. Now, why do you not learn our faith? You are a man of wit, of learning, and of noble qualities. I have need of men such as you."

A strange mixture of emotions flickered through Roland as he heard this. He is proposing that I convert to Islam and betray my people. If I say no, will he have me killed, like our poor men-at-arms?

He felt sweat break out on his forehead, even though the night air was chill.

I could never embrace Islam. These contending religions all seem to me equally true and equally false. But I would rather die than betray Louis.

Baibars sat expectantly, looking catlike in the wavering lamplight. The night breeze blew through the drapery, and the silent guards and slaves shifted their feet. The whole room seemed to be waiting.

Roland composed himself, smiling at Baibars to show that he had no fear. "Will you kill me if I do not submit to Islam? Make a slave of me if I do?"

Baibars waved the suggestion away with a large, powerful hand, fingers twinkling with pearls and diamonds. "I despise those who accept Allah out of fear of death. As for being a slave, I am a slave, as all Mamelukes are. Yet I am also commander of the Sultan's army. Sole commander, now that Fakr ad-Din is dead."

Ah, Guido was right, Roland thought. Baibars is pleased that I killed Fakr ad-Din.

"I was not born a Muslim, any more than you were," Baibars went on. "I had wit and strength when the Turks bought me." He raised a clenched, glittering fist, and his voice seemed to shake the walls. "But Islam has multiplied my powers a hundredfold. Allah blesses all who serve him faithfully."

He is really trying to convert me, Roland thought. Feeling somewhat safer, he shook his head. "Lord, as my mind is shaped now, I cannot be a strong believer in any religion."

Baibars's face darkened. "A doubter, are you? Doubters weaken themselves, and their presence in an army weakens its will. Perhaps the great victory Allah shall grant us tomorrow will stamp out your doubts."

The tight knot of fear in Roland's stomach loosened, and he felt muscles ease all over his body. If I am to see tomorrow's victory, I can hope to live at least that long.

Baibars said, "I send you back to your fellow Christians. Stay alive as best you can. I may have some use for you in the future."

He beckoned to the guards standing behind Roland, and they came forward to take him away.

Three young women in long embroidered cloaks, their faces hidden behind translucent veils, smiled at Roland with their black eyes as the guards pushed him out of the room. He stumbled down the corridor, followed by the sound of drums, reed pipes, tambourines, and stringed instruments striking up behind him. Baibars carouses, he thought, and makes my captivity the more bitter. All around him now he could hear the rejoicing of victorious Mansura. They were dancing in the palaces and singing in the streets.

When he said Allah would let him win again tomorrow, Roland realized, he spoke with such assurance that it never occurred to me to doubt him. What will become of the King and all the others?

He was like a man who had been made to walk for uncounted hours at the very edge of a cliff. Again and again, facing death, his mind and heart and body had been forced to their highest pitch of fury, terror, and grief. Now he had no strength left. He had encountered Baibars the Panther and lived, but he felt no joy, only a dull ache of sorrow for those who had died this terrible day and pity for all others, including himself, who must go on living and suffering.

Chains clashing, Roland stumbled back into the prison room, now plunged into total blackness. From all around him came snores, mutterings, the groans of sick and wounded men. Once, a scream. Some man must be dreaming of what he went through that day. Sure that he would never find Guido and Perrin in the dark, Roland sank down into the first clear space he found on the floor. The men on either side squirmed closer to him for warmth. The stench of human excrement assailed his nostrils, but he was too tired to let it bother him. Exhausted and aching both in heart and body, he fell into a fitful sleep, like a man in a fever.

He felt fingers prodding his arm and shaking him. "Roland, Roland." It was Guido's voice. Roland opened his eyes slowly. It seemed as if he had just closed them on darkness, but now a weak gray light was filtering in through the barred window that had looked out on yesterday's butchery in the garden courtyard.

"We must talk," said Guido. "There will not be much more time. I thought I might never see you again when they took you away."

Roland sat up, his mind shrinking from full awareness of what had happened to him yesterday. His entire body, his right shoulder most of all, ached from yesterday's fighting and from the cold, hard floor.

"Baibars himself sent for me." Roland described his meeting with the Mameluke. "In my judgment he is more than a match for any of our commanders."

"The Tartars are warriors without peer," said Guido gloomily. "They have conquered half the world."

"Baibars spoke of 'the late Sultan.' "

"Then it is true that Ayub is dead. His eldest son, Turan Shah, will claim the throne."

They spoke in low voices. The men all around were sleeping, except for one who got up, stumbled to a corner of the room, and let go a stream of piss against the wall.

"I can understand poor Robert d'Artois wanting to charge into Mansura," Roland said. "He was a hotheaded man. But how could experienced leaders like Longsword and de Sennac let Amalric talk them into such a disaster? It was plain madness."

Guido said, "That madness is what gives knights their power over the rest of mankind. Being willing to ride straight into the arms of death—that is what makes knights different from commoners. You have more than a touch of that madness yourself. You rode into Mansura with the rest of us."

Roland found himself thinking of Diane. "Diane was always ready for death. Sometimes she seemed to want it. But she did not want the kind of power over others that knights have."

"Many of us are like Diane," said Guido.

Something in Guido's voice sounded strange to Roland. "Many of us? How can a Catholic Knight of the Temple of Solomon be like a Cathar preacher?" Roland remembered how he had once feared that Guido would discover that Diane was a Cathar. How long ago that now seemed.

"Solomon's temple harbors more secrets than you might guess," said Guido. His voice was so soft that Roland had to strain to hear him. "I have permission to share some of that hidden knowledge with you. Roland, not all Knights Templar are merely what they purport to be. There exists within our order, another, secret order."

The light filtering in through the narrow window was brighter now, and the prayer callers in the towers of Mansura's mosques began their cries, reminding Roland that he was the prisoner of people who hated his kind, with good reason, and might at any moment decide to kill him.

Guido's words made Roland want to draw back. He felt almost reluctant to hear more. He might, he suspected, learn things he would be better off not knowing.

"Guido, are you telling me that you are a heretic?"

In measured tones Guido said, "I am not a heretic. A heretic disagrees with the Church over this or that point of belief. I have left the Church far behind. I gave up everything when I joined the Templars—the little wealth I possessed, the love of women. I vowed to follow the orders of my superiors. I tell you in simple truth that I do not miss my past life. With my fellows, I have known, through the light imparted by my secret order, such bliss as no other Christians—except, I imagine, a few saints—have experienced on this earth." He gripped Roland's arm and stared into his eyes with a burning intensity. "Roland, I live in that state now, even as I talk to you."

Roland looked deeper into his friend's eyes and realized that what he was seeing was joy.

"You are a troubadour yourself, Guido," Roland said. "You must know that those who practice courtly love attain the bliss you speak of. But we find it *through* the love of man and woman, not by giving up love."

"Of course. But it is also possible to achieve the heights by constraining the appetite for physical love. There is one Light, but we need a window to see it, and in that window are panes of many different colors. Courtly lovers, Templars, Cathars, the masons' guild, and many others have their representatives in our order. We have even forged secret links among Christians, Moslems, Jews, and men and women of other religions in far-off countries most people have never heard of."

Roland was astounded. A secret organization of so many different kinds of people spread across the world, yet all sharing the same hidden knowledge of the inner light he had discovered as a troubadour—the vision made his head reel.

He said, "Nicolette once told me that de Gobignon believes there is a network of heretical plotters who are working to overthrow the kings of Christendom and the Pope and his prelates."

Then he caught his breath. In his excitement he had forgotten himself. He had never before told Guido that he had talked privately with Nicolette. Well, what matter now? If Guido could be trusted with Diane's secret, he could be trusted with this one as well.

Roland went on, "I thought it was a fantastic tale Amalric had invented to justify his ambition. Are you telling me now that there is such a network?"

Roland heard voices and the tramp of boots in the courtyard outside the barred window, in that terrible garden. Was there to be more killing now?

Guido glanced at the window and sighed, as if he were thinking the same thing. He leaned forward to speak in a still lower voice.

"De Gobignon is partly right, but the truth is so different from what he imagines that he might as well be entirely wrong. There is an alliance, and it is secret. It must be kept secret, for if any king or prince of the Church learned what is truly at the heart of the Poor Knights of the Temple of Solomon, we would all go to the stake. But our goal is not to overthrow those in power, as the count imagines. We seek knowledge, we protect it, and we pass it on to our friends. Instead of a web of conspirators, you might think of us as an invisible university."

Roland's mind spun dizzily. Before his very eyes Guido had turned into a giant or a magician. I thought I knew this man, and I thought I knew the world. Now I find out both are so different I can scarcely believe it.

"We do act to defend ourselves and our friends," said Guido, "and so may at times strike at powerful enemies. There again Amalric is partly right. Our order has watched over you from the time you were at the court of Frederic, who is also one of our initiates. That is why I took the part I did the night Perrin was attacked, and why I have aided you since then."

"Frederic?" said Roland, surprised. "But he is not at all like you. He is so—unscrupulous."

Guido spread his hands. "Many panes—many colors, as I told you. What we have in common is a belief that humanity can be far greater than it is and a hunger for more knowledge of the world around us."

"I always wondered why you were so quick to befriend me and to go on such an un-monkish adventure as running down highwaymen."

"We had long been planning to invite you to join our alliance, Roland. Not the Templars, with their vows of poverty and chastity, of course," he added quickly, with a smile, "but a branch more suited to your temperament. Because of your friendship with King Louis, we had to be very cautious. We had to be absolutely sure of you. Now, because there is so little time, I must speak openly to you."

The growing light and the noises outside were waking some of the men in the room. Men stumbled over the bodies of others to relieve themselves in the privy corner. They talked in dull, dispirited voices. Guido stood up and drew Roland to the side of the room where the fewest were gathered.

"My friend, there is one thing you must know. Only I, and no one else, can tell you."

He paused and took Roland's hand in his own strong grip, his eyes fixed on Roland's.

"It was I who killed Diane."

A black curtain swept over Roland's eyes, and he tottered.

Guido took his arm to steady him.

"You? How?" Roland stammered.

Guido helped him to sit down.

"It was the hardest thing I have ever done in my life, even though it was an act of love. You do understand that, Roland, do you not? I killed her because it was the only way I could help her."

Roland felt tears burning his eyes and running down his cheeks.

He stammered, "Yes—yes—I myself wanted to do it. I thought of it often after I learned that she was captured. But I had not the strength. I loved her too much. Or not enough."

"You loved her body, and so you could not harm it. She and I knew that she was not her body. How else do you suppose she could have withstood those weeks of torture? How I longed to rescue her from that, but there was no way. I could only save her from the final agony of fire, and only with an arrow. I could not even weep for her as I killed her, for fear the tears would spoil my aim."

"But how did you ever manage to do it—to kill her and escape?"

"I was with a delegation of Templars in Béziers. Our order has often been criticized for our lack of interest in persecuting heretics. So my brothers and I went to Béziers ostensibly to demonstrate our sympathy for the holy work of Friar Hugues. You might have seen me there, but fortunately you did not. If you had, you would have hated me, and I would not, at that time, have been able to tell you the real reason I came. Count Amalric had stationed all his men in the plaza, leaving many of the towers on the city wall unguarded. I slipped into an empty tower that overlooked the plaza. Afterward, dressed as I was in a Templar's mantle, I simply let myself appear to be the first one of the pursuers who found the archer's hiding place, the discoverer of the bow and arrows. I went back to my brother Templars, and half the people who saw me in the tower forgot me in their excitement. We Templars look so much alike with our beards and mantles. The idea that someone from the clerical party on the church steps might have done the killing was so farfetched it occurred to no one. Only Hugues would have had a devious enough mind to think of such a thing, and he, poor fellow, was gone."

Roland, battered by shock after shock, could only shake his head dazedly. Here he had worried about Guido discovering Diane's identity, and all along there had been a secret link between them.

But why did he call Hugues a "poor fellow"?

"Surely you are not sorry you killed Hugues, are you?"

The Egyptians were shouting orders at one another in the courtyard, and in the corridors of the house Roland heard the approach of jingling mail and clanking weapons. The sun was fully up now, and Baibars's cavalry must be attacking what was left of the crusader army. Would he win the victory he expected?

"I do regret killing him," said Guido. "It was done on an impulse of rage. I could not hold back when I saw him thrusting that torch at her face. My act caused much evil. Amalric's reprisals killed hundreds and hurt thousands horribly. I could not surrender myself to Amalric, because that would have exposed the order and done even greater harm."

He paused, and Roland saw tears standing in his dark eyes. His shoulders seemed bent under some great weight.

"Having injured so many innocents, I have a great debt to pay."

Roland knew that their conversation might be interrupted at any moment. So he asked the question uppermost in his mind.

"Why did you care so much about Diane? Is it because the Cathars are part of this secret alliance you tell me of?"

"Only some Cathars are part of it. Most do not know of it, just as most Templars know nothing of it. Diane was told about it after she survived the massacre at Mont Ségur. She became an unknowing link between the Cathars and the Templars. In that chain, I was her superior. I met with her secretly."

"When you brought Perrin to our house the night he was hurt, did she know who you were?"

"She never knew that her superior and Guido Bruchesi were the same person. I always met her at night and hid my face. I came to know her, though, and love her."

"You loved her?" Roland stared into the dark eyes.

"Yes, Roland, I loved her." Guido squeezed Roland's arm gently. "Pledged to chastity as I am, my love for her was a thing of the spirit. My God, she was a beautiful person! How could anyone with a heart and soul help but love her?"

"Yes—I know—" Roland stammered.

"It was I," Guido went on, "who insisted, perhaps unwisely, that she remain at your house in Paris when she begged me to let her leave."

At the reminder of those days in Paris Roland felt a pang of regret so sharp his tears flowed afresh.

Guido said, "She loved you desperately, Roland. She was on the point of breaking her vows and giving herself to you after Nicolette discovered her at your house."

Yes, she did, Roland thought, remembering that she had said "I love you" to him that day in Paris when they parted forever.

"Then how could she refuse my love?" he asked.

"Saying no to you was the hardest thing she ever did in her life. Perhaps even harder than bearing those weeks of torture. From the time you were boy and girl together, she had never stopped loving you."

A great joy and peace came over Roland. Then it was *not* wrong of me to love her. She loved me, too.

"But why did she not accept me if she wanted me that badly? Why did she have to leave me?"

Guido shook his head. "If she had taken you as a lover she would have destroyed herself. I do not accept the Cathar doctrine that there are unforgivable sins, even for those who call them- selves 'perfect.' But I could not convince her of my view. If she had broken her vow of chastity with you she would have felt so guilty that the rest of her life would have been spent in an earthly hell. As it was, she knew that you loved her, she loved you, and yet she was true to her faith to the end. In a way, her life and death *were* perfect."

Guido's words were healing old wounds that had never been closed. Chained and imprisoned, Roland still felt a new comfort, a new calm. Guido had given him a great gift. He put his hand on Guido's and gripped it hard.

The iron gate of the prison room crashed open, and Sahil the eunuch glided in, followed by his troop of guards. He held a scroll in his hand. He looked about the room until his hollow eyes fell upon Guido.

"That one. With the white mantle. Take him."

Shocked, Roland levered himself to his feet, all pain forgot- ten. "No!"

Guido rose beside him and patted his shoulder. "Be quiet, Roland. There is nothing you can do. I told you I had a debt to pay."

Perrin came over to them and stood at Roland's side, holding his other arm. "May you return instantly to the Light, Master Guido," he said with quiet reverence.

"Oh, I shall," said Guido with a tranquil smile.

Roland looked desperately around the room.

"There are only six guards here," he shouted to the captive knights. "There are hundreds of us. Let us stop them!"

He glared at the sad, tired faces. No one moved.

Sahil spoke swiftly to his guards. "Hold that man. If he speaks again, beat him." Two black-skinned warriors with daggers in their belts seized Roland. On fire with rage, he tensed himself to pull his arms free and fight them.

"Master," said Perrin gently, "there is little we can do with our ankles chained. Even if we overcame these guards, the rest of the Egyptian army would simply come and slaughter us."

Sahil stared hard at Roland. "If the Emir Baibars had not taken an interest in you, I would send you to the headsman as well. If you attempt again to stir up your comrades, I will do it."

The whole room seemed to Roland to grow dark. They were going to take Guido, this marvelous man, his friend, and kill him, and there was nothing he could do. He slumped in the grip of the guards, feeling hardly strong enough to hold himself up.

"Why are you taking him? Why?" he sobbed in anguish. "He is as good a knight as any in this room."

"Roland," said Guido, "they are killing all prisoners who cannot pay a ransom. It is against the rule of the Knights Templar for any of us to ransom ourselves. They kept me alive last night so I could treat the wounds of the knights who might be able to pay for their freedom."

"He must die," said Sahil, "because the Knights of the Temple have vowed their lives to making war on us." He spoke in a tone that, in a strange way, sounded respectful. "And they are better fighters than the rest of you Christian dogs. It is a tribute to a man such as this that we make a point of killing him."

Roland stood looking at Guido, unable to speak. Madness, madness. Why do people kill and kill, for no reason at all?

Guido turned to Sahil. "May I give my friend here a remembrance of me?" The eunuch shrugged and nodded.

Guido slipped his hand inside his torn mantle and took out a rolled-up sheet of paper. "Roland, last night I tried one more time to be a troubadour. Try to keep this about you, and if it pleases you, set it one day to music."

"I will, Guido," said Roland, his voice quavering as he took the paper.

"Keep what I have said locked in your heart," said Guido, calmly drawing his tattered and stained white mantle around him. "When you go back to France a call will come. Do not mourn for me. Lend your warrior's heart and poet's mind to the great work Diane and I have lived for. Then we will live on in you."

He held out his arms to Sahil's guards and let them lead him away.

The Egyptians holding Roland let him go, and he collapsed, weeping, to the floor. Perrin sat beside him, his hand on Roland's shoulder. The gate of the prison room clanged shut.

Watching Guido go to his death so serenely, Roland remembered the martyrs of Mont Ségur and his vow to them that he would work to put an end to such murder. So far he had accomplished little. Now, perhaps, if he got out of here alive, he could link himself to Guido's order and achieve more.

But that would not bring Guido back. His heart was a ball of pain. He hugged his knees to his chest, trying to draw his body tightly together so that it would hurt less. He buried his face in his arms and sobbed bitterly, the paper with Guido's poem on it clenched in his fist.

XXVII

THE CRUSADE WAS OVER, AMALRIC THOUGHT, WHETHER LOUIS REAL-ized it or not. He sat on a big, brown war-horse on the riverbank opposite Mansura and watched the last remnants of the crusader army hastily retreating. They were crossing the bridge of boats built seven weeks ago while knights and Mamelukes had been battling on Fat Tuesday on the south side of the city.

Amalric glanced behind him at the remainder of his army, about two hundred knights and eight hundred men-at-arms. Half the number he had brought with him from the Gobignon domain. But the losses had been for good purpose.

He remembered the tears Louis had shed as he realized that he had to abandon the ground his brother and so many others had died for.

Here is where I want it to end, and soon, with Louis and his other two brothers dead in the mud. Dead as Robert. Dead as that bastard de Vency.

Saint Dominic, I wish I could have seen de Vency's body. Did they burn it, I wonder, or just throw it in the Nile?

If only Louis had decided to stay and fight it out. There would have been a good chance then that he and his brothers might already have been killed. The fortified camp Louis built on the Mansura side would surely have been overrun soon.

Was it only seven weeks since that Fat Tuesday battle? It seemed more like a lifetime to Amalric. Well, he had fought, endured, and stayed alive. And there had been some pleasures, such as watching men who might have been obstacles to him fall. Raoul de Coucy. That gave Amalric a warm feeling. Enguerrand, who had managed to stay home, would now be seigneur of Coucy, and Enguerrand hated the King just as much as he did.

And William de Sennac, killed only a few days after he had survived the fighting in Mansura's streets, and nearly all his white-cloaked Templars dead, too.

The men retreating across the bridge of boats were far from the strong, brave knights who had marched south from Damietta last autumn. It had been weeks since the galleys from Damietta had brought any fresh food. But why? No one he had spoken to knew. Only this morning Amalric had heard of a barrel of rotten salted beef being sold for eighty silver livres. Back home that would buy a first-rate destrier.

Amalric's chest swelled as he felt the strength and health in his own body. He knew how to care for himself. Some foolish barons had shared their provisions with the less fortunate and were now as starved and sick as their poorest men-at-arms. Amalric had kept his food and money for himself and for the men he valued most, such as d'Etampes and Maurice. Thank Saint Dominic for Maurice, who could slip out of the camp now and then and come back with fresh fruit and meat.

The retreating men shuffled and stumbled over the bridge. Many of them looked too weak to swing a sword. They were riddled, Amalric knew, with fever, scurvy, and the flux, maladies that had killed more of Louis's men than the Mamelukes had.

And what of the Mamelukes? He eyed the still unbreached

walls of Mansura. Behind those walls, he knew through Maurice's contacts with the Egyptians, ever greater numbers of Saracens were gathering, coming in from the farthest reaches of the Sultan of Cairo's empire.

Movement under the walls of Mansura caught Amalric's eye. He saw banners unfurl and heard the Saracen drums and war cries. Those heart-freezing yells were now as familiar to him as the sight of death.

Our damned fool engineers, they have not even started to cut the ropes that hold the bridge together, thought Amalric. It looked so inviting, lying wide open before the rapidly massing Egyptian army. Amalric could now hear fear in the shouts of the crusaders as they, too, caught sight of the Saracens pouring out of Mansura.

"*Allahu akbar!*" A great shout reached Amalric from the other side of the river.

What a loathsome din. Thousands of Saracens were howling, backed by hundreds of pipes, trumpets, and drums.

First to come onto the bridge were bizarre-looking men dancing and singing, in black and white robes with long beards. Some stopped every few steps and twirled on their toes so rapidly that their robes billowed out like huge white flowers. Behind them walked tambourine and flute players.

These mad priests—"dervishes" Maurice called them—often led a major Saracen attack. Amalric felt a chill on the back of his neck. Sorcerers!

Now Egyptian foot soldiers with long spears marched onto the bridge. Behind them the Mameluke cavalry came trooping, yellow and green banners waving above their spiked helmets.

Suddenly he could no longer see where the Egyptian vanguard began and the French rear ended. Bodies were tumbling into the river. The water was being stained red. Clouds of Saracen arrows were arching into the sky and falling on the crusaders.

Guy d'Etampes rode up. "Have we had any change in orders from the King, monseigneur?"

"No," said Amalric. "And we cannot afford to wait for his command. Give the order to ride past the old camp and stop again when we are on the road to Damietta."

Without waiting for a response he wheeled his horse and headed off northward.

He had to hold back his horse almost to a walk to give his men on foot—which most of them were—a chance to keep up. In the past few weeks horses had become more valued for eating than for riding.

He glanced at the site where the crusaders had first camped on arriving before Mansura. Servants, priests, and other camp followers were swarming like ants whose hill has been kicked open, striking tents, loading bundles on their backs, and fighting over the few remaining donkeys and camels.

"Wait, monseigneur, will you let us ride with you?" some of the rabble called.

He ignored them.

He rode past galleys tied up along the shore, eyeing them covetously. He could be in Damietta in less than two days if he could commandeer one of those. But Louis, damn him, had insisted on loading the galleys with the sick and wounded. Well, they would be lucky if they got away before the Egyptians fell upon them.

He rode on. He had left the camp a good distance behind when d'Etampes, who was bringing up the rear, trotted up.

"Monseigneur, it appears that our army has turned to stand and fight."

Amalric's stomach burned with anger. He had no time for d'Etampes and his stupid reports. He wanted to get himself back to Damietta and safety. That was what counted.

But now he would have to make at least a show of concern.

He looked over his shoulder and saw that some knights and archers had formed a defensive line around the galleys. Fools, he thought. The Saracens will annihilate them.

"The King commanded a retreat," he said curtly, "and retreat we will, unless he calls me back."

And not even then, he thought to himself. If Louis should live through this day—and I pray he will not—and he calls me to account, I shall just say I received no message.

They rode along in silence, d'Etampes on one of the few war-horses that had not been eaten, Maurice on Amalric's other side on a gray palfrey that the wily old man had managed to find somewhere. Before them rode an equerry with the purple and gold Gobignon banner. The Gobignon contingent retreats in good order, Amalric thought with satisfaction, considering what we have been through.

By Saint Dominic, I will see Nicolette again. The thought of her made his groin ache. He had had no woman in months. The filthy, brown Egyptian women disgusted him.

Nicolette, and no more troubadour coming between us, he exulted. That is all over forever.

The shouts and clanging of fighting drifted to Amalric's ears like a reproach. He was ill at ease with what he was doing—riding away from battle. But knightly conduct or not, what was the purpose in staying? Louis's army was outnumbered, and the men were too weak to fight. Saint Dominic grant there are no more Saracens waiting up ahead for us.

His troops were not the only ones fleeing such unfavorable odds. Looking back, he could see small bands of men breaking away from the fighting and hurrying up this same road.

He ground his teeth as, one by one, the galleys loaded with the sick and wounded sailed by, moving swiftly downriver with the brown current. Sailing to Damietta loaded with useless ones, he told himself, while he and his men must plod along the road.

In silence he rode, his followers strung out along the riverbank behind him.

At mid-afternoon he heard himself hailed and turned to see a perspiring, terrified-looking priest on a donkey.

"If you please, monseigneur, will you have your men clear the road? The party of His Excellency the Patriarch of Jerusalem is behind yours and must hurry on."

Damn! Amalric thought. More lost time. But he could not deny the right-of-way to the most eminent prelate on the expedition. Grudgingly, he passed the order to d'Etampes.

Amalric recognized the Patriarch, a wizened old man wrapped in a black traveling cloak. Even though he was nearly eighty, he kept up easily with the rest of his party without assistance. Clustered about him on horses and donkeys were a flock of priests and monks, most of them, Amalric noted contemptuously, with white faces and wildly staring eyes. They know that the Saracens have especially ugly ways of killing Christian priests, he thought. Two Templars, perhaps the last of the lot that had ridden under William de Sennac, rode on the flanks of the party.

The Patriarch made the sign of the cross at Amalric and his men as he passed by them. Amalric touched forehead, breast, and shoulders in response, but shuddered as he did.

I have done everything I could to destroy this crusade, to bring about the death of the King and his brothers. I have Robert's blood on my hands. Can a blessing do me any good, or am I damned?

A little later, as they rode on, Guy d'Etampes said, "The Oriflamme."

Amalric looked back to see the gold banner bobbing over the river road half a league or so behind them.

"I told you the King intended to make no stand," said Amalric.

"He is able to escape because others are making a stand," said d'Etampes. There was a hint of disapproval in his voice that angered Amalric. He forgets, he would be nothing without me.

"I do not think that knight is wholly loyal to you, monseigneur," said Maurice in a low voice. "I would keep an eye on him."

In the late afternoon, a messenger from the King reached Amalric. The King's party, the man reported, had stopped at a village a league back. The fighting, he said, seemed to be dying down. The King requested Amalric's presence at a council.

The village was a collection of mud brick huts with thatched roofs, abandoned for now by its *fellahin* inhabitants, who had probably fled behind Saracen lines. It smelled of human and animal dung. The Oriflamme was planted above a gray-brown house that looked like a small box made of clay. There was not even a door, just a brown curtain through which Amalric pushed.

The sight of Louis filled Amalric with secret delight. The King sat on a pile of blankets, his long body bent double, holding his belly, his gaunt face dripping with feverish sweat. His cook, Isambert, a sturdy man, stood beside him with folded arms. A small group of barons, all looking exhausted, was gathered around the dark room.

Count Charles d'Anjou sat on the dirt floor of the hut near the King. Amalric grew wary at the sight of Louis's shorter, darker brother. Knowing Charles to be more practical than Louis—and far more clever than the late Count Robert—Amalric felt he must be especially on his guard in his presence.

"God has seen fit," Louis said in a weak voice, "to give me the flux. But I am happy to see you looking strong, Amalric."

He means it, the idiot, Amalric thought.

"Count Amalric," Charles said, "the King should not be riding, should he? There is still one galley left. Tell him he should go by galley to Damietta."

Amalric tensed, fearing that Charles's advice might get Louis out of danger.

"As long as my army marches, I will march," said Louis with his usual quiet stubbornness.

"Gallantly spoken, sire," Amalric said heartily.

Charles rolled his eyes in despair.

Alphonse, the youngest of the royal brothers, a slight, sandy-haired youth, sat staring at the floor, as if trying to keep his mind off the conversation.

"We have little enough occasion for gallantry left, my good Amalric," said Louis. "I have decided to ask the Saracens for a truce. I intend to plead with them to halt their attack on us, permitting us to withdraw in peace to Damietta."

Why in God's name should they do that? Amalric thought. Does he think this is a tournament? They have us now. They can annihilate us and take Damietta at their leisure.

"What will we offer them in return, sire?" he asked.

"If they destroy us here, they will lose thousands of their own men doing it," Louis said. "We are weak, but we are desperate men. There are still perhaps ten thousand of us, and each of us will kill many of them before he falls. On the other hand, I will suggest that if they let us return to Damietta we might reach some final settlement of this war."

Louis sighed sadly. Then his face went white and he clutched at his stomach.

"My Jesus, the pain!" He reached out a shaking hand to Isambert, who hauled him to his feet and half carried, half dragged him out of the hut.

He cannot even walk, thought Amalric. He must be near death. He felt himself breathing harder with excitement. And I am already Constable of France. So close, so close—except for Louis's brothers.

Charles d'Anjou made a grimace of distaste, as if the King's illness embarrassed him. "What think you of my brother's idea of a truce, Count? It seems to me we have no choice but to try it."

How to answer?

In his mind, Amalric could see the royal palace in Paris. Could see himself dominating a council of those who would rule the country after this disastrous crusade. He ached with a longing to make that vision real.

Louis could be dying, but Charles and Alphonse both looked healthy enough. He had to be rid of them.

So, first, no treaty with the Saracens. If they agreed to bargain, everything he planned could be ruined.

"As I have said before," he declared, "the Saracens will think we are even weaker than we are if we ask for a truce. It will convince them that this is their great chance to wipe us out, and they will fall upon us ferociously. Whereas if we really resist they might decide that the cost of defeating us is too great. They might then withdraw, leaving us to make our way to safety."

Charles opened his mouth to reply when another voice broke in.

"If I had only myself to think of," said Louis from the doorway, his voice barely audible, 'I would happily make a last stand here, with a few brave companions such as yourself, Amalric."

A fine line to tread here, thought Amalric. I must encourage Louis to fight, but not let him draw me into it.

Louis hobbled back to his place on the blankets, leaning heavily on Isambert. "The rest of the army might escape while we held off the Saracens. We could die like Roland and his men, and perhaps be remembered in song."

Amalric started, then realized that Louis was only maundering on about the ancient hero Roland. De Vency, that dog of a troubadour, would be remembered in no one's songs.

Louis went on, "But my knights and men came with me to liberate Jerusalem, not to die in a fruitless struggle against impossible odds. I have always accepted it as my duty to lead men to their deaths when necessary, but I have no right to waste lives when I can preserve them."

"Well said, brother," Charles put in.

Alphonse did not even look up, but went on staring fixedly at the dirt floor.

He is only a boy, and he is terrified, thought Amalric. This is his first war.

"Besides," said Louis, "if we fall here, there will be no one left to defend Damietta. Those of us who cannot fight are going there in galleys. Our ladies are there. What if those helpless souls fell to the Mamelukes?"

Horror widened the eyes of Charles and Alphonse, both of whom, like Louis, had wives in Damietta.

However this turns out, Amalric thought, proud of his strength, I will be in Damietta protecting my wife.

"Sire," he said fiercely, "everything we have fought for, all the lives we have lost already, all will be for naught if we give up now."

Tears appeared on Louis's cheeks. "I know, Amalric, I know, I know. Oh, the pain I feel, being the one who made all this happen. All these men dying in vain. It would be a happy release for me, too, to die in battle now. But my life is not my own to dispose of. No, I must do what seems best for my men, and seek a truce. Here is Philip de Montfort, recently come to us from Tyre, who will speak to the Egyptians for me."

De Montfort, an elderly knight who had been born and reared in Outremer, stepped away from the clay wall and bowed to the King. De Montfort's mustache was white, in bright contrast to his dark brown skin.

"Go, good Philip," Louis said, "and Jesus give you eloquence."

De Montfort bowed again and hurried out.

"I must go, too, sire, and see to my men," said Amalric, his voice choked with fury.

Louis waved his hand feebly in farewell.

Mounting his horse outside the crumbling hut, Amalric studied the positions of the two armies. A man on horseback could see for leagues in this flat land. The sun would be down in two hours or so. The crusaders had marched a good distance north from Mansura, so that Amalric could just see its walls, pinkish-yellow on the horizon. Mounted knights and archers on foot held a line south of this village where Louis sheltered himself. Facing that line spread the vast Egyptian army, led by the Mamelukes, thousands of mounted men, tens of thousands of men on foot, their spears like the tops of a pine forest. If they mount a final attack and encircle us, thought Amalric, it will finish us.

As he rode back to where he had left his men, Amalric cast about in his mind. I must get away from here safely, he thought, and I must make sure the King and his brothers are killed.

He had said those words to himself many times before, but this time somehow he saw the full reality of it.

Louis's death is right, Amalric said in his mind, as if he were defending himself before God. It is needful. The kingdom must be saved from chaos. Christendom must be protected from heresy.

The Gobignon troop had set up tents by the side of the road. The men sat wearily on the ground, some cleaning their weapons, some talking, some just staring into space. D'Etampes walked among them, chatting with this one and that. He looked up questioningly when Amalric dismounted, but Amalric turned away from him. He'll be no help, he thought.

Old Maurice was waiting for Amalric in his tent. Of late, Amalric had found himself relying more and more on the veteran's counsel. Now, sitting on his camp cot, he told Maurice about the proposed truce.

"Would it not be for the best if this heresy-loving king did not return to France?" asked Maurice, casting a sideways glance at Amalric.

The old man seemed to know Amalric's thoughts without his even speaking them. Nor did he seem to find them shocking. But his cringing manner was tiresome. Why can he not look me in the eye? Amalric wondered. Damn him, was he so beaten down by his Saracen masters that he must ever cower like a whipped dog? He glowered up at Maurice, who stared over his left shoulder.

"From what you know of the Turks," Amalric said, "are they likely to give the King leave to march unscathed back to Damietta?"

Maurice shrugged. "It depends on who is commanding. Baibars would no doubt prefer to destroy this army here and now, once and for all. Turan Shah, the new Sultan, is more of a bargainer, as his father was. He will want to accomplish the most with the fewest losses.

Even though Maurice's manner encouraged him, Amalric felt reluctant to say any more.

"What if a band of crusaders were to launch an attack on the Mamelukes while the truce talks were going on?"

Maurice considered this and shook his head. "It might provoke the Saracens to strike back. But"—he smiled at Amalric— "who could be found who would want to commit suicide by attacking the Mamelukes now?"

"Not I," Amalric agreed. "If I do not get out of here alive, I have accomplished nothing."

"If the crusaders surrendered instead of talking of a truce," Maurice ventured, "then the King and his brothers would fall at once into the hands of the Mamelukes."

Amalric felt as if he were seeing a sunrise.

"And then what?" he asked, his heart quickening with excitement.

"While the Saracens are rounding up their prisoners, some of us might escape."

Amalric pictured almost the entire crusader army being taken captive. Can I make such a calamity happen?

What other choice is there?

"If they take all these men prisoner, what will they do to them?"

Maurice shrugged. "Quite possibly they will kill them all, monseigneur. It would be the surest guarantee that *these* crusaders, at least, will never trouble Egypt again."

I cannot do it, Amalric thought. Let thousands of French

knights be killed and say I am doing it to save the kingdom? And anyway, how? I cannot *make* them surrender. Or can I? he asked himself, as he thought of a way.

"The deaths of so many men," said Amalric, recoiling from the prospect. "A terrible thing."

And many of them *good* men. Men who think the way I do about things.

"They are going to die in Outremer anyway, monseigneur," Maurice said softly. "One way or another. If now now, then later on."

That is not so certain, Amalric thought. If there were any way at all to get our men back to France, Louis would find it.

But if Louis gets his truce, I will never get revenge for Hugues or my father. I will see the kingdom taken over by heretics. I will end my days as a slave to Louis.

He struck his fist into his palm, and the loose chain-mail gloves dangling from the sleeves of his hauberk clattered. I have come this far, I cannot lose it all now. It will not be my fault if the Saracens kill them.

"Whatever happens to the men after they are captured, that is not your doing," said Maurice softly, again seeming to know Amalric's secret thoughts.

"I must do what I must do," Amalric said suddenly. "For God and for France."

"Yes, monseigneur," said Maurice, looking away still.

"Very well then." Amalric plunged on quickly now. "Maurice, ride through the army and cry that all our men are to lay down their arms. Tell them the King has ordered it. Tell them surrender is the only way to save the King's life."

"Why should they do it because *I* tell them to, monseigneur?"

"They will do it no matter who tells them," said Amalric. "They know the King has sent the Sire de Montfort to treat with the Mamelukes. Confused, frightened men will obey any voice that speaks with conviction. And you know how to speak with conviction." Besides, he thought, if this plan should fail, the surrender order must not seem to come from me. I can always say I had no idea what Maurice was doing.

"I will go at once, monseigneur." Maurice turned to leave.

The tent flap flew aside and Guy d'Etampes rushed in, trembling. He stared at Amalric with the eyes of a madman.

Maurice edged away from him.

"Traitor!" d'Etampes spat at Amalric.

Amalric felt his heart start to pound. This eavesdropping

young fool must have heard everything. By Saint Dominic, I shall be destroyed. Louis will hang me.

"Go, Maurice," said Amalric, quietly but urgently.

D'Etampes drew his sword. Holding it level with both hands, he pointed it at Maurice.

"Stay where you are!"

My vassal. How dare he? Drawing his sword against me.

Amalric sprang from his cot, and his long, three-edged basilard was in his hand before d'Etampes could begin to turn. He threw himself on the young man, grasping his neck with his free hand. D'Etampes was wearing his hauberk. The blow would have to be to an unprotected spot.

D'Etampes, struggling, looked at Amalric with horror and disbelief as Amalric drove the dagger like a spike into his eye.

He screamed with pain and shock.

Amalric forced the young man's head down with his other hand, pushing the point into his brain.

D'Etampes's scream stopped abruptly and he went limp.

Amalric pulled the dagger out with a jerk. A rush of blood followed it. The young knight collapsed on the carpet without a sound, his sword still in his hands.

"And he dared to call me a traitor, a man who could turn against his seigneur like that." Breathing heavily, Amalric wiped the blade of the basilard on his tunic before putting it away.

Maurice, his lips sucked in, stood looking down at the dead young man.

"Well?" Amalric challenged him hoarsely. "Never seen a man killed before? Come awake, man." Can I trust Maurice? he asked himself. What if he goes out there and denounces me?

"You have put your life in forfeit, too, you know," he reminded Maurice. "Ever since you brought in those Arabs to destroy the stone-casters."

"Of course, monseigneur," said Maurice in a low voice, turning his eyes from d'Etampes's body and looking toward the doorway of the tent. He sighed and spoke more briskly. "I was just gathering my wits. Shall I get rid of the body for you, monseigneur?"

"No. Get on with spreading the cry for surrender." Once the army surrendered, no one would know or care who had killed d'Etampes.

Amalric stood staring down at the handsome profile, his legs trembling as they sometimes did after a particularly pleasurable carnal embrace.

My God, what have I done? It all happened so quickly.

The wounded side of d'Etampes's head was down, and only the spreading puddle of blood showed what had happened.

Why did you make me kill you, d'Etampes? I liked you. There were times I thought of you as a younger brother, someone who could be to me what Hugues was.

But Hugues was cleverer than you. He would have understood and would have helped me. You were either too stupid or too pigheaded. A shame. And I just might have let you marry Isabelle after all.

"I will ride north," he said to Maurice, "and wait for you when I am a safe distance from here. I wish we could catch up with those galleys."

"We are safer traveling on shore, monseigneur," said Maurice with a certainty that puzzled Amalric. The old crusader bowed and left.

Moments later Amalric heard a horse galloping and Maurice's voice raised in a loud shout. "Lay down all arms! Yield yourselves! The King commands it!"

Amalric threw blankets and discarded clothing over d'Etampes's body. He put on German steel shoulder guards and a breastplate over his mailed shirt, and replaced the helmet he had been wearing with a lighter one veiled with white linen to protect his head from the sun.

He unlocked a small chest and drew out a bag that contained all the silver and gold coins he had left. He buckled on his longsword and tied the money bag to his belt.

He did not call to anyone to help him. He could not bear to talk to any of his men.

He tried not to think about what he was doing, but shame burned in his heart. Deserting, leaving them to fall into the hands of the enemy. Was this not the most despicable thing a seigneur could do? Guilt fell on him like an enormous stone.

He straightened his shoulders, trying to throw the stone off his back. No, I must injure these men now, so that later on I can do greater good for many more people.

Carrying his shield, hanging his battle-ax around his neck, he went out. Now he would have to tell an equerry to saddle the one fresh horse he had left.

"What is happening, monseigneur? Are we really surrendering?"

"Get that damned horse ready."

"Will you lead us into battle, monseigneur?"

"Be still!" Amalric shouted as he threw himself into the

saddle. He wheeled the horse, a big black Flemish charger, and set off at a trot for the river road.

From upriver, where the bulk of the army was gathered in milling confusion, came shouts of "Down arms! Surrender!" Amalric paused at the top of a low rise to watch. He could not see Maurice, but he could tell where he had been by the sight of men stacking spears and swords, by the sudden fluttering of white flags made of torn cloth. The setting sun, tinged deep red by a sandstorm over the distant desert, cast a fiery glow over the defeated army.

Amalric heard a roar of triumph swell up from the lines of Mamelukes that moved to enclose the crusaders. He saw the yellow banners move forward and the sun flash on scimitars.

He became aware suddenly of the danger of his own position. There was nothing between him and the oncoming Mamelukes but an army that had just laid down its arms. He dare not stay.

There was one sight, though, he had to wait for. Louis. Amalric held the black war-horse steady, peering at the cluster of tan-walled, flat-roofed huts where Louis and his brothers had taken shelter. The Oriflamme, shining brightly in the glow of sunset, hung over the center of the village.

Now the banner was in motion. A man on horseback, a crusader, had picked it up and was riding this way with it. Trying to save it from the disgrace of being captured by the Saracens. The rider's faint cry of "Saint Denis!" reached Amalric's ears above the din.

A spearhead of Mamelukes, cutting through the crusaders unopposed, had almost reached the village. They fired a volley of arrows at the fleeing rider with the Oriflamme. The horse stumbled to a stop, and the man fell backward out of the saddle. Like a tree cut down by a woodsman, the war banner of France toppled into the mud beside the Nile. A groan of grief went up from the Frenchmen who saw the Oriflamme fall.

Amalric turned away. If only I could have had the glory of saving it. He spurred his horse up the road a few paces, but could not resist the urge to look back again.

A Mameluke had reached the Oriflamme. He swung down out of his saddle, seized the banner's staff, and lifted it out of the mud. With a long scream of triumph he galloped back to the Egyptian lines waving the red and gold banner wildly.

Not a man among the French moved. That, thought Amalric, shows how completely they are defeated.

Mamelukes on horseback, Amalric now saw, crowded into the

village where Louis was. A thrill of terror and delight went through Amalric. *Perhaps I shall see his head raised up on a pole and carried off in triumph like the Oriflamme.* He was suddenly struck with the thought that if Louis were killed he could turn and ride back among the crusaders, rally them, and lead them to victory.

What a mad notion.

Then he saw Louis. The King's blond hair gleamed above the turbans and spiked helmets crowding around him. Many hands seized him. They were lifting him up. They set him on a war-horse, and he sat rigidly, like a man in fetters. Doubtless they had wrapped chains around him. Slowly his horse moved through the crowd of Saracens, back toward Mansura. Charles and Alphonse, also mounted, followed. Mameluke horsemen in green cloaks positioned themselves around the royal brothers.

It was over.

Amalric felt as if someone had struck him with a hammer. He remembered the first time he had ever killed a man—a peasant he had found poaching in his forest at Gobignon. He had run the man through with his sword, and then been astonished by how quickly something so terrible could happen, something that could never be undone.

In just the few moments it had taken him to ride from his tent to this little hill the great French army had succumbed. Four long years Louis had spent putting that army together. Another whole year to move it from France to Egypt. Nearly another year of bloody campaigning. And now all over, in the blink of an eye.

And Amalric had done it, and the army was forever past saving. His body froze with the horror of it.

There was no outcry from the French knights at the sight of their King in chains, but Amalric saw a man kneel in the mud. Then more were kneeling. Soon the entire crusading army was on its knees, watching in silence as their King was led away.

Tears welled up in Amalric, and he rubbed his eyes with his bare hands, the empty mail gloves clinking.

"Oh, dear God!" he muttered to himself.

Why am I weeping? This is what I wanted, what I have worked for.

Louis got what he deserved, he told himself. He took a deep breath, clenched his fists on the reins, and turned his face away from the unmanning sight of all those poor wretches being dragged off to captivity.

He pulled his stallion's head around and set out on the road to Damietta.

The riverbank ahead was mostly empty. Here and there he passed groups of women and servants who had been part of the crusader camp, trudging north, trying to escape. The Bedouins will get them if the Mamelukes do not, Amalric thought.

I am all alone.

A strange sensation. All of his life he had never gone anywhere without an entourage, often an entire army. From the age of five he had been the Count de Gobignon. And now he was traveling alone, fleeing for his life in an enemy country. True, he was fully armored, carrying both a longsword and a battle-ax, but he felt naked and helpless.

Because I deserted my men.

He thought of them, two hundred or more knights from the house of Gobignon, whom he had left behind to perish.

But if I had led them into battle and they had all died fighting? A leader cannot feel sorry for the men he loses.

Just after sunset he came to a heap of dirt and logs the crusaders had piled up across the mouth of an irrigation canal to dam it so they could cross it more easily. Beyond this artificial hill he reined up and waited. Not likely that the Mamelukes would pursue any who escaped this far north.

One man, at least, he could take out of this disaster with him. Of all of them, Maurice had proved the most valuable. He was bold, despite his age, and he knew the country. Amalric would wait here for him.

Time passed slowly as he sat on the ground beside his horse in the twilight. Why the devil did I not think to bring something to eat or drink with me?

A group of the commoners he had passed earlier, appearing a few at a time out of the darkness, gradually gathered around him. No doubt, he thought, they felt safer in the company of an armored knight. None had any food. There was none to be had in the camp when they left it. One had a wineskin, and Amalric drank deeply of the sour wine and then chased them away.

"You are wasting your time. Your only hope is to get as far from the Turks as you can. When I ride on, I am not going to wait for you, and you will not be able to keep up with me."

He saw fear and resentment in the shadowed faces of the servants and camp followers, but none dared to speak out. Slowly, single file, they set off along the river road.

What is going on back at Mansura? he wondered. If Maurice

does not reach me by moonrise, I will have to go on without him.

He heard the hoofbeats of a horse ridden hard. A dark figure clattered through the stony bed of the gully that had been a canal and reined up before him. Peering into the gloom, Amalric saw that it was Maurice.

"You need not fear pursuit, monseigneur. They will be occupied for hours with the slaughtering of the foot soldiers."

"Saint Dominic!" Talons of remorse sank themselves into his innards.

"It was only to be expected, monseigneur. They cannot spare food for so many. They have not yet started to kill the knights and the barons. They may give them a chance to send home for money to ransom themselves. The common men die happy, thinking that by their sacrifice they have saved the life of their King."

Maurice's words jolted Amalric. Ransom? If that happens, I am undone. I will not achieve my purpose at all.

"What of the King?"

"He still lives, as far as I know, monseigneur."

"Would they let him ransom himself?" The thought of Louis buying his way out of captivity and walking again among the living and free infuriated him. No, that must not be.

"They must know that he is the chief cause of this crusade that has ravaged their country," Maurice said. "They will probably either behead him or hold him prisoner for the rest of his life."

Amalric let out a deep breath.

A full moon rose over the Nile as Amalric and Maurice rode quickly on. The common folk stumbling north did not even look up as the two men on horseback passed. After some hours Amalric drowsed in the saddle, assailed by images of good, brave men falling unarmed under Muslim swords. It was Louis's fault. Didn't I advise him to fight on instead of run begging to the Turks for a truce? Those men would at least have died with their swords in their hands. And who led them to Mansura in the first place?

He was almost asleep when Maurice slapped his arm. "Off the road, quickly, monseigneur."

Instantly he was alert. By moonlight he saw the white and black horizontal stripes of Egyptian sails on the river ahead of him. He and Maurice turned their horses into a clump of shrubbery and palms and watched as a dozen long, narrow boats sli toward them over the shimmering water. But how did they get north of Mansura, where our galleys are supposed to control the river?

Amalric realized with horror that he could be trapped between Mansura and Damietta. If those on the galleys saw him and Maurice, a volley of arrows could well be the end of them. Though the desert night was cold, sweat dripped down his sides.

The Saracen ships glided past, propelled by many oars as well as by sails, the voices of the warriors on board carelessly raised in merry shouts, song, and laughter.

They know they have nothing to fear, thought Amalric.

When the voices of the Saracens were only a distant murmur upriver, Amalric and Maurice spurred their horses on. They rode without further incident until dawn.

As the sun appeared over distant brown hills to the east, their way was blocked by two knights with drawn swords. White mantles. Templars.

"The Constable of France!" exclaimed one of the Templars when Amalric identified himself. "You are most welcome, monseigneur. We are escorting the Patriarch of Jerusalem back to Damietta, and God knows what enemies lie ahead of us. Did you see those Saracen ships? Where did they come from?"

They took Amalric to the Patriarch, who was resting in a grove of olive trees, and Amalric knelt and received the old man's blessing for a second time. The Patriarch's party had left the crusaders long before the surrender and knew nothing about it. When Amalric told the old man the news, tears ran down his bony cheeks.

"Surely God has sent you to help us. But how did you escape, my son, when all surrendered?"

"The King urged me to ride with all haste to Damietta, your excellency," Amalric improvised, "to take command of the defense."

"We must hurry on, then," said the old man. "We not only have to fear Bedouins before us, but Mamelukes behind us."

The Templars shared their provisions with Amalric—bread and dried beef as hard as Egyptian bricks, and wine that had turned to vinegar.

The party set out just after sunrise. Amalric prayed they would encounter no enemies. It was now a whole day and a night since he had last slept, and he felt too weak to fight. His eyelids burned, and his arms were too heavy to lift. He was barely able to hold himself in the saddle. He raised his tired eyes and saw that the sky was cloudless, as it almost always was here in Egypt. It was April—they had celebrated Easter only a few days before the retreat—and in this part of the world that meant suffocating heat. He dreaded the day's ride.

His companions seemed stronger. The Patriarch and the Templars had rested part of the night, they had brought food with them, and they were used to this climate, having lived most of their lives in Outremer.

Later in the morning he opened his half-shut eyes when he heard a note of fear in the voices around him. Ahead of the party a strange humming sound filled the air and black birds the size of geese rose and fell. One of the Templars rode ahead while the party waited in silence.

When he came back, his eyes were haunted and his face was sallow under his deep tan. "The field ahead is full of dead men. They have all been beheaded."

"Who are they?" asked the Patriarch.

"Christians. They have been stripped, and their skin is white. We must ride past them, your excellency. There is no way around."

The members of the party drew cloaks over their noses and mouths as they rode past the field of slaughter. The bodies had been exposed for many hours. The hum Amalric had heard, now almost deafening as they passed, was the sound of millions of fat, black flies, sharing the feast with the great vultures of Africa.

Amalric glanced at the corpses and then turned his face toward the river. If he were to go back to Mansura he would see a sight like this, and there the blood of the dead was on his hands.

He cringed from that thought, even as he kept his gaze away from these bodies.

A sudden notion struck him. Maurice will have to die. He knows too much.

But no, not while he is still so useful.

Around a bend in the river Amalric saw another sight that made him gasp. The riverbank and the shallows were strewn with wrecked galleys, their sails blackened tatters, many of them burnt to the waterline.

"Our sick and wounded," said Amalric. "They took them off these boats and slaughtered them in that field we passed."

"Remember, I said we would be safer on shore, monseigneur," said Maurice. "I suspected something like this when no food reached us from Damietta for so many weeks."

"Those Egyptian ships that passed, going up the river last night," said one of the Templars. "They did this. But how did they get between us and Damietta?"

"Baibars must have sent his galleys down another branch of the river and then transported them overland to the Damietta branch," said Maurice. "A difficult feat, but the Egyptians have light ships that can be carried in sections on camelback."

"May God have mercy on all our poor, lost men," said the Patriarch of Jerusalem. "They are surely in the bosom of Seigneur Jesus now. We should give them Christian burial."

"We few could not bury all these bodies in a month," said one of the Templars sadly. "And it is not safe to stay here, Your Excellency. We shall be in peril of our lives until we reach Damietta."

"Damietta is not safe either," said Amalric. "Who is there left to protect it?"

"See there," said Maurice. He pointed to a flat-bottomed barge floating in a slime-coated green backwater, half hidden by a thick stand of papyrus reeds. "That boat looks in good enough condition to carry us down the river. We can collect some oars from the other galleys, and the current will help us along. We could be in Damietta this very night."

Yes, thought Amalric. And then there will be no one to stop me from taking all the power I want—the power to depart for France, first of all, and leave Louis with no Damietta to use in bargaining for his life. If he lives even now.

Let us get to Damietta. Take the barge. It will mean having to leave this fine horse behind, but I am too tired anyway to ride any farther.

A Templar said, "There may be more Saracens on the river."

"Almost certainly all the Saracen ships have gone upriver to Mansura," said Maurice.

Slowly they rode toward the barge. "Is the crusade over, then, count?" asked the Patriarch. "We began with such high hopes and so many thousands of stout fighting men. Is all lost?"

"Yes, it is, your excellency," said Amalric, making his voice sound heavy with grief but feeling grim pleasure despite his weariness. "All is lost."

His chest swelled, and his limbs felt lighter. Fatigue and exultation together made him dizzy.

He looked with satisfaction into the watery eyes of the Patriarch. You thought surely you would get your bishop's throne in Jerusalem back, did you not, you old fool? All is lost for you, but not for me. My greatest victories are all ahead of me. And tonight, in Damietta, I shall be with Nicolette again.

XXVIII

THE QUIET HERE IN MARGUERITE'S BEDROOM AND THE QUIET OUTSIDE helped keep Nicolette calm. Sunday afternoon is peaceful, she thought, even in a Muslim city. For many minutes now she and Marguerite had enjoyed a companionable silence as they did their needlework together.

Keeping her hands busy with sewing eased the tension Nicolette felt, but fear for Roland and the King still lurked in her heart. There had been no news for weeks.

She was altering, to fit herself, a green silk dancer's gown she had found in the Damietta bazaar. She liked the Saracen style. Marguerite's work was of a more pious kind. Nicolette glanced at the heavy satin bishop's cope spread out on the bed, which Marguerite was embroidering with gold thread, resting the hoop on the huge curve of her belly. When that is finished, it will be worth a fiefdom, she thought. And embroidered by the Queen of France, that makes it priceless.

I wonder if she will finish it before the baby is born.

A change in the sounds of the city disturbed her. Why do I hear shouting in the streets?

Marguerite heard it, too. She dropped her embroidery frame and reached for Nicolette's hand, gripping it so hard that pain shot up Nicolette's arm.

"Nicolette, something terrible has happened. I can feel it."

They waited, talking in frightened murmurs as the cries came closer. It is a messenger, Nicolette decided, and he is telling his news to everyone he meets along the way, and the news is bad.

Soon the uproar had reached the palace, and now women were screaming and crying. Nicolette's heart clenched like a fist.

The door of the Queen's bedchamber was pushed open by Sire

Geoffrey de Burgh, an eighty-year-old knight whom Louis had charged with guarding Marguerite's person. There was a man behind him.

For a moment, Nicolette stopped breathing. She saw a tall knight with a sun-darkened face partly covered by a blond beard. It was a face she knew well, and yet it looked so ghastly it frightened her. Amalric.

He brushed past de Burgh, his heavy steps making the floorboards quiver, and knelt at the Queen's bedside. Another man slipped into the room and stood against a wall. Maurice, the old crusader Amalric had found here in Damietta when he first entered the city. How, she wondered, did that strange gray man come to be with Amalric now?

"Count Amalric," said Marguerite in a small, trembling voice. "You are welcome. What news do you bring us?"

It is a wonder she recognizes him, Nicolette thought. He was much thinner. Above the beard his heavily tanned face was bony. The blond hair hanging down to his shoulders in lank, greasy locks was doubtless crawling with lice. He was armored from head to foot. The steel of the square ailettes that protected his shoulders was dented, and his purple and gold surcoat was ragged. Even though he was on the far side of the bed she was aware of how his unbathed body reeked.

His stare transfixed her and she felt a cold dread in the pit of her stomach.

"Nicolette."

His eyes were bloodshot and set deep in hollowed-out sockets. They were cloudy with weariness, but behind the fatigue was a strange glow that frightened her.

What terrible things had he seen and done?

He returned his gaze to the Queen. "Madame, my news is quickly told, but grievous. The King, your husband, charged me to bring word to you. I begged him to let me stay with him to the end, but he commanded me to leave."

"The *end*?" Marguerite's voice was shrill with terror. "My God, is Louis killed?"

Nicolette suppressed a scream.

Amalric went on implacably. "I saw the King taken by the Mamelukes and carried off in chains, madame. He and his two brothers. As to whether he is still alive, I do not know."

Nicolette turned to Marguerite. At this moment her greatest fear was not for the men, lost somewhere in this horrible country, but for the woman beside her. This shock might do terrible injury to Marguerite and her child about to be born.

Nicolette jumped up and caught the Queen just as she fainted. Nicolette eased her friend back against the lace-edged pillows.

And then she turned to glare up at Amalric. So callous. Why did he tell Marguerite so brutally?

Keeping a tight rein on her anger, she forced herself to speak courteously. "I beg you, monseigneur. If you have more to say, say it gently. The Queen could give birth at any time."

"I come from a place where gentleness is unknown," Amalric answered coldly.

Amalric's eyes still held that glow of triumph. *Why*, she wondered, when he comes from disaster?

Then horror wrenched at her stomach as she understood. He has got what he wants. The King is lost.

And Roland? How will I ever find out?

We are all lost.

As she stared at Amalric, fear and anguish churning inside her, she massaged the Queen's deathly cold hands.

"It is dangerous to upset her in this condition," she said. "Please."

"She is in far worse danger than you imagine," Amalric coolly returned. "The Turks are on the way. The quicker she realizes that, the sooner we can get away from here."

Get away?

Nicolette fought panic. But the men—we do not even know what has happened to them. We cannot leave. What is he saying?

A white-bearded man wearing a cylindrical black hat and a black robe entered the bedchamber. A large silver cross with a double crossbar hung around his neck. Nicolette had seen him many times in Damietta before the army left. It was the Patriarch of Jerusalem. Surely he will not want to flee from here, she thought, feeling a little more hopeful.

"Is Madame the Queen able to travel?" the Patriarch asked Nicolette after she had kissed his ruby ring.

"Travel where, your excellency?"

It is true, she thought, feeling tears sting her eyes. They want to abandon Damietta.

"There is no Christian army between this city and the Saracen host," said Amalric. "All the crusaders are taken or slain. All."

There was a shriek from the doorway, followed by an outburs

of hysterical sobs. Nicolette turned and saw a group of ladies clustered there.

"Shut that door," said Amalric harshly.

Maurice went to the cedarwood door and firmly closed it.

But the damage is already done, Nicolette thought. By now the whole city knows.

I want Roland here. I want him *here*.

Her vision blurred, and she put her hands on the Queen's bed to steady herself. Oh, let him be alive. Please let him be alive.

Marguerite had come out of her faint. She looked up at Nicolette, her brown eyes overflowing with tears. She struggled to sit up, and Nicolette held her and soothed her.

"The Muslims have always allowed Christian knights and barons to ransom themselves," Marguerite said in a weak voice. "We must offer at once to pay for the King and his men."

"If they are still living, madame," said Amalric evenly.

God, I would like to kill *him*! Nicolette thought. He is *trying* to hurt her.

But Marguerite seemed to have found some inner strength. She sat a little higher in bed and looked unwaveringly back at Amalric.

"We must have faith, Count. My husband is too good a man. God would not let him be killed."

Amalric hesitated.

"You may be right, madame," he said after a long pause. "We shall offer to ransom him and the other barons. Once we are back in France, I shall see to collecting the money myself. By Saint Dominic, I will empty my own treasury to win our King Louis back." He struck his palm with his fist.

At the sound of her husband's name Marguerite began to sob quietly.

"To be honest, though, madame," Amalric went on, "I cannot hold out much hope. There are no people more treacherous than the Saracens. They could take ransom money from us and still kill the captives. They have no more mercy than wild beasts. On our way here we found the headless bodies of thousands of our sick and wounded."

"Oh, Mary, mother of God!" Marguerite's weeping became louder.

Nicolette sprang to her feet and glared at Amalric across the bed.

"Will you stop!"

Amalric's blazing eyes swung to her. "Be quiet," he said through his teeth.

"Nicolette is only trying to protect me, Count," said Marguerite. Her woe-filled eyes turned to Nicolette. "But it is all right, Nicolette. I must know everything. I have to make the decisions now."

How proud I am of you, Marguerite, Nicolette thought.

"How did this happen?" Marguerite asked, looking pleadingly at Amalric. "Our army was so strong. The King did everything to make it so."

Amalric shook his head. "Ah, madame, I fear he was misled and betrayed. He and all the other brave knights who followed him here. We did not lose the war here on the battlefield but at home in France. It is the conspirators and heretics in our own country who have won." Again he pounded his fist into his palm. "I will make it my life's work, after I return to France, to avenge our royal family and all the poor men who died here in Egypt."

Staring across the bed at him, Nicolette thought how much the fire in his blue eyes reminded her of Hugues. It was frightening.

The Queen looked bewildered at what he was saying.

"I do not know what you mean, Count Amalric," she said. Her pale hands rose from their resting place on her swollen belly, then fell helplessly back.

"No need to concern yourself, madame," said Amalric with a faint smile. "The important thing is for you to realize that there is no one to defend you here in Damietta but a handful of knights, most of them elderly, and a few unreliable Genoese sailors. We must take ship at once for Cyprus."

"Would you have her give birth at sea?" Nicolette exclaimed. "It could kill her."

"Would *you* have the Queen give birth in a Saracen prison?" said Amalric gratingly. "Or a harem?" he added in a horrified tone that did not sound sincere. He turned to Marguerite. "Give the order, madame, and we shall start boarding the ships at once."

Still weeping, Marguerite shook her head. "I cannot sail away and leave my husband. I must think what I can do to help him. I need time."

"Every moment of delay will make your position more dangerous," said Amalric.

"I see that," said Marguerite. "But I am not going to abandon Louis. I am afraid, Count, but I am not *that* afraid."

Marguerite sank back into the huge silken pillows.

"I need to be alone now," she said. "To think and to pray. And to rest." She turned to Nicolette. "Nicolette, your husband needs care. I give you leave to see to him." She added in a desolate voice, "You can thank God you have a husband to see to."

The Egyptian men who usually carried Nicolette's sedan chair had run away, she discovered. Amalric sent for a horse from the Queen's stable. When a page brought it, Nicolette climbed up behind him and they rode the short distance to the Saracen mansion he had claimed for himself when they took Damietta. Maurice said he would follow them on foot.

The locals who had been working in Nicolette's household also had vanished. Her French servants were trembling with terror. Agnes, who loved a man who had gone off with the army, was red-eyed and unable to speak.

Calmly and firmly Nicolette ordered Agnes to bring wine and to have a tub filled for Amalric in the bedroom.

She helped Amalric undress, forcing herself to do all a dutiful wife should for a husband who has returned after a long absence from a terrible war. She washed his body with precious perfumed soap from Spain. She washed his hair and cut it, combed the lice out, and even picked the nits out with her fingernails.

He said nothing, seeming caught up in his own thoughts.

The Queen's women and my own have men they love at Mansura, Nicolette thought, and they do not know whether they are alive or dead. But they at least can weep, or scream, or faint. I must keep my fear for my beloved locked in my heart.

Roland must be alive. If he were dead, I would know it. I would feel it. Or I would have dreamt it.

By the time Amalric was bathed, he had downed a flagon of wine. He fell naked on the bed he had had shipped here from France. His body, never exposed to the sun, was pale as ever. Red insect bites dotted his skin, standing out against the white. His muscles were hard and lean like stretched ropes, and the bones of his big frame showed through everywhere. He eyed her, and for a dreadful moment she thought he was going to make her submit to him, but his eyes closed and his mouth dropped open. Breathing heavily, sprawled on his back, he lay motionless. Nicolette spread a coverlet over him.

Now she was alone.

She started to tremble, then jumped to her feet and ran out of the room as if the Turks were already pursuing her.

How can I find out whether Roland is alive or dead?

How did we suffer such a defeat?

And how did Amalric alone escape?

Her temples throbbed, and she pressed her hands to her aching head.

Night fell, and still she paced the tiled floors of this strange, sprawling house that had once belonged to an emir. When she walked in the garden a warm breeze from the sea rustled the long sleeves of the cool white linen gown she wore.

She had to do something. But all I can do, she finally decided, is lend my strength to Marguerite. She is the only one now who can save the King. And whatever helps the King will help Roland, if he is still alive.

No, we must not give up Damietta. I must stop Amalric from persuading her to do that.

But how?

Just thinking of Amalric's power made her feel weak. Constable of France. What choice had Marguerite but to listen to him?

She shuddered with a realization. There was a way to turn Marguerite against Amalric. She would have to tell her. Everything. Amalric's ambition, the hatred of heresy that possessed him, his belief that Louis was ruining France, his wish that the King might die.

She will never believe me. What if she turns against me, not against Amalric? She will denounce me, and he will kill me.

Oh, dear Goddess, oh, sweet Jesus, what am I going to do?

She buried her face in her hands, frantic.

Suddenly she saw Roland's face before her, heard the words he had spoken to her long ago when he invited her to go up to the secret room at the bookseller's with him. *Risk it.*

She squared her shoulders. All right. I will tell her.

Having decided, she went upstairs to the bedroom and lay down on the bed as far from Amalric as possible.

For the rest of the night she was awake more than she slept.

When she heard the birds calling in the marshes around Damietta she knew that dawn was coming, and she got up again to dress herself in a dark brown tunic and a gray surcoat. Nothing gay or bright would do in this city in mourning.

She busied herself calming and comforting the servants. She and Agnes held hands and wiped away each other's tears. She

looked in on Amalric once before she left, during the hour of
Prime. He looked as if he might sleep through the day. He had
hardly moved all night long.

She hesitated at the doorway to the mansion. Until now she
had never hesitated to walk through the streets of Damietta, even
to visit the bazaars. From time to time, Marguerite and some of
the other women chided her for her boldness. Perhaps having
been a stranger in northern France for so long, Nicolette had
learned not to fear strange places. And so she had ignored the
warnings.

But then Damietta had been behind the lines of a conquering
army. Now things were altogether different.

She heard a crier in the minaret of the one mosque the
crusaders permitted, calling the Muslims to morning prayer.
Did she hear a new note of triumph in his voice?

I *will* go out, she decided. I have my dagger, and it is not far
to walk. I will not let my fears imprison me.

She felt drops of sweat on her brow and wiped them away
with the back of her hand. The day's terrible damp heat was
already rising. It is only April. If I spend another summer here, I
shall die anyway, Saracens or no.

She walked to the palace, not wanting to arrive before Marguerite might have had a full night's sleep. Sullen-looking Genoese sailors gathered around the outer gate glared at her. She kept
her eyes decorously down, pretending not to see them, but her
stomach was churning. Those ships anchored offshore, the ships
that had brought them all here, were hired from Genoa and
manned by Genoese crews. They cared nothing for France or the
crusade. Money alone interested them. What if, with this defeat,
they decided to leave?

We would have to go—or be left at the mercy of the Muslims.

When Nicolette entered the bedchamber, Marguerite was crying.
Sire Geoffrey de Burgh, who slept on a pallet at the foot of the
Queen's bed, saluted Nicolette and left them alone.

"Oh, Nicolette, I do not know what to do," Marguerite
sobbed. "Louis never talked to me about any of the plans he
made for the war. Now, if I do not do the right thing, he and all
those other men may die."

"Has there been any message from the Saracens?" Nicolette
sat on the edge of the bed and took Marguerite's hand.

"No." Marguerite shook her head woefully. "The first sign
we see of them may be their army surrounding the city."

"Marguerite, back in the days of Saladin, a woman named

Isabella of Toron held a castle with only eighteen knights against a whole Saracen army. You have at least fifty here.''

Marguerite wiped her face with her kerchief. "Oh, I know, I would not be the first woman to command a city under siege. Eleanor of Aquitaine did it, too. But I am no Eleanor. Tell me, how long did this Isabella and her knights hold out?"

"Five days."

Marguerite laughed, as Nicolette had hoped she would.

Nicolette looked out through the iron arabesques that barred the window. This room was probably part of the Egyptian governor's harem, she thought. What would it be like to be the slave of a Muslim, subject to his lusts? She would cut her own throat first.

"Nicolette, I will not leave Egypt without Louis. I want to hold this city until I can deliver him. But I know so little about warfare. The count—the Constable—your husband seems certain we should abandon Damietta. And we cannot depend on the Genoese. Admiral Lercari has asked me again and again to release their ships."

Nicolette's heart beat hard in her chest. Now is the time.

She reached for Marguerite's hands, holding them in both of hers. The Queen's hands were small and cold.

"Marguerite, about Amalric's advice—I have to tell you something terrible. You will find it hard to believe. Amalric does not have your good and the King's good at heart."

She held Marguerite's gaze with her own, watching fear, bewilderment, and suspicion flicker through the Queen's eyes. If only I could read her mind. If only she could read mine, and know that what I am telling her is the truth

After a silence Marguerite said, "In God's name, what are you saying?"

"My husband is very ambitious. And you know how he hates heretics."

"Nicolette, you are not making any sense. Louis has rewarded your husband's ambition. He has made him Constable. He listens to him. Amalric is Louis's cousin. Louis's mother loves him. And what do heretics have to do with this? Amalric spoke of heretics, too, yesterday. We are fighting Muslims, not heretics."

Sweet Goddess, it is going all wrong, thought Nicolette. She wished she could call her words back.

The royal bedchamber was growing uncomfortably warm as noon approached. Only the seaward breeze coming in through the grilled window kept the room from being stifling. Nicolette knew she ought to call in a page to fan Marguerite, but they had to finish this talk alone.

What shall I say next? O Goddess, give me eloquence.

"Amalric blames Louis. You remember, the Pope declared the Emperor a heretic, and yet Louis would not fight the Emperor. Well, Amalric has turned against the King. He has said so to me."

"But those disagreements are all in the past."

"Not for Amalric. He never forgets that heretics—as he believes—killed his father and his brother. He never wanted to go on this crusade. Now he just wants to get back to France. To destroy everything your husband has worked for—the prosperity of the common people, the equal justice, the general peace."

Marguerite looked bewildered, hurt. "But why? Anyone can see the good Louis has done."

"Amalric cares about two things only, the nobility and the Church. He wants the country run entirely for their benefit. And most of all, for his own."

Marguerite shook her head as if to clear it. She pulled her hands away from Nicolette's and wiped the sweat from her brow. Nicolette wet a linen cloth and patted the Queen's forehead and wrists with it.

"But we are not back in France arguing about how the country should be run," Marguerite said. "Louis is in the most terrible danger, and we must all work together to rescue him. Why are you tormenting me with these old disputes?"

I am just making life more difficult for her, Nicolette thought. Despair drove her to cut to the very heart of the matter.

She put down the damp cloth and leaned across the bed, bringing her face close to Marguerite's.

"Marguerite, please, listen to me. Amalric wants your husband to die!"

Marguerite shrank back. Her mouth fell open, her brown eyes grew huge, and she put her hands over her round belly.

"No!"

Appalled at the enormity of what she had just said, Nicolette managed to choke out, "I swear it is true. He has felt that way for years."

"For years? Then why have you never said anything before?" Nicolette saw anger growing in Marguerite's eyes.

"Would you have believed me? Would you trust a woman

who accuses her own husband of treason? A woman who, as you well know, loves her husband's enemy?"

"But you let this go on? You let my husband befriend a man who is plotting his death?" The horror and rage were mounting ever higher in Marguerite's face.

My God, thought Nicolette, am I upsetting her more than Amalric did yesterday?

"I did not say he was plotting the King's death," she said, forcing herself to speak calmly. "I have no proof of that. I said he wants the King to die. In the long run he hopes either to make himself King or to control whoever wears the crown."

"If this is true, he must be mad. If it is not true, you are. Will you accuse your husband to his face?"

Nicolette felt as if the floor had disappeared beneath her feet. She pictured herself facing Amalric before the Queen, perhaps before a court of clergy and knights. Her word, the word of a wife, against one of the greatest barons in the realm.

She stood up and went to the window. Through the iron scrollwork she looked down into the palace courtyard. The same little group of Genoese seamen were squatting on the tiles. Like Amalric, they want to force us to leave, she thought.

She turned to face Marguerite. After looking at the bright sunlight outside, the bedroom seemed shadowed to her, and she could barely see the Queen on the bed.

"Yes," she said, because she could not say anything else. "Yes, I will say it to his face. If that is what you want."

Marguerite shook her head. "I do not know what I want. I need help as I have never needed help in my life before, and you are telling me that the strongest man at my side is a traitor."

Nicolette stepped closer to the bed and saw that Marguerite's face remained deeply flushed with anger.

I have made everything so much harder for her, thought Nicolette miserably. I have failed to convince her, and I have ruined our friendship. Now Amalric will have his way.

When Marguerite spoke again, it was in a cold fury.

"Would you have me govern this city, hold it against the Saracens and try to ransom my husband, all the while suspecting that Amalric de Gobignon is a traitor?"

Marguerite pressed her hands against the bed and with difficulty pushed herself until she was sitting bolt upright. Nicolette reached out to help her, but Marguerite waved her away.

"Why, oh, why," Marguerite went on, "did you keep this

from me until now? I thought we were friends. I thought I knew everything about you.''

"I never told you because I knew it would be almost impossible for you to believe me. You have before you no proof, only my word against one who is the King's own cousin. Would the King himself have believed it, if such a rumor reached his ears, even if it came from you, Marguerite? Dear friend, I have only one reason for telling you now. The King's life is in such danger I cannot keep silent. Even if you cannot believe me. Even if you make me confront Amalric. Even if you throw me in prison or he kills me. At least I have spoken out. And now, you must decide.''

Marguerite stared at Nicolette.

An eternity seemed to pass. Nicolette sat with her hands knotted in her lap. She could hear the gruff voices of the mariners below, talking to one another in Italian.

Marguerite spoke. "Nicolette, in all this horrible Outremer, you are the only one whose counsel I can trust. You must tell *me* what to do.''

Nicolette went limp with relief. She reached out her arms to Marguerite and held her, feeling the Queen's tear-wet face pressed against her cheek. Our love for each other is strong, she thought. It may yet save us.

They wept in each other's arms until they both quieted. Nicolette sat back and tried to pull her scattered thoughts together.

She had not thought beyond speaking out about Amalric. Somehow, Marguerite, once persuaded not to trust Amalric, would do the right thing.

But what was the right thing? Marguerite did not know, any more than she did. With a jolt of fear she realized the burden of saving their loved ones still rested as much upon Nicolette herself as upon her Queen.

She thought, and spoke.

"The only advice I can give you is that as long as you hold Damietta, you have something to trade for the King's life. You must not give this city up. And you *can* hold Damietta. We have fifty or so knights. They may be old, but they must be good at their trade or they would not have lived so long. We have servants and pages and common people who can be armed. Perhaps we can get the Genoese to send some crossbowmen ashore. With these we can hold it for a time, at least. And you can send messages to Cyprus, to the Christian strongholds in Syria and Palestine. More knights will come. The Templars and the Hospitalers will send knights. With the Queen of France in such peril, what chivalrous man could stay away?''

Marguerite took Nicolette's hands. The Queen's grip was stronger now.

"Yes," said Marguerite, "as long as we have those ships we are not lost."

"Send to Queen Blanche and tell her what has happened. Tell her you will need ransom money. The Templars guard the treasury of France, and they have banks throughout Outremer. They can transmit the money for you."

"Of course!" Marguerite exclaimed.

"You must also send word to the Sultan, let him know you are willing to bargain," said Nicolette. "Perhaps the Patriarch can go to him under a flag of truce."

"Yes." The color was coming back into Marguerite's cheeks. But then she paled and her face fell. "What can I do about your husband? Must I confront him? Accuse him? Have him imprisoned?"

"For now I think not," Nicolette said. "You have no proof of his malice. Only my word, and that is not enough to convince others. You will divide our forces if you act against him now, and we have little enough strength as it is. But you must not let Amalric take command of the city. *You* must speak, in the King's name, and leave no doubt that everyone here is under your rule.

"I know—you can appoint Amalric commander of the city's defenses. That will make it clear that he gets his authority from you. It will make the defense of the city a matter of his honor. That might hinder him from doing anything to undermine our resistance to the Saracens and force us to leave. And if he does, you have the proof you need to move against him."

"It will be hard to face him and not let him know I think of him as an enemy."

"You can do it," said Nicolette. "I have been doing it for years," she added bitterly.

"I will call the chief men in the city together today, Nicolette," Marguerite said, suddenly fired with determination, "and tell them that as long as the King and his brothers and the remaining crusaders are in the hands of the Egyptians, we will hold Damietta."

Then Margeurite again looked uncertain. "Do you really believe we can do it, Nicolette? With a few old knights, a crowd of half-pirate Genoese, and a baron who wants to usurp the throne?''

"We have ourselves, Marguerite," said Nicolette, taking both the Queen's hands in hers. "Are we not women of Languedoc?"

"Yes!" Marguerite's smile flashed, and the sight of it brought tears to Nicolette's eyes. "I will show them all, Nicolette—the Saracens and the Genoese and our people—and Louis—what a Queen a woman of Languedoc can be."

XXIX

"GOD, I NEED FOOD," AMALRIC GROWLED AS HE AND NICOLETTE entered the main hall of their Egyptian mansion. "I have not had anything decent in months. And then that silly woman's summons woke me and I had no time. Bring me bread and cheese and fruit at once, and put the servants to roasting a beef. And wine, a jar of that good Cypriot wine."

Quietly, Nicolette gave orders to the servants as Amalric sat heavily on a divan.

The servants set a table before Amalric, and Nicolette seated herself on a gilded footstool across from him. She felt as if she were in a cage with an angry wolf. He attacked everything brought to him, gulping his wine between huge bites.

Nicolette picked at the fruit. She had no appetite.

But everything had gone as she had hoped. How proud she had been of Marguerite as she firmly told Amalric and the other chief men in the city that she had no intention of giving up Damietta.

Amalric had blustered, as Nicolette knew he would, but to her delight Marguerite had stood her ground. Lercari had demanded a written guarantee of more payment for his ships and men. Marguerite had called for pen and parchment, scribbled a note, and tossed it at the Genoese admiral as if he were a beggar.

Nicolette almost smiled at the memory, but she dared not in front of Amalric.

Now, as he chewed his way through a joint of beef, Amalric slowed down to pause and glower at Nicolette.

"You had something to do with this, Nicolette."

She tensed. She had feared this—that he might suspect her.

"With what, monseigneur?"

"By Saint Dominic, do not play innocent with me. This morning when I was awakened you were already at the palace. No doubt giving Marguerite the benefit of your good counsel."

"It is my duty to serve the Queen, and she needs me now more than ever."

"When I went to bed yesterday I was certain that I could convince her today—with help from you—that we should sail for Cyprus at once. Today I wake up and she is preparing for a siege. Who changed her mind, Nicolette?"

She could not take her eyes off his big hands, holding the beef bone and dripping with blood. She could feel those hands around her neck, squeezing.

"The Queen makes up her own mind, monseigneur. But she did ask my advice."

"And what did you say to her?" asked Amalric with menacing softness, putting down the chunk of meat.

Nicolette steeled herself. *I cannot show fear. I must pretend this is just an ordinary conversation.*

"I said that instead of just giving up Damietta she should use it to bargain with the Saracens. We could offer to surrender Damietta if the King is freed."

Almaric's hand shot across the table and seized her wrist. The touch of his fingers, wet from the meat, made her skin crawl.

"So it *was* you. You have ruined everything. From now on I command you, as my wife who owes me obedience, to tell the Queen only what I order you to say."

God, how she hated him.

She jerked her arm, and her wrist slid free.

"You cannot blame a woman, even one who is Queen, for not wanting to abandon her husband, monseigneur."

He eyed her.

He is wondering how much I understand, she thought.

"It is a foolish waste of lives and of treasure to cling to Damietta," he said. "The army is lost."

The thought of Roland and King Louis and so many other good men suffering and dying while Amalric calmly stuffed himself with beef infuriated her. "Is it not enough that you left the entire army to be taken captive? Left all your own men back there? Even your faithful vassal, d'Etampes? All but your toady, Maurice. Must you desert your comrades altogether?"

The blood drained from his face under the deep tan, and he

stared at her, lips drawn back from his teeth. "Are you calling me a coward?"

"No—no—" Her voice trembled as she realized, terror-stricken, how dangerously she had spoken in her surge of anger.

He pointed a grease-stained finger at her. "It is that troubadour. That is who you are thinking of when you talk of my comrades. You have never really forgotten him, have you? You fear for him." There was mockery in his voice.

"I fear for all the men killed or taken captive, all of them, whether I know them or not."

Amalric leaned toward her, his wide grin baring canine teeth.

"I have the pleasure of putting your fears to rest, madame. Your former lover, the troubadour, is dead."

For just a moment her vision clouded. Then she clenched her fists under the table, digging the nails into her palms. I will not show anything. I will not let him see that he has hurt me.

"I say again I mourn for all the dead at Mansura." She kept her lips from quivering.

"It was just as we were retreating from Mansura on Fat Tuesday," he went on, as if she had not spoken. "De Vency and his equerry ventured into a courtyard, perhaps looking for a bit of loot to carry off. A swarm of Egyptians who had lain in ambush on the rooftop fell upon them. I saw them go down under dozens of flashing daggers. Then more Egyptians, Mamelukes, were upon us. I myself barely escaped."

Her head spun. I do not believe it. He has made up this story. He does not know.

If Roland were dead I would know it.

But the story Amalric told her was so full of particulars. It *sounded* true.

She drew in her lower lip and bit down on it. "You seem to have a talent for escaping from dangerous places, monseigneur."

He rose from the divan, his eyes wild, and stood crouched across from her, his hand resting on the hilt of his dagger.

Heart beating wildly, she waited for him to spring at her.

Then, slowly, he relaxed. "You are trying to goad me. You want to hide what you feel from me. I am happy that his death hurts you. But now you can forget him."

His expression began to change. His eyes smoldered with a look that was part pain, part desire.

"If only you could love me, Nicolette, as I love you. You will never know how I longed for you out there. Even in the midst of that nightmare, with the dead and dying all around me, I kept thinking that I was coming back to you.''

"I am honored, monseigneur," she said faintly.

"Honored?" He smiled bitterly. "The devil with honored. I need you, Nicolette." He reached out the hand that had been holding his dagger. "Please. It has been so long."

Oh, no, she thought. Oh, no, no, no. How could I bear it, when he has just told me Roland is dead? She fought to keep her face and body under control.

"Nicolette, I must have you. Now."

She would scream if he touched her. She would rather be burned alive.

"I do not—I do not want to, monseigneur." ·

He stepped around the table and took hold of her arm. His grip was not very hard, but she felt the terrible strength behind it. He smelled of meat and wine.

"Please, Nicolette. Be kind to me. I have been back a day and a night, and I have yet to feel your arms around me. By God, I have suffered and bled for months in this stinking country. I have fought my way back to you when all the other French knights were captured. I had hoped you would welcome me back. It has been very long for you, too, has it not? Have you not missed me? Have you never wanted me?''

With an enormous effort, she resigned herself. She had to let him do as he wanted, so that he might make the mistake of trusting her more.

"Very well," she said in a low voice. "But clean your hands first."

"Anything madame asks," he said with a wry smile. He let go of her to splash some water in a basin and rinse his hands in it. He dried them on his purple and gold tunic. Then he took her hand and in silence led her upstairs.

Their chamber had been part of the emir's harem. An entire suite on the second floor was closed off by a heavy wrought-iron gate. Amalric had had their bed placed in the largest of these rooms. Now he led her to the bed, and she lay down.

I will turn myself to stone, she thought, and try to flee this agony within.

But when he entered her, it hurt, as it always did, because her body did not want him, and she knew that she was not stone but flesh. She waited for it to be over, thinking of him gloating over Roland's death, and hating him for it. When he groaned and relaxed, she could bear the intimacy no longer. Quickly she twisted out from under him and turned on her side, sinking her teeth into her fist.

In her mind she saw Roland's dark, smiling face, and her body was rigid with grief.

"He really is dead, you know," said Amalric, showing an awareness that frightened her. "I saw him fall." He got up and adjusted his clothing. "I will leave you to enjoy your deep sorrow in private. There is much for me to do." His voice took on an ironic tone. "After all, I am in command of the defense here."

After he left the room, she turned over on the bed, biting the satin bedcover to muffle her sobs. She lay there for what seemed like hours, wanting to scream aloud but not wanting to be heard.

I must get out of here, she told herself at last. She pushed herself up and, moving like a person under an enchantment, took a dark, hooded silk cloak out of her clothes chest and put it on.

Her face was expressionless and her eyes dry as she stepped through the arched doorway of the mansion. She smelled the salt on the cool breeze from the north and for a moment wished she were at sea, escaping from this horrible land.

Just as she was crossing the courtyard to the outer gate she heard running footsteps and Agnes's voice calling her. She stopped and turned.

"Madame, it is not safe to go out."

Nicolette looked at Agnes. Her eyelids were red, her cheeks sunken in. Oh, poor friend, what have I led you into?

"I will be safe enough," Nicolette said quietly, impatient to leave.

Agnes took a deep breath. "I will go with you, madame," she said, swallowing hard. "If you want me to."

How much courage it must have taken for her to say that, Nicolette thought, feeling a rush of love for Agnes. Poor thing, she is terrified. But she would face the whole Egyptian army at my side, if I asked her to.

"I am not going far," Nicolette lied. "Go back inside, Agnes. I will be fine."

After she went out the gate, she drew a veil like a Muslim woman's over her face and raised the hood. She glanced up at the burning African sun. It was mid-afternoon. She would have to be back before dark.

She was relieved to see that the gateway through Damietta's triple walls was still open. That must mean that the Saracen army was not yet approaching. The sergeant in charge spoke roughly, warning her that the gate would be closed at sunset. He evidently took her for a woman of low degree or even a Saracen woman.

She had but one thought in mind, to mourn for Roland. But she could not let Amalric, or anyone who knew Amalric, see her sorrow. Leaving Damietta, with the Bedouins prowling outside, was even more dangerous than walking in the streets, but she had to be alone with her grief.

She went down to the river. She knew no Arabic, but the Egyptian boatman understood her gestures and the offer of a Cypriot silver drachma. She indicated that she intended to row out alone, and the Egyptian shook his head and shrugged. He probably thinks I am mad, she thought, but that coin is worth more than his skiff, and why should he care what happens to me?

She started to row upriver. Under the afternoon sun the muddy water was the color of brass. She had not been to the island since that night with Roland last autumn, but she thought she could find the place again.

The river was quiet. She was rowing against the current, but the Nile's flow was not strong in April. She left the walls of Damietta behind and slid past small Egyptian villages with their waterwheels turned by buffaloes, and dovecotes on the roofs of the gray mud huts. Canals branched off the river, and she recognized one and turned into it, rowing by islands formed by the crisscrossing network of waterways. The island she wanted rose higher than the others and was crowned by temple ruins.

There. She saw slender white columns, broken off near the top, rising above the reeds. She grounded the boat and climbed out. Her deerskin boots sank in the soft earth as she pushed through the reeds to the temple, built ages ago when pagan Greeks had ruled here.

From the slight rise at the center she had a clear view, beyond the flat marshes, of the walls and towers of Damietta.

She walked into the circle of columns and dropped to her knees on the marble floor. She looked for and found a carving that she and Roland had talked about the night they came here. It had fallen from the temple roof and showed a naked young man facing three naked women and holding out an apple to one of them. Roland had said the one receiving the apple was the Goddess of Love. She reached out and with her fingertips touched the smooth shoulder of the young man.

"Roland!" she screamed. "Do not leave me!"

She lay on the marble, sobbing until her throat hurt and she was too hoarse to do more. She wept and thought of Roland and wept still more as the sun slowly descended and the shadows of the columns grew longer.

Oh, Roland, I cannot bear it. I cannot believe you are gone. Our souls were united in Love. They must still be linked. Would I not feel it if you were killed?

For a moment she allowed herself to hope.

But despair took over again. He must be dead. When so many thousands had died, how could he still be alive?

Then she heard footsteps. Voices.

Her heart stopped. Her body froze. The voices were speaking Arabic. Sweet Jesus, the Bedouins!

She shrank into the shadow of the fallen temple wall. On this little island there was no place to hide. And they probably had already seen her boat. She could hear the men coming closer, their footsteps crushing the low shrubbery, their voices getting louder. She wrapped her arms around herself in terror. In her grief she had given no thought to her danger. But if these were Bedouins, the same who had been murdering unwary crusaders, first they would rape her, and then they would take her to Cairo and sell her, and she would spend the rest of her life as a slave whose body belonged to any man who owned her. And she had not even thought to bring a dagger with her, to defend or kill herself.

A tall man in Bedouin robes emerged from the reeds.

Though he was dressed as an Arab his long mustache was red and one of his eyes was blue—the other white as an eggshell, and a scar ran through it from brow to cheek.

The reeds parted again and a second man appeared. He stared at her in amazement.

"By Saint Christopher! It is madame the countess!"

Her hood and her kerchief had fallen away during her spasms of grief, so Maurice had no trouble recognizing her.

She read a succession of feelings in the wizened face—surprise, dismay, anger, and calculation. Why is he here? And who is this Arab, or whatever he is?

She climbed to her feet and made herself stand straight and face the two men. Muslims despise women who let their faces be seen, she thought. This Bedouin probably thinks I am a whore.

The one-eyed man took a few steps toward her, speaking to her in a low but commanding voice, in his own tongue. His mouth was a lipless slash under the red mustache, and his grin was frightening.

"Maurice, you are my husband's vassal. Protect me." She hoped the trembling of her knees would not be visible under her gown.

"Be careful, madame. This man is the chieftain of a powerful tribe. Be polite to him. Do not anger him, and he will not hurt you."

The Bedouin asked Maurice a question, and Maurice's answer seemed to Nicolette as fluent as if he had been born in Egypt, although his toothless mouth muffled his words. He spoke softly and with respect that bordered on fear, the way he might speak to a great seigneur. Nicolette caught the words "Countess de Gobignon" in the midst of the long string of Arabic phrases.

The one-eyed man looked surprised, then laughed a little and shrugged.

He reached out with his right hand and grasped her face. His hand was huge, and the palm and fingers were rough.

She wanted to pull away, but she felt paralyzed, transfixed by the gaze of the single blue eye. She thought of tales she had heard of one-eyed giants who lived somewhere on the shores of the great sea.

His fingers slid over her cheek with surprising delicacy, then he smiled at her and turned away.

She heard Maurice softly release his breath.

The tall Bedouin spoke to Maurice, and Maurice in turn addressed Nicolette. "I have some business with him, madame. Wait here, and when we are done, I will take you safely back to Damietta."

He and the chieftain walked around to the side of the island facing Damietta. They stood looking at the city and talking in low voices.

That one-eyed man is a scout for the Saracen army, thought Nicolette, and Maurice is telling him about our defenses. He has lived thirty years among the Muslims and must have become one of them.

Anger choked her. He might have helped destroy our army at Mansura. Helped kill Roland. She shook with rage.

The sun hung low over the flat marshland. Nicolette thought of trying to run for the boat, but she knew they could catch her.

When they were done talking, she saw Maurice bow to the Arab, touching his right hand to his forehead, lips, and breast. Almost like the sign of the cross, Nicolette thought. The Bedouin bowed to Maurice with a flourish of his hand, turned, and plunged into the reeds. A moment later Nicolette heard a horse's hollow footfalls on the bridge over the canal from this island to the next.

Maurice returned to her. She braced herself, ready to fight or run if he attacked her. She watched his hands closely, alert for a move toward her or to the dagger in his jeweled scabbard. He is old, she thought. He cannot be as strong as I am. But he *looks* strong.

"It is good that you came by boat, madame," he said. "I walked out, and it would take us hours to walk back. By that time they will have closed the gates. May I row you back, madame?"

She tried to think what to say to him as they walked toward her boat. If I question him he may kill me. But he must expect me to demand an explanation. If I say nothing at all, he will be convinced I plan to denounce him when we get back. And then he will surely kill me.

"That man is the chief of a tribe," Maurice said, "a tribe that owns many sheep. I have just made an agreement with him that will put meat on your table even if there is a siege. Is that not splendid?" He eyed her searchingly.

If I call him a liar, he can still kill me, she thought.

"I suppose, then, my husband knows about this—agreement?"

"I have done this sort of thing for him in the past, madame. That is why he came back to you looking as fit as he did. You can ask him about the fresh-killed lamb and beef I bought him at Mansura. Old soldiers know how to forage. But, as it happens, he does not know about this meeting today, and I think it best to keep it that way for now. It would not look right for the commander of Damietta to be getting provisions from the Bedouins. If I get caught at it, he can swear on the Sacred Host he did not know anything about it. Do you not think that is best?"

He swept a clump of reeds aside, and there was her little flat-bottomed boat. In the distance the rippling water of the canals reflected the setting sun like gold filigree. Maurice steadied the skiff for her as she got in and climbed to the seat in the stern. Without hesitation he stepped knee-deep into the muddy water and pushed off, then slid nimbly in, dripping, to seat himself amidships at the oars.

"My life is in your hands, madame," Maurice said gravely as they drifted down the canal toward the Nile. "The Christians in Damietta are mad with fear. If you say I was spying, they will hang me without asking for my side of it."

And that is exactly what I will do, she thought. If he is foolish enough to let me live.

Maurice rowed in silence, head bowed. When he looked up at her again, it was slyly and with a hint of disrespect.

"Perhaps Madame has secrets of her own to keep. Such a beautiful spot for lovers to meet, that island, is it not? You ought to tell me, if you do not want the count to know about your visit, so that I will be careful not to speak of it."

She cast her eyes down, avoiding his shrewd gaze.

"We understand each other, Maurice. We each have things we would rather not have the count know about. Perhaps you can do me a service as well. Besides getting meat from the Bedouins, are you able to get information?"

"Anything madame wishes."

Her stomach muscles tightened. I am taking a chance. He could use it against me.

"Could you find out for me what knights are still alive as prisoners at Mansura?"

"Is madame interested in learning about any particular knight?"

"If you have any news of the captives, bring it to me, and I will decide what further questions I have for you."

They were in the main channel of the Nile now, the brown walls of Damietta looming on the riverbank. They spoke no more, each absorbed in thought.

If Maurice is really helping the Saracens, Damietta might fall if I fail to denounce him. I will have murdered all of us.

Dear God, now I shall have to watch Amalric and Maurice both.

She felt weak, crushed by fear. Why must this all fall on me?

But there was no one else. She would have to struggle on alone.

XXX

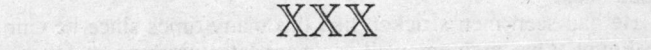

Roland had lost track of the days, but he thought he must have been a prisoner of the Mamelukes for about two months when he was marched from the house of Lokman to the walled camp outside Mansura.

He stumbled through the gateway in the mud-brick wall. Inside he saw a small cluster of brown huts like all the others he had seen along the Nile. But here were no Egyptian peasants. Instead, everywhere were men of France, hundreds of them, maybe thousands. His heart sank.

Two months—that was all it had taken Baibars and his Mamelukes to reduce the rest of Louis's army to this.

"Ah, Jesus!" Perrin whispered.

The men were tattered, thin, filthy. Some paced, some stood staring into space. Most sat on the dusty ground. They wore whatever rags were left to them after the Egyptians had taken their armor. Worst of all, Roland thought, they did not seem to care about anything. Only a few even bothered to look up when Roland's group straggled into the compound.

Roland found himself remembering the glorious June day in Paris two years before, sunlight dazzling on helmets, thousands of knights on magnificent chargers, the Oriflamme gold against a blue sky, the deafening cheering of the crowds, the King in his glittering armor. And he looked again at these defeated, despairing men. And then he wept.

"In the name of the Voice comes brightness," Perrin said suddenly that night.

"Saint Michel! Be still!" Roland snapped, recognizing the Cathar saying.

"The lord of this world has me fast in his power," said the jongleur, slurring his words.

Roland looked around the dark, crowded hut to see whether any of the captive knights had heard. He saw no sign.

Perrin must be talking in his sleep, Roland thought. He reached

395

out a hand and gave him a shake. "Keep talking like that and you will get us killed," he whispered.

Then a dread suspicion struck him. He put his hand on Perrin's forehead. The jongleur's brow was so hot Roland jerked his hand back.

He had seen men stricken like this many times since he came to Egypt. One moment well, an hour later writhing in fever, a few days after, dead.

He seized Perrin's hot hand in both of his and squeezed it as hard as he could.

"Fight it, Perrin," he whispered fiercely.

Fear turned his body as cold as Perrin's was hot. There was nothing he could do. There was no food, no medicine, no one left who knew anything about illness. Oh, Guido, why did they have to kill you?

He stroked Perrin's forehead, rubbed his burning hands. His helplessness was torture. Is this all I can do—sit here and watch him die?

He looked around at the other knights in the hut. Could any of them do anything? Each sat enclosed in his own silence.

I can count myself lucky even to be with him, Roland thought.

They were together only because Perrin had been kept with the knights at the house of Lokman. The commoners captured when the rest of the army surrendered were being held in another brick-walled enclosure a small distance away.

In the days that followed, the whites of Perrin's eyes turned deep pink, a yellow crust formed on his lips, and he kept sweating away the little flesh left on his bones.

Roland sat with him constantly, numb with fear. He begged for extra bowls of the watery mash the Egyptians brought twice a day in buckets and tried to force it down Perrin's throat, but the jongleur could not swallow.

Though he had never had much trust in God, Roland found himself praying.

At midday, a week after their arrival in the camp, Roland stepped out of his hut for air. The entire camp stank, but less so outside.

He noticed a small crowd gathered at the wall. Some of the men were shouting angrily. Curious, Roland went over to them. A young knight was standing on the shoulders of two other men, watching something. He climbed down just as Roland pushed his way into the crowd. He was white with fear.

"They are killing the sergeants and the men-at-arms," he said. He wiped his nose with the grimy back of his hand. "You can hear screams from within the stockade where they are holding them, and a cart just came out from there with a pile of bodies. Bodies with no heads."

Just as at the house of Lokman, thought Roland.

His sorrow was deep inside, tormenting his whole body, like the constant hurting of an infected wound.

A man with a filthy, bloodstained bandage tied around his face said, "The worst of it is, our men have no priests to shrive them before they die. The dogs of Saracens cut all the priests' throats the day they took us."

"It will be us next," said the man who had been looking over the wall.

"Not at all," said a dark-bearded knight who somehow had managed to be better dressed than the rest of them. "That treatment is only for commoners. Surely even the Saracens have more chivalry than to butcher knights as they would peasants."

Rage clouded Roland's vision. Fists clenched, he shouldered his way to stand in front of the bearded knight.

"Messire, I shall thank you not to speak scornfully of men who are dying because they have served us faithfully," he said, keeping his voice soft.

"I do not know you," the well-dressed knight said loftily, but what he saw in Roland's eyes put fear into his own.

"I know him," said the man with the bandage. "And he knows more of chivalry than you ever will, monseigneur. Good Christian men are being murdered over there, and if you think yourself too grand to grieve for them you can at least show a decent respect."

"It is true, though, we will have to buy our way out," said the man who had been looking over the wall. "Monseigneur the Count Pierre de Bretagne has already made an offer to the Saracens on behalf of himself and those of us who are his vassals."

"My seigneur was William Longsword," said the bandaged man with a heavy sigh. "There is no ransoming your way out of the place where he is gone." He gripped Roland's hand. "Walter of Salisbury. You let me keep my horse and arms at the King's tournament, remember?"

"Oh, yes," said Roland. My God, he thought, that was an age ago and a world away. It was sometimes hard to believe that France even existed.

Jean de Joinville took Roland's arm. Like everyone else in the prison village, de Joinville's face was all bones. We look like the dancing skeletons in the church carvings, Roland thought, except that we do not dance.

"The King sent me to fetch you, messire," de Joinville said.

De Joinville led Roland to a mud-brick hut no better than those occupied by the rest of the knights.

"What a palace, eh?" de Joinville said with a melancholy smile. "Two rooms. But he only has to share it with his brothers and their men."

A rumor had reached Roland that the Saracens had offered to hold the King and his brothers in a mansion in the city, but Louis had insisted on being with his knights. No doubt, thought Roland, that pleased Charles and Alphonse not at all, since they had to go where Louis went.

"Sire Roland." Louis's voice came weakly from the darkness as they entered. "Have you heard? They are killing our foot soldiers."

As Roland's eyes adjusted to the dim light, he saw that he was in a bare room with walls of brown plaster and a floor of trampled dirt. The King was seated against the far wall on a blanket-covered pile of straw. The faithful Isambert, as much Louis's friend as his cook, stood beside him like a pillar. If the barons and knights looked like living skeletons, the King looked like Death himself. All he needed was a scythe.

"I have just come from some men who were looking over the wall, sire," said Roland, seating himself on the dirt floor at Louis's gesture.

"We can save lives if we act quickly," said Louis. His hands were trembling, and his teeth were chattering.

Roland had heard that the Sultan had sent his own doctor into the village to treat the King's bloody flux, and the worst of the illness was said to be over, but Louis was still terribly weak.

"What can we possibly do, sire?"

Louis held out a hand to Isambert, who helped him up. He stood shakily but without support. At once, Roland stood up, too.

"I am going to the Sultan," said Louis. "I shall beg him to let me ransom all my men." He put a hand on Roland's shoulder, his grip surprisingly firm. "De Montfort is down with the tertian fever. You must come with me to convey my words to the Sultan."

"No, sire!" de Joinville cried, anguished. "You must not risk your life."

"Have I not been risking my life all along?" said Louis calmly. "Have I not asked every one of you to do the same?"

The guards at the heavy, makeshift wooden door recognized the King, and after conferring with their superiors let Louis and Roland out of the prison compound. They ushered them to a pavilion just outside the entrance, in which Sahil the eunuch sat on silken cushions, surrounded by his assistants. All the Egyptians rose and bowed deeply to the King, pressing their hands together before their chests.

"What does the thrice-honored King of the Franks wish of us, O knight of the emerald?" Sahil asked.

Not surprising that Sahil remembers me, Roland thought with amusement.

"Tell him I must speak to the Sultan at once, as one monarch to another," Louis said to Roland.

Sahil's eyebrows twitched on hearing this, as if to comment on the absurdity of a man in Louis's position making demands, but he bowed again.

"I shall send word to my lord."

Roland was grateful for the wait in Sahil's tent, where the air was cool and clean and smelled of rose petals. Yet his mind kept returning to Perrin. Even now his fever could be getting worse. What if he dies while I am gone? He found it hard to respond to Louis's attempts at conversation.

Two Saracen warriors with drawn scimitars strode into Sahil's tent. Their gold-trimmed breastplates and helmets identified them as men of the *halka*, the Sultan's Mameluke bodyguard. They spoke to Sahil and motioned Louis and Roland to come with them.

King Louis, Roland noticed with admiration, walked with as regal an air as if he were in his own palace.

The Sultan's men marched them briskly through the Egyptian camp, whose warriors turned to stare in openmouthed curiosity at the tall, serene figure of the captive King of the Franks. The tents they passed were arranged in orderly rows, not scattered about at the whim of their owners, as in French camps.

Roland felt abashed, ashamed even, among the Mamelukes. These so-called slave warriors had crushed Christendom's best knights.

Their guards led them to a tent-palace, a series of huge,

interconnected domes of yellow silk stretched over frames of lightweight wood. The plank floors were covered with thick carpets woven in intricate designs of red and gold, blue and green. The pavilions and their silken cushions and bright hangings looked graceful and comfortable. Moment by moment he felt dirtier and clumsier. We are barbarians compared to these people, he thought.

Roland had lost count of the pavilions they had passed through when Louis and he came to the largest dome of all, where a semicircle of a dozen turbaned men faced them. The light cast by brass lamps glinted on jeweled sword hilts and corselets inlaid with gold. A spicy odor of incense masked the smell of burning oil.

Roland had to force himself to look directly at these men. He and the King were facing their conquerors, the rulers of Egypt.

In the center of the group a stout man with the dark, heavy features of a Turk reclined on the red, green, and yellow cushions of a gilded divan. His lips, thick and red in the midst of his glossy black beard, curved in a supercilious smile. He reminded Roland of the well-dressed knight who had spoken unconcernedly of the deaths of the foot soldiers.

A Mameluke officer standing to one side of the tent said, "You must kneel to the anointed of Allah, His Majesty Turan Shah, the Sultan of Cairo."

Knowing it would be death to show disrespect, Roland fell to his knees, but Louis only bowed deeply.

"Tell them, Roland, that the King of France may bow in courtesy to a brother monarch, but he is forbidden to kneel to any but his holiness the Pope."

This is the end of us now, Roland thought, but he translated without hesitation. To die at the side of his King would not be a bad death. As he spoke, he noticed Baibars sitting beside Turan Shah. A small smile played about the Mameluke emir's wide mouth.

Turan Shah shrugged off Louis's response. "My father told me that Emperor Frederic did not kneel to him either. Of course, they met as equals, not as conqueror and prisoner." He looked about him at the Mameluke commanders for appreciation. Several of them nodded and chuckled, but Baibars was expressionless.

He does not play up to the Sultan as the others do, Roland thought.

Turan Shah took a grape from a gold platter beside him and popped it into his mouth. There were two or three jeweled rings

on each of his fingers and one on his right thumb. He gestured to
Louis and Roland to seat themselves on the carpet.

The audience proceeded with a slowness that felt maddening
to Roland, desperate to get back to Perrin. Louis showed no sign
of impatience, though Roland was sure that he too must be in
agony. His men could be dying under the scimitar even as he sat
here. The Sultan ordered food and wine to be brought. Louis,
barely recovered from the flux, declined the fruit, but he quickly
tore a flat, circular loaf of bread into small pieces which he ate
with relish, washing them down with wine. Turan Shah also drank
wine, as did most of his officers, but Baibars did not. Strict
Muslims, Roland recalled, drank no wine, and it was water
Baibars had served him at their first meeting.

Roland found himself admiring the one-eyed Mameluke more
and more. Have a care, he warned himself. Baibars's qualities
make him the most dangerous of the lot.

"Now," said Turan Shah, when the repast was finished,
"why does the King of the Franks honor us with this visit?"

Louis pushed himself to his feet, Roland rising to help him.
"Your warriors have been beheading my poor foot soldiers.
They have killed hundreds of my men already. These are helpless men who laid down their arms and surrendered to you in
good faith. Had they not surrendered it would have cost Your
Majesty's soldiers many lives to overcome them. They do not
deserve to be butchered like animals. I implore Your Majesty to
order the killing stopped."

"What killing is this?" the Sultan blustered. He turned to
Baibars with an appearance of anger.

Roland's stomach turned with disgust. The Sultan's air of
surprised indignation seemed transparently false.

"Why," said Baibars without a trace of embarrassment, "does
not my lord Sultan recall? As you ordered, the Christians who
cannot ransom themselves are being slain. First, of course, being
given the opportunity to save themselves by converting to Islam.
Your Majesty said that we could not feed so many Christian
captives." Baibars's voice was cold and matter-of-fact.

Turan Shah gave him a poisonous look.

"That was the famous Baibars the Panther who spoke,"
Roland said to Louis after translating the emir's words.

Louis bowed to Baibars. "I have just been told that you are
he Emir Baibars who led the Sultan's army to victory over
mine. You have given me grief that will last me a lifetime, but
ou are a puissant foe and a master of warfare. I salute you."

Baibars rose and bowed when Roland translated this.

"I accept your compliment on behalf of my Sultan, O King," said Baibars smoothly. "His was the victory. He commanded our troops here at Mansura. In him the blood of his ancestor, the great conqueror Saladin, on whom be peace, runs true. I am but his slave."

"Indeed, you are my slave, Baibars," said Turan Shah haughtily, "as are all Mamelukes."

Baibars's expression did not change, but there was a subtle shift in his posture as he stood over the Sultan. Roland sensed rage controlled by great inner discipline. He remembered with a chill the prayer that had been repeated in churches throughout Christendom for the past several years: "From the fury of the Tartar, good Lord deliver us."

Baibars bowed to the Sultan and sat down, and the other Mamelukes in the pavilion turned their eyes to stare at Turan Shah. Those eyes were utterly impassive, but their hatred for the new Sultan was as palpable to Roland as the gold on their breastplates. Turan Shah seemed unconcerned, perhaps even unaware.

The Sultan leaned forward and smiled at King Louis. His teeth, Roland noticed, were stained brown, and several were missing.

"You must understand, O King, that my people have suffered great hardship on account of this war. We have fought you for almost a year. Crops have not been sown or harvested. We have not enough food for all our prisoners. Is it not more merciful that your men die quickly by beheading than a slow, cruel death by starvation? After all, what use are they to you now?"

"I guarantee on my honor as King of France to pay a ransom for each and every living Christian you now hold captive," said Louis, throwing his head back, his blond hair shimmering in the lamplight.

As he translated Louis's words he saw that the Mameluke lords looked gravely approving.

But Turan Shah smiled contemptuously.

"Is your care for your foot soldiers and peasants and grooms so great that you will give us the castles and cities you Christians hold in Palestine and Syria?"

"Do you mean the places that neither your mighty ancestor nor his worthy descendants have been able to capture?" asked Louis blandly.

Turan Shah's face darkened at the thrust, and Roland saw Baibars smile faintly.

"They are not mine to give," Louis went on. "Those strongholds belong to the Templars and the Hospitalers and to the crusader barons who hold them."

"It appears you do not want freedom very much for yourself or the remnant of your army," said Turan Shah. "Perhaps you would be more willing to pay the price we ask if we were to put you to the torture."

Roland could not believe he had heard correctly. For one monarch to torture another was unheard of, even for Muslims. Roland looked from side to side and saw that the Mameluke officers were staring at the Sultan.

When he translated the Sultan's words, the King appeared unmoved.

"I am your prisoner, and you may do what you wish with me," said Louis quietly and without the least trace of fear.

Expressionless, Turan Shah leaned back against his cushions and sipped at his wine.

At last he set down the golden goblet and threw up his hands. "Very well. What will you pay for your life and the lives of your men?"

Saint Michel! thought Roland. Has the King won?

Louis said, "Anything you ask, within reason."

Baibars spoke suddenly. "Do you truly mean to buy the lives of every least man we hold prisoner, as well as your nobles and knights?"

"All," said Louis firmly. "Not one shall pay a ransom for himself. They came on this crusade at my bidding, and their ransom will be paid by the treasury of France."

Turan Shah leaned forward, pointing a fat finger at Louis. "One million bezants for all your men, great and small."

"Agreed," said Louis promptly.

Turan Shah clapped his hands and looked round at his officers delightedly. "By Allah, this Frank does not haggle!"

Haggle? thought Roland. If the Sultan had expected haggling he did not know this King.

"You are open-handed with gold, as becomes a monarch," said Turan Shah. "Shall the Sultan of Cairo be any less generous? Behold, I forgive you part of the ransom. You shall only pay eight hundred thousand bezants." He looked again at his officers, and they nodded grave approval.

"I am most grateful," said Louis.

Turan Shah held up a finger. "But, because you are a king, it is not fitting that you should buy your own freedom with money. A sovereign must trade land for his person."

"I agree," said Louis, again without hesitation. "In return for my freedom, you shall have Damietta."

Turan Shah glowered. "Would you be so brazen as to give us what is already ours?"

"It would cost you dear to take it back," said Louis serenely. "My Queen holds it for me, and she has many knights with her, and our fleet of over a thousand ships with sailors and crossbowmen. Before you could overcome those forces, more knights will be coming to our aid from France and Outremer. To have the gates of Damietta opened freely will be worth far more to you than the wretched person of Louis Capet."

Even as he repeated these words in Arabic to Turan Shah, Roland felt a thrill of admiration. To think Amalric had been trying to deprive France of this King!

"I know full well that Damietta is a toothless camel," said the Sultan, "but I wish to spare my people and my treasury the strain of further warfare. We must discuss these things more, but in principle we are agreed."

"What of the killing of my men?" asked Louis anxiously.

Baibars raised a pacifying hand. "I ordered my warriors to put up their swords, O King, when our gracious Sultan agreed to grant you an audience."

Turan Shah's eyebrows lifted in surprise, but he said nothing.

Baibars went on, "The killing will not be resumed as long as this bargain holds."

Roland was breathless with joy. Hundreds have been saved, and we may go free, he thought. I may see Nicolette again.

But then despair leaped at him again, like an enemy attacking from behind. Perrin, what of Perrin?

Louis was speaking again. "Before I take leave of Your Majesty, I have one last request, a very small favor."

"It shall be granted," said the Sultan with a sweeping gesture.

"You are most kind," said Louis. "This knight who interprets for me here is what we call a troubadour—a singer of songs. If, in your generosity, you could provide him with an instrument—a lute, say, or a harp—so that he could play and sing for us, it would comfort us greatly in our sorrow."

A great lump swelled in Roland's throat. Saint Michel, do not let me cry in front of these Saracens.

"It shall be done," said Turan Shah, as he dismissed them with a wave of his hand.

On their way back to the prison compound, Louis said suddenly, "Pray that I was right about Damietta."

"How could you be wrong, sire?"

"I know nothing of what is happening there. My Queen is with child, and her hour is come. How can a woman in that condition, her life in danger, her husband a prisoner, not give way to panic?"

"She will have good advice, sire."

"Will she? Who is there with her? The Genoese undoubtedly will want to go home. The elderly knights will advise her to flee. And perhaps they will be right. Perhaps it would be better for her and for the kingdom if they were to flee now."

My God, Roland recalled with sudden horror. Amalric could well be in Damietta. The knights who surrendered along with King Louis had told him Amalric had been seen taking flight on the road to Damietta even while the Count's man Maurice went through the army and told them to lay down their arms. When he heard that, Roland realized that Amalric had betrayed the entire army. In Damietta he would be able to betray them again, this time to certain death.

Louis went on, "That man Turan Shah ordered the killing of our foot soldiers just so that he could drive a harder bargain with me. If he finds a way to take everything we offer and give back nothing, he will surely do that. He will take Damietta and the million—or eight hundred thousand—bezants and kill us all, if he can."

And if Amalric can do anything to make that happen, he will, Roland thought, his newfound hope receding.

The Sultan's soldiers brought them to the tent of Sahil the eunuch beside the gate of the prison compound. Sahil came out, followed by two servants. One knelt before the King and held out a black satin coat. The other handed Roland a long, narrow object covered in dark red silk. Roland unwrapped it. There in his hands lay a cithern, its neck fretted with ivory, its pear-shaped bowl of polished golden wood.

"Presents from the Sultan," Sahil said with a smile.

Roland held the cithern and plucked its strings with its ivory pick. Perhaps I can, in the smallest way, ease the pain for all of us, he thought.

Louis wrapped the coat around himself as they walked back to his cottage. "Maybe this will stop my confounded teeth from chattering. Everything depends on Damietta, de Vency. Marguerite must hold Damietta for us or we are lost.''

One of the knights with whom Roland shared a hut came up to them, bowing to the King.

"We have been looking for you, de Vency. Your jongleur is in a bad way. You had better come now, if you can."

"Is your man ill?" said Louis. "Forgive me for taking you from his side. Of course you must go to him at once."

The hurting in Roland's heart made him want to cry out. With a hasty bow to the King he began to run toward his hut.

In the gloom of the little hut Roland threw himself to his knees beside Perrin. He was thankful when the jongleur rolled his eyes toward him and smiled weakly.

Perrin tried to raise a hand, but it fell back limply to the rag pallet on which he lay.

Anxiously, Roland scanned Perrin's wax-white face and trembling body for signs that he was better. He laid the cithern down on the dirt floor and took Perrin's hand. It was hot and dry.

"I am glad you could come, master," Perrin whispered to Roland. "I am not going to be awake much longer. The fever is coming back. It will take me this time. I am not strong enough to fight it."

Roland tightened his grip on Perrin's hand, wanting to pour all his strength into him. "You must hold on, Perrin. The King has struck a bargain with the Saracens. He is going to ransom us. They are going to let us go. Just fight the fever a little longer, and we shall be free."

As if to confirm what Roland had said, a shadow appeared in the doorway of the hut. Roland looked up. It was the King. The men crowded into the hut started to scramble to their feet, but Louis motioned to them to be still.

"Is it true about the ransoming, sire?" one of the knights asked Louis.

"Yes, my friends, it is true," said Louis. They whispered excitedly among themselves.

But Roland shook with rage at his own helplessness. Why cannot somebody help me? The King. Or God. Or Diane? Is she waiting for Perrin on the other side? Do not take him, Diane. I need him.

"Live, Perrin," he whispered. "Live, my friend. Please live."

"Master," Perrin gasped. "There is something I want to tell you."

"What is it, Perrin?"

"When you do get back, to Damietta or to France, remember one thing." His clawlike hand tightened on Roland's. "Do not seek vengeance. Not for me. Not for her—I mean Madame Diane. Not even for the King and his army. In the end the Adversary will claim his own."

Does he mean Amalric? No vengeance on Amalric?

At the thought of Amalric, Roland's body seemed to burn as hot as Perrin's. I only wish I could kill him a hundred times over. For all of us here.

Vengeance? Yes, for you, Perrin, most of all. I never paid him back for what he did to you. And now you are dying because he betrayed the army.

"We need not talk about this now, Perrin."

Perrin grinned. The smile was gap-toothed. Like many of the crusaders he had lost several teeth over the last year.

"We will never get another chance to talk about it, master. It is important. Let me have my say."

"Yes, Perrin." Roland wiped the tears away from his face. He felt a strong hand on his arm. It was the King, trying to comfort him.

"Master, to hurt your enemy as much as he has hurt you, you would have to become as bad as he. You would damn yourself."

"I do not know who this enemy is," said Louis, "but that is well and wisely said. I truly believe that a wicked man is punished more by being what he is than by anything that good men can do to him."

Perrin groaned and rolled his head from side to side. His forehead glistened with sweat.

Roland's shoulders sagged in despair. He is going. Ah, God, he is slipping away from me, and I cannot stop him.

Louis moved to sit on the dirt floor beside Perrin. He drew Perrin's head and shoulders into his lap and wiped his wet forehead with a torn piece of blue silk.

"Time to think of *your* soul, good Perrin," said Louis, peering with large, grave eyes into Perrin's fever-flushed face. "Alas, all our priests are martyred. There is none to hear your confession, but if you repent of your sins and make an act of contrition, God will hear you."

"I need no priest," said Perrin, and Roland braced himself for what he knew was coming. "If only there were one here who would give me the consolamentum."

There was silence, the kind of silence that follows the shatter-

ing of a precious vase. Roland glanced over his shoulder to see if
any of the other knights in the hot, dark room had heard. But
they had all withdrawn to the far side, perhaps wanting to give
Perrin privacy in his dying and any confession he might make.
Only Louis and himself had heard the damning name of the last
Sacrament of the Cathars.

The surprise faded from Louis's long face, and he looked
sadly at Roland. "He is already delirious."

Before Roland could reply Perrin spoke again through trembling
lips. "I am not delirious, sire. I want to proclaim the truth once
before I die. I am a son of the church of Jesus Christ, known as
the Cathars. Sire, a heretic is dying in your arms."

Roland expected Louis to spring to his feet with a curse, but
the King continued to hold Perrin's head and to wipe his brow.

"Do not hold my being a Cathar against my master, sire,"
Perrin went on. "Good Catholic that he is, I never dared tell
him."

Louis shook his head. "That a Cathar should wear the cross.
It passes belief."

"No need to send me to the stake, sire," said Perrin with a
slack-mouthed smile. "I am burning up already."

The feeble joke was too much for Roland. He pressed his
hands to his face. Sobs battered their way out of him.

"Stop, master, stop," came the faint whisper.

Roland took his hands away from his face and found himself
looking into Perrin's hot blue eyes.

"Do not mourn so," Perrin went on.

Roland had to strain to hear the voice that sighed through
cracked, crusted lips. "You know we long for death. Now I
shall meet Madame Diane in the Light."

At these heretical words Roland noticed that Louis shut his
eyes as if in pain. But he never stopped his gentle wiping of
Perrin's brow.

"May you find the happiness your faith promises," Roland
said softly.

"Sing for me, master," Perrin gasped. "One last song."

Perrin's breathing had slowed. It was heavy and rhythmic, like
waves rolling to shore, Roland thought, and the song came to
him. He picked up the cithern.

> "Above the rocks, upon the wind
>   The lonely seagull cries.
>   The anchor up, my little craft

Slips out now with the tide.
>   Look not for me at the merry board,
>   My face is set to sea.

The mourning dove flits through the trees.
I hear her plaint no more.
The shore is fading fast away,
The waves will sing to me.
>   Look not for me at the merry board,
>   My face is set to sea."

Roland sang on, because a strange notion had seized him that when he stopped singing Perrin would die. He kept his eyes on his fingers as they moved over the frets. As the moment to begin the final chorus approached, he looked again at Perrin. The young jongleur's eyelids were half shut and his quivering lips whispered gibberish as his head lolled in the King's lap.

"The fever has him," said Louis as Roland ceased his song. But the hand holding the crumpled blue silk tirelessly stroked Perrin's face. "There is nothing we can do now but wait."

"Sire, no one could ask you to stay any longer," said Roland. "What you have done for him and for me has already gone far beyond kindness."

"I will watch with you. I am not needed anywhere else. No one awaits audience with a defeated king," Louis said sadly.

Some of the other knights stepped closer now. They formed a ring around Perrin, Roland, and the King. It is as if Perrin were dying for all of us, Roland thought.

"Perhaps, sire, you would lead us in a prayer for him," one said.

"Our Father, Who art in Heaven . . ." Louis began in a strong voice.

Moments later, as the criers in the minarets of Mansura's mosques were calling Muslims to prayer, Perrin ceased to breathe.

The throbbing ache in Roland's breast begged for the relief of tears, but he had no tears left. He could only sit, staring at his friend's body.

Ah, my poor, poor Perrin. You chose the wrong master. I brought you suffering only. You should have followed a wealthy troubadour, or become a troubadour in your own right. You could have had rich patrons, worn silk and satin, slept on fine linen with your pick of handsome women. You had the wit and skill for it. Why did you waste your life with me? I did not merit such faith, such love.

Oh, Perrin, Perrin, how could God be so cruel?

Louis stood up, pushing himself slowly and painfully to his full height.

He must be terribly cramped from having sat so long with Perrin's head on his lap. And he is still a sick man, too.

"Come, I will help you bury him," said Louis.

"You cannot, sire," Roland started to protest.

"I can and I must," said Louis, and he bent his long frame to reach down and take Perrin under the shoulders.

The knights from the hut followed Louis and Roland as they carried Perrin's body to the burial pit. As they walked through the prison village more knights joined.

See, Perrin, you have a king to carry you to your grave, and hundreds walk in your funeral train. That much being my man has gotten for you.

Under the eyes of Egyptian archers standing on the wall, a party of knights with wooden spades was filling in part of a long, deep trench. On the first day of their imprisonment here Louis had asked permission for the crusaders to bury their dead— instead of having the bodies of those who died of starvation, disease, or untreated wounds thrown into the Nile. From then on, each day's dead were brought to this trench, tenderly laid in it by comrades, and covered up with the rich earth of the delta before the African heat could start them rotting. Knights chosen from a roster kept by the King himself used the shovels granted them by the Saracens to lengthen the mass grave.

After Louis and Roland had set Perrin's body down beside those the burial detail had just started to cover, Roland stepped back to take a last look at his friend.

He stared at the still, pale face until his eyes blurred.

He turned away from the motionless form and followed the King climbing out of the pit. Louis took a shovel from one of the grave diggers and handed it to Roland.

"Do you want to cover him?"

"Thank you, sire." Roland took the shovel. But he could not bear to throw dirt down on Perrin from above. He went back down into the trench and dug with his fingers in the soft earth and let the dirt trickle from his hands over Perrin's face.

*   *   *

The knights who had followed them to the graveside had dispersed. The sun was a huge red ball resting on the smoldering horizon.

"Sire, how can I thank you?"

Louis stopped walking, turned, and put his hand on Roland's shoulder. They stood on the winding, dusty path leading through the dun-colored, flat-roofed huts. All about them, ragged, gaunt men, faces burnt to dark brown leather, walked aimlessly about.

"Your Perrin was a comrade in arms," said Louis. "Never will I turn my back on any man who fought beside me in this crusade."

"Few Catholics would show such kindness to a heretic, sire."

A look of pain shadowed the large blue eyes. "I may be violating the law of the Church. I can only hope I am being true to the spirit of my faith."

A perverse urge to test Louis seized Roland. "He did lie to you about one thing. I knew he had converted to Catharism. He told me long before we left on this crusade."

The suffering in Louis's eyes grew deeper. "Why do you press me so?"

"You know I am a son of Languedoc. Your people destroyed my people."

"Yet you follow me."

Roland nodded. "Yet I follow you, and have led others, like Perrin, to follow you also, to their deaths. Every man I brought with me is dead now. And that is why I try you."

They stood looking at each other in the heart of the prison village as the sunset reddened the dust around their feet and the specters that had once been crusaders shuffled past them.

Full of mingled grief and dread, Roland waited for Louis to speak. How he answers me will tell me if I threw away Perrin's life, and Martin's and the others, and mine, or spent them well.

"Walk with me," Louis said. "I do not want to speak of these things here in the open."

As they trudged along the path that led to Louis's cottage, a group of men stopped the King.

"Is it true we are to be ransomed, sire?"

Louis held up a warning hand. "Pray that it be God's will, my men. Much could yet go awry. But I have talked to the Sultan, and we have come to terms."

The men began to cheer.

"This is a time for prayer, not for celebration," Louis reproved them gently. "Pray for me, that I may be given the grace to find a way to free us."

"God hears your prayers sooner than He hears ours," said one knight heartily. "When you are not talking to the Sultan, sire, put in a word for us with the Almighty."

"What are the terms, sire?" another asked. "Many of us spent all we have on men and equipment for this crusade. We have little left for ransom."

Louis shook his head. "Not one man is to pay his own ransom. The whole sum will come from the royal treasury."

They gasped in amazement. "Never has there been such a king!" said one, and the others chorused agreement. The men nearest him began to kneel and reach out to touch him as if he were a holy object.

Louis reddened and drew back from them.

"On your feet, messires, if you please. This is unseemly. Pray, I tell you again, that all goes as I hope it will."

"If anyone can make it happen, sire, you can," someone called.

What faith they have in him, Roland thought, even though he has led them only to defeat and captivity.

"I will do whatever God lets me do," said Louis with his head bowed. He started again to walk toward his hut, and despite his evident embarrassment, kneeling knights lined his path. As word of the ransom proposal spread, more and more knights came running. Even more embarrassed than the King, Roland followed him a dozen paces behind, so that the knights would be on their feet again before he passed them.

Roland caught up with Louis as he stepped into his cottage. The King's back stiffened.

Moving to Louis's side, Roland saw the royal brother Charles throwing unpainted wooden dice with Isambert the cook. With three quick strides Louis kicked their little piles of silver coins in all directions. The deniers rang against the gray brick walls of the cottage and sparkled on the brown dirt floor. He stooped down and seized the dice and threw them out the door.

"Hey, brother!" the stocky Charles cried, jumping to his feet. "I spent hours carving those dice."

"Spend your hours doing something useful," Louis scolded. "Help to bury the dead. Our poor men are dying out there while you gamble."

"I cannot do anything for them," Charles grumbled.

"Go among them," Louis cried. "Show them that you care about them. Go on, get out of here."

Muttering, Charles charged out the door, pushing Roland aside.

Isambert scrambled around the small room, gathering up the coins.

"Whose money is that?" asked Louis grumpily, seating himself on the pile of cushions and blankets that was throne and bed for him in this mud brick palace.

"Mine, sire," said Isambert. "The Count d'Anjou borrowed some of it from me to play, but I was winning it all back."

"May Our Lady give me patience," Louis sighed. "Do not encourage my brother in vice, Isambert. He needs little enough help in that direction."

"When you begin preaching again I know you are feeling better, sire," said Isambert with a grin.

Louis smiled back at him.

"Leave us now, Isambert. There are matters I must discuss with this gentleman."

When they were alone, Louis invited Roland to seat himself on the hard-packed dirt floor and said, "I know only this. Your Perrin was brave and true, as you are brave and true. As for the state of his soul and what you knew about it, you must answer to God."

What kind of man was this, who buried a self-confessed heretic with his own hands, then flew into a rage at his brother for playing with dice? Thousands who followed him were now dead. How could a man who cared so much about right and wrong live with that?

"We all have a great deal to answer to God for, sire," Roland said tiredly.

Louis smiled sadly. "Still testing me, Roland de Vency?" Then his cadaverous face turned solemn. "Do you truly think God is angry at me? I was dying, six years ago, when the vision of Jerusalem came to me. If God had not wanted me to go on crusade, he could have let me die then and there. I cannot believe God gave me back my health only so I could lead a whole army to death and defeat. God cannot be so cruel."

"You know what the Cathars say about the two Gods, sire," Roland said.

Louis raised his hands in horror. "Do not repeat it. That is blasphemy. There is only one God, and He is a good God. I know it. I believe it. Suffering is part of His plan, and His plan is good."

Roland shrugged. "Many of these same men suffering here with you, or their fathers, crusaded in Languedoc and destroyed it. Perhaps God has chosen this way of punishing the French for what they did in Languedoc."

"That is not possible," said Louis.

"Sire, you heard Perrin mention the name Diane. She was a woman I loved, a Cathar woman. She was the kindest, the gentlest woman I have ever known. May I tell you what happened to her? Amalric de Gobignon's brother, Hugues, had her tortured for weeks and then tried to burn her at the stake. An arrow sped by a merciful hand ended her life. Sire, in Languedoc thousands suffered as Diane did. It was your barons, your knights and priests who did those deeds."

"I know," Louis said, his voice mournful. "I know. I cannot understand how Christian men could have strayed so far from the teachings of Jesus. I could not stop what they did. But by this crusade I hoped to heal those wounds. You know that. That is why you are with me. Still, I accept the blame." He bowed his head. The sun had set, and the room was in twilight. The Saracens gave them no lamps or candles. Roland could not discern Louis's features below his palely gleaming hair.

He had faced the King with all the doubts he had felt ever since he had entered Louis's service. Louis had heard and answered.

"Thank you for letting me speak so freely to you, sire," he said.

"Thank you for all your good service to me, Roland," said Louis. "In the past and in time to come."

In the darkness of the hut, Roland heard a movement and felt a hand, thin and cold, but firm, take his.

As night fell over the prison camp, the two men sat together in the silence of friends.

XXXI

Through the window of the Queen's bedchamber Nicolette heard men's voices in the courtyard below. She sat upright in the big chair, her fingers gripping its arms, her body rigid with dread.

Only two weeks ago, on just such a quiet Sunday afternoon as this, she had heard the shouts in the street that accompanied Amalric's return. She remembered how he had burst into this very room, his eyes gleaming with secret triumph. She remembered hearing the news that seared her heart. And Roland? Alive or dead?

Today, two weeks later, she still did not know.

Now she heard boots tramping through the hall below, and then the tread of heavy feet on the stairs.

Why must they come now, whoever they are? she thought. They will wake the baby.

Exhausted as she was after the agonizing hours of Marguerite's labor that had begun before dawn, she pushed herself out of the chair. She must make these men be quiet.

She went to the newborn infant beside Marguerite's bed. Geoffrey de Burgh had hammered his cradle together out of scrap wood. She looked down at the pink face. The tiny Tristan had not stirred.

But the rough voices and the footsteps were coming nearer. The Queen, too, Nicolette saw, was still sleeping, a small figure in the great royal bed.

Oh, poor Marguerite! Nicolette thought. For the past two weeks she had been waking up screaming, dreaming that Saracens swarmed into her room to rape her, and kill her and the baby cradled in her belly. After one unspeakably awful nightmare she had asked Nicolette to stay at the palace and sleep in the royal bed with her.

If she heard this commotion, Marguerite would surely think the Saracens were upon them. She must not be upset anymore, not after her sufferings of the past hours.

Nicolette ran to the door and pulled it open. De Burgh stood there with his back to her, facing a group of men. She recognized them, from their flamboyant silk caps and capes, as Genoese shipmasters. At their head was their commander, Hugo Lercari, who called himself admiral, a title the Genoese had borrowed from the Arabs. With scowling eyebrows and a short, thick beard, he looked more like a highwayman than a nobleman.

"These men insist on seeing the Queen," de Burgh said angrily. "I would like to have turned them away, madame, but I thought it might be too important for me to take that on myself."

Fright took a cold grip on Nicolette's heart as she realized what the shipmasters were doing here. Just yesterday Nicolette had been walking with Amalric on the city battlements. He had urged her to break down the Queen's resolve to hold Damietta, and when she answered that she could not sway Marguerite, he had declared he had a way of his own to make the Queen see reason and leave. She knew that he had planned to visit the fleet this morning. This could mean the end, the deaths of King Louis and all those good men.

I must do something, she thought, but what? Desperately she tried to think of words that would turn the Genoese away.

She took a deep breath. "Admiral Lercari, surely this can wait a bit. The Queen has just given birth. She is asleep. In the name of chivalry, I beg you to let her rest, at least until tomorrow."

Lercari's face hardened.

Nicolette flinched inwardly. She knew that he had only to give the order and his fleet would sail away, leaving all the crusaders still alive to end as bleached bones in the desert.

"I know the Queen has been brought to childbed, madame," he said, speaking French in an accented growl. "But we cannot delay another day. Lives are at stake. We are delighted to learn, as we hear, that she has given birth to a son and that both are well." He turned and nodded to the men with him, and they grumbled assent. "That is one reason why we come to her now. There is no longer any danger that she might go into labor at sea. It is safe to move now."

Time, Nicolette thought, I must fight for time.

"Admiral, many women take sick and die after they give birth. Would you have the Queen's life on your hands? You would not want to answer to King Louis for that, would you?"

Lercari's impatient expression told her he never expected to see the King a free man.

Lercari smiled unpleasantly. "First we cannot leave because

she is about to have a baby, now because she has had the baby.
Next we will hear she is pregnant again.'' The shipmasters
laughed coarsely.

"How dare you!" De Burgh's hand was on his sword hilt.

In a panic, Nicolette seized the old knight's arm.

"No, Sire Geoffrey." She looked into the aged eyes pleadingly. "Christian men cannot afford to fight one another with
Saracens outside our walls."

De Burgh nodded, to her immense relief, and let go of his
sword.

"Madame," said Lercari, "I say only this to you. If the
Queen is not aware of her danger, we are. The Saracens are now
camped only half a league away. You can see their tents from
the city walls. Their galleys sail down the river within bowshot
of Damietta whenever they please. They know you have only a
few hundred men here, and only a handful capable of really
fighting. An Egyptian fleet from Alexandria might attack our
ships at any time. We are here to make our intentions known to
the Queen. If we cannot have an audience, we will sail away this
very day without speaking to her." He frowned at her, bringing
his heavy brows together. "I was given to understand you would
assist me, madame, not put obstacles in my path."

This was Amalric's doing, Nicolette thought. How I long for
the day when I can expose him for what he is.

She stepped back and bowed her head.

"Give me a few moments to prepare the Queen to receive
you, messires."

Marguerite had slept through the argument at the door. Nicolette
gazed down pityingly at her. She lay on her back with her head
turned to one side, looking as helpless as a child. Softly Nicolette
called her till she awoke. Then she told her about the men
outside.

"Nicolette, I cannot face them now. What can I say to them?"

Nicolette seized her friend's hands and held them tightly,
wishing she could pour strength into her. "Listen to their reasons, then ask for time. Every day we can delay them is a
victory for us."

Marguerite pressed her lips together and painfully pushed
herself up in the bed. "Arrange the pillows so I can sit up
straight. Bring me my blue and gold brocade robe and bind up
my hair. Give the baby to one of the maids and have her take
him to another part of the palace."

A short time later Nicolette opened the door and the seamen

trooped into the room, looking abashed at the sight of the wan Queen. They bent the knee to Marguerite, and Nicolette held her breath as Lercari began to speak.

"To come to the point quickly, madame, I have learned from one I trust that there are no more provisions in reserve in Damietta. Counting the oarsmen, I have nearly ten thousand men out there on the water. Ten thousand men to feed daily—even the galley slaves have to be fed once a day, or they will not have the strength to pull our oars. I am responsible for all those lives, madame, and I do not intend to let them be lost. So I have come to ask you to prepare to leave."

No food in Damietta? Nicolette's stomach clenched violently. If Lercari is right, we cannot hold out.

Amalric, she thought. It is he who told Lercari that there is no food. But our provisions? All these months we have kept the warehouses full. Did Amalric destroy them?

"This cannot be," Marguerite spoke up. "I know of no shortage of provisions. There are ships on the way from Acre and Cyprus. We have plenty of gold with us to buy more food, Admiral, I can assure you of that."

Lercari shrugged. "If madame goes to the marketplaces of the city, she will see that there is nothing to buy. You do not even know whether your appeals to Acre and Cyprus have arrived, much less whether any help is on the way. And the need is upon us now."

The finality in his voice was to Nicolette as a dungeon door closing. She and Marguerite would never see Roland or King Louis again.

"But, Admiral," Marguerite pleaded. "We cannot give up now. We have heard from the Sultan. He demands a ransom of eight hundred thousand bezants, and the surrender of Damietta. The treasury of France can supply the money, and more if need be. We have sent for it already. Only a little while longer and those brave men that you brought here will be free. They will embrace you as brothers when you carry them home. How can you turn your back on them now, when we are so close to rescuing them?"

"Forgive me, madame, but we are not that close to rescuing them. The Saracens love nothing better than haggling. You might have to go on talking to them all summer and still get nowhere."

"But that is why we must stay here," said Marguerite, holding out her small hands in appeal. "Think how much longer the bargaining will take if we have to conduct it from across the sea."

Lercari shook his head in brusque dismissal. "Madame, we cannot wait. My men are sickening just from being confined on board. Now they will start to starve. You are asking more than you have a right to, madame."

"More than I have a right to?" There was anger in Marguerite's voice, and her dark eyes flashed. "In Jesus' name, what kind of Christians are you? This is no ordinary war, and no ordinary king. If you turn away from us in our need, I promise you, Admiral Lercari, God will remember it. Your city will feel His wrath. And the world will remember, too. Do you want the name of Genoa to stand for cowardice and treachery?"

At the mention of God's wrath one of Lercari's captains crossed himself, but Lercari glowered. "Madame, if a man spoke thus to me, he should answer for it."

"You are very good with threats to a woman who has just borne a child, Admiral," said Marguerite.

Lercari's face turned red under his olive skin.

"We are not cowards or traitors, madame," said Lercari sullenly. "We are good Christians and do not want to desert your husband and his men. But against famine the strongest of us is helpless. What would you have us do?"

She has him now, Nicolette rejoiced. But can she hold the advantage?

Now Marguerite's tone changed, as if she were making a concession. "Give me a little more time, Admiral. Let me look for provisions. Perhaps some people are hoarding. Perhaps there are supplies in the city we do not know about. I will pay whatever I have to. I promise you, your men will not go hungry. Give me a day at least."

Lercari bowed. "A day, madame. Yes, certainly, you can have that. But if your search for food fails, I expect you to be more agreeable to our leaving."

It is hopeless, thought Nicolette. If Amalric has told him there is no food, he surely must have seen to it that none will be found.

Then she remembered Maurice. Could he really have made an arrangement with the Bedouins to get food for their household? Could he arrange for much more food, backed by the Queen's treasury? And if he could—would he?

"If there is no food to be had, I will understand your position, Admiral," said Marguerite quietly. "Now, I am very tired."

Lercari and his men genuflected once more and backed out.

As soon as they were gone, Marguerite put her face in her hands and sobbed bitterly.

"Oh, Nicolette, it is impossible. What difference can a day make? My poor baby, he will never see his father. And I, I will never see my Louis again."

Nicolette threw herself across the bed and took the Queen in her arms. "There is a chance, Marguerite. I think perhaps I know a way to get what we need."

With her heart in her throat, Nicolette hurried through the palace. She crossed a garden in the rear, yellowing because all water was being conserved for the expected siege, and entered the stables where the dozen or so horses left in the city were under day and night guard to protect them from the hungry of Damietta. In the little room where she knew he was stationed, she found Maurice sitting at a table throwing dice with one of the stable guards. Both men sprang to their feet.

"I need a private word with you, Master Maurice," she said, searching the faded blue eyes for a hopeful sign.

Maurice dismissed the guard, each scooping up his small pile of coins and dropping it into his purse.

"I hope madame does not object to a bit of gambling," Maurice said with a grin. "Since the Count put me in charge of protecting the horses, I have had little to do but sit in this room. Things will get livelier as people get hungrier, I suspect. How may I serve you, madame?"

She sat down at the rough wooden table and gestured to him to sit across from her. She told him of the Genoese threat, but as she talked, she found his face unreadable. She had not spoken privately to the old crusader since the day he found her in the ruined temple. Still, her discovery that he kept secrets from Amalric had left her with a sliver of hope.

When she finished, he laughed. "Just because I can get some fresh food for the family I serve, does madame imagine I can feed a whole city?"

"We need to keep a few thousand people alive till help arrives," said Nicolette. "You can reach the Bedouins, and the Bedouins could supply us for a time. Is that not true?"

"Well, yes, you might say that," Maurice admitted. "But madame must know it would greatly annoy two powerful men, the Sultan Turan Shah and your husband, Count Amalric."

"The Bedouins can get through the Sultan's lines, can they not? For enough gold?"

"And what of Count Amalric, madame?" said Maurice with a wry smile. "I am his man, am I not? If I played him false he would kill me, would he not? And he is right when he says that the Christians in Damietta would be better off if they left at once."

"Do you not care that the King, *your* King, and all those good men, crusaders like yourself, will surely die if you do not help?"

Maurice stood up, turned his back on Nicolette, and walked to the doorway, where he looked out on the dying garden. He knotted his scarred hands together behind him. She had turned to stare after him, wondering what was in his heart. She noticed for the first time that seen from the rear his short, powerful frame could be taken for that of a much younger man.

Without facing her, he said abruptly, "Women should not meddle in matters of war and statecraft."

"Would you like to lock us up in harems as the Saracens do with their women?" she demanded, growing angry.

Still with his back turned he said, "You know nothing about Muslim women."

"And you seem to have forgotten everything you ever knew about Christian women," she retorted.

He half turned. The bright afternoon sunlight behind him silhouetted his face.

"You are taking a terrible chance talking to me like this, madame. What if I were to tell your husband how you are working against him?"

She somehow managed to hold down her fear.

"I am quite certain he would kill me," she said, "Do you want that on your conscience?"

He came back into the shadows of the hut and leaned toward her across the table.

"I know he is capable of killing you, madame. No, that is not what I would want. I admire what you are doing for the Queen." He turned and walked away from her again, seeming to want to hide his feelings. "And for the King and his men. Your loyalty is very beautiful."

There was good in the old man. She sensed it.

She rose to her feet, pushing the chair away.

"Master Maurice," she said to his wide back, "if Damietta is abandoned, I swear I will contrive some way to stay behind. I will run away from the city or I will hide until the fleet is gone."

"Your husband would track you down," he said.

"Not if it might cause him to miss the ships," she said briskly. "But I will not turn away from those men. I would not be able to live with myself back in France if I did that." She finished breathless, shocked at her own foolhardiness.

Maurice whirled around and stared at her. "By Heaven, you mean it."

"Yes."

He shook his head. "Meeting you has hurt me, madame. You remind me of how much I have indeed missed the women of France all these years."

"Then you will help? In spite of the count?"

"Madame, I have seen your husband do things that make me ashamed I was born a Frenchman. And in his service I, too, have done much that I regret. It is possible that now I could do a little good to make up for it. Though the Sultan would like nothing better than to see Damietta abandoned, there is another party among the Egyptians who may be able to help me with provisions. Thwarting Turan Shah, and receiving the gold your Queen will pay for supplies—both could interest them greatly."

Nicolette felt like a caged bird suddenly set free.

"I knew you could do it, Master Maurice."

"I have not done anything yet, madame. And even if the Queen manages to hold Damietta, the crusaders still may not come out safely. There is a good chance that Turan Shah, after he gets the ransom money, may still order the prisoners massacred."

She fell back into the guardroom chair.

"Is the Sultan capable of such gross treachery? Is there not some chivalry even among the Saracens?" If the Sultan could take the ransom and then kill the captives, there was no hope.

"Madame, there is great chivalry among the warriors of Islam, but even Turan Shah's own officers do not consider him a man of honor," Maurice said. "Since Sultan Ayub's death, Turan Shah has been replacing veteran Mameluke generals with his favorites, men who think as he does. And he persecutes the Sultana, Spray-of-Pearls, his father's chief wife, a lady whom the Mamelukes hold in high esteem. Many there are who despise this new Sultan. That is why perhaps I can help you."

She eyed Maurice. He seemed to know too much about the intrigues of the Saracens to be but a captive slave. Could he have turned Muslim during his captivity and now be spying on us?

"Oh, please, Master Maurice. Without you we have no hope."

"You must not expect too much of me, madame." Maurice sat down and tapped his short, calloused fingers on the table, thinking. Then he looked up at her.

"Madame, you know how frightened of the Egyptians the Christians here are. If they find out that I have been in contact with the Bedouins, you must promise to speak up for me. At whatever risk to yourself."

"I promise," she said firmly, holding his eyes with hers.

"Swear by whatever you hold most sacred."

"I swear by—by Love."

His gray eyebrows lifted. "A pagan oath?"

"We must be open with each other, Master Maurice. Do you think less of me?"

He shrugged. "I think, when it comes to belief, people have no choice. If something seems true to us, we are compelled to believe it." His eyes were the color of the sea on a gloomy day, as if he recalled an old grief.

Moving stiffly, de Burgh pulled open the door, and the Genoese shipmasters trooped into Queen Marguerite's bedchamber. Hugo Lercari swept his scarlet cap from his head and made a deep bow.

I should not hate him, Nicolette thought. He is only doing what many in his place would do. But she could not help herself.

Nicolette stood with Beatrice and Jeanne, the wives of the King's brothers Charles and Alphonse, at the head of the bed. As Marguerite had ordered, each woman was dressed in her finest. Nicolette wore a pale blue silk gown with a wide belt embroidered with gold thread. Her Byzantine mantle of brocaded purple satin was too heavy for this hot day, but she knew it gave her added dignity. On her head she wore her silver coronet. Marguerite was seated beside the bed in a great heavy chair she had ordered her servants to bring up from the audience hall downstairs. She wore the small gold crown she had brought with her from Paris for state occasions. In her arms she held her baby. She had finished nursing him only a short time ago, and he was sleeping.

"Messires," Marguerite said, her eyes sparkling, "I present to you the newest heir of the house of Capet, Jean Tristan."

Amalric pushed his way into the room behind the Genoese captains. His eyes, full of baffled rage, met Nicolette's briefly. His gaze traveled over her finery, and he pressed his lips together.

How lucky that I am not living with him now, she thought.

"Tristan," Hugo Lercari repeated. "But that means 'sad soul.' A melancholy name, madame, for such a handsome young man."

"He was born on a sad day, admiral," said Marguerite.

"May these unhappy times end speedily," said Lercari. "And may your son's royal father soon have the pleasure of looking upon him."

"Sooner, I trust, because of what we have accomplished yesterday and today," Marguerite said, handing the baby to her sister-in-law Beatrice, who carried him to his cradle. "Have you been to the warehouses today, Admiral Lercari?"

"I have seen with my own eyes, madame, that the warehouses and granaries are again full. I am amazed. Never before, I think, has a city under siege been able to buy provisions from its besiegers."

"That is not quite what happened, Admiral," said Marguerite with a laugh. "The wandering herdsmen of this part of the world acknowledge no ruler. They are at war with anyone or no one, depending on how they feel. They are Muslims, of course, but gold speaks more directly to them even than religion. With this good knight acting as my buyer, I was able to persuade them to part with provender for us." She gestured with a smile toward de Burgh, who bowed, his eyes twinkling with pleasure at the small deception in which he was involved. "Messires, I have spent three hundred sixty thousand silver livres, funds of the crown of France, to put to rest your fears of starvation. In return, the crown of France expects you to stay as long as you are needed."

"You and the Sire de Burgh have performed a miracle, madame," Amalric said, staring balefully at the elderly knight. "But at what cost? What money is left now to pay the ransom with?"

"The ransom money will be here soon, count," said Marguerite. "It is being transmitted to us from the royal treasury in Paris with the help of the Knights of the Temple."

"The Templars!" Amalric burst out. "If the fate of the captives depends on the Templars, we are in a sorry pass indeed."

"The Knights Templar have always been among the most dependable friends of the Kings of France," said Marguerite coolly. She turned to Lercari. "And what of the Genoese captains, Admiral Lercari? Can we count you now among our staunch supporters?"

Lercari bowed. "My apologies for disturbing you yesterday, madame, especially as you lay in childbed. It was terribly rude of me. But my crews are *my* children, and I was anxious for them. It seems we were mistaken about the difficulty of obtaining food and the danger of starving." He glanced casually at Amalric, who abruptly turned his back and strode to the side of the room to stare out a wrought-iron window grille.

"We will be happy to stay, madame," Lercari went on.

"Then we can rely on you as long as we can pay you," Marguerite said sweetly.

At least he has the grace to look embarrassed, thought Nicolette, as the shamefaced admiral dropped his eyes.

The shipmasters bowed and backed out of the room, and Nicolette thought, We have won a little time for our men. But only till the food and the money run out. And Marguerite has spent everything she had on those supplies. If help does not come soon, or the bargaining drags on, this will all have been for nothing.

XXXII

"To leave my sweet country,
   The home of my fair one,
   Has darkened my life.

   Farewell, my beloved.
   I fight for the Lord God,
   But still we are one.

   With my body I serve God,
   Yet my thoughts are all with you,
   With you is my heart."

ROLAND DEFTLY PLUCKED OUT THE CHORUS OF THE SONG TWICE MORE on the cithern, bringing it to an end. His hearers did not applaud, only nodded and muttered quiet appreciation. In the faint light of a half-moon hanging low on the eastern horizon he could see tears on the hollow cheeks of some of the men gathered around him at the stern of the prison galley. They loved to be reminded of the women they had left behind.

And Roland knew that the depth of his own longing for Nicolette had lent ardor to his singing.

He felt almost as if he might call to her and she hear him. They were, their guards had said, only five leagues from Damietta, at a town called Fariskur. The dealings for their release were going so well, Turan Shah had told King Louis, that he was pleased to move them in these twelve cargo galleys closer to Damietta and freedom.

Interpreting for the King, Roland felt only distrust for Turan Shah. He was sure the Sultan had moved them nearer to the Christian-held city to make their captivity the more painful, and so force more concessions from the King. And near Damietta or far, Turan Shah could still butcher them all.

Enough brooding, Roland told himself. The men want more music. He played the opening notes of a new song but then paused as stirring amidships caught his attention.

He saw a tall figure step on deck from the gangplank. A steel helmet topped with a spike glistened in the light from torches on shore. A long scimitar in a plain leather scabbard hung from the embroidered scarf wrapped around the man's waist. The Mameluke now began slowly to walk down the deck of the long, slender Egyptian war galley.

It was Emir Baibars.

Roland saw the ragged men who crowded the deck of the galley fall back as he strode through them, but they moved with reluctance, and they gave the tall Mameluke only a little room. The captives stared balefully at Baibars, and he looked back at them, swinging his head from side to side unceasingly as he walked. No doubt he had to do that, Roland thought, to see as much as men with two eyes did.

Is it madness or courage that lets him walk alone among us without fear? Roland wondered. They could swarm over him and bear him to the deck before he could even draw his scimitar. The men did not know, of course, that this was the commander who had defeated and captured them. He did not wear the gold ornaments that went with his rank, only the simple red silk surcoat of an ordinary archer. It seemed, Roland thought, a sensible disguise.

Now Baibars stood before him, a small smile on his dark face. "Come with me, Roland de Vency."

Roland felt a tremor of fear. Would he come back alive? And why had Baibars chosen to summon him by coming in person?

Hating to part with the beautiful cithern, Roland handed it to Jean de Joinville, who was near him.

The other crusaders tensed and moved closer to Roland protectively. Their fingers twitched, and they whispered to one another.

Baibars said, "Tell them I promise not to harm their precious singer. Tell them I want to talk with you about music."

Roland repeated Baibars's words in French, and then followed the tall Mameluke to the gangplank. He could hear the jingling of the iron mesh Baibars wore under his surcoat. At least he had taken that much of a precaution. Roland noticed that the Mameluke guards at the head of the gangplank neither spoke to Baibars nor looked at him. Doubtless when in disguise he forbade his own people to recognize him.

Roland's stomach felt hollow. What does he want of me? It has to be something terribly important for Baibars to come himself, alone, like this.

Baibars paused before descending the gangplank to gaze in the direction of the Sultan's compound.

Roland looked with him. The Sultan's yellow tents glowed warmly from the lamplight within. They were set on a gentle, grassy slope and surrounded by silken walls hung on wooden poles. From the midst of the tents rose a wooden tower in which Roland had several times seen Turan Shah himself standing, surveying the river, the nearby town, and the prison galleys.

"We shall walk beside the river," Baibars said as they descended.

"You should have sent for me," Roland said as they walked along a narrow towpath of hard-packed earth, their backs to the Sultan's tents. "You risked your life going alone among those men."

"I could have sent for you," Baibars agreed, "but the quieter way was to come for you myself."

Roland's heartbeat quickened, but he tried to sound casual. "The quiet way, that is the Panther's way, is it not? I still remember when you came as a horse groom to Damietta. I know only one other man of exalted rank who goes as freely among the people as you do—King Louis. Only he does not go in disguise."

"Then it is he who risks his life, more than I."

"Not so, because they love him," said Roland.

"My people fear me," said Baibars. "I consider that more reliable. But much as I terrify them, they love to tell stories about me."

Ever since he arrived in Egypt, Roland had heard about Baibars's exploits. Many of them involved disguised entry into other men's harems.

"I am sure you made up and spread some of those stories yourself," Roland said, hoping Baibars's genial mood would last.

Baibars laughed. "You have too much wit for a Frank. You must be part Arab."

They came to a grove of date palms, and Baibars stopped in their shadow. Beside them the Nile murmured in the night. Ahead of them in dark rows Roland saw the tents of the Egyptian army. Campfires twinkled into the far distance. There must be tens of thousands camped there, ready to march on Damietta at a word of command. The sight filled Roland with dread for Nicolette and the Queen.

"I have a very important question to ask you, singer of songs. Your King meets almost daily with the Sultan, and the Sultan's spies watch him closely. I cannot approach him. You must tell me his mind."

Roland's whole body went tense. Tell him what the King has confided to me—such as his fear that the Queen may flee and leave us stranded here? But if I do not answer Baibars's questions, what will happen to me, to all of us? Roland could almost feel the cold edge of a scimitar pressing on the back of his neck.

No, the only way to deal with Baibars was to be forthright.

"I will not tell you anything I do not think the King would want you to know."

"Of course." Roland saw Baibars's hand wave in the shadows. "You need not have said that. We are both men of honor."

Roland brushed at a mosquito that was humming near his ear.

I believe that, he thought. But how can he be a man of honor and conspire against his Sultan?

"I have had occasion," Baibars said after a brief silence, "to read a message sent to our thrice-honored Sultan from a person in Damietta. It was sent secretly. It was from him who commands the Christian defenders of Damietta, Count Amalric."

Roland felt white-hot rage. "Amalric de Gobignon is treating with the enemy?" So he *had* made his way to Damietta.

"Not all the enemy," said Baibars. "Only with the Sultan, and that in secret. Who is this Amalric? What sort of man is he?"

A succession of images of Amalric rose in Roland's mind—Amalric's ordering the slaughter of the Cathars, bringing the mace down on Roland's shoulder, presiding over Diane's burning. Hatred almost blinded him. And then he heard Perrin's words: *Do not seek vengeance.*

"You will not get a balanced answer to that question from me, Emir Baibars. That man is my greatest enemy in the world. Perhaps my only enemy."

"Truly? I cannot imagine having only one enemy. What has he done to you?"

"He has caused the deaths of many who were dear to me. And I have loved two women in my life. He had one burned at the stake. The other is his wife."

"Ah, his wife. A most beautiful woman."

Roland was stunned. "You have seen her?" he asked eagerly. "When? Is she all right?"

"A wife belongs to her husband. If you have loved this man's wife, you wrong him, not he you."

With an immense effort, Roland made himself relax. Baibars would tell him only as much as he wanted to about Nicolette, and pressing him would only antagonize him.

"I will not argue the point with you, emir."

"You still have not told me who this Amalric is and what kind of man he is. Is he a very important man, or does he hold his present place as commander of Damietta by chance?"

"Were we in France and not trapped here in Egypt, he might be the second most powerful man in the kingdom."

"More so than the King's brothers?"

"The King controls his brothers completely. Amalric, as Count de Gobignon, has a realm of his own that he rules over, almost as a king in his own right. As to what sort of man he is, Amalric is intelligent, courageous, cruel, ambitious, and treacherous." It occurred to Roland with dismay that he could well be describing Baibars himself. "I believe he deliberately tricked our army into surrendering to you."

Baibars chuckled. "Then I am grateful to him."

"Does a victory on such terms truly please you?"

"On any terms, victory pleases me." There was that dread word again—*mansura*.

Roland spoke his thought of a moment ago. "In that respect, you and Amalric are alike."

Baibars chuckled again, but there was no warmth in the laugh. "You are all going to die, you know." There was a carelessness in his tone that belied the horror of his words "Probably tomorrow."

Sudden panic gripped Roland, but he wrestled with his terror and fought it down. He told himself there must be more to this. Baibars would not have gone to the trouble of seeking him out for this clandestine meeting just to terrify him. And why would Baibars have told him about the letter from Amalric if Roland and all the others were going to be slaughtered on the morrow? Baibars surely wanted something.

Roland forced himself to sound unconcerned.

"Is that all you brought me out here for, lord? To tell me that?"

Baibars grunted, and Roland heard approval in the faint sound.

Baibars said, "The message from the noble Amalric to the thrice-honored Turan Shah asks the Sultan to kill all of you, from the King down to the least servant. Amalric promises that the Sultan shall have all the money he asks and the city of Damietta, without any other conditions, if he does this."

Rage surged through Roland's body like a burst of Greek fire. And amazement followed, that Amalric should be capable of treachery and murder on such a scale.

"That devil!" Roland whispered.

Baibars put a firm, steadying hand on his arm.

"Now, as you know full well, this is a better offer than your King has made to Turan Shah."

Yes, Roland thought, Louis had promised to pay half the silver at once and the other half only after all Christian prisoners were freed and safely on Christian land. And Louis, with that sublime self-assurance of his, had demanded that Turan Shah free not just his own men but all Christians held captive by the Egyptians, even those they had been holding for many years. It had been plain from the expression on Turan Shah's face, Roland recalled, that Louis's terms had not been received well.

Baibars went on, "This Amalric says, when the money is brought to Damietta from across the sea, and when he knows the King is dead, he will open the gates of Damietta to our warriors. They may do as they please with all Christians in the city, granting Amalric alone safe passage back to Christendom."

Roland's breath came in ragged gasps. Amalric would turn over the Queen, the King's baby son, the Patriarch of Jerusalem, all those faithful knights and servants, to the Saracens to rape and torture and slaughter. And Nicolette, too? The man is not human! Perrin, this is beyond revenge. No revenge would be enough.

"There is nothing that can be done to that man," he said after he got control of himself, "no punishment cruel enough to match his evil. I have always doubted whether there was a Hell but if there is a just God, which is also hard for me to believe there would have to be a Hell for a creature like Amalric. I wish only that I could send him there."

Baibars's voice struck harshly at him from the shadows. "Do not question God in my presence, infidel. I paid a high price for my knowledge of Islam, and I will not hear God mocked. If you are not sure whether you believe in *your* God, then you are the more fool for having invaded my country."

The sudden rebuke served to calm Roland's rage a little. "Very true. But I did not come here to serve God, only to serve my King. Can you show me this message Amalric sent to your Sultan? I myself believe what you tell me, because I know Amalric, but for the King I must have proof."

"You are a bit slow," said Baibars, and Roland saw his teeth gleam in a grin. "Perhaps you *are* only a Frank. Of course I cannot show you the message. It had to be delivered to the Sultan at once lest he suspect others had seen it. I do not want your King to know about it. Open and innocent as he is, he would be sure to reveal his knowledge when next he meets the Sultan, and then I and all who are allied with me will be destroyed."

Then it *is* a struggle between the Sultan and Baibars, Roland thought, staring out at the great, slow-running river touched with moonlight.

"Will your Sultan make this agreement with Amalric? Take advantage of such treachery? Can he meet with the King and bargain with him as he does nearly every day, and still plan his death and the deaths of all his men?"

"Oh, yes," said Baibars. "This way he will have the silver, and with your King and his surviving warriors dead, he can be sure the Franks will not trouble us for another generation. And he will recapture Damietta without a fight."

Roland, in agony at the thought of Nicolette's peril, asked, "What can you tell me of the people in Damietta? How are they faring?"

"They are as well as people in a besieged city can be. There is little food, and the weak and ill are dying off. Indeed, the Queen has ordered a great trench to be dug in the heart of the city, before the palace of the governor, for the burial of the dead—and those who will die.

"The Queen has given birth to a son. Turan Shah has told your King about this, I believe."

"Yes, he did," said Roland. "The King was overjoyed." He added bitterly, "But he did suspect that the Sultan might betray him."

"Your King shall not know that he suspected rightly. Not yet," said Baibars. "As the Christians in Damietta do not know which crusaders are alive and which are dead. Turan Shah has not permitted that information to reach them."

Then Nicolette probably thinks I am dead. If only I could get word to her.

"There is no need for such cruelty," he said, angry in his frustration.

"Our Sultan thinks your people in Damietta will cooperate with him more eagerly if all of them hope they have living loved ones whom they can help to set free. They would have run out of food altogether and abandoned Damietta, but I arranged, through agents of mine, to reprovision them. In return for this, a large sum of money from the Queen's treasury was transmitted to me—ten times what such a supply of foodstuffs would ordinarily cost. Of course, she had no idea that it was her husband's conqueror whom she was paying so extravagantly. Or that she was only buying back food that had been previously spirited out of the city by this Count Amalric."

"Why did you send the food?"

"It suits my purposes for things to remain as they are. I do not wish the Christians to give up Damietta before the bargaining is concluded. And the money, many thousands of bezants, will be useful to me."

"Who could not use such a sum?" said Roland ironically.

"I shall not keep it long," said Baibars. "But I do not wish to speak of that now."

Roland felt him drawing closer. He tensed, knowing that Baibars was about to reveal his purpose.

"Listen, singer," said Baibars in a lower voice. "You must swear to me that you will not speak a word of what I am telling you to anyone. If I even suspect you have spoken, my vengeance will be terrible."

"Perhaps I will decide that the King must know of this. What if I refuse to swear?"

Roland heard a movement, the clinking of the chain mail Baibars wore under his red surcoat. Then there came the hiss, from Baibars's right side, of a blade being slid from its scabbard.

I must show him I am not afraid.

"You are left-handed," Roland said with forced casualness.

"So am I. My left hand has been my sword hand ever since Amalric destroyed my right shoulder in a tournament."

"You heard which side I drew my sword on? How keen a

you. I hope I will not have to slice such a clever head from its shoulders. Will you swear now?"

Roland sighed. "I will swear, not because I am afraid of your sword—I have felt myself to be a dead man for months—but because I do not think you would put me in the position of betraying the King."

"You understand me well," said Baibars approvingly. "Among the people I was born to, those you call Tartars, the spoken promise is forever binding. I take what you have just said as your oath, and I will hold you to it.

"Hear, then. Many Mameluke lords are offended at the way Turan Shah has dealt with them since he became our Sultan. They, together with his father's chief wife, the lady Spray-of-Pearls, guarded the empty throne until he could come from Syria to claim it. They kept the old Sultan's death a secret from everyone—especially you invaders. He thanks us by demoting our emirs and replacing them with his cronies. Now he has charged the good lady Spray-of-Pearls with misusing the Sultan's treasury, while he himself wastes the wealth of Egypt on his debaucheries."

Something in the warmth with which Baibars uttered the name of Spray-of-Pearls suggested to Roland that his feeling for her was more than simple loyalty to a former Sultan's widow.

"It seems the Mameluke lords have many grievances against their new Sultan," Roland said carefully.

He heard voices calling in a singsong behind him. He turned and saw torches flaring up on tall poles around the silken walls of Turan Shah's tent palace. Guards were calling the hour.

"What would your King Louis think of these grievances of the Mamelukes?" Baibars asked, his voice low but vibrating with intensity. "Suppose certain high officers decided that the Sultan had used them ill and deserved death. Suppose they sent him to the afterworld. How would your King deal with the executioners?"

Instantly, Roland understood. Whether Baibars acted or not, whether Louis and the crusaders lived or died, might depend on what Roland said now.

He stood utterly immobile as a huge, cold, hollow space grew inside him. No man should ever hold so many lives in his hands.

If the Mamelukes rebelled, overthrew their Sultan and killed him, would Louis deal with them?

Turan Shah is the lawful prince, descended from a line of Sultans going back beyond Saladin. Even when sovereigns are enemies, there is a bond of understanding between them. The

King has been meeting with Turan Shah every day. The Mamelukes are upstarts, slaves at that, not even natives of this country. Would not the King despise them? Might he not refuse to traffic with them?

But that would be the end of us. He might sacrifice his own life, but would he send the rest of us to our deaths just because he did not want to deal with rebels? And certainly, if he knew the Sultan was conspiring with his own constable and cousin, he should be happy to see Turan Shah done away with.

But what if he did not believe the Sultan guilty?

Roland felt an enormous silent pressure from Baibars. He had to speak.

"The King would have no choice but to deal with whoever is in authority over the land of Egypt," he said. "Even if they had killed the Sultan." He hoped there was conviction in his voice.

Baibars grunted skeptically. "A man who thinks he lives by heavenly law, as your King does, always has a choice. Even if the choice leads to his death. Monarchs are often outraged when lesser men rise against their rulers. Louis might scorn to deal with men whose hands were red with the blood of their Sultan. I ask again, companion of Louis, what would your most Christian King do?"

A clammy sweat broke out on Roland's forehead. Oh, Jesus, I have been a troubadour these many years, and yet now I cannot find the right words. I do not know what the King would do. He might decide we should all be holy martyrs. Die and go straight to Heaven.

The moon was high now in the eastern sky, and Roland could almost see Baibars's face in the shadows. But it was like a mask; he could read no expression.

"He would not sacrifice the lives of thousands of men for a principle," Roland said.

"He has done that already," said Baibars, "leading his army to Egypt."

"But he thought it was God's will that he would win," pleaded Roland. "Now he knows we can stay alive only if you are merciful."

But Baibars is not merciful, he thought. He remembered the tale he had heard of the Christian captives paraded through Cairo with the heads of their comrades hung around their necks. Baibars might himself kill us all. He might even strike a bargain with Amalric.

Roland still felt pressure, but now it was building up inside him. What was Baibars going to do? He had to be prepared.

"I will not tell the King," he said, "but I have to know what you intend. You must tell me enough so that I can protect him."

Baibars laughed.

"Even if I did tell you my plans," Baibars said, "how could you rely on what I said? You know you cannot trust the word of a Saracen."

Coming from Baibars's lips, the Christian word for the Muslims sounded strange to Roland. It made him even angrier that Baibars should joke when Roland, the King, and all their comrades, helpless prisoners, were about to be slaughtered. And, my God, I am the one man in the crusader army who has never wanted to make war on these people.

In his fury he suddenly reached out and seized Baibars's right arm. He felt a powerful pull as Baibars tried to jerk free, but he hung on.

Baibars did not move.

After a moment of silence, he said in a very low, flat voice, "Let go."

Roland released his arm, and Baibars rubbed it.

"There was a time when I could not have stopped myself from killing you. But I understand that fear and desperation drove you to lay your hand upon me. And they made you very strong."

"I am sorry," Roland said, feeling sure he had blasted all hope for the crusaders' lives.

Baibars said, "As they said in the tribe I was born to, my heart speaks to you. I must tell you that I do not know what I will do. Only Allah knows that. There is nothing you can do now to help your King or yourself, nothing that will not put you in more danger. You will just have to play upon your strings and sing your songs. We must await the time, and what it brings. Perhaps you will all at last go free. Perhaps you will all die. Perhaps I will have to kill you myself, when the Sultan orders it, if I decide that time is not right to disobey him. If I must do that, Frankish poet, I will do it with sorrow."

As he walked with Baibars back to the prison ships, Roland thought, This man beside me may be dead, too, before tomorrow ends.

Baibars turned away from him at the bottom of the gangplank.

As Roland moved slowly to board the prison ship, he felt a light touch on his arm and heard Baibars speak softly to him.

"Whatever happens will be as Allah wills. We are nothing. All power is His."

XXXIII

AMALRIC LISTENED TO THE WAILING CRY THAT CALLED THE MUSLIMS to evening prayer and wished he could hang the damned Saracen doing that weird caterwauling. He felt oppressed by this room in which he and Nicolette sat, a library, part of the harem area of the house. On bookshelves lining the walls stood neat rows of leatherbound volumes and boxes of scrolls. I should have these fed to the kitchen fire, Amalric thought. There was something almost obscene, he felt, about such a huge collection of books. Were not books a source of contamination, breeding heresy and rebellion? Did not much of the evil spreading through Christendom spring from these very Saracen and pagan writings?

He looked at Nicolette, sitting at a table in the center of the room, turning the pages of a large volume under the light of a filigreed lamp hanging from the ceiling.

"Do not tell me you can read the devils' writing," he tried to joke with her.

"No," she said quietly, "but there are beautiful pictures in many of these books."

Her remote, self-possessed manner churned up a fury within him. She was betraying him. He was sure of it. Maybe now was the time to get the truth out of her. He remembered how she had been when he first came back, anguished for the lost army and trembling in fear of what the Muslims might do if they took this city. Then when he had told her of de Vency's death he had felt certain her spirit was totally crushed. But it was not. He could still see her at the meeting with the Genoese, after those sneaking Bedouins sold the Queen provisions—the same provisions Amalric had sold *them* for a mere tenth of what they got from Marguerite. When that snake Lercari went back on his word, yes, he had seen triumph in her eyes, he would swear it. And if not for that stroke of bad fortune, he would already be safely on Cyprus.

Looking at her now, the first time she had been at home with him since the day after his return to Damietta, he felt her beauty move him, as it always did. But he felt no lust to bed her.

What he needed most was to relax enough to sleep, to stop asking himself all night long, Would Turan Shah cooperate or betray him? Would Louis somehow return to accuse and destroy him? Visions of the King, Robert d'Artois, and the others he had betrayed tormented him like demons. An outcry last night from the sentries on the walls had turned his bowels to water. He had imagined the crusaders free, coming back. This morning on the street one of his hired men-at-arms had spoken to him from behind, and his body had gone rigid, his hand leaping for his sword hilt. Yes, it was good Nicolette had been sharing the Queen's bed. God only knew what he might have uttered in his sleep.

And now the moment was almost at hand. The great chests of silver were sitting offshore on a galleass whose sails were painted with the splayed red cross of the Templars. Maurice had gone to the Sultan with Amalric's message and had come back saying that Turan Shah would act in a day or two.

Suddenly he felt a longing to see his children. Was not today the first of May? Back at Château Gobignon they would be dancing around a Maypole. He ached to feel his sweet Isabelle's arms around his neck. Well, if all went as planned, Simon might one day be King of France.

Curse Nicolette, why could she not share with him so magnificent a dream?

He watched her turn another page and smile at the brightly painted picture she saw there.

"I suppose you would be satisfied to stay here for the rest of your life, madame, woolgathering over these Saracen books."

She looked up, surprised. "Not at all, monseigneur. Now that the ransom money is here, our men will be back with us soon and we shall leave. With that I am content."

Does she think the troubadour is still alive? Did she not believe me? He felt himself grow hot with fury. She must still hope to see him again. Why else would she be so infernally serene?

And she had given the Queen the strength to stay here. Yes, and he would make her admit it, too.

"Are you pleased, madame, because you think you have succeeded in betraying me?" His voice came out louder than he had intended, almost a shout.

"I have no idea what you mean," she said coldly, laying her hands flat on the open book and staring at him.

"Indeed? I instructed you to urge Marguerite to flee this city.

Of all her women you are closest to her. Yet with every passing day she becomes more stubborn. And those fresh supplies, I think you had something to do with them. You should have been at my side, and instead you were giving aid to my enemies. You are a faithless woman.''

Her lips drew back from her teeth. "Faithless? You accuse me, when everything you have done has been for the death of your own King and comrades?''

The red rays of the setting sun streaming through translucent sheets of horn in the tall windows glittered on the names of books written on leather in gold leaf. He hated the wriggling Arabic symbols, because they hid their meaning from him.

How much has she told Marguerite?

Hugues was right. I should have gotten rid of her long ago.

But I could not bear to. Why was I so weak?

No, not weakness. It was love. Always. I can command armies, even topple a great king, and yet fail at every turn to win this one small woman.

"Have you never understood me?'' he demanded. "This king is destroying us.''

"If you really believe that, you are mad,'' she answered, staring at him. "I have little knowledge, perhaps, but I believe King Louis must be one of the best men ever to wear the crown of France. And you speak against him only because you yourself want to take his crown.''

My enemy, Amalric thought. She has always been my enemy. He felt as if she had driven a dagger into his side. How could she be my wife, how could she bear my children, and yet see *nothing* as I see it?

"I do not care about being king. But I want a man on the throne who respects the Peers of the Realm and who will stamp out heresy.''

"You are lying, Amalric,'' she said with strange gentleness. "Perhaps to yourself. Because what you are doing is so foul that you cannot admit it even to yourself.''

He felt himself trembling with fury. How dare she, a woman who has betrayed her own husband, sit in judgment on me?

He felt the muscles of his arms and hands swelling and tightening. He wanted—to kill her.

"It is not the King you care about,'' he said through clenched teeth. "Your thoughts are ever on the troubadour, de Vency.''

If only I could throw his severed head down before her.

"For Roland de Vency and for me, our King comes first," she said calmly.

Her boldness was intolerable. Now, he thought, now I will tell her the things that will destroy her.

"It was I who killed de Vency!" he roared. "I led him to his death. I saw the Egyptians lying in wait on a rooftop over a courtyard in Mansura, and I sent him in there to be ambushed. *I*. What say you to that, madame?"

Nicolette felt as if he had run her through with his sword. She almost expected to see her blood spurt out over the book beneath her hands.

She had known, somehow, ever since Amalric had first described Roland's fall, that he must have had a hand in it. Until now, though, she had been able to think that Amalric might have made it all up. Now he was admitting murder. That had to be true.

What to say? Nicolette thought. Does he actually expect me to say *anything*?

She saw Roland's beloved dark face in her mind, and she put her hands over her own face. She heard her own sobs, loud in her ears.

She remembered the last time Amalric had spoken to her of Roland's death. She had held her grief in, waited till she could get out of the city. Now she did not care. He could do nothing more to her. The silver was here, under Templar guard. In a few days the King would be free, and then he would punish Amalric.

She took her hands away from her face. Let Amalric see her grief. That way she could hurt him, too. See, Amalric, no one will ever sob like this for you.

Finally she looked up. His face terrified her. The whites of his eyes were stained red. Breathing in short gasps, he had the look of a maddened bull.

He suddenly rushed at her. With one swing he struck her face and knocked her to the floor.

She heard herself scream. The room seemed to be rocking. She drew herself into a ball, fists over her face, knees and elbows together. A part of her mind braced her for the sudden thrust of steel she expected at any moment.

"Get up! Get up, God damn you!" he roared.

She lifted her head. Pain throbbed in her temples, and she was so dizzy that the books and scrolls on the walls seemed to be revolving around her. She felt something trickling down her lower lip and chin. She touched her fingers to it and looked at the tips, red with blood. She made herself look up at him as he stood like a colossus over her.

Slowly, trembling and in pain, she pushed herself to her feet.

Swaying unsteadily, forced to look up at him even when standing, she said softly, "You have killed him, have you? Well, then it is time I told you a secret. You may have tricked him into an ambush, but you could never beat him in a fair fight. He is better than you. And do you know why?" Hoarsely she whispered the words: *"Because he is your brother!"*

He said nothing, staring at her as if she were raving.

He does not understand, she thought.

Still dazed by his blow, she leaned over the book she had been reading, her palms flat against the table. Her long black braids, coming undone, hung down to brush a bright painting of a pair of lovers embracing in a tent under a blossoming tree.

"You have no idea what I am talking about, do you?" she said with a wild little laugh. "Well, you had best listen. Years ago, when your father rode into Languedoc against the heretics, he was given a conquered castle as a prize. The rightful inheritor of the castle was a thirteen-year-old orphan girl, whom he raped."

She went on to tell him the whole tale just as Roland had told it to her, under the ancient oak north of Chartres. As she talked, she watched Amalric, eager to see him crumble. She watched his face change expression, at first angry, then red with shame. She saw his eyes wander as he began to think about what she was saying, comparing it with what he had heard. She saw him grow pale with shock.

"So you see," she said, "all these years you have been deluded. You thought heretics killed your father, and your hatred of heretics has poisoned your whole life. When it was really a band of young men of your own faith, fighting for their homeland."

She watched his face twist with nausea.

He stepped backward, putting a hand out to steady himself against a bookshelf. His chest rose and fell spasmodically.

Trembling, she waited, hoping to see him collapse.

Instead he straightened his back. His face became a passionless mask. "You weave a tale skillfully, madame," he said lightly. "A good story to amaze children."

He would not be so easy to overthrow. What other means did she have to wound him?

After a moment, she felt a fierce exultation. She smiled at him. "You do not believe me?"

He eyed her almost with fear.

"What proof is there?" She could hear the strain in his voice, the effort to sound casual.

"None," she agreed. "You think it is a tale for children, do you? Well, let me tell you about another child."

Her voice no longer sounded like her own. It had become the screech of a demon.

"Simon is not your son. He is Roland's."

Terror seized her as soon as she said the words. She had let out the secret of her life, and in doing so, risked Simon's. With dread, she watched Amalric.

His eyes seemed to roll up into his head. He put his hand on the table and held himself upright.

Then his eyes opened, and a fire blazed in them. His face reddened, swelled, and twisted until he looked like a creature from Hell.

"You just killed your son, Nicolette," he snarled. "Your bastard child. The moment I get back to France, that child will be dead."

"No, no!" she screamed.

"Whore! Filthy, rotten whore! Do not say no to me!"

He stopped, choking. He stood there with clenched fists.

Simon! she screamed inside. What have I done to you? She felt the blood still trickling from her mouth, but she did not bother to wipe it away.

"In spite of everything you did, the King and all with him are lost," he said in a lower voice. "Dead men."

A certainty in his tone told her he was not feigning this to torment her.

"No," she whispered, terrified. "They are to be ransomed."

"They are to be killed," he said. "I have promised the Sultan everything he wants—the ransom money, the city, and all the Christians in it—if he kills the King and his men." He spoke quietly, reasonably, compelling her to understand that he was telling the simple truth. "I have arranged it all."

She saw a huge black ocean wave racing toward her. She stood paralyzed before it. The wave rolled over her, covering her with darkness. She was drowning. She put her hand to her bleeding mouth and swayed back and forth.

"Oh my God! Oh my God!"

"It is too late for you to call upon God, whore."

"And you? Who do you call upon? You are worshiping the

Devil, Amalric. Only he could drive a man to the things you are doing."

God, why did I never kill him? I could have stabbed him while he slept, poisoned him.

"You call my faith Devil worship? That is what the heretics say."

In the grip of horror as she stared at him she whispered, "Yes, call me a heretic. That is what your rapist brother Hugues would say, is it not? The world is well rid of him." She bared her teeth in a grin, knowing she had hurt him again.

He moved toward her, hand lifted to strike.

She remained motionless, defiant.

And then she sprang at him. She went for the hilt of the basilard, the three-sided spike that hung at his right side.

She had to reach across him, and she was not quick enough. His hand seized hers in an iron grasp, but rage gave her strength.

She had the dagger halfway out. His powerful fingers were crushing the bones of her wrist, grinding them together.

She brought her head down and sank her teeth into his hand, biting in frenzy.

He roared his pain.

For an instant his grip loosened and she jerked at the dagger. She almost had it free.

Then his other fist smashed like a hammer against the side of her head.

Again he pounded her skull.

She hardly felt the third blow as she slid to the floor.

He laughed and picked her up as if she were a heap of bedclothes. He pushed her back against the reading table, pressing his body against her, bending her backward.

She felt a hard pressure against her legs. Then he reached down and drew up her skirt.

"This is the beginning of a humiliation that will last the rest of your life, Nicolette," he said through gritted teeth.

She fought him with all her strength, arching her back, throwing her hips from side to side, kicking. She managed to hold him off for a moment.

"Go on, fight me," he laughed. "Better than having you lie there like a dead woman, as you usually do."

"No," she gasped, writhing in his grasp. "My God, you are not going to do this. I would rather you killed me."

He pushed her back and forced her legs apart. "I know that, Nicolette."

She screamed helplessly. She tried to rake his face with her nails, but he pinned her arms to the table.

It was over in an instant, like the rutting of a stallion. He leaned against her, panting, and she drew her head back.

"Pig!" She spat in his face.

He hit her again with his hand, open hand, cutting her lip in another place. He drew back from her and threw her to the floor.

In spasms that shot stabbing pains through her, she vomited on the beautiful Arabian carpet. It felt almost as if she were expelling her defiled insides.

Eventually the clenching of her stomach subsided, and she lay on the floor and wept.

Amalric went to the wrought-iron grille that locked the harem rooms off from the rest of the house. He had the key in a pouch at his belt. Avoiding looking back at her, he locked her in and strode off.

"Maurice! Maurice!" he bellowed through the corridors of the mansion.

He felt as if he were writhing on an iron spike thrust through his bowels. A voice within him bewailed his loss—a wife and a son. Now he would have to kill Simon. But it was she who had decreed his death.

At that instant he saw the face of de Vency in the child.

But—Oh God!—de Vency's face is *my* face. His head swam with the shock. My father, murdered by de Vency's stepfather. And my father *his* father. Impossible! Lies. I am ill. I would not give these lies a thought if I had not lost so much sleep. I should kill her now.

If only I could find de Vency's body, cut out his heart, and force her to eat it.

A woman in a dark blue gown appeared below him on the stairs.

"Monseigneur." She bowed. "I heard you call."

He focused his eyes on her. A thin, ravaged face that had once been pretty. Brown eyes, full of fear as she looked up at him. Agnes, Nicolette's maid.

Damn! he thought. She must not talk to Nicolette. Nicolette will tell her everything.

His rage turned against Agnes. Another damned Languedoc woman, like Nicolette and Marguerite. She must know all about Nicolette's infidelity. She probably carried messages between her and the troubadour. She might even know about Simon.

He could not bear to think she might.

"Yes," he said. "Madame needs you. Come with me."

Without waiting, he turned and started back into the second-floor corridor. He heard her steps behind him. He waited till he was passing an empty room.

Then he whirled and seized her throat.

His thumbs crushing her windpipe cut off her scream. He dragged her into the shadowy room. She struggled against him, beating him with fists he did not feel. He watched her face turn dark. He looked at a mosaic on the wall. He fixed his eyes on it, his arms rigid, his hands tightening, tightening.

She seemed to take forever to die.

When her body was limp and unmoving, he let her drop to the floor. He put his hand on her breast. There was no heartbeat. He tore a hanging down from the wall, threw it over her, and left her there.

If only I could show her body to Nicolette, but there is no time for that.

He found Maurice on the first floor and told him some of what had happened between himself and Nicolette.

The old man looked at Amalric in puzzlement. "But why, monseigneur? Why did you tell madame so much?"

"I told you, we quarreled. Do not question me, damn you. Just make sure that she is kept locked up and quiet until we know the King and the rest of them are dead. And there is something else you must take care of for me. I had to kill Nicolette's maid."

Maurice's hand went to his chest, and there was shock and pain in his eyes. *Saint Dominic, did he care for the damned girl?*

But all he said was, "Does Madame Nicolette know?"

"No. I want you to get the body out of the house before anyone finds out about it. It is in a room upstairs."

Maurice nodded slowly, turning his face away from Amalric. "It will be easy, monseigneur. When the dead cart comes around after dark, I will put her on it. I will tell the other servants she just collapsed suddenly. They will be afraid to get too close to the body. She will be buried in the big grave in the center of the city, with no questions. People are dying every day."

"Do it, then. Make sure no one finds the body before you have rid us of it."

Maurice kept his head turned. "But why did you have to kill her, monseigneur? She did not know anything, did she?"

"Do not question me, God damn you!" Amalric shouted.

"No, monseigneur," Maurice whispered as Amalric walked away.

In the early evening twilight Amalric took his war-horse, one of the few left in Damietta, and rode through the streets. He passed the long burial pit before the governor's palace, into which Agnes would soon disappear. He turned and rode to the south gateway, the largest of the four in Damietta's triple walls. Leaving the destrier in the care of a guard, he climbed to the top of the gate tower.

His steps were slow, legs hard to move. Somewhere inside him a voice cried out in anguish, Simon! Simon! The pain ran down his backbone, filled his body.

And I had thought he might one day be king. He wondered if he would go mad, suffering so, losing everything in one night.

Standing on the stone platform of the tower, leaning against a sandstone merlon, he stared at the Nile. The marshlands were black and the river a glistening purple. Somewhere, up that river only a few leagues, were King Louis and his men, about to be slaughtered. Nicolette should see them die. God, I wish she could. What can I do to pay her back in full?

Go back now and kill her? God, I have loved her for so many years. Such a waste. That traitorous bitch.

No, I will take her back to France. She can learn of my triumph while she withers in a dungeon. And I can torture her at my whim. She must watch the death of that bastard she and de Vency conceived. Oh, my poor little Simon, I loved you. He felt grief rising in him, choking him.

Then a new idea came, so cunning he found himself exulting. I will force *her* to kill Simon. Torture a person enough and they will do anything.

But what about that heretic woman who died with Hugues? He tortured her endlessly. And she never gave in. Yes, and we knew de Vency was her protector, though we never proved it.

By God, de Vency is the cause of all of it. What I would give to have him alive again.

But de Vency—my brother?

He looked up at the huge stars that seemed to hang right above his face like so many mocking fireflies.

"No!" he roared.

He smashed his fist against the rock. The pain shot up his arm, and it felt good. He pounded his knuckles into the unyielding merlon again and again until his fist was as numb as the stone itself.

And then he seemed to wake, as if from a nightmare.

What am I doing?

It is she. She is driving me mad.

Take her back to France? No, how can I? I shall have to kill her here. But first she must suffer. Must suffer as much pain as she has caused me.

Yes, she should see her beloved Marguerite raped and that baby's brains dashed out against a wall. And then I could give her as a slave to the Saracens. Down on her knees for the rest of her life.

No, no. She is clever, she might trick some Egyptian into treating her kindly. But I could mutilate her. Disfigure her so that she could be nothing but a whore for the lowest brute.

Well, there is time to plan. I swear that before she dies I will have vengeance in full measure.

XXXIV

ROLAND GRIPPED THE RAIL OF THE PRISON SHIP. A SUDDEN FLURRY of movement in the Sultan's compound had caught his eye, and he quivered with tension. All morning and afternoon, after the previous night's talk with Baibars, he had felt cold with dread.

Now it begins, he told himself. But what? The Mameluke uprising? Or the massacre planned by Amalric?

Jean de Joinville, standing beside him, exclaimed, "My God, they are killing a man. Who is it?"

Robed figures were rushing out of the central pavilion. The warm yellow light of late afternoon flashed on gold ornaments and the bright steel of curved swords.

Roland and de Joinville leaned over the railing to see better. A Turk was running ahead of the others, red, green, and blue raiment billowing around him. He was clutching his wrist. His free hand, held out before his chest, was covered with blood. He ran toward the riverbank, awkwardly because of the way he was holding his hands. As he came closer to the galleys, Roland could see his face. His eyes were wide with amazement and terror, his mouth open.

It was the Sultan of Egypt, Turan Shah.

"They are killing their Sultan," Roland exclaimed as he clapped de Joinville on the back. "Go and tell the King." De Joinville hurried down the deck.

A group of warriors in flowing white robes, swords drawn, followed Turan Shah down the grassy slope to the Nile. Roland recognized most of them as the high Mameluke officers he had seen before in council with the Sultan. In their center walked Baibars, taller than the rest. Their stride was unhurried, purposeful, inexorable.

Where was the Sultan's bodyguard?

Roland remembered Baibars saying he was giving away the money paid him for Damietta's provisions. So the bodyguard must have been bought off. They are actually going to do it, he thought—kill Turan Shah. For the moment he was hopeful. But still he felt afraid. He had seen too many seeming victories turn suddenly into disasters.

Now Roland spied men of the Sultan's bodyguard in their gilded breastplates spreading tumult through the royal pavilions. Instead of rushing to the Sultan's aid, they were hacking at the ropes and poles that held up Turan Shah's tents, and some of them were cutting down screaming, fleeing courtiers and retainers. Roland saw a bearded head sail out over the lawn like a rock shot from a catapult and land at the bottom of the slope.

He felt no revulsion. Saint Michel, he thought, have I seen so much horror that it is all one to me whether a bird or a man's head flies through the air?

Turan Shah was at the base of the tall wooden tower from which he had enjoyed observing his prisoners. Three elderly men, their black gowns and turbans marking them as mullahs, expounders of Islam, were already crowded on the tower's platform. Turan Shah dragged himself up the narrow wooden steps, leaving a trail of blood. As he reached the top, the mullahs shouted at him, waving their hands. They seemed to be telling him to get out because he was endangering them.

The Mameluke officers gathered around the base of the tower, conferring among themselves and waving their swords at the Sultan, challenging him to come down. Baibars stood apart, aloof, his arms folded, master of the scene of panic and murder spread out before them.

The galley rocked and hundreds of feet pounded on the deck as the captive crusaders crowded the railing to watch. Some were laughing, even cheering the Mamelukes on. De Joinville came back to stand beside Roland.

"The King is ill with fever again, but he is getting dressed," he said.

Roland wondered how the King would feel when he saw what was happening.

The Mameluke officers called to the three mullahs, urging them to come down, showing by reverent gestures that the holy men had nothing to fear. The teachers conferred among themselves, then hurried down the steps. Turan Shah clung to his perch. The Mamelukes bowed to the mullahs, who walked briskly away, not looking back.

A soldier of the Sultan's bodyguard came down to the tower holding at arm's length a white ball the size of a man's head. Roland recognized it as a bladder made from a cow's stomach. There is Greek fire in that, he thought, his neck prickling. Then the Mameluke emirs backed off, and the soldier swung the bladder around his head and expertly let it fly up toward the tower platform. The bladder struck and exploded into flame.

"Did you ever see a prettier bonfire?" de Joinville chortled.

Roland did not answer, thinking of other great fires he had seen—at Mont Ségur, at Mansura, his stone-casters. This whole uprising, too, was a kind of fire, and it might well spread and consume them all. When these Mamelukes finished with Turan Shah, what then? Roland had a momentary vision of their racing toward these galleys, the steel scimitars turned on himself and his friends. His hands felt empty, his arms weak.

Now Turan Shah was running down the steps. The Mamelukes crowded to the base of the tower to receive the Sultan with their blades.

His feet at a level with their heads, he suddenly leaped from the tower toward the river. He struck the ground hard, rolled, and picked himself up. He must have hurt himself, because he was limping badly. But he had gained a few precious moments, and he reached the water's edge ahead of his pursuers.

In spite of himself, Roland was beginning to feel pity for the Sultan. He could feel the pain of the man's hurts, his desperate longing for life.

Turan Shah turned to face the men who were trying to kill him and shouted angrily at them. Roland could imagine what he was saying. He was their Sultan, raised above them by Allah. To strike at him was to strike at his great ancestor Saladin.

"The dogs!" It was the King's voice, trembling with rage

"He is unarmed. They have not even enough honor to let him defend himself."

Roland turned. The King's long face was twisted with anguish. He was pale and trembling, and Roland took his arm as he tottered to the railing and continued to hold him, afraid Louis might fall over the side.

Then Roland heard a scream from the river's edge and looked back to see an emir's sword bite deep into Turan Shah's side.

"Stop it, you swine! Stop!" the King shouted. "You will answer to God for this."

Now there was no need to keep Baibars's secret.

"Sire, the Sultan has been plotting to kill us. He planned to take the ransom money and Damietta and kill us all anyway."

Louis turned to stare at Roland with his large eyes. "I have always thought that he might, but how can you be sure?"

"Baibars himself told me in secret last night."

"The Sultan is still trying to get away!" came de Joinville's amazed shout from beside him. Louis and Roland turned to look again.

Turan Shah had turned away from his attackers and was facing the river. The scimitar was still caught in his ribs. Half falling, half diving, he threw himself into the muddy water.

Near the spot where the Sultan had jumped in there were longboats pulled up on shore. Leaping waist-deep into the river, the Mamelukes launched one of them and piled into it. Three of them stood up and poled it swiftly into mid-river, laughing and shouting like men enjoying a day's hunting.

Roland's pity for the Sultan grew. Why could they not just let him go? Then he realized why that was impossible. Alive, Turan Shah would find forces loyal to him and counterattack.

Anxious to see what would happen, Roland ran to the riverward side of the galley. Hundreds of others were doing the same. The old wooden ship listed dangerously as all aboard crowded along one rail.

Turan Shah had swum straight out into the river. Roland marveled that with such terrible wounds he still had the strength to do that. There was a trail of blood in the brown water behind him. Perhaps, thought Roland, he really did inherit some of Saladin's might.

Where is the King?

Not seeing him at the railing, Roland turned. The King was kneeling on the deck, his eyes shut, his hands clasped before him, his lips moving in silent prayer. The sight of Louis praying for his enemy filled Roland with awe.

But Heaven protect us, thought Roland, smitten with a sudden pang of fear. If he pities the Sultan so, will he be willing to deal with the Mamelukes? He just called them swine. What if he insults them and they understand it? They will butcher all of us.

A shout rose from the watching crusaders, like the cry of spectators at a tournament. Roland looked back at the river and saw that the boatload of Mamelukes had caught up with Turan Shah. Almost tipping over, they were reaching for him with grappling hooks, beating him with their poles, and striking at him with their swords. Roland could hardly see the Sultan himself in the midst of the spray thrown up by his frantic thrashing.

The crusaders on the galleys were now falling silent, horror replacing their amusement.

The Mamelukes dragged Turan Shah up against the boat, stabbing at him with their swords. One held him by his wet, long, black hair as they poled the boat back to shore, pulling his body.

Roland could not tell whether the Sultan was alive or dead, but there was a cloud of red in the water all around him.

The crusaders crossed the deck again as the Mamelukes pulled their Sultan up on the bank and the robed figures with their bloody swords gathered around the body. The silks of the Sultan were now but shreds, their once bright colors obscured by blood and mud.

Baibars, scimitar in hand, strode down the bank. He gazed down at Turan Shah for a moment, and Roland thought he saw the Sultan move. Suddenly Baibars lunged, driving his scimitar into Turan Shah's chest. The fallen man quivered from head to foot, then lay still. Baibars gathered up part of his white robe to wipe the blood from his blade, leaving a dark red smear. He deliberately marks himself with the Sultan's blood, thought Roland. After a long look at the other Mamelukes, Baibars sheathed his sword and walked away.

One emir raised his scimitar high and brought it down on Turan Shah's chest with a shout. Then he fell upon the Sultan and plunged his bare hand into the wound. Soon he was on his feet again holding aloft in both hands a lump of meat dripping red.

"Sweet Jesus!" said de Joinville. "They have torn out his heart."

Roland felt his stomach heave, and he quickly turned away. A bitter bile came up in his throat, and he covered his mouth with his hand. No, he had not become as hardened as he had thought.

"May God have mercy on his soul," said Louis softly. He had returned to the rail to stand beside them.

May God have mercy on all of us now, thought Roland. His knees trembled as he realized that all too soon they too must face these same Mamelukes.

Roland saw Baibars standing alone on the hill, where the Sultan's tents burned around him. He surveyed the scene, smiling. What happens to us depends on him now.

The descendants of Saladin will rule Egypt no more. There ought to be a sad song in this, ugly and bloody though it is.

Roland's spine froze as he watched the Mamelukes rejoice. They shouted and sang in the high wailing way peculiar to Saracens. They danced around the butchered body, led by him who held up the Sultan's heart, and waved their swords. Mameluke guards marched a small group of musicians to the riverbank and made them play their drums, tambours, and hautboys.

Suddenly the blazing wooden tower crashed in upon itself, and there was a moment's silence. Then the shrieking and laughter broke out again, wilder than before.

Soon, Roland thought with dread, they will remember us.

Roland saw Baibars standing silently watching all this, looking pleased but not taking part. At one point the emirs hailed him with drawn swords, and he acknowledged with a bow. Then he turned and strode off into the rapidly falling evening.

He had killed the Sultan and stained his robe with blood to show the emirs that he was one of them, but he remained apart now to show that he was above them.

His departure frightened Roland. Somehow, with Baibars present, Roland felt safer from the madness that possessed the Mamelukes. With Baibars gone, they might do anything.

Even as he thought this, he saw some of the emirs pointing at the prison galleys. They were a terrifying sight, their pale robes spotted with dark blood, their teeth glistening in their black beards like the fangs of wolves. Singing, chanting, shouting so wildly Roland could not understand a word they uttered, the whole group, a dozen or more, marched to the gangplank of this ship, where the King and his brothers were held.

Roland was surprised that he could still feel such a sharp pang of terror.

As they strode aboard the galley, the Mamelukes seemed to

him in the grip of a frenzy. The defenseless, tatterdemalion crusaders fell back. Led by the emir carrying Turan Shah's dripping heart, the Mamelukes tramped down the deck, straight for the King.

The blood-lust upon them, what was to stop them now from murdering an enemy ruler? Not us. We can slow them only as long as it takes for them to cut us down.

Even so, Roland, de Joinville, and a few others formed a protective half circle in front of Louis.

Saracen torchbearers ran up to flank the emir carrying the Sultan's heart. He held it high, and Roland felt another wave of nausea. He was gently but firmly pushed aside by a hand on his shoulder from behind, and then the King was standing next to him, though still leaning on him for support.

The Mameluke emir made a mocking bow, holding out the heart as if it were some choice delicacy. "What reward will you give me, O King, for the heart of your enemy? He died by fire, water, and iron. If he had lived, he would have murdered you."

Roland translated, turning to Louis, who stared coldly down at the Mameluke, the bones of his face casting deep shadows in the torchlight.

"Tell them I have nothing but scorn for those who murder their sovereign lord," said Louis.

Roland froze. As he had feared, the King's sense of honor was now going to be the death of all of them. There was such tension in his spine that he could feel his head quivering from side to side.

"Our King says he respected your Sultan as a brother monarch," said Roland, "and he is anxious to know what your lord's misdeeds were, that they merited his death."

"Does your master think to put me on trial before him?" said the Mameluke angrily. "I saved his life, and I expect a reward. Very well!" He threw the heart down on the deck with a sodden thump.

Roland quickly turned his head away from the sight.

The emir shouted, "We know how to treat ingratitude! Line up, all of you, and lie down on the deck."

Roland's limbs turned to water as he translated this for those around him. We are dead men, he thought. In a moment they will cut us to pieces, just as they did Turan Shah.

Roland now saw many more Mamelukes, of the middle and lower ranks, boarding the galley to reinforce the emirs. The officer who had addressed Louis turned and repeated his orders to the other Mamelukes.

With blows and menacing gestures with their swords, the Saracens conveyed the command to the crusaders. Groaning and wailing, the weak, sick prisoners sank to the deck.

Two of the Mamelukes seized King Louis and started to pull him away from his men.

Roland pushed his way to Louis's side, ready if need be to throw himself on the scimitars that swung in his direction.

"Do as they say, Roland," said Louis. "If it be God's will, we shall live through this night."

They took Louis off in the direction of the tent on the afterdeck in which he and his brothers were quartered.

The rest of the crusaders were forced to lie on their backs in rows, one man's head beside another's feet. On either side of Roland were Count Peter of Brittany and the Sire de Joinville.

"Roland, will you hear my confession?" de Joinville called.

"I am not a priest," Roland answered, embarrassed by the request.

"It matters not. I will tell my sins to you and make a good act of contrition, and perhaps I shall go to Heaven when they chop off my head."

De Joinville then babbled out a list of sins. He had not confessed, he said, since the Saracens massacred all the priests last month at Mansura. Roland tried not to hear him, and in his fear for Louis and for himself found it easy to turn a deaf ear. Then when the knight finished, Roland at de Joinville's insistence forgave him and even made the sign of the cross, feeling foolish.

"Now I will hear your confession," de Joinville offered.

"You are kind," said Roland, "but I would rather make my peace with God in my heart."

Before the blade falls on my neck, what ought my last thoughts to be? I must feel glad and grateful that before I died I was given the grace to love two of the loveliest women who ever walked the earth.

And he composed himself to wait for death.

So passed the watches of the longest night of Roland's life.

The thousands of birds that nested in the reeds along the banks of the Nile raised their chorus to the dawn, and Roland began to see light around him.

The sun was high in the sky when he heard the emirs coming back. He listened, his body tensing, as they gave orders in the distance. Now the slave-warriors of Egypt would fall upon them with their swords.

A voice called in Arabic, "Where is the Frank called Roland?"

Wondering if this was to be his last moment, Roland sat up to look into the eyes of a Mameluke guard with a spear.

"You are to come," said the guard. "Your King orders it."

Moving one stiffened limb at a time, Roland slowly pushed himself to his feet. The King was still alive! His eagerness to see Louis gave him strength.

He saw now that the Mamelukes were allowing the crusaders to sit up and to stand and move about. Following his guard's gesture, Roland limped, step by painful step, to the middle of the ship.

King Louis, wearing the black coat the Sultan had given him and surrounded by emirs in clean white robes, stood at the head of the gangplank.

"It appears we are to enter the lair of the Panther," said Louis. "When he growls, you must be my voice."

As they descended the gangplank, Roland saw that during the night the fallen tents of the Sultan's compound had been taken away, and the top of the grassy slope was now occupied by a smaller tent, cool white in the morning sunshine. Before the tent stood two poles. From one hung a yellow banner inscribed with black Arabic letters: "For the safety of the faith, slay the enemies of Islam."

On the other pole was the scarlet and gold Oriflamme of France. Louis groaned aloud and wept when he saw it. He had to stand a moment to get a grip on himself.

Roland had not seen the Oriflamme since he was captured at Mansura. The sight of it hanging in captivity brought tears to his own eyes. True, he had been a reluctant crusader, but this banner had become part of his life. It stood, not for the glory of warfare, but for King Louis and his visions.

And now, could there be accord between Louis, a zealous Catholic, and Baibars, a fanatical Muslim? Would Louis's pity for the late Sultan and scorn for his murderers provoke him to insult Baibars? The thread by which their lives hung was so slender.

Roland's body stiffened with apprehension as he followed Louis into Baibars's tent. It was a single spacious chamber. Four poles of dark, gleaming wood held up the roof. The floor was covered with Arabian carpets. Baibars, in red robe and yellow turban, was seated on the carpet, leaning back against a jeweled saddle. A small mahogany chest lay beside him.

The one-eyed emir stood to greet them, then bowed them to

places on the carpet. A mullah, perhaps one of those who had escaped from the Sultan's tower last night, was seated before an open Koran on an ornately carved reading stand.

As Louis and Roland seated themselves, he finished reading, "Sun, moon, and stars, each in its own sphere doth journey on." He closed the book and stood up. Baibars bowed reverently to him, and he left. Louis and Roland were alone with Baibars.

"Before we speak of serious matters, please join me in a morning repast," said Baibars. He clapped his hands and the blond boy Roland had seen waiting on Baibars at Mansura entered, bringing sliced melons, a plate of oranges and dates, and cups of cool, clean water. There was a small bowl holding ground-up salt and a tray of flat, round loaves of bread. The sight of the tray raised Roland's hopes.

"He offers you bread and salt," said Roland in French. "That means you are his guest. Once you have eaten his bread and salt, he is obliged by the Muslim law of hospitality not to harm you."

"I shall eat at once," said Louis with a smile, salting a slice of melon and biting off a chunk of bread. Baibars watched with a knowing grin, apparently amused that Louis so quickly ate the bread and salt. It relieved Roland to see both men in good humor.

"Thank you, Daoud," said Baibars, and the youth bowed and left.

"A handsome lad," said Louis. "He could be French."

"English, actually," said Baibars with a smile when Roland translated this. "It was his good fortune to be taken as my slave after the battle of Gaza. He was young enough to absorb the teachings of the Prophet, and now he is entirely one of us."

"What a shame that such a fine young man is lost to the true faith," said Louis.

Roland translated reluctantly, and Baibars laughed.

"True faith? O King, can you still speak of yours as the truth faith when you have suffered so grievously? Thousands of your men are dead, and your hopes of victory lie in ashes. Do you still believe in the God in Whose name you fought?"

"I am still His servant," said Louis.

"If Allah had tried me as your God has tried you," said Baibars, cocking his head slightly so that the gaze of his single blue eye was fixed on Louis, "I would surely have renounced Him."

"Even as you murdered your Sultan when he displeased you?" said Louis quickly. "You seem to be rather lacking in loyalty, monseigneur."

Roland's limbs went cold. Baibars, his honor questioned, might fly into a rage.

This talk must not break down before it had even started. He could not translate the King's words.

He said to Baibars in Arabic, "God sometimes gives us trials and lets us suffer defeat to test our submission to His will, my lord."

Baibars nodded. "But God makes Himself known as the true God through the triumph of His followers upon earth. Allah has long tested the faithfulness of the people of Islam. Did He not allow you Franks to come here and take Jerusalem and hold it for over a hundred years? Then He sent the great Saladin, on whom be peace, to take it back. And after Sultan Ayub graciously restored it to Christian hands when entreated by your Emperor Frederic, Allah permitted *this* unworthy slave, when the Christians provoked us beyond endurance, to capture it again. Now the time of our testing is over. Allah has granted His people many great victories. This, our triumph over your crusade, is only the latest. Soon He will allow us to drive every last Christian from the sacred soil of Islam. Then all men will know Allah is the true God, the one God."

It was painful for Roland to sit quietly and follow this argument, translating it sentence by sentence, all the while fearing as he did for his life. He waited in trepidation for Louis's answer.

"Indeed?" said Louis. "My God grants me a greater gift than victory in war. He allows me to know what is right. When, with His help, I do what is right, I need not care whether my efforts meet with earthly triumph or defeat."

As Roland translated this, Baibars looked surprised. "A strange religion. You believe that the great prophet Jesus the Messiah, was executed like a common criminal. You make war, calling it your God's command, yet you do not expect Him to grant you victory. How can you know this is right when you have no sign of it?"

Almost what I might ask, thought Roland.

"I need no outward sign," said Louis. "I have a sign in here." He touched his fingertips to his narrow chest. "God helps me to believe."

Roland found himself thinking of Diane, who had suffered abominably and gone to the stake for what she believed.

Baibars was speaking, but Roland was absorbed in his own thoughts. If a teaching is true, does my death, or my killing someone else, make it any more or less true? Could it be that

believers die and kill for their faith because they are not sure
that what they believe is really true? "For the safety of the faith,
slay the enemies of Islam." Yes, because faith, when confronted
by doubt, is always in danger.

"Your mind is wandering, Frank," Baibars said to Roland
with sudden sharpness. "Translate for your King what I have
just said."

"Emir Baibars asks if you believe that God will ultimately
give Christianity victory over Islam," Roland said quickly to
Louis. "Sire, why not ask him whether our two faiths could not
live side by side in peace, without one triumphing over the
other?"

A new kind of excitement seized him, heady and powerful.
How many ordinary men had ever had a chance like this? These
two men held the future of nations in their hands. He had to let
them know how much he longed for an end to this war or he
would never forgive himself.

Louis looked surprised at Roland's suggestion. "But if two
religions teach contrary things, one must be right and the other
wrong, and the one that is right must eventually win out."

"What are you saying to each other?" Baibars demanded.

Roland translated the exchange between himself and the King.

"Your King is quite right," said Baibars with a smile. "There
can only be one truth, and in time all peoples must come to
see it. Your King and I agree on that. We disagree only on
which of us upholds the truth. I believe with all my heart that
one day the whole world will embrace Islam."

Again Roland felt driven to speak his own thoughts. "But,
Emir Baibars, a victory in combat only proves which man is the
better fighter. It does not prove the truth of what he fights for.
In our country we have abandoned trial by battle. This King
before you has forbidden it. You yourself said that fear makes
poor converts."

"True enough," said Baibars. "But the ultimate victory of the
warriors of Islam will be proof that Allah is the true God."

Roland's hopes for an agreement were sinking.

"You see," Louis said to Roland. "War is the only argument
they understand. That is why we must make war on the Saracens.
Tell him that I still believe that the whole earth will one day be
Christian. One defeat does not shake my faith."

"I would not expect it to," said Baibars. "It is because you
are a man of such faith that I trust you. Because I trust you, I
offer you freedom on nearly the same terms you agreed upon

with the late Sultan. I know that in your eyes I am a rebel who has murdered his lawful lord. Will you keep your word with me nonetheless?''

Roland was almost breathless as he translated and waited for an answer. He held himself rigid as Louis sat staring at the intricate black and red pattern of the carpet on the floor of the tent.

Louis looked up somberly. "At this moment I would bargain with the Devil himself to rescue what is left of my poor fellows.''

Tactless, thought Roland. Anxiety made his heart flutter.

"God has willed that you be in command here," he said in Arabic, "and I will happily bargain with you to rescue what is left of my poor fellows.''

Baibars's thin lips curved in a smile. "I took the risk that your answer would be something like that when I decided to strike down Turan Shah. If you were not willing to deal with me, I would have to kill you. Had I more strongly suspected that I would not have your cooperation, then I would have preferred to let Turan Shah live long enough to do the killing, as he planned, so that the dishonor would have been his, rather than mine.'' Baibars's eyes turned to Roland as he said this.

Roland's heart lifted with pleasure. Then I did help save the King's life. I said the right thing to Baibars last night.

"You are justifying killing your sultan because he would have killed me," said Louis. "But the truth is you would have let him kill me. You overthrew him only because you want to be sultan yourself.''

Roland felt his palms go cold and wet as he translated this. Why must Louis keep goading Baibars? Was this his way of retaining self-respect while captive to a man he thought a criminal?

"I will not be sultan," said Baibars, spreading his yellowish hands in a fending-off gesture. "The Mameluke general Ai Beg, who is senior to me, will wed the lady Spray-of-Pearls and reign in Cairo. We have agreed. So ends the dynasty of Saladin. A pity, but fate is fate. Turan Shah did us many injuries. It would take too long to tell you all of it. If the servant has a duty to the master, so also the master has a duty to the servant, and Turan Shah failed his servants many times over. He rewarded fidelity with contempt and punishment. And that is why we slew him. But he was plotting to kill you and all of your men. He had been guaranteed that he would get the ransom money and Damietta even so, you see.''

Roland was elated and anxious both. Now, at last, Louis will learn the truth about Amalric.

Louis stared at Roland, surprised and bewildered, as Roland repeated Baibars's words in French.

"Guaranteed? What do you mean?"

"The Frankish nobleman who is in command at Damietta promised this. After your death he would yield the city."

Louis's sun-browned, grimy skin turned pale. His lips worked, but he was unable to speak.

"What Frankish nobleman?" he said to Roland in a low voice after a moment.

"He means Amalric de Gobignon, sire, who escaped at Mansura. It seems he has taken command of Damietta."

"And he says Amalric conspired against me with the Sultan? Can he possibly be telling me the truth?"

"Yes, sire, he is saying that the Count de Gobignon wants to bring about your death. And I am certain he speaks the truth."

Louis grunted. "I know you and Amalric are old enemies, but I cannot believe there is any French knight so vicious, so traitorous."

And so close to you, Roland thought, feeling sorry for Louis.

"We can ask the emir for his proof."

"Yes," said Louis, distraught. "Go ahead, ask him."

For answer, when Roland put the question to him, Baibars opened the chest on the carpet at his side. He took out a bundle of small scrolls and handed a pair of them to Louis.

"I learned of these letters from the man who carried them back and forth between Turan Shah and the traitor Frank. Unknown to either of them, that man was, and is, my trusted servant. This is the first letter. Like all the others, it is written in Frankish and in Arabic. The Arabic is a translation prepared for Turan Shah by his scribe. The original was written in his own hand by Count Amalric."

"Amalric!" When he heard Baibars speak that name, Louis began with trembling fingers to untie the ribbons from the scrolls without even waiting for Roland to translate Baibars's words.

"Jesus, sweet Jesus!" Louis whispered as he read. Tears were forming in his eyes as he looked up at Roland.

Shaking his head, Louis said, "He offers the Sultan everything— the money, the city, and all the Christians in it. Even my wife. My son. Oh my God! Everything and everyone, as soon as he is assured of my death. I cannot believe it! He must be possessed by the Devil."

"Perhaps," said Roland. His heart twisted in pain as he saw Louis's face. If they were not in the tent of an enemy lord, Roland would have taken Louis in his arms to try to comfort him.

"My own cousin. Roland, what could I have done to him to make him want to do this to me? To my wife, my child. To his comrades. How have I hurt him, driven him to this? This is worse, so much worse, than anything I have suffered from the Saracens. If Turan Shah had killed me, his crime would have been nothing compared to Amalric's. My God, my God!"

"Even Jesus had a Judas," said Roland, trying to think of some way to console Louis.

"Do not compare me with Seigneur Jesus," said Louis with sudden anger. "That is blasphemy." In a quieter tone he added, "But this treachery is as foul as Judas'."

Baibars said, "Your King is very upset."

"This perfidious lord is his kinsman," Roland explained. "And a man of great importance in our country. The King has never before experienced such a betrayal."

"Then life has not prepared him well for kingship. Ask him, does he recognize that the letter comes from the Count Amalric? Does he wish to see more?" Baibars indicated the pile of scrolls in his lap as Roland translated.

"Amalric is one of the few barons who knows how to write," said Louis. "His mother, my father's sister, insisted upon it. I do not recognize the writing as his, because I do not know his hand that well. But the seal is his. The three crowns. I have seen that ring on his finger a thousand times." He covered his face with his hands.

"Sire, I have known for a long time that Count Amalric hated you and wished to do you harm."

"Then you, too, have betrayed me!" Louis shouted, his big eyes glaring in sudden rage. "Why did you never tell me?"

Roland felt his face burn, just as if the King had slapped him.

"Sire, you spoke of bad blood between Amalric and me. If I had told you what I thought I knew, or suspected, you would have thought I was maligning the count out of my own ill will. If what I say now is not true, punish me as you see fit."

Louis sighed. "You are right. I remember what Amalric did to you at the tournament, and I heard tales of other things. He suspected you of loving his countess, did he not?"

"I do love his countess, sire," said Roland quietly. "That was another reason why I could not speak against him to you.

Much of what I knew about his intentions I learned from her, and if I spoke of them it would have put her in danger.''

"I did suspect there was something between you two," said Louis with a sad smile. "The giving of the scarf at my Queen's song contest was not so innocent after all, was it? How long ago that was! Yes, I would never have believed you if you had accused him without proof. He and I quarreled about many things, but I always thought I could depend upon him." He looked at Roland with the eyes of a wounded child. "I trusted him."

"This betrayal shocks you greatly," said Baibars, who had sat listening to the exchange in French between Roland and Louis.

"We are not so used to treachery in those close to us as apparently you are here," said Louis sarcastically. Roland flinched within as he translated this. But Baibars laughed. The King's air of moral superiority seemed to amuse him.

"Turan Shah was as different from you, O King, as a jackal is from an eagle. That is why I am willing to make a treaty with you. But I would add one more condition to the terms you and Turan Shah agreed upon."

"What is that?"

"Turan Shah did not think of it because he did not expect you to live. I ask you to swear on oath that you will not attack Islam for twenty years. I am convinced that if you take such an oath you will keep it. You are the most powerful monarch in Christendom, and also the only one who insists on continuing these foolish wars against us. If you give me your word, I know we will have twenty years of peace."

"Why twenty years?" asked Louis. "Why not ten or a hundred?"

"I will tell you in all honesty. It is the real reason why I wish to send you back to your people. I need those twenty years to make Islam safe against the Tartars."

Roland's head spun. Saint Michel, what did the Tartars have to do with all this? He knew that Baibars himself was a Tartar, and that the Tartars had briefly invaded Europe nearly ten years ago, annihilated huge armies of Christian knights, then had mysteriously disappeared again. Were they coming back? And had his fate really been decided by a savage nation almost totally unknown to him?

"I see!" Louis exclaimed. "And if we Christians allied ourselves with the Tartars, between us we could destory the empire of Islam. You are asking me to forswear a great opportunity."

"It is an opportunity you would be foolish to seize. I myself am a Tartar of the Kipchak nation, O King. Allah willed that I be captured by Turks as a boy, and so I became a civilized man and a Muslim. The Tartars believe it is their destiny to conquer the whole world. If you helped them against us, they would swallow you up next."

"It was not so long ago we waited in terror for them to invade France," mused Louis. "Very well, Emir Baibars. Done. Twenty years of peace between us."

Roland's heart beat faster. He felt himself smiling.

"It will be twenty years anyway," Louis continued, "before I can raise another army big enough to liberate Jerusalem."

Another army in twenty years? God, Roland despaired, how many of us have to die in Outremer before we realize we do not belong here?

Baibars's wide mouth curled in a grin. "You have saved your life, O King. I could not have let you go free if you had not promised me those twenty years. Let me send for scribes, and we will write all the conditions down and sign them."

Roland's heartbeat sounded like thunder in his ears. Thank God! Thank God!

Louis held up a hand. "Wait, emir. What of Damietta?"

Baibars smiled, a little cruelly, Roland thought. "You have promised to give it to me, O King. You must deliver the city to me before you or any of your men can go free."

Louis looked from Baibars to Roland. "But you say Amalric is in command there. My Queen and my son are in his power, and thousands of other unarmed Christians who accompanied us. If he learns that you have not slain me, and that I know of his treachery, he might murder them all. Or certainly use them as hostages."

"I will send a party of emirs to demand the delivery of the city," said Baibars airily.

"You know he will refuse your emirs entry," said Louis. "Their coming alone will be enough to let him know his plan has failed. He might even attack them, hoping to provoke your retaliation against us here. He will surely hurt the helpless ones in his power. Please, let me send a group of my barons. The men under Amalric's command will recognize them and let them in. Then they can denounce Amalric and take command."

"My emirs, I am afraid, would not permit that," said Baibars. "I control them, as yet, with difficulty. Some would still prefer to kill you all, as Turan Shah intended. And to those willing to

keep you alive, the person of each of your great lords is worth
many thousands of bezants. They will not risk letting them go."

"Let *me* go, sire."

Roland had spoken so suddenly that he all but looked around
himself to see where the words had come from. They hung in the
air, in a silence in which Baibars and Louis stared at him. He
felt his heart beating hard, not with fear but with eagerness for
battle.

Louis looked doubtful, but in Baibars's harsh features, Roland
saw approval. Roland translated his offer into Arabic.

Baibars nodded. "I understood at once, from your face and
your voice, what you were saying."

Excitedly, Roland urged his idea on Louis. "I can bring the
news of the treaty to Damietta, arrange for the evacuation of the
noncombatants, and open the city to the emir's men."

"But first," said Louis, "you must deal with Amalric."

Baibars leaned forward, his good eye narrowed, and Roland
translated for him. He nodded his head.

"I understand your need to do this thing," he said. "But if
you fail, and the Count Amalric holds the city against me, that is
the death of my agreement with your King. The emirs insist that
I get at least as much from you as Turan Shah had demanded. If
we cannot achieve that, I do not know what will happen."

There was another silence. All three of them, Roland thought,
knew too well what would happen.

Louis said, "You are half starved, weakened as all of us are.
You would be no match for Amalric."

Roland felt a moment of self-doubt. Was he risking all their
lives just to satisfy his yearning to fight Amalric?

No, he suddenly realized with surprise, it was not that. One
man, alone must go to bring the King's message and Baibars's
terms. And only he understood Amalric well enough to be ready
for any counterattack he might make.

And besides, who else could rescue Nicolette from Amalric?

"I will not have to face him alone."

"How do you know that? He will have the support of the
whole city. No one in Damietta understands what is happening."

"Of course, sire. But I will carry a letter from you that
appoints me as your emissary, details Amalric's crimes, and
conveys your order to surrender the city. We will make careful
plans before I leave. And I have no doubt that Emir Baibars
here knows more than we do of the forces in the city and their

disposition. He, too, can advise me on who will work with us. He can also give me a letter.''

But most important for me, Roland thought, is that I must meet Amalric.

He no longer yearned for revenge. In these past weeks he had known such sorrows that the desire for vengeance had been burned out of him. Perrin was right. There was no retribution for the things Amalric had done. To attempt to inflict pain on that scale would make him into what Amalric had become. Roland longed only to meet Amalric, to strike him down. His wish had the simplicity of an arrow's flight.

He looked questioningly at the King. Louis's great blue eyes held his, and he could feel the King trying to penetrate his soul.

Roland held his breath.

''God go with you then,'' said Louis, putting his hand on Roland's shoulder.

Roland expelled a deep sigh of relief. And then came a sinking feeling. Can I do it? Can I really do it?

Louis turned to Emir Baibars. ''What do you say, Emir Baibars? Shall this man of mine go up against Amalric?''

Baibars nodded. ''I agree. He must go alone and enter the city before this Amalric can stop him. It is the only way.''

''You must try to find the loyal people in Damietta,'' said Louis. ''Get help as soon as you are inside the city.''

Baibars drew a heavy seal ring from his finger.

''I will give you a token by which you can command the help of my man who is in Count Amalric's service.''

Roland took the ring, hoping he would be able to keep it as a memento of one of the most remarkable men he had ever met. If I live, he reminded himself wryly.

''How will I know your man?''

Baibars smiled. ''You already know him. He calls himself Maurice.''

Roland was stunned. He heard Louis gasp beside him.

''Maurice!'' Roland almost shouted. ''I always thought he was a traitor.''

''It was he who spread the false command to surrender at Mansura,'' said Louis in a desolate voice.

''He is no traitor,'' said Baibars. ''He has been a good Muslim for almost as many years as you have lived.'' His face hardened ''Now perhaps you see that neither you, O King, nor the Coun Amalric, nor even you, troubadour, ever had a chance of accom plishing your desires. All along it is we who have been in control.'

Yes, but soon now it will be over, Roland thought. And I can go home. We can all go home. If I overcome Amalric.

His heart filled with joy. Whatever happened, even if he were to die, he could hope for at least one last sight of Nicolette.

XXXV

"FOR ALL I KNOW, MADAME, THE CRUSADERS MAY BE DEAD BY NOW," said Maurice flatly. "I hate to hurt you so, but you asked, and that is my honest answer." Apologetically he set down the tray of melon slices, eggs, bread, and wine he had brought for her breakfast.

"In other words, you know nothing." Nicolette felt angry enough to slap him. True, he had been kind to her in the last two days; he seemed genuinely to regret acting as her jailer. But because of him she could not warn the Queen against Amalric.

Where is Agnes? she wondered. If only I could see her, I could slip a message to her and she could get out to Marguerite with it. How is she being kept away from me?

She thought of trying to overpower Maurice and escape. He was an old man, after all. But he looked strong. No, instead of fighting him, she would talk to him. Somehow perhaps she could move him.

"I do not understand you, Master Maurice. You helped me deceive my husband about the provisions. Why will you not help me now? Whom do you really serve?"

He shifted his feet and then pointed to the other chair in Nicolette's bedroom. "May I?" He sat down at her nod, facing her across the black marble table.

She leaned forward eagerly. This was the first time he had sat down to talk with her. Now if only she could find a way to reach him.

"There is nothing you can do to hurt me now, madame," he said. "And I have a need to confess my sins—if sins they be. Confession is one thing I missed all these years in Egypt. You think you hate me now for doing your husband's bidding. You may hate me more when I tell you what I really am.'' He smiled sadly.

"Do you care what I feel about you?'' She prayed that he did. In that lay her only chance.

He nodded thoughtfully. "I told you once, madame, you remind me of the best part of the life I left behind, when the Saracens took me prisoner. But much of that life, as I remember it, was very bad.''

Ah, she thought, just as I've suspected.

"You are a Muslim,'' she ventured.

He bowed his head in acknowledgment. "You understand, madame, that if you are a commoner, they do not let you live unless you accept Islam. And even then only as a slave. Most of my mates went to their deaths, praying. But when I was facing the executioner's sword, a thought came to me. You would probably say the Devil put it in my mind. But what had the Church ever done for me, really? I had been hungry all my life. A few years before, my aunt and uncle and cousins were all burned as heretics. There was much so-called heresy among the weavers, you know. Then those cursed friars talked us into marching off to Outremer. Said it was God's will we should fight these people on the other side of the world who had never done a thing to me. I went, I guess, partly because I believed them, partly because I now hated my home. All I remember now about the crusade itself was being seasick and losing my teeth, being eaten alive by fleas and being so frightened all the time I could never keep my food down. And then, for the Church, I was supposed to let them cut off my head. All of a sudden I found myself saying, to Hell with the Church—begging your pardon, madame. I would try being a Muslim. There was nothing more I could lose. I suppose you think I was a damned coward.''

She quaked within. All this time we had a Saracen spy in our house. He could have cut our throats in our sleep.

But he did not. And the only important thing now is to get to Marguerite.

Who is Maurice's real master?

"It does not sound at all like the act of a coward,'' she said. "In your place I might have done the same thing. The Church has not been kind to me, either, or to people I love.''

Maurice nodded. "Ah, yes, you are a woman of Languedoc, are you not? Well, the fact is I learned to love Islam. I had many masters, some of them cruel and some kind, but all of them took seriously the duty of instructing me. I got an Islamic name,

Mukaddam ben Faris. Islam made sense, Paradise, you see, is a place of comfort and good food and beautiful women. Heaven as the Christian priests described it always sounded dull. I liked the Muslim rituals, the praying five times a day, the duty of giving to the poor, the pilgrimage, even the fasting. I even got used to not drinking wine, though not all my masters were strict about that. One of my owners was a carpet merchant. I helped guard his caravans. He took me to Mecca with him, and I kissed the sacred Black Stone in the Kaaba. I have been to Jerusalem, too, which is more than your King or anybody in his army can say. It is just as holy a place to them—to us Muslims I mean—as it is to Christians. The friars never told us that. I worshiped there in the Dome of the Rock, where our blessed Prophet ascended into Heaven. I have lived a good life here, madame, better than I could have at home. I learned to read and write—in Arabic, think of it! I owe my good health to the Arab doctors, who know more about illness than any Christians. Muslims eat better, too; our clothing is more comfortable; we are cleaner than Christians. Do you know that we bathe every day? Can you imagine how Christians smell to us? Muslim women smell sweeter than Christian women do, excepting yourself, of course, madame. I have married three women here in Egypt. You are allowed to do that, as the Prophet did not like to see women left unprotected. All in all, I have been very happy.''

She felt moved. Was she the first Christian he had ever poured his heart out so to?

"How could you do all that as a slave?" she asked.

"Even the slaves are better off in Islam, madame. A slave can be rich and powerful. The Mamelukes are slaves. Even the great Baibars is accounted a slave. In fact, because I had been a soldier, it was eventually the Mamelukes who took me in. Life became even better for me then. The Arabs and the Turks, people born Muslims, they do not trust converts, but the Mamelukes are all converts, so it did not matter to them that I had once been a Christian. Eventually, I came to serve Baibars himself. He wanted to know everything I could tell him about the Christian part of the world.''

If only everyone she loved were not in such deadly peril, Nicolette would have been fascinated by Maurice's tale. But it was his people who were about to slaughter King Louis and the others.

"You serve Baibars, the Saracen general everyone fears so much? The one they call the Panther? You know him?''

Maurice chuckled. "You have met him, too, madame."

"What do you mean?"

Then she remembered the Bedouin chieftain. Yes, she had heard once that the Panther had only one eye. "The Bedouin! He was spying on the city."

Maurice nodded. "Scouting it. It is his way. He must see everything for himself. He loves to go about in disguise, like the great Caliph Haroun al Rashid of long ago. You enchanted him, madame."

Nicolette, shaken at how close she had come to being kidnapped, took a sip of wine. It was heavy Cypriot wine, and it burned her tongue.

"So Baibars set you to spy on us?"

Maurice's eyes were two pale blue fish caught in nets of wrinkles. "It was my idea, madame. I volunteered."

"Whatever for? To destroy your own people?"

"Madame, the more I came to love Islam, the more guilt I felt that I had converted only out of fear. I doubted my own sincerity. I needed to prove to myself I had truly become a Muslim. Your crusaders landing here seemed the perfect opportunity. If I could live among French Christians once more and risk my life for the triumph of Islam, that would prove my conversion was a true one."

I should hate him, Nicolette thought. But I cannot.

"It cannot have been easy after you joined us for you to remain true to your new faith."

"When I first saw Count Amalric—such a big, handsome nobleman, the first free Christian I had seen in years—I wept. I surprised myself and was afraid. Could I do such grievous harm as I intended to this man and the army that had come with him? But as I got to know him, I realized he was the perfect unwitting ally in what I had set out to do—to bring about the defeat of the crusaders. The better I came to know him, the more I loathed him. It got so I could not look him in the eye for fear he would see my true feelings." His face darkened. "To think, he tried to turn me against King Louis by calling him a lover of heresy. Never knowing how many of my family had gone to the stake."

Staring into his watery blue eyes, Nicolette felt the need to escape growing in her until it almost burst its way out of her body. She rigidly averted her eyes from the key dangling from his belt, the key that could unlock the harem gate.

He may be right. Louis, and whatever remained of his army of crusaders, may all have been killed by the Sultan already. But I must keep trying to save them.

"You do not have to serve Amalric any longer," she said. "You have accomplished all you set out to. The crusade is over. What have you to gain if the Sultan massacres all the captives?"

Maurice shook his head, smiling grimly. "The Sultan will not, madame. The Mameluke emirs killed the Sultan at sundown two days ago."

She gasped and dropped the bit of bread she had been holding. "Then who rules? What is going to happen to the prisoners now?"

"It is the Panther who will decide. I have had no message from him since the Sultan's overthrow. My standing order is to obey the Count in all things, unless I hear otherwise from Emir Baibars. That is why I must keep you here."

She clenched her jaw angrily. If only she could get help. In God's name, where is Agnes?

"But you do not have to treat me like a criminal, Maurice. You have kept me locked in here for three days. I need my maid. At least let Agnes come to me."

Maurice turned his face away. "You cannot see her. Those are my orders."

"But she must suspect something has happened to me. Has she not she asked questions about me?"

He stared down at the black table. "The count has given it out that you are ill and that the sickness is easily caught. He found duties for Agnes at the Queen's residence."

But she would insist on seeing me, Nicolette thought. She probably did, but Amalric bullied her out of it. So I must get out of here without help.

And soon. Baibars. Again she remembered that single penetrating eye, that iron-hard hand on her cheek.

"Does Baibars intend to kill the King and his men?"

"He has not told me. But he is a man of his word, not like Turan Shah. He respects your King. As I do. I believe he would not want to kill the captives unless he had to. But if he decides he must, he will act without hesitation and without mercy. That is the way he is."

She heard a call from the street. A wagon that collected the bodies of those who had died during the night was going by. Desperately, she tried to think.

If only she could tell the Queen all she knew now about

Amalric. Marguerite would remove him from his post and have him arrested.

She recalled the arrival of the Templars four days ago, fifty grim-faced knights, all looking alike in their plain steel helmets with their long beards, white surcoats, and red crosses. They rode small Arabian horses, flanking a dozen ox-drawn wagons groaning under chests of silver. At the sight of them tears had come to her eyes, and for the first time since Mansura, she had felt a little safer. She had heard the cheering Christians tell each other as they rode by that one Templar was the equal of ten ordinary knights.

So now, she thought, we have enough loyal men to overcome Amalric's hirelings. We could warn the Saracens that we will not yield until the King and his men are delivered to us alive.

She fixed her gaze on him. "Master Maurice, if Amalric learns that the Sultan is dead and that Emir Baibars plans to free the King and his men, he will find some way to prevent it. Killing those captive men would be a foul deed that would dishonor not only your master but Islam itself. We must stop Amalric now."

"I wish I could," said Maurice, looking pained.

Nicolette reached across the table and seized his rough hand in both of hers. His eyes widened in surprise, and he started to pull away. Then he let her hold his hand. His weathered face reddened.

"Amalric could attack Emir Baibars's emissaries. He could load the ransom money on a Genoese galley and take it away. Master Maurice, if you were strong enough once on your own to change gods, you must be strong enough to act now on your own, without orders."

She released his hand, and prayed with all her being that her appeal would move him.

He sat silent for a long time, frowning at the table. Finally, he looked up. "What can I do?"

Tears of relief sprang to her eyes.

"Take me to the palace," she said quickly, terrified that in the next instant he might change his mind. "Take me to the Queen. I will tell her everything."

He uttered a little laugh of dismay. "You will get me hanged."

"No, no, I shall not tell her about you. Let her think you are a good old crusader who saw through Amalric and is helping me. She will probably reward you, if you want to wait around long

enough. But after we have gathered our trustworthy men and
deposed Amalric, you can leave for the Saracen camp."

"You make it all sound so easy, madame. Count Amalric has
many of the palace guard in his pay, you know. He himself may
be at the palace right now."

"Get me past them and help me to talk to the Queen alone,"
she said. "Sire Geoffrey de Burgh is always at the Queen's side.
He well help us get in."

Maurice shook his head. "He is no longer with the Queen.
The Count placed Sire Geoffrey in charge of the guards on the
city walls. All the men in the palace now are your husband's."

"You said Agnes is at the palace. She can let us know when it
is safe to try to get to the Queen."

Again he hesitated, and her heart stopped in fear. It was so
quiet in the room that she could hear his breathing. His gaze
wavered, and he shut his eyes for a moment.

He reached out and took her hand, and the suffering in his
faded eyes frightened her.

"Madame, be strong. I have to tell you something terrible."

She felt as though her heart had stopped. "What?"

"Agnes is dead."

She felt herself swaying in her chair. Maurice sprang to her
side and held her steady.

"Oh my God. No. Oh, no, not Agnes." Sobs bubbled up in
her throat.

"Yes, madame," he said gently. "She is gone. And there is
more I will tell you if you can stand to hear."

She trembled against him.

"Yes, tell me," she sobbed. "What happened to her?"

"Your husband killed her. To silence her."

Dazed, she listened as he told her how Amalric had strangled
Agnes and left her body in a room right here on the second floor,
telling him to dispose of it.

"Before I put her body on the dead cart, madame, I prayed
over her. Muslim prayers, but they were honest. She lies buried
now in the great grave before the palace."

"Oh, Agnes" was all she could say. Even her tears had
stopped. She felt so empty inside.

My poor loyal friend. Why did I have to drag you to this
wful place with me, only to have you die so horribly?

"He did not have to do it, madame. There were a dozen other
ays to make sure she would not make trouble."

"He did it because he hates me so much," she said in a lifeless voice.

Maurice put his hands on her shoulders and stared into her face.

"You cannot blame yourself, and you cannot give up. When a man's comrades fall in battle, he cannot stop to mourn. He must go on fighting. You are in a battle now."

Yes, she thought. And suddenly hatred boiled up inside her. There is only one thing I can do for Agnes now. Avenge her.

I swear by your memory, Agnes, I shall destroy Amalric.

She stood up, her chair scraping on the floor.

Maurice shook a clenched fist. "We shall repay the count for what he has done to your poor Agnes. Get your mantle, madame, and let us go to the palace."

She kissed his withered cheek lightly.

"Muslim or Christian, Master Maurice, you are a good man."

Amalric stood at Queen Marguerite's bedside, making an effort to be courteous that was almost beyond his strength. Seething, he bowed to her, his mail clinking softly, his battle-ax swinging heavily from his belt.

"Madame, with your permission I shall make my daily report on the condition of our defenses."

He waited with irritation as she adjusted the position of the stinking infant in her arms. As she looked up at him at last, her face appeared so bony, and there were huge dark rings under her eyes. She had never been as pretty as Nicolette, he thought. Now she was beginning to look like a crone.

"Speak, messire. If we can do nothing else, we can keep our walls in good order and our men alert."

Rage boiled in him. How dare she presume to inflict these platitudes on him, pretending to be *his* commander? Oh, how he longed for the moment when he could crush her with the truth.

But when, in God's name, would that moment come? For two days he had eaten little; for two nights he had hardly slept. If he did not have word from the Sultan today, surely he would go mad.

Even as Amalric made his report, knowing that he would make sure the defenses were of no consequence, his mind wandered. A devil kept whispering in his ear, What if the Sultan betrays me?

He had thought it through. He would hold the city for a while at least. Long enough to provoke the Sultan into massacring the captives. He had enough men in his pay to take the Templars by surprise—they would hardly be suspecting an attack from their fellow Christians, to whose aid they had come—and seize the ransom money. *And then, when I hold the treasure, Turan Shah will agree to terms.*

And if the Sultan did not cooperate by killing Louis and his men, he could at least hold the Queen and her son and make his escape, taking them with him. Some Genoese would take him away from here, if he were paid enough. The Genoese were all pirates anyway. Then, with royal prisoners, the treasure, a band of hired followers, he could find a stronghold for himself somewhere and carve out a domain here in Outremer.

But whatever else, Nicolette must die. *She knows too much.*

He was done talking about the defenses, and the Queen thanked him.

"How is Nicolette?" she asked.

Saint Dominic damn her! Can I not have even a moment's peace of mind?

He shook his head. "She seemed weaker today when I left her, madame. The priests do not seem to be able to do anything. They say this is the quartan fever."

"I miss her so, and am so very worried for her. Perhaps I could visit her."

Yes, perhaps I could lock you up along with her.

"Do not think of it, madame. You are not strong yourself yet. And your son—you would risk both your lives if you were to catch her fever. Her poor maid has already died of it."

"Agnes? Oh, how awful!" Marguerite made the sign of the cross. "So many have died. God forbid anything should happen to Tristan. If only Louis were here to see him."

"I have no doubt he will be back with you soon, madame."

Amalric was in an agony to get back to the battlements. Turan Shah's messenger must come today. *He must!*

"I am so afraid for Louis," she went on, tears sparkling in her brown eyes. "The Saracens could already have killed him, and we not know about it."

God grant that they have. O Lord, when will this woman let me go? If she keeps me here another minute I will take that baby and break his neck.

"I feel in my heart that all are well, madame."

"I know you must long to see Louis as much as I do, Count Amalric. His very presence is such a blessing. He often spoke to me of how burdensome the crown is. But I never fully understood what he meant until he was captive and I had to hold in my hands his fate and that of all the crusaders. What a relief it will be when he is back. You must miss his leadership, too, Count, do you not?''

His leadership? The leadership that had ruined France. The Devil piss on his leadership!

"I find my own leadership quite enough for me," he said curtly, before he could think.

Startled, she pulled the baby closer to her bosom. "Of course, you are used to managing your own domain, Count," she said, wide-eyed. "Still, you are not a king, and the view from the top of the mountain is very different from what you might see a few steps below."

Me, below Louis? He see better than I? The more Marguerite talked, the angrier he became. By Jesus, I have had enough of this silly Provençal woman and her mad, psalm-singing husband.

My time is coming, he told himself. In a few hours at most, I will be turning the city over to the Egyptians. They will seize the treasure and take everyone prisoner, everyone except me. I will return to France. Then, with the King and his brothers dead, with nearly every great baron of fighting age lost, old Queen Blanche will have to ask me to join the regency. How she will thank God that I was spared to assist her. I do not need to take the crown. Not yet. To be first among the Peers of the Realm, to control the throne, that is enough for now.

So I can speak my mind to Marguerite now.

"Did you ever see a mountaintop covered with clouds, madame? I would liken your husband's vision to that. Look about you. The army is destroyed, and the Saracens are at our gates. And what happens to France, may I ask, if the English or the Germans decide to make war on us now? I warned him against this. I urged him to obey the Pope, to stay home and fight the heretics in Europe. None of us really wanted to go on this crusade. But he was so sure that being King made him wiser than all of us. Well, madame, the outcome has proved him an idiot."

Her face flushed, and she drew herself up in bed, clutching the baby so tightly he began to cry.

"How dare you speak so of your sovereign lord?"

"I dare, madame, because he gets his power and authority from the barons. From me. We are his equals, and Count de Gobignon is as weighty a title as King of France."

"I suspected as much," she whispered. "You are not loyal to him at all. You are his enemy."

"Nicolette has been talking to you, has she not? I tried to be your husband's friend, but he would not listen to me. If he had, we would not be here. And as for you, if you had attended to me instead of to my wife, you would be out of danger now." He had to raise his voice to make himself heard above the brat's wailing.

"Because I did not listen to you, we are about to ransom my husband and his companions. Then we will *all* be out of danger. And you may be sure he will hear how you have spoken of him this day."

She lifted her chin, straining her skinny neck. She must suppose she was giving him a regal look.

Amalric stood, his chest heaving against his coat of mail. The silly fool! I could shatter her right now, tell her she will never see her husband alive.

No, better not. It may be hours before I hear from the Sultan, and in that time she could do me harm. Those damnable Templars.

Still, I no longer need to pretend I respect her or her witless husband.

"Say what you like to Louis," he said with deliberate discourtesy. "I care not."

Marguerite gasped, outraged, but at that moment someone hammered on the oaken door.

Amalric turned, the mail skirt of his hauberk swirling heavily around his knees, and went to the door.

"Monseigneur," said a guard, panting. "A messenger has come from the Saracens."

The guard now was one in Amalric's pay. No more than a boy, he had for armament a long carving knife stuck in a dirty silk sash at his belt. Before Amalric hired him, he had been a cook's helper for one of the barons killed at Mansura.

Amalric's heart warmed with delight. He drew in a huge, deep breath. At last, at last! Thank God!

"Where is he?"

"A Saracen boat brought him to the landing by the west gate. He showed a message with the Sultan's seal and we let him in. He is coming to the palace on foot. I ran ahead to tell you."

"Bring him to me at once!" Marguerite called from her bed, her voice shrill with anxiety.

"Yes, of course," said Amalric. "Excuse me, madame." With a curt bow he strode out the door, pushing the guard aside.

"Stand you here," Amalric said in a low voice after closing the door firmly behind him. "See that no one enters. Or leaves." He jerked his head at the door. "You must keep *her* in there."

"But, monseigneur, how do I stop the Queen if she wants to go out?" asked the boy, wide-eyed.

Amalric reached into a leather scrip at his belt and took out a key. Quietly, he locked the bedroom door and dropped the key back into the pouch. He congratulated himself on his forethought in ordering Sire Geoffrey de Burgh to relinquish his duties at the palace and to turn over the key to him a few days ago. Through the door he could still hear the baby crying.

"There. Now you can just tell her that in truth you are unable to let her out. Or make no reply at all if she calls to you."

He paused, realizing that the young guard was staring at him dumbfounded. The boy would not be willing to hold the Queen of France prisoner without some justification.

"It is only to protect her," Amalric explained. "She is in poor health from her recent childbirth, and the city will soon be full of Saracens. She is headstrong and must be kept from endangering herself. You know how it is with women."

Amalric gave the boy a man-to-man clap on the shoulder that brought a glow of pride to his young eyes.

He felt a quivering in his chest and a hollowness in his stomach as he hurried through the corridors of the palace. What will the Sultan's messenger say? The mail he wore felt light as silk as he rushed down the stairs. Great God, take my side in this. Let Louis be dead. For Hugues, for my father, for all the wrongs we Gobignons have suffered. Give us the victory, God.

But why was the Sultan's man coming on foot? Why the devil could he not have ridden? Why must I be kept waiting an instant longer?

He passed through the audience chamber, where some of his men were gathered, along with a little cluster of priests in black soutaines. They were talking excitely to one another, falling silent as he walked by. They have heard the news, he thought, and are wondering what it portends. Well, soon enough they will know.

He felt a sudden pain in his chest. Priests would be slaughtered today, along with ladies and knights. He, Amalric de Gobignon, good son of the Church, would have brought it about. But at least they will all die martyrs' deaths and go straight to Heaven.

Still, he avoided the eyes of those he passed.

Giving his arms a shake to settle the mail on his shoulders, Amalric strode out the palace door. At the foot of the steps stood his big, dark charger, tethered under guard.

Amalric hurried down and handed his helmet to the guard. He drew the hood of his coat of mail over his head and laced it tight around his face and neck. Best be well protected—you cannot trust the Saracens. Then he took back the conical steel helmet adorned with its wolf's head and donned it. He undid his battle-ax from his belt where it hung beside the basilard and slung it from the saddle. He put a foot in the stirrup as one of his men held the horse for him, and sprang up.

I am strong as ever. I can still leap on a horse's back in full armor.

He unhooked his freshly painted shield from its mounting on the saddle and slipped his left arm through the straps. Let the Sultan's messenger see the three crowns of Gobignon on their royal purple background. The crown of Clovis, the crown of Charlemagne.

And the crown that is yet to come.

He dug his spurs into the horse's sides, and the huge animal trotted across the courtyard, men scattering to left and right before him.

He slowed the horse with a tug on the reins and walked him into the plaza. The noon sun of Egypt beat down on his head. The glare from the white dust, from the blue and white tiled walls of the mosque across the way, bedazzled him. The only dark spot in the vista before him was the gaping rectangular burial pit. Even now a cart loaded with bodies was trundling into the plaza, the drover cracking his long whip over the backs of two large oxen. It had cost lives to protect those beasts from the hungry. They were carrying to the grave people who would have eaten them.

Squinting, he could make out the eight-pointed red crosses on the surcoats of two Templars standing guard before the mosque, where they held the treasure.

I must warn the Sultan about them. They will fight to protect the silver.

The messenger. Where is he?

Amalric saw a tall man in white Saracen robes enter the plaza out of the street that led from the west gate. Jewels glittered on the scabbard of a scimitar at his belt. His face was dark, shadowed over by a white hood.

Amalric spurred his horse and started to ride toward him. The man saw him and stopped. He stood waiting for Amalric to approach.

Why does he make me come to him? This is not courteously done. Amalric slowed to a walk.

The messenger raised both hands to his hood, dropping it back.

Amalric stared and gasped, his mailed hand falling to the handle of his ax.

De Vency.

A fire seemed to engulf Amalric's body, and he saw the figure across the plaza through a red glow. Was this a creature of the Devil, risen from the dead? In Mansura, he had seen the troubadour, in his black surcoat on his chestnut war-horse, falling under an avalanche of knife-wielding Egyptians leaping down on him from a rooftop. How could he have survived that?

By joining them, that is how. I always suspected him of loving infidel ways. But can he truly be coming now as the Sultan's emissary? Or has the Sultan betrayed me?

The effrontery. Standing there, in nothing but robes. No armor, not even a helmet, no horse, carrying one of those ridiculous crooked Egyptian swords.

Amalric's eyes quickly traveled over the nearby streets and buildings. No sign that de Vency had hidden allies lurking about. He spurred the war-horse lightly, and walked it close enough to speak to the troubadour without having to shout.

"So, messire, you live. But it appears you have given up your country and your faith to save yourself. Though you never have really had a country or a faith, have you?"

A sardonic smile crossed de Vency's dark features. "You could teach me much about faithlessness."

Amalric gripped his ax, tensing himself to ride his enemy down, then stopped himself. What if the Sultan had sent him? Perhaps when all the other prisoners were slaughtered this dog converted to Islam to save his life, and then the Sultan had no one else to convey his message in French.

"Well, traitor, it is evident from your robes and scimitar that the Saracens think highly of you. Do you bring me a message from the Sultan?"

He peered at de Vency. Are my father's features hidden somehow in that ugly face? Or, he thought with a sudden pang, my son's?

Messenger or not, I'll kill this bastard before this hour is out. I'll throw his head down before Nicolette.

Bastard indeed. My father's bastard. Can it be?

"There will be no message from the Sultan, Gobignon. He has been sent to Hell, and by his own people. There are new rulers in Cairo. No, I bring you the command of one whose death you sought, one who lives to doom you—Louis, your King."

Amalric's mind reeled. Louis alive? And the Sultan dead? And de Vency to tell the whole city what happened at Mansura? People will be gathering at any moment to hear what news he brings. I've got to kill him at once.

"The King commands that you surrender the city to the Egyptians now," de Vency was saying. "And that you surrender your person to me."

The sight of the troubadour standing there in the Saracen robes gravely making demands was ludicrous. Light-headed from the strain of the past days, Amalric roared with laughter.

"What a jest! That prating fool Louis has never before made me laugh so."

And now de Vency must die, and quickly. Amalric seized the handle of his battle-ax.

No, from horseback a lance would be easier to aim and have a longer reach. He wheeled his horse with a savage pull on the reins and galloped back to the palace gateway. A small group of his men was gathered there.

"Get me a lance there, a battle lance. And be quick."

Roland was surprised that what he felt on first seeing Amalric was pleasure. At last they would fight to the death.

Perhaps this is what I was born for. Of Gobignon blood, raised to destroy the house of Gobignon.

He watched Amalric ride back to the palace and call out to the men there. A moment later a servant came running out with a lance. Amalric reached down, took the lance, and couched it. He pulled back on the reins, making the war-horse paw the air. When its front hooves came down hard, kicking up clouds of white dust, Amalric kicked it with his spurs and it charged.

Roland heard a creaking sound and the crack of a whip and took his eyes off Amalric long enough to see a slow-moving ox cart with blue-white human arms and legs showing through the slats in its side. God, they must be dying off here as badly as in our prison camp. Now, growing accustomed to the blazing light in the unshaded plaza, he saw that a huge trench had been dug out for the dead between the governor's palace and the central mosque. Oh, Nicolette, he prayed, be well.

The ox cart was crossing Amalric's path. He heard Amalric cursing at the drover, shouting for him to get out of the way. The drover stood up and frantically cracked his whip, longer than the height of a man, over the oxen. Their pace increased only slightly. He will never get them to move fast enough, Roland thought. But I have to use this somehow.

He surveyed the plaza. Before the great mosque he saw two Templars, their shields hung around their necks. They had stepped away from the entrance to see Amalric's charge. I will run to them, Roland thought. They must be guarding the ransom money. I must get the King's message to them.

The drover leaped with a terrified yell from the body cart, barely escaping impalement on Amalric's lance, his whip falling to the ground.

Amalric at the last moment pulled his charger up short.

The Templars, seeing Roland come toward them, drew their longswords.

Roland cursed the Saracen garments he wore. They must think he was the vanguard of an Egyptian attack. But he dared not throw down his sword, not with Amalric so near.

"I am a Christian, a crusader. I bear a letter from the King!" Roland cried.

Amalric had circled the cart, he saw, and was lowering his lance for another charge.

"Roland!"

The clear, high voice stopped him as if he had been struck by an arrow. There, beyond the Templars, running into the plaza from the east, was Nicolette, a short, gray-haired man with her. Amalric's henchman, Maurice. No, Baibars's man. What is she doing?

"What letter? Bring it here!" one of the Templars shouted at Roland.

Hoofbeats thundered in his ears. He turned to see bearing down on him the great mass of horse, man, and lance.

At the last moment Roland jumped aside.

Amalric shifted his lance point, but not soon enough.

Roland fell, and he heard Nicolette scream as he rolled in the dirt.

He picked himself up, and Nicolette ran toward him.

The Templars ran forward, one stepping into Nicolette's path, the other facing Roland with drawn sword.

"Roland, my love, you are alive!" She held her arms out to him and across the stretch of plaza that separated them he could see tears glistening on her face.

He forced himself to tear his eyes away from that lovely face he had yearned for so many months to see. Where was Amalric? The charge had carried horse and rider out of the plaza, down a side street. Now Amalric had reined the horse and was galloping back.

Roland frantically pulled the scrolls from his belt. "I have been sent by King Louis and Emir Baibars. Here are letters from them." He held them out, and the Templar took them with one hand, though with his other he still distrustfully warded Roland off with his sword.

"That man, Amalric de Gobignon, has betrayed the King and the whole crusade," Roland went on, even as Amalric bore down on them.

The Templar hastily thrust the scrolls into his own belt. He quickly swung his shield from his neck to his arm.

In an instant Amalric loomed above them.

Roland waited till the lance point was barely a yard from his chest, then threw himself to the dirt. The ground shook under drumming hooves as the great horse galloped by.

Thank Saint Michel I am wearing no mail, Roland thought, or I would never be able to move fast enough.

Rushing on, Amalric was now headed straight for the Templar with the letters. The warrior-monk held up his sword with one hand and shouted, "Halt!" standing square in Amalric's path.

Amalric ignored the command, his lance aimed straight at the Templar's chest. The Templar raised his shield, blazoned with the eight-pointed red cross, and braced himself. The lance struck the shield with a clang, throwing the Templar to the ground. He scrambled to his feet and swung his sword wildly at Amalric.

Amalric's horse reared and then ran on.

Eyes wide with terror, Nicolette ran to the doorway of the mosque.

Roland, wanting to draw Amalric away from her, moved in the direction Amalric had just come from. How can I fight this man with nothing but a scimitar? I have not the strength to go on outrunning him.

The two Templars, swords out and shields high, backed toward Nicolette and the mosque.

The old man, Maurice, remained standing in the open. Amalric, now at the west end of the plaza, jerked on his reins, slowing his horse's gallop, and pulled its head around toward Maurice.

"What the devil are you doing here with her?" Amalric roared at Maurice.

Maurice spread his empty hands. "I serve you no longer, Count Amalric. The Sultan is dead. Emir Baibars is in command, and he wants the King and the crusaders to live."

"Traitor!" Amalric shouted.

"No traitor," said the old man with quiet pride, "but Mukaddam ben Faris, servant of the Panther, Mameluke and thirty years a Muslim."

Amalric gave a yell of anger and spurred his horse, pointing his lance at Maurice's chest.

Maurice, though Amalric was almost on top of him, managed to sidestep the lance point.

Amalric threw down the lance, the long wooden pole ringing on the hard-packed earth, and snatched his ax from his saddle.

Maurice ran for the mosque, but Roland could see that the old man was misjudging Amalric's expert control. In an instant Amalric wheeled his charger about and was running Maurice down. Leaning far out of the saddle Amalric swung his ax. The blade bit deep into Maurice's shoulder and chest, and Amalric dragged him a short distance before he jerked his weapon free.

Roland heard Nicolette's scream from the doorway of the mosque. She was running out to the fallen, bleeding Maurice.

"Get back, Nicolette!" Roland shouted.

Ax high over his head, Amalric was riding straight at her.

Roland leaped for the lance Amalric had dropped, picked it up, and drove it at the horse's side. It struck, the force of impact knocking Roland to his knees. The horse whinnied in pain. Roland had not weight or strength enough to penetrate the charger's mail coat, but he had hurt it and thrown it off stride.

Nicolette flew back to the safety of the mosque doorway, where one of the Templars stationed himself in front of her.

Amalric galloped away, circling the burial pit to the north. Roland could hear him shouting to his men at the palace gate to bring him another lance.

"Has the Count gone mad?" said the Templar standing near Roland.

"Read the letters!" Roland cried.

Nicolette rushed out of the doorway again and knelt by Maurice. Knowing he was not strong enough to wield the lance to good effect on foot, Roland threw it into the pit and hurried to her side.

"No tears, madame," the toothless old man whispered. "I am bound for a Paradise that offers many more delights than yours does." Blood trickled from his nose and mouth, and his head fell back. *"Allahu akbar,"* he sighed.

Roland put his hand on Nicolette's shoulder as she shook with sobs.

"Nicolette, in God's name get yourself to safety," he pleaded.

"What is happening?" said a Templar, coming up behind them and interrupting them. "Who are you, messire?"

Roland turned to face him. The Templar was many years older than Guido had been, with a flowing white beard that glistened like silk in the bright sunlight.

"I am Roland de Vency, and I was one of the captives at Fariskur. If you will look at those messages—"

"Look out!" the other Templar called, and Roland again heard the terrible drumming of hooves. Amalric, charging down on them, had a new lance now, aimed at Roland.

Roland stood to meet Amalric as the templar pulled Nicolette to safety.

He felt no fear. Instead he had the strange sense that all movement around him had slowed. Only inside him did everything move swiftly.

Amalric, riding toward him through clouds of white dust and shimmering heat waves, was like a knight riding through water. Roland could distinguish every movement of the charger's legs, thick as young trees. He stood perfectly still until the glittering steel head of the lance was perhaps an arm's length from his chest. Then he stepped to his left. The movement was almost leisurely, and he saw the lance point follow him, but it was slow, slow, and it slid by, barely grazing his right shoulder.

Then Amalric was gone, and the dust around Roland was settling. His heart was still hammering, and he felt the fatigue in his starved limbs. If I am to win, he thought, I must finish it quickly.

He drew the dusty air deeply into his aching lungs. Looking about him, he saw the body of Maurice, lying where he had fallen, saw Nicolette standing between the two Templars in the tall, pointed doorway of the mosque, saw people all around the plaza watching from rooftops and walls, saw the deep pit in the center. Saw the drover's long leather whip lying where he had dropped it when he fled.

The pounding of the war-horse's hooves was growing louder. Roland darted to the whip, picked it up, and ran to the edge of the trench. He flexed the whip and drew back his arm.

Again he felt that strange clarity and sense that time had slowed down. The exhilaration of it reminded him of moments of blinding light Nicolette and he had known at the peak of Love.

Horse and rider were looming over him. He darted out of the way, crouching, and then lashed the whip at the charger's racing forelegs. Galloping, the horse had both legs together. The whip coiled itself around the horse's shins, and the animal gave a terrified whinny and went down head first, with that same strange slowness. The war-horse and the man on it were gone.

There came a clattering metallic crash from the burial pit. The horse, as Roland had hoped, had toppled over the edge. He ran to look in.

What he had scarcely dared hope for had come about. He saw the horse struggling, its huge eyes rolling under its steel chauffron. Beneath its heaving body Amalric lay motionless. His helmet had been knocked off by the fall, and the side of his face was bloody. His head was partly buried in the mud at the bottom of the pit. One of the horse's legs was bleeding heavily, and it was bent in the middle of the shin. Poor creature, he thought.

"Roland."

He turned.

"My goddess," he whispered.

His entire body seemed to tingle, and hot tears ran down his cheeks. Her eyes, too, were overflowing with tears. He could hear her panting, as if she had run a long, hard way.

"I never thought I would see you again," she sobbed. "I cried for you every night."

His heart was still beating hard, but in a different rhythm now, slower and stronger. "And did you doubt the power of Love?"

"No," she said softly, "but I doubted that we would ever meet again in this world."

Slowly, almost as if they had a will of their own, Roland's arms reached out to her. My hands must touch her face. I must hold her against me.

Just as the tips of his fingers were about to come to rest on her cheeks, she screamed.

His heart gave a great leap in his chest.

He heard a scraping sound, steel grinding against earth, behind him.

Nicolette, her eyes with terror, was looking past him.

Amalric stood at the edge of the grave, holding his battle-ax high. His surcoat was filthy. A long gash in his cheek was bleeding freely. But his face was aglow with the frenzy of battle.

"Get back to the shelter, Nicolette," Roland said softly. "Hurry," he urged her through clenched teeth. He dared not take his eyes from Amalric, who advanced a step even as Roland heard Nicolette run back to the mosque. Left-handed, he slid the scimitar for the first time from its sheath. He remembered Baibars praising it as Damascus steel, but even that would not cut through Amalric's chain mail.

"No doubt it pleases her to dishonor me by embracing you in public," Amalric growled. "But thus she gives me the right to kill her publicly, when I have done with you."

While you live, you will never be done with me, Roland thought.

Amalric took another step toward him. "Tell me, mincing troubadour, do you really claim, as she tells me, to be my father's wayside brat?"

"No offspring of the wayside," said Roland, "but the son of a lady of good family whom your father—my father—took by force. He was as cruel and dishonorable as you are."

From the open grave came the agonized shrieks of the wounded horse and the thumping of its hooves and body against the earthen walls of the pit.

"It is a lie," declared Amalric, baring his teeth in a grin. "You do not favor my father in any way. And for slandering my father, I am going to make you suffer before you die."

"Yes, there is little resemblance," Roland retorted. "And in my heart I am in no way like Stephen de Gobignon. The man who reared me was a better man. He was your father's slayer. If you still doubt me, then think—why would I speak of such shame? Only because I must, because it is the hateful truth. My having the same blood as yours makes me despise part of myself."

Amalric shook the battle-ax. "Taunt me as you will. Soon enough you will be rotting in that pit. It will be as if you had never lived—my father's son or not."

Roland waited warily for the attack that must come. He could see the lust to kill in the set of the face under the wolf's-head helmet.

Amalric moved slowly toward him, one step, then another. He hefted the double-bladed battle-ax, still streaked red from Maurice.

The scimitar felt heavy in his hand, awkward. It had been a month since he had held a sword of any kind, and he had lost much of his strength. Could I even swing that battle-ax of Amalric's?

He felt the tension mount inside himself like a bow bent to its limit. He watched Amalric come closer with a delicate, almost gliding movement. His mail and his spurs clinked faintly in a vast silence that had fallen over the plaza. Roland waited.

Until his enemy sprang.

As Amalric sent the huge battle-ax whistling through the air in a horizontal arc, Roland jumped back. He could almost feel the heavy blade slicing into his belly.

As the ax reached the end of its swing, Roland gathered all his strength and brought the scimitar down on Amalric's right arm. Amalric grunted. The blade would have gone right through the bone had not the arm been protected by mail. The blow had hurt him.

Amalric grasped the ax with both hands and swung it again at Roland's waist.

Roland leaped backward, then struck with the scimitar at Amalric's hands, but missed.

Amalric swung again, driving Roland farther back.

Roland glanced over his shoulder. The plaza was ringed with spectators. He could see Nicolette in her dark silk mantle in the mosque doorway.

He danced back, away from another whistling slash of the battle-ax. Amalric caught the counter-stroke of the scimitar on his forearm but seemed unhurt by it. Was Roland fighting a man of iron?

Roland's thighs and calves ached. His feet felt heavy. His left arm throbbed from wrist to shoulder.

They had come to the end of the mass grave now, and Roland turned as he backed away from the ax so that Amalric's back was to the mosque and they were circling around the east end of the pit.

He had to put all his remaining strength into one last attempt. He watched for his chance.

Amalric swung the battle-ax again, his blue eyes, on either side of the nasal bar of his helmet, fixed on Roland. But his arms were stretched far to his left by the weight of his mighty weapon.

Roland leaped.

He launched himself with all the power left in his legs and threw his arms around Amalric. For a moment the battle-ax was immobilized, and Amalric seemed to be losing his balance. Roland felt the steely mass of his enemy toppling backward. Suddenly, there was no ground beneath his feet. Clinging to Amalric, he felt himself falling into the pit. His left hand was clenched achingly tight around the haft of his scimitar.

They crashed together into the sodden earth at the bottom. Amalric landed under Roland, on his neck and shoulders. Amalric's mailed weight came down like a boulder on Roland's arms and hands.

To his horror, Roland felt his grip on his scimitar broken.

The impact of the fall dizzied Roland in his weakened state, and Amalric twisted himself under him and rolled over on top of him. Empty-handed, Roland lay on his back as Amalric knelt astride him and raised the ax.

I am dead, Roland thought.

The hilt of Amalric's dagger, hung at Amalric's right side, caught his eye. His left hand shot out and seized it. Amalric let go of the ax with one hand and tried to grab Roland's wrist, but not quickly enough.

Gripping the handle of the three-edged spike in both hands, Roland drove it upward, the point penetrating just where the mail around Amalric's throat stopped, under his chin. Roland felt the basilard pierce flesh and bone. He pushed upward with all his strength, driving the dagger deeper and deeper into the head.

Amalric screamed.

Roland did not listen. He pushed and pushed on the basilard, staring up at the blazing blue eyes, the fine-boned nose, the chiseled mouth. Amalric's arms went limp, and the ax fell away into the freshly dug earth. The fire went out of the blue eyes. The great, mail-encased body collapsed, a dead weight on Roland.

He let go of the basilard and heaved the body off to one side. He rolled away from Amalric, coming to rest in a sitting position with his back against the wall of the mass grave. Above him he saw a narrow strip of pale blue sky framed by walls of red dirt. Halfway down the trench Amalric's horse still whinnied and struggled.

I ought to get up and kill that horse out of mercy, Roland thought. But I have not the strength. Saint Michel, will somebody please do it?

He looked again at Amalric, who lay on his back with the hilt of the basilard jutting from under his chin. Blood flowed from the wound and soaked into the brown earth.

He looked at Amalric's torn, dirty surcoat, the emblem of the three gold crowns repeated over and over again on a purple background. No crown for you, Amalric.

Exhausted, drained, Roland studied the contorted dead face, framed in steel and pierced by steel.

A mighty man. I never had a real brother. What made him the way he was?

He heard movement above.

"Oh, Roland, Roland, Roland," was all Nicolette said.

"I am alive. And he is dead."

Nicolette's head was only a dark silhouette against the pale sky, but he knew she was weeping.

"Get someone to help me out of here," Roland said. "And call for an archer to end that poor horse's suffering."

She turned and spoke to someone. Then she was over the edge and scrambling down to kneel beside him. She looked at Amalric briefly, then shut her eyes and looked away. She pulled Roland to her and pressed his head against her breasts. Her silk mantle had fallen away, and her long black hair fell around his face.

He felt pain in every muscle. But new strength as well. He wrapped his arms around Nicolette, feeling with delight her straight back and slender waist.

"Can you climb up here? Come, I will give you a hand." It was the white-bearded Templar. He pulled the mail mitten off his right hand and reached down to Roland.

Roland stood. He looked about the pit and found the jeweled scimitar Baibars had given him. God, he thought, reliving the fear, when I lost this I was sure it was the end. He wiped the dirt from it against his white robe and slid it back into its scabbard.

Nicolette knelt beside Amalric and gently pressed her fingers to his eyelids to close them. Tears trickling over her cheeks, she shook her head.

"He died believing his cause was just," she said. "He was sure of that."

"Most men die so," Roland said. "When they think about it at all."

"And he let his love for me blind him."

Love? Surely she could not believe that Amalric had ever loved her, or anyone else. But there was nothing Roland could say.

"You go first," he told her. He held her at the waist and helped her up the sloping earthen wall until she could reach the Templar's hand.

When she was over the top, he turned and looked at Amalric. "Farewell, brother," he said.

He turned away and reached for the Templar's hand.

Nicolette stood waiting for him.

He took her hands in his and stared into her huge dark eyes.

"That which delights both woman and man is praise to Him Who made them," he said softly.

"I pray you pardon," the Templar interrupted. "But is it seemly, messire, for you and the count's wife to cast such fond looks at each other when you have but just now made her a widow?"

Nicolette smiled, though she was still weeping. "Oh, most seemly, brother Templar. More seemly than you can know."

"Sire Roland," the Templar went on, "we have read the letters you bring, and we see that you act with the King's authority and that he condemns Count Amalric as a traitor. Still, there is much that we must learn from you. You have killed the commander of Damietta."

Still holding Nicolette, Roland nodded. "I will explain it all, brother Templar. And if I do not satisfy you, then hear the King when he comes, as he shortly will. Now I must have the letters back, that I may take them to the Queen."

"We have good report of you from our late Brother Guido," said the Templar, handing him the letters.

"I have wept many a time for him," said Roland sadly. "Come, Nicolette." Holding her hand, he walked with her around the grave, toward the palace.

He dimly saw and faintly heard people greeting him on all sides, and he responded mildly, but took little note of them.

"It is claimed, is it not, that true Love cannot exist between husband and wife," he said to Nicolette. "Still, I would have you for my wife, if you will accept me. And I believe that Love will be with us all our lives long. What say you, *mi dons*?"

She smiled up at him. "I say that we have done so many impossible things already, it should be no great feat to keep Love alive. Even married. I will not let you be apart from me ever again."

The baking sun beat down on his head as he walked. Now he saw Queen Marguerite in the gateway of the palace, waiting to meet them. All had changed so, in so short a time, that he felt dizzy with the wonder of it. He walked slowly, feeling a radiant joy all around him, to present the two letters he had carried here to Marguerite, and to tell her that Louis, their King, was safe and would soon return to her.

XXXVI

ROLAND TURNED HIS ATTENTION FROM THE RIVER TO GAZE BEHIND him, at the walls of Damietta. A dozen large Saracen banners, dark silhouettes against the flush of the early morning sun, hung in the windless sky above the battlements. They reminded him that Mameluke scimitars were poised still over them all. Tension clawed at Roland's stomach. *The Mamelukes have everything now—the city, the treasure, and the King. We are only hours away from being free, and yet Baibars with a word could destroy us all.*

He wondered how the King felt, seeing these Saracen banners. He stood beside Louis in front of a tent the Egyptians had set up on the bank of the Nile. Louis wore the black silk coat the Sultan had given him, the only decent garment he had left. Roland was in French clothing borrowed from the Sire de Burgh, including a dark blue tunic, with the jeweled scimitar Baibars had given him at his waist. It seemed a good sign that the Egyptians had let the few knights in the city keep their weapons. *But then they know they have nothing to fear from us,* Roland thought wryly.

They stood where the Mamelukes had brought Louis by boat shortly after sunrise. Now they watched silently as the Templars arrived with chests filled with coins loaded on ox carts and piled the chests inside a large tent. He saw the Egyptian galleys loaded with the remnants of the army slowly being rowed down the river and mooring along the bank.

"There is Baibars," said Roland, recognizing the tall figure in a long red robe coming down the gangway of the first galley. Egyptian soldiers on shore bowed low.

Soon Baibars was facing them, and Roland and Louis bowed to him. His gilded helmet, partially covered by a green turban, flashed in the sunlight.

"I wish I could have seen you kill this Count Amalric, Sire de Vency," he said with a smile. "I am told it was a magnificent fight."

"So it may have been, to watch," Roland said wryly. "For

490

my part, I pray that I may never have to have another fight so magnificent.''

Baibars laughed. "You are a brave man, but perhaps you have not the true warrior spirit.'' Then he frowned. "I am sorry we lost Mukaddam ben Faris. That old Frank was one of my best men and very dear to me.''

"I believe we are much in that man's debt as well," said Roland.

Baibars held out his hand. "I must have back the ring you were to show him. It was given me by a lady very dear to me.'' Roland, disappointed, took the heavy ring from the pouch at his belt and gave it to Baibars. He remembered hearing the same fond tone in Baibars's voice when he spoke of the Sultana, Spray-of-Pearls.

"Do not look so downcast, Roland de Vency. The scimitar is far more precious than this antique ring, and it is my gift to you. You have earned it well. I hope that one day you will show it to your grandsons and tell them how you came by it.''

"It served me well," said Roland with a bow.

In French he summed up for Louis what he and Baibars had been saying.

"Where is Amalric buried?'' Louis asked Roland.

"At the Queen's command we left him where he lay, sire. His own dagger still in his head. The gravediggers just shoveled earth over the body.''

"Let him be forgotten. When we return to France we will expunge his very name from our records.'' He shook his head as if to cast out the memory of Amalric. "Will the emir enter this tent to see the treasure my kingdom presents to his?''

Baibars stepped back respectfully to allow the King to go into the tent first. Roland followed the two leaders. Within, all appeared ready for the counting. At a long table six Egyptian scribes and six Lombard clerks brought by the Templars sat facing each other. A row of Templars stood before the treasure-filled chests. Baibars approached and they stepped aside, allowing him to open one of the oaken boxes. He thrust his strong fingers in among the silver coins, lifting up a handful and letting them trickle back into the chest.

"Explain to him that these are *livres Tournois*, minted at Tours, a larger and heavier coin than the gold bezant," said Louis.

When Roland repeated this in Arabic Baibars smiled. "I know the value of every kind of Christian coin. I also know that these men"—he gestured at the Templars—"guard the royal treasury of France."

Among the Templars was the one with the shining white beard. He nodded almost imperceptibly to Roland.

Baibars, leading them outside again, said, "You have endured crushing hardship with calm and courage, O King of the Franks. Do you know that there were those among the Mameluke emirs who admired you so much they wanted, were you to convert to Islam, to make you Sultan to replace him whom we slew?"

Louis shrugged sadly. "It is easy enough to bear hardship. A donkey can do that. It is the duty of a ruler to accomplish much more."

From his sorrowful countenance, Roland could tell that a great heaviness was upon the King.

They stood in the open air now. Saracen guards with round shields and drawn scimitars formed a ring around the pavilion at a respectful distance. A Genoese galley with a red cross painted on its sail now had entered the river and was maneuvering to anchor downstream from the prison ships.

"Just so," said Baibars with a harsh laugh. "I persuaded the emirs that they were mistaken in you. I reminded them that, believing you were following the command of God, you led a great army to disaster." He paused and fixed his blue eye on Louis. "You must take care to remember what happened here if ever again you think you are hearing the voice of God."

Louis drew himself up to his full height. "I am a slave of my God, just as you are a slave to yours."

Fear beat upon Roland's heart as he translated this. Thank God the women had left Damietta yesterday for the Genoese ships.

Baibars never seemed more like a panther about to spring than in that moment. "Would you make war on us again?" It came as a soft growl.

"I have given you my word that I will not make war on you for twenty years," said Louis.

"But it seems you have learned nothing from this defeat," said Baibars thoughtfully. "Besides the emirs who wished to make you Sultan, there were those who urged that I do as Turan Shah had intended. Perhaps I should have listened to them."

The terror grew stronger in Roland. His left arm quivered with the urge to reach for his scimitar.

Instead, he reached for words.

"The kingdom of France is very large and very difficult to

govern, Emir Baibars," he said. "And much can happen in twenty years." Baibars knew, he remembered, that King Louis was the only ruler left in Christendom who still believed in crusading. "I do not think we will trouble you again."

He held his breath.

Baibars looked from Roland to Louis and back again, swinging his head. "Ah, well," he said, after a pause, "I promised the lady Spray-of-Pearls I would honor the treaty I made with you. She has taken pity on you. You Franks may not realize it, but you have been saved by two women, the Sultana and Queen Marguerite."

Roland sensed that the moment of greatest danger had passed, relaxed a bit. *Three* women, he thought. Nicolette, too.

Baibars took a scroll from his belt and handed it to Roland. "Read this to your King. One of our poets composed it for this occasion."

The scroll was of a heavy Egyptian paper made from the reeds that grew along the Nile, cream-colored, covered with the calligraphic right-to-left black strokes of Arabic letters. As he read, he translated. Grasping the import of the cruel words, he wanted to stop, but he looked up at Baibars and saw that diamond-hard single eye commanding him to continue.

> "Bear to the lord of the French these words
>   Which are traced by the hand of truth—
> May Allah reward you for having destroyed
>   The followers of Jesus the Messiah.
> You thought to be master of Egypt—you believed
>   You would meet here only drums full of air.
> And you led your warriors to the gates of death
>   Where the tomb gaped open for them.
> Where are the twenty thousand, your men?
>   Dead, wounded, and captive!
> If you wish to come again to Egypt,
>   Know that the mansion of Lokman still stands,
>   With its chains and its eunuch awake!
> May your God be merciful to you
>   For all that you have accomplished."

Roland looked up at Louis when he had finished and saw tears standing in his eyes.

"Your poet is right, Emir Baibars," Louis said. "I need God's mercy more than anyone else does."

"Truly, you are a holy madman," laughed Baibars. "You should be a prophet, not a king."

"Was not your Prophet also a ruler of men?" asked Louis.

Baibars shook his head. "That does not mean ordinary men like you and me can be both. None can compare with the Prophet."

He gestured, and a warrior in a gilded breastplate brought forward a long bundle wrapped in silk. "Permit me to give you another parting gift, O King of the Franks, one less bitter than that poem." Baibars unrolled the bundle ceremoniously. It was the Oriflamme.

Louis clutched the banner to him, weeping, and kissed its scarlet fringe. "Thank you, thank you. I thought never to see it again. May God bless you for your kindness."

"See that you never risk it in battle here again," said Baibars brusquely. "May Allah render to you the mercy you hope for." He bowed, turned, and walked away.

Roland walked with Louis as, the Oriflamme cradled in his arms, the King descended the bank of the river to board the Genoese galley that was waiting for him. Mameluke officers accompanied him. Roland heard a whistle on the galley deck, and in an instant the railing was lined with Genoese crossbowmen, their weapons trained on the Mamelukes.

"The Genoese do not wish to risk losing me at the last moment," said Louis with a smile. "How else can they be sure of being paid for their services?" He stopped at the edge of the plank the sailors had pushed out to shore for him. "I have promised Baibars to wait on this boat until the money is counted. Go back to that tent and help oversee the work." Roland dropped to one knee, kissed his hand, and left him.

At the tent Roland saw that the counting of the silver was beginning. Such a huge number of coins, he knew, must be counted by weight, or else the crusaders would be here until the Nile flooded. He watched as the Lombard clerks counted the first fifty silver coins into one pan of a large scale, while the Egyptians carefully added weights to the other until the scale balanced. Then the Lombards swept the coins off into a chest and poured more on the empty pan, this time without counting them, till the scale balanced again. Even this procedure, Roland realized, might take days.

Sire Jean de Joinville and Sire Philippe de Nemours were there, and they greeted Roland happily. The three would observe the counting on the King's behalf, and they settled themselves in chairs behind the Egyptian scribes.

De Joinville untied a scarf and picked out a brightly painted egg and gave it to Roland. "The Mamelukes gave us these before we left the prison ship. They said it would be shameful not to feed us before letting us go, and the painting on the eggs is to honor us. A pleasant custom, is it not?" The egg was hard-boiled. Roland, who had eaten nothing yet that day, peeled away the prettily colored shell with regret—but quickly.

The white-bearded Templar beckoned Roland, then drew him out of the tent.

"I bring you a message from an old friend," he said in a low voice.

"Who?"

"Our brother Guido."

Roland's heart fell as he remembered Guido being taken out to the executioner.

"I was with Guido just before they killed him," he said.

"He is not dead," said the Templar solemnly. "That is what he wants you to know."

Roland shivered. Was this Templar mad or merely uttering a pious commonplace?

"How do you mean that?" he said sharply.

"We have our allies, even among the Saracens," said the Templar. "It was time for Guido to become a new person. When he left you he was taken to the Ismailites. Do you know who they are?"

"Yes, the followers of the Old Man of the Mountain. At his order they kill kings and lords by stealth, and they inflame their minds with foul potions. What would Guido have to do with such debauched murderers?"

The Templar smiled. "You know only what their enemies say of them. They kill tyrants and persecutors. And they do not kill the brothers of the Temple."

Roland remembered the arrow that had ended Hugues de Gobignon's life and was silent.

"As for potions, has not brother Guido told you there are many ways to see the Light?"

"Yes," said Roland grudgingly.

"Do not be quick to judge, then, until you know all," said the Templar. "I tell you this much because Guido has said you can be trusted. You may repeat it to none, not even your lady."

"I have already sworn so to Guido. May I see him?" said Roland eagerly. Guido, alive!

The white-bearded Templar shook his head. "He bids me tell you he has much work to do farther to the East. There is knowledge to be passed on and knowledge to be acquired. Perhaps you will go to the East yourself one day and meet him there."

Roland stood silent, remembering Guido. What a great and good friend he was.

So the Templars were linked to the Ismailites, the so-called *Hashishiyya*. And the Cathers to the Templars. Would he ever learn all about this web of secrets that seemed to spread under the surface of the world like the roots of a great tree?

"Thank you, brother Templar, for bringing me this joyful news. If you should see Guido again, tell him I am writing the song he asked for."

"You will hear from us when you return to France."

Together they went back into the counting tent.

Let this be my last sight of Egypt, Roland thought as he stood beside Louis on the stern castle of the galleass *Montjoie* watching the brown and green coastline grow smaller in the light of the setting sun.

Louis sighed heavily. "Where did I go wrong, Sire Roland? I thought I had a vision. I believed that if we could restore the reign of Christ to Jerusalem, God would give us a new earth. I actually thought God had chosen me to turn the world from a vale of tears into a place of happiness. I was a presumptuous fool. Yes, sinful, and God intends for me to suffer as I do. The loss of all those lives must be my punishment for believing that I could change mankind's destiny."

Roland was thunderstruck, that the reach of Louis's vision was so vast. He had never realized that anyone could have such a dream. But then he remembered his vow at Mont Ségur and thought, I have wanted to change the world, too.

"Sire, to have seen such a vision is more than is granted most men. To have struggled for it is everything, whether or not you succeed. And you may still be destined to create that new world, not through recapturing Jerusalem, but by working as best you can to build a new Jerusalem in your own kingdom." And I can help you, because that is a dream I can share with you with all my heart.

Louis leaned on the railing to steady himself against the rolling of the ship's deck. "You know, Baibars offered me a safe conduct to Jerusalem, that I might at least see the holy city before I go home."

"Will you go, sire?"

"No," said Louis sadly. "I am not worthy to set my eyes upon the Jerusalem I could not rescue. As Baibars's poet said, all I can ask is that God be merciful to me for all whom I have led to their deaths." He put his hand on Roland's shoulder. "I want you to write out a translation of that poem for me. I plan to read it every day for the rest of my life as a penance, to remind me to be humble."

Here, despite his errors, is one of the best men alive, Roland thought. "Yes, sire."

"And I want you to write another poem for me. An answer, as it were, to Baibars's poem. Tell me why this crusade failed. Tell me what I did wrong. Tell me why God let it happen."

Roland was aghast.

"Sire, you ask more than a poor poet like myself can possibly do. I cannot explain God's ways."

Louis put his hands on Roland's shoulders. "If that Egyptian poet could break my heart, perhaps you can mend it."

"I shall try, sire."

The breeze ruffled Louis's thinning hair. This is the first time, out here on the water, thought Roland, that we have felt refreshed in almost a year.

Something on deck caught Louis's eye. "Sweet Jesus!"

"What is it, sire?"

"At a time like this!" he exclaimed.

He rushed to the steps leading down to the main deck and clattered down.

Roland saw the King's brother Charles at a table by the mainmast. Facing him was Sire Jean de Joinville and between them a backgammon board. Gold bezants were piled up on the table.

Louis fell upon his brother. "How could you?" he shouted. "You know gambling is a sin. And on this day of all days, when you should be thinking about Robert, and all our dead. Go to your cabin and get down on your knees and do penance!"

Charles sat staring at Louis, his mouth hanging open.

Louis lifted the table, dumping the coins in de Joinville's lap, then carried the table and game board to the rail and threw them over. A moment later Roland saw the brightly painted board bobbing astern.

De Joinville caught the coins up in the skirt of his tunic and hurried away, throwing a wink at Roland, while Charles, under Louis's furious stare, stalked off to the forward castle.

"Oh, God, forgive me!" Louis cried. He sank to his knees by

the railing, threw his arms around the polished oak, and sobbed convulsively.

Roland wept himself. The suffering in Louis's face was like that in a statue of the crucified Christ.

Roland was about to go to him when someone brushed past him. Marguerite. She knelt beside her husband. Louis turned his agonized face to her. He put his arms around Marguerite and they knelt there weeping together.

Roland felt a light touch on his arm. He turned and saw Nicolette. As he moved to her, she drew him gently away toward the stern, leaving Louis and Marguerite alone together.

Once they were by themselves, Roland lifted his arms to embrace her.

"Not yet, Roland." She held up her hands. "We must be seemly."

He took her arm courteously. "Come walk with me to the after castle."

They stood looking at the ship's wake, the breeze blowing the galleass away from Egypt and cooling their faces. The coast of Africa now was a thin black line between violet sky and sea.

"If you want to weep as the King does, here I may hold you in my arms," she said softly.

"All the men I brought with me are dead," said Roland, "and I grieve as much for my ten as Louis does for his thousands."

She laid her hand on his.

"Roland, it still feels strange to be free of Amalric, to be leaving Egypt behind, to be together with you. I cannot see what our lives will be like. Can you?"

"I want to live in Languedoc and do what we can to rebuild our country. You will want to have your children with you, and we may have to fight Amalric's family to get them."

She squeezed his hand harder. "Yes, Roland, I must have them back. I have missed them so much." She laid her head on his chest. "Simon—he is still so little. He needs us."

He put his arm protectively around her shoulders. "The King will help us."

"We can live at my family's estate," she said. "It is mine again. Will it please you to be seigneur of a small domain?"

"I do not know yet what will please me," he said, drawing her closer. "What I have done since I met you was at the bidding of Love, and for a vow I made to the martyrs of Mont Ségur. My vow still holds. It is part of what I am. But I cannot slay all the murderers, and I cannot change all mankind. I can write songs, though. I think that in the end songs may change more than swords can.''

And, he thought, I have the seed of that poem the King asked me to write. The pilgrimage is itself the goal. Whether we arrive or not, we must journey toward the Light.

It had become quite dark, with the suddenness of African nightfall. They would not be seen here on the after castle of the galleass. He pressed her to him.

And he looked up at the stars that were coming out one by one and whispered to her, ''All things that are, are lights.''

Historical Afterword

Louis IX: After the Mamelukes released him he remained in the Middle East, strengthening and unifying the crusader principalities there. He never saw his mother, Queen Blanche, again. She died in 1252, while Louis was engaged in complex treaty negotiations with the sultans of Cairo and Damascus. It was another two years before Louis felt his work in Outremer was done and he could go back to rule France.

He was much concerned with justice. He banned trial by combat and made it a law that a murdered man's family must wait forty days before taking vengeance.

In 1256 Louis prosecuted the odious Enguerrand de Coucy for hanging without trial three young equerries accused of poaching in his forest. De Coucy, with the support of most of the great barons of the realm, refused to cooperate in the investigation and trial. Louis pressed on against heavy opposition from the nobility, and Enguerrand was convicted and fined 12,000 livres, some of which went to endow perpetual masses for the souls of the men he hanged.

Louis's reputation for fairness was so great that he was asked to settle quarrels all over Europe, and he arbitrated between the dukes of Lorraine and Burgundy, between the kings of Hungary and Poland, and between the King of England and his barons.

The tragedy of his failed crusade weighed upon Louis and made him a much sadder man than he had been in his youth. He kept his promise to Baibars and waited exactly twenty years before launching another crusade. This one was even more unpopular than Louis's first crusade had been, and such old comrades as de Joinville flatly refused to go.

Louis's brother, Charles d'Anjou, had by this time managed to make himself King of Sicily and dreamed of a Mediterranean empire. So he persuaded Louis to try an even more roundabout approach to liberating the Holy Land than he had before, besieging Tunis in North Africa. The Muslims remained secure within their walls while fever spread throughout the French army. Louis's son Jean Tristan, the baby born at Damietta, succumbed. On August 25, 1270, Louis had himself laid on a penitential bed of ashes and there died.

Charles d'Anjou had his brother's body boiled in wine to separate the flesh from the bones. The bones were sent to the abbey of Saint-Denis near Paris, traditional burial place of French kings, while the heart and entrails went to the great cathedral of Monreale at Palermo in Charles's kingdom of Sicily. In 1297 Louis was proclaimed a saint by the Catholic Church, the only King of France to enjoy that honor, which perhaps would have greatly embarrassed him.

BAIBARS: He did not quite reach his goal of driving every last Christian out of the Middle East, but on the way to it he accomplished much else. On September 3, 1260, at the Well of Goliath near Nazareth, Baibars won one of history's decisive battles, defeating the Mongols for the first time since the rise of Genghis Khan and saving Islam from a Mongol conquest. When the Sultan of Cairo failed to reward him properly he drove a spear through the Sultan's back and made himself Sultan.

Baibars now turned his attention to the Christians and systematically conquered stronghold after stronghold along the coast of Palestine and Syria—Caesarea, Haifa, Jaffa, Belfort, Antioch, Krak des Chevaliers, Montfort. Before he could quite finish off the crusaders he died suddenly in 1277, some say of poison. Some even say he mistakenly drank poison he had prepared for another, but Baibars was surely too clever to do that.

In 1291 the last crusader city, Acre, fell to Baibars's successor, al-Ashraf Khalil, and the era of the crusades was at an end.

The Mamelukes ruled in Egypt for centuries thereafter, continuing their practice of adopting slave boys and training them to be warriors. In 1798 another French army invaded Egypt, and the Mamelukes, recalling the defeat of Saint Louis, rode out against them expecting easy victory. But the world had greatly changed. At the Battle of the Pyramids the French artillery shattered the Mameluke cavalry, and the country was subdued in a matter of weeks by a general almost as talented as Baibars— Napoleon Bonaparte.

THE TEMPLARS: The Order of Poor Knights of the Temple of Solomon was founded in Jerusalem in 1120 by six knights led by Hugues de Payns of Champagne, for the purpose of guarding the routes of pilgrimage to the Holy Land. By the middle of the thirteenth century the Templars had become exceedingly powerful, with hundreds of command posts across Europe and Outremer. Kings and nobles gave them large grants of land. They developed a banking system, and the royal treasury of France was kept at the Paris Temple. The grand master of the Templars was almost a sovereign in his own right.

The Templars maintained strongholds in the Middle East until the last crusaders were driven out. In 1291 the Temple in Acre fought on for several days after the Muslims army took the city. The Templars then moved their headquarters to Cyprus.

Alarmed and attracted by their enormous wealth, Louis IX's grandson, Philip the Fair, turned against the Templars. He took them by surprise on the night of Friday the thirteenth of October 1307, arresting their leaders all over France, including Grand Master Jacques de Molay, who was visiting from Cyprus. The royal prosecutors charged that the Templar initiation ritual required candidates to deny Christ, spit on a crucifix, and kiss the backside of a superior. They were also accused of sodomy and making secret treaties with the Muslims. The evidence against them was obtained under torture, but with the cooperation of Pope Clement V, many Templars were burned at the stake and others imprisoned for life, the order was suppressed throughout Europe, and its property in France seized by the crown. When Jacques de Molay was burned in 1314, he cried out that King Philip and Pope Clement would join him before the Divine Tribunal within a year. In less than a year the King and the Pope were both dead. Within fourteen years all of Philip's direct heirs had died. The house of Capet, which had ruled France since the tenth century, was no more, and the throne went to the Valois family.

Historians still disagree about whether there was any truth in the charges against the Templars. Some have suggested that the Templars held Gnostic beliefs, others that there was an order within the Templars whose secrets were known only to an inner circle. The Templars have been claimed as predecessors for the Freemasons, the Ordo Templi Orientalis, and the Ancient Illuminated Seers of Bavaria.

During the French Revolution the last King of France, Louis XVI, was imprisoned in the Paris Temple, from whence he went to the guillotine.

THE CATHARS: Catharism traces its roots to such primitive Christian sects as the Gnostics, who taught that direct communication with God is possible for each person, and the Manicheans, who believed that good and evil have equal power in the universe. Because Catharism originated in eastern Europe, Cathars were also known as "Bougres" (Bulgars). From the word Bougre, because the Cathars were accused of encouraging homosexuality, comes the term for anal intercourse, "buggery."

Catharism became widespread in Languedoc during the twelfth century, and by the thirteenth century had so many adherents that Pope Innocent III began to take steps against it. He commanded Friar Dominic de Guzmán, later Saint Dominic, to found the Order of Preachers and do missionary work in Languedoc to combat Catharism. In 1209 the Pope proclaimed a crusade against the Cathars, declaring them "worse than the very Saracens." Attracted as much by the prospect of looting the rich lands of southern France as by the desire to make war on a rival religion, barons and knights from all over Europe invaded Languedoc under the leadership of Simon de Montfort. Catholics and Cathars in Languedoc united in defense of their homeland, but were overwhelmed, and the crusade officially ended in 1229, when Raymond VII, Count of Toulouse, surrendered in Paris to Queen Blanche and the boy-king Louis.

From then on French armies occupied Languedoc, and the Inquisition, most of whose functionaries were Dominicans, carried on the work of stamping out the rival religion. By the middle of the fourteenth century Catharism had all but vanished. But religious dissent endured and eventually gave rise to the Protestant Reformation.